Other Books by Author

A Colorado Cowboy Romance Story:
My Texas Streak
Call Me Home [Coming 2020]

Assassins' Guild of Obseen:
Vision of a Torn Land (Prequel Book)
The Cost of Redemption

The Crystals of Syre:
Book 2: Revelation [coming 2020]

D1522670

The Crystals of Syre
Book One: Awakening

By Lindsey Cowherd

All Rights Reserved
Copywrite 2019
9781075847967
Published by Lindsey Cowherd
Cover art by SelfPubBookCovers.com/Shardel

"Those who don't believe in magic will never find it."—
Roald Dahl

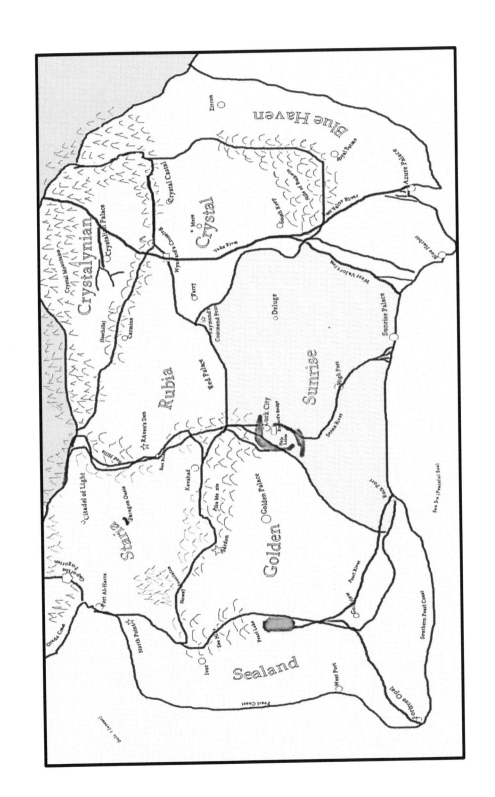

The Kingdoms of Syre

(Note: this only notes characters from each kingdom that are mentioned in this book; further characters will continue into Book 2)

"Six Companions" refers to: Anibus Farryl, Patrick Kins, Jacen Novano, Rio Ravesbend, Merchant Roland Seagold; apprentice Sage Cooper

Crystal:
Royal Household:
King Lanar Starkindler; wife: Queen Lestial
Children:
Heir: Prince Lance Starkindler; Second son: Page Starkindler;
Third son: Zeek Starkindler; Daughter: Zerra Starkindler

Crystine Cavalry:
Commander Matar; Second-in-command: Wix; Lieutenant: Madden
Other:
Decond (orphan; farrier hired by Crystine)

Staria:
Royal Household:
King Maushelik; wife Selene (deceased; former Duchess of Port Al-Harrad)
Children:
Sole Heir: Prince Al'den Reddiar Maushelik

Military:
First Guardsman Meeg Thorson
Captain Sean Woodman, Starian cavalry
Liuetenant-commander Terrance, footsoldiers

Starian Court (mentioned)
Lord William and Lady Rosetta Greyson; Lady Diane Levine; Lady Selena Durrow; Lady Kaitlin Lepree; Lady Rosa Quartlett; Zale Herth
Other:
Saida Newdon (business woman)

Sheev'anee
Shi'alam: Sheev'arid; son: Terrik, daughter: Zyanthena; cousin: En'ril Savam'eed
"Three" Kala: Shík Savam'eed; Shík Cum'eri; Shík All'aum
Other clansmen:
Kor'mauk Siv'arid; cousins: Kor'ar and Kor'moon Siv'arid
Cum'ar All'ani
Sid Tem'arid

Re'shaird Aerrisson (clan Sheev'arid)
Shytin (Sheev'arid retainer)

Kavahad
Lord-governor Darshel Shekmann friend: Viscount Markus LaPoint; cousin: Jeremy Freedman
Advisor Abrus
Kavahadian Cavalry
Commander Raic; Second Commander Gordon

Port Al-Harrad
Governor Thornhoff

Rubia:
Royal Household:
King Chível; wife never mentioned
Children:
Sole Heir: Prince Derek Chível; (his heir: Miguel)

Other:
Lord Protector Yory Selèv

Mertinean (military)
Commander Ethan Kins; son: Patrick Kins
Commander Tyk—Raven's Den;
Commander Grant—Raven's Den
Lieutenant-commander Curtis Marx (under Comm. Kins)

Sunrise:
Royal Household:
King Raymond Sunrise; wife: Queen Sylvia
Children:
Heir: Rowin Sunrise; Second son: Connel Sunrise

Other:
Lord Protectors: Rio Ravesbend; Elis Thorpson

Sunarian army
Commander Loris Ravesbend; Second-in-command Bradon
Thane Cornell

Blue Haven:
Royal Household:
King Jarod Eldon; wife: Queen Elise Eldon-Tomino
Children:
Heir: Prince Jace Eldon; Princess Éleen Eldon-Tomino;
two daughters (not mentioned)

Other:
Lord Nexlé of Zircon; son: Carrod Nexlé (Lord Protector to Princess Éleen)

Golden:
Royal Household:
King Argetlem; wife (deceased)
Children:
Sole Heir: Prince Kent Argetlem
Other:
Lord Protector: Liuetenant-commander Eric Sloan

Golden military:
Lord-commander Ivance (Sardon, capitol)
Lord Aeronson (royal advisor; former lord-commander)
Commander Charles Hadley; Colonel Jared Deed (archers)

Sealand:
Royal Household:
King William Fantill; wife: Queen Kesnia
Children:
Heir: Par Fantill; daughter: Celeste

Other:
Lord Protector: Lord Gordar Farrylin; cousin: Priest Anibus Farryl
Sealand militia
Commander Averron; Lieutenants Marcus and Tennet

Prologue

§

The Crystal Kingdom
(102 SC, Snow Thaw)

I.

Before one of three raging fires, stood a stocky, plump woman; she was kneading dough to make homemade bread for the evening feasting. She paused long enough to brush her greying hair away from her sweaty, beat-red face, then tackled the mound of dough with a renewed vengeance. A hum left her throat as the cook settled back into her work. The song was picked up by the other woman in the kitchen, who was readying a tray of pastries. Together, they let the song pass their time as they worked and used the rhythm to steady their kneading.

On a usual day, more than twelve other kitchen staff would have been humming along too, making the kitchen thrum in a joyful round, however, the time was still in a lull from post-lunch as the staff took their short reprieve before the evening's feast preparations. Only the two women, the head cook—who was too stubborn to rest when work was to be done—and the other, the Lady of the House, had remained to make batches of desserts for the night's events.

The Lady of the House untied her apron and set it aside. She breathed out a happy sigh at a job well done as she watched the pastries begin to bake in the fires. The joy turned sour, however, as she turned to regard her daughter. The youth sat on a tabletop near the windows. There was a look of longing in the girl's eyes as she stared out at the inviting landscape of high-mountain pines and spring wildflowers that called through the pane's portal; the expression had been seen too often by the queen of late. "She is sulking again, do you not also think, Sava?" The Lady of the House asked the old cook. She ignored her daughter's brandy-eyed glare at the inference.

"Oh, not at all, My Highness." Cook Sava answered cheerfully. "She's just a sufferin' the fever o' youth. She'll grow out of it, but, for the time bein', she just needs a little time for herself."

"I am not so sure of that." Queen Lestial replied, exasperated by the girl's dalliance. She turned back to her daughter and put a hand on her slender hip. "Zerra, it's the eve of your thirteenth birthday, and—and per usual—you're just sitting there doing nothing of any importance! Most girls your age are busy perfecting their stitches or practicing their etiquettes or penmanship. Yet, here you are staring off into space." The princess turned away from her mother with a sour expression. "Zerra! Why do you look away? I am talking to you." Queen Lestial let out a sigh in frustration. "You are not thinking of your brothers' sword practices again, are you? You know that you can never lead such a life."

"Highness!" Cook Sava scolded, unafraid to confront her queen. "She is young! Leave rest her dawdling; she will outgrow it. B'sides, your pastries are nearly browned. Come set 'em from the fire."

Still perturbed, Lestial turned back to her cooking. Cook Sava smiled smugly at her victory and shared a secretive wink at the girl before turning back to her own loaves of bread. "You know, I think we've outdone ourselves on His Majesty's return feast, Highness. He should be greatly pleased with the lemon pastries and the duck soup. Now, all we need are these apple-snap cakes."

"Do not fret." Lestial calmed the cook, "Lanar will understand if he does not get his round cakes."

"Yes, I know, Highness, but I'm not his head cook for nothin'. He will have all his favorites…"

Zerra barely listened to the older women banter about the dinner feast. She, unlike her mother, had no interest in cooking. There was no foreseeable way she would understand why the queen liked the laborious task—especially when being the Lady of the Castle meant she was not required to work in the kitchens. A soft sigh escaped Zerra's lips as she surveyed the groves of fir trees that grew along the cobbled lane in the courtyard below. They pointed the way to her real passion. The ninety-horse stable was just visible through the trees, its normal bustle lost in the green screen of the forest. Oh, how she would rather be there than in the stifling kitchens!

Annoyed and bored, Zerra began to count pinecones in the trees across the way.

As if the Stars wished to grant the princess's silent desire, a tall-statured and fair-haired youth came galloping down the lane—interrupting her count of one-hundred-and-twenty cones. He reined his fine-boned, steel-grey steed to a stop below the kitchen's window and yelled up to his sister. "Hey, Zer, hurry down! Father was seen by the river crossing. He will be here soon! We ride to meet him."

It was all the prompting the princess needed. "Coming!" Zerra yelled back, happy for the alibi to go to the stables. She spun away as her brother, Lance, turned his horse around. Ignoring the queen's disapproving call, the princess flew out of the kitchen and through the halls to the eastern stairwell. Without slowing, she bound down the long staircase, through the main grounding, and out to the courtyard, heading ever toward the barn where her three brothers were waiting.

Nearing the stable, the princess called out, "Vale!". She grinned when a towering, black stallion answered her call. The great courser sidled up to the twelve-year-old and stood in quivering anticipation as Zerra reached up to grab a handful of his flowing mane and swung herself up onto his broad back; Valed Darkness had been the princess's mount since she had been a little girl; she was very comfortable around him—and, perhaps a little too feckless—unfazed by his towering height.

Lance guided his horse beside the tackless black and flashed his sister a smile. "I thought this would be a good excuse for you to escape the kitchens."

"It was. Thank you, brother." Zerra grinned as she settled onto the stallion's back, relishing in the feeling of his muscles bunching underneath her in a sign of readiness and power. On cue, Vale was spinning about to set the pace as the four siblings rode south toward the orchards that connected to the creek road. Her other two brothers rode abreast of the other siblings' horses and shared smiles at their sister's characteristic ill-behavior.

Zeek, who was the closest to their younger sister in age, gave Zerra a sympathetic look. "Mother was that bad, huh?" He teased. He could tell that Zerra had been lectured again. "She will come around in time, I am sure of it."

Zerra nodded, though she knew the prospect unlikely, then motioned to her brother's horse, wanting to forget her torturous afternoon in the kitchens. "How is Causinova doing?"

"Very well, since you worked with him." Zeek leaned forward to stroke his light-chestnut charger admirably. The horse arched his neck in pleasure at being praised and struck the ground all the harder with his enormous, platter-sized hooves. Zeek laughed at Causinova's exuberance. "Yes, he has been doing exceptionally well."

"Well, good for him!" Page huffed from the other side. The other Starkindler siblings looked over to see Page's dark bay, Moon Dancer, crow-hopping down the lane, overexcited at their excursion. "Stop it!" Page growled and pulled his horse's head up. He glanced sheepishly at his sister and brothers. "She only acts up now and then but often enough to make me wish for a gelding. "Mooney" here is quite temperamental these days."

"You calling her that is why she acts this way, you know. Ladies like to be treated well." Lance teased from his place next to Zerra. He let loose a laugh at his brother's grimace and guided their posse onto the creek road.

The Starkindlers lapsed into a comfortable silence, as they cantered along, passing the last of the peach groves. The road stretched away, then, across a waving pasture of wild oats and continued until it reached the creek. The four royals pulled their horses up alongside the calm waters at the end of the lane and allowed their mounts to graze in the shade of the weeping branches of the willow trees that grew along the embankment.

The sound of coming hoof beats down the road played out just as the four horses caught their breaths. Vale pricked his small, stallion-ears and rang out his challenge to the trespassers. The shrill whinny of Victory, the king's courser, echoed the black's. Only Zerra's calming hand on her stallion's neck kept Vale from rushing at the other horse, who came prancing proudly up to the group in all his gleaming, bay glory. King Lanar stopped him safely away from the other stallion and flashed an appreciative smile at his four children. "This is a great surprise after a long ride. And a feast for mine sore eyes,"

"Still rhyming away, are we?" Lance teased as he hopped off Starwind. King Lanar echoed his eldest son's laugh as he leaned down to hug him. He straightened then and extended his hands to his other sons, who affectionately took his callused hands in their own. The king grinned at them and lifted his handsome face to include his daughter in their reunion.

Without another word, the young men broke from their father's grasp and climbed back onto their mounts. A final, delighted gleam passed through the king's eyes as he motioned the procession onward, back to the enormous Crystal Castle beyond. The three princes joined their father at the front of the line, excited for news from the front. King Lanar, having long been away, obliged his sons with tales of his adventures on the battlefield.

None of the brothers seemed to notice the princess, as they were enraptured by king's exciting stories, so Zerra hung back from her family and cued the stallion away from the procession. The duo disappeared onto a different path through the cherry groves. In quiet relief and finally alone, Zerra let the happy banter drift away behind her. "All right, Vale, let's have some fun!" The stallion flicked back an ear then snorted happily at the suggestion. He leapt into a long-strided gallop. The two of them sped off, dodging trees and jumping irrigation ditches that ran in perfect rows down the lane. It felt amazing to feel the wind whip Zerra's black hair away from her face; she grinned at the sheer joy of riding and spread her arms out as if to embrace the lazy sun.

Yet, in what seemed no time at all, the stable came into view, and the pair was forced to slow to a dainty walk (so the ladies at the court would not complain of Zerra's reckless joyriding). "Sorry, boy. My mother has harped on me about appearances. She would skin us both alive if she heard about us in her ladies' court." Vale bobbed his head, as if he understood, and resolved to the sedate walk required as he clopped across the cobbled courtyard. The stallion stopped by the stable entrance at last and stood sedately as a groom hurried out to meet them.

"M'lady, may I take y'er horse?"

Zerra glanced around cautiously and noted there were only stable hands around. "No, Jeremy, I think I will tend to Vale myself today. Could you keep watch for the king? His Majesty and the Crystine will be here soon." Jeremy nodded and tried to help the princess steady herself as she slid off, but Zerra waved his touch away. The stable boy backed off, flushing in shame. "Oh, Jeremy, don't be angry with me." Zerra begged softly, as she turned to him.

"I'm not, M'lady." Jeremy reassured her. "I's just forgot you've no wish to be treated like the other ladies. That t'is all." Zerra smiled at him and began to turn away; however, Jeremy grabbed her arm. Quickly he released his grasp, knowing it was an affront to touch royalty and gave a bow of apology. "Sorry, Y'er Highness. Ah...Lord Carrod arrived today. He may seek you out. I just wished you t'know."

Zerra frowned, unhappy to hear the young man's name. She disliked the lordling from Blue Haven. "I thank you, Jeremy. Please warn me, if you can, if you see him approaching."

"Yes, M'lady." He shared, with a knowing grin. "I'll come sprintin' if I see 'im." Jeremy turned away, then, to take care of an unruly chestnut colt. He left the princess to take her stallion to his stall.

Vale followed along placidly as Zerra hurried ahead of the great stallion and collected her grooming equipment. Trained, Vale continued past Zerra to enter his stall, all without his usual antics. His young owner smiled sympathetically. "I know, I hate this stupid dignification as much as you do. Luckily, our guests will be gone by tomorrow evening." Vale waffed softly and turned to his hay as the princess picked up a curry comb to brush the sweat from his body. She rubbed the stallion's coat in circles then exchanged the curry for a soft-bristled brush. She finished his grooming by working through his draping mane and tail with a deer-bone comb.

Just as Zerra was finishing, Jeremy came running up and ran his finger across his neck. He disappeared in a flurry. Glancing down the aislway, Zerra saw why. She instantly recognized the burly Havanese youth who strolled down it. "Dang!" She whispered and ducked back inside. Vale glanced at the princess quizzically as she went to hide behind him to crouch in the corner—and not a moment too soon. At the next breath, Carrod's heavy footsteps paused outside the stallion's stall.

The young lordling's husky voice, which changed dramatically as he spoke, ruined the quiet of the stable. "Oh, Vale! Move your blocky ass away from the door!" Zerra watched as the young man placed a ring-studded hand on the stallion's hindquarters and shoved. Vale pinned his ears and snorted at the offense, as he lifted his hind leg to kick outward. The hand disappeared in a haste, and Carrod's voice resounded again. "Stop that, you blockhead!"

Zerra was sure Carrod would have said more, if not for other footsteps nearing. To her relief, Lance's voice followed. "What are you doing here, young sir? Step away from Valed Darkness's stall! The king would be furious to see you harass his prized stallion such as you are."

"I am looking for your sister, Highness."

"Well, she is not here, now is she?" Lance replied, harshly. "Princess Zerra will be found in the castle. If you had the wit about you, you would know to look for her among the nobles and not the grooms!" If Carrod answered at all, Zerra did not catch it, but she was glad to hear the heavy footsteps of the young lord leaving. A few minutes later, Lance's hand touched the stallion's hindquarters, moving him away, and the prince entered the stall. He ignored his sister as he stroked the black horse and spoke to him. "He's rude, isn't he? I apologize in his stead, Vale."

The stallion turned to sniff in the prince's pockets, looking for treats, then turned away to the princess when he found none. Zerra touched her hand to his velvety nose before standing up.

"And you are lucky to have the protection of the stallion. Even my words on your whereabouts can not proceed the rumors of your skulking around."

"I know." Zerra looked shyly away from her brother's brown gaze. "Unfortunately, Vale is not able to come to the banquets or be present at court to chase away my unwanted stalkers."

"The princess will have to make do with her protective brothers instead." Lance answered seriously though there was a twinkle in his eyes.

"Yes, if she must." Zerra fell into her royalty role once again.

"And now, we mustn't tarry if we are to be presentable for the banquet."

Zerra reluctantly agreed with her brother, and they stepped out of Vale's stall. Lance offered her his arm, and the two siblings walked out of the stable to face what they knew would be a long, drawn out evening.

A flustered maid flew up to them, as they walked through the main anteway. "Where have you been, Princess?! The queen is in a frenzied at your disappearance, and the time is so pressing!" She pulled the reluctant Starkindler away from her brother. The maid scurried, with princess in tow, up the main flights of steps, and turned left to the queen's chamber. They burst into the room in unruly fashion, further unsettling Queen Lestial. "I have brought her, My Highness."

"And in such a haste, for thee was late." The Crystal Kingdom's queen frowned in disapproval.

"It is not she you are to blame." Zerra drew herself up under her mother's strong gaze.

"Indeed, she is not," Lestial agreed, "It is not she who flees to the stables when work is asked, nor is it she who should care that thee is inappropriate for the royal banquet."

Zerra stood proud under her mother's held wrath. "I went to receive my king."

"If you were one of his sons it would be deemed appropriate, Zerra, but you are his only daughter. You are not fit for man's business." Zerra held her tongue at her mother's harsh words. If the queen expected an outburst, she was not indulged. "So, she has learned to hold her tongue?" Lestial murmured. "Very well. Now, let's see..." She scrutinized her daughter. "You smell of horse and sweat, eh, and pieces of straw are stuck to you." Her nose wrinkled in disgust as she picked out the stall bedding from Zerra's dress. "Oh, it won't do! Go get in the bath and be quick about it! The time is pressing and you are unfit to be presented."

Zerra sighed and followed the maid to her bath where she was promptly washed. She was given no time to dally in the warm water, nor in getting into her party flock, which was fitted to her much too tightly. Then, it was off to the hairdresser where her black tresses were buffeted around as the dresser expressed her opinions on its style. The lady finally decided on a braided crown, encompassed by a nest of tiny, tightly twisted buns. Blue and white flowers were added at the end to contrast with Zerra's black hair.

"There now, Highness, let Her Majesty inspect you."

Zerra plodded back to her mother's chamber and stood still as Lestial inspected her once again. "You could do with perfume and a little powder." Queen Lestial commented as she ran her slender fingers over Zerra's sapphire dress. "Yes, yes. And your white diamond necklace." She shooed her away again so Zerra could be appropriately swaddled. When Zerra reappeared the third time,

Queen Lestial's eyes lit up in approval. "Oh, yes! That is so pretty. My, do you look so grown up!"

Zerra glanced in the mirror beside her and gave a withering look. She looked like a fancied, pale-faced puppet. How could anyone stand this?

"Oh, come now, darling." Queen Lestial hugged her daughter from behind. "You look just alluring."

Zerra groaned at the word. "Alluring to whom? Only a dullard could be attracted to this." Her mind was on Carrod.

"Zerra! I swear," Lestial reprimanded, "You look very sophisticated. Most ladies at court are even more lavishly attired than that, and we can't have you too under-dressed. That would be awkward."

For whom? Zerra thought but kept the comment to herself. "Very well, mother. I guess I will head down now." Zerra paused only long enough for her mother to give her a kiss on a cheek before she rushed out the door—much to Lestial's chagrin.

Her brother, Zeek, stood outside. Zerra paused to take in her brother's handsome attire. He had also been decked out in blue; the velvet shirt looked dashing against the coffee color of his erdskin pants and leather boots. The prince's black hair had been slicked back into a warrior's ponytail that hung neatly to his shoulders. Of the four Starkindler siblings, both Zeek and Zerra bore their father's dark features, while the other two had Lestial's fair ones. Zerra thought it made her and Zeek appear mysterious and aloof, which was probably, in part, why they were less apt to being in the social light. (People did tend to avoid brooders.) Zeek bowed to his sister, in mock curtsey. "Prince Lance had requested I escort you, Princess Zerra."

"My thanks, Prince Zeek." Zerra returned and accepted her brother's right arm. Together, they strode through the hallways and down the grand staircase, attempting to be stately. Guests glanced up from the ground floor, their eyes held on the prince and princess as they paused on the last landing. A few gasps arose in the room, and young men and women flocked to the stairwell to get a closer look at Zerra.

"Keep walking." Zerra ordered from the corner of her mouth. "Give them no chance to ogle longer than possible." Prince Zeek chuckled but followed her instructions without pause, though the "oglers" flocked around them. They were able to reach the spacious ballroom with easy speed.

Zerra's eyes wandered across the enormous room as she took in all the new details set out for the celebration feast: Bright tapestries hung on the walls, painting scenes of the past histories of the Crystal Kingdom. As was customary, the largest tapestry was of the Eight Kingdoms of Syre; it hung centermost of all the other hangings, there so guests could feel included during events. The princess loved to study the rich colors of the tapestries as she ran her fingers over the names of places around the Crystal Kingdom or the other eight kingdoms that made up Syre. Zerra frequently day-dreamed of future visits to such places are Blue Haven, Rubia, and Sunrise, or the farther kingdoms Staria, Golden, and Sealand. Of course, there was also the forests and ruins of the lost kingdom, Crystalynian, to the north—though no one dared venture into the Forbidding Forest anymore... Some guests, she knew, came from these fairytale kingdoms. It was, perhaps, the only real and exciting reason to attend such events as balls.

In additional decorations about the room. Flourishes of colors had been set over the tables and pillars, made up of many assortments of wildflowers from the mountain pastures of the Kingdom's lands. Rich carpets had been placed underneath the tables' feet to cushion the stone floor. Comfortable pillows and cushions adorned the large, flat stones around the ten blazing fireplaces against the walls; the fires would continue to be a gathering place this night, for, though it was spring, the nights in the Crystal Kingdom—which nestled itself in a mountain valley—were still a bit chilly. Finally, to add to the simple beauty, the cooks were already dining the table with colorful meats, cheeses, breads, and greens.

Zerra's eyes took all of this in in a single glance; she was pleased with the sight. Despite the princess's dislike of such affairs, she did love dancing and eating delectable foods reserved for such occasions. If it wasn't for the dreadful dresses and suffocating etiquette, she would have reveled in the night's celebration more—especially when the castle looked so stunning. "May we join our brothers, Prince Zeek?" Zerra asked as she spotted the said siblings near a fireplace surrounded by other young nobility. Zeek obeyed wordlessly.

Lance glanced up as his younger siblings approached. With the movement, the others gathered around him turned to see who came near. Lance smiled at his sister. "And here is my porcelain princess."

Zerra joined in his laughter over their secret joke. "Yes, my darling brother, I am indeed "*painted to perfection*" this night." She allowed Zeek and Lance to steer her to a blue silk pillow. Once she was settled, she glanced around at her brothers' unfamiliar friends. "I do not believe we have met."

Prince Page handed her a glass of wine then began introductions, starting with the young man to her right. "This here is Lord William Greyson of the kingdom Staria and his sister, Lady Rosetta."

Zerra nodded politely as they were introduced but struggled to hold back a chuckle at the formalness in her brother's voice. Since they were not really considered nobility—in title— just of noble birth, there was no real need for such formalities. Only Page could give introductions with a flair that allowed their guests to feel privileged.

"Next, may I give you Lords Brédon Serliv and Markus Pride of Rubia." Both boys, though from different houses, were tall and thin with near-white hair and ice blue eyes that glistened warmly at Zerra. The princess had a feeling, as she smiled back at them, that they would be pleasant to speak with and help ease the dullness of the evening.

Page waved his sister back to their present introductions and motioned to the next person in the circle, a young man dressed in Sealand blue. He sported interesting golden eyes. "Lord Gordar Farrylin of Sealand, cousin and Lord Protector of His Highness Prince Par Fantill—whom you already know." Gordar was quick to give his hello and back away, allowing room for the other Sealander to come to the fore. Prince Par, like his cousin, was slenderly built, with golden-blonde hair tied back in a warrior's tale. He was one of the eldest of those gathered. His ocean-blue eyes showed sympathy for Zerra. He was the only guest there that the princess had met previously, and he knew, well, how annoyed she really was over the court formalities. Smiling kindly, Prince Par took her hand and brushed a kiss above her gloved knuckles. Zerra felt herself blush under the white makeup.

"And this is Highness Éleen Éldon-Tomino, eldest daughter of King Éldon and Queen Asilla of Blue Haven." Page continued, ignoring the other prince's overly-familiar hello. Éleen curtsied gracefully before averting her eyes shyly to the floor.

"Welcome to the Crystal Palace." Zerra said to the pretty girl with a smile, in hopes of settling the older girl's nervousness. Éleen peeped up through her brunette bangs to return the look. The smile seemed less guarded.

"And lastly," Page called Zerra's attention away from Éleen. "I would like to present to you, His Highness Prince Rowin Sunrise of the Sunrise Kingdom."

Zerra had not noticed the handsome youth standing on the other side of Lance. Just his title alone surprised her, for never before had the Sunrise royalty graced a celebration outside their own kingdom, yet it was his appearance that shocked her even more. Where the other youths wore fine clothing, his was even richer. His maroon tunic was tailored to precision to accent his lean but muscular frame; his leggings, embroidered in gold-thread, made the Starkindlers' erdskin pants unseemly. Rubies adorned a thin circlet of silver around his head, and rings of similar stone adorned each of his slender fingers. The outfit easily accented his dark chestnut hair and midnight-blue eyes, making him a dashing figure to look at. Zerra could have gagged.

Rowin seemed not to care about his appearance—or he was just too used to it. He bent down on a knee, in Sunarian court fashion, and kissed Zerra's hesitantly outstretched hand. "My household is graced to be invited to this celebration, Princess Zerra. May your father continue his victory on the front lines at the Crystal-Rubian border." *"And, may the princess have an enjoyable coming-of-age."*

Zerra glanced up, startled, at the prince's telepathy, but she stopped herself from blurting out her astonishment. She realized, of a sudden, that Rowin must had inherited his mother's, Queen Sylvia's, rumored gift of telepathy.

"Yes, princess, I am indeed a telepath, as has been rumored. I bid you not to be frightened of this." He released her hand, and only seconds had passed between their little exchange. Zerra stared at the Sunarian prince as he stepped back to his former position by her eldest brother.

After Prince Rowin returned to his spot, Lance informed Zerra of the whereabouts of his best friend, the Prince of Staria. "Prince Al'den sends his regrets for not making this night, sister." He said, bending over to whisper in her ear. "The fighting against the maunstorz has gotten a bit rough, and there were concerns that a Starian party would not make it safely here. He sent ahead a gift for you and a letter of pardon. I put it in your room."

"Thank you, brother." Zerra whispered back. "Send my regards for his safety, and my thanks at his generosity, when next you write him. I do miss his not being here."

"Will do." Lance gave her an affectionate peck on her cheek and straightened to join in the conversation with his friends.

Zerra sat quietly on her pillow as the others talked and gossiped. For her, their conversations were idle and little important compared to horse breeding or the attacks of the maunstorz to the north and west; such talk as was deemed inappropriate for a lady at court. Therefore, the princess kept to herself. Her brandy eyes wandered around the ballroom, seeking out faces she knew. Zerra noted which nobles were present and who had accompanied whom. Nearly all of King Lanar's soldiers were present, as well, decked out in court-acceptable vestments. Her eyes finally rested on Carrod. The young lordling was standing amongst a group of older nobles, looking, for the most part, ignored. Zerra smirked, happy to see the sight. There was no way could Carrod leave to find her without the disapproval of his chosen companions.

Servants scurried over to the small group and bade them to follow to their seats. The youths split and made their ways to the dinner tables. All about the room, knights and nobles were being directed to their places so that the king and queen of the Crystal Kingdom could enter the great hall.

Once everyone had found their chairs, the main doors were pushed aside and King Lanar and Queen Lestial walked in, regal heads held high and hands clasped affectionately. Everyone continued to stand until the rulers took their places at the head of the main table and motioned for the room to sit. Neither royal gave a speech, only enough words to bide their guests to enjoy the night. The feasting began soon afterward, in a flurry of reaching hands and a flood of talking. Food was offered by polite retainers, who hovered behind the guests. Soon everyone's plates were heaped with delicious smells and tastes.

Zerra was one of only a few at the royal head-table that didn't indulge in the fine cuisine before her. She ate tiny mouthfuls, as appropriate of a princess, and silently pinned for the simple but palatable meals Sava cooked for the soldiers. A polite tap to her right snapped Princess Zerra out of her thoughts.

"You okay, sis?" Zeek whispered as he glanced around the table to see what she had been staring at.

"Yes, I was just lost in thought." She picked up a piece of bread to show she was back to the present.

Zeek gave her an amused smile. "Do share, little sister, or perhaps not? At least join in the conversation if you can. Maybe with Prince Par across the way or our new guest His Highness Rowin Sunrise to your left? He had been glancing this way, but, I believe, he is too intimidated to speak with you when you scowl in such a way." To prove his point, Zeek mirrored her look, teasingly. "It looks better on me don't you think?"

"Hardly," Zerra chuckled, "But I will try to look less menacing, big brother. Perhaps, you are right that I should court friendlier ties with the Sunrise family."

Again, Zeek gave her a mocking scowl. "Just don't get wooed, young lady, by his rubies and callings of gold."

"Like I would." She answered sarcastically before turning away from her brother. Taking an inaudible intake of air, Zerra sucked in as much confidence and courtesy as she could muster, then pasted a smile on her face as she turned to the Sunarian prince.

"How is your dinner, Highness Sunrise?"

Rowin turned to smile at her with all his Sunarian charm. Perhaps because she had finally spoken to him or maybe he really was enjoying himself? "It is absolutely superb, Princess. In fact, it is the best cuisine I have tasted in a long while." He paused to courteously wipe his mouth on his linen napkin. "And how about you? Is the food satisfactory?"

"Yes, it is wonderful." She answered with her best sincere smile. Inwardly, though, Zerra felt like gagging on her court-friend politeness.

Rowin nodded then took a sip of red wine to wash down his meal. He rose a finger in the air to show he had a thought to share as he gulped down the drink. Replacing his cup, the prince brushed a ruby-studded hand in the air charmingly. "I heard a rumor in the stables earlier, that you are the rider of the Crystal Kingdom's allegedly undefeatable black stallion. Is that a fact?"

Zerra hesitated and glanced to the head of the table where her father and mother sat. They would not be happy to know the grooms had told their guests that their only daughter rode more than their tamest horses, and most especially their prized black stallion; however, Zerra then remembered her annoyance at her mother for being reprimanded for riding the said mount. "Yes," she stated boldly, "I do ride Valed Darkness. I am the only one, besides my father, that he will let astride him."

Rowin's eyes sparkled in amusement at her matter-of-fact tone. "Then you must also be involved in his breeding. I have heard he is bred only to the best of mares."

"Yes." Zerra answered, beginning to be suspicious. "He is matched carefully to each mare so that the offspring is hardy and athletic. His lines are seen in many of our top horses, including our racers and war coursers."

"I have heard nothing less." Rowin answered politely. "The reason I am asking all this, is that my mother and I are here to buy blue-blooded war horses and chargers for our military down south. Ever since I saw a Valed Darkness offspring in action at the Deluge Market, I have been hoping to have one of my own."

Zerra rose a hand in alarm to stop the prince. "I must warn you; my father rarely gives up an offspring of Vales', nor does he breed the stallion to any mare. If you are looking for high-class war horses, you would be better off breeding or buying from Victory's line, father's war courser, or from Glorified or King's Randsome, our other stallions. You would have a better chance of getting breeding rights for them, in any case."

"Oh, I see." Rowin's smile faded. "I never realized how right our stable-master was. You see, for years now, I have been selectively breeding some of our mares so that I could get a filly fine enough to rival the Crystal Kingdom's breeding lines. I had hoped, if His Majesty saw her, he would change his mind about breeding Valed

Darkness to only his stock. I see, though, that my work will not pay off." His words came out as a mutter, and, it seemed, he had forgotten he had an audience. With a defeated shrug, he said, "Well, the other stallions are also respectable. Even that mix will strengthen our cavalry."

Zeek leaned over then to eye Prince Rowin. In the process, he bumped his sister. Zerra noted the twinkle in his eyes that alerted her to pay attention. "Did you say you breed horses yourself, Prince Rowin?"

"Why, yes," Rowin straightened with pride, "I even brought my best prospect, Blue Galeon, with me."

"The dark bay mare in the eastern wing of the stables?"

"Yes, that is her." Rowin beamed. "A beauty, is she not? She is out of Royal Blue and sired by our own stallion, Gallantry, by Léoso. I raised and trained her myself, since she was foaled four years ago. I had seven other horses as well, but she overshadows the rest with her charisma and versatility. She has both strength and speed—a rare match these days."

"Indeed, she is a jewel. I saw her earlier and had to stop to see her closer. You have an eye for horses, if you have others like her at your stables."

"Why thank you, Prince Zeek." Rowin puffed up from the praise." Yet, it seems my work will fall short of my expectations. Are you sure there is no way I can get Galeon bred to Valed Darkness?"

"I will have to discuss that with the king." Zeek replied, "But, I have not seen a mare like that in some time. Father might reconsider... Either way, I want you to know, you have my support."

"I am grateful, Highness." Rowin eyed Zerra accusingly once Zeek turned back to his dinner. "You should go see Blue Galeon before we leave on the 'morrow. Perhaps, you will change your mind, princess, if you see her." Without another word, he turned to talk with his mother and another guest.

Zerra was left to glare at him. *Boy, is he rude!* Zerra thought and sighed. *This is going to be one long evening.* Annoyed, she picked at her food and wondered who she would have to talk with next. Luckily, she was saved from speaking to anyone else, as King Lanar stood up and raised his glass for silence.

The room quieted. "As you all know, tonight is a celebration of two glorious occasions. First, I would like to congratulate my soldiers and loyal friends who helped us win another victory at the border. We have, once again, thrust back the guerilla attacks of the maunstorz." A loud cheer echoed through the room. King Lanar allowed it to last a little while before he rose a hand for silence once again. "And is my daughter's eve night for her coming-of-age. As is customary, I have appropriated a gift to bestow on her. My daughter, Princess Zerra Kareen Starkindler, would you rise and accept my gift?"

Zerra's eyes widened and she glanced at her brother. Usually, it was only the male heirs that received a gift on their coming-of-age. Zeek smiled encouragingly and motioned for Zerra to stand. She did so with some hesitation and received a round of applause. Zerra came to stand by her father's right side.

"Tonight, my daughter will cross over into adulthood. With that, she will gain new responsibilities; however, all of her life, I have watched her grow toward this moment. I have seen that she is more than ready and I welcome the fact that I will have her by my side, just as she is right now." King Lanar turned so he was addressing Zerra singularly. "Zerra, I am so proud of you this night. Since I first saw your face, I have been waiting for this moment. Now it has come. May this coming-of-age be a memorable one for you for years to come. Berneisse!"

"Berneisse!" Everyone echoed enthusiastically.

Then, King Lanar motioned a servant forward and lifted a necklace from the case he bore. "This is for you, Zerra Starkindler. May you always treasure it."

The silver-chained necklace held a single stone. It was unpolished and naturally cut. Though it was not anything like the royal jewels, Zerra saw in it an unfathomable beauty. Under its obsidian facets danced a shimmering, soft-golden light that was there one moment and a different place the next. It pulsed through the obsidian stone in a way that reminded Zerra of a heartbeat, and, as the stone rested over her collarbone, she felt a warmth, as if the stone was alive. "It is exceptional, father, thank you." Zerra breathed with delight.

"And someday I will tell you of its history and worth." King Lanar whispered conspiratorially before straightening and raising his arms to his audience. "And now may we celebrate! Remove the tables and roll back the carpets! We are going to party all the night long."

Another cheer rose and the guests hurried to comply with the king's orders. In no time at all, the floors were cleared. Musicians took up the eastern corner of the great hall., and the first song began in earnest. Couples strode out to the dance floor while unpartnered women crowded to the walls and awaited invitations from charming men to bring them to the flurry of the floor. Among those along the wall was Zerra, though her reasons were far different from the others. Silently, she was trying to steel herself from the party—though in truth, she stood little chance of that.

Much to her chagrin, Carrod Nexlé came pushing through the crowd toward her. Zerra grimaced as the burly youth came nearer but she managed to paste a smile on her countenance before he reached her side. "Good evening, My Lady." Carrod greeted her and kiss her hand. "You look absolutely stunning tonight, princess."

Zerra almost made a disgusted face but was able to catch herself. "And you look very congenial, as well." She replied and cringed inwardly. *I can't believe I just said that!*

Carrod's face lit up at her remark. "So, would you care to dance then, My Lady?" He lifted a hand in invitation.

No. Zerra wanted to blurt out, but she could not think of an excuse that would be good enough to get her out of that mess. "Well...um..."

"There you are, princess! I was worried you had forgotten your promise." Zerra whirled around to find Prince Par Fantill standing behind her. "You weren't trying to smuggle out of our dance, now were you?"

Carrod stared, flabbergasted, at the Prince from Sealand. "She p-promised you a dance?" He choked out flaccidly.

"Yes, and I apologized that she led you on, Lord Nexlé. As a princess, she should know better." Par tossed her a disapproving frown, though a playful wink followed it from the eye hidden from Carrod. "Now, if you will excuse us, Lord Nexlé, I wish to reprimand her in private."

Par pulled Zerra away through the crowd. Once they were far enough to be out of earshot of the lordling, Zerra spun to face the Prince of Sealand; however, before she could get a word out, he continued his teasing. "Are you blushing, princess? I can't tell underneath all that white paint."

"You..." She growled but was again interrupted by the prince.

"Are very welcomed. I saw how flustered you were and decided to step in before he completely ruined your evening."

Zerra almost wanted to continue with her angry retort, but she let loose a defeated sigh instead. "I thank you. Belatedly."

"Oh, come now, Zerra! You know it worked out for the best. You don't have to dance with the charming creep anymore."

"Yeah, because he thinks I am to be your *betrothed*. How could you lead him on like that?" Her anger flared instantly back to life.

"It is better betrothed to me than him, I would say." Par actually seemed serious. Zerra glared at him. "Oh, please tell me you have thought about it?" Her eyes narrowed further. "Think, princess. It is your coming-of-age night. Everyone knows, and that is why there are more young men here than normal."

Zerra glanced around and realized Par was right. Just like that, her anger was squashed. "Now my evening is ruined." She groaned and leaned against the nearby pillar, utterly deflated. Many young girls were given proposals at their Berneisse. How had she forgotten the custom? *Why can't they just leave me alone? I'm too young to care about all this "dutiful" princess stuff. It totally sucks.*

Par's blue eyes softened in sympathy. "I am sorry, Zer, but I couldn't leave you ignorant of that fact."

"It was my ignorance."

"Still...you should not become glum tonight. After all, it is your Berneisse." He paused. "So...is my dance card still filled?"

Zerra couldn't help chuckling in relief. "You are indeed a good friend, Prince of Sealand, though your methods are a bit rough. I gladly accept." She took his outstretched hand and followed his lead to the floor to join the reel already begun. For the next two-and-a-half hours Prince Par, Zeek, Lance, and Lord Brédon took turns dancing with Zerra.

By the end of the second hour, Prince Par stepped her though a slow waltz then escorted her to the side of the room. "I will need to retire soon," he informed her.

Zerra's elated eyes dulled at his words. "But it is still so early."

"Yes, but my family is heading back to Sealand tomorrow, and I need a good sleep for the trip. However, I would like to have a little more time with you. Perhaps, we could venture in the Queen's gardens?"

Zerra accepted. "There will be few people there, especially unwanted ones." Her mind flashed back to Carrod. "It should be quiet enough that we will not be disturbed."

"Great." Par grinned.

The Queen's Garden was indeed expansive. It was the largest room in the castle, laying four acres across; there were twelve paths, twenty-five different plant quadrants, and seven waterfalls surrounding a large, spring-fed lake. Giant evergreen and weeping-willow trees loomed over the cobbled paths, and artful bridges covered the wandering streams; colorful flowers dotted the grassy carpets of the garden.

Zerra led the way, unhindered by the dark, and Par followed her closely. They strolled without speaking, enjoying the quiet of the wandering streams which was soon shattered by the thunder of a nearing waterfall. The pathway Zerra had chosen ended abruptly. It emptied into a small glade at the base of a cascading fall. On floating feet, Zerra raced ahead to her favorite spot under the oldest willow tree in the garden; she disappeared behind its draping veil. Par smiled at her "unladylike" behavior and followed her in more sedately. He parted the falling branches and entered Zerra's hidden domain. "So, this is where you disappear to when we play hide-and-seek."

"Just one of my many hiding places." Zerra replied.

"Is that so?" Par chuckled and settled down in a sofa of reeds. Zerra gave him a quizzical glance, a passing thought at his behavior. She shook her head to rid herself of it and sat down in a billowful of skirts. "So, is your Berneisse enjoyable?"

Zerra shrugged and plucked a blade of grass to twirl idly between her fingers. "It is as good as to be expected."

"But not as you had hoped?"

"No," she sighed, "But what I had hoped for was not appropriate for a "young lady" such as myself."

"Ah, I hear your mother's words. She is still set to see you molded into a maiden, I see. Sad that is."

"Sad? Huh?" Zerra asked. Par leaned back onto his elbows and grinned at her without supplying an answer. "Par, what do you mean by sad?" She urged and added in warning, "Don't make me angry at you again."

"Perhaps, I'd like to see you get a little miffed."

No sooner were the words from his mouth did Zerra launched herself at the prince. The royal found himself pinned to the ground in a billow of sapphire pleats. He gaped in shock then let out a pleasant laugh that shook his whole body. "This is what saddens me, Zer, your mother trying to take that tenacious spirit from you. It is the one I have come to love the most."

It was Zerra's turn to gasped. The words flustered her; however, she had no time to react as the prince took advantage of the breach in her concentration to flip her onto her back and properly pin her. Par smile was impish as he stared down at her. "So, I can surprise you after all."

"Yes, when you talk of such things as that." Zerra growled.

"And I am not joking, princess." Par's countenance turned sober. He blocked a punch aimed at his stomach.

"You are a jerk, just like every other young man here tonight." She pushed against the older boy's chest. "Get off of me! Now!" She ordered, beginning to feel trapped in a not-so-good way. Her panic made her struggle more furiously.

"I will not, Zerra."

Finally, out of breath and subdued, Zerra ceased her struggle and laid back. She turned her head away from Prince Par's handsome face. "You are no different from them." She repeated.

"But, you know, you don't really mean that." Par touched her cheek and brought her head back around. "I, like your parents and brothers, want you to be happy, Zer. Others you could have, this I know, but would you really be happy with them? Strangers. I am giving you a choice. You do not have to decide now; and I do not want to pressure you with this, but, at least, take the time to think it over."

"But you are six years older than me, and...and there are many others you could choose, that must be more acceptable to the Sealand crown."

Par smiled at her with the same warmth Zerra had always remembered. "Age makes no difference once you grow old enough to see it. And my parents adore you, you know all this. I have thought this through a long time, Zer. I do not want anyone else. Just you. If you trust me, I will wait for you to decide."

Words said, the fair-haired Sealander pushed himself away from the princess, stood, and strode out of the concealing branches of the willow tree. Zerra lay there in the dark, trying to separate the turmoil of her thoughts and calm the rapid beating of her heart; the price had thoroughly shocked her. Yet, she knew her parents would approve a marriage between herself and Sealand. The two royal houses had been life-long friends. And, her brothers would be elated to have the prince in the family.

But—what of herself? Would she be happy? Marriage had never been one of her fancies—and to Par? She liked him all right, to be certain—after all, she had known him most of her life—but...Zerra still felt *so young*! The age gap between them had always been a little daunting. She looked up to the Sealander as an acquaintance of the family. Yet, Zerra knew there was only one question Par wanted her to answer: did she love him like he loved her? Or could she grow to love him...in *that* way?

"This princess thing really is a pain in the derriere!" She growled. Sighing in frustration, Zerra lofted herself up and pushed aside the willow tree's leaves. She stalked to the edge of the stream. It was only as she neared, that the form of Par's body took shape, startling her that the fact that the prince was still so near. "I thought you had left." She squeaked out and tried to ease her anxious heart.

"And I thought you would leave," Par's voice came out softly, "But then Serein's song told me you were not leaving but coming nearer."

Zerra paused, confused at the word the prince had used. "Who is Serein?" She asked as she joined Par by the water's edge.

Without explanation, Par reached into the collar of his shirt and lifted a necklace from around his neck. He held the silver chain in front of him and allowed the beautiful, glowing brilliance of its sapphire to pierce the darkness. A sweet ocean song poured from the stone. A moment later, it was answered by a mysterious nighttime call. Shocked, Zerra clutched the black stone at her breastbone. Her stone called again, and the two songs melded in the night.

"Serein calls to yours." Par said, his voice still quiet. "She calls herself that. Apparently, it means "water holder" in our ancient Landarïan dialect."

"The *stone* told you that?" Zerra asked, not sure if she was more skeptical or incredulous.

"Yes, and yours should do the same. It is some power they hold inside themselves. One day, I am sure your stone will talk to you and tell you its name."

Zerra glanced into the dancing facets of the black stone and watched the unusual light as it thrummed out into the darkness. "And I had thought it just a simple stone my father gave me..." she murmured.

"As did I on my Berneisse. My father promised he would tell me of its significance one day. I assume that means about what Serein really is, for she is certainly more than a simple, precious stone."

"Strange...my father said the same thing tonight, when he handed over this necklace. What do they know that we do not?" She asked, hoping Par would have an answer.

The Sealand prince shrugged. "All I know is that the stones are somehow connected." He turned his blue eyes to stare into Zerra's. Their sudden intensity brought a heat to her cheeks and her heart to pounding in her chest. The prince shifted toward her, until he was a hairs-breathe away. He paused for just a moment, as if uncertain, before pressing his lips to Zerra's. In the short time they kissed, Zerra realized the depth of the love the prince had for her.

Once the moment passed, however, Prince Par looked away, suddenly shy. "I am sorry. I should not have done that." Par averted his gaze to the water in his discomfort.

Zerra chuckled softly. "Now even I do not have that audacity! But you should not apologize for something you meant to do— especially if you are to do so again."

Par spun his head back around, shocked. "What!?"

Zerra grinned and stood up. "Maybe someday, I will be able to love you as much as you love me, Prince Par Fantill; but, until then,

I want you to know, I will be waiting for the right day to accept your proposal. And that day will come. Be prepared to woo me." Turning, Zerra fluttered away into the night, leaving Prince Par by himself to ponder her words.

II.

"You will hold, please, Royal House of Sealand!"

Prince Par, beside his father and mother at the head of the procession, craned his body around in the saddle to look back at the familiar voice. Beside him, his cousin also turned to see, while King and Queen Fantill exchanged knowing glances and ordered the line to halt.

Princess Zerra came sprinting across the courtyard. She was wearing rider's clothing of a comfortable leather tunic, and pants, and workmanlike field boots. Behind her ran a distraught hairdresser, still screaming at the princess to come get her hair finished—though it would have to be completely redone from her rushing to stop the Sealand procession. Ignoring the lady, the princess ducked through the crowded courtyard to slide to a stop beside the prince's large courser. "Good, you weren't gone yet." She huffed slightly.

Par chuckled in amusement and reached down to take the princess's hand. "You will be in trouble, as usual, for this escapade, princess."

"Who cares," Zerra shrugged and laughed along with the older boy. "I just wanted to see the royal house of Sealand off."

"We are very appreciative." Queen Kesnia thanked Zerra. Her eyes, though, had a look of knowing for whom the send-off was really for. "We will always welcome such courtesy at Seaside Fortress Opal. Please come calling at any time."

"We will. Thank you, Your Highness." Zerra politely accepted the queen's invitation.

Queen Kesnia nodded and waved the procession forward. Par's father caught his son's eye before he moved off. "Do not be long, son. We will wait on the southern roadway."

"Yes, sir." Prince Par bowed to his father and stepped his mount out of the way to let the others by; though, much to his annoyance, Gordar joined him.

As the line went past, Par looked to the princess to say, "Shall we ride through the orchards?" Zerra nodded, and, with Par's help, she swung up behind the prince to settle onto the courser's back. Ignoring his cousin, Par cued his mount to a canter and headed out of the bustling courtyard.

They turned away from the main road and into a stand of peach trees in bloom. Cantering leisurely, the two royals enjoyed the spring sun's warmth and the smell of morning dew that permeated the air. The trees were just blooming; the delightful waft of their sent mixed with the smells of dawn. It was a delight, that solitude of the moment.

Unfortunately, though, the stroll ended too quickly. They came to the end of the orchard and found an open wheat field sprawling out in front of them. The field had been left sallow, so Par held little thought of getting into trouble with King Lanar for tracking up the plot, however the empty land was a reminder of where they had come out; it was disappointing that they had ridden so far. Up ahead, Par knew, they would reach the south road and the place where he would have to part ways with the princess.

Indeed, the field ran into the southern road far too fast. Par sighed and eased his courser to a halt. Lord Gordar stopped his mount a few paces away, being ever the courteous Lord Protector. Par was still annoyed with his presence, however, and wasn't afraid to show it. Gordar stared back unblinking. "It looks awkward for a prince not to have his Lord Protector, Your Highness, even in these lands."

Par started to retort, but a hand on his arm stopped him. "He is right, you know. It was smart of Gordar to accompany you in the courtyard." Zerra did not have to tell him to be grateful.

"Since when did you start following protocol?"

"Since you tried to make us official to the court." Zerra replied, jutting her chin out. "Rumors have been flying around all morning."

Par was shocked. News had traveled that fast?! The gossip in the Crystal court was as fast as in his mother's court back home. Unsure what to say, Par was left speechless.

"She does not exaggerate," Gordar continued. "No disrespect intended, Highness, but I did not want you to look foolish back there."

Par pursed his lips at his cousin's sense. Finally, though, he relented. "No disrespect taken, cousin." He glanced away then and spotted the Sealand royal procession exiting the grove of trees. Everything was moving too fast! "I will miss you, Zer."

Zerra nodded solemnly. "And I you. During these times of war, there are no assurances when we will meet again...I just pray it is soon."

A chuckle sprang from Par's lips. "Anibus would have loved to hear you say that, just now."

"Yes, I am sure he would." Zerra smiled at the mention of King Fantill's nephew, Par's closest friend, and a priest-acolyte of the church of Estaria. A year older than Par himself, the young priest had been orphaned at three-years-of-age and raised in the palace with his cousins, up until his induction into the priesthood. "Send my best regards to him." Zerra asked of Par before she turned to Gordar. "And you, keep the prince from harm, Lord Gordar."

The golden-eyed lord bowed, as graceful as a swan. "He will be kept safe, My Princess—except for his pride, I am afraid. But no harm will come to him until your return to us. That I promise you, Princess." With his vow spoken, Gordar spun his horse away and galloped back to the line, leaving the two friends alone.

"He is one true to his word." Par commented to himself, watching his cousin's retreating back. "Do you know what kind of hell you have just imprisoned me to?"

"Less than what you will get from me if ill finds you." Zerra promised with a rueful grin. She added teasingly, "My betrothed-to-be."

Par followed suit in the shared joke before sobering. His eyes got that intense look in them, like the night before, and he leaned forward to kiss Zerra one last time. His hesitation was still there—and he decided to peck her on the cheek instead of her lips—but the feelings he had shown the other night were still hanging in the air. As he pulled away, Par's warm smile returned. He helped the princess down to the ground. "Happy Berneisse, Princess. May you be well, until our paths meet again."

Zerra watched the procession pass and disappear beyond the forest edge of mountain pines. Inwardly, she wished the Sealanders a safe and swift travel back to the distant coast. Once the line was completely out of her sight, the princess turned away and started the long jog back to the castle. However, just as she reached the line of peach trees, a loud neigh rang out in hello. Turning, Princess Zerra found Valed Darkness galloping down the line toward her. Farther back were two riders, one Zerra recognized as Zeek on Causinova; the other, she was unsure of, was riding a bay courser.

Vale slid to a stop in front of his young master and lowered his neck so Zerra could stroke his broad forehead. Sighing happily, he leaned into her firm strokes and directed her to an itchy spot at the base of his neck. Zerra laughed as Vale stuck his lip out, stretching his head high. He wiggled his lip in pleasure as she found the best spot. "You're such a ham, you know that?"

"Hey, you going to join us?" Zeek called from behind the black stallion. He and his companion halted their coursers a short distance from the pair. Zerra glanced to her brother's associate and found him to be Rowin Sunrise. "We're going up to the high mountain lakes, if you want to tag along." On second thought, he added, "We'll be gone all morning and maybe half of the afternoon. You'd be away from the castle most of the day."

They were just the words Zerra loved to hear. Anything that kept her from "women's work" was high on her list of things to do— even if she ended up in hot water when all was said and done. Practicing stitches be damned, she was going to join her brother on his excursion! With practiced ease, she swung aboard Vale.

Once seated, they surged forward like one being, both alike in body and mind. Leading the way, the pair raced through the wheat field and around the eastern side of demesne around the Crystal Castle. They headed for the wildlands to the north. Behind, the two princes' coursers pounded hard on Vale's heels; yet, they began to fade back as the stallion continued his unrelenting pace as he entered the pine trees that formed the northern forests trekking into the mountains. Soon, Vale and his rider left the other horses behind, and still, their pace did not slow. They thundered up a steep mountain side. Only when they reached the top did the great stallion finally stop.

The view from where they stood was breathtaking. All around the stallion and his rider sprawled snow-encrusted mountain peaks that pushed through a thick blanket of wispy clouds. Tundra grass covered the hard ground, and lichen-covered granite rocks dotted the landscape. Tiny flowers, in sparse clumps of white, blue, red, and purple, peeped out of the thin tundra grass, while budding mountain-willows covered the basins between the peaks and glassy lakes at the hollow of the bowls. In the distance, the giant chain of mountains disappeared in a blue haze, teasing the beholder on how far their beauty actually stretched.

Zerra took the short time she had to herself to relax on her horse's muscular back. She breathed deeply of the crisp, mountain air. Her heart pounded in her chest, beating out her wish for this freedom to last forever, that she would not have to worry about court life again, but the arrival of the two princes broke her revelry. Zerra sighed as Zeek reined Causinova beside Vale and pointed out the high mountain meadows to Rowin.

As she waited for her brother to finish, Zerra studied Rowin's mare, who could only be Blue Galeon. Galeon was, indeed, a finely bred mount. With a perfectly chiseled face, intelligent eyes, and well-flared nostrils, she was stunning. Her neck arched beautifully from a deep chest and broad shoulders, and long legs, as perfect as could be, looked powerful and ground-eating; Blue Galeon had the look of a grey-hound, long and lean. As a mare, she lacked the muscular build of Valed Darkness, whom was also bred for speed and power but all of Zerra's visions of a dainty little mare were dashed. In short, Blue Galeon was everything a fighter looked for in a charger broodmare.

Zeek turned to his sister, once he finished telling Rowin about the pastures. "Rowin wants to see the summer pastures up close to make sure they are adequate enough for Galeon, during her stay."

So, father must have agreed to breed her. Not that that is a surprise. "Very well. Vale and I know a quick trail to take, but you must follow closely because I won't slow down."

"Don't worry, My Lady, we can keep up." Rowin assured her. Zerra glared at the Sunrise prince and squeezed Vale into a canter. "Did I say something to offend her?" Rowin asked Zeek in confusion.

Zeek grinned, "She doesn't like being called a lady by most people. She's sensitive about that."

"Oh, I didn't know." Rowin frowned at the departing rider. "I will remember that next time..."

Zeek noticed the cautious glance Rowin had given his sister. "Zer really isn't a mean-spirited person. She is just not suited to be a court maiden. If you don't remind her of her position, she really is quite enjoyable to be around."

Rowin still looked uncertain, but he did let a polite smile light his lips. "I will remember give that a try; however, if we do not hurry after her, I will never be on the princess's good side."

"Agreed." Together, they asked their horses into a faster pace and caught up with Zerra and her tall stallion. In an almost companionable silence, the three of them came down the easy slop Zerra had chosen and galloped across a flat tundra basin to another trail. Their path led over another ridge and dropped into a large cirque. Lurking in its shadows were over two-dozen blue-blooded horses. They were the harem of Valed Darkness, and the large cirque was his wild domain.

At the sight of his mares, the black stallion bellowed his return and rushed forward, by his own will, to join his herd; Causinova and Blue Galeon pranced in excitement at seeing more horses but held back, as their riders told them to. Zerra vaulted off Vale as he slid to a stop beside his favorite mare, Sun Glory. She left her four-legged friend to join her brother and his guest as they untacked their coursers and let them free. They two princes joined the princess near the banks of the lake.

They sat tensely as Blue Galeon was approached by Sun Glory. As usual, Sun Glory, being the lead mare, decided if she accepted the new arrival into the herd. After some squawking and pawing, Sun Glory turned away from the taller mare and returned to munching grass. Blue Galeon wandered to the edge of the herd and settled down nervously to eating. Satisfied that there would be no fighting amongst the herd, the three high-born youths turned away to talk.

"This place looks well-suited for her needs." Rowin commented lightly. "I will not worry about her being here."

Zeek nodded his agreement. "We will give her the best care possible. King Lanar will send a watcher daily to check on the horses, and we will bring them in, if the weather turns ill."

"And, does Vale stay with his herd or do you separate him, after a time?"

Rowin's question, though directed to Zeek, was answered by Zerra. "He comes and goes as he pleases. No fences can hold him and no hand can tame him."

"Then why do you ride him?" Rowin tried not to show he was pointing out the fact that she was a girl and a princess. His challenge was blatant.

Zerra recognized his bias for what it was and scoffed at the prince's disdain. "I ride him only because he lets me. He has always been that way. Only the king and myself have been able to sit on his back."

Rowin recognized her quick temper from the night before and his own flared to life because of it. "So, what you are saying, is that the Crystal Kingdom's prized steed is really just a wild, untamed creature? I brought my prized mare to be bred to a rogue? This is unspeak-."

"Then take her and your insolent self back to your kingdom and leave us be!" Zerra sprang to her feet with fire in her eyes. "That "creature" you are looking down upon, of a sudden, is better than any courser you will ever come across. Do not forget, it was that fact that you wanted your mare here in the first place!" She turned her back on the two princes—one fuming, the other in angst—and ran to the herd of horses.

Vale left his companionable place beside Sun Glory to comfort his human friend. Zerra stroked his satin neck, to reassure the stallion that she was not angry at him, and whispered into his mane, "They never understand how truly amazing you are. If only outsiders could know you as I have come to...but, not now. Lend me one of your own to carry me away, to a place far beyond social graces." Vale seemed to nod, as if he understood her words, and nickered to his mares.

A fine-boned, steel grey came prancing out of the herd and flitted over to Zerra. She halted and lowered her finely chiseled, dished head to whuff the princess's hand. Zerra smiled and softly rubbed her hands over the mare's forehead and across her bright eyes, to soothe the lines there. "Rain. An honor that you would carry me." Rain nickered softly and raised her head. She arched her delicate neck and stood as still as a statue until Zerra was sitting atop her back. With a departing toss of her head, the spirited mare wheeled around and cantered away from the harem. They disappeared over the cirque's lip, with a parting flicker of Rain's silken tail.

Princess Zerra did not bother to give her brother and his guest a backward glance.

Prince Rowin watched her departure with a mix of surprise and anger. "Is your sister always so volatile?" He sounded both astounded and repugnant.

"Only on certain subjects." Zeek explained in his sister's defense. "Being a lady and anything to do with Valed Darkness would be on the top of that list."

Rowin had the sense to look embarrassed at the slight. "I only questioned the domestication of your prized stallion, not your sister's abilities with him."

"Valed Darkness is the best courser you will ever see; just as Zerra said. No other horse has been able to beat his speed and stamina. That is why people bring their best horses to the contests each Planting Time and Harvest-Gathering Time, in hopes that one of theirs will beat our champion. As of yet, Valed Darkness is undefeated. This fact is also why his offspring are so highly valued. You know these facts; it is the reason you sought out the stallion for the traits he passes onto his young. Do not let your knowing that Valed Darkness cannot be ridden by anyone but two people, diminish your opinion of his breeding capabilities."

Rowin felt thoroughly chastised but he had the mind to hold his tongue—lest he say something that insulted the Starkindlers more so. "Really, it is not my business what you do with him—only as long as he produces a blue-blooded offspring."

"That he will." Zeek promised. He stretched then stood and offered a hand to the other prince to help him rise. "I don't believe word of this incident will reach the king, but you should try to patch up the mess with my sister. Zerra is easy to forgive but forgets naught. Her tongue may be sharp, yet her influence with Valed Darkness can affect your breeding with Blue Galeon. You best not forget that." Zeek rose and whistled. Causinova trotted over at the signal. Zeek began to pile the two saddles on the horse's withers and back, slinging the two bridles over his shoulders.

"What are you doing?" The Sunarian asked.

"We're walking back," Zeek answered indirectly, "To give you time to think over things." Without embellishing, he started back across the pasture, pausing only at the cirque's edge to wait for the prince. "Besides, Prince Rowin, it's a great way to go sightseeing."

Rowin kept his grimace from his face. "You have weird ways of paying back insults, Starkindler."

Zeek shot him a firm smile. "It is not I who will pay you back your insult. My sister's dislike of you tends to lead her to indelicate reproof. Settle your issues with her before you leave—else, it may be a long while before she is on speaking terms with you; however, that may be hard to do, as I doubt Zer will let her presence be seen before your departure this afternoon."

Rowin understood the warning and hoped that he would get the chance to apologize to the princess. It was not that he was especially wanting to make any extenuations with the princess, but if it made Zeek happy and facilitated their friendship, then it was a small order. However, the afternoon came and went. Rowin did not get the chance to make amends, before the Sunrise departure. The princess's slight was answer enough of how she felt about the Sunarian royal. Rowin had to make do with his apology to her brother and thankfulness that the situation did not turn into anything; as, it seemed, the no one had gossiped of the event to the Royal House of the Crystal Kingdom. In relief that his Blue Galeon would stay on a a brood mare, Prince Rowin bid the northern kingsmen good-bye.

It was only after the Sunrise Kingdom's procession was well beyond the Crystal demesne that Zerra returned to the keep. She and her brother did not say a word about the tiff between Rowin and herself. It seemed the princess was willing to let bygones be bygones. With that unaddressed offense, the princess's Berneisse came to a mediocre end.

III.

Three months passed in quietude, with the fighting at the border just a distant reminder of the troubles outside the Crystal Kingdom. The four Starkindler youths spent their time training their war coursers. In usual fashion, the brothers secretly helped their sister learn the skills of bow and sword. As for the king, he returned often from the battlefield to see his family and report about the stalemate at the edge of the kingdom. For them all, the focus was not on the war so much as on the upcoming tournament, held on the eve of the new moon during Planting Time*.

[*Side note: The eight divisions of the year in the Syrean calendar: Deepest Snow, Snow Thaw, Planting Time, Flowering Time, Growing Time, Harvest-Gathering, Levies and Storage, First Snow (each 1.5 month/8 weeks long)].

The complacent mood was not to last, however.

In the stillness of an early summer morning, the beat of drums rang through the forest pines, accompanied by the clash of metal. Birds shrieked away from their quiet resting places in the pine boughs, and small forest creatures scampered nervously at the prelude of the marching feet. The enemy army broke from the forest, at the edge of the farthest peach orchard, its evil shape breaking the tranquility of the day.

Lance and the others had been practicing swordsmanship in the wheat field, under the watchful eye of their father, back from two weeks on the border. They had been hard at work, preoccupied with not getting hit, and it took some time to notice the danger nearing. Zerra was the first to notice the far-off army; her perch on Vale's back giving her more of a view of the landscape. She gave a terrored start at the sight of the unexpected enemy flags and choked back a cry. "Father, it-it's an army!"

King Lanar paled and rushed to his horse shouting, "Hurry, back to the castle! It's the maunstorz!" He heeled Victory between his sons and the army as they hurried to mount. His attempt seemed futile, since the army could easily hack him down—single, defiant obstacle that he was.

"Father, we must go!" Zerra begged as her brothers rode past. "You cannot take on the whole army by yourself!"

Lanar consented easily enough and whirled to follow his sons and daughter. They rushed to the safety of the orchard and galloped through the rows toward the castle. "We must find Matar and signal the Crystine." Lanar ordered as they ran.

Vale quickly overtook the other mounts with his longer legs and inherited speed. Soon, the pair disappeared up the main lane to the castle. Zerra knew every second counted if they were going to defend the keep. She crouched lower, becoming a part of her companion and edged him to higher speeds. They broke into the courtyard, scattering attendants and grooms in their wake. Vale skidded to a halt at the center of the yard, and Zerra yelled out her warning. "The maunstorz, the maunstorz have broken through! They are at the Northern road. All men to arms!" Everyone stopped and stared at the princess as if they had not understood her words. The whole place became deathly silent, leaving her voice to echo through the yard as she repeated the warning again and again.

Finally, Commander Matar appeared, dressed in his leather tunic and battle armor. "All men to arms! Come on you dullards, we must defend the castle!"

Zerra nodded her gratefulness at the veteran fighter and cued Vale up the main steps of the castle. She burst through the wooden doors, scattering the sentries there, and pounded through the anteroom. Servants stopped in astonishment as Zerra rode in on her dark mount, yelling for men to go to arms. The pair streaked right past the gaping attendants and bound up the main staircase.

Queen Lestial met them at the top with her hand on her hips. "Now you've done it! Running that animal through these halls. Out with him now!"

Zerra ignored her mother's furry. "The maunstorz are attacking! Father needs his broadsword from his chamber." Lestial turned a deathly white shade and hurried passed her daughter and horse to see the danger for herself. Zerra heard her yell orders to the servants below and saw them scurry for anything to protect themselves. "Let's go." The young girl nudged Valed Darkness down the long hallway and up a stone stairway.

They reached the third level and turned left to the king's private study. The princess slid down from Vale's back and thrust the heave oak door aside. She rushed through, into the oak-furnished room, and surveyed the tapestried walls for the black scabbard of Sorengraand. The broadsword hung beside a seven-shelved bookcase near the fireplace. Zerra stretched for it and nearly dropped its heavy weight as it slid free of its pegs. Burdened, she stumbled back to Vale's side and propped it against his left foreleg as she swung herself back aboard. Zerra hauled the broadsword up onto her lap and asked Vale back around. They took off again, back down the stairs and through the near-empty halls.

The black horse and his young rider bound out of the front doorway into a fray of warriors. The courtyard was in total chaos. Beyond the shouting of the Crystine soldiers, the sounds of a battle drifted back to the princess. She searched through the crowd but found neither her father nor her brothers among the horde; however, Commander Matar was ordering soldiers to horseback near the stables. She kneed Vale through the throng toward him, letting the stallion's powerful bulk shove the men aside.

Matar glanced up as she approached and frowned. "You must leave this area. We can't have you in the way."

Zerra glared back. "The king needs his broadsword." She indicated to Sorengraand in her arms. "He only had a short-sword in the field."

Matar paled as he realized what that entailed. "He can't possibly survive without more protection." The commander yelled for another man to take his place organizing and directing the soldiers. As another veteran took his position, he ran up to the towering stallion—ignoring the black's laid-back ears and cocked leg—and jumped aboard behind the princess. "He was just outside the wall a moment ago."

Zerra did not need to be told twice, though her black courser did; the stallion pinned over the uncomfortable, armored stranger on his back. Zerra coaxed him a few steps forward, begging him to go faster. Finally, the stallion seemed to realize her urgency was precedent, though he still gave a baleful snort at the affront. He charged through the gathered warriors, then, to the thrown open gates.

Two sentries there tried to stop them, for they were trying to get the solders in to close off the entrance way, but Matar ordered Zerra to push through. He shouted at the sentries to let others pass and ordered the nearby horsemen to group up and follow. Once outside, they turned right and galloped down the length of the high castle walls toward a small group of soldiers holding a maunstorz party at bay. Among the group, Zerra spotted her father and brothers hacking and shooting at the enemy. Lance caught sight of the black steed racing toward them and ordered the soldiers on the side closest to them to open up a breaths-width for the horses to pass through.

Vale slid to a halt beside Starwind, and Matar leapt off with Sorengraand in his hand. Zerra maneuvered herself so she was protected by her brother. She stretched for his bow and quiver. Zerra let loose a volley of twelve arrows into the enemy force before she ran out. Lance pushed her head down as the enemy shot back and knocked arrows away with his sword. "I can't hold for both of us for long!" He warned as the front line of Crystine soldiers were pushed back. Zerra nodded and pushed back a wave of fear at his words.

Suddenly, Matar was back. He jumped up behind the princess again and unsheathed his sword. "Do as I say and we may yet survive," he yelled in her ear. Zerra swallowed, feeling numbed, and took hold of the dagger he handed her. At his next order, she kneed Vale forward in a charge with the rest of the mounted soldiers. The line in front of them hacked at the enemy, breaking a small hole through of the maunstorz force. "Protect the king and the princes! We must get them back to the keep." Matar boomed out and the solders renewed their vigor from the three directions they defended. The western edge plowed through the enemy, allowing just enough space for the royal family to head back toward the gates. The rest of the cavalry followed.

Men all around Zerra and Matar were being hacked down, but the veteran kept them safe from the enemy blades. He urged her to work Vale up toward the front, and they edged through to the outside to stop a maunstorz interception force. Then, it was all over and the tiny group of fighters were passing through the front gates.

The tired band flowed into the courtyard, where it was finally cleared of soldiers. The Crystine had reached their places atop the wall, leaving only young squires and pages to take the lathered horses from the king's men. Zerra looked around her and saw many deep wounds on the soldiers. One was leaning off the side of his horse, spitting blood and wiping fervently at a gushing gash across his face. When he straightened, Zerra realized he was trying to cover the mess where his left eye had been. Sickened, she turned away only to see more men with wounds of their legs and arms and one man with just a stump where his fighting hand had been.

"Don't throw up of me." Matar commanded as he wrapped an arm around her to steady the princess. "You should go to the infirmary. You will be of more use there. Your horse is safe with me." To lighten his blow, he added, "You did well out there, girl. Be proud of that."

Zerra slid down from Vale's tall back and leaned against his massive shoulder to steady herself. When she finally regained her senses, she glanced back at the stern face of the commander. "Vale won't listen to anyone else. You'll end up fighting him more than the enemy."

Matar gave her a look that said, "I know." He touched the stallion gently, in a kind of assurance. "He and I know each other well enough, plus he is not going to try anything stupid in this hell— he's too smart for that." Zerra would have argued further, like the fact that her steed was tackless, but Zeek came over to drag her back to the castle. As she was led away, Matar shouted at her, "He will see you after the battle safe and sound, on my word, Princess!"

Zerra nodded numbly and turned away to join her three tired brothers in their climb up the main stairs. Page looked the worst, with a steadily bleeding gash in his shoulder. He sagged weakly against Lance, who seemed fine, even with a painful-looking cut above his right eye. Lance took his time guiding his younger brother up the steps, making sure to keep Page talking, so he wouldn't pass out with each jarring step. Beside Zerra, Zeek trudged wearily, cleaning his sword on a small cloth to distract his disturbed mind. Zerra read the lines in his face and realized her brother shared the same shaking cold as she did. After all, they had never seen battle until that day. Now that they had, Zerra understood why soldiers never talked about it much.

"You okay, sis?" Zeek asked, noticing her brooding countenance.

"Fine, I'm fine." Zerra managed to croak out. To show he understood, Zeek wrapped an arm around her shoulders and walked with her. "Is Page going to be all right?"

Zeek nodded. "I believe so. His wound looks minor, not at all as bad as it appears. He just caught the edge of a blade is all."

Is all. Zerra thought while they walked through the broad wooden doorway into the anteroom. Zeek must have seen the doubt shadowed in her eyes became he rushed to add, "Really, it's minor. If the sword had struck Page square on, he could have lost his whole shoulder."

"That didn't help." Zerra tried to joke with a forced smile. Zeek shrugged helplessly with an embarrassed look of his own.

The princess balked at the doorway leading to the infirmary. Even though the battle had just started, there was a soldier in each bed and seven more laying or sitting down, where room could be found. The nurses and maids were hustling about trying to take care of the wounded, but they were already taxed to their limit. Queen Lestial hurried over to inspect her sons, aghast at their appearances. She finished her inspection of Page's arm and wiped her hands on her bloodied dress. "Come on, let's get you cleaned up." She paused to look at the other two princes, though, lingering to be sure they were all right. "You two don't need to be here. Go somewhere where you're not in the way of the nurses."

Lance and Zeek left silently, numbed in the aftermath of their battle. Zerra watched them go, longingly, then turned back to her mother, knowing she would have to work. Lestial silently approved and motioned for her to help Page, as he hobbled over to an empty corner. Zerra steadied her elder brother, as their mother prepared him a bed, then lowered him down onto the thin pallet of blankets. More soldiers hobbled in as the two women settled Page into a comfortable position. Queen Lestial sighed raggedly and hauled herself to her feet to help, leaving Zerra alone to care for her brother.

Zerra dipped a cloth into herbal water and pressed it against her brother's injury. Page hissed in pain but held the cloth in place as his sister took her dagger to his shirt. Once the bloodied strips of cloth were removed the princess dabbed away the drying, crimson blood. She wet the rag again.

Between their silence the siblings became aware of the groans of the other soldiers and the loud grumblings of the newcomers. "They've broken down our defenses, My Queen. There is very little we can do, except try to hold our walls. Their numbers are great. Eventually they will overwhelm us. I fear we are at a loss." An old veteran of the Crystine army was telling Lestial. His companions voiced similar assessments, proving how truly unprepared the Crystine had been. Around the room, the princess heard similar words of, "How did they even get past our lines and without warning?" Everyone from the castle who heard became more troubled as the hopelessness of the situation filtered in.

The siblings exchanged a glance at the news. "Our kingdom will be lost." Page stated, his voice echoing Zerra's feelings of doom. "We never expected the maunstorz to reach the castle, let alone break through our outer defenses."

"It wasn't anything we had predicted." Zerra agreed. *It seems too impossible. How could they have gotten through the forces by Wynward's Crossing or did they get through at Tarry? Messengers should have come with a warning, at the least.* Her thoughts strayed to the possibility of an inside spy, but that thought seemed even more farfetched than the invasion. *However, this is war.* Page's groan brought Zerra back to her task. Concerned, she realized her brother had been going into shock. Now, he was a stark white color, cold to the touch, and was beaded with perspiration. Cursing, Zerra dipped her cloth and wiped her brother's face before covering him with more blankets.

A tiny, pained chuckle escaped Page's lips. "It's great to see a princess curse. You would have made a great soldier."

"You're not thinking straight." Zerra countered, to hide her surprise. Page had always scolded her endlessly on acting unladylike. He had, in fact, angrily told her off a number of times for it; for him to suddenly laugh about it seemed unusual. "Here, you need to drink this."

Page stared at her solemnly, fighting his pain and ignoring the offered medicine. "I mean it, Zer. I know I chastised you for it countless of times but only so you wouldn't be shunned by everyone at court—that's important you know, appearances I mean. Yet, it was always something I could count on you doing."

"Don't start any dying speeches on me," Zerra warned, "I am not ready to lose a brother."

Page chuckled again, only to finish with a hiss as his wound burned. "I'll try not to, sis. I'd miss your petty arguments, after all."

Zerra smiled in spite of her growing sense of despair. Could her brother really die from such a wound? She didn't know, for she was no physician.

A loud thunder of feet in the hallway surprised everyone in the room. Sensing something was wrong, Zerra grabbed her dagger and rose into a defensive posture beside her brother's bed. Just as she did, a large group of eighteen maunstorz blocked the entrance way. Their eyes were an eerie blood-red color that matched the dull gleam of human blood on their dark armor. The look was haunting beneath oil-slicked, spiked hair and the tattoos that some had across their arms and faces. Hissing victoriously, the front maunstorz, their leader, sauntered into the room. His eyes took in the room hungrily. The look paused on the princess guarding her brother in the corner.

"Cvesoth zerek nevser shevnk!" He crowed and pointed at the two siblings. "Take them and search for the others. Zepthanial had uses for them." The leader's voice sounded ragged in the common tongue but Zerra knew what he had said. Whomever this Zepthanial was, he wanted her brothers, and maybe herself, for reasons she was sure included much harm.

Queen Lestial knew it too. In fear, she threw herself between the maunstorz and her children. "You won't ever have them!" Her words seemed to reveal she had a secret about what the maunstorz wanted, but Zerra could only guess at what her mother was trying to warn her against.

The leader hissed out an amused laugh. "Our great Mansocan had no use for you, Queen Lestial." To his warriors he said, "Kill her."

It took a moment for the words to sink into Zerra's mind. Once they did, however, Zerra realized what that entailed. She also realized her mother stood defenseless against her own killers. "No!" The princess screamed and pushed past her mother just as the first maunstorz brought his sickle-shaped sword down. She blocked the powerful blow and rushed in to stab the creature in the throat. Unthinkingly, she turned to her next opponent and blocked his sword too; however, she had never fought so many opponents before and was quickly subdued. The leader laughed at her rebellion and had her hustled away, but not before he had her witness her mother's death: Queen Lestial stood stone-still, except for her constant swallowing. A warrior raised a weapon behind her and ran it through her back and out her abdomen. The queen gaped in pain but refused to give them the pleasure of a cry. It seemed as if the minutes passed slowly before the queen slouched, lifeless, to the ground. The warrior kicked her body off his sword as if she was garbage and advanced to where the prince lay. Another maunstorz followed him and helped lift the prince, cursing under his breath from the jostling of his wound, to his feet.

Zerra was half-dragged and half-carried to the courtyard where she was dumped into a pile with her brother. In shock over the suddenness of her mother's death, Zerra didn't notice when they were joined by her father, Lance, and Zeek. When the still-warm body of the queen was thrown in front of them, however, her eyes did clear to take in the harsh reality.

"There's your queen, *oh powerful* king!" The leader spat on Lanar's face with pleasure. "Oh, how defiant she was." The maunstorz laughed as if it was the greatest joke they had ever heard. "And so proudly did she stand as my man impaled her on his sword."

Lanar's muscles clenched on his jaws but didn't respond nor did he look at the lifeless form of his wife.

Satisfied, the king had gotten his message, the leader motioned for his gathered army to collect the royal family. "We march them back to Xerconvith. Leave the Crystine swine to rot here in their courtyard. Their corpses will signal to all the kingdoms their coming doom."

The princess was prodded to her feet beside her brothers and marched down through the bloodied courtyard. In sudden impulse, she glanced back and found Commander Matar staring after her, from his fallen place at Valed Darkness's hooves. An arrow protruded from his thigh and blood covered him from head to toe, but there was a fire in his eyes that seemed to tell her to be strong. Even after she vanished out of his sight, his intense, midnight-blue gaze played in front of her. *So, we will go to this Xerconvith far to the north and west.* Her heart hardened with resolve, even though the pain over the loss of her mother made her chest constrict. *I cannot fall. People need to know of the cruelness of these maunstorz. I swear, if I can escape, they will pay!* Her vow echoed inside her head long after they were marched from the kingdom of her homeland. With it, the image of the Crystine commander spurred her resolve into a hard drive for survival. Somehow, the maunstorz would pay.

IV.

The oppressive heat from the noonday sun, pressed down on the floundering group of captives and the enemy army. The dry, desert air sucked away their moisture, leaving cracked and burned skin and ever thinning bodies. The princess and her second eldest brother were the worst off, barely able to trod along in the back of the procession. Page was becoming delirious from a fever; Zerra was no better off, having suffered from helping her burdened brother along—their captors having thought it quite amusing that only she, the female of the group, should get to shoulder her brother's weight.

Slowly, the princess's resolve was weakening...and the hours seemed to meld into one long struggle. She could no longer remember her count of how many days they had been prodded along, she was so exsiccated. It seemed like an eternity ago since she had drunk of the sweet, mountain air and felt the cool breeze on her skin.

Finally, Zerra's step faltered, and she tumbled to the burning sands. She struggled to rise, only to find her shaking legs would not hold her. In despair, she looked to her brothers and father—but they seemed to be held in a trance. Zeek met her gaze briefly, and sluggishly still at that, but was prodded on by a sharp sword. The maunstorz leader came to look down at her in mocking disgust. "She's done for. Leave her. Mansocan does not need her, anyway. The other should survive by eating her share of the food; we need him to, at least." He waved his warriors on and bent down in front of the princess. "We'll let the predators have a go at you—if ye don't die of heat exhaustion first." His laugh echoed hollowly in her ears.

The band trudged on and soon disappeared into the haze of the desert. Zerra sat dully where she had fallen and gazed after them long after they had vanished into the haziness of the horizon. Then, she closed her eyes to the heat of the yellow sun, feeling as if her entire body—down to her very bones—had become fire and dust. Letting go her exhausted breath, she allowed the Aras Desert to consume her into unconsciousness.

It was said that, at the beginning of time,
the Stars created for the eight kingdoms
each a secret weapon, a Stone of Power
with majiks beyond the imagining.

Morning Star created the diamond, Sheveth,
and gave it to Prince Menol of Rubia.
Evening Star then made a sapphire, Serein,
and presented it to Faliss of Sealand.

In turn, Yellow Star gave the citrine, Amun,
to Prince Al'rever of Staria,
while Red Star created a ruby, Kevel,
as a gift to Prince Rishard of Sunrise.

Next, North Star gaze Jezzen of
Blue Haven the jade stone, Bellor,
and South Star gifted the crystal, Ravel, to Perin
the eldest of the Crystal Kingdom's princes.

White Star gave the Golden
Kingdom's prince, Lormond, a pearl, Sevén.
On the last day, Black Star gave the obsidian stone, Vauldin,
to King Trev'shel of Crystalynian, at the high-seat of Syre.

With the last gift, a promise of power
was given for which none of the others could hold...
Though the wisest claim that these
powers will one day bring life to the
Kingdoms of Syre. Others say that they are what
cast the maunstorz on the world...

Part I

§

(Year 110 SC, Growing Time)

Chapter One

§

Meeting

It was considered the most exciting bar to enter when traveling through the Crystal Kingdom, and it was the best place to find whatever you were looking for—especially if what one sought was either pleasure or the Crystine Guard. The tavern itself was rebuilt, for the invading maunstorz had burned it down years ago, during their rampage.; the maunstorz had been successfully pushed out of the kingdom by the Crystine soldiers. Yet the marks of the enemy pillage remained. Men, mostly battle-hardened soldiers and farmers, consistently filled the casinos and bar room of the tavern looking for pleasure, solitude, or an occasional strike of good luck. Often, there was at least one of the original Crystine soldiers—of which only two-hundred-and-fifty still remained after the horrible conquest of the Crystal Kingdom's castle. These men usually occupied the booths at the back of the tavern reserved for that elite group.

This day was no exception from any other. The place was packed full with men discussing how great—or miserable—their lives were as they guzzled down their whiskeys or beers. Dancing girls flitted about the room, teasing the customers or cheering them on in their gambling. Shuffling around in the revelry was a handful of Crystine soldiers. They had entered Harry's through the back door. Pushing past drunkards, they made their way to their customary round booth in the back-most corner. Harry himself came around the bar to order their drinks, then he hurried away to leave the veterans to their peace.

Commander Matar, sitting in the center, shifted his lanky frame to survey the room. His deep, midnight-blue eyes took in every detail of the tavern before shifting to the young man beside him. "You said they would be here," he spoke softly to his companion.

The dark-haired man, with a coppery complexion and stunning, brown eyes that marked his desert blood, answered in return. "As they have said, so they have done. The flower of Evalaus was seen at the window."

Matar relaxed his chiseled features to show he had found humor in the younger man's words. "Count on a Tashek of Staria to answer cryptically. At least we know that they have come inside."

"Commander," the desert man bowed his head in way of agreeing. They quieted as Harry brought their drinks. Terrik sipped his mead as he waited for their host to leave then he picked up the conversation again. "Zyanthena reported following them here from Mere. They traveled lightly and were a mixed bunch, six in number. She was uncertain of their origins, however, and had some reservations about them. She was going to ask around to see if any of the border camps remember them crossing."

"Your spy network is lacking a little it seems."

"We can do only so much, Commander. Even we have our limits, as you know. When we are not allowed closer than 'scope distance from our quarry, it is harder to ascertain such details as you've desired from us. But, if you find our skills deficient, you can assign others to our job, Khataum". Brown eyes flashed his irritation. "I would be happy for the reprieve. We've been sent hither and yon for many moons turning. As it is, the Tashek have only so many resources here in the Crystal Kingdom; the rest are spread thin across the North. The Shi'alam explained all this when you sent to him for aid."

As usual, Matar was not certain how to take the Tashek's words. Was he complaining or being matter-of-fact or curt? It was so typical for the desert people to mask their emotions behind long, interlaced sentences so as to confuse the listener to their true meaning. The Crystine commander considered the Tashek masters at saying nothing and everything at the same time. For most outsiders, it made their heads' hurt—but they were very good at their job.

Matar had only just met Terrik Sheev'arid, son of the Tashek leader (called a Shi'alam) two fortnights passed. Though when he had been a younger man, he had lived among the desert warriors for a good handful of years, Matar found the Shi'alam's son especially hard to cipher. He declined further comment and turned to speak to his other soldiers, knowing Terrik would watch the room; the Tashek's eyes missed nothing.

A few minutes later, Terrik leaned over to whisper, "Zyanthena has returned. She will have report from the posts at Wynward's Crossing and Mere. Maybe she found out more about our visitors."

Matar turned to see where the woman had entered. Terrik whispered her position to him, and the commander found her, after a second look, camouflaged at the entrance. Though Zyanthena Sheev'arid posed a striking figure at most times, the desert woman could also use her smaller stature to disappear into a crowd. Matar hardly recognized her in a disguise of a plains-woman from the Golden Kingdom. Her raven hair was hidden from sight in a hood of glistening gold; the color made her look older than her twenty-one years. Terrik purred appreciatively at his clansman, showing just a little of the affection he had for her.

The Tashek woman was intercepted at the doorway by Sesha, the lead dance girl. The two women spoke with Zyanthena constantly shaking her head and pointing at a back table. Once she won their argument, Sesha led her to a small, corner table. The dance girl turned away with an annoyed look on her lovely face.

"She must have been trying to recruit Zy'ena as a dancing girl again." Matar commented with a light chuckle and returned to his ale.

Terrik glanced at his clansman once more before tearing his eyes away. "Zee told me, once before, that she doesn't comes here because of the drunks running around acting stupid; however, I think she was more worried about the dancing girls being wonton and half-dressed."

Wix, Matar's second-in-command, let out a bellowing laugh. "Why would she be scared of women? She's the toughest bitch I know."

Terrik glared at the veteran, somehow offended by the remark. "Men she can beat up for their insolence. Women, however, are too soft, a conundrum of breakable glass and wells of tears."

The Crystine soldiers burst out laughing, and Wix slapped the man beside him in the back. "The kid's got a soft spot for the lady, Madden; spoutin' poetry in her defense."

"Yeah," Madden joked back, "Too bad Z' don't notice. She'd find it amusin', I bet."

Terrik scoffed at the remark and said in his defense, "Zyanthena is my sister. It's my duty to speak for her."

"Yeah, but she's not blood. Adopted isn't that what ye said?" Madden threw back. "That means she's open game, boy." The soldier patted an imaginary booty, overly-enthusiastically.

The group burst out laughing again. Terrik's eyes burned cold, but he was left with no reply sharp enough to do himself justice. Finally, though, Matar waved them down. "Enough or all of you can take a turn washing the Crystal Castle top to bottom with the pages."

The soldiers settled down and quietly returned to their drinks.

Terrik turned his gaze back to the cloaked Zyanthena, waiting for some signal they used to communicate. Conversations droned on in the tavern. A few minutes passed then the Tashek woman lifted her hand, as if to rub a temple, and she crossed her fingers a certain way. "Zyanthena says they are here sitting at the table by the eastern wall." He waited again as she dropped her hands with another signal. "The party is as reported. Six in all and armed."

Wix bent over near Madden to tease the Tashek again. "I think they make that up."

"Yeah," Madden agreed, "Too few signals to be real."

Matar glared at them for silence. "Tell her to go visit with them," he told the Tashek. "She will meet them outside at noon and bring them to us."

Terrik signaled the response back and watched as Zyanthena leaned back in her chair, pretending to stretch, then rose from the table.

§   §

Zyanthena acknowledged her Tashek brother then ignored his brandy-eyed stare as she continued with her assignment. Terrik, she knew, would be watching her every move until they left Harry's Ruby.

Their potential clients were seated at the other, round-table in the back, a sign that they were wary of the place. Zyanthena noted the fact in her mind as she wove her way toward them. Keen brown eyes assessed the six men at the booth. The two at the sides of the curved booth were most likely soldiers. The younger one on the left was from Blue Haven, she surmised, for he sported the thinner bone structure, the tall height, and brown hair of a Havenese. His clothing was less disguised than it should be for a man under cover—the dark blue of Havenese dye was evident and the blue and white crest, in the shape of a flame denoting his claim to the Havenese militia, was left in plain sight. The other lad, however, must have had more experience in the field; he could still be marked as a soldier, but Zyanthena had a harder time placing him. Her guess was that he was from the Sunrise army, maybe even of high rank. The man had chosen the look of a wilder but the shine of his gold buckles and the beautiful artistry of his weapons gave away his social class. At least he had dressed sensibly; Zyanthena approved of his style over the rest of his companions'.

The other four men seemed to be of lesser standing—or that was what they wished to portray. The man next to the Havener was dressed as a merchant. Expensive-looking clothing adorned his lanky frame; though, in truth, the garments probably cost a doc at a local store. The high rise of his forehead and pointy chin mixed alluringly with his chiseled facial features and dark chestnut hair. There was something about his features that made the Tashek woman surmise he was from the Sunrise Kingdom; yet, it was the look in his deep midnight-blue eyes that pulled a cord of familiarity in Zyanthena mind—if she could place where the thought had come from... Perturbed, the warrioress decided to ignore the feeling. She stored it away for a later time.

Next to the Sunarian merchant was a youth who sporting similar facial features of pointy chin and high forehead of most Sunarians. This man had auburn hair and hazel eyes. He looked to be the merchant's apprentice or perhaps his slave (as was common in Sunrise) and was barely into adulthood. Zyanthena frowned at that thought, for she had always disliked the Sunarian practice of the upper-class taking slaves. Her own people abhorred the custom.

The final two men, could be written off as veritable. After all, one was a priest of Estaria, decked out in the usual robes and impresa of his religion around his neck. The Estarian priests were trusted by nearly all Syreans. His companion was just as familiar—a hired guard of Rubia, one of many seen frequently in the kingdom because of the shared border between it and Rubia.

It was the priest of Estaria who noticed the Tashek first.

Zyanthena waited for the group to quiet their chatter before nearing their table. She turned to the Sunarian guard on the right; the one the priest signaled to speak with her. The desert warrioress offered a greeting of hello and peace. The man returned it. "I know you by the crown of eldlaus wings," Zyanthena murmured the phrase they had decided to use. "I am Zyanthena of the Sheev'anee and Tashek scout in the Crystine. I serve under Commander Matar." In respect the man should have answered with his name and rank but Zyanthena saw him pause, as if ready to lie.

"I am Anibus of Sealand, Tashek," the priest's voice called her attention. He pushed back the cowl of his midnight-blue robes to reveal his face. The lines of the Sealand royal family were easily written there, framed by his long, brown-hair and blue eyes. "My companions wish not to be known—for now at least—not until we are away from this place."

Zyanthena felt herself pause at the priest's down-to-earth character; it was a rare commodity in the life of war. Finally, though, she nodded acceptance. "I will meet you outside, near the smithy." She kept her orders short and simple. "Do not leave right away. Matar will meet with you after the high of noon." Zyanthena turned away then without waiting for a reply. She walked away through the crowd. Sidling up to the bar, the Tashek ignored the patrons there as she waved down the barkeep.

Harry came over to her, recognizing her as one of Matar's men. "Hi, little missy...ah, Zy'ena, dear." He used Zyanthena's informal name, by her behest, since he could never quite pronounce the full name accurately; Zyanthena had taken pity on the man after three failed attempts. The heavy-set bartender asked, "What can I do for you?"

"Just a mead, please." She replied. "More, I was more wondering if you had wish for news?"

"That's my lass!" Harry joked as he passed her a pint. Zyanthena gave the bartender a dark look. She may have decided weeks before to not complain about the bartender's pet names—knowing it was common place in Harry' pub—but they still bothered her to no end. Tashek were not known for nicknames that were shallow or "cutsie", as Sasha professed them; however, it would be a waste of her breath to mention her dislike. "Hm, let's see now. I hear them maunstorz have retreated into Staria; seems we have ye to thank for that. Or, is it that I heard wrong?"

"You heard true." Zyanthena bowed her head in thanks, as she lifted the tankard of mead and took a sip. "Not that I will take credit for the last advance, mind you. The Tashek and Crystine cavalry were able to push the maunstorz back passed the Red Hills. Fifteen were lost in the advance, but we were able to take down ten separate war parties. The enemy still relies on small collections of fighters to infiltrate the border, an error much to our advantage. I was the one to come across the last three camps, all hidden near Wynward's. They should not be that close for some time now."

"Thank goodness, little missy, you always get 'em good and beat!" Harry cheered genuinely and turned to serve a stuporred patron before returning again. "I keep tellen' everybody about your holdin' the Crossing for a half-day by yourself. Most find your feat incredible an' noble. I—." Harry cursed and had to turn away to yell at a drunken farmer. He turned back. "I know I ask every time, but have you any guess to the war's end? And, too, have you thought more on what your plans will be after? Last time I asked, you had no idea on either account."

"Alas, I still do not. If it is possible to defeat the maunstorz, a long reprieve will be appreciated by all but this war just seems to drag on into the next year. There is no foreseeable end to it." Zyanthena paused to taste the honey mixture in her glass before moving on to Harry's other question. "As for myself, I have no clue as to what my future holds. The Stars refuse to tell me." Harry chuckled, for he had learned that Zyanthena, though Tashek, did not follow her people's religion very piously. "But you know, the wilds have been calling of late. Maybe this war is losing its hold on me." She shrugged. "After all, what real use is a Tashek when there is no fighting about? We are born for war. The Starian kings have used us for centuries to fight their battles."

"More good than you realize, little missy." Harry patted her hands affectionately. "Remember, little lass, Tashek are very lucky. Both to themselves and others." He winked.

Zy'ena let go a mocking chuckle. "Yeah, I'll bet you made that up." She finished off her mead and threw two pence on the bar. "I have scouting to do so I best be going. Give regards to Eliza."

"Will do. You take care now, missy. The Stars do watch over you."

Chapter Two

§

A Request from Fortress Opal

The smithy's furnaces were searing hot that day causing young Decond's usually fluid movements to slow and become pudding-like. His master, drunk as always, had passed out in the back by the cool water barrels leaving the seventeen-year-old to work the day away.

Today, the second day of the week, Decond would be molding more shoes for the cart horses. It was promised to be a quiet day, uneventful; the kind of day he wished he could sneak off to the pubs to find a girl or try to catch a friend or two with a few pranks; however, the arrival of a few clients kept him chained to his job.

Anibus had taken his group to the smithy as instructed. It was almost noon but the priest saw no sign of their contact. The only other person around was a young smithy working a piece of metal by the furnaces. The lad looked up, none too happy at the interruption, and came over to the companions. Anibus bowed as he neared.

"What can I do for you?" Decond asked as politely as he could spare.

The priest of Estaria answered back kindly. "We have a horse that threw a shoe coming up the pass through the Buckwin Hills. Could you, kind master, reshoe our horse?"

"The cost is four decets," Decond told them truthfully—he had heard priests knew when you were lying. "A high price because of the war. I cannot lower it."

"That is fine," Anibus answered gently and handed the amount to the youth. "Jacen," the priest called to a Havenese man, "Could you bring the sorrel here?" The man called Jacen left. He returned with a fine brown courser that shined like a copper pense.

Decond took the horse's lead like he had been handed a fragile piece of glass. "What a fine animal," he cooed as he got to work constructing a shoe.

Anibus nodded in kind. "A horse of very fine breeding though I had to pay a fair price to get him." Decond nodded to show he had heard as he lifted the hoof, cleaned it, and leveled it out. With great care, the youth rasped then clipped the hoof wall smooth and reformed the wall to its correct shape.

Decond was just finishing the last nail when another customer appeared; coming to the smithy riding a tall, medium-boned stallion. The entire group turned to watch the horse and rider's approach, entranced. The grey stallion was magnificent, moving like a ballet dancer, light of foot and well balanced. With a stately neck, he looked high-schooled. His rider slowed the great steed to a halt and dismounted. Decond left the shadows and the visitors in the smithy to greet the new customer. When he neared, he recognized the pretty woman "Zee! Wow, how long it's been?! What are you doing here?"

The raven-haired woman hugged the youth in greeting. "My master wishes for Majestic to have new shoes."

"Of course, my lady. New shoes coming right up." Decond lead the grey stallion to another open stall. As if he suddenly remembered his other guests, Decond turned to Anibus. "Sorry for the interruption gentlemen. Your horse is finished. May I introduce you to my friend, Zee. Zee this is—." Decond paused and waved her to the priest when he could not give a name.

Anibus extended his hand to the woman and smiled warmly into her eyes. The eyes! Anibus noted the sharp, brandy color, the only facial feature he could have picked out on their hooded contact's face. Here she was, uncloaked, in a fine, red-velvet servant's dress! "Hello, miss. What a fine steed you have. Is he of the Farwind linage?"

"Why yes, gracious priest. My master has quite a few war courses out of that line." Zyanthena's smile was truly dazzling; it made her remarks seem all the sweeter. "I see your sorrel is of no lesser breeding. If I am not mistaken, he is a Landarïan horse from the coast of Solé near the royal palace?"

Anibus could not help raising his eyes in surprise. "You are very observant, miss." The priest led his gelding near so Zyanthena could study him closer. "This is Capet a courser out of the city Opal. He's as close as you can get to a royal-bred horse in my home area. Of course, even Landarïan blue-bloods are not as well-bred as those from the east. Majestic shows true breeding."

Zyanthena seemed pleased enough with Capet's looks. However, when she spoke again the subject wasn't close to the subject of horses and their breeding. "May I ask you gentlemen what brings you to the Crystal Kingdom? You certainly do not look like men in search of pleasure."

Anibus caught the warning in her eyes, and he knew he had better give a legitimate answer in front of the smithy, Decond. "We were really looking for a place to break from the rigors of war. My merchant friend and I, being familiar with the area, volunteered to take these men to a haven somewhere in the back country. These men have seen many battles and have been given only a month's leave. Their commanders suggested we ask after the Crystine to find boarding. Would you, miss, have any ideas on where I might be able to meet with the Crystine?"

Zyanthena seemed to approve of his story. "I cannot tell you if the Crystine would have room for men such as yourselves, but my master, whom owns much of the lands west of the Crystal Castle, may have empty beds for you; though, I would suggest meeting with the Commander of the Crystine at the Castle. Only he can give you permission to stay on the lands around the demesne, and he will want to know your business here. Since the...loss of our King and his sons, the Crystine commander has become the highest authority in the kingdom. Would you, kind priest, like to have a word with him?"

Anibus glanced at the others and realized most had not recognized the woman as their contact. They were giving him unsure glances. Jacen, at least, nodded his acceptance to the proposal. The priest of Estaria turned back to the woman. "I think that is a grand idea, miss. Your master sounds like just the kind of host we're in need of. Thank you."

Zyanthena smiled. "Good. Once Majestic is reshod, I will take you to the Crystine then my master's keep."

§   §

The party of seven left the little smithy and headed west out of the town. Zyanthena led, with Anibus riding next to her; the others followed along skeptically. Once the small band had left the sight of the village, their beautiful contact turned off the main trading road and paused in a clearing beyond. Anibus followed obediently though the others expressed their unease with their guide.

"Calm yourselves." Anubis soothed. "Zee is taking us where we need to be."

"But this is not the way to the Crystal Castle. This woman may be leading us into trouble," the Sunarian merchant argued. "Remember, we have been warned to watch out for miscreants and bandits."

Zyanthena kneed her horse around to flash a very cutting glare at the man. Her countenance took the men by surprise and caused a few to back their horses away. "Only a royal ass could say such a thing of a Tashek!" The desert woman noticed the nervous glance from the other Sunarian man—the apprentice—but dismissed it as being out of concern for the protestor. She centered her attention fully on the Sunarian merchant. "For your peace of mind, sir, since you are obviously too dense to think of this on your own, I am Zyanthena, scout of the Crystine, and your only contact to reach Commander Matar."

The merchant man watched the angry glare of the Tashek. "If you are our informant then why not take us directly to the castle? This direction goes to the town, Newash, west of here."

Zyanthena stared at the rich merchant for a long time before turning her horse away. As she passed by Anibus and the Havenese man, Jacen, she muttered, "If he so much as insults me again on this trip, I will knock him out. I have not time to tell a Sunarian every precaution Commander Matar wishes me to make."

Jacen and Anibus shared a concerned glance but the priest nodded at her order. "We will tell our friend but nothing rash need to be done over such a petty misunderstanding."

"Then, keep his mouth shut." Zyanthena hissed, still annoyed, and cued her horse into a trot.

The rest of the trip was uneventful, much to Anibus's relief. Zyanthena was a good guide hurrying in open places to reach the safety of the pine trees. She tread carefully and pointing out areas of concern to their mount's feet. It was clear she knew the land well. With an ease that the Tashek were known for, she led them straight around the wild country to the Crystal Castle's back pastures. As the snow-colored castle came into view, the Tashek slowed the horses to a walk. "I will take you no farther," she told Anibus. "My master wishes for me to remain here. Up ahead is the stables and courtyard.

This road leads straight there. Leave your mounts with the men and go into the castle. Commander Matar will meet you in the war room."

"I thank you, Tashek." Anibus bowed his head. "Shall I give your commander a good word about your assistance?"

Zyanthena averted her eyes, as if ashamed of such a request. "No, priest, my commander will not need such a word. He will know what I have done when he sees you." The Tashek turned her grey stallion and quickly left the group. With her absence, the other men relaxed their tight postures. Only Anibus watched the desert woman leave.

"She is pretty intense if you catch my drift." Jacen said, as a way of averting the priest's eyes from the parting rider. "Come now, Anibus, our message to Matar is still awaiting its delivery."

"Yes, I know." Anibus smiled at the warrior. "Lead on, my friend, lead on."

Another Tashek met the small group at the castle entrance. He smiled disarmingly and bowed as they climbed the stairs. "Welcome to the Crystal Castle. I am Terrik Sheev'arid. My commander has informed me that your time is pressing."

"It is," Jacen replied. "We carry word from the Fortress Opal and North Point." He pulled out a sealed parchment and passed it to their greeter. "May we see Commander Matar?"

"Commander Matar feels as you do." Terrik answered oddly but went on say, "He will see you right away."

Terrik floated ahead of the others, his willowy frame lost in the flowing contours of his desert garb. To the visitors, who had not been around the desert people much, the Tashek seemed an entity from another world. Most of the group hung back but Terrik pretended not to notice their behavior. "In here, good sirs." Terrik waved his coppery hand toward the entrance of the war room. "Commander Matar will receive you alone." The men filed past quickly. Once they had all passed into the war room, Terrik turned to block the doorway from visitors.

A middle-aged warrior sat at the far end of the long table, his hands steepled in front of him in a calculating manner; his midnight-blue eyes shown intelligently under barely salt-and-peppered, deep-chestnut hair, cut in a military length; his body was encased in the light armor of the Crystine cavalry. Surrounding the commander was the near-empty war room. Most of its former glory had been lost to the maunstorz pillaging; however, the eight stones that represented the old kingdoms had not been picked out of their pillars.

The true opulence of the room, the stone-inlaid pillars started their tale to the commander's right then went on around the oval. The first was inlaid in quartz crystal from Mount Alon, behind the castle. The words King Perin and Queen Kella, first rulers of the Crystal Kingdom, were etched below on a glossy stone base. Continuing on were the other kingdom's pillars, inlaid in their colors and first rulers respectively: King Al'rever and Queen Dest of Staria, inlaid in topaz stone; King Lormond and Queen Savala, set in mother of pearl, for the Golden Kingdom; King Rishard and Queen Leanna in Sunarian ruby; King Faliss and Queen Quartney in Sealand's sapphire; and King Monol of Rubia and his consort, Doris, in diamond; and, in the final pillar, was the plaque for Crystalynian. Instead of the kingdom's first rulers, the names King Trev'shel and Queen Kestral—last to govern the province before its fall—were chiseled in a rare assortment of black and white obsidian.

The companions halted to study the dead kingdom's plaque. It was the last, surviving emblem of Crystalynian—all others had been destroyed in maunstorz raids or had not survived the horrible, earth shaking destruction of the kingdom itself. Realizing they were gaping, the six men turned quickly to their seats hoping they had not angered their host.

The fifty-some-years-old veteran was not irritated, however. He had learned to let visitors stare at the stone plaques in the war room, to his advantage; not only did it allow Syreans to admire the plaques of their kingdoms, it gave the Crystine leader a chance to study them unobtrusively. Today it seemed, Zyanthena had brought him a priest, three Sunarians, a Havenese, and a Rubian—just as she had reported. "Welcome to the Crystal Castle. I apologize for its bareness, but, alas, the maunstorz have stripped it of its former glory."

"We are sorry to hear of this plunder." Anibus replied sincerely. "But rumors gave us some warning. The rumors are not why we have come, however. Other business is more pressing."

Matar sat back in his chair. "Quite to the point you are, young priest. I like that." The commander shared a wink with Terrik, as the Tashek turned to the hint in the man's voice. "But even as time is pressing, Terrik and I are still sticklers for knowing the names of our guests."

The Estarian priest replied, "I apologize for such rudeness, Commander, Tashek. I am Anibus Farryl, cousin of and nephew to the royal family of Sealand. Beside me are: Jacen Novano, eldest son of Commander Barret Novano of Blue Haven; Rio Ravesbend, son of Commander Loris Ravesbend of Sunrise; and Patrick Kins, eldest son of Commander Ethan Kins of Rubia." The three soldiers stood and saluted respectfully. Matar returned the greeting from his chair, nodding with familiarity at the names of the three commanders' sons. Being a commander himself, he had made sure to keep tabs on the other kingdoms' war leaders. Anibus continued, "To my left is Roland Seagold, a merchant from Sunrise, and his assistant Sage Cooper. They have some training in weapons but were mainly here as our cover to cross the borders between kingdoms."

Again, Matar nodded. A merchant could very easily be traveling with guards to avoid unnecessary exploitation of their goods. With the Estarian priest along, it added to the Sunarian practice of religion and state being closely connected. However, there was something in the air of arrogance that the merchant man put off that sat wrong with the Crystine commander—or, maybe, it was the lack of the devious glint one would expect to go with such an attitude. Matar found himself wondering if he was reading the young man's strong jaw wrong. Undecided, he tucked away the tidbit for when he could speak with the two perceptive Sheev'arids alone.

"Welcome again." Matar repeated, a smile lighting his face. "You all know who I am I assume, so there is no need to introduce myself." He seemed fairly cheerful about the prospect. "Now, to the point. What is so urgent that a motley group of young men have asked to see this old, forgotten war veteran at the far eastern corner of Syre?"

The companions shuffled restlessly, perturbed at the commander's question, but it was still clear that Anibus was their leader. After a moment's pause, the priest spoke up, his words both shocking and unexpected. "My king, Majesty Fantill, sent me here from Fortress Opal. My companions, though they have traveled with me since Deluge marketplace, are not privy to the information I will now share."

Matar looked surprised at the last statement, but motioned for Anibus to continue. "What does King Fantill have for me?"

Anibus recognized the respect in the man's voice and hoped it was a good sign. "First, I must warn, my story may be a bit unbelievable to your ears, but I must say it, as it is the truth as I know it." The young priest paused to suck in a breath then plunged into his unusual tale. "I am an acolyte at the church in West Port, serving under the Eminary himself. Not but eight weeks past, I was called from my room to His Reverence's presence. The Eminary had had a vision, he said. In this vision, a force of darkness, with gleaming red eyes, ascended over the northern kingdoms of Syre, swallowing them in its wake. The people cried in their pain and suffering as they were killed but none were saved from this horror. Yet in the dream, there came a rainbow, small at first but growing. It came to block the advancement of this evil. As this rainbow grew in power, it forced back the darkness. Eventually, His Reverence said, it won.

"After this, the Eminary sent me to King Fantill, to warn him of this vision. Not but a day later, the Sealand forces at North Point received word from King Maushelik of Staria that an enormous force of maunstorz were seen marching passed Port Al'Harrad. King Maushelik believed them to be heading for North Point." As the maunstorz have a habit of ignoring cities of trade to go after those with military occupation, it was a safe guess. "Another force was spotted to the north of the Gap of the Forgotten, moving closer to the Citadel. King Maushelik doubted he could be of assistance to North Point because of this secondary threat. Upon hearing this, I was sent eastward to ask if any of the eastern kingdoms would come to Sealand's aid. So far none will come, but I ask of you," Anibus hesitated, knowing how outrageous his story was but also knowing the price for not saying his request, "Will the Crystine prepare itself for war?"

The companions seemed as unnerved as Commander Matar felt. Visions were an unusual cause for such rushed actions; however, Matar was not the same as the other leaders. The Crystine commander had lived among the Tashek of Staria (who heeded such unnatural signs), had fought alongside the Starian king (whom he felt was very wise), and had been through many battles (including the one when Crystalynian had been overthrown).

The last battle of Crystalynian had been preceded by such sinister warnings, and Matar was well aware of the powers, whether of unearthly means or from men, that had been called upon during that final battle twenty-five years before. The Eminary, a young lad at that time, had had a prophecy about the destruction of Crystalynian then, too. Hearing Anibus's words, he felt a chilling repeat of that very time. Matar's face became grave. "I've no idea which is worse an omen: that two kings fear a threat as large as the one that took out the Eighth Kingdom of Syre or that the words were spoken from a man of reverence."

Anibus rose his eyebrows, surprised at the remark. It had not been what he had expected the commander to say.

"I assume King Fantill chose you because of your familiarity with the Crystal Kingdom and with the Eminary. That you have attracted companions such as these shows me that the Stars have wanted this information to reach me safely." The group seemed astounded that a highly-respected war veteran sounding so pious. Terrik, still at the door, did not seem the least surprised, however; the Tashek did call him their Khataum—or "warrior of the Stars"—for that very reason. Matar continued thoughtfully. "Oh, what poor times this is that we must once again band together against a large army of maunstorz—and with such ill omens! The last time such came to pass, an entire kingdom fell." His expression changed in an instant. "We must prepare swiftly. We are to leave at dawn."

"So soon?" Rio asked, stunned.

"Yes, and even that is too long." Matar stood with renewed conviction. "If two kings, Maushelik and Fantill, and the Eminary believe an attack of that size is imminent, then I believe them. I won't be caught with my pants down again. Zyanthena!" Matar called out.

The beautiful Tashek woman did not appear at the doorway, though her voice floated through the room as clearly as if she had. "Yes, commander?"

It was only when Matar looked up to the woman's high, window perch that the startled young men realized where the ghost-voice was coming from. The Tashek's smirk showed how satisfied she was with the ruse. "Zy'ena, you know the news. Spread it to the Crystine. We leave at cavalry speed at first light. Also," Commander Matar added quickly, though the Tashek had not moved to leave, "Send word to Sunrise to take their soldiers to the border. King Raymond has been clear that he has no wish to move his men passed his lands, but they should be close enough to counter any attacks that get through us. And, tell Commander Kins that we are on our way to Wynward's Crossing. We will meet him there."

"Yes, sir." The Tashek bowed her head then was gone just as silently.

Anibus studied Zyanthena's chosen listening stoop amid the buzz of his companion's conversations and Matar's commands. With a shiver of awe, he realized that the desert woman could have easily stalked into a room to kill someone as she could to eavesdrop. No wonder the Crystine employed the Starian nomads into their service; they were better than even the renowned soldiers of the Crystal Kingdom! It was another sign that King Fantill and the Eminary were worried about the maunstorz—if they were desperate enough to send for fighters such as these. His trip to procure such forces suddenly made the eminent attacks feel less surreal and more ill-fated.

Chapter Three

§

To Wynward's Crossing

That night was filled with the Crystine soldier's packing. The six guests were sent away to private rooms, ordered to rest, while the rest of the castle was in a melee of activity. All was finished well before dawn.

Zyanthena Sheev'arid supervised the last of the supplies, relieving Commander Matar so the veteran could sleep a few winks before the journey. As soon as she was sure the packing was complete, the Tashek woman gave command to her brother and hastened to the Crystine commander's chambers. Her silent footsteps and chosen dark-colored robes made her seem like a haunting shadow flitting through the cold, stone hallways.

Matar, however, was not fooled and knew the warrior had arrived. The tingle up his spine was all he needed to feel to know she was present; it was so like a predator staring. The commander didn't move a muscle as the desert woman came to stand a few paces behind. He sat in a meditative trance for as long as he dared, trying to contain the last amounts of energy that he could before rising to face an exhausting day. The minutes ticked by while impatient shadows slowly lost their hold on the room and the coming of the dawn lite his walls in reds and gold. "All is gathered," Matar finally spoke out, certain.

Zyanthena replied, though the statement needed none. "Yes, Commander. Even the kingdom's finest warhorses have been gathered from the mountain pastures. All is ready for great haste."

"And so it must be." Matar agreed as he turned toward the young woman. "Do I have your mind today?"

Zyanthena answered the Tashek question with a courteous bow of her head. "Yes, Master, as always, I will lend my opinion to the point that I can."

Matar flashed a fond smile her way. "I thought you would, though it never hurts to ask. I've already spoken to Terrik about it but wished your own thoughts as well."

"It is his right as senior to offer his advice before mine."

"Good." Matar answered, relieved. Ever since the two Sheev'arids had become a part of his forces, he had felt a tension playing between them over dominance. Zyanthena may not be one to say so outwardly, but the commander felt she resented being overlooked by her adoptive brother. Even the Tashek, as disciplined as they were, could have their grievances. He continued, "You both have seen our guests enough to judge. What say you about them?"

Zyanthena's sharp eyes studied the veteran, as if trying to determine what her commander wanted of her. "The priest is true. He will not be a problem. He has picked his companions wisely."

Matar prompted, "But you have no any doubts?"

"On loyalty? Or their story? No. Though for personal gains, some of them may be hiding their truths. The knights seem to be their part, but the Sunarian folk can be...mask wearers."

Matar met her brandy eyes with his serious, deep-blue ones. He knew the woman would have caught onto what he had suspected, she was just being too cautious to say it. "You have a guest in mind that should be kept an eye on?"

"You know it as well as I, Master, whom seems suspicious. But, suspicion is not enough to convict a certain fox of fowl stealing."

Matar laughed at the Tashek's pun. "Then we will have to keep a watch on our food stuffs until we are sure, my Night Fox."

"Yes, Khataum."

"Now," Matar stood, switching subjects as he did, "I have a different matter to ask about."

Zyanthena fluidly closed the gap between them to assist the Crystine leader into his light armor. "And what would that be, Master?"

"Just a simple domestic problem."

"Domestic? Sir, you make me feel like a housewife!"

A brazen laugh echoed from Matar's chest. "Never, Zy'ena, you are certainly not that. No, what is wrong is that we will have too little time to reshoe our horses once the fighting begins. Using your connections, I assume you can find us an able farrier within the hour?"

"That is all you ask?" Zyanthena joked, a rare moment of humor coloring her words. "No make-shift shirt patching or cooking chores?" She quickly sobered, however. "I think I know just who you want. He is young but his master has been too drunk to perform so the lad has learned the craft through time and effort. He is an orphan, from what I remember, and will not likely be missed."

"Sounds like our man." Matar agreed.

"Then I will seek him out and rejoin you before you leave the demesne." Zyanthena promised.

The tall commander nodded his satisfaction as the Tashek finished buckling his armor. Turning, he met the young woman's fiery eyes. "What would I do without you here, Zyen?" He asked with a fond smile. "I fear none of the men could replace you, even if there were a hundred."

"If there were that many, Master," Zyanthena replied seriously, "They had better guard you as closely as I or better. We would fare badly to lose you."

"You are too kind to this old man." A waning smile lite his tired features.

"You are neither old nor not without need of kindness." She answered the remark truthfully.

Matar chuckled at the woman's sincerity and turned away to collect his helm and sword from his bedroll. "Come now, my Night Fox, we have the day to conquer."

Zyanthena murmured a "yes, master", and fell into step by her leader's right shoulder. They trudged down the Crystal Castle's old halls in silence, collecting the last of the night's peace and calm; however, once they reached the main floor, the arrival of the six guests broke their comfort. Zyanthena noted the guests step into the hallway ahead of them and slowly began to hang back from the Crystine leader. "If you will excuse me, Khataum, I would like to attend to my assignment." Matar nodded permission and the desert woman flitted away with a final reply of, "I will meet you at Wynward's Crossing with the farrier."

Anibus noticed the Tashek's departure as they neared. He admitted, in afterthought, it was a sign of trust that the wary, desert woman allowed the visitors to be with the Crystine leader unattended. "Commander Matar." The Sealander greeted the veteran, with the companions following suit.

"Priest. Friends." Matar replied in turn. "You appear at just the right time. My soldiers are ready to depart and have selected new mounts for you. With haste, we make for North Point. We should arrive in a half-moon's time."

"That is better than we had hoped." Anibus commented, grateful for the news. "The Crystine's speed will be much appreciated."

Matar led the group outside. At the steps, his force waited for his appearance, all mounted on the Crystal Kingdom's war steeds. Majestic, the royal courser Zyanthena had ridden the day before, was ensconced in light tack of a supple, golden leather; the commander's spare weapons and saddlebags tied deftly out of the stallion's way. The grey nickered a greeting and pulled his handler toward his master. The sight was an amusement to all but the poor stable boy assigned to the charger. Chuckling, Commander Matar turned back to his guests as he finished greeting his mount. "I have given you all fresh horses for the journey. Terrik will show you to the ones we chose. Your own will be safely guarded here until you can return for them."

The six guests nodded at the sense of the leader's decision. After all, their horses had traveled the full length of eastern kingdoms of Syre, and Anibus's the full long length. The promise of riding the famed Crystal Kingdom's horses was also an added enticement; no other kingdom had horses as fine as these. Quickly, they moved to where the Tashek waited, eager to discover which horses had been chosen for them.

Terrik smiled charmingly in good morning and motioned to the horses lined up behind him. "The mounts are the best this kingdom has to offer. Please, treat them better than you would a queen. Now, Mr. Novano," Terrik indicated for Jacen to step toward him, "You will ride Sapphire, one of the mares directly from the line of Valed Darkness. May she carry you swiftly and far." Jacen could not hide the admiration in his eyes as he was handed the reins of a seventeen-hands-high courser of deep grey-blue coloring. As he was to see, Jacen would not be the only one to be impressed by the Crystal Kingdom's generosity.

The Tashek motioned the next horse forward and called Patrick out. "Son of Kins, as your father rides a horse of royal Glorified's bloodlines, so shall you. I give you Candor, as is your right." And, so, Patrick was handed the reins of a golden steed very similar in stature and color to his father's own warhorse.

Terrik continued onward, waving Rio to follow him. "As a gratitude to your family for helping us hold the boarder, we have decided to let you ride our own prince's mighty Causinova, for, as you know, without his master, the warhorse had hardly had any attention. The romp will do him good." Rio handled the large chestnut's lead reverently and shared a look of awe with his comrades. It was rare that anyone besides royalty would ride such a prized animal and Prince Zeek's warhorse was well-known. Rio couldn't believe his luck.

Sage Cooper was hailed next, to the side of a lithe liver-chestnut mare. "Cauza is the first filly of Victory, our king's courser. She will not falter under any foe you may encounter. Treat her well." Terrik moved on as Sage rubbed the mare's neck gently.

"Merchant Roland, I reserve for you one of our Tashek and Valed Darkness crosses, Zahara. She is as fast as lightning and as willing as they come. Keep her from harm and she will see you home." The light-boned bay eyed Roland Seagold; her gaze speaking of unimaginable intelligence. She was everything a man of a merchant's stature, or higher, could ever want. Roland thanked the desert warrior and stroked the mare with a hand of familiarity toward their kind.

Lastly, the Tashek led the priest to his mount. Anibus, having been a close friend to the Crystal crown because of his ties to the Sealand royal family, recognized the fleet mare instantly. "Rain." He murmured to himself and ran his hand reverently down her silky, grey neck.

"Ah, you know her." Terrik's eyes twinkled in appreciation. "Matar said you might. She is Vale's favorite mare. She should be brave for you during the journey."

"She is blessed by the Stars." Anibus said, then paused to wonder why he had spoken such. Terrik seemed to agree, however, so the priest let it pass. "Thank you, Tashek. These horses are truly gifts. We will care for them with the upmost of respect."

Commander Matar waited for their guests to mount before calling out his orders. "Crystine, Tashek, my friends, we have been called to aid Sealand and the western lands of Syre against an imminent maunstorz attack. Today, we march to Wynward's Crossing to meet with Commander Kins. Together, we should be able to cross Rubia without suffering many losses to the enemy. May we reach North Point before the full moon's turning, with Stars' speed." The Crystine and Tashek repeated the final words and the force was on the move.

Decond brushed his autumn-gold bangs from his eyes, feeling them bunch in sticky, damp clumps behind his ears. He sighed, tired from the work, and looked at the large pile of metal bars he still had to shape into horseshoes. "That lazy old bastard should be doing this. He's been too drunk this last month to do anything, except to go relieve himself." As if to argue, the drunken farrier's snoring became really loud and grating. "Yeah, fine, go back to bed you damn drunkard!" Decond growled under his breath and continued pounding his latest iron bar.

"Sounds like you and the "man" are having quite the talk."

"Stars!" Decond jumped back in surprise. He dropped his tools and metal piece. "Zee, I told you before not to sneak up on me!"

Zyanthena hid a smirk as she came around the furnace. "As I recall, I told you I don't sneak. You just happen to be pounding a little too loudly."

"Right." Decond replied sarcastically and bent down to retrieve his things. "So, um, what are you doing here this early in the morning? You know I only started my day half an hour ago."

The Tashek came to stand near the seventeen-year-old. "I just came to see if you wanted a job."

"A job?" Decond ran his hand over his hair, a motion unconsciously done. He was often checking that the ponytail was holding; it wouldn't do to have his shoulder-length hair singed off by accident! "You mean like washing dishes or cleaning horse crap?" He was teasing because he assumed his friend was joking. After all, what would a rich man want from an orphan, anyway?

Zyanthena looked at him, seemingly intrigued at Decond's lack of believing her offer. "We are in need of a good farrier. There's plenty of horses and the pay is good," she repeated the request.

"Right." The young man chuckled and started to finish his pounding, but something in the woman's tone stopped him. He turned back to her. "You're not joking, are you?" He dropped his tools on the workbench beside the fire. "You never joke." Decond turned to the desert woman, giving her his full attention.

"The man I serve is in need of a good farrier. One who would not mind travelling a long distance nor the hard work involved. Other metal-works that may be in need of repair, so our hire must be resourceful when the need arises. Having with no ties to a place or family would be best." The Tashek waited for the lad to find his thoughts. Decond couldn't though; for the proposal seemed too outrageous. Just eight years ago, he remembered becoming an orphan. To survive, Decond had taken the only job offered to him by the aging, tankard farrier. Now this young woman, his friend of two years, was telling him he had a chance to work for a well-to-do nobleman. "I...ah. Stars, Zee! You sprang that on me quick."

"It is after dawn." It was the closest thing to an apology Decond had ever heard Zyanthena say. The desert woman shrugged and turned to walk back out to the front of the shop, leaving her friend to his thoughts. Decond watched her go. He found himself comparing her to a mountain cat, the way she padded quietly away. Man, was she beautiful!

The snoring of the old man brought Decond's attention back to his work. Reality struck him as he looked around the musty, heat-ridden furnace room; he wasn't getting the good deal here—the old man was, sleeping all day and getting paid for Decond's work. The young man did all the labor and cleaning and client relations, yet, in the end, the farrier got all the dough. Decond kicked the side of the clay furnace in disgust and dashed out to the front. "Zee!"

Zyanthena was leaning casually against her black steed. She grinned at her friend. "I knew what you would decide. Come, I will help you load up what tools you need on my packhorse, and we'll get out of here."

§ §

It was passed noon by the time Decond had packed what equipment he wanted. Zyanthena frowned on this, as they were wasting precious time, but her attempts to speed him up were thwarted. The seventeen-ear-old argued the use of every tool he picked out and, in the end, there were too many important tools required for the job. The list of reasons finally caused the Tashek to relent and wait impatiently next to her war charger. Even by the end, though, she never once regretted picking young Decond for the job.

When they finally left, Decond's weighted-down packhorse made Zyanthena recalculate the time it would take to reach Wynward's Crossing. She sighed, resigned to the new schedule, and led the way at a steady pace slow enough to not tire out the packhorse. Her brother and tribe would tease her for being so late, but Zyanthena know Matar would not care—as long as she made it to the Crystine safely. Still, the desert woman had hoped to take a much-needed break to check her weapons and light armor and to give Unrevealed, her black mount, a well-deserved grooming. It would have to wait.

Zyanthena kept to the small deer paths just below timberline, leading the way she knew would be hidden from maunstorz prowlers. Though the Tashek knew that the main roads would be all right, her warrior upbringing urged her to take the concealed routes. Decond didn't seem to notice the unusual trek, however, he was too busy enjoying his new-found freedom. Zyanthena was relieved over that. She had had to take other people on off-road trips but had found most travelers were a big pain in her derriere, complaining the entire way about the uneven footing. Decond's cheerful mood was heartening.

The two spoke a little but were mostly content with the comfortable silence that fell between them; however, when Zyanthena spotted the flicker of campfires through the mountain pines that evening, she stopped the young man; he would need some heads-up on their arrival into the army camp. "There are some things you will need to know before meeting my master."

"Okay." Decond smiled cheerfully and sat with his arms folded, waiting.

Zyanthena could not help her affectionate smile at his calm attitude. She shook her head, a chuckle on her lips. "I could tell you the world was coming to an end and you would still smile." She continued before the youth could offer a retort. "I just want to warn you that I am more than I appear. Down there," she pointed to the camp, "Is the Crystine Calvary and Rubian mertinean."

"The Crystal Kingdom's militia?" Decond frowned. "Why are we with them?" He looked at the Tashek, not comprehending her identity.

"Commander Matar is my master."

The youth's ice-blue eyes widened in shock. "The leader of the Crystine! You're a soldier?"

"A Tashek scout, actually."

Decond expression froze. The young man looked Zyanthena over, as if seeing her for the first time. The lithe woman sat her black charger with ease, though, because the horse was Crystal bred, Decond had missed the details that marked Zyanthena as a desert folk. Now, he saw the signs: her skin that was a touch darker than normal (though not as dark as most Tashek) and her black hair and brown eyes that were typical of the people of the sands. The form-fitting desert garb, which she now wore openly, was adorned in dark colored bead and talismans. A woven belt held a lethal kora blade. How had he missed that? Decond wondered at the sight of the weapon. He shook his head ruefully and glanced back down at the military camp. "You aren't trying to enlist me, are you?"

"No." Zyanthena's serious expression broke that absurd notion. "I brought you for the reasons I explained. We have no farrier for the Crystine horses. A sudden call to arms causes us to travel a long way, to the west, to Sealand. Your services will be greatly needed and the pay will be more than you have been earning—unless you have changed your mind?"

Zyanthena looked the same as ever—except for the desert scout detail. Decond relaxed with that thought. "If it's just farrier work, I can handle that. No weapons, though. Ever." He paused, wondering if the Tashek would ask him about the declaration. She didn't. "It's going to take a while to get used to you being a Tashek, and here I thought you a servant of a wealthy nobleman!"

The beautiful warrior shared in her friend's amusement. "I am glad I am not; I can assure you of that." She waved them ahead. "I'll see what I can do to remedy how you perceive me, however, right now we need to find Commander Matar. Follow me."

The six companions had set up their tents as close to the command tent as the Tashek would allow. Thought they were exhausted from the Crystine's hurried ride, all six stayed on their feet, to double-check equipment and get their supplies in order. Under the ever-watchful eye of a Tashek warrior, they brushed the fine horses they had been given as they waited for Matar to call them to his tent.

The sun was setting, but still the commander of the Crystine had not called; Roland and Jacen were becoming concerned—from what Anibus could tell. The priest studied his companions thoughtfully, noting that only Rio and Patrick appeared relaxed. If they were, he knew he had nothing to complain about. *We are all just tired and restless. I'm certain Commander Matar has not forgotten us. He must have a lot to discuss with the other commander, especially after the news we carried.*

Suddenly, Rain tensed under the priest's hand. Anibus tore his eyes away from his friends to see what the mare had noticed. The grey stared down the main lane between the army tents, her nostrils flaring and quivering as she caught the scent of the three shapes coming down the way. "You know them, lady?" Anibus asked.

Like a shadow, the companion's Tashek guardsman coursed to the two horsemen. Anibus watched as the man paused beside the tallest mount then sprinted toward the command tent. The two mounted horsemen continued forward and stopped by the light of the companions' fire. The six friends wandered over as soon as they realized it was Zyanthena Sheev'arid. "You do them honor by taking such care of your mounts so," she said as way of greeting.

Anibus came forward in his own hello. "The honor's all ours." He answered smoothly. Then, noticing the Tashek's companion, he asked, "Would you two care for rest and drink or food?"

Zyanthena seemed taken off guard at the courtesy. She glanced at her master's tent, as if looking for an answer, then she turned to study the young man beside her. "Perhaps a little for this man here. I wish for only water and oats for my steed. Master Matar should call us soon."

Anibus nodded and took the young man's horses as the farrier hopped off. He looked weary. "Go, eat. I will take care of them." The youth nodded, too tired to protest. He trudged to the fire and accepted the food and water Sage handed him.

The Tashek woman watched for a moment, then deftly dismounted. She walked to where Anibus had taken the other two horses, her black charger following on his own will. "Thank you for offering such. Decond is more tired than he will admit, and kindness is not usually shown him."

Anibus held the water bucket still as Decond's horse drank. "Is that so?" He replied. "That seems a sad statement." Zyanthena nodded and stroked her stallion's satin neck. She seemed not to notice the priest's eyes on her. *She is different from before, less tense. Is the young man the cause of this or is it something else?* "Here, this water is as fresh as it gets." Anibus handed the Tashek the watering bucket. As the desert woman's horse drank, Anibus filled another bin with oats. He handed this to the woman then stepped back to the other two horses.

Zyanthena's touch seemed reverent as she brushed her charger's glossy, black coat. The stallion, in turn, would nuzzle the woman gently between bites of grain. It was obvious that both trusted each other and their affection was mutual. Anibus found himself staring at their bond with a surprising envy. Zyanthena caught him staring. Instead of glaring, however, she waved the priest over. "You take much joy in watching others." The woman reprimanded gently, though her voice carried no anger. "Perhaps, you could put those skills to better use. I, like all Tashek, am fond of horses. Alas, we have a good eye and knowing touch about their kind. I have seen you have a similar talent; few handle Rain so well. So, tell me, Priest of Estaria, what do you think of my stallion?"

"I...ah." Anibus cleared his throat nervously. Not often did a Tashek acknowledge other people's horse skills (or so he had heard). He was a little flustered. Zyanthena looked over at him from the corner of her eye and gave a small, encouraging nod. She prompted him to go on and tell her his opinion as she walked to the black charger's other side and continued brushing Unrevealed.

"Well... he is an impressive mount, about eighteen-hands-high, I estimate, and built like a distance runner. His legs are clean and well-angled, even his shoulder to forearm is not too steep. The long croup and powerful hindquarters give the impression of a forward-reaching gait and the lift of the withers suggests he can use himself fully and efficiently. Combined with a naturally arching neck, I'd say, he could collect himself well. He doesn't have the look of a Tashek mount, though."

"No," Zyanthena agreed. She was quiet a few breaths as she studied her stallion herself. "You have a nice eye for conformation, and you are right about him not being a desert horse." She paused to give the holy man a bemused smile. "You have passed my test thus far—but you are not done. A Tashek, if gifted, could mark the bloodline of each animal. Could you do the same?" She asked, but not in a mocking way. The woman's teasing tone suggested to Anibus that he had overlooked a vital detail in his assessment.

Glancing over the black horse again, the Sealander searched for clues to the stallion's breeding. Zyanthena would not have made him guess if it was not easily ascertained. "Am I allowed to ask questions in this game of yours?" The woman chuckled and nodded as she continued to brush the sweat marks from the stallion's coat; she was enjoying herself too much. "Was the sire or dame from the Crystal Kingdom?" Zyanthena nodded. "Both?" No, was the head shake. "Is the sire a well-known horse?" Yes. Anibus walked around to the black's head and looked into the large, liquid-brown eyes carefully. "He has the look of a king." He commented and noticed the Tashek perk up. "He must be a colt out of Valed Darkness? I can make out no other lines than that."

Zyanthena came up alongside Unrevealed's cheekbone and laid her hand there. "Correct you are, Priest of Estaria. Unrevealed is out of Valed Darkness. His dame is a Sunarian blue blood—the only horse from outside the kingdom that the king ever allowed to be bred to Vale. Her name is Blue Galleon, and she was Prince Rowin Sunrise's personal steed. Since the maunstorz invasion of the kingdom, the Sunarian prince had not asked her to be returned." Zyanthena paused to put her brushes away. "I know I am honored to be this stallion's rider. Matar says Unrevealed takes after his sire. Only I have been able to ride him, so it makes sense to let me use him as my mount."

Anibus stroked the velvety black nose of the stud. "It is interesting—the history of this horse. Valed Darkness had been rumored to pass along that selective-rider trait. You are blessed." He flashed the desert woman a smile.

Tentatively, Zyanthena returned it. "You make a good Tashek." She remarked and was about to say more but a call in keshic turned her attention. "Thank you for this discussion, priest," She said as she turned back. "I would like to talk more, but later. Master calls us to his tent. Gather your companions and meet there." The warrioress turned away to her duties. In a turn, she looked like an unapproachable Tashek scout once again. Anibus found the quick transformation curious and a trifle sad. Yet, he had no time to dwell on the exotic woman and her idiosyncrasies. "Come," He called to his companions and Decond. "Commander Matar calls us."

Chapter 4

§

War Councils

The six companions ducked into the lighted command tent and looked around. Already, many high-ranked officers, both Rubian and Crystine, occupied the main space between the entranceway and map table. The back wall was lined with solemn-faced Tashek warriors, their arms crossed and hidden into the contours of their robes. Commanders Ethan Kins and Matar were quietly discussing the map. Both straightened when they noticed the companions had joined the gathered.

Commander Kins brought himself to his full six-foot-three height and surveyed all of the men, and handful of women, occupying the tent. His striking, emerald eyes, identical to his son's, glimmered strongly in the firelight. They reflected the unease his features masked. "I believe you all know why you were called here. Recent events have caused us to pull you from your posts a more urgent purpose." Ethan paused, hearing his men whisper complaints against leaving Rubia's northeastern flank undefended. "There will be none of that!" He snapped harshly causing the mertinean soldiers to stiffen and salute. Kins continued as he paced in front of the soldiers. "No one likes the situation, I least of all; however, Wynward's and this border are well defended. Another front is not, and for this reason all of you have been summoned. Lord Farrylin will explain."

A tall, golden-haired, and clean-shaven Sealander stepped forward from his corner in the back. He bowed to the two commanders then turned his striking golden eyes on his audience. His tenor voice carried smoothly through the room. "Mertinean, Crystine, and Tashek, I am Lord Gordar Farrylin, Lord Protector to His Highness Par Fantill of Sealand. I have come directly from North Point baring disturbing news. Eight days ago, my Highness's scouts spotted a force of Maunstorz marching down the coastline. The force numbers close to ten thousand strong. We are only a force of eight thousand..." He paused to let the room absorb the facts. "How they came to circumvent Port Al-Harrad, we are uncertain, but we are sure that we are hard-pressed to fend off such an army. We are worn down from long days fighting raids on our northern borders. A fourth of our force is wounded..." Gordar turned back to Kins and Matar. "Sealand calls for any aid your forces can spare. My Highness realizes the distance you must travel to reach our front, but Sealand swears to try and hold the line until reinforcements arrive. Please, will you come?"

The men were stunned. Gordar's speech had not been eloquent, but it had shown how desperate he thought the situation was. Finally, someone stepped forward. Everyone realized it was Terrik Sheev'arid. "Lord Farrylin, your plea is heard. My people, for one, will answer. We do have one question, though: have King Maushelik or King Argetlem sent any support?"

Gordar shook his head. "Alas, neither has, honorable Sheev'arid. King Argetlem had sent no reply, last I had heard; King Maushelik sent word that his own forces have been confronted by another force of the enemy. His army is matched in strength, but no soldiers can be spared to help us. He did promise that if such an opportunity presented itself, he would send relief."

Terrik's brows knit together in consternation. "This is ill news you bring, Lord Farrylin. The Tashek will disperse and aid Staria's honorable king as well as Sealand. I will have falcons sent to the other tribes to inform them of these attacks."

"Sheev'arid, I thank you for the assistance you grant us." Gordar bowed deeply.

Matar stepped up beside Terrik and motioned the Tashek back. "The Crystine cavalry had already agreed to aid you, Lord Farrylin. All in thanks to Priest Anibus's request." Matar paused as Gordar turned to glance at his cousin. Apparently, he had not been aware that King Fantill had sent his relative ahead of him. "My soldiers will travel, with Star's speed, to North Point. We won't leave Sealand to its fate."

The Sealander returned his attention to the commander. "Sealand is indebted to you." His eyes blazed with gratitude.

Commander Kins had hung back patiently, as the other leader announced his call to aid. When neither the lord nor Crystine said anything more, he, too, stepped forward. "My forces will also join Sealand's defense. Too, I have sent out riders to warn the other kingdoms of this threat. The Maunstorz have not released a force of this size since...since Crystalynian fell twenty-one years ago. Syre cannot afford to lose another kingdom. All of Syre will need to overcome our differences to defeat this threat. Let us four—Sealand, Rubia, Crystine, and Tashek—be the first to show Syre how it's done!" Ethan extended his right hand and clasped it firmly to Gordar's offered forearm. Matar and Terrik joined in just as the command tent erupted in a fierce war cry.

All of the soldiers' voices grew stronger as they left the tent to inform the rest of the camp. The scent of real war was in the air. The camp came alive in excitement. Finally, some of Syre's people were ready to retaliate in full force against the enemy. Though the army wasn't the largest gathered in Syre' history, it was the first one constructed since the fall of Crystalynian. The Maunstorz would find it a more difficult task to take down a kingdom this time around...

§ §

The winds picked the sand up, creating golden sheets off the top of the dunes. All about, the desert seemed alive and rich in gold—expect where the large foreboding shape sat out in the distance. This dark blemish held the prince's attention, keeping him unaware of the natural beauty around him. "They come again. How much longer can we, or Syre, stand?"

"My Prince!" A Starian guard came riding up the dune. The man stopped his mount and saluted his leader. "Prince Al'den, word from the Citadel."

"Go on." Al'den encouraged, though his gaze wandered back to the disturbing sight near the Gap of the Forgotten.

"Highness," the guard bowed as he continued, "The King received word from Raven's Den. All of the mertinean and Crystine stationed at Wynward's will go to Sealand's aid. The Tashek among them will travel half to North Point and half to us, curtesy of Clan Sheev'arid."

"That is good. Give token of our appreciation to the Shi'alam when he arrives. Also, send word to the nearest clan that we can hold for a fortnight if need be but appreciate the speed of any aid." The prince paused. "Unless my father has already instructed, of course. Was there anything else?"

"No, my prince."

Prince Al'den nodded and waved the guard away. "Inform my father of the enemy's position." The guard bowed and began to back away. "Also," the prince added, "Tell my father I will be returning shortly."

"Yes, Highness."

The guard cantered away leaving Prince Al'den to his thoughts. The Starian had much on his mind. He was the eldest of the princes of Syre and the most knowledgeable of war tactics; a trait that would serve him well in the coming days ahead; however, his thoughts were disturbed by the number of enemies they faced. Too, old memories of his long-time friend Lance Starkindler, long taken by the maunstorz, haunted the prince. He would have gladly fought to keep his friend and the Starkindler family alive and well had he known about the attack on the Crystal Palace. As it was, Staria had heard too late, themselves having been harried by the enemy and diverted. Lance and his family had not been heard from again. "And now it is our turn, but this time around the enemy does sneak to our gates. Peculiar that they do not but come in small numbers." He gazed across the sands lost in thoughts of the past and future. "Your family would not have fallen had the enemy come like this." Al'den said, thinking of Lance. "I promise, I will not give up until those monsters are erased from our world." The winds swirled golden grains of desert sand around the prince, as if to say "*we heard your words, you must keep your promise*". Prince Al'den caught some of the sand in his hand and felt its fine texture filling his palm. "This battle will be long and it could end poorly, but...it will end this time. I will make sure of that."

§ §

"Damn them all to hell!" The king roared as he entered his army's command tent in a fury. "What are they thinking leaving the North undefended! That leaves our boarders wide open to maunstorz attacks. Bloody, selfish fools!"

The tent was deathly quiet; the king's advisors too stunned by their liege's abrupt entrance to answer. King Raymond of Sunrise, a man of average but broad bearing and a countenance usually pinched in demanding lines, snarled at the aggrievement and began throwing off his outer garments, nearly clubbing a slave unconscious when the man reached forth to help. The tent's other occupants shifted uncomfortably, hoping their king would not notice them and throw his fury their way. Having rid himself of his robe and jacket, King Raymond swooped up a chalice of ale and went to lounge on his cushioned throne. "Commander Ravesbend, Bradon, a private audience."

The dismissed men hurried away, visibly relieved. They left the two called advisors to face the infuriated king. Bradon, a man of short stature and balding head, eyed the door longingly but came to hover out of his majesty's reach. He bowed meekly and waited for the Sunrise's commander-in-arms to join him. Unlike his smaller second-in-command, Loris Ravesbend was not intimidated by his liege's smoldering nature. Loris stepped close to Raymond Sunrise's raised dais, keeping his strong but artistically long and shapely limbs relaxed. The two commanders made an image of a mouse and a wolf waiting silently below their leader's perch.

"You have heard the preposterous call-to-arms of our northern allies. They claim Staria and Sealand are in greater need of their defenses than us!" King Raymond snarled at the thought. "Tell me, how much at a loss are we with the Rubian mertinean moved from our border? Are we to take command of the northern defenses now, too?!"

"Ah," Bradon cleared his throat and shifted nervously; the answer he and Ravesbend needed to give clearly countered their majesty's opinion. Arguing with this king was not a good idea, if one was to keep their head.

Loris spoke instead, keeping his second out of Raymond's wrath. "My Liege, our forces are not burdened by Rubia's decision nor the Crystine's. Their forces are merely being moved closer to the enemy's lines, meaning the maunstorz will be farther from us. We have no cause to be overly concerned. Just keeping your force here at the Command Front will be enough to keep our Northern border safe. Also, King Chível did not ask us to journey north to aid his force in Rubia. I take this to mean he is keeping enough mertinean in his lands to prevent maunstorz harrying." Bradon was mortified by the time Loris finished. He tried to huddle behind the taller man, hiding from the rebuke he knew would come.

The king said nothing.

Bradon snuck a glance at the ruler. King Raymond's cold eyes were staring, either stunned or angry (the man could not tell which), at Commander Ravesbend. It felt to Bradon that he was caught in a stare-down between a mountain cat and a wolf, a feeling that unsettled his stomach.

The two men continued to let the silence build in the tent until it felt like an invisible band would snap. Commander Ravesbend kept his cobalt-blue eyes lock with the king's, though fairly neutrally, and hoped his king would consider his advisement—silently praying that his majesty would not stick stubbornly to the opposition or strike out a blow.

"You know the consequences if you are wrong." King Raymond stated bluntly. "May you hope yourself right in this action, Commander—for your family's sake." He lifted the jewel-ensconced chalice and drank deeply of the ale, delighting in the liquid's burning down his throat. A sly smile lite the ruler's face as he waited for Loris Ravesbend to plea for his family's safety. The commander only bowed, however, and waited for the king to say anything more or dismiss him. *He is as arrogant as ever,* Raymond thought, annoyed. "I have nothing further of you." He waved his commanders away.

"Your men will be stationed here for the time being. None can take leave until I am satisfied that this danger is gone. I will be returning to the capitol at dawn. You are dismissed."

The two leaders bowed and backed away. Bradon waited until they were well out of the king's ear-shout before speaking furtively with his commander. "Is it not too much to ask you to agree with the king on something? The men will know this confinement order is punishment for your pigheadedness against our king."

Commander Ravesbend rose a hand to stop his second-in-command from further words. "The decision I made was right, even if it comes at a price. I respect my men enough to stand against an unwise choice. It is better than being sent to Raven's Den or the Red Palace or elsewhere beyond the border. I will not have my men worn thin by the maunstorz wearying raids."

"Yes, but, sir, the men know you and the king disagree often. Over half would follow you over him any day. That bodes ill if the king ever decides you need to be …made example of. A full revolt would not be good."

"And I hope my men respect me enough to know I would never approve of that." Loris replied. "I am gambling with my family's life as well as my men's. I hope they see and understand that. The maunstorz will not attack us here. Make them aware of that. And one more thing," Commander Ravesbend stopped Bradon. "Tell them that this camp will go on as usual, and I will make an example of anyone who does not perform up to snuff."

§ §

North Point was not only being pounded by maunstorz that day, it was also being hounded by a westerly front from the Pearl Coast. The cutting wind and rain pelted the soldiers still at their posts and managed to creep its way into the command tents. It soaked clothing and equipment alike. Three thousand of the Landarïan forces were still huddling against the rain in the trenches; others, having just finished their shifts against a full battalion of maunstorz, were finding wet beds to fall to sleep upon. Though the enemy had pulled back, giving the men a needed break, the storm had not abated. The whole situation was a dreary, bone-chilling wait.

A figure walked among the weary ranks, hunched against the wet gall. He tried to keep himself looking strong for his men, though he could not keep the tired lines from his face. His damp, blond hair had come loose of its ponytail to batter his ocean-blue eyes mercilessly, but the man was too exhausted to bother to rebind it. Enough effort went into walking down the line to check on his forces. It was a bother to toy with a silly swath of hair.

"My Highness!" Sealand's head-commander came running up to the man. "Prince Par, please you need rest."

Prince Par Fantill turned his back to the wind and glanced at the old veteran from the corner of his eye. "You know I cannot. These men have had to endure this weather and battle a long while. For them, I will not leave."

"They would be disheartened if their prince fell from ill or exhaustion. Please, Highness, they will understand if you take a short rest."

The heir of Sealand would have argued the point further had not a messenger arrived. In resigned haste, Prince Par allowed the two men to escort him back to his tent so he could read the scroll his runner had sent. His commander forced him into a chair and started to boil some water for tea as the messenger laid smooth a scroll in front of the royal. The Sealander accepted the offered pieces of bread, meat, and cheese his men forced on him as he read. Then, it was all silence in the tent, except for the howl of the wind pulling on the tent, as the prince poured over the message.

"What does it say, Highness?" Commander Averron asked as he handed Par his tea.

"It is a correspondence from Lord Gordar." There was relief in his voice. "He arrived at Wynward's Crossing eighteen days after he left us. He reports that the Crystine have already grouped to come to our aid. It is understood that Priest Anibus had met with them about the situation ahead of his arrival. The mertinean will march with them; half of the force from Raven's Den will be here within the coming days. The main force of Crystine, mertinean, and Tashek should be here within a fortnight. The Crystine are debating sending a force in advance to help us hold on. With all this, hopefully, the maunstorz will be repulsed." The prince paused and he skimmed the rest of the document. "There is no mention of other reinforcement. I assume that means that the other kingdoms have yet to either know or decide on a course of action. So," he paused wearily, "Only Rubia and the Crystal Kingdoms send any aid."

"But someone is coming!"

Prince Par straightened his aching body and nodded to his commander. "It seems so, Averron. We may be given some respite soon. Stars know we need it!"

Averron smiled, his hope restored. "With your permission, Highness, I would like to tell the men. It would help morale."

"Yes, we should tell them." Prince Par rose, feeling a little of his old energy return from the promising news. He vowed to stay on his feet a little longer. After all, his men deserved their highness's support, and he had never seen men fight so bravely in his name. It was odd for the heir to be so cheered. He could not keep the thought that bay that it wasn't so long ago that he had lived a luxurious life, pampered in the Fortress Opal in the south. Just one battle, where he had fought alongside the men that served his father, and overnight he had become a war cry. *I'd rather be here with these men who look up to me and I them then spend six years in easy, boring royal graces.* Leaving his dry tent behind, Prince Par glanced around at the soldiers of his army. *Yes, I would rather be here with these honest men, standing in this Stars-forsaken rain than sitting, talking about the flowers of mother's gardens with another flirting lady.* He chuckles at the folly and followed Averron. *Stars! What a prince I am, choosing soldiers over women. Still, I am glad I can finally give my men some good news. Once this is over, I will give them much better—it's the least I can do.*

§ §

The sun was setting, casting the golden-encased palace in glaring brilliance. The large courtyard, that surrounded the majestic building lay empty of visitors. Its white marble was waiting for the evening wash crew to come scrub away the grim acquired during the course of the day. Lanterns were being lite within the many rooms of the Golden Palace, its inhabitants far from done with their own business. Whereas the outside of the gold-ensconce palace seemed serene, inside it was becoming heated in a haste-called-for debate. The cause was from a lone runner returning from Sardon with news from the North.

"Your Majesty, we cannot help them at this time." A royal advisor, Lord Aeronson, was saying to his king. "All of our defenses are at Sardon. Having them there causes great strain on us as it is. If we were to march them northward, our people would feel abandoned and must suffer rationing."

"But I, nor any of you, cannot ignore this threat—even if it comes from the North. The force of maunstorz described to me shows they are capable of cutting open Staria and Sealand's defenses. What then? The Golden Kingdom would be in their path." King Argetlem couldn't stop his restless pacing, which was enough to cause discord in and of itself. The medium-heighted king straightened his eschewed, golden robes and ran a weathered hand over his tire, cyan eyes. He forced himself to sit down at the council table with his advisors. "I apologize if I seem pressed. I, always a man of action, find this news quite disconcerting." He paused, taking a deep breath to calm down. "We must discuss our options thoroughly. Lord Aeronson, you spoke of us being strained. I assume you mean financially?" He turned to his son to his right. Prince Kent who, though a prince, was viewed more as the kingdom's lead economics overseer. "Prince Kent, my son, what have you to say on this?"

Prince Kent rose from his chair to his full five-foot-nine frame. He straightened his tailored clothes carefully, like a fretting young lady, and shook his chestnut bangs from his blue eyes. Just his scholarly presence called the lords' and advisors' attentions. "I do give warning, father, council. My words are only economical however, and not political, so you may not heed them as fully." The gathered chuckled at the absurdity of the statement. All knew Prince Kent's assessments of the Golden Kingdom's economy were highly regarded province-wide. His worlds would strongly sway the council in this situation. Prince Kent continued, "Being that it is Harvest-Gathering Time, much of the crops are being stored away for First Snows. What is being consumed is handed out as equally as is able among the people. The towns were allowed to keep more of their own spoils this year, so the larger cities have relied on out capitol's own fields to supply them. If the army is moved, much of the food-stuffs will have to be sent with them. That strains our citizens even more. It would be better to keep the balance as it is. If we go to Staria or Sealand, then we will need to take more from the towns we already allotted from." He paused as he realized his speech lacked its usual eloquence. "I suppose that what I want say is that, economically, our kingdom would suffer if we need to be put on military alert. However," Kent set his matching eyes on his father's, "Politically, we would benefit from helping Sealand or Staria."

King Argetlem motioned for his son to sit back down, then he stood. "You did, of course, my son, touch on our problem. Do we help our fellow kingdoms, as is politically advantageous, or do we withhold support and see what comes? With First Snows approaching, we cannot take either decision lightly. So," The king clapped his hands. "What say you?"

The councilmen looked among themselves, all having opinions but unwilling to share. Prince Kent rose, seeing the reluctance, and put forth his answer. "I say we withhold our troops for now. There had already been rumor of troops rallying in Rubia and, maybe, even in the Crystal Kingdom. They have the better fighting forces, in any case. Our troops should remain at Sardon, on military alert, and wait for further developments. Perhaps, this unusually large maunstorz force is just to test Syre's patience. Rallying too quickly may prompt more of an attack."

Lord-Commander Ivance stood then, his highly decorated military coat shimmering in the lantern light. "The maunstorz need no prompting, Your Highness." He bowed his greying head at Kent to show no disrespect was intended. Turning, he addressed King Argetlem. "They took down Syre's strongest kingdom at the height of its power twenty-five years ago. Crystalynian fell, completely destroyed and abandoned four years later. Eight years ago, the enemy tried again with the Crystal Kingdom. We lost the Starkindler family before the Crystine were allowed to relinquish it again. *Let,* mind you—no disrespect to the Crystine. So, they've set their sights on Staria and Sealand now. Very easy to win with the rumored numbers they have." He paused to take a breath in his passionate speech. "Yes, we can station our troops at Sardon, but then we abandon our fellow to maunstorz knit-picking. And, the damn Sunarians certainly aren't going to help, you all know that! Probable not even the Havenese, who follow whatever the Sunrises do. Is this how the Golden Kingdom wishes to repay the kingdoms that protect our northern boarders from the maunstorz!? Stars, I hope not!"

The council was quiet after Lord-Commander Ivance's passionate speech. The aging commander knew too much about the enemy he spoke of; he had fought with King Trev'shel of Crystalynian during that year's final war. The Golden leader was not one to skirt around the quarter-of-a-century's old history, despite many in the kingdom who wished the event long forgotten. Others on the council were unwilling to risk the citizens in the war against the maunstorz skirmishes; some would go as far as to act like the war in the North was not happening.

The king knew all this. Argetlem sighed worn out and waved the council's attention to him. "I believe it is decided, then, that, our best interests are to withhold action events conspire further. For now." He heard the relieved mutterings of some of the advisors. Disappointed at this, he gave Ivance a wan smile. "I am sorry, Lord-Commander but you will withhold your troops until further orders are sent. However," he contradicted, "I will send my son with a royal military procession to the Citadel of Light to speak with King Maushelik and assess the situation in person. I would risk my only son and heir to keep our neighboring kingdoms in good graces. Lord Commander Ivance, I give you leave to commission the men to accompany my son—minus your own person; I still need you here." Ivance nodded stiffly. "Anything else? No? Then go and prepare what you must. The hour has turned late and I will not keep you further from your duties."

§ §

The midmorning sun was a wonderful delight to the royal hunting party. If a stranger had happened to pass the procession at that moment, they could have sworn the party was unaware of the war eleven hundred miles to the northwest. Indeed, they weren't. The news came galloping to the king and his family by a sullen-faced carrier near midafternoon tea-time.

Kind Éldon frowned at the young man for disturbing his family's outing. Annoyed, he said, "And what is so pressing that you must disturb me at my Royal Estate?"

The lad flinched but bravely answered his king, "A message from Zircon, Your Majesty. Arriving with urged and discreet orders to be sent to Your Excellency immediately."

"Urged you say?" Feigning to be amused, the king waved the youth away. Taking the scroll, the king observed the seals, noting one to be from Lorde Nexlé at Zircon, north and east of the Royal Estate; the other was the raven and sword seal of the Crystine Commander. Interesting. King Eldon broke the seals and unrolled the starched paper. His family—wife, son, and two youngest daughters—crowed around to await the news. Éleen, the king's eldest daughter, hung back. Rarely did she involve herself in the others' pushy anticipation.

A hush fell over the family. All waited for King Éldon's summary. After skimming the parchment, Jared rolled it back up and met the curious eyes around him. "Commander Matar of the Crystal Kingdom writes of war at the northern boarders of Staria and Sealand. He requests Blue Haven's support in keeping the maunstorz out of Syre."

The guards, military all, shifted restlessly at the news; however, it was Prince Jace who asked the question they all longed to say "So, does this mean there will be open war in Syre and not just in the North?"

"No, "Jared replied too quickly, "It only means Commander Matar fears open war and is taking actions against it. The battle is near the Gap of the Forgotten, in Staria, and on the Oracle Coast— far, far away from here. We have no concern with this."

"No concern?!" Queen Elise argued, having always done so when her husband dismissed situations with political advantage. She flashed her pretty, blue eyes and set her jaw, ready to get into a heated debate. "Do I need to remind you of our petition from last Planting Time about Éleen? It would be a bad political farce if we have offered Staria a bride-gift then not send some kind of reinforcement. It looks diplomatically flippant!"

As the argument was sparked, it was apparent that the royal couple had completely forgotten their children and guards were present. More than one of the guards looked as if they would have left the scene had they any reason to—for fear of hearing information not intended for their ears. Only Princess Éleen noticed the discomfort of the men; her siblings clearly enjoyed hearing court intrigues playing out in front of them. She stepped forward to stop the spectacle before it evolved into something worse. "If Blue Haven is wishing to look diplomatic, father, mother, then why not send me and a sufficient force lead by Lord Nexlé to the Cathedral of Light? We could support Staria's case and benefit our kingdom with my presence."

King Eldon and the queen paused in mid-argument and turned to stare at their eldest daughter. Then, a brooding gleam came into the queen's eyes. "Yes, that would be a perfect solution. Prince Al'den would not only enjoy the support of our troops, he could see with his own eyes the delight we offered. Staria would have to be erringly rude to not accept us then."

Éleen was too relieved that she had stopped the pending argument to be bothered by her mother's rude, taciturn politicking. Even her siblings' snub remarks had no influence on her mood. "All right then, I will go prepare for my journey. May I depart as soon as Lord Nexlé is prepared?"

Kind Éldon barely acknowledged his daughter. With the situation resolved, he dismissed it from his mind. "Of course, of course, child. Go. Have a wonderful time. Write back of your success—of Blue Haven's success. Only come back if you have won the prince's heart." Without a backward glance, he and the rest of the family turned to their prepared tea, leaving the princess to ride her horse back to the estate accompanied by one guard. Unnoticed by them, however, Éleen was pleased to be leaving the smothering confines of her hypercritical family. For once, she got to travel! *Staria, here I come.*

Chapter 5

§

The Company Divided

Dust blew in great clouds, having been trod up by the passing Rubian foot soldiers and Crystine horses. The cloud spread the distance of a mile, almost the entire length of the crawling army. Anyone for leagues could have marked the slow advance across the Rubian grasslands.

Ahead of the Crystine cavalry cantered the Tashek horsemen, scouts all. Most paced the main contingent as they waited for their turn to go on scouting runs. Closest to Commander Matar jogged Zyanthena, having returned from her fourth run. Still antsy, she and her horse alike looked ready for more action. "This pace is torrid." The desert woman murmured, her complaint carrying to those nearest her: the six companions, Decond, Matar, and Terrik.

Matar smiled wryly and reined his mount around a sharp gouge in the ground. "You would complain even if we were traveling at cavalry pace." Zy'ena gave him a withering look that only caused the Crystine commander to chuckle. "You, of all people, know we cannot leave the mertinean behind. The discourtesy to them would cause great distension. And, you know full well that the mertinean must march at the pace of the wagons."

Zyanthena frowned, her sour energy bringing her fiery Tashek mount to a lively walk as he sensed her distress. The desert woman crooned to him and ran her fingers through his mane as she relaxed her emotional turmoil. Once steed and rider were settled, she returned to her conversation with her master. "I am well aware of the mertinean's reliance on their supply wagons, but it costs us too much precious time. Send our Tashek force ahead at least. We scout for you because it is asked, but it is a wasted effort when we are in friendly territory. What point is there to misspend us and the horses on pointless runs when we know exactly where our enemy is? It's a disgrace of our skill."

"In your opinion," Matar countered, "Your brother does not share your complaints." Zy'ena turned her sharp, brandy eyes to her sibling. The older Sheev'arid kept his gaze directed forward, however, making him unaffected by his sister's heated stare. "We have decided to wait until Raven's Den before we decide things further."

Having great respect for her master, Zyanthena ended the argument, though there remained a simmering atmosphere around the Tashek woman. Frustrated and needing to be in action, she guided her black charger away front the slow procession. Her intent was to go off again to search the long, spreading grasslands. A call to wait, however, brought her short of her intentions.

"Tashek. Sheev'arid?"

Zyanthena halted Unrevealed and turned him around to acknowledge the lord of Sealand as he cantered his steed near. "Your Grace." She bowed her head politely.

Gordar waved his hand dismissively. "Please, I prefer Gordar in informal company. And, I consider you an equal; in respects to the stories I have heard of you, Zy'ena."

Zyanthena begged to differ but, in Tashek fashion, she did not argue the point—wasted breath that it would be. Instead, she turned Unrevealed westward, allowing Gordar to fall in beside her. "The winds blow curiously today to send a Lord of Sealand running after the tresses of a desert kyesh."

Lord Gordar chuckled and answered her question. "Indeed; yet times call me to beg you to continue pushing for your request." Zyanthena's expression hardened, causing the Sealander to flush. "I apologize for overhearing your argument. It's just that I, too, wish to reach North Point by swifter means. The situation I left behind was desperate." Zy'ena's eyes gleamed with understanding. "It is for that reason that I wish for you to persist in your request."

"And the Lord of Sealand believes I have more power in such a request than him?" Her words seemed to be directed to her unbridled, fiery steed. "I have less pull that the man whom asks."

"Perhaps, but it would be ill-mannered of me to make such a request when the mertinean has given Sealand much of its support already."

Zyanthena frowned at the rationality. Her irritation boiling once more to the surface. She replied, quite pointedly, on the mertinean's support. "They would have been a greater help had they kept more of their men at Raven's Den and not marched to Wynward's Crossing two moons ago. The maunstorz have awaited such a blunderous move. They attacked the north-eastern provinces at a time we were thus inconvenienced."

Lord Gordar had the sense to look embarrassed for Zyanthena's sake. He cast his golden eyes to the following procession. No one seemed to have heard, though. Still, he checked again before signaling they move farther away from the group. "Many know of your opposition to that move, including those of King Fantill's court; however, this is not the place to bring it up. In that case, only you and Prince Maushelik disagreed of all the councils. Even if you find yourself correct now does not make you right then."

"You look suspicious." Zy'ena muttered.

"I should be. Your talk is near-treasonous."

The Tashek chuckled. "I have no king to be treasonous to. Tashek have no masters. We offer our loyalty only when it has been proven in turn. Matar carries that title because I respect the military expertise he offers me; King Maushelik does because of the treaties he holds with the Sheev'anee."

"You do not need to explain your world to me. I only came to ask you to keep pushing your vendetta. I am not here to argue the wisdom—or lack thereof—of the mertinean's rush to support the Crystal Kingdom's border. Would you do such?"

Zyanthena's features softened. She realized her keshic culture's ways were more concerning than comical to a lord such as Gordar. Downcasting her eyes to show her remorse, she said, "I can try, Your Grace, but you would be wise to council the priest, Anibus, on your matter. No one—not even the Sheev'anee or mertinean—would deny his request."

"Aye," Lord Gordar nodded agreement, "My cousin does seem to be a wise choice to change their opinions."

"Perhaps, Your Grace." Zyanthena bowed her head. "Tonight, I will help you speak to the priest of Estaria."

Gordar nodded his head once to show his agreeance. "I would be honored to have a Sheev'arid eat at my fire."

"It is settled then. Good day, Your Grace, and a leisurely journey." Without further ado, Zyanthena bowed to the Sealander and cued her black courser away, to scout the region.

Lord Gordar held his steed back as the impatient pair galloped away. "There is the reason why some of the more conservative political coterie call Matar's "shadow fox"" too impulsive." He shook his head to shake any unsettled emotions he may had acquired in the discussion with the Tashek woman.

"Zy'ena must have been very fervid to mark your face in such expression, cousin."

Surprised, Gordar focused his attention back to the present to realize he had rejoined the military procession, or more specifically Anibus and his companions. "Ah.... only on the point of her bluntness, Ani. She is certainly not one to curtsy around a flitting dandy."

Anibus nodded reined Rain closer to Gordar's steed. "Just as long as she is being civil to your person." The knowing shine of Anibus's blue eyes showed he suspected a different story.

Gordar wished to relieve his cousin's concerns, as the two relatives were well-versed in each other's council; however, he was unsure of the priest's companions. "She asked to be invited to supper tonight. Would you care to join me, too?"

"Hm." Anibus consented, though he shot Gordar a look of caution. "Be wise of those under the heavens, cousin. There are those that would find her request improper."

"I am aware that this steps behind the drapes, Ani, but ask that you understand the view I see from."

"Oh, I understand more than is assumed. I pray to the heavens daily to keep all those who need it safe from their follies—including my own when I agree to dine with a cousin far from chaste in my teachers' eyes."

"You jest cruelly, Anibus, for a man I could blackmail for more than enough mischief in his day."

"Aye," Anibus flashed an amused grin at his cousin, "And ne'er a day passes when I repent for such wild pursuits as you and Par led me though. I do not forget and will remember to tread carefully tonight. Especially when you give me a look like that."

"But innocence is all mine, Ani. Tonight is only a friendly meal among friends, nothing more. No disrespect to the commanders or kings here or afar. The heavens will certainly know that."

"Stars, I am certainly in league with calamity! Tonight, for good or ill."

It was late into the evening when the last of the mertinean's wagons rolled into camp. The sky had darkened to deep purple over the Red Hill tops the army had chosen to settle under. Dozens of individual campfires were already started, most heating the tired soldiers' suppers.

Separate from the main encampment was posted the Sheev'anee and their precious mounts. All the desert peoples' horses were feed and groomed, none of the desert folk wasting their efforts on their horses for their own relief. Only one of their tents stayed empty, the one reserved for Zyanthena. Terrik made sure to place fresh water and feed in his sister's tent before he walked his rounds about the Tashek encampment. He was used to his sister's long absences and always took time to make sure her and her mount's needs were met. Yet, Terrik wished fervently that his willful adopted-sister would come back quickly from her scouting run. It was useless anyway and only an excuse to vent her impatience on the empty duty.

A tired sigh escaped him as Terrik finally allowed himself to sink into the comfortable folds of his sleeping pallet. His retainer, Shytin, handed him his hot meal and a cup of tea before stepping back to give his superior some space. "And Zyanthena?"

Terrik shook his head, "Zyen will not be joining us yet. Set her super near the fire. I'm sure she'll be back soon enough to want it."

"Sir." Shytin bowed and backed away to attend to his job.

The elder Sheev'arid leaned back wearily on a tent post as he chewed his dinner. He was just finishing his last bites when the sound of a light horse's barefoot hooves thudded up to the tent. Terrik straightened himself from his seat as Shytin rushed by to see to the horse and rider. A moment later, Zyanthena's delicate shadow slipped through the main entrance. The heavy blue cloth closed softly behind her. Terrik started to rise in respect but Zy'ena waved him down. In haste, the vivacious woman rid herself of her outer armor and heavier weapons, throwing them in a careless pile on her pallet. Terrik got the sense that she was anything but ready to sit down and eat a quiet meal, but before he could ask her to settle, Zyanthena told him of her plans.

"I am going out to check on Decond. Please, do not worry about saving any repast for me. I am sure I will find something among the Crystine."

"But, Zyen, surely you would find better fare here? Eat, please, before you go."

The look Zyanthena shot her brother was sharp. "I mind not the soldiers' grub. It may not be as palatable but it is still sustaining. No, I will eat with Decond."

Terrik gave an extra loud sigh to Zy'ena's retreating back. "If you weren't such a lovely kysh'aunen [female-dog] I don't know how I'd ever get past your incivility." Of course, Zyanthena was already too far away to respond to the crude mark. "Kyesh!" [woman]

Zyanthena had heard her brother's crude remark but quickly batted it aside as sibling pestering. Terrik was tired, as he usually was these days, and rarely had a good thing to say. Besides, Zyanthena found she was later than she expected herself to be in reaching Lord Gordar's tent. Though it usually didn't bother her, she hoped the Sealand lord would not take offense.

The path Zyanthena had chosen wove past Anibus's own tent— on purpose, as she always was, to see how Decond fared. The soft-eyed priest was not around, having already left to dine with his cousin, but young Decond was in. The autumn-haired youth sat up quickly from his intense ceiling studying; the motion of the tent flap alerting him of a visitor. Zyanthena stepped in and smiled warmly at her friend. "So, Anibus has granted you space in his personal tent. Honorable."

"Aye." Decond smiled back and waved Zyanthena to the seat he was clearing off beside himself.

"I am sorry, but I have little time here." Zyanthena saw her words wounded the boy. He was, most likely, feeling lonely after she had cast him aside to be watched by strangers. She came near to lay a hand gently on his shoulder. "Decond, my friend, I do poorly by you." The seventeen-year-old shook his head to disagree but Zyanthena forged on. "I do. Here I've cast you away from all you've know just to leave you among boisterous military brogues. I can't even promise you a moment of my friendship."

Her words seem to touch the boy deeply, for he could not even answer her. Instead, he turned his eyes away to stare intensely at the weaving of the priest's ornate blankets. Zyanthena was afraid he was trying to hide his tears. Kindly, she wrapped her arms around Decond's strong shoulders and pulled him into her embrace. "I apologize for not being here as you need me. I had hoped Anibus would be kind to you, but I understand that there is a different need between him and me. I will try to do better for you, Decond, I will." The young farrier nodded and pulled himself from her embrace; this time there were traces of tears in his eyes.

But, just as quickly, Decond's disarming smile spread across his face. "I had a good day otherwise, though. Five horses lost shoes, so I was busy enough."

Zyanthena cocked an eyebrow, surprised at the change in her friend. "Well... I am glad to hear you didn't spend today idling away, what with the mertinean's slow pace." The raven-haired woman stood and proceeded around the tent, lazily making her way for the door. "I hope you are being fed. You have eaten?"

Decond shook his head. "Anibus told me to wait 'til you arrived. He assumed you'd stop by and instructed me to "escort" you to dinner. Apparently, His Grace Lord Gordar, has asked us to dine with him tonight."

"Indeed". Zyanthena hid the consternation she felt at hearing that. Anibus was not a fool, but she was surprised he wanted young Decond apart of their unauthorized concourse. Was the priest warning her he was aware of Zyanthena's distension with Matar and Terrik? Or, was Anibus trying to keep her from such an insubordinate by including Decond? Anibus certainly knew Zyanthena cared about the youth. *I hear, priest.*

"So," Decond asked, not noticing Zyanthena's sudden quietness, "Shall we go?"

"Yes. I am sure I have kept His Grace waiting long enough." Zyanthena answered as cheerfully as she could. "Lead on, my chivalrous escort."

"Oh, dear me, that was such a dreadful plan!" Anibus exclaimed, shaking his head ruefully at the tale Lord Gordar had reminded him about. "It didn't turn out so well, either, if I remember right."

"No, it did not." The Sealander replied as he sipped his mead to rewet his throat. "The cook found out we had used her flour to make the apparitions, and King Fantill ordered us to wash all the soldiers' boots and tack just for scaring them so."

"Ah, I remember," Anibus chuckled at the memory. "But Par go it the worst. He had to take five all-hours classes with Head Priest Röme just to learn why a prince should not treat his father's soldiers so."

"You were so amused, bantering about it for days afterward. But, of course, the king put a stop to that by sending you to West Port, to the covenant there."

Anibus sobered immediately. "Yes, to start a life learning to be a pious and respectable priest. That last diabolical was too much for His Majesty."

Gordar cast his cousin a look of sympathy. "We were all too much, I'm afraid. After you were called away, King Fantill "suggested" I accept an apprenticeship with Commander Averron. A year and half later, Par proposed to the princess of the Crystal Kingdom; on order of his father I assume. King Fantill certainly knew how to end our mischief."

"That he did." Anibus answered quietly. He shook his head, his eyes seeming somewhat distant. "Those were fun times." The priest's blue eyes returned to shine gratefully at his cousin. "I'd almost forgotten. The covenant being such a sober place, I've rarely had a good laugh 'til tonight."

"Ah, don't get too sentimental on me, cuz. " Gordar teased. "I'm afraid the good mead has gone to your head!"

"Better than strict Estarian doctrine, I say!" "I'm sure they'd appreciate you saying that."

"And I am sure they would not." A feminine voice reprimanded them.

Lord Gordar almost sputtered on his drink. He turned around, surprised and ashamed, to offer a welcome to Zyanthena and Decond. "Lady, sir."

Zyanthena gave a short chuckle, unable to hold her seriousness in the face of a blushing Sealander and embarrassed priest. "Pardon me, Your Grace. I know I should not eavesdrop and should have asked your soldiers to announce me, but I wished not to bother them." The alluring Tashek unraveled herself from Decond's nervous grasp and glided over to join the two cousins at the oak table. Decond hesitated, flustered at the unusually relaxed display between lord, priest, and warrior, but he finally joined them—at Anibus's kind beckoning. He started to bow to Lord Gordar, the man being of a higher station, but the golden-haired man waved him to a seat.

"No need for formalities in our small company, lad. I know my cousin and I tire of such formalities and Zy'ena is less than pleased with long graces." Zyanthena nodded approval. "So, tonight Decond, you may share with us as equals."

"Y-yes, Your Grace." The seventeen-year-old quickly took the offered seat, settling his lanky limbs onto ornate chair as delicately as he could muster.

Gordar, meanwhile, called out to his one servant to bring out their waiting meal. A moment passed before the old man came through the side flap, loaded down with a pot of mashed vegetables, turkey and herbs, a basket of bread loaves and cheese. Lastly was a small tankard of Havenese wine. In a flourish, the man had all items set out in front of the diners. He was quickly away.

Anibus grabbed the small stack of dinnerware on the chest beside him and diligently began to sever the others. "Oh, you've quite outdone us, cousin, having this fine fare tonight. And Havenese wine! I haven't had that in years!"

"It is still your favorite, I hope."

"Oh, yes." Anibus grinned. He finished distributing the plates and began to pour the wine. The group was silent for a breath as the priest finished; each person savoring the unique and flavorful taste of Gordar's cook's delightful food.

Very little was said throughout the meal, just small talk about politics, fine wines, and good horses—all of which Zyanthena and Gordar could argue extensively upon. At the end, however, the conversation turned more toward its original intention, for the dishes were cleared and the effects of the fine wine took hold of tight-lipped characters.

Zyanthena started the conversation. "Your Grace, you have spoken to Anibus about your request?"

The cousins and Decond had been jesting with each other on a topic of hunting, but Zyanthena's words sobered them immediately. "Yes, Tashek, we have spoken about it at great length while waiting for you."

Zyanthena read the reluctance in the Sealander's eyes. "The priest does not agree, hence his using a bait on me." She meant Decond without involving the boy.

"I only set it for the restless soul I see in you."

"Anxious soul, priest." The Tashek repeated flatly. "And Lord Gordar's plight is not a restless situation, I presume, or your prince's".

"I refer not to them, as you know, Zy'ena." Anibus answered calmly. "You are under oath to respect Commander Matar. This goes against him. Yes, I long to help My Prince as much as Gordar, but your involvement may put us on uneven terms with the Crystine and Rubia."

"Then don't directly involve me."

"If it were so easy, lady." Gordar interjected. "Matar would know where such a request comes from."

"But perhaps your master would re-evaluate at Raven's Den? He seems to find that a reasonable town to leave the mertinean to their pace. Or had I not heard correctly?"

Zyanthena narrowed her eyes at the priest. Standing, she strode over to the map case Lord Gordar kept by his bed. She returned with the map of Syre and smacked it down on the table between Lord Gordar and Anibus. "And the time that would cost, priest! We have just barely reached the end of the Red Hills, not even a quarter of the distance to Carmine. It will take us six days to reach the city; and may five more to Raven's Den. The Tashek alone could make it in five days; with the Crystine, perhaps, six at most. Decide how much you care about your prince."

"Don't you fear your Tashek, Zyanthena, will try something?"

Matar glanced at the mertinean commander in surprise, caught off guard at the sudden turn on their conversation. Until then, the two commanders had shared a simple meal in relative ease as they discussed their options, the weather, and their armies. The Crystine commander had known Ethan Kins would bring the subject up eventually; he had just hoped it would have been later. "I expect her to." Matar answered.

"Oh?" Commander Kin gave Matar his full attention, enticed. "You want her to stir up discord at our slow pace?"

"On the contrary, I hope she does not do that. But I do expect her to make a point about how little time we have, yes. She is one of the best warriors I have ever worked with, and she knows Sealand has precious few days to receive our support. I promised Anibus—a priest no less! —that I would hurry to his kingdom's defense, yet here I am sitting two days-worth cliques behind. Zyanthena is right to be offended at this arduous pace. It goes against the promise I made to Anibus and against the natural fashion of the Tashek. The Sheev'anee would have been to Raven's Den by now. "

"But to disband with us could offend Kind Chível. That must worry   you?"

"Yes, damn politics! I stay because it is expected for us to stay with your forces that helped us at the Crystal border, but—."

"Your Tashek do not like it—the waiting." Ethan interrupted so Matar did not have to say something slanderous about Rubia's king. "I see their restlessness; Zyanthena being one of the most active. If they did not have a vow with you, they would be long gone to King Maushelik or Prince Par."

"Undoubtedly. They are warriors of action. Their horses are bred to travel long distances faster and more effectively than any alive today, and their skills in battle are reputably the most superior. They really should be going ahead."

"Then why not let them?"

"What?" Matar wondered if he had heard the other man right.

"Send the Tashek ahead of our own forces." Kins repeated. "It will allow Lord Gordar to feel we're supporting Sealand and keeps our forces from otherwise inevitable conflict. Besides, it will assuage Zyanthena's restlessness."

"She really does rub you, doesn't she?" Matar jested, causing the Rubian to chuckle. "It could work, I guess. We could ask them to send back a Tashek scout to tell us the situation. It would be highly beneficial."

Commander Kins nodded in agreement. "Tomorrow morning, then, we will announce our decision. The Tashek move at first light."

Early dawn brought tired men to their feet, each knowing it would be many days yet before they would feel any comfort. One by one, tents were torn down, the pace quickening as the chilly morning air pushed back sleepiness. Campfires were doused once each man got his meal; the dying smoke trails rose to the brightening sky.

Out of the morning mist, the Tashek warriors joined the camp. All looked fresh and dangerous. Their mounts pawed on the cold earth in anticipation. Included in their ranks, rode Zyanthena, no traces of the wine or late-night discussion on her countenance. She and the other desert nomads looked impatient at the army's slow pace.

Commanders Matar and Kins rode up through the mertinean ranks, the Crystine in a uniform line trailing behind. They stopped alongside the Tashek horsemen. No one spoke as the mertinean organized its line, and the six companions, accompanied by Lord Gordar and Decond, joined the commanding ranks. Even the day seemed to pause as the silent anticipation grew. Why were the commanders no issuing any orders?

Finally, Commander Kins cued his mount forward to address the men, his golden steed tossing its creamy mane in response to being allowed to move in front of the ranks. "Soldiers, desert warriors, and guests," Ethan Kins began, "We are marching as fast as we can to aid Sealand, but there is fear our speed may not be enough to save His Highness. Therefore, Commander Matar and I have decided to send a small contingent of volunteers. The Tashek will escort those who wish a quick travel to North Point. Two scouts will return to report to us in Raven's Den. I ask that any able and willing horsemen join the Tashek."

The army glanced about in surprise. Would all of the Crystine leave with the Tashek? But, no, not a single Crystine soldier left their ranks to join the desert warriors. A different horseman did, however.

"I will travel the pace of the Tashek so that I can meet with My Highness again." Lord Gordar stepped his Sealand mount in front of the commanders. "Tell King Chível I do this not to spite him but because I fear for My Prince."

Commander Kins nodded acceptance.

"And we will go as well." Patrick announce coming to the fore of the companions. He confronted his father as bravely as he could. "We wish to hurry to Sealand's aide."

The elder Kins was slow to respond, casting a critical glance at the six companions. "I cannot grant all of you to leave. Merchant Seagold, you and your men are under protection of the king; Priest Anibus, it is against Rubian law for us to allow to you to be escorted to a battle ground; and Decond is needed here." Ethan paused letting his news sink into unwilling ears. "But," he continued, "I will grant permission for Kins, Novano, and Ravesbend to join the fore."

The companions hesitated before Patrick and Jacen took their mounts across the gap to the Tashek. Rio apologized quietly, saying he would stay to guard his friends. Ethan Kins granted both actions, bemused at the sudden comradeship the newly formed group shared.

"Anyone else?" He called out. No one moved to answer. "Very well. Mertinean, Crystine, we march out to Carmine. Tashek, Stars' speed!"

A hastened bustle preceded the Rubian commander's words. In short time, the slower army was organized and ready to move. Beyond, on the outskirts, the Tashek were huddled in a circle—Gordar, Patrick, and Jacen included—listen to Terrik's orders.

"We move as fast as our mounts can carry us." The Sheev'arid was telling his group. "We could send scouts, but I feel it will slow the pace and tire the horses. So, go with caution but speed. We must reach Sealand in six sun-counts or take passage by the stars to speed our time. Use the mounts' fatigue to gauge the pace—do not overwork them!" The Tashek chanted out agreement. "I elect Lord Farrylin and Siv'arid Kor'mauk as leaders of this journey. I will stay behind with Matar as representative." The Tashek shouted out agreement and broke. Everyone, that was, except Zyanthena. Terrik's sister stood looking stood looking at her brother with misgiving.

"I choose Kor'mauk because he is more reserved." Terrik started thinking his sister angry at his choice. He found he could not read her expression.

"A wise choice, but not the best." Zy'ena answered emotionlessly. "I should stay with Master. The Tashek need you leading."

It was for Terrik, then, to look surprised, but not for long. "No," he said quietly but sharply. "Matar needs a Sheev'arid who is ever loyal to him. You go before I say worse."

Zyanthena's brown eyes flared. "Master knows I am most loyal to him. It is you who thinks in treachery." Angered, she asked Unrevealed away, leaving her harsh words behind.

Terrik watch her leave, half in vexation and half brokenhearted. "I do love you, Zyen. That is why I protect you. Stars' speed."

Commander Matar looked startled to find Terrik riding up beside him on his chestnut mount. The Tashek ignore his questioning stare and acted as if it was the most normal thing he could do. "Zyanthena is to be one of the scouts to return to us. She and Unrevealed are the most appropriate choice to make the time and distance."

"Then it is good for them to be a part of the force making up our time." Matar agreed, "Though it is an assurance to have you remaining. I'm embarrassed to admit that I have come to appreciate having a Tashek to watch my back"

"Yes, Master. I will watch it against any foe—no matter how close they are to you."

Chapter 6

§

Breakfast in Deceptive Company

"Look, My Highness there shines the monolith Bel'falor that marks the edge of your kingdom with Sunrise. We should make it to the royal palace by dawn tomorrow morning."

Princess Éleen looked out her coach's window at Lord Carrod Nexlé's call. Her china-blue eyes locked onto the distant, jade-stone structure. She had seen it before, as a small child, but the ancient pillar still held her fascination as it had all those years ago. "Ah, it's beautiful! Tell me, Lord Nexlé, have you heard its story?"

"I'm afraid I have not, Highness." Carrod replied smoothly, though he, like many Havenese children had heard the tale. "If you would be so kind as to enlighten me?"

"It would be a pleasure." Éleen answered politely. "In ancient times, many say as far back as the end of the First Age, our ancestors delved into the realm of majik and devilry. Bel'falor was one of their majiks. Some believe it was created to call down the forces of maunstorz from the Stars, others that it had a far less foul purpose; however, all agree it carried magical powers. As the stories go, our ancestors continued to use majik though the Second Age. Bel'falor and other monoliths became their central focus of these powers. On the eve of the turning of the Second Age, it is believed the people called out of the monoliths eight Stones of Power, directly given from the Stars. The energy used to create these stones drained the monoliths of their majik—the consequence for asking such a price from the Stars. To this day, Bel'falor and the other pillars are as cold as the night the stones were cast."

"That was a brilliant fabrication of the tale, My Highness."

Éleen shot the tall man a withering glance. "It is not even close to being an amateur bard's tale and certainly not flourished in its telling."

"But, My Highness" Carrod protested, "You make it so simple and lovely. Anyone would be thrilled to have you relive the story."

"Probably not." The princess countered quietly. "Most people spurn majik these days. Bel'falor with all its beauty is considered refuse of a time long forgotten."

Lord Nexlé, politely pretending not to hear the princess's mutterings. He guided his dapple-marked bay ahead of the princess's carriage. Éleen didn't register he had left her company; she was too busy contemplating the past and majik and curses and other invidious things. History had an odd way of coming to the surface even centuries past...

"Your Majesty." A nervous page said, coming into the firelight so King Raymond could acknowledge him.

"What is it?" The Sunarian ruler snapped from the disturbance to his evening tea.

"Majesty," the man shrunk back a little and held out his message. His hand shaking. "Th-this had arrived by fast courier from the Azure Palace."

The king growled in his throat and snatched the scroll away. He waved the man back and quickly broke the seagull seal. The jade wax and ribbon fell away into the embers of the nearby fire, becoming singed and unrecognizable in moments. The grumpy ruler skipped over the flourished pleasantries, bored with the flattering words. Finally, his eyes found the bulk of the letter:

...and so I write to inform you, Your Majesty of the Sunrise Kingdom, to implore you to allow my daughter Princess Éleen safe and comfortable passage through your lands. She travels with the graces of myself and King Maushelik of Staria. Princess Éleen will arrive on your boarder the morning after you receive this letter. My greatest appreciation for your assistance...

Other words followed but Raymond skipped over them, finding nothing more of value. "Selfish bastards these other kings are." He muttered under his breath and took a long, impolite slurp from his teacup. "But, I must appear the generous Sunarian king my people say I am. Yes, that I will do for you, my dear King-man. I harbor your daughter, give her safe passage in these dangerous times and you are indebted to me for future needs." A rough chuckle rasped the king's throat. "Man!" King Raymond called his servant back to him. The cowering subject scuttled into the firelight and bowed as quickly as his shaking body allowed. "Prepare a room for Princess Éleen Éldon-Tomino. Make it cozy. I am sure her journey has been trying on her delicate nature. Too, arrange a wonderful meal for her arrival—delightful Sunarian teas and pastries to relax the travel pains away. Make it in the southern garden, overlooking the seashore. Use the blue chinaware and ivory. Oh! And make sure the linens and silk ae new. Arrange a florist to have Irises and Star tulips freshly set about the table."

"Yes, Your Majesty." The poor man was sweating as he tried his best to remember the king's growing list. "Will that be all, Your Majesty?"

"Yes, ah...no!" Raymond snapped his fingers together as he thought of one more thing. "Alert Connel he will be joining us at breakfast tomorrow. Make it eight o'clock sharp in his best burgundy. Now out, out!"

"Majesty."

King Raymond took no notion of the lesser man as he scurried away. The king was smirking, scheming his good fortune. "Most likely, the princess is set to show the Havenese support to the North. I have not that wretched heir of mine to send, but Connel can do to win the princess's favor. She will certainly carry our support to Staria. Or other arrangement can always be made..."

"My Highness, we have arrived at the Sunlight Palace's outer gates."

Princess Éleen groaned and set herself upright from the uncomfortable position she found herself in. She had not realized, when she had ordered her guards to continue through the night, that it would cost her body many pains—mostly in places she did not want to think about. Diligently, she pushed the sleep from her mind and began to rearrange her appearance, hoping it did not look as she felt it did. "Thank you, Lord Nexlé. For your quick pace, we will have time to stay an extra while and recuperate."

"My Highness, there is no need." But, Éleen could hear the relief in his voice as he protested the courtesy. She kindly ignored it and set her eyes to taking in the magnificent, ruby-studded archgates leading into the palace's courtyard. All about, servants bustled from one task to another, many working to keep the marble flagstones bold-white and polished. Another dozen were at their daily tasks of trimming the exotic foliage to certain measurements while still keeping them as healthy as possible. There was no sign of any soldiers or courtmen along the path, leading Éleen to suspect they had taken the southern gates (she had heard they were rarely used) into the complex. The southern entrance avoided the rest of the city, being set nearly on the coast but away from the wharf that lay to the west. Sadly, she would miss the sprawling sight of the "city of jewels".

As her coach stopped at the gem-ensconced stairwell, a royal procession rushed forth, all banners unfurling, to line her inevitable passage. Silence followed as Éleen's stunned guards slowly came out of their state of surprise. Lord Nexlé was the first to let go of his awe, quickly dismounting to assist his princess out of the carriage. In his eyes, Éleen noticed, were the words and relief "*the letter got through*".

The Havenese smiled her warmest smile at Carrod and slid her arm into his. "Well done," she mouthed and nodded in the direction of the palace. The other guards were quick to fall into formation behind Lord Nexlé and their princess.

At the top of the stairs was another surprise. Instead of a common page or the chief of the household, the princess and her escort were met by Prince Connel, second-in-line to the Sunarian throne. The twenty-year-old flashed a disarming smile and gave a courtly bow. "Your Highness," he began in a suave baritone, "I hope your journey here was pleasant. Seeing as it is morning, would you accept a quiet breakfast with His Majesty and myself before retiring to your rooms?"

Princess Éleen was sure neither she nor her men really wanted to stay on their feet but policy, and the enticement of some genuine repast, was enough to lure the strength back into her posture. "With such hospitality as you have shown, we cannot refuse, but, please, Your Highness, may my men be given a warm meal and retirement? Lord Nexlé and I would graciously see to your request, however."

Princess Éleen was quite aware her words did not sound as formal as they should—and she had rushed the last sentence so as to not seem rude.

Prince Connel, however, took her discordance all in stride, as if he had never heard a catch in her acceptance. "By all means, Your Highness, my men will make sure your escort is well-taken care of." As if on cue, servants arrived and motioned the tired soldiers toward the nearest entranceway. Once they disappeared, Connel waved his two charges in a different direction. They continued down a side lane leading around the towering palace. If you will, His Majesty King Raymond waits for us in the southern gardens. He wishes you to relax and eat a pleasant meal before finding rest in your quarters. Your possessions will be taken to your rooms during this time."

"Your household is very kind." Princess Éleen returned the younger royal's polite words. She suppressed a tired sigh and squeezed Lord Nexlé's arm to assure herself she was doing fine. Carrod smiled encouragingly at her and clasped a hand over hers. Relieved, Éleen returned her attention to Connel, who was courteously pointing out the sights and history of the Sunlight Palace.

§ §

The southern garden was famed as the most beautiful in the Southern kingdoms—and not without reason. Its allure was, in part, due to its advantageous view of the Sen Sia, the peaceful ocean; plus, the Sunarian court had made a point to allot most of the kingdom's garden revenues to this location. Huge sums had been spent on exotic plants and rare foliage, just to excite visitors with Sunrise's beauty. It was resplendent enough that it guaranteed a win of favor with any gullible young lady. [A fact King Raymond had used countless of times before and hoped to procure again with the young princess of Blue Haven].

King Raymond stood against the elaborate railing near the dining pavilion, his back to the entrance of his son and guests. He made sure his stature was tall, stern, but not unpleasant (one should not be overly stoic) and knew he would make a strong impression on the Haveners. After all, Raymond had many plans for this encounter, why not decorate it up with the best?

A scuffle, and Prince Connel's rich baritone voice, alerted the Sunarian king to his guests' arrival. He did not turn, for he wished to make his guests wait—only for a moment. Yet, he did cock an ear to listen for the princess's gasp of delight. None came. King Raymond scowled and bid himself ten more breathes before he pasted a smile on his face and turned to greet the young woman.

Princess Éleen was more delicate than paintings portrayed her. Amidst the pastel colors of roses, star-brights, and trilliums, there was a certain allure to the woman that travel had not replaced. King Raymond could not have been more pleased if the Goddess of the Evening danced in. The Havenese princess would be glorious pawn to play with. "Your Majesty." Princess Éleen curtsied as the king approached her. She offered him a graceful hand. "I am pleased to be accepted so venerably, Your Majesty."

"Oh, quite the contrary, my dear." King Raymond collected her gloved hand and kissed a knuckle. He continued his polite smile as he led her over to their breakfast table. "I am very honored to be blessed with the company of such a delightful guest. My son and I have not had the pleasure in some time now, what with war in the North and all. Your charms are sure to send these grey clouds that hang about us away." Raymond helped the princess to her seat and waved this son to sit across from her. Finally, he acknowledged the escort, Lord Nexlé, "And Lord Nexlé, how wonderful it is that you are the one accompanying Her Highness. I pray your father is doing well?"

"Yes, Majesty, he is quite well." Carrod bowed and waited for the king to take his seat before he found his. "He is handling King Eldon's affairs from our estate in Zircon."

"Good, good." Raymond muttered, keeping his face cheerful, despite his loathing of courtly etiquette. "Ah, do enjoy this breakfast, Princess," he continued, returning to Éleen.

"Yes, Your Majesty, I shall. Thank you kindly." Princess Éleen graced the three men with a perfect smile, well-schooled. She proceeded to pick up a strawberry pastry delicately between her gloved thumb and forefinger. The prince watched, as if enraptured, as she nibbled off an end and, somehow, didn't drop a single crumb. A delighted smile formed on her lips. "This is a fine pastry, Your Majesty. My deepest compliments to your cook."

"Indeed." King Raymond answered, though he was more pleased by his son's interest than the Havenese princess's remark. "Please, enjoy each as you can, Princess. My cook will be most delighted to hear your council on his delicacies." Princess Éleen nodded and took her time to sample the pastries before her, as well as, savoring the fine assortment of teas.

Lord Nexlé ate his breakfast in silence, observing the great Sunarian king and the princess discuss the finer points of the meal. He did not like the overly-charming way the Sunarian was flattering the royal woman, but it was not his place to intervene—only Princess Éleen could do that, and she did not seem to mind the attentions the ruler bestowed her.

"I see you are a military man, Lord Nexlé." Prince Connel politely brought Carrod into the conversation. The Havenese man could see the prince really didn't care what he said, as his eyes were only for Éleen; but, Lord Nexlé took the invitation nonetheless. After all, neither of them had been asked to partake in the royal's "scones" debate.

"My father is commander-in-arms for King Eldon, as is customary for my family. His Majesty requested I accompany Her Highness in my father's place, whilst she leads our Havenese force to Staria." He kept out the fact that his father was horribly crippled from a war injury—the real reason the former Nexlé had not ridden as an escort.

"Indeed." Prince Connel feigned interest. "A high task for one such as yourself."

Carrod sucked back a reply that the prince was unqualified to speak about what was "qualified" for a protection detail. Instead, he replied, "The king would not trust his eldest daughter to anyone he thought incapable of the job of protecting her."

"As I am sure." Connel interjected, cutting off any more remarks Carrod might have. He sipped a cup of tea and smoothly changed the subject. "So, the maunstorz have become more daring these last few months. Have you any news on that front, Lord Nexlé?"

Carrod shifted back in his chair taking a moment to think over his words. The prince felt the pause and switched his gaze from Éleen to the young soldier, his attention suddenly becoming very attuned. "News has it that the fighting on the Rubian-Crystal border had become quite fierce. Concern over the sudden interest at Wynward's Crossing forced King Chível to send aid to the Crystine, though there was opposition to this decision. The Tashek force pledged to the Crystine Commander Matar believed the sudden maunstorz push was a route created to push other agendas."

"You mean to act as a decoy?"

"Yes, I do; though, that is not how I heard the Tashek stated it." Lord Carrod replied and continued on his narrative. "Not a week after the arrival of King Chível's mertinean, the maunstorz gave retreat into the Crystal mountains, leaving behind them the scattered forces of mertinean and Crystine. The Tashek attempted to follow; however, an unusual snowstorm forced them to return to the Crystal Kingdom."

"And the border has been quiet since."

Carrod nodded. "A month has passed since the maunstorz unexpected retreat. One month of no battles or any other skirmishes. It was too odd a coincidence to be anything but suspicious." The Lord's brow knit as he thought. "And then the raids began again against the Crystine. Not battles, per say, but they were enough to cause unrest on the north-eastern border."

"And then the two big battlements showed up at "The Gap" and down the Oracle Coast."

"Uh huh. The Tashek had been right. The maunstorz had been planning on scattering Syre's Northern forces so that they could push a force through Staria and try an attack into Sealand or any of us in the South."

"You should be cautious when throwing opinions around so casually." Connel eyed the Havener in warning, his eyes wandering to his father. "Some believe the North does not need the South's support against a few maunstorz."

Carrod knitted his eyebrows, angered, "Ten thousand maunstorz in no small force! That these are nearly nineteen-thousand attacking the entire North should be a cause for all our concern. Never has there been this number of enemies. The South needs to rally against these maunstorz. For, if they get through the Northern lines, there is nothing stopping them from coming here."

"We can handle that when—and if—the time comes; which is unlikely." Prince Connel replied arrogantly. "We can handle any maunstorz force. Yet, until such happens, it is not our problem."

Carrod shook his head in disbelief, controlling his rage. "This is all of Syre's problem, Your Highness! It's foolish to think it is not."

King Raymond had overheard Lord Carrod's last comment—and he was not very impressed. "Lord Nexlé, when last I recalled, I am King of Sunrise." Carrod looked taken aback. "And as king, I have studied the amount of resistance the savages have shown thus far. Pitiful by all accounts. So, if I say these is no concern with the maunstorz force in the North, then then there is no concern. Any judgement otherwise is out of line."

Lord Carrod bowed his head in meek acceptance. "As you wish, Your Majesty. There was no detraction in my words, merely a count of how the others kingdoms view the attacks. You are, of course Majesty, correct about your kingdom."

"Indeed, I am." Raymond replied shortly. He had a deep scowl on his face that darkened his features to an uncomfortable severity. It lasted long enough to cause tension to rise in the air. Then the king shifted and the air seemed to clear. "Well, princess, lord, I do hope you have enjoyed your breakfast, but I am sure you are very tired after your journey. I will pardon you now so that you may hasten to rest."

"Thank you, Your Majesty, Highness. Your courtesy is greatly appreciated." Princess Éleen stood and accepted the king's leave, giving her hand for the ruler to kiss good-bye. She curtsied to the prince and motioned Carrod to her side. Both hastened away in as smooth a fashion as they could manage behind a cowering servant. They needn't have bothered, however, for King Raymond ignored their departure.

"Ignorant, stifling fool!" Raymond muttered. Prince Connel calmly overlooked his father's cursing. The two Sunarians sat in the beautiful mid-morning silence, oblivious to the splendor of the day. Finally, Raymond spoke again while still gazing darkly out across the sea. "She will make a good catch for you son. She is mild and genteel and only as witted as a dog—perfect to be a Sunarian queen. You should be sure to be with them tomorrow when they leave. Not only can we appease the North with your presence, we can capture you your queen—with your charm, of course. This is best."

"Indeed, father, as you wish." Connel replied and stood from the table. "With your leave, then, I will go prepare."

Raymond waved carelessly, lost in thought. "Just return home quickly, my son. The people need their prince, and it is best that you be where they can see you—especially while your brother is off playing 'soldier'."

"Yes, father." The prince bowed. "I will be back—with all your requests."

§　§

Princess Éleen waited until all of the king's servants and her own had left the room before turning away from the window to address Carrod. "The king is a cunning man." She stated, though her words were drenched in sarcasm. "He had you baited quite well with his son."

Lord Carrod gave Éleen a withering glance; yet, he could see the sympathy behind her reprimand. "Indeed, My Highness. I apologize for the impertinence I caused."

"No need, dear Carrod," Éleen answered. "We must be more conscious of our tongues is all. Tomorrow we will be away."

"Yes, My Highness." Carrod stepped closer to Éleen and tentatively took one of her hands in his. "You are always so calm, Princess. It is a quality I deeply admire. I will watch myself better."

A smile played on Éleen's delicate lips. "I am very happy to have you as my escort, Lord Nexlé. It makes the miles more bearable. Now, please, get some rest. We need all we can get."

"Highness." Carrod bowed and turned away from the Havenese princess.

Éleen watched him depart before turning back to the large window and its view. In truth, her eyes were too far-seeing to notice the beauty of the sea. "In a fortnight, I will meet my betrothed," she whispered. "I pray, dear Evening Star, that he is much kinder than my dreams depict." But the silent scene did not answer her. The princess sighed and looked down at her hand, to find it had unconsciously wrapped around the pendant the Prince of Staria had gifted her upon their betrothal agreement. The citrine stone glistened gently in the morning sun, as if capturing a sense of calm elusive to Éleen—until she looked at the stone. "He must not be that bad, Mother, (Estarian religion, Mother is the sky that houses the stars) if he was nice enough to give me this pendant. I do pray that it is so." Éleen clutched the stone tenderly to her chest. "Please, may he be someone I can learn to love."

Chapter Seven

§

Sacrifice

"Make way for His Royal Highness!" A Starian guard called out to the crowd as the procession of Prince Al'den's soldiers marched through the populated streets, clearing the way to the Citadel of Light. The one-hundred-count of horses and riders that followed shortly afterward rode as hard as they could through the scattering citizens. They continued hard-bent toward the main courtyard and dismounted quickly. Already there in formation, the foot-soldiers saluted as their prince touched ground.

Prince Al'den ignored the men, too preoccupied with concerns outside of the fortress. He rushed up the stairs, two guards hustling behind him, and did not bother to issue any orders; he expected his commanders to know the needs of the cavalry. "Call King Maushelik!" He ordered as he strode toward the war room. "I will meet my father by the maps."

The Starian king was already in attendance over the said maps when Al'den hurried through the ornate yellowwood doors. He turned as his son neared and motioned his three advisors to step away. "You come from surveying the Gap?" The question was spoken calmly but the prince saw his father's long, greying beard tremble in apprehension for what was to come.

"Indeed, father, I do." Al'den bowed formally but quickly. "I regret my haste, but I wish to be gone from here as soon as you say the word. I fear the maunstorz are on the move again. They are heading here and not continuing east as first predicted."

King Maushelik stiffened but motioned for his son to continue. "The count, my son?"

"Eight thousand remain. Our forces have been able to hold the Gap for these past twelve days, until word could reach us. Considerable damage was done to our northern lines. This morning, the enemy forces have regrouped farther in the Gap of the Forgotten. They are using their pyre smoke to cover their movements. Commander Sheen, fearing a trap, called the troops back to safer lines. His retreat did not stir the maunstorz to action—yet. Sheen thought that, perhaps, they are following the pattern they have preferred for years, retreating and attacking us elsewhere. I do not think, knowing their numbers, that that will be the case."

"Hm." King Maushelik narrowed his eyes and stepped away from the map table. He motioned for Al'den to walk with him as he took a pass around the room. "This would seem a stroke of relief for us, but for the warning in my heart. I fear as you do. The enemy would not just retreat with nearly eight thousand men still strong."

Al'den nodded gravely. "I am wary of this move. Perhaps, they feel Sealand is the weaker target and more vulnerable to attack—."

"Which they are."

"—but I, too, doubt they are receding to swing around toward Sealand. The maunstorz have ways of playing these cat-and-mouse games, but I, for one, do not think this is their motive in this advancement."

"You are wise to be vigilant." The Starian king agreed, "I think we are best to not be passive this time around. They are not here for raiding."

"Your thoughts then, father?"

King Maushelik turned to wave at his three war advisors, all of whom had kept out of the way while the king and prince deferred. "We have been discussing the options open to us. You have been busy on the field while we have whittled away in here. You know the strength of your men. Do you think you are capable of more fighting, this time as offenders?"

Prince Al'den paused, a frown forming over his face as he considered all the tactics open to them. "Fight them head on, you mean? We could, father, but the cost could be high if we forced it too long. What have you in mind?"

The Starian king gazed levelly at his soldier-like son, his best battle commander of his armies. "You, of all people, should know what is left to do." Al'den's heart constricted as he came to the conclusion his father was asking for. The king continued without waiting for his reply. "All the times Syre had spent fighting the maunstorz, most of our attacks have been defensive against raids and guerrilla tactics. They were a small bother to us, minor infringements on our way of life. However, there was a time—back when Syre had leaders daring enough to challenge them openly—when the maunstorz had to amass. We beat them down." Maushelik paused for dramatic effect and rallied his voice louder to the men who accompanied them. "Since the fall of Crystalynian we have become a weak nation, quivering like dogs that the maunstorz kick at their leisure! Now, I did not ride alongside King Xraxrain all those years ago to let some bathetic, blithering monsters control us as they have for so long! They have grown bold again with our failure to respond in large force. Until now. Now, I say, is the time to fight back with all we have." Maushelik turned back to his son, eyes blazing. "If our soldiers and cavalry can fight, then we must. We give them no quarter—not anymore. I will send for what aid can come but you and your men will have to fight with all you've got—and more. Can you, son of my soul?"

Prince Al'den sucked in his breath and controlled the fluttering of his heart. How long had it been since he had seen his father so aroused, so full of vigor? Since before the love of his life had died? Before the time when he had been injured and lost the good use of his leg? But, the Starian king had never been a man of poor conviction; he had fought those battles of old and come out the other side. If any knew how to lead an army to battle, it would be the king and his son. Al'den knew his father had trained him for a day like this one. "My troops are capable, My King. I have had word, too, that the Tashek are racing to our borders. With Stars speed, they will have eight-days ride to our aid. Word has been sent to Kavahad too, of need of Lord-governor Shekmann's army. We can hold the lines until all support arrives. Once the horsemen and Kavahadians join us, the maunstorz will be quick to fall."

The king of Staria could not have been prouder of his brave son. Even if he, at thirty, had not seen a battle as big as this one, King Maushelik knew the steel his only son and heir was made of. The prince would not disappoint and would make a name of himself in the days to come. The king fought back his tears; he could not afford to let any of his underlings see them shed. "Our kingdom will not forget this bravery you and your men show. We will honor their sacrifice. To arms! All of Staria to arms!"

The two-hundred-count of Tashek horsemen came to a halt through unspoken command; most shifted nervously in their saddles. All around the horsemen, the Aras Desert stretched endlessly; the last stands of grass and trees having disappeared a short distance back after the crossing of the Senna river. Yet, it seemed the Tashek had stopped at an invisible line. A line one they seemed reluctant to cross. *What was going on?* The three non-desert soldiers glanced at each other uncertainty.

Finally, Zyanthena cued Unrevealed forward and turned him to face the company. "I know that this is the border of the lands belonging to the Shekmann, and I am fully aware that we, the Sheev'anee, have a pact to stay off his lands," she paused, looking wild and daring, "But at a time like this, with people losing against hordes we can only imagine, I dare us to push the horses through these lands. Chancing this takes us the shortest distance to Sealand."

Kor'mauk nudged his mount out of the line to take his rightful place as leader beside Zyanthena. He motioned for the fiery woman to stand down. "We hear your words, Sheev'arid, and the rightness of them. I, too, agree with your haste. To go around the Shekmann estate will take too many days from us—but, we should be extra vigilant against their guards' watch. Keep the horses to an easy trot. If dust is spotted, we make a run for it."

As soon as Kor'mauk commanded action, the Tashek responded. Horses were urged forward once again. Kor'mauk turned his mount and joined the force at his place in the middle. Zyanthena let the long line of horses trot around her steed and joined the three stragglers.

"The purpose of your stopping seems atypical for such skilled warriors." Jacen remarked to the desert woman.

"To outsiders, it does indeed." She seemed embarrassed for her people. "Two generations ago, Lord Shekmann and the Tashek had some…unsavory incidents between each other. It left both sides angry and resentful. This grudge has continued on down to the Shekmann grandson, new Lord-governor of Kavahad. We have an ordinance, signed by the king himself, to never trespass on his lands." The unspoken inflection in her words made the three travelers wonder what Zyanthena was leaving out of the tale.

"What kind of dealings would keep Tashek warriors off a lordship's property during a time of war, where speed and time are critical?"

Zyanthena glanced at Lord Gordar, attempting to keep her own bitterness from showing on her face. "The old man Shekmann had a love for war and women. In generations past, he plundered Tashek camps, killing the men and horses, and enslaving the women as prostitutes. His son, Lord Alord was less war hungry but just as equally perverted. Tensions ran high enough to make the Sheev'anee attack the city Kavahad. Unable to protect his city from our retaliation, he agreed to a written contract created by King Maushelik to leave the Tashek alone if we stayed off his "designated" lands. This pact has kept our peoples from each other's throats, and no worse actions have been required. Peace has ensued well enough by the contract, even if peace has not been achieved. However, the Shekmann grandson does still feast upon the pleasures of his city's women—so I have been told. Such acts keep us vigilant. If townswomen can still grace their Lordship's bed... then it would not be hard to venture him pursing his family's past transgressions at some future point."

"So...the Tashek violate a treaty that could result in another war in Staria? This one among the king's own people?" Gordar reiterated.

The desert woman nodded, "It is a risk we will take for Sealand. Keep your guard up. The evening light sometimes enhances billowing dust, and I, for one, am more worried of our own stirrings than that of Kavahad's guard."

§   §

The Tashek finally let their horses rest a few hours into the night. Though the temperatures were less demanding than during the day's beating rays, the horses were showing some signs of fatigue. Having great concern from their mounts, the desert warriors agreed to an hour's reprieve. Zyanthena, however, remained mounted on Unrevealed, electing to stand watch with unnerving vigilance.

Lord Gordar strode up to the black's shoulder and touched the stallion lightly as he surveyed the silvery desert land, reveled in the moonlight. Though the dunes stretched silently onward, he, too, could sense an unrest in the wilderness. "Do you feel we are slipping through unnoticed, Tashek?" he asked softly.

Zyanthena did not avert her gaze from the dunes; but, she did answer the lord. "The winds were such today that I am concerned. That aside, I have not seen any signs to be alarmed about."

"Yet...?" Gordar's golden eyes held the question.

"Yet," Zyanthena did look at him then, "I feel an uneasy wind. We should continue west right now, even at the expense of our horses. We risk much by stopping this long."

"You argue many commands." The Sealander pointed out.

A tiny smile formed on the Tashek's lips. "It is in my nature, Your Grace. I can be no other way."

"Indeed, one cannot fight one's nature." He agreed. "I feel it wise to follow your advice, just so you know, Zy'ena." Gordar told her out of respect and turned away.

Zyanthena followed his retreating back until Lord Gordar disappeared among the horses. *You ae a wise advisor yourself, Lord of Sealand. I respect you, too.*

§   §

At the end of their hour-rest, Kor'mauk weaved his way to Zyanthena's side. One other accompanied him. Zy'ena turned her eyes away from her constant watch to acknowledge the leader's footsteps. "Zyanthena, I feel it is time to report back to Sheev'arid Terrik and Commander Matar. I am entrusting you and Arimun to this task, as you both have the strongest horses. Inform them that we make good time to North Point and we will reach the base of the No-way Mountains in another three days. With Stars' speed, we will reach our destination on one or two days after. You will return to us at Sheev'arid's leave."

The desert woman bowed her head to hide a flash of anger. She had been hoping to reach the fighting, but her brother must have alerted Kor'mauk to her restlessness. She could not disobey the direct order. She and Unrevealed stood as patiently as they could stand as Arimun mounted. With a nod, the two desert warriors turned their steeds southeasterly and cantered off.

The smell of early morning found the two horsemen just seven miles north of the East Bridge. Zyanthena had reined them down to a sedate trot by that time. She signaled Arimun to ride up beside her. "We will rest ten cycles-count at the Senna crossing, enough time to water the horses and eat a short repast. I feel that we should angle ourselves toward Raven's Den and travel just easterly in hopes that the mertinean and Crystine have passed Carmine." Zyanthena paused, though she had more to instruct, and took a wary sniff in the air. Unrevealed stiffened beneath her and craned his neck in the direction of the East Bridge. "I smell a campfire." She murmured to Arimun.

The other's jaw clenched as he and Zyanthena met each other's eyes. Arimun's held fear. "We made no fires." But, the smell was too close and too fresh to deny its existence. "This is not—." *Good*, Arimun was about to say when a volley of arrows rained down to their right. They drove into the sand mere feet from their mounts' hooves. Unrevealed half-reared and snorted uneasily, while Arimun's liver chestnut wheeled around, frantic to escape. The two steeds slammed into each other in their fright.

"Hold steady!" Zyanthena ordered and kneed Unrevealed around so she could see where the arrows had come from. One-hundred-and-fifty yards away, on top of a small dune, appeared a full mounted cavalry. Zyanthena cursed. "Kavahad. Hurry, we go north!" She wheeled Unrevealed around, knowing Arimun's scared mount would follow her black stallion. Behind them, the Kavahadian cavalry galloped after, arrows still flying. "Cross the Senna!" Zyanthena yelled to Arimun, as the desert man caught up. "Our only chance is to reach Rubia." The Kavahadians should not follow them there—in theory.

However, unlike the Tashek horses, the Shekmann's cavalry was fresh and had not already travelled nearly six hundred miles at war-pace. Even for Tashek mounts, the sudden chase coupled with the long miles were taking its toll. Zyanthena felt Unrevealed's stride change. She glanced back at his right haunch to see an arrow embedded into his powerful flesh. Even then, his stride was becoming choppy and short. "Go, you must reach Rubia!" She yelled to Arimun, who had slowed to keep pace. The desert man looked scared to death as he glanced between the Kavahadian cavalry, still thundering after, and his Sheev'arid leader.

"But, Zy—."

"Get moving your ass!" Zyanthena hissed, feeling the cavalry bearing down. They had closed the distance the Tashek horses had procured. "You must reach the Crystine. I feel I must take my chances here; I cannot create more harm to Unrevealed by running him. Now go! Go!" Arimun's terror about the Shekmann's wrath helped convince the warrior to sprint away.

Zyanthena was too preoccupied with bringing Unrevealed to a halt to notice if the Tashek man was getting away safely. Once she had the stallion stopped, Zyanthena was off his back and at the injured hip. Unrevealed held it up gingerly, his blood mixing with his lathered hair. Despite the fear forming in her throat, Zyanthena's concern for the stallion overrode her common sense to flee the approaching cavalry. There was no way she could think of killing Unrevealed and herself—even if it would save them from the inevitable torments at the Shekmann's hands. Shaking, the warrioress focused on her mount and pushed down her growing terror.

The cavalry, minus the few who continued pursuit of Arimun, slowed and surrounded Zyanthena and her mount. The circle closed, arrows and spears pointed promisingly at the woman's heart. "Hold!" The commander called as he pushed his courser through his men's horses. He reined his mount to a halt in front of the desert woman. "Well, what a tasty surprise." His dry, sarcastic voice rang out. "We have a Tashek trespasser."

The warrioress slowly took her hand off of Unrevealed to pull her sari from her face. The men seemed taken aback, gasping in surprise at seeing her feminine features. "I am a scout of the Crystine from the Crystal Kingdom." She said, knowing that would be her only defense to what would surely be a quick death. The commander looked uneasy. To prove it, Zyanthena carefully reached up to where she had tied the raven and sword emblem in her hairpiece. Slowly, she lifted the emblem Matar had given her, its silver metal shimmering in the morning sun.

With a distasteful expression, the commander leaned over to take the emblem from her hand. "You are long way from the Crystal Kingdom." He stated, showing his doubt.

Zyanthena replied, "The King of Sealand had requested the Crystine's aid in a battle against the maunstorz at North Point. The enemy numbers ten thousand strong, and Sealand requires reinforcement from anyone he can get." She did not add that the Crystine were still at least six days behind in Rubia.

"An unusual story, quite an exaggeration. I'm inclined to include unbelievable. A Tashek all the way in the Crystal Mountains?" The men laughed at the absurdity.

Zyanthena tried to quiet the ponding of her heart. "You may send message to North Point or Fortress Opal for conformation. You will find I speak true." Nervousness at the mention of a king's involvement flashed over the faces of the cavalrymen Zyanthena could see. She knew the men dare not kill her if she spoke the truth; the repercussions of killing a king's scout would be severe.

"You are to be taken to Lord Darshel on this matter. You are our prisoner until proven otherwise. Stant!" He called and pointed to Unrevealed. Suddenly understanding the commander's meaning, Zyanthena jumped in front of the man's aim, unwilling to let the soldier shoot her black stallion. "No!" She yelled. Stant, the soldier, snarled at her block. "You cannot harm one of the Crystine's war horses." She turned her icy, brown eyes to the commander. "To do so is punishment by death by order of the Crystal Kingdom doctrine."

The Kavahadian commander looked both annoyed and perplexed as he took another—and true—look at Unrevealed. The black stallion did not look like a Tashek's normal mount, that was to be sure. Even the trigger-happy commander could not deny that. "The animal is injured. There is no way he can make the trip to Kavahad."

"The arrow can be removed and the wound sealed." She argued, not letting her position as their prisoner deter her. Silence reigned as the man deliberated. Finally, the cavalry commander nodded and waved his major to stand down. "Do so quickly, vermin. We march in twenty minutes."

The cavalry backed their horses away, giving Zyanthena a few extra breadths of space. Two guards remained; the others got off their horses to stretch and check their equipment.

Ignoring the watching eyes, Zyanthena turned to her stallion and began to take off his light weight saddle cloth and travel packs. She cued the black to lay down, of which the tall steed obeyed with some effort. Then, Zyanthena began to remove the arrow in his hindquarter. Agony was in her hands and throat, as the warrioress readied a dagger to cut around the embedded weapon, but her hands were steady as she sliced as little as she could around the arrow shaft and tip. Though the removal took long, tedious minutes, Unrevealed lay relatively still—as if he knew any movement would cause him harm. Zyanthena release the breath she had been holding as the arrow came out clean. Quickly, she rinsed the wound with her last quart of water and gently packed it with powdered herbs. She completed her doctoring by applying an erdskin patch, covered in a sticky tree resin, over the wound. This she pressed into the stallion's black coat, where it held firmly when tested. "May it hold long enough." Zy'ena whispered as she replaced her medicines into the pouch at her waist.

The cavalry commander had watched the whole proceeding with inconspicuous curiosity. When he saw the prisoner had finished, he signaled to his men to remount and walked over to Zyanthena's two guards. "Take all of her weapons and belongings and noose the horse. Stars only know how she can control him without anything on his head! Bind her hands. I was all precautions taken with the Tashek."

The lead guard ran his hands lecherously over Zyanthena's body, feeling her up just as much as he looked for weapons. The Tashek stood as impassively as she could manage against it.... barely; though her mind was turning over all the things she would do to the man, it she could. Finally, the man had collected what he searched for. He stood aside, smug at her distasteful glare, whilst a second cavalryman tied her hands together. At least this Kavahadian had the sense to look nervous as he did so. This second man motioned for Zyanthena to return to Unrevealed.

The black stallion had righted himself so he lay more on his belly, his powerful legs curled delicately beneath him. The guard seemed unsure how to proceed; he was obviously pondering how to remount the desert woman, and which way got it done quickest. The warrioress rolled her eyes and stepped up to Unrevealed, swinging her leg over his supple back and sat down on him. With a simple cluck, the stallion rose, tripping some, to his feet. The guard gawked. "It would be advised that you pick up my saddle and bags."

Zyanthena warned the cavalryman, keeping herself calm by issuing the order. "I will remember your face if you do not."

She made sure the young man was the only one to hear the threat. The Kavahadian nodded, nervous at the implications, and rushed to pick up her belongings. These he hiked with him to his own mount, a safe distance from the Tashek prisoner.

Another cavalryman sidled his horse alongside the much taller Crystine courser and looped a lariat around the stallion's neck, up behind his ears and throatlatch. Unrevealed tolerated the abnormal hindrance with as much dignity as his rider had taken her body search.

The commander met Zyanthena's gaze then, his arrogant gloating glinting in his eyes. "To Kavahad!

Chapter Eight

§

Some Relief at Last

One day passed Carmine, the mertinean and Crystine ran into an unexpected rainstorm that brought the heavy wagons to a halt in the think, sticky mud. Frustrated and drenched, the army created make-shift tents to keep somewhat drier and wait out the storm.

Huddling together for warmth, for fires would not stay lit in the gale, the four companions—Roland, Rio, Sage, and Anibus—shared hunks of "road-tack", a hardened type of bread, and pieces of fruit.

"The weather seems to be siding against us." Rio muttered, cold and impatient. "It seems the Stars do not wish to aid us in reaching Sealand as quickly as possible. I'm almost wishing I'd just risked it with the Tashek, seems better than wasting my days in the rain."

"You stayed as our escort." Roland Seagold reminded with more authority in his voice than was needed. "Rain or no rain, though, we will reach North Point and help aid Sealand in victory, rest assured."

Priest Anibus glanced between the three Sunarians, as if working through a complicated puzzle. His disapproving frown seemed to answer some question in his mind, not at all to his liking. He shrugged it off. "The Stars are not doing this to punish us." He said to his religion's defense. "And, I'm sure the rain itself will lessen with time." As if to prove his point, the crazy downpour slackened to a light misting. Anibus smiled as if to say "see" and peered out their tent's flap to the rest of the army.

Beside him, though, Rio was still grumpy. "So, it stopped raining, priest. We still have to pull the wagons out of this muck. Ask your deities to do that."

Anibus pulled himself back inside to reply. "My words have nothing to do with this, but I see four good, able men that can help in regards to the carts." The men groaned in answer. They stretched their already over-worked muscles before heading out into the muddy camp. Anibus waited for all to pass by him before pulling Rio back in to whisper a warning to him, "And you, Captain, need to keep your merchant's attitude in check before he is seen as something he is not." Rio's eyes widened in shock then they narrowed with suspicion. Anibus nodded silently and released the military man's sleeve. "If I've noticed, others will as well. That could be more attention than he is looking for."

Rio nodded solemnly. "Just keep your peace, priest. He, and more importantly I, trust you."

"Prince Par! Prince Par!" An excited Averron came bursting through the prince's chamber door, crashing the old wood against the stone wall of the fortress. Par startled awake from his study desk, where he had nodded off. He cast wearied eyes his commander's way. Just as quickly, worry etched onto his face as he stood in fear of bad news.

"Speak Averron, what has gone amiss?"

"Amiss, Highness? Naught anything of the like! You should hurry and see. The mertinean banners fly to the east!"

"Raven's Den! That should be Commander Tyk." The prince rushed by his commander, barely stopping to grab his outer jacket and sword. The two men hurried to the eastern ramparts and looked out across the green carpet of beach grasses to the moving shape of the mertinean army beyond. "Prepare the fortress to accept them." Par instructed his war commander. "Then get word to the men still on the field. This news will very much renew our hopes against the weary beating of the maunstorz."

"Aye, Highness. Quickly, sir."

Prince Par gazed out at the distant flags one last time, hope finally showing on his face. "Stars preserve us, this is certainly good news!" He said in thanks and rushed off in Averron's wake.

A long, anxious thirty minutes later, the company of Raven's Den was filing into North Point's outer courtyard. Prince Par strode to Commander Tyk's horse and took the reins personally, a broad, relieved smile on his face. "Commander Tyk."

"Prince Fantill." The roughened commander returned respectfully and saluted. "Commander Kins asked us here ahead of the main mertinean army in hopes of gifting you with some relief until the main force and Crystine arrive. We may be just a small force, Prince, but I know we can be of some help to you."

"Even this count is welcome, Commander." Par assured. "My men are wearied from constant fighting. Your men bring relief and greatly needed encouragement. We are very grateful."

"Well then," Commander Tyk ruffled his burly frame and straightened his uniform. "Let's get those men to the front lines. I've got an itching to kick some maunstorz ass."

"Do your men not need some rest first?" Prince Par asked, surveying the group of one-thousand soldiers. Commander Tyk puffed his cheeks as if to guffaw the notion. "Dear Prince, my men came to relieve you of fighting! We will not have your men squandering their reserve energy on our account. Now lead on; I want to see those red-eyed bastards for myself."

§   §

The front lines of the Sealand army were littered with corpses, arrows, and large, broken clumps of dirt. To Commander Tyk, the field was in terrible disarray, but reminded him distinctly of his own lines on the Rubian-Starian boarder. "I see they do not let you claim your dead here, either."

Prince Par shook his head sadly, "Indeed not, Commander. They fire on us even during the night and especially when going out to our soldiers. It's too risky to try and save our wounded; it just leads to more men needing rescuing. I lament at the toll it's taken on me and my men to see our comrades suffering out there in the cold and rain, just to die on the 'morrow."

"That sounds like them, those bloody bastards! They don't follow the rules of war. If you're not careful, they'll hollow the will right out of you. It is the worst part about this war with them."

Prince Par chose to say nothing in return. Deep inside he, too, already felt a piece of his soul was disturbed by the fighting. The only question he really wanted to know was: *how much longer must things go on?* But, of course, the Sealander did not speak so aloud. Instead, he called out orders to his troops for the weariest watchers to go get some rest as the fresher Raven's Den soldiers marched to replace them. A heartened applause broke out from the worn army at the blessed relief. Silently, Par prayed that it would be enough to hold the lines until more help could come.

A heavy clasp on his shoulder brought Prince Par back from his introspection. "I'll leave my men in the hands of your Commander Averron. I'd like a look at your maps, if you'd allow, Highness."

"This way." Par nodded and waved the other man toward the keep. The map room lay in slight disarray, much to the royal's dismay, but the mertinean commander turned a blind eye to it as he pulled out the map he needed and spread it across the table. "So, this is local North Point." He mumbled to himself as he studied it carefully. After a pause, he spoke again, "So, has King Maushelik sent word to you?"

Prince Par sighed, trying to hold back his fatigue. "No, Commander. From what I have heard, the Gap of the Forgotten is overwhelmed with near-equal numbers of the enemy. This has, of course, occupied all of King Maushelik's time. The only message we have had on that account was the one giving us permission to cross into Staria's border—it if comes to it."

"I just do not understand those savages! Not once have they overtaken a trade-city, like Port Al-Harrad to the north. It has far more importance, strategically, than North Point."

"I cannot begin to understand them, either." Prince Par agreed. "However, I have come to believe that they attack places of military might. To them, such places could be more or a threat; ones they would wish to neutralize. Their strategy did take out our most influential military kingdom, after all… I say we should pray and be grateful that they have not touched our trade, for without such cities and supplies, we are as good as done."

"Indeed, prince, indeed."

Chapter Nine

§

Of Detestment and Desire

Kavahad looked like a large outpost from the outside. It had enormous log walls and the towering spires of the keep could be made out beyond. Zyanthena eyed the place warily, her people's distrust of the Shekmann rulers coloring her opinion of the place. Around the keep were only small acres of fields, as the desert did not harbor crops well in its dry environment. There was a steady stream of people, carts, and livestock coming in and out of the entrance gates. The cavalry commander called out to the citizens that they were coming through. The crowd parted and the Kavahadian cavalry trotted passed into the inner town. The streets were unpaved; the thirty horses kicked up the dust from the streets, causing the townspeople on foot to keep back or suffer the cloud of dirt. There were some curious glances cast up at Zyanthena and her large, black mount. Most were scared of the Tashek, and they held their stares for only a short time before Zyanthena's cold glare forced them to look away. The Tashek made sure to make a defiant impression.

The commander led the force up the long streets to the inner walls surrounding the Shekmann's keep. He called out and the iron-welded gates were slowly raised. The cavalry moved forward into the main courtyard. They stopped at the staircase leading to the keep and dismounted. The soldier who was less intimidated by the warrioress came up beside Unrevealed and started to reach upward to pull the woman down. The Tashek let loose a threatening growl and slid down herself before he could get his lecherous hands on her body. Startled, the man backed away then puffed back up as his sense of superiority came back. He pushed Zyanthena toward the stairs while his partner took hold of Unrevealed and started leading him away to the stables. The black stallion nickered for his rider, but the first soldier pushed Zyanthena onward roughly, ignoring the large courser. A large handful of the cavalry members came to surround the Tashek and her escort as they continued into the keep.

Inside the keep, the commander turned their group into what Zyanthena believed was the lesser hall, for it did not seem quite as elegant as a hall should. The room was long, stretching many squares deeper than width-wise, giving the lord ample time to assess any visitors as they proceeded to his dais. So, this man was cautious and likely trained in the art of war more than politics. If he was anything like his father or grandfather before him, Zyanthena knew she would expect Lord Shekmann to be a tyrant.

There were very few occupants in the room—just a few courtesans, a clerk, six soldiers, and a group of young women dressed in town-spun dresses. Lord Shekmann sat on his large chair on the raised dais looking down at the young ladies as they answered whatever questions he asked of them. As the cavalry members neared, Lord Darshel rose a hand to quiet the women and turned his attention to his commander. "I see your outing was not without some excitement, Commander Raic."

"Aye, M'lord." The commander came to proper salute then waved his hand back toward Zyanthena. "We found this trespasser and one other coming southeast from the Aras Desert with the morning sun. We raced after and caught this one. The other escaped past the East Bridge."

Lord Darshel rose to his full height of six-foot-one and glided cat-like down the dais steps to inspect the warrioress. She straightened in defiance and narrowed her brandy eyes, hoping to intimidate. There was almost the hint of a smirk on the man's chiseled face—almost—but it was quickly replaced by an angry scowl as he took in the rest of Zyanthena's character. Head-to-toe, the desert woman looked every inch of her Tashek heritage—except for her lighter skin and her empty belt where her scabbard and kora sword had been. Forcefully, Lord Darshel tore off her sari, unveiling her beautiful and untamed features and long, flowing black hair. Zyanthena's eyes sharpened considerably.

The Shekmann lord did not bother to notice how absolutely attractive Zyanthena was through his abhorrent displeasure. "A Tashek! Of all the bloody, stomach-turning creatures to catch running on my lands..." He cut off in anger and started to turn away.

"She claims to be a part of the Crystine, M'lord." Raic reported, despite the fact he might incur his leader's wrath by talking out of turn. He held out the raven and sword emblem to support the claim.

"It seems the Crystine travel to North Point to aid a battle between the Sealand army and the maunstorz."

The emblem was grudgingly accepted by the Shekmann, but he whirled back around on Zyanthena before really looking at it. "And that excuses you?" Lord Darshel's eyes flashes, openly enraged. "My family has kept to the treaty for seventy-five years! It was not even accepted that it be pardoned during the last war, the one involving that kingdom to the northeast, and you fucking think you can just ignore it now for one tiny battle!"

Zyanthena downcast her eyes in an effort to cool the lord's fury, a position that played up a weakness in herself that she did not really fee but hoped would help her. She used her softest and most neutral voice to allure to the image further. "It was indeed a great ignorance on my part, Your Lordship, to have tread on your lands so rudely. If it would please His Lordship, I may make amends with a sincere apology and be on my way quickly to the Crystine—with promise to never touch his said lands again."

His backhand to her right cheek came out of nowhere, Darshel's response to her "plea". "I know of no Tashek courtesans whom can talk so sweetly." In other words, there were no Tashek that were diplomates or politicians. "And I've been fore-warned that the females of your kind are very deceptive."

Zyanthena's head had been whipped around to the right. She took the few seconds the new position allowed to evaluate the other occupants in the room. Though all seemed shocked at their lord's behavior, there were no compassionate looks for Zyanthena, either. There were no friends here. She slowly straightened and ignored the throbbing of her face. "You know nothing of us." She hissed quietly, barely audible. Louder, she said, "For one whom spouts off about our treacheries, you do not condemn yourselves your own cruelness. I was doing my duty to those I've sworn allegiance to; your men cannot say the same."

"My men are every bit loyal to me."

The warrioress's eyebrows twitched in expression that she did not agree. "Commander Matar of the Crystine will vouch for me."

Lord Darshel's mouth turned to a hard-lined smile. "I'm sure he might, whenever he might arrive. Your people, however, will undoubtedly not. Shall I tell them you send your dearest regards?"

This last he whispered slyly into Zyanthena's ear. To the small group of watchers, Darshel said, "Oh, but forgive my lack of curtesy, Tashek." He flourished his hands as he stepped back up to his chair and sat down. "My name is Lord Darshel Shekmann, and to whom do we have the pleasure of entertaining?"

All present seemed interested in the question. Zyanthena almost lied. Almost. "Sheev'arid, Zyanthena, Your Lordship."

Lord Darshel smiled, triumphant. He eyed his clerk to make sure the man had written the name down. "I'm sure your people will be happy to hear what you have done." *Doubtful,* Zyanthena thought. "But, until they send a reply, you belong to me—as proposed in the treaty. You're in my territory now, prisoner." He motioned Commander Raic to come to him and whispered in the man's ear, "You know what to do with her. Make sure she is humiliated."

"Do you wish us to have our way with her first, M'lord?"

"No. Leave her to me. She'll find out why her people avoid the Shekmann."

"Aye, M'lord."

Zyanthena was taken into a side corridor, where she was gagged and blindfolded. Numerous twists and turns later, she was stopped, pinned against a wall, and forced to stand legs uncomfortably wide. Wrist and ankle chains were shackled to her limbs, stretching her further against the harsh wall. All footsteps but one pair departed. There was the sound of a knife being pulled from a sheath. Zyanthena was too terrified to move as the soldier tore away her Tashek clothing. The man snickered and ran his fingers across her exposed belly, enjoying how she tightened against the unwelcomed touch.

"Be just like that, Tashek, and our lord will enjoy himself immensely." It was the soldier that had already felt her up, now enjoying the full view of what had only been imagination. Zyanthena feared he would take her right there as she felt he lusted to do, but the large hand fell away. The man walked away leaving Zyanthena with the darkness, and painful chains, and the rough wall to remind her of her captivity.

§ §

Zyanthena untangled herself from her semi-awake state to then wish she hadn't. The sounds of unabated lovemaking so close and overzealous could no longer be ignored. Repulsed, she thought of retching. She shifted in the chains, feeling the clay wall where it had bitten into her back. Unsuccessfully, she tried to adjust her arms and legs to redistribute her weight. A sharps ache from her limbs answered in return but there was no room to give them a break. Nearby, the noise crescendoed as a young woman's voice reached its peak and she cried out her ecstasy. The man grunted too and then they were both left panting. Zyanthena clenched her jaw, refusing to picture whatever disgusting scene had transpired. She begged, silently, that whomever it was would leave it at that.

The sound of footsteps padding closer alerted the Tashek woman to the man's presence just moments before he removed her blindfold and gag. Lord Darshel's smug, handsome face met Zyanthena's as her eyes adjusted to the semi-bright candlelight in the room. The tall, brawny lord hadn't bothered to cover his sweat-soaked body. Zyanthena couldn't help wrinkling her nose at the musk from his lovemaking. She looked away to the brown wall beside him.

Lord Darshel chuckled. "Not so tough now, are you?" He leaned closer and rested his hands on either side of Zyanthena's head, his arms long enough to keep himself out of reach if the Tashek decided to head-butt him. The desert woman shrunk back into the wall despite its rough texture biting into her skin. "I figured this would disarm you quicker than anything else." He gloated. "After all, beyond whatever breeding you are, you are still just a woman; though, for a wandering savage, you're not half bad." Dark, emerald eyes appraised Zyanthena's battle-hardened body, moving slowly lower.

That time, Zyanthena felt anger rise and swell within her. "You are your father's son. Only a Shekmann could be so skanky." She had meant it as an insult but realized, too late, that it amused Darshel to no end.

He laughed. "What is one person's disgust is another's desire. My family is very good at what we do. By this point, the townspeople practically beg me to take their young women to bed."

"Revolting." She hissed. Her brandy eyes wandered to the left, where Darshel's bedchamber could be seen beyond the small alcove she was held in. A young girl, little over the onset of womanhood, lay naked upon the large mattress. She slept deeply, her body still glowing in the aftermath of the lord's lovemaking. Zyanthena recognized her to be from the group of townswomen from the lesser hall in the morning.

"Since my grandfather's time, a townswoman is given to the lord every night. We make them happy and give their family hopes of glory, should their daughter conceive an heir."

"And how do you know you don't have a horde of bastards running around?"

"My physician has special teas he gives them to prevents pregnancy. So far, it has worked for over one-hundred-years. It would be by my choosing only that I would ever have a son." He puffed up as he gloated. "And, I have other methods of course. We [my family] are the masters of the Art of Love."

"Pervert." Zyanthena replied. She doubted Lord Darshel could gloat any harder. "And you believe such actions could disarm one such as myself? I've had worse humiliations."

Darshel fixed her with a broad smile, fully amused. "You may be a warrior, Zyanthena," He pronounced her name suavely, "But underneath that hardened exterior, you are nothing more than any other woman. Your body will want what your mind says it can ignore. Eventually, the thoughts must bow to the instinctual. In the end, *you will* beg me."

"You are too full of yourself."

Another chuckle. Darshel pushed away and moved over to a table full of delicacies. He ate pieces of sweetmeats and biscuits, eying Zyanthena for a reaction. He returned to her holding a piece of mouth-watering boar. "If you play nice, you could even share my dinner. Twelve hours of no food must make you a little hungry."

Zyanthena did feel the empty pangs in her belly but the burning anger in her soul fueled her pride. "I'd rather eat with your dogs."

"Suit yourself," he shrugged. "I can always arrange that, but…. I'd rather like to see you beg. There's something so fascinating about the breaking down a woman's hard-won ideals. Tomorrow then." Lord Darshel ate the boar and turned away. "May your night be very cold as you remember I could have kept you warm…" He walked back to his bed to snuggle the young woman in his fine bedsheets. Soon, he was asleep.

§ §

Zyanthena shivered most of the night, the slight breeze from an open window keeping her from any relief. Dawn was just lighting when she finally allowed her eyes to close. Not long after, however, Darshel and the girl woke her with a morning lovemaking session. Zyanthena suppressed a groan. They finished what seemed an hour later, and some servants led the girl away. Lord Darshel washed himself and put on his cloths before returning to pester the desert woman. He smelled so clean and refreshed she was instantly revolted. The Tashek felt the desire to rip his throat out and steal his clothes—just to be rid of her discomfort. She could not repress a shiver, however, despite the effort she took to cover it. Lord Darshel, of course, noticed. He reached a hand out to clasp the fingers of her left; they were ice cold. Without a word, Darshel turned away and left the room.

A maid servant came in a few minutes later, a jug of hot water, a basin, and a towel in hand. Keeping her eyes down, she began to clean Zyanthena's skin, the hot water warming the Tashek's frozen body. Once the maid finished, she collected her things and set them by the doorway. She spoke to someone, then returned with a light cloth, which she expertly adorned Zyanthena with, clipping it so that everything the Tashek would deem needed covering was appropriately swathed.

Two soldiers entered as she finished. They attached a chain-choker around the Tashek's neck and unlocked her wrists and ankles. With a bob of his head, the lead soldier indicated Zyanthena should step toward the door. Together, the threesome entered the hallway and were met by four more guards. They all turned down the keep's east wing.

The hallway had round–topped windows on either side; golden rays of sunlight streamed through, lighting up the earthen-colored walls and blue-painted tiles. At the end of the hallway, glass doors opened up to the outside. The group stepped out into a lush garden of vines and exotic flowers. Zyanthena halted at the sight of the desert paradise.

"It's a stunning view." Lord Darshel agreed from his place at the balcony's wall. He motioned the guards back, except for the one holding the Tashek's chain. Darshel took the lead and waved the soldiers away. "They think I am unwise trusting you outside alone, but I assured them Tashek hold no honor in running away."

"Not when we know the way. I cannot say for a place I know nothing about."

"I'll remember to not show you around then." Darshel turned away to look across his yard. Zyanthena' stood complacently by his side. It felt good, absorbing the heat of the sun into her thawing body. Yet, the warrioress watched Kavahad's young lord from the corner of her eye, not quite sure she trusted the comfortable silence he allowed. It felt deceptive. Yet, the aristocratic Starian did nothing to cause any suspicions. Finally, unable to decipher anything, she took to following where the lord's gaze was occupied.

Lord Darshel had felt her imploring eyes on him; it was hard not to when the Tashek's sheer presence commanded such control; he had never seen such in a woman before. If Zyanthena was indeed one of the Crystine's Tashek agents, he could see where she could have been influential in battle. Her brandy eyes were very perceptive. He found himself wondering what they saw in him. His mind flashed back to the memory of her naked body. If his guard had slipped the night before; and he had tried to persuade her to go to his bed; his prisoner would have tried to kill him, once the opportunity presented itself. He could feel that promise in her eyes just then, but Lord Darshel was not a stupid man. Some things took time—and care—and some things were too dangerous for one's health.

"A pigeon was sent from the Crystine this morning." He began and felt the Tashek stiffen at his side. "Your commander has heard of your capture. He and a small force are coming here at horses' speed to speak with me. It seems you do have some pull with this Crystine man." Zyanthena did not say anything in return but Darshel had the feeling she was giving him an "I told you so" look. "They will arrive tomorrow morning. You are my guest until everything gets settled—one way or another."

"Guests are given food and their own bedchambers." Zyanthena pointed out.

"True, but guests are *usually* invited." There was a hint of anger in his voice. "I'll give you food, since you should not look famished in front of your commander, but you will remain locked in my bedchamber. Seeing and hearing things you've deprived yourself of will be good for your disposition." Then, a sly thought came to Lord Darshel, one that got him what he desired. "Why don't we make a deal?" He saw Zyanthena's eyes slide over him. "If you sleep with me, I will let you go. Just like that. That is all I ask of you, just one night."

The look of disgust on her face was priceless. "I'll wait for Commander Matar to wipe that smirk off your face. By tomorrow morning, I will be free of you."

Darshel took up her challenge with a smug grin. "We'll see, darling, we'll see."

§ §

Lord Darshel woke before the morning light and carefully untangled himself from the pretty brunette he had bedded the night before. He had been restless all night, his thoughts on the Tashek woman close by. He walked to the alcove where he had chained her. Although he had allowed the desert woman to stay clothed, he had made sure her wrist and ankle chains were stretched tight. As Darshel neared her in the half-light, he found Zyanthena's eyes already trained on him, glaring. There was no way to suppress the amused grin that formed on his face. "I admire you for your unbridled spirit. It seems that it is not easily broken." He reached out and touched her cheek and was rewarded with a cringe. "But you are scared of me, too, woman. Such contradiction…Today, we will see which side the Stars favor—yours or mine. I've got half a mind to not let you go; perhaps, they will listen to my prayers."

"I doubt you are that religious." Zyanthena retorted. "You'll see. I will be walking out of here, free, in two hours."

The morning came slowly. With it came Commander Matar and a handful of the Crystine. Darshel invited the small group to join him in his private study, knowing it would make the confrontation seem less official. Once Commander Matar and his men were seated, he called his soldiers to bring Zyanthena—without her chains. The Tashek woman had schooled her features into a calm mask, though her eyes looked brighter with expectation.

"I am glad to see my letter reached you quickly." Lord Shekmann began as introduction. "I am sure you are aware of the situation your Tashek had caused between her people and mine."

Commander Matar nodded and waved to the Tashek man at his right. "This is Sheev'arid, Terrik, leader of the Tashek in my forces. He has filled me in on the treaty between Kavahad and the Tashek—and its implications." Lord Darshel studied the desert man with surprise. *He has the same sur name as Zyanthena. Relative? An interesting fact.* Matar continued, "Terrik has also mentioned that the treaty was imposed by King Maushelik." He waited for Darshel to nod. "If that is the case, I have no authority here. I must defer my judgement to clan Sheev'arid." This last part, Commander Matar said to Zyanthena, apology written on his face. "I am much in need of Zy'ena's skills as a warrior in my forces, but I know my place, Lord Shekmann. I cannot cause more trouble when my position does not allow it." Matar turned his face away from Zyanthena, unable to look at her as her features went from confusion to desperation—a look he thought never belonged on the woman's beautiful face. He hated himself for being just coward enough to not protect his favorite warrior.

Zyanthena stood suddenly, distressed by her commander's words. A guard grabbed her arm but she twisted about and caught hold of his own. She turned his wrist painfully. The other guards caught hold of her just as quickly and wrestled the desert woman to the ground. She cursed but could no longer move.

Lord Darshel looked to the other Sheev'arid to see his reaction. The man looked ashamed at Zyanthena's behavior. "And what judgement does clan Sheev'arid give on this matter?"

Terrik slowly took his eyes from his sister to meet the Kavahadian man's question. "The Sheev'anee counseled that they do not wish to disrupt the peace that has been held since the treaty was woven. The winds have warned bad omens if the treaty is broken. They have ruled that Lord Shekmann can decide what punishment he feels is fit for the trespassing of Sheev'arid Zyanthena. Until she has fulfilled her contract, included but not limited to a punishment of death, she is repudiated from clan Sheev'arid."

Lord Darshel could not believe his luck. It seemed the Stars were on his side after all. "Well, I apologize for the long ride you had to take to deliver such news as this." He stood and the others followed suit. None looked at Zyanthena. "I will say that I have already condemned Zyanthena. It is left to her if she agrees to my proposal. However, I assure you, Commander, Sheev'arid, that no harm will come to your Tashek fighter."

The Crystine began to leave. Commander Matar turned only once to nod a good-bye to Zyanthena then he walked away. The Tashek woman struggled against the guard's hold and called out once to her brother, the last to leave. Terrik paused and spoke over his shoulder, "Whatever he has asked of you, Zyen, you had better do it quickly."

"You know not what he asks!" She yelled after him, but Terrik had already slipped away. Zyanthena felt the hope she had held that morning slip away. Angered, she struggled furiously all the way back to Darshel's quarters and on through the process of being chained up. She was left alone, thrashing against her restraints, for the remainder of the day.

Chapter Ten

§

The Stars Do Hear

"Hold steady!" Prince Al'den called out to keep some kind of order in the chaotic fighting. His main line of cavalry repaired their formation as best as they could and followed their leader for another charge at the maunstorz. The Starian army had been re-engaged with the enemy for two days. They had created a significant amount of damage to the enemy on the first day of fighting—mostly because the maunstorz had not been expecting an attack of that nature. The surprise did not last forever, though, and Prince Al'den had found it increasingly difficult to cut into the opposition's lines. New maneuvers had to be conjured up just to keep ahead in the battle. Victory seemed far away.

Unfortunately, Prince Al'den could see the toll wearing down his men. He was afraid he had overestimated his army's willpower. "A miracle might be needed right now." He breathed as he swung his sword across a maunstorz face, leaving it a bloody mess. His destrier reared at another foe, striking out with a front hoof to catch the man chin to sternum. The large horse nipped out, bringing another man down to be pummeled under large, shod hooves. Prince Al'den assisted by covering the warhorse's flanks. "This way!" He shouted again, clearing his men from the muddled enemy lines to regroup and charge anew; a rush of Starian foot soldiers covered the retreat of the cavalry. The reformed formation of horses swung around, quickly charging into a horde of footmen with spears. A few horses were impaled but most got through the front lines, getting deep into the maunstorz army. The hacking and stomping began all over again.

The fighting continued on late into the afternoon. Prince Al'den kept his forces from scattering, which helped to protect his men from unnecessary losses. Yet, the Starian royal could tell their chances were slowly decreasing. More and more often, Prince Al'den found himself praying to the Red Star—the deity of war and conquest. If there was any hope left it would not come from a human source.

"Your Highness!" A messenger cried out to the prince during one of the army's many regroupings. Prince Al'den reined his mount around and motioned for the man to speak quickly. "Sir, a large sandstorm has been spotted to the southeast. The king orders everyone back. It will reach here within the quarter of the dial. Hurry sir!" Prince Al'den looked in the direction of the storm and saw the looming cloud forming, dark and sinister. He made a quick prayer of thanks to the Red Star [of the Southeast] and called his forces to retreat. He signaled the cavalry to cover the foot soldiers.

Once the men on foot were far enough away, the Starian whistled his men to a full-gallop retreat, leaving the maunstorz—who had a fear of horses and thus no animals of means for such speed—to run after. The enemy seemed unaware of the dust cloud that was nearly upon them all.

The prince was the last one to reach the large gates into the town of the Citadel of Light. He galloped through just as the large wall of sand hit. His men closed the gates right on his horse's heels, blocking out the storm. "My son!" King Maushelik called out as he guided his grey courser through the large throng of men and horses. Prince Al'den turned his destrier and gave a small bow to his father. The aging king reached out to grasp his son's forearm. "I was worried you would not make it before the storm."

"For a moment so was I." Prince Al'den confessed, raking his fingers through his short, dark-brown hair to rid it of the gritty sand. "I only pray this storm wreaks havoc on the maunstorz. It would give us a much-needed break. Which reminds me, father, I need to go to the temple before I do anything else."

The Starian king did not ask where Al'den's sudden sense of devoutness came from. "As you need, son. The townsfolk will help fend for the men and my physicians will care for the wounded. Make sure you take this reprieve to rest and eat. You will need the strength."

"Father." The prince bowed then got down from his destrier and handed him to a stable boy. He walked through the quieted side-streets to the temple on the southern reaches of the town. As he kneeled by the stone alter, Prince Al'den felt the weariness of the battle crash upon him. He staggered and fell forward onto his palms, pressing his forehead to the floor. For many long breadths he stayed that way, listening to the silence within the temple walls and the muted sounds of the whirling sands hitting from outside.

Finally, Prince Al'den stirred.

He began a quiet chant to the Stars, thanking them for their aid and asking them to continue giving himself and his men the strength to hold through the war. His baritone voice sang louder as he came to the end and let it stop. The room went silent. Standing, Al'den felt more refreshed and clearer. "Thank you, Mother." He finished and bowed once to the altar of the Stars.

§   §

Nighttime came but still the sandstorm did not abate. Whispers came up from the more superstitious men and women of the town that the storm was a sign from the heavens. Unlike the others, however, Prince Al'den found the omen helpful more than evil. He had eaten and rested, waking refreshed by the setting of the sun.

Currently, he was walking the southern ramparts of the city wall, having already checked his men on the others sides. There had been nothing to report; it seemed even the maunstorz did not fight during a sandstorm.

"Sir." One of his men ran up and saluted. "We could be wrong, sir, but there seems to be movement to the south. It is hard to see through the sand, but we have been ready 'case there are maunstorz prowling."

"Lead me." Al'den ordered and followed the man down the wall. The Starian archers had arrows at ready, pointed out in the dusk at something. "Hold." Prince Al'den commanded. "I do not want to fire unless I know for sure that it is the enemy, not something else out there."

Slowly, the darker shapes took form into a group of horsemen, their mounts struggling through the blowing winds. As they neared, Prince Al'den counted the lines of five horses abreast to twenty deep—one hundred soldiers? From where? "Get the South gate open! Someone direct these men inside." Soldiers scrambled to obey his orders. "Archers, keep sharp, but under NO circumstances does anyone fire."

When the one-hundred horsemen were safely inside the city's walls, Prince Al'den's archer commander went down the rampart stairs to meet them. Two men—a man slightly younger than the prince and a grizzled lieutenant-commander—dismounted to meet with him. They spoke for a moment, and Prince Al'den watched as his man bowed, of a sudden, to the younger man before turning and hurrying up the stairs.

"Highness." His man bowed quickly. "It is Prince Kent Argetlem and his Lieutenant-Commander Eric Sloane of the Golden Kingdom."

Prince Al'den could not hide his surprise. "This is an unusual but welcome turn of events. Help his men get their horses into the southwestern stables. I'll tend to Prince Kent and Commander Sloane personally." He asked the rest of his archers to continue watching the wall then headed down to where the Golden Kingdom's men were standing. Nearing, he saw just how filthy the men were from riding through the sandstorm; even the horses needed a good dusting.

Lieutenant-Commander Sloane recognized Prince Al'den immediately—despite the fact that the Starian did not look much like royalty in his basic armor and desert-colored robes. "Your Highness." The older man went to one knee respectfully, as did all of his men behind him.

Prince Kent frowned, confusion on his face, as he glanced between his bowing men and the six-foot-two Starian. "Highness..." He murmured. "Prince Maushelik?" He asked then.

"Al'den, if you please, Prince Kent." The Starian extended a hand to clasp the other prince. "It is a surprise you and your men came here through the storm, but you are also very welcomed. My men will see to your horses and men. If you and Lieutenant-Commander Sloane would like to accompany me to the Citadel?"

"I—we—would be happy to." Prince Kent began, "But, I am not sure how King Maushelik would feel to have half the desert dragged into his parlor." To prove his point, the young man tussled his head, shaking loose a dust cloud from his chestnut hair. "The Sheev'anee in Paragon said we were crazy to travel into the storm. I had begun to agree with them."

Al'den chuckled and mirrored the other prince's smile. "Yes, the Sheev'anee are wise about knowing the weather patterns. It is smart to listen to them. As for King Maushelik, my father had his parlor soiled by me this afternoon. One more dusting is not going to hurt much of anything. A good bath for you and your men wouldn't hurt either. You will feel better once the travels of the road are cleaned away."

"Thank you kindly." Prince Kent said. "A bath does sound mighty good right now."

"In that case, follow me."

§ §

Clean and refreshed, Prince Kent changed into the garments the maid had laid out for him—which fit despite the fact that he suspected they belonged to Prince Al'den. Satisfied, he left his rooms and followed a man-servant down to a private dincr, where Prince Al'den and Lieutenant-Commander Sloane already sat, talking earnestly about the war with the maunstorz. They stopped as the prince came in. Prince Maushelik rose to welcome Kent to the table.

"It's not much," Prince Al'den indicated to the food of fresh fruit, bread, and a platter of meats and cheeses, "Because we are rationing the city in case we are unable to get supplies, but I hope it helps you regain your strength from your trip."

Prince Kent wondered if the other man was testing him to see if he would pull a "spoiled prince act" or if Prince Al'den was just used to being to the point—he decided both were a little true. "What is good enough for you is good enough for me." He decided to say, keeping neutral about it. "And thank you for the clothing."

Prince Al'den waved a hand to signal it was nothing. "Those fit me when I was nineteen, so it's not like I have much use for them anymore. You looked to be about the same size as I was then, so I had Sarah get them out of the closet. Why she kept them, I've no idea, but I am glad they fit someone."

"You have him looking like a prince again." Sloane joked. "We ae not used to seeing our Highness in armor and travel gear. To see him like this is a great relief."

Prince Kent made to protest but Al'den could see the younger man was pleased to be in courtesan clothing, too. It was, also, good to see another royal-born conversing comfortably with his inferior— a big plus in Al'den's book. "So, I take it you are not much for fighting then?" He asked courteously.

"No, not really." Kent admitted as he selected what foods he wanted on his plate. "Lord Commander Ivance has taught me some swordsmanship and dagger moves but my only real love of weapons is archery. Usually, though, I am too busy keeping checks-and-balances to the kingdom's budget to practice."

"Our prince is the most respected Economic of the kingdom." Sloane filled-in with pride." He has increased the Treasury by sixty-five percent more than anyone else in the Golden Kingdom's history."

"Impressive." Prince Al'den agreed. He was not one much for numbers and monies, though he always kept a check on the kingdom's accounts.

"And you?" Prince Kent asked, to hide his embarrassment at his man's words of praise. "I am sorry to admit, but I know little about you."

"My Highness," the Lieutenant-Commander looked surprised. "Prince Al'den is the best military strategist in all of Syre! He was also the Fighting Champion at age fifteen, a child protégé, and undefeated since that time. Only the war has prevented him from competing in recent years." Now it was Prince Al'den's turn to look self-conscious.

"Really?" Kent eyed the tall Starian as if trying to see the champion in the desert royal. "And how do you know so much about Prince Maushelik, Sloane?"

"I competed against Mr. Sloan that first year, when I was fifteen." Al'den shrugged his broad shoulders. "I guess he was impressed enough to keep tabs on me." The Lieutenant-Commander nodded to confirm. "But my strategies, for which I am renowned, are actually tactics I invented with the late Prince Lance Starkindler of the Crystal Kingdom. He and I were best friends since a young age and very much into creating new moves for the armies."

"I apologize for making you remember a painful memory."

"Not at all." Prince Al'den countered. "I am very grateful for these memories. They keep me going when this war gets too grim. I just have to remember how it was before and know that I want the future to be just as happy and carefree as it was then. If not for me than the children I might have."

Prince Kent felt his respect for the older prince grow. There was something in the Starian's conviction that pulled at a longing in his soul. He was suddenly very grateful that he had taken the long trip instead of staying home, in safety. "If you have no objection, Prince

Al'den" he said, surprised to hear himself saying the words, "I would very much like to become your friend."

Lieutenant-Commander Sloane looked shocked that Prince Kent could speak so rashly; the two princes had just met, after all! Prince Maushelik, however, looked thoughtful as his ice-blue eyes assessed the scholarly prince before him. Whatever he saw made him smile. "I would be very honored to have a friend like you. But, if we are going to be friends then I insist you call me Al'den—no prince or former titles. And, do expect me to cause you some trouble now and them." He finished with a hint of humor.

"Trouble was always my middle namc." Prince Kent grinned. "And, I'll be just plain old Kent, with a little taste for the flare."

The Lieutenant-Commander shook his head at the princely nonsense and left them soon afterward, with the excuse that he wanted to check up on his men. In truth, he felt his presence would deter the two men from speaking freely with each other. The princes didn't seem to mark his leaving; they were getting on so well. They talked for many hours into the night, learning about one another. Both had been raised as only children. Al'den had never had a sibling, for both his father's wives had born stillborn sons; this had been long after the prince had been out of swaddle-clothes. Kent had had a younger brother, but the boy had been found dead in his crib when Kent had been three-years-old. Besides their similar childhoods, the princes shared a love for astronomy and mathematics. Prince Kent was well versed in trade and the economy and could spill out any fact, price, or educated opinion about the market that Al'den had a question about. Adversely, Prince Al'den was more knowledgeable about geography, weather, and the sea currents (despite living in the desert), which he added to Kent's trade ideas between kingdoms.

They were so engrossed in their discussion that neither prince noticed the elder king who came into the room. "So, this is where you have been hiding out."

The two princes sprung from their chairs and bowed. Prince Al'den answered his father. "Not hiding, father, just conversing. This is Prince Argetlem from the Golden Kingdom. He and his men arrived through the storm just after dusk. They have ninety-eight archers to add to our force."

"Yes, I heard." King Maushelik neared and waved the princes back to their seats. "I spoke with Lieutenant-Commander Sloane an hour ago about the capabilities of his men." He didn't add that Prince Kent should have been present. "Mr. Sloane also informed me that Clans All'ani and Tem'arid from the Sheev'anee are going to arrive at the wake of the sandstorm. We should have three-hundred-some Tashek warriors to add to the fighting. Speaking of," he paused to eat a piece of fruit from the tray beside his son, "The storm should be breaking soon. I suggest you both get what little sleep is left for you. I will send for you when we convene the council." The king turned away and walked to the door. He paused at the steps to add, "And Prince Argetlem, a very gracious welcome to the Citadel of Light. I am grateful for the assistance your kingdom had given. Please, pass on my thanks to your father."

"Yes, Your Majesty." Prince Kent bowed deeply until the king was gone. He gave a sigh as he let go of the breath he had held. "I cannot believe I was so discourteous as to not see King Maushelik upon my arrival!"

Prince Al'den waved the comment away, lightly. "Do not worry too much about it. My father knew you were with me. Though he may have looked stern, I could tell he was pleased to see us getting along so well. He has been worried that I have had no good friends to speak with, equally since Lance passed."

"Yes, but—."

"But nothing." Al'den stood and waved Kent to follow. "He is very understanding, and, behind that facade of his, my father is a very kind man. He will forgive such slips of etiquette. But, we should listen when he calls for us to sleep. We have a long day ahead of us. Come, I will walk you back to your room."

"Thank you."

Prince Al'den returned Kent to his rooms then wandered down the hall to his own. He sat at his desk, thinking about the interesting turn of the day. Finally, though, his eyes closed in weariness and he fell asleep against the tall back of his chair.

And, slowly, the sandstorm outside of the city walls dissolved to a whisper.

The All'ani and Tem'arid tribesmen arrived with the dawn, just as the last wisps of sand settled to the desert ground. They came quietly through the city; even their desert mounts gave near-inaudible passage. The group of three-hundred-strong horsemen lined up before the Citadel of Light and waited to be greeted.

King Maushelik came first down the fortress steps to meet them. One lone rider stepped forward and bowed to the king atop his chestnut mare. "Welcome, Sheev'anee," Maushelik began, "We deeply express our gratitude at your arrival, as we have been in need of assistance against the maunsturz."

The Tashek made a humming noise, as if to clear his throat. "The Tashek have come because the Stars foretell that there is a tall warrior here, of the Yellow Star, that is in need of our assistance. He called for us yesterday."

The king looked baffled. Tashek were known to be cryptic but not usually to that extent. "I'm not sure of what you refer—."

At that moment, Prince Al'den, followed closely by Prince Kent, came jogging down the stairway. As if on cue, the entire Tashek cavalry made their horses bow. The Starian prince halted in surprise and wonder.

"Prince Maushelik," The leader addressed, "I am All'ani, Cum'ar. The winds ruled that we should serve you, Prince of the Yellow Star. The Stars said you called, and so we have come."

Prince Al'den was too stunned to respond. Luckily, Prince Kent stepped in quickly, himself being ever the diplomate. "He, Prince Maushelik, is very honored for your assistance, All'ani." He bowed deeply with his arms outstretched from his sides, palms up, in a Tashek version of the deepest respect. Cum'ar looked pleased with the gesture and that the man knew it. He returned the greeting. "And he is grateful for the assistance the Stars have given."

"Yes," Cum'ar bowed again. "The Stars do hear all of your prayers." Prince Al'den looked into the desert man's amber-brown eyes as the Tashek spoke, knowing the words were for him. "They are elated that you chose to trust in them. Your piousness is not without reward. All they ask is that you continue to call on them, and they will continue to help you."

"I will, All'ani." Alden spoke loudly enough for those closest to hear, but his bow, very deep and respectful, was witnessed by all. "Our Citadel is open to you. Please, ask for anything and it will be given."

Cum'ar made a final bow to the three royals then straightened. His countenance was excited and predatory. "I believe, Prince of the Yellow Star, that we must post-pone your hospitality. Right now, we have some hunting to do."

"Yes, All'ani, Tem'arid, we do." Prince Al'den turned to his father. The king nodded in understanding and permission. "Father, King Maushelik, let us go fight the maunstorz again. I am more confident that ever that we can win this battle."

"Then go. Protect our kingdom well." *My son.*

Chapter Eleven

§

Trilliums and Blackberries

The Havenese procession stopped at Luck City to recuperate from the long travel and to await news from the Citadel of Light. They stayed at the king's royal estate just outside of the city; Prince Connel insisted that the property was the most beautiful in all of the Sunarian country and that Princess Éleen must see it.

It had been dark when they had arrived, so the Havenese had been unable to see the land; however, the expansive vacation residence was state-of-the-art. The interior was made of a rare high-mountain pine tree that grew only in the interior of the Noway Mountains in Staria. Its rich honey-colored wood was off-set by ruby-satin chairs and Sunarian curtains, all stitched in gold. Ornate tables and chandeliers were scattered elegantly throughout the rooms, leaving an impression of harmony and peace amidst the Sunarian finery. Even the bedrooms had mirrored the theme of the house, with plush mattresses adorned in royal-red silk sheets and heavier, satin coverlets. Each bedpost was made in the same rare pine of the walls; each bed intricately carved in Sunarian scrollwork. There was no doubt that the place was owned by Sunarian royalty.

Princess Éleen rose early, the golden rays of the sun coming through her room's windows teasing her awake; she had wanted it that way the night before and had made sure to dismiss the house maid before the curtains could be closed. By doing so, the princess was able to see the beauty of the land first thing. The sight of the wild greenness of the Sunarian countryside was as breathtaking as the prince had promised.

Princess Éleen touched a hand to the window pane in awe, as if she could reach out and feel how lush the green grasses were or hear the waters from the Halo Lakes lap against the pebble shore. "I'm going to be there soon." She whispered the promise and turned way to put on a light dress, cloak, and serviceable shoes.

It seemed she was the only one wake, which made it easier for the princess to hurry through the halls to reach the outside. Within minutes, she was alone in the peaceful morning sunshine. Following a well-worn path down to the lake, she was serenaded by the cheerful singing of robins. The mist had just begun clearing from the lake, revealing the large, serene waters. Éleen inhaled deeply of the sharp, earthly coolness of the early morning and turned her head to the sun. "There is something so magical about this place," she mused.

The princess had been born in the kingdom mainly occupied by beaches and grasslands, very little of it had rolling hills or mountains. Though Sunrise was similar to Blue Haven, it boasted the beauty of the largest lakes in Syre, which sat at the altitude of three-thousand-feet above sea level. The only other time Éleen had been to a higher elevation was at age sixteen, when she had been invited to the Princess Starkindler's coming-of-age party; however, unlike the high mountains of the Crystal Kingdom, the rolling hills around Luck City were lush, full-on green, and the air had a forgiving warmth to it. Contented, Princess Éleen began a casual stroll along the side of the lake, stopping occasionally to touch a lovely wildflower or observe a bird fly. She got lost in the wonder around her and stopped thinking of the time as it flew by.

Éleen was just stooping down to observe a deep-pink trillium when a voice spoke behind her. "I see you are enjoying the countryside."

The princess jumped at the sudden appearance of Prince Connel but quickly composed her surprise with a curtsy. "Your Highness."

"Please, Ms. Éleen, call me Connel when we are in private." The prince shook his light-chestnut hair from his blue eyes out of habit and noted what the princess had been looking at. "The trillium is our family's flower. It grows everywhere in Sunrise, but especially here. It is said that trilliums represent "modest ambition", whatever that is supposed to mean," he shrugged, "But they are a pretty flower are they not?" Before the Havenese woman could respond, he reached down to pick the flower she had been observing and handed it to her with a little bow. Éleen took the flower shyly, not used to such attention. The prince seemed pleased. "There are also wild blackberries and sometimes strawberries along the hillocks. It is the perfect season for them. If you'd like, I can lead you to a patch. There is one just over that hill, heading back to the main house."

Princess Éleen was not sure about the request, but the prince seemed genuinely content to show her around. She accepted. The

Sunarian gave a broad smile that lite up his comely face and softened the hard angle of his jaw. In answer, he waved her back down the pathway and began talking lightly about the flowers and plants, of which he seemed to know a lot about.

The prince had not lied about the blackberries. They were so large and ripe that the princess could not help exclaim in delight. Connel picked one and offered it to her, enjoying the glowing smile she returned as she plucked is from his hand and savored the berry. "These are so good!" Princess Éleen commented. She began to pick a handful but soon didn't have enough hand-space to hold them. She began to pull up the front of her dress to collect them better.

"Ms. Éleen, please stop!"

"But I would like to take these back to share with everyone."

"Yes, that is fine, but your dress will get ruined. Here," Connel pulled out a fine, silk handkerchief. Princess Éleen baulked at using such a nice cloth, but the prince piled her berries into it before she could overly protest. "See? Now you can take back enough for everyone, and that pretty yellow dress of yours stays nice and clean." Blushing, the woman began picking more berries, hoping the young royal could not see the heat on her cheeks. Connel joined her and soon the handkerchief was as full as they could get it. "There, that should be more than enough for a feast," the prince smiled and bobbed his head back to the house, seen just beyond the small field. "Shall we return? Everyone should be awake by now."

"Yes, please."

As they neared the main house, Lord Carrod came out to lean against the railing, a scowl on his face as he saw the two royals conversing and smiling so casually together. Prince Connel nodded a hello as he walked up the three steps to the deck. The Havenese lord gave a small nod in return, without the smile. His face changed, however, as Éleen showed him the berries. Her happiness seemed infectious.

Lord Nexlé followed the two royals into the dining room where the others were already partaking of the pancakes, sausages, and eggs. The group became livelier over the ripe blackberries, and soon everyone had their share of the bounty. Princess Éleen looked pleased.

A courier arrived just as breakfast ended. The maid let him in and he hovered by the room's doorway until Prince Connel waved him near. The man bowed to the seated prince and offered the piece of paper before stepping out of the way. The room quieted as the Sunarian tore open the correspondence and skimmed the writing. Finally, Prince Connel pushed back his chair and stood so all could hear. "Well, it seems that we are advised to go no further than Kavahad if we continue on from here. The fighting at the Gap of the Forgotten is still fierce. Going further would endanger us unnecessarily."

"May I see that?" Lord Carrod asked. The other man passed the letter over.

"This was signed by Commander Kins of the mertinean! He says our messenger reached him as his men crossed the East Bridge. Commander Kins states he is surprised Princess Eldon-Tomino is among our procession and askes that, for her sake, we wait until the fighting had ceased before heading to the Citadel of Light."

Prince Connel gave Carrod a look that said, *you're so dumb to say all that out loud; it was so ungentlemanly of you to announce all that with princess in the room. Where is your respect?*. Out loud, Prince Connel said, "Well, it would be better to wait here than to continue to Staria. Kavahad is a small desert outpost and not very comfortable to wait out a war. Staying here will give everyone and the horses needed rest and will be suitable for our needs."

Lord Carrod could not hold back his look of distain. "I believe, Highness, that the decision is up to Highness Éleen."

Éleen looked surprised to be put on the spot; but then, resolutely, she squared her shoulders. This was her royal procession, after all. "Yes, it is my decision." She stood then. "And, I think we should stay her for now." Prince Connel smiled, victorious. "But only as long as it takes for the Lord of Kavahad to respond to the letter I will write him. Our main reason for this journey is to support Staria, and I, for one, would prefer to do that in Staria's border. If we cannot reach the Citadel of Light, I would prefer to be as close as we can get. Now gentleman, if you will excuse me, I have a letter to write."

Prince Connel lifted a hand as if to stop the princess's leaving but the Havenese woman curtsied politely and stepped around his reach. The prince barely hid his annoyance. Lord Carrod cast him a gloating sneer behind the royal's back and followed his princess out into the hallway. They walked to her room without a word between them.

Once they were alone and the door was shut, Lord Carrod muttered frankly to his charge. "I do not trust that Sunarian leech."

Princess Éleen shot him a look of warning. "He is a decent man and very amiable. Do not be rude to his hospitality."

Carrod's eyebrows rose and he argued back in a hushed voice. "Amiable?! Highness, all Sunarian royals are as slippery as snakes. They play admirable hosts while behind your back they scheme and plan discord. The only things they are out for are themselves. I urge you caution, My Lady. Prince Sunrise is not to be trusted."

"I know their history as well as you, Lord Nexlé." Éleen retorted, sharper than she intended. "I do not need you sheltering me from the politics I already know."

"Just so you haven't forgotten." Lord Carrod finished as forcefully as he could. "Do not dismiss the man you are going to be betrothed to just because you have yet to meet. He may be more enticing than this lying dandy who's been leading us around."

At the rebuke, Princess Éleen's hand instinctively clasped the pendant hanging around her neck. Its smooth surface settled her emotions. "I understand what you are saying, dear Carrod; and I have not forgotten why we are traveling; but is it wrong for me to have some fun and laugh a little? Prince Connel may be just this side of trouble, but I have been having a good time with him."

"Just as long as you understand what is and is not acceptable with him, My Lady. That is all I ever ask."

"Yes." Éleen gave a soft, apologetic smile. "Thank you for your concern." She straightened and said with more conviction, "I know you have my best interests in your heart." Lord Carrod bowed to her, glad he had gotten his message through. The princess turned away, then, to the desk in the room, where she had set a stationary set and inkwell. "Now, I do need to write this letter. Please, give me the room."

Chapter Twelve

§

Afflictions

Lord Darshel had left Zyanthena alone for one full day and night since the Crystine's departure. He had even avoided his bedchamber because of her thrashing and cursing. However, the next morning had been too quiet. Darshel knew he should check up on the Tashek.

The desert woman made no sound as he strode into his quarters. Even as the tall lord neared her in the alcove, she did not stir. He found Zyanthena hanging, her hair covering her face and all her body weight held up by her arms and chains. The picture she painted disturbed Darshel. "Oh, come now! Where's that fire, Tashek?" He goaded as he reached out to brush back a lock of her long, black hair. His hand touched feverish skin. Perturbed, Lord Darshel stepped closer and retested her temperature under a hand. He *tsked.* "This isn't good," he murmured. His eyebrows knit with concern. The lord called out for his maid to fetch the physician then he turned back to his captive warrior.

Lord Darshel unlocked first the feet chains then each of her wrists, balancing the woman's weight against one broad shoulder to do so. As Zyanthena crumpled forward, Darshel noticed the bloody marks on her back that stained the white cloth dried red. So, in her angry thrashing, the rough walls had broken open her skin possibly leading to infection. "Is this your doing, woman?" Darshel wondered. "Do you feel so forsaken that you would rather die?" He carried her unconscious body to his bed and gently laid her down. Reaching over, Darshel collected a basin of water and a towel from the stand beside the headboard. He wet the towel and dabbed it gingerly against the blood-soaked cloth at Zyanthena's back.

The physician arrived just as the Kavahadian was beginning to tear the dress from her body. He nodded his approval at the lord's work. "Smart to wet the clothes before peeling them off her cuts. It prevents further injury. This little lady sure did a number on herself."

"If it was intentional," Darshel replied. The doctor gave him a look that said he doubted any other story. "She's running a fever, too. It feels quite warm to me."

"I'll be the judge of that. Now, step aside and let me have a look at this lady."

Lord Darshel respected his physician. Doctor Murnin had been with his family for years, and he was the only man, besides Darshel's deceased father, that the Kavahadian lord let boss him around. The physician never once refused to treat a person and his results were always first-rate. Whatever was wrong with Zyanthena, Darshel was confident she would pull through.

"She's a fine one," Dr. Murnin commented as he stepped back from his examination. "It's been over forty years since I've treated one of her kind. Interesting people, the Tashek are, and hardy too. They heal quicker than us—something to do with a healing trance they know. I think she may in be one now."

"How would you know?" Darshel inquired. To him, she looked unconscious.

"Oh... just how slow her breathing is; not natural that. But, what do I know?" The old man shrugged and turned to his bag of medicinals. "What I do know is that her fever is not caused from the trauma to her back. I think that the real reason is something else burning her up from the inside. Did something happen to this woman recently? An argument or fight or anything like that?"

Lord Darshel suppressed a grimace. "Her people forsake her to captivity all from the treaty between them and us. She learned of it yesterday."

"Well, it's shaken her spirit up real bad." The doctor gave him a scolding look, like he had when Darshel was little. "She's burning up with resentment."

"What? Wait, one damned second!" Darshel sputtered, seeing where his doctor was going with his diagnosis. "You are saying her illness is caused from an emotional upset, when we can see, *for a fact*, that her back has been torn open?! Are you nuts?"

Doctor Murnin placed two bottles of liquids on the nightstand then clipped his bag closed. "What I know, sonny, is that this woman had just been ripped apart in the worst of ways. Now, she's a beautiful rarity and I can fix her beaten body, but as far as for her heart and soul, that's beyond my ability. You can ignore me if you wish but she isn't going to heal entirely unless you address that side of her, too—and I'm not talking about your kind of loving." The man eyed Darshel knowingly. "I'm leaving two medicines here, plus an external liniment. This first bottle is to be applied to her back, to heal her wounds and prevent infection. This second one is to be taken internally to bring down her fever. Have her take it by the hour once she wakes. And this," he handed Darshel a pot full of a sticky, brown substance, "I want you to massage into her joints, especially her shoulders—to relieve any pain being chained up for days might have caused. You understand all that?"

Darshel forced himself not to squirm in the man's gaze. "Yes, I got that."

Doctor Murnin nodded, satisfied. "Okay then, well... I'm off to treat other patients. I will swing by again tonight."

"Thank you, Murnin."

Lord Darshel returned to Zyanthena's side after seeing the physician out. The maid had left a clean dress beside the Tashek and had covered her in a light blanket; the Kavahadian was surprised at the girl's generosity. He made a note to speak with this maid...

Tired of just standing and staring at the desert woman, Darshel came to sit down beside the Tashek and pulled her to a sitting position. He propped her against his shoulder as he gently dabbed on the first liquid over the wounds on her back. Though they all looked like deep marks, Darshel had to admit Murnin was right that they did not look infected—yet. However, the raw injuries would definitely hurt for at least a week. It was probably a good thing that the Tashek was unconscious.

Finished with the medicinal, Darshel covered the area with a clean cloth then redressed the warrioress, silently relieved she was not awake to protest his administrations. He lowered her back down to the pillows. Next, Lord Darshel picked up the pot of liniment and gave it a skeptical sniff. The brownish goo smelled both strongly earthy and overly aromatic. He wrinkled his nose. "This stuff better work." The maid had been smart enough to have the foresight to give Zyanthena a sleeveless dress; Darshel could easily reach all sections of her arms without having to work around the clothing. Hesitating at the first dab into the sticky mess, Darshel look one last breathe, then dove into the task.

§   §

Zyanthena slowly came back to awareness, fighting her feverish state. She became alerted to the feel of strong fingers stroking a substance into her right arm. The movements were deliberate and practiced. The feeling was so gentle and pain-relieving that Zyanthena almost didn't want it to end—except she was beginning to have thoughts that the touch belonged to someone she was less than enamored with. Forcing calmness upon herself, the warrioress let herself drift up into a wakeful state and took in the sounds around her.

§   §

The maid came back into the room with a bowlful of broth made from beef stock and wild yam powder. She gave a little curtsy as she neared her lord. "Doctor Murnin said this broth should be taken by the patient now, to help her regain her strength."

Lord Darshel took his hands from of Zyanthena's arm and stood to wipe them on a clean towel. "I am sorry but she is not awake yet."

"But she is, M'lord," the maid replied," Her eyes are open and she's lookin' right at us."

Surprised, Darshel turned to study the desert woman. Sure enough, her brandy eyes, dulled by the fever and her mental state, were fluttering then slowly steadying onto his person. "Well then…by all means, let us get some of her medicines and some food into her." The maid nodded and set the bowl on the bed stand. She walked over to help Darshel prop Zyanthena up against the headboard and puff up the pillows as support. Darshel took note that the Tashek did not protest the assistance, nor did she bother to cover the pain she felt. He pulled up a chair next to the bed and handed the fever-reducing medicinal then the bowl of broth to the maid as she feed them to the desert woman. Zyanthena took both without question.

"Thank you…Tika." Lord Darshel told the maid as she finished. The girl seemed pleased he had remembered her name. The lord motioned for her to follow him out into the hallway. "I have noticed that you have taken all of the shifts to care for this Tashek. Thank you. But I do wonder why none of the other maids have come to relieve you…?" He prompted.

"Ah...M'lord," the girl looked down shyly, "The others are terribly afraid of her, My Lordship. They do now want to go anywhere near her. I don't really see why though, sir, the woman hadn't done anything when I've been around. In fact, I think she is the nicest lady you've had in the keep, M'lord."

Lord Darshel smiled to himself at the thought of Zyanthena being called a lady. "Well tell the other maids I do not want them up here, since you have been doing a fine job. I excuse you from all other work so that you can take care of this Tashek. And, here is my gratitude for you doing the job." Darshel pushed a silver coin into her hand. The girl looked stunned; the coin was worth over one month of her wages! She stammered a thank you and waited for the lord to dismiss her. "Return when you can. Zyanthena needs constant watching for the time being and I am needed elsewhere." The girl curtsied and hurried down the hall to dispose of the used dished.

Lord Darshel returned to Zyanthena's side. "It was good to see you can still eat, Zyanthena...or should I call you..." he searched his memory for the name Commander Matar had spoken, "Zy'ena?" He had hoped the desert woman's eyes would flash at the name, but if it was the fever or the fact that she felt defeated, she reacted very little to his words.

She did respond, however. "Zyanthena is the formal name given to me and used when I am being addressed by the council or during other important events. Zy'ena is the common version of that and the one most preferred because of its ease." She finished with, "Your Lordship."

"You know, I liked you better when you were all spite and fire."

A very tiny, unenthusiastic smile floated across her lips. It did not carry to the rest of her face. "That was before I was officially chained to you, Your Lordship."

"Yes; I have heard Tashek do not do well with capture. They usually waste away in their cells." At least that was what his father had always said. "But, it seems unlikely when your people have such spirit in them. It's a stupid action to squander all that talent just because of certain circumstances."

"Certain circumstances?" She asked with some greater force. "My people are going to be fighting and some dying, while I stay chained up here useless to them. I should rather die, seeing as I am no longer considered part of the Sheev'anee."

"I would never have expected you to sulk. You are quite pathetic." Lord Darshel stated, hoping the sound of his voice would lull the Tashek out of her woefulness. There almost seemed to be a flash of anger in her eyes. "If you are dead, you cannot return to them. Now, I do not know if it makes any difference to you, but whenever we finally get a call from King Maushelik to help at the Gap—for I believe there will be a call—then I will need every able-bodied fighter I have. If that includes a Tashek, then so be it, but I am not going to take you if you are unable to perform." Zyanthena looked away as she thought over the Kavahadian's words. He could see a flash of her old self come back into her countenance. It wasn't much, but it would do for the time being. "I really do not care what you decide, Tashek, but do remember, my offer still stands." He leaned forward to look her deeply in the eyes. "One night and you are free of me." Zyanthena felt well enough to look disgusted. "And if not, I have other uses for one such as yourself. Until then, Miss Tika will make sure you recover properly." He stood and turned toward the door. "Now, I have other duties I need to attend. If there is anything you require, Miss Tika will help you." He finished just as the maid returned. Lord Darshel gave one last, very alluring smile and strode away.

The day passed in a feverish haze to Zyanthena. She easily dozed off between the hourly doses of medicine. The girl, Tika, seemed content to sit by her bedside all the day, occasionally changing cold compressed on Zyanthena's forehead, at other times working on an embroidery piece. When the Tashek was awake, she would chat idly about random things, at first shyly but then more freely as the sick warrioress prompted her with comments about her chosen subjects. Zyanthena had not been around many women for a handful of years; not since she had been out scouting and fighting with the men. She had spent many months proving to even her own people that she was more useful on the battlefield than left behind at the tents. Above all, Zyanthena doubted the girl could have harmed a fly... And so, the day plodded along while with the two females keeping each other company.

Doctor Murnin and Lord Shekmann returned with the start of the night. The physician seemed pleased to see Zyanthena sitting upright in the bed, a fact confirmed after finding her fever gone. "Well, you are out of the woods—so to speak. A good sleep tonight and I believe you'll feel more like your normal self. How's the rest of you?" He inquired and stooped closer, gently pulling Zyanthena forward to get a look at her back. The Tashek let out a hiss against the fiery pain in her muscles, alerting the doctor to her other complaints. "You hurt where dear?"

"Just moving, sir," she responded shortly. "Muscle aches and nothing more. The back is fine."

"Well, most of you is not *"fine"*." He said, shooting Darshel an accusing look. "But, as I've heard you are a soldier, these injuries must not seem too bad. I'm still gonna leave your medicines here for a few more days, just to help you get back on your feet. If anything, and I mean anything, comes up you say immediately." Zyanthena nodded, dossal as a lamb. "Now, how is your appetite?"

"I feel like I could eat something," she responded.

"She ate two heaping bowlfuls of broth, Doctor." Ms. Tika filled in politely.

"And they went down okay?"

"No problems."

"Then I give the patient leave to eat some solid food. Not too much, mind you, as you do not want to overdo your body. And if you can manage a short walk, it may do you some good—but only if it does not hurt you." The Tashek woman gave another nod. The doctor looked satisfied with everything. "Well, okay then. I'll be back tomorrow on my rounds. Until then, keep getting well."

"Thank you, Murnin." Darshel told the physician. He motioned to Tika. "Doctor, if you and Ms. Tika are in need, my kitchens have prepared a lovely dinner of pot pie and roasted vegetables. Pease, help yourselves before going home."

Doctor Murnin waved a thanks as he left the room. Tika was right behind him, grateful to be dismissed, but she did pause to give a departing curtsy to her lord and to say good-night to Zyanthena. With the two people gone, the room seemed more oppressive.

"Well," the dark-haired Kavahadian began, "I guess you have been declared over the worst of your illness."

"And you have yet to get over your affliction," Zyanthena muttered.

Lord Darshel chuckled at the words. "So, you can be sassy after all. Doctor Murnin believed you to have lost your will, what with your people's decree. It's good to know he can be wrong about something."

The Tashek's face fell upon hearing the words. Her eyes turned sad and distant. Lord Darshel had not expected the reaction; it seemed his taunt had drained the life out of the woman. He came closer to perched beside the desert woman on his bed. A small flash of anger flitted over her eyes then was gone. "Our peoples have been at odds for nearly a century. It is astounding that the peace between us had lasted so long despite the hatred. Yet, I have been astonished at how your people have decided to deal with this situation. I would have expected them to revolt at the capture of one of their own. Instead, they gave you up so hastily that I wonder if they even thought it through."

"It shows you know so little of my people."

"That is true." Darshel answered honestly. "Half of what I do know came from my father, who very much despised your kind. The rest...well, let's just say it came from a long string of myths and conjectures about your people..." He looked away, his face thoughtful and very handsome in its strong-featured way. "It seems that the discourse between us is from a lack of understanding more than anything else. Which is why I'm still nonplussed about it." He looked back.

"Politics." She stated shortly. Darshel raised an eyebrow confused. "It may be hard for you to comprehend that Tashek could have politics, but we do. We try to do what's best for the Sheev'anee as a whole. If a single person screws up, it can be disastrous for many. So, it is up to that individual to fix their own mistake. That is why they left me behind. Why compromise a people to war when one person can be punished instead."

"That seems cruel and arrogant.... What if that person at fault was very important, say a great leader? Would the same apply?'

"Of a course." She replied coolly. "No leader leads by himself. There is a council and designated clan second-and-third-in commands for such situations. But, again, if one's men are loyal enough that leader may be "rescued" from himself by the sacrifice of another. In the end, it is still all politics."

"I'd say, and that left you in the first category." Her lack of response meant yes. Lord Darshel studied the Tashek's face, still intrigued at the beauty of it. Even competing against the fatigue that accompanied a battle with an illness, Zyanthena was really something lovely and exotic. *Had he really been lucky enough to get the prettiest woman from the savage desert nomads captured and in his keep?* By impulse, he leaned forward ready to reach out and touch her face.

"One more inch, Your Lordship, and I will break your wrist in two."

Lord Darshel froze at the threat, his hand inches away from her cheek. Her brandy eyes were hard and serious as she stared back into his emerald ones. They promised everything her words said. "You forget who is in control here." He returned the threat, hoping to hide the pounding of his heart.

"You still gave me the choice. You do not touch me unless I say."

He sighed and leaned away. "So stubborn you are. You could be rid of me tonight but you still cling to that clouded form of dignity you wear like a knife. You are so close to your freedom—and yet you choose your cage."

"A fact you keep me from forgetting."

"Yes well, you deserve the reminder." He flashed a disarming smile and stood. "My cooks have prepared us dinner on the balcony. If you are up to it, I can help you over."

Zyanthena's eyes looked calculating. "I will eat with you..." Darshel started to reach out to help her up, "But, under my own power," she finished with a glare.

Unassisted, the desert warrioress pushed back the covers and came to her feet. She walked steadily enough, but it was obvious by the time they reached the table that the exertion was taxing. Zyanthena didn't bother to hide her relief at being able to sit. She collapsed heavily into the chair. Lord Darshel shooed his servants away and proceeded to dish up their dinners himself before taking his own seat. He kept quiet for many long minutes, watching the desert woman from the corner of his eye as they ate their food. As they neared the end of the meal, Lord Darshel finally spoke, "It's good to see you can eat. Doctor Murnin will find that news a relief."

Zyanthena looked at him for the first time since she had started eating. "You just can't help making small talk, can you?"

He chuckled. "It's the polite thing to do." The lord answered suavely. "But, I guess you are not used to that, since you have been around soldiers. No matter. I do want to talk with you, though." Zyanthena looked guarded. "About you and your horse. I went through you bags; just to be sure we had gotten all your weapons, mind you. They should be back in the alcove. Everything is there— I made sure of that—except this." The Kavahadian lord pulled an item from his pocket and dangled it from his hand. "I was intrigued that a Tashek warrior would own a necklace, especially one made of such an interesting stone as this. You don't seem the type to wear such." The obsidian stone, unpolished and coarse in contrast to the smooth silver chain, looked dull and lifeless in the candlelight. Yet, Lord Darshel could see a look of panic in the Tashek's eyes, as if he had taken a very precious thing from her. "It seems to be the only personal item you carry with you. I'm curious as to why that is?"

"It is considered rude to go through other's things," she retorted.

"Not when you are my prisoner. Now, will you answer my question?"

"I am its keeper."

Lord Darshel waited for more, but the desert woman did not expound. "That does not answer anything."

Zyanthena scowled and looked away. "It's complicated…. the story, I mean."

"Indulge me." He sat back, taking the necklace with him.

Brandy eyes chased after his hand, worried, but finally Zyanthena seemed willing to speak. What she told the Shekmann seemed inconceivable. "The Sheev'anee are the "Guardians of the Truth" and have been since the Second Age of Syre. A part of the histories we hold foretell of eight precious stones that can control the Tides of Fate. These "Stones of Power" were said to have gone missing during the last generation, only three have definitive whereabouts. The Obsidian stone is one of those." She pointed at the necklace. "The Stones of Power will awaken for the ones they are intended to be used by. That obsidian is supposed to go to the heir of Crystalynian.

The Shi'alam gave it to me for safe keeping until its wielder can be found."

"An interesting story. I assume there is much more to it than that; however, it seems implausible. The heir of Crystalynian? Stones of Power?" He laughed at the absurdity of it. "I knew your people had whims of magic and the like, but this takes the cake!"

"You mock our ways yet do not take into account all the tales across Syre that tell of similar majiks—some used not thirty-years past. And, who is to say that there is no heir of Crystalynian? Was the kingdom not destroyed by a natural disaster? People do survive those things."

"Touché, touché." Darshel waved her defense down. "So, you have been given this obsidian stone for safe keeping?"

"Until the heir can be found, yes."

"But why you? Why are you the one chosen to carry it? Are you that high up in the Tashek hierarchy to be given such a task?"

A smirk was his reply. "I am a Sheev'arid, Shekmann." The look he returned showed that the Kavahadian did not know what she meant. Zyanthena sighed. "My father is Shi'alam, the leader of the Sheev'anee. I am very "high up" as you would say."

The lord's eyebrows rose as he realized the implications. A gleam lite his eyes as he calculated the leverage he had just procured under this woman's capture—leverage against the Shi'alam and King Maushelik. Yet, Lord Darshel's look changed to a more thoughtful one as he held up the necklace to the candlelight. Its soft gleam within the unpolished obsidian stone held a certain fascination. *A "Stone of Power"? This?* Darshel had heard stories of such majiks himself, but never believed them, and yet, the Sheev'anee did. *And this stone?* It was in a raw form, as if it had just come from the earth. *How could it be so old?* Not a scratch refined its dark surface. Finally, Lord Darshel leaned forward and offered it to Zyanthena. "You should wear it instead of keeping such an item in a pouch. Less easy to lose something of value from around your neck. Besides, I think it will look pretty on you."

The last comment almost made Zyanthena defy him and not put it on; however, she treasured the necklace, the one order from her father that made her seem still graced in his eyes. It had been too long from her neck already. With practiced familiarity, the desert woman brushed back her long hair, slid the chain around her neck, and clasped it. The obsidian stone rested coolly against her warm skin.

Lord Darshel seemed satisfied. "It does indeed suit you." The words sounded sincere. "I see you have been wearied from tonight's exertions. If you are ready, I have prepared a bed for you to sleep on in the alcove. I do apologize but I still don't trust you to run away—or slit my throat while I sleep—so I will have you chained up at night. If you are up to it, tomorrow I will take you to see your horse. Though he had behaved himself well enough, I am sure he is better for you."

Zyanthena's eyes brightened at the prospect but they were quick to narrow in suspicion. "You are treating me differently because of who you now know me to be."

"Leave it to you to jump to that conclusion." Darshel said as way of not answering. "Shall we, then?"

The warrioress responded by standing and, even though she looked fatigued, the Tashek made it back to the alcove on her own shaky legs. The sight of the plush mattress was a welcome relief, even though it involved being chained up. Zyanthena sank to the bed unceremoniously and barely acknowledged the Kavahadian lord as he shackled her wrist. Very soon, she was asleep.

"She must be tired to ignore me so easily. I do not think I have seen her go to sleep while I have been around." He murmured to himself as he turned away to his own bed. It had been changed and washed down while he and Zyanthena had eaten. Lord Darshel sat down on the large mattress, his eyes still wandering to the sleeping desert woman across the room. "I must be a fool." He declared softly. "Here I have spent the whole day worrying over a woman my people would call an enemy, and I have not thought once today about whom I would bed tonight or the city I need to govern." A huff-like chuckle left his throat. "An affliction indeed! Father, you would really look down on me now, if you were here." The lord-governor finally laid back on his mattress and covered his face with a hand. He groaned. "I thought I was the one doing the tormenting, but having that woman here is torture. If this keeps up…" Lord Darshel could not finish the thought. "Stars! Something better give soon or I do not know what havoc will reign down between us."

Chapter Thirteen

§

Vanishing

Day seventeen of the fighting in North Point began foggy and cold, but, at least, it was not raining. Commander Tyk's men had been as good an omen as Prince Par had hoped for, making the losses to both his men and the mertinean much less than there would have been. Yet, Par could not help cast a worried glance to the east each morning, wondering what had become of his cousin and the promised mertinean and Crystine soldiers. Every day there was no sign of the others was one more day Par felt himself slowly losing faith that North Point could hold back the maunstorz.

"We need your focus here, Highness." Commander Averron spoke from the prince's right.

Prince Par pulled his thoughts back and turned to his man. "I apologize for my distress. Is it my turn for the run of the field?" Since Commander Tyk's arrival, the three men had been taking shifts in the field with the men, to keep up morale as well as dictate orders. It had been the mertinean commander's idea; after all, they knew they were in the fight for the long haul and wanted to make sure at least one leader was refreshed enough to make informed decisions that many lives depended upon. Prince Par had been on his break and had just woken up to thoughts of how it was going on the battlefield.

"The fighting has picked up again, My Prince. Tyk was afraid they are getting more desperate, now that their numbers are down a few thousand. He asked if you would come with the reserve company. This may be it, sir."

Prince Par did not like the look in his commander's eyes. Never before had the man admitted they might be on the losing end. Quickly, he donned his armor with Averron's help and hurried out to the courtyard. The reserves were already lining up. They gave a quick, practiced salute to their prince. Par returned it just a fast and ordered a march out of the front gates. With no time to prepare for what could lay beyond, the group rushed out—into chaos.

The maunstorz had pushed a suicide-like advance through the front ranks. They held a large, unnerving hole deep into the Sealand army. The defending soldiers fought back desperately, trying to restore the lines that had broken, but there were too many enemies rushing in to hold off the threat. Prince Par saw the problem immediately and ordered his company to charge into the weakened section of the fray. The group came running with voices yelling and swords poised at ready. The two forces met in a clash of metal.

Prince Par swung at a maunstorz man trying to finish off a Sealander. His stroke cut cleanly through the man's side, rendering him useless. The prince kicked the man away and whirled around to block a club aimed at his face. He parried around the next blow and aimed for the man's neck. The sword sliced cleanly through and the man crumpled. Par gritted his teeth against the gore and forced himself to continue defending his falling men. His forces managed to move deeper into the fray, almost making up for the lost ground.

The dead from both sides began to pile up, making hazardous footing underneath already wearied feet. Hours passed in a dizzy blur as Prince Par, Commander Averron at his side, continued to hold their hard-won position.

A battle horn called retreat from Commander Tyk's side, a signal that gave the Sealander pause. Prince Par risked a glance to the left to see the grizzled veteran stumble back with his men, a horrible would in his shoulder. The mertinean covered their retreat well, but the Sealander prince felt his heart stop as a large wall of refreshed maunstorz came pounding up to the lost line, howling victory.

"Averron! Hold this line. Marcus, Tennet to me!" Prince Par called two subordinates to him and rushed toward the failing line. Nearly fifty soldiers hurried after, weapons at ready, trying to get to the mertinean before the maunstorz engaged them. The two forces clashed, metal ringing sharply against the cooling air of dusk. Prince Par swung his sword around in desperate thrusts, his aching arms protesting every motion. Too fatigued, the prince and his men found that they could not hold back the advancement. Yelling an order, Par hoped they could keep the line long enough to get the rest of the North Point forces to the safety of the fortress walls. The men with the prince looked scared at their impending doom but held true as the rest of the army retreated back. Everyone fought as hard as they were able.

Eager, sensing victory, the horde of maunstorz pressed their enemy, an eerie battle cry rising from their throats. Many were bloodied forms from hundreds upon hundreds of cuts along their unarmored bodies—but those eyes, which were the same cast of fresh-red as their wounds, shown bright in anticipation. The lead savages crowed loudly, licking their lips, knowing only too well how intimidating their features were to their enemy.

And, indeed, Par was terrified. Today, he just might meet his maker.

The Sealander force was pushed against the wall, unable to reach the safety of the fortress gates. The remainder of the army already inside the walls were frantically trying to help their prince's forces. They threw pots of flaming oil, rocks, and arrows into the enemy fray; however, Prince Par could not see any escape for his men.

"Highness, please take hold of the rope!" Tennet called from Par's back.

Par glanced at his man for only a moment, "No, Tennet! I would rather die with all of you than be skewered to the fortress walls. Leave the rope. Come and fight!"

Just as it seemed the prince and his small group of men were finished, the ground began to shake. At first, the maunstorz did not seem to notice, but, as the thundering got louder and closer, the entire mass of savages seemed to lose it cadence. Suddenly, a large herd of charging horses came from the east, plowing straight into the body of maunstorz. The momentum of the charging animals took the cavalry all the way to the heart of the enemy, opening up a large hole in their forces. In a matter of moments, Prince Par and his men were protected by a wall of horse flesh.

"We got you covered, My Highness." Familiar golden eyes flashed loyally from under a silver helm of Sealand before turning away to confront the maunstorz.

Prince Par panted in exhaustion now that he found himself at a reprieve from his attackers. Stepping back to lean against the wall with his men, the Sealanders watched as the over three-hundred-strong Tashek cavalry pushed the maunstorz back. In only a handful of minutes, the entire front third of the enemy was killed and the rest were scattering into a retreat from the skilled desert horsemen.

Prince Par could not have been more stunned at the short work done by the Tashek.

By nightfall, the exhausted army of North Point collected their dead under the watch of the Tashek, setting flame to the bodies, and amassed inside the safety of the fortress walls. The large number of Tashek and horses clumped together in the large southern courtyard, the desert steeds standing calmly next to one another despite how closely they were crowded together. Most of the Tashek stayed with their mounts caring for them before attending to themselves. Only eight Tashek, accompanied by Patrick Kins and Jacen Novano, left the quiet of the courtyard to join the commanders and prince atop the northern wall.

Prince Par turned away from the sight of his burning dead and the blue of the surrounding evening to greet the Tashek. He bowed gratefully as the desert men addressed him, much to their surprise.

"It is we who should bow to you, Prince of Sealand." The lead man said.

Lord Gordar, whom had not left his cousin's side since the battle ended, stepped forward to introduce the Tashek to the prince. "This is Shi'alam Sheev'arid of the Sheev'anee and his three kala Shík Savam'eed, Shík Cum'eri, and Shík All'aum." Prince Par made sure to show deference to the Shi'alam as the man was considered to be the rank of a king to his people. To the others, the Sealander bowed his head politely. "And this is Kor'mauk Siv'arid of the Sheev'anee," Gordar continued, "and Kor'moon and Kor'ar Siv'arid, who follow under Kor'mauk."

Lord Gordar had become aware of the many rankings within the Tashek on the long travel. The desert people usually followed complicated ranks of honor depending of family name and age that defied even royalty's long twists and turns. Both Kor'moon and Kor'ar, he had found out, were first cousins to Kor'mauk, while Siv'arid himself was the third nephew to the Shi'alam. Lord Gordar, however, know the intricate ranks would be lost on his fatigued cousin, so he held off from the explanation.

Prince Par did not forget to be diplomatic, though, even in his weariness. "I am deeply indebted to you, Shi'alam, for bringing Tashek support. I do not believe I would be standing here now, thanking you, had you not arrived when you did."

The Shi'alam looked out at the burning pyres, his face stern but for the sadness in his eyes. "If the winds had carried us faster, we would have prevented such deaths. But your people will rest peacefully with the Stars." Prince Par, surprised at the tenderness in the Tashek's words, could only offer a "thank you" to the Shi'alam. The senior Sheev'arid continued, "The maunstorz will regroup. They have need to re-evaluate their attack. They have always tread carefully when a number of Tashek are on the field. Your North Point will hold strong."

"Thank you, Shi'alam. If you have need of more guard, some of my men ae more rested than others. Do not hesitate to call for them."

"Your offer is generous but unnecessary." The Shi'alam replied. "My men are fresher than yours and more alert. It is our responsibility, as your reinforcements, to allow you all recovery. We will be fine as we are."

Prince Par bowed one last time, too drained to argue. He prayed, inwardly, that he was not making a huge diplomatic blunder, then allowed his cousin and the two other Syrean soldiers to lead him away to the mess hall.

§ §

The mess hall was crowded with Sealand and Rubian solders, all trying to take advantage of the time they had to eat a meal that did not consist of bread and cheese. Others, those that had been fighting longest, looked like they would fall asleep where they stood, so Commander Averron came around the room and ordered wearied soldiers to their bedrolls. Under his command, the hall was able to clear enough that most of the men could sit at the long tables. With the mass dispersed, the tired Sealand commander found his seat and waiting meal next to the patched-up Commander Tyk.

A few minutes later, Prince Par Fantill came into the dining hall, accompanied by his Lord Protector and two of the soldiers that had come with the Tashek. The entire room of men stood at their leader's arrival. All saluted. Prince Par paused, surprised by the respect shown him, and waved his men back to their meals. Slowly, the soldiers sat back down and the royal-blood and his small troupe continued over to the commanders' table. Prince Par sat heavily beside the two veterans and allowed Lord Gordar to get him a dinner bowl. "I see you are okay."

Commander Tyk nodded. "Indeed, Highness." He grinned devilishly and clasped his hand to his shoulder. "Nothing another round with those bastards won't fix. I'm not apt to getting caught by a saber again."

The prince gave a tired laugh and accepted the bowl of soup and beer tankard his cousin brought him. As the other Sealander settled into the seat beside him, Par waved his hand toward the other two companions. "My apologies, sirs, as I did not ask your names. There was no disrespect intended to you."

"No, Your Highness, we understand." The taller, brown-haired man said, bowing respectfully from his waist. "With fathers that are generals to crowns afar we understand military ranks well; the Shi'alam is well above our stations. I am Jacen Novano, son of Berret Novano, former General of Blue Haven's royal army."

"And I am Patrick Kins, eldest son of mertinean commander Ethan Kins of Rubia." The soldier's emerald eyes twinkled in amusement as Par realized who the other soldier was. "My father wished you to know the mertinean and Crystine are travelling as quickly as they can but at army speed. They have not forgotten you."

"Thank you, Kins. I am glad to meet you both." Prince Par's respect for the two mentioned commanders rose. It was rare for generals to allow their sons to be as carefree as to join up with the legendary Tashek during war time. The two sons must surely have their fathers' deepest respects to have been given rein to do so.

"Commander Kins gave us the option to go with the Tashek so as to reach you more quickly." Gordar explained to his cousin and prince. "Great haste had been made since Wynward's Crossing. Jacen and Patrick had been with a small group of companions that reached the Crystine before I did. Our cousin, Anibus, was among them. I think King Fantill had known of our plight and sent him ahead to find us relief."

"That's almost how it happened." Patrick interrupted, sensing the lord's uncertainty. After all, he and his companions had not exactly explained how their odd group had come together. "Priest Anibus had been sent east by the Estarian Cardinal. I think he said the Cardinal had had a vision that the Crystine and Tashek would lead our people to victory, or something like that. Coupled with a letter from King Fantill, I guess, made the matter urgent enough to send Anibus to the Eastern Syrean kingdoms. Anyway, we—Jacen, me, and another—met the priest at the Deluge marketplace." The prince opened his mouth to get clarification but the Rubian plunged on anticipating the question. "I had been a guest of Novano's since last Levies and Gathering Time. We had gotten an invitation from Rio Ravesbend, a friend of ours, to meet at Deluge for a jousting tournament. During our outing, we ran into Priest Anibus and he told us of his orders to go to the Crystal Castle. Seeing as the Crystal Kingdom was still being attacked by maunstorz, we thoughts it made sense for use (the sons of generals) to go along with him for protection. With the influence of another colleague, we were all able to pass through the Sunrise-Crystal boarder and make our way to the Crystine."

"That is an interesting turn of events." The prince commented. "If you had known you would be all the way across Syre by the end of the month, would you have taken up such a challenge?"

"It is not what our fathers would have liked, to be sure, Prince," Jacen joked, "However, I have been quite content with our travels thus far. The excitement is as much as I could have hoped for."

The men all chuckled at that. Then Commander Averron brought the group back to more pressing matters. "Highness, what did the Tashek have to say?"

Prince Par sullened. "The Shi'alam says he and his men can protect us for one night; as gift to us for holding out for over two weeks unaided. He did not want us on guard-duty. Looking around, I would have to agree that our men cannot be counted on to do such, in any case. Our men are beyond exhaustion. One night would be more worth it to them right now than all of my father's gold."

"Aye, I would agree with you." Tyk assured in his gruff voice. "Your men may not have been at war as long as the Tashek, but then, the Tashek have not been hounded by ten thousand maunstorz either. The Shi'alam know this well. His knowledge of the enemy will keep us safe passed the dawn. Take the man up on his offer."

"You will have no argument for me, either." Averron said, seeing the uncertainty in his prince's eyes. "All I have heard about the Tashek has been good. They are true to their word—and their battle skills." He stood and gave a quick salute before collecting his bowl. "By your leave, My Prince, I would be to bed. You too, Highness. Everything will be less troubling by tomorrow." Commander Tyk stood as well and bade the younger men good-night. His departure seemed to be the cue for most of the men to finish and find their own bedrolls.

The North Point fortress became quiet as its men settled in for sleep. The soft moonlight lite enough of the land that the Tashek, whom stood at alert, had no need to light any fires. In the quiet of the night, the wearied men were able to find sleep, despite their fears of another attack by the maunstorz. It seemed some kind of peace had settled over the land. Some balance had been met.

§   §

The morning fog from the ocean slowly dispersed as the rising of the sun cast its rays upon the land. The calm from the night seemed to linger as the refreshed Sealand and mertinean men woke from their beds. The vigilant Tashek kept their places on the walls and watchtowers as the rest of the army prepared. Still, there seemed to be an unusual peace to the day.

Kor'mauk Siv'arid strode purposely though the keep to the prince's chamber and called out his entrance. Lord Gordar greeted the man and waved him inside. "Prince Fantill, Lord Farrylin, it seems an unusual event had occurred over the night." The two men looked perturbed. "The Shi'alam did not wish to make a scene so he asked me to bring you to see for yourself. Quietly."

Intrigued but concerned, the prince and his cousin followed the desert man back to the northern wall, where the Shi'alam had met with the prince the night before. The Tashek leader was found much as he had been, still staring out the battlefield. However, following the Sheev'anee's deep gaze, the two Sealanders immediately understood why the Tashek had been secretive.

The maunstorz army was simply gone!

"What—?!" Prince Par breathed. The entire five-thousand-plus army had left no trace of themselves on the ocean seagrass. The land looked nearly untouched as if it had not been ground down by the ten-thousand-count of savages for two weeks. "That can't be! Where did they go?"

The Shi'alam shook his head. "My men have searched all over these lands, even deep into the Noway Mountains to our east and up and down the coastline. There are no footprints leading out in any direction. The area they occupied these past weeks is clear, as well. There are no fires, no left equipment, nothing. It is almost as if they were never here."

"That is not even possible!" Lord Gordar declared.

Shík Savam'eed shifted beside his leader; his face betraying some knowledge the Tashek knew that most Syreans did not. He spoke softly in Keshic, the Shi'alam bending his head to listen. The two Tashek argued something that seemed very important. Finally, Sheev'arid rose his hand to silence his man. He said something shortly, before turning back to the prince and his protector. "Are either of you aware of the legend of the Prism of the Stars and the eight precious stones that contain this light?"

Prince Par shook his head. "I am afraid I have never heard of such. It is a Tashek legend?"

"Well, it is not a knowledge known for a hands-count of time. The truth of the Prism was hidden since the Second Age of Syre. Even your Estarian priests, who should have kept the history, have forgotten their duty... At the beginning of the Third Age, only those people who had direct contact with Keepers of the Stones kept the knowledge of their existence. This included the kings (or queens) of the kingdoms and their descendants. However, after the fall of Crystalynian, it seems even those royals have withheld this information from their heirs."

"Hold on one second!" Lord Gordar interrupted. "You spoke of the Second Age. That was an age of "majik'!" He spoke with trepidation, as most Syreans thought of the occult as dangerous and evil.

"Indeed, it was. It was the Golden Age of the Syrean Count. Where your people fear the past, mine remember it in a different light. The eight Stones of Power were gifts from the Stars to all of Syre. Powerful majiks that built this land into something magnificent. But, as with all power, there is always a price. The Stones were misused and the great kingdoms of Syre were broken apart into the eight factions. These became the kingdoms of today. Your people's folly ruined the best thing you had and erased the gifts of majik. The mysteries were hidden from you, feared throughout the kingdoms as devilry."

"But what has that got to do with the events before us?!" Prince Par demanded. He enjoyed history for what it was worth but, with five thousand maunstorz unaccounted for, he was not in the mood for a lesson in Syrean antiquity.

The Shi'alam paused, considering how much he wanted to reveal to an unwilling audience. "There is much you are not ready learn, I can see that, but I will tell you what we suspect. One of the stones, a pure crystal, had the ability to take objects from one place to another many miles away in a matter of seconds. If this is the power that was used, then there is a great deal to be concerned about."

"I refuse to believe something so nonsensical!" Prince Par declared. He looked back to the empty field. "My men will search the area again. Those maunstorz could not have gotten far. We must find then before they harm innocents. Lord Gordar, call a meeting. The commanders need to know what is going on."

"Yes, My Highness."

Prince Par turned back to the Shi'alam in defiance, daring the man to argue. The Sheev'anee leader stared back and bowed his resignation. "My men will search into the Aras Desert. Some will remain to help guard this border. If the maunstorz are there, we will find them."

"Thank you, Shi'alam." He bowed his head to be respectful and sprinted away to his meeting.

Shi'alam Sheev'arid watched the prince's retreating back. Shík Savam'eed shook his head angered, a movement that echoed his leader's own exasperation. "For one of the wielders of the stones, it seems wrong that he denies his role."

"Yes." The Shi'alam agreed. "And in his innocence, the prince is unaware that it was his sapphire, Serein, that made it possible for Ravel to be used." He shared a knowing glance with his brother-in-law. "Ravel's teleportation power only works if there is another crystal at its focal point to guide its actions."

"But, how could it be in use? Who is the crystal's wielder?"

Shi'alam Sheev'arid shook his head. "Alas, even I do not know that. One thing is for certain, though, we need a Guardian to watch over the Prince of Sealand at all times until he can return to his father and learn about Serein's powers. She is active; he just doesn't know it yet."

Chapter Fourteen

§

Held in Secrecy

The Crystine and mertinean had reached Paragon Oasis just as the worst of the midday sun was beginning to beat down. It was eight days since the army had been subjugated to the rainstorm and with the drying heat of the Aras Desert many of the men were wishing for the cooling liquid instead. It had been a hard decision for Commander Matar and Kins to push on from their last stop to reach the small paradise during full daylight, but the two leaders had felt that they were close enough to the blessed oasis to risk heatstroke. They had been lucky. Only three men had fainted during the trip.

The four companions found a small corner to themselves where they fell into an exhausted pile. Even Decond, now a fifth member to their little party, had been given permission to rest until the heat lessened. The young farrier climbed up one of the palm trees and knocked down five, ripe coconuts and brought the armload over to his new friends. Elated, Rio made short work of cutting them open. Refreshed, the companions leaned against the palms enjoying the shade of their leaves and their food.

"Ugh, who would want to live in this heat?" Roland complained, opening his tunic to try to get cooler. "I don't understand why Starians choose to live here."

"You would be surprised what some people like." Anibus countered gently. "Not everyone finds comfort in the southern plains. In Deep Snows, you would probably enjoy yourself here."

"I'm not sure I could ever get used to all this sand."

"I don't know, sir," Sage spoke up, "I kind of like the untamed beauty of this land. It is so wild and free."

Roland Seagold studied the younger man beside him, seeming to puzzle through a difficult problem. The page averted his gaze under the man's strong midnight-blue eyes. "Yes, the Aras Desert does suit you." He finally said. Sage looked up in surprise. Roland continued, more thoughtful. "Maybe there is something to this land after all. I guess I will have to keep my mind more open."

"That's good to hear, sir." Rio complimented. "Sunrise needs more broadminded individuals. Too many of us are closed off from the rest of Syre. There is much to be missed in that condition."

"Agreed."

Again, Anibus was aware of the power triangle between the three Sunarians; however, it seemed that, now that they were outside of their normal circles, each was finding new ways to express who they were. The priest was excited by the process; no longer were they chained to the roles they played in society, being as equal as free men. Perhaps, the repercussions would have a great influence in the Sunrise Kingdom...

Young Decond, still not quite sure of his place among the companions, fidgeted with his shirt tail. He was tired from the long journey but too restless in the heat to sleep. As the others began to doze, Decond wandered off, not really caring where he ended up. Paragon Oasis was the largest haven in the Aras, which was why it was so widely known as a resting spot, but there was little else beyond the stand of trees and watering pits. The small pools and their stream were flanked by a forest of palm trees that stretched over a quarter of a mile against the rest of the barren land. As the seventeen-year-old neared the water, he came upon the Tashek Terrik Sheev'arid, the only desert warrior to stay with the Crystine. The desert man turned to see who was there before looking back to watch his horse drink.

"Hello, young farrier." Terrik said in greeting. Decond muttered his reply and hesitantly walked closer to the bank. The Tashek did not send him away or invite conversation, so Decond stood quietly a little way off, studying the small, find-boned desert horse. Terrik finally seemed to notice the keen look in the youth's eyes. "Saulyn is a fine animal, yes?'" Decond nodded bashfully. "He is the grandson of Sheen, my family's finest runner." The Tashek seemed to sense that Decond was unfamiliar with Tashek blood-lines. He politely changed the subject. "My sister, Zy'ena, is the one who hired you. She had a good eye for talent. You have done a fine job with the army horses and repairs."

"I...thank you." Decond ventured a small smile.

"A youth with your strength would be a good swordsman." Decond's eyes widened in surprise—and apprehension. "I'm nonplused that no one has said such to you before. Here you are among a throng of army men and none have offered you those words. Blacksmiths are good with weapons, as they are so intimate with them, creating such craftsmanship out of cold metal. You should take advantage of your close proximity to these war veterans, at least to learn the basics of defense. If it wasn't for the heat of the day, I would introduce you to old Smitty right now, but then our farrier would suffer of heatstroke." There was a sense of amusement to Terrik' words and Decond almost wondered if the desert man was teasing him. After all, how could he wield a sword? Terrik continued, unaware of Decond's skepticism. "Or, perhaps you would be better with the battle-ax? I've never handled one myself, but they seem interesting enough." Terrik paused, as if to consider the prospect.

In the silence, the two men became aware of the cry of a hawk. Terrik Sheev'arid glanced skyward, searching out the bird. An odd chittering left the Tashek's lips, answered by the hawk again. The desert warrior raised his right arm and a few moments later, a beautiful short-tailed hawk swooped down and landed on Terrik's arm in a flurry of brown feathers and sharp talons. It finally settled and chirped out a message in high-pitched, long cries. Terrik crooned to it, settling its nervousness, before unwrapping the small note attached to its leg. He balanced the bird on his arm as he awkwardly unfolded the letter and read its contents. Whatever was written had Terrik turning away in haste. "Excuse me, farrier. I must report to Commander Matar." The Tashek was away, then, his chestnut steed following loyally behind.

Sensing that there was going to be some action, Decond followed the Tashek from a distance, tailing him all the way to the command tent. He observed the desert man step into to tent and waited a few seconds before crouching low to the ground and nearing it from the side. Decond waited, holding his breath as the Tashek spoke with the commanders.

"Commander Matar, Commander Kins. I have a message from North Point."

"Go ahead, Terrik, tell us. There must have been some major occurrence to send a hawk over a rider."

"Yes, Khataum. This note says this: Somehow the entire maunstorz force at North Point has simply vanished. Be alert to their presence any place. Send the main force to the Cathedral of Light. We continue our vigilance here." The Tashek man paused and the rustling of paper was heard. "There is a separate message for you, Khataum."

"Read it to me, please."

"Commander..." The desert warrior hesitated, then continued. "To Commander Matar: I believe Ravel may be involved in this phenomenon. If this is true, the enemy had a powerful weapon. Take care of yourself and your men. Shi'alam Sheev'arid."

"Ravel?!" Commander Kins said, astonished. "The Crystal Stone of Power?! Its hasn't been used for over twenty-five years! How could the maunstorz have gotten hold of it?"

Decond had never heard of Ravel but the word rolled off of his tongue sweetly. With baited breath, the young farrier strained to hear more.

"Unfortunately, I am not surprised that the maunstorz have the crystal. Ravel was entrusted to Lance Starkindler."

"And he was taken, as was his family, when the Crystal Kingdom was overrun." Commander Kins finished.

"Exactly. Either the prince is alive and being coerced into using its powers or the stone has found a new wielder..."

"Yes, but," Commander Kins sounded perturbed. "I thought all the crystals lost their powers?"

Terrik spoke up. "No, that is not exactly true; however, to understand why the stones' powers have diminished takes a lot of explanation."

"Tell him." Matar commanded. "Ethan knows some of the Stones of Power. He can be trusted with the history—and it's better if he knows all."

Terrik must have consented because he bid the men to sit and began speaking about a piece of history Decond had never heard. "To help you understand the power of the stones, I must go back to the waning of the Second Age. Majik was a way of life for Syreans, however, during some horrible event with a young prince gone power-hungry, the populous became whole-set against the use of the Stones. Suddenly, anything majik seemed abhorrent. Royals clashed and the Syrean head family split apart into the eight factions [kingdoms] of today. To protect the people, they ordered all traces of majik: books, charms, teaching, objects—basically everything—to be sent to Crystalynian [the original capitol] and guarded. Powerful majik was used to make the people "forget" what had happened, making the Second Age appear hazy in the memory and written books. Only the Estarian church and the Tashek, the Guardians of the histories, were allowed to retain the knowledge. The rulers passed the stones as heirlooms to their children, secretly teaching the chosen wielders about their powers.   A council was formed at Crystalynian in secret to continue learning about the Stones of Power, and so the process went. But, twenty-seven years ago, the maunstorz appeared and began to attack Syre—starting with the seat-head of the kingdoms. They purposely targeted the capitol and destroyed it. Believing, perhaps, that the people were right about majik really being the root of this evil, the kings ended the council and stopped passing on the knowledge of the Stones. Some of the stones were lost, a few stayed with the royal heirs, but all were said to have gone dormant. None worked after Crystalynian fell."

"But if Ravel is working..."

"Then the others may also begin to reawaken. The stones choose their owners. Once found, they will activate, usually producing a song or having an inner light about them. Unfortunately, the Sheev'anee do not feel that the people are ready to have this majik back in their lives."

"This must not get out to anyone." Commander Matar warned Ethan Kins and Terrik. "The Tashek have kept this secret for over two hundred years. If they deem the populous unable to handle this news, then it must be true."

Terrik continued, "The worst part is that only the whereabouts of the stones Kevel and Vauldin are known. Three—Serein, Ravel, and Amun—were promised to stay with the Sealand, Crystal, and Starian royal families. But this promise was before Crystalynian's fall. There is no guarantee that any of the heirs have the stones. The other three could be anywhere, including buried in some forgotten nook."

"This situation seems to be out of our hands." Kins commented. "If the Sheev'anee cannot account for these stones, then it seems we have no choice but to wait for another activation. If I remember anything of the Stones of Power, it was that they could call to each other, right? If we could get either of the two stones we know about to come back to life, could we not seek out the others?"

"If only it was that easy." Terrik sounded wistful. "You see, Commander, the obsidian stone Vauldin was thought to be given to the rightful heir. Yet, at present, it had not activated."

"Who holds the stone?"

Terrik sidestepped the question by saying, "It is held by one of our own. A direct descendant to Queen Kestral, who was part Tashek herself. If the stone lies dormant, then we do not know to whom it is to belong."

"And Kevel?"

"Is safe but, again, had not found its wielder." Matar answered the question. It seemed, to Decond that both Commander Matar and Terrik were withholding information from Ethan Kins. Even as a trusted confidant, it seemed some truths were not ready to be voiced.

Commander Kins sounded exasperated. "Well then, *again,* it sounds like the situation is out of our hands. Saying that, we should focus on what we do know and what we can do. Right now, there are no maunstorz reported at North Point and there arc at the Citadel of Light. If we join King Maushelik's forces, we could crush a large group of those bastards! I want to get them before they up and vanish, too."

"I agree." Matar responded. Decond could hear the two army veterans get up and walk about the tent. "We rest here until the day cools then head north. We could make the Citadel well before the next night gets cold."

"I would like to request a small part of the force goes to North Point to help look for the maunstorz." Terrik interrupted.

Commander Matar didn't miss a beat. "Of course, Terrik, you have my leave to take thirty rides with you. Just because there seems to be no threat at North Point doesn't mean we should assume we won't get caught by them when we least expect. I will let you have the pick of my men. When you reach the Shi'alam, give him my regards and tell him we went north, as he instructed."

"And the stones?"

"Will be held in the strictest of confidence." Matar assured. "Neither Ethan nor myself will say anything without a Sheev'anee present."

Decond had not realized the Tashek had left the tent until he was suddenly and quite literally thrown on his backside with a dagger to his throat. Terrik, who only shortly before had been civil with Decond, looked ominous. Roughly, he dragged the farrier to his feet and pushed him toward the command tent entrance. The two leaders looked up from the Syrean map in surprise as Terrik propelled the seventeen-year-old inside. Matar opened his mouth to protest the maltreatment. "He was listening in on every word." Terrik said darkly.

Commander Matar took in Decond's scared visage, seeing no treason in his eyes. "Terrik," he responded calmly, "This boy is no enemy."

"He heard everything."

"Is that true?" Matar addressed Decond, no animosity in his voice. Decond gulped and nodded mutely, scared to deny anything. The aging veteran sighed and gave Terrik the signal to stand down. "So he knows. Who is an orphan going to tell?" He rose a hand to silence the Tashek. "You cannot erase what is already in the mind. I'm happier it is Decond than someone else. If it is such a worry for you, then keep the boy in your confidence."

"Then he must go with me."

"Would that console you?" Terrik nodded. Matar hesitated, seeing fear still in the farrier's eyes. "Decond," he began and lowered himself to the boy's eyes level. "Do you understand how important it is to keep what you heard in silence?"

"Y-yes, sir." Decond forced himself to calm down, mirroring the leader before him. "Magic is a feared thing. It is not spoken of openly, even under dire circumstances."

Matar nodded, satisfied. "You will go with Terrik, then. We will take your farrier in exchange for Decond." The veteran rose and eyed the desert warrior. "You will not harm the boy under any circumstance. And," he added quickly as Terrik began to turn to leave, "You will teach him how to be a Guardian of the Prism of the Stars." The Tashek spun back, looking unhappy about the order. "Decond knows now, so I say he needs to be instructed into our circles. As one high-up in the Sheev'anee, you know everything there is about the stones. Consider him your new apprentice."

"Khataum…." Terrik began to protest.

"*I said teach him.*" Matar ordered. "He is an orphan with no family, no ties. He will make a good asset to the Tashek. Now, we have to prepare for our march later today. Go now as your winds tell you. We will meet again as the Stars' allow."

§ §

A very nettled Terrik Sheev'arid led his new charge to his tent. Decond trailed behind, holding his breath for another angry onslaught. He was still rattled over having a knife to his throat and by the events afterward. The desert man's tent seemed foreboding, though not because of its rich blue color or spaciousness. More, it was because of the aura surrounding the Tashek.

An older man, a retainer of about fifty-summers-old, seemed not the least bit shaken over his leader's temper. The man went about his tasks closing the tent flaps to keep in the unusual but welcome coolness and preparing some repast. The retainer paused only once to point Decond to a place to sit—on the opposite side of the large tent from Terrik—before continuing his work.

Finally able to let off steam, Terrik spoke to Shytin in keshic. The other man answered some question and brought the Sheev'arid a bowl of stew. He said something else then grabbed a bowl for Decond. Terrik seemed about ready to stop him from giving the farrier food but Shytin responded with a last word that changed the desert man's mind. Decond took the food timidly and watched as the retainer disappeared into another room of the tent.

"Shytin manages my equipment and property." Terrik informed Decond shortly. "He asked if you had need of him bringing any of your stuff over. I told him to speak with Anubis. I assume you do not have much."

"Ah, yes...sir. I mean no...sir." Decond fumbled. "I mean, I have a bit of farrier equipment and a pack horse but nothing much of a personal nature."

Terrik nodded absently. "He will bring everything."

Silence stretched between them. Decond shifted nervously and nibbled at his food. Across from him, Terrik ate his bowl with little thought of it, his eyes lost studying the weave in a blanket on his cot. It was only as the last spoonful was finished from his stew that Terrik felt a need to speak again. "I hope you realize that you know nothing of our ways or our Guardianship of the Prism of the Stars. It's only because you happened to hear a small, very important tidbit back at the command tent that you have any claim to it."

"I don't want it." Decond managed to croak out. "If I could take back overhearing, I would; I just want to be a lone, orphan-farrier boy that I am."

Terrik stood, still vexed, and came to crouch in front of Decond. His brandy eyes bore into the boy's as if they could read his soul. Unnerved, the youth felt himself shift away but the Tashek reached out and grabbed his arm, preventing the movement. Decond froze and started to count the seconds as the intimidating warrior stared at him. Slowly, Terrik's eyes softened and he leaned back to give Decond some breathing room. "My father would say there is no such thing as chance. The Stars align things just as they are meant to be. Why they asked for our paths to cross so fatefully, I cannot begin to guess, but if you are to be a part of the Guardianship, I cannot refuse the order."

"Do I really have to? Can't I be released to my work? I won't ever speak of what I heard."

"No. What you heard was too significant. Besides that, I cannot go against the direct order of a high-ranked Guardian." Decond's eyes told his question. "Yes, Matar is one of a few non-Tashek Guardians. He says you are to be welcomed into our circles; I cannot dispute him. Your fate has been decided." Terrik stood. "There is much you will need to know. For now, however, I need you to swear to secrecy on all that will be revealed."

Decond became suspicious. "Is there something I need to do?"

"Eventually, yes, you will need to mark yourself." The Tashek rolled back his sleeve to reveal an elaborate tattoo made of eight stars coming out of a prism. It was surrounded by a circle of ruins, written in keshic. "Until then, you need to make an oath—in blood—of your agreed secrecy. After, once you show you are committed to the Guardianship, you will be tattooed."

Decond balked at the mention of a blood-oath, especially when Terrik returned with a small blade he had prepared. "This will be quick and relatively painless." Terrik assured. He paused, holding his hand out, and waited for Decond to give him his own. Clasping the boy's fingers, he spread Decond's palm. "Repeat these words:

Sheev'anee Alklem Ernom; Guardian of the Heavenly Prism."
Decond fumbled with the keshic. Just as he muttered the last syllable,
Terrik ran the blade quickly across the farrier's palm, drawing blood.
Decond hissed but found the pain less than he had expected. He
watched as Terrik sliced his own palm with his dagger and clenched
his fist tightly. The Tashek then opened his hand and reached out to
clasp Decond's. The blood mixed with their contact. "We are now
blood-brothers in the Guardianship. Your silence protects us all."

Chapter Fifteen

§

Losses

The Tashek cavalry waited as the Starian army scattered to assemble. Foot soldiers lined up on the eastern side of the military guard, snapping to attention, metal smarting together. The archers of the Golden Kingdom came next, adding their one-hundred bows to the Starian two-hundred-and-fifty. Lastly, came the prince and his five-hundred-and-sixty count of horses, trotting forward to line up just out of the way of the Tashek.

Prince Al'den cued his destrier forward, coming to stand beside All'ani Cum'ar. The two leaders nodded to each other, then the Starian prince rose his hand to signal a quiet to all his men—not that any were talking in their nervousness. "The Stars gave us a reprieve yesterday with a sandstorm, giving us enough time to regroup, as well as, to be given aid by the Tashek All'ani and Tem'arid and the Golden Kingdom. Now rested, we go back out to face our enemy. I do not want to promise you a quick end, but, with this help we have received, I am more convinced of out victory than ever before. Men, we will prevail!"

The Starian forces raised their voices in a loud cheer. Using the tension and excitement, Prince Al'den motioned for his and Cum'ar's cavalry to head out. The large group of horses trotted down the long, main road toward the main gates; the entire army falling in behind. The townsfolk came out to line the streets, summoned by the shaking of the ground from the hundreds of horses and marching of the army. These people joined the cheering, showing their support to the soldiers.

Prince Al'den bowed, relieved to see such support from his city. He understood its importance for keeping the men motivated to protect their homes. With over two weeks of fighting, it was imperative to have something to keep the men strong. But, as the prince led the army out of the enormous outer walls, he sobered. Seeing the looming maunstorz force also preparing for battle in the shifted dunes beyond was a bitter reminder of their situation. Prince Al'den gave a signal and the two cavalries split apart to follow along the tall, stone walls that protected the Cathedral of Light. As one long line, the entire cavalry rode forward, making a defensive line for the rest of the army. The foot soldiers followed, forming ten lines deep, spears and shields held at ready and swords and daggers in easy reach. The cavalry and army continued to march forward until there was enough room to allow the archers adequate enough room for shooting. Once the entire army was set, Prince Al'den rose his hand and halted the lines.

An uneasy quiet settled over the field.

A fair distance away, the enemy lines began to come forward, forming a dark, ominous shape against the dawn. As they came closer, taking a stance closer to the Cathedral of Light's walls than ever before, an eerie chant began to grow, and then sound like human screams. The sound rose hauntingly in a way meant to scare the opposing army. Joining the sound came the clashing of metal, drumming out a beat.

Prince Al'den had never heard the maunstorz make such noises before; however, he refused to let his army be baited into fear. He passed along a command to stand firm and waited, sword raised, until he could begin to see the red eyes of the enemy. Shouting and dropping his arm, the Starian signaled his archers to fire. Arrows went aloft, signaling the beginning of the battle.

The first wave of arrows landed amidst the middle rows of maunstorz; the eerie cries became replaced with those of pain. Another volley was released before an opposition could be mounted. Soon, though, the maunstorz were angered and the dark mass charged ahead. Prince Al'den motioned his archers to stand down and yelled out to the cavalry.

Leaping forward, all eight-hundred-and-sixty horses returned the charge. The outer horses sped up as the long line neared the enemy, forming a large horseshoe. Wrapping around the large maunstorz force, the wall of horseflesh rammed into most of the front lines and cutting deeply into the enemy. Immediately, swords began swinging, both to protect the brave mounts and to continue harrying the enemy.

Prince Al'den, with Cum'ar alongside, cut a deep hole into the horde. The Starian hacked away, swing after swing, protecting his large bay, as the destrier struck out at the men around them. Cum'ar yelled out to the royal that the foot men had reached the fray and that the prince should fall back a bit to stay amongst his forces. The prince nodded and cued his horse to sidestep closer to Cum'ar's smaller mount. Together, the two men defended themselves and their mounts as they slowly pushed back, closer to the Starian army.

Suddenly, a burly maunstorz broke out from the rest of his men and charged the two Starians, swinging a wicked looking mace on a long chain. Prince Al'den took notice of the three black stripes on the man's bicep that signaled the man to be about a general's status, which, therefore, seemed to denote that the enemy was a man of great skill amongst the barbarians. Al'den warned Cum'ar and tried to get his destrier out of the way, but there was too little space to turn and run. The enemy sneered and sent his spiked mace flying toward the prince.

There was no way of blocking the blow. Al'den felt his world slow.

Cum'ar yelled something and had his chestnut ram into the destrier's shoulder. The mace swung into the tall destrier's neck, cracking it and injuring its windpipe. Blood sprayed into Al'den's face, blinding him, and he felt his mount fall to the ground. All'ani Cum'ar was off his mare in an instant and in front of the downed prince.

The maunstorz general bellowed a victorious laugh and jerked the mace from the dead horse's flesh. He puffed up his wide bulk intimidatingly at the slim warrior before him and began to swing his weapon again. Cum'ar nudged the Starian at his feet. "Prince Al'den." The royal responded that he was all right as he took a defensive crouch by the Tashek's knee. He wiped the blood from his eyes with a gloved hand. Confident that the prince was unhurt, the Tashek raised his kora and waited for the enemy to loose his weapon.

The mace flew at Cum'ar not a moment later. Stubborn to leave the prince in its path, All'ani Cum'ar stood his ground, turning just enough to deflect the sinister weapon to his right. The force of the blow against his sword made Cum'ar hiss in pain, however, and Prince Al'den struggled to stand so that his defender was not so limited in his fighting. "Get to the other side of your horse!" Cum'ar yelled over his shoulder as he braced for the next swing. Battle trained, Al'den responded without thought, giving Cum'ar the room he needed to fight. And fight he did.

Unencumbered, All'ani Cum'ar was able to roll out of the way of the next attack and into a striking range of his sword. The maunstorz general was not quick enough to get out of the way before the kora blade sliced thinly into his hamstring. Battle-high, the angered enemy-man kicked out at the Tashek, catching him in the ribs, without noticing the damage he had incurred. The desert warrior took the blow as best as he could and rolled out of the kicking range. He was quick to his feet and rushing back into striking distance. Still seething, the maunstorz general flung his mace around, but the spiked head fell too far outward to do any harm. Taking the few seconds the heavy mace took to lift again, Cum'ar aimed for the general's vulnerable flank. He almost sliced into the man, when the general dropped his heavy chain and batted the kora away with his forearm. Cum'ar swung back again only to have the maunstorz land a punch to his solar plexus. Briefly out of breath, Cum'ar stumbled back, giving his opponent time to grab up a battle ax that had been discarded by a downed man. The Tashek sucked in what air he could as he dodged the first ax swing. He re-engaged with the maunstorz, and the two matched fighters began a dangerous game of perries-and-thrusts.

Prince Al'den watched the two fighters attack each other viciously, in an evenly-matched duel. He struggled to decide if he should help the Tashek or continue his own fight elsewhere—and if he left would Cum'ar would be okay? A challenging bellow from a maunstorz charging him decided Al'den's course, however. The prince turned to this new attacker. He raised his sword to block a wildly swung pole arm. The fight ended quickly, as Al'den found the man's skills to be little better than a common farmer's. He dispatched the man as mercifully as he could and headed off to face another enemy.

Other cavalry men had also gone to the ground, either from their mounts having been injured beneath them or to let the horses run away from the fighting. These men effectively sliced through the enemy, gathering around their prince to follow his lead. The foot soldiers, too, gravitated toward Prince Al'den and some of the horseless Tashek that danced around the field. Bodies and the wounded piled up at their feet, but it was obvious that the Starian army was slowly overtaking the enemy horde.

Needing to give more direction to his men, Prince Al'den reached out to an abandoned Tashek horse and climbed atop the fiery little steed. His new vantage point allowed the royal to survey the fight. A good portion of the cavalry was still ahorse, the men being led by Al'den's Captain, Sean Woodman. The horsemen had taken the right and left sides of the field, using their horses to keep the maunstorz from spreading out and funneling them toward the foot-soldiers and archers. The maneuver worked perfectly to contain the enemy and Al'den could see that the rest of his army had an easier time holding their position. Lieutenant-Commander Sloane's archers had joined the main army, some of his men still firing off arrows, while the others protected their unit's backs. With both the distance and close-range weapons being used, a large swath of the enemy was being pushed back and taken down. Following the cue from the archers, the foot-soldiers pressed ahead, forcing the maunstorz to retreat farther away from the Cathedral of Light.

Prince Al'den rose his sword to signal to the men around him to follow his lead. Judging the best place to re-enforce his army, the Starian pointed his men toe the left and regrouped foot soldiers plunged into the wall of maunstorz trying to overtake the smaller section of cavalry. Re-committed, the Starian army pushed forward.

Left behind, Cum'ar and the maunstorz general found themselves in an empty pocket, the rest of the fighting seeming to have left the two opponents to their own duel. The burly maunstorz was slicked with his blood and sweat, showing he was tiring from the Tashek's constant harrying; however, All'ani Cum'ar did not lose his head over the small sign of victory; keeping his stance guarded, he spun and perried around the bigger man. The desert man blocked the battle ax aimed at his left shoulder and followed the change of direction to block the next strike. Seeing an opening, Cum'ar ducked in to take the man's armpit, severing the tendons and, hopefully, the blood vessels nestled deeper within. He ducked out and circled, waiting to see what damage he had inflicted.

Though blood flowed down the general's side, it was not enough to prove that any large blood vessels had been damaged. The left arm hung useless against the red-slicked side, however, and Cum'ar took the new advantage he had to begin for a more aggressive attack. He leapt closer and swung his kora left-right-left, hacking into the maunstorz's defensive and forcing the fighter to back away. The enemy man valiantly blocked the assault but his energy was failing. Cum'ar struck out more often as his chances for victory grew. With one final feint then an upper cut, the maunstorz general sputtered, tensed, then slumped to the ground. Cum'ar was left, panting hard, before his opponent while the rest of the Starian army continued their own battles around him.

§ §

It became clear, as the day continued, that the Starian army was wining. The maunstorz army was reduced to a few thousand men and pushed a safe distance from the Starian capitol. Sensing their inevitable defeat, the enemy force tried a full-army retreat; however, the Starian cavalry quickly out raced them and corralled them in against the main force. In a short while, the last of the warriors had been dispatched. The fighting came to an anti-climactic stop.

Prince Al'den glanced across his tired army; the celebration of their win feeling very empty, just like the weak cheers that circulated between his men. Soldiers dropped to their knees, weapons forgotten, as the exhaustion of their long weeks at war took over the receding adrenaline. The prince cued his horse forward through the corpse-laden sand, so that he could survey the losses, as well as, greet those of his men that had survived. The Starian royal was not sure if he should feel so relieved to find his best commanders still alive, as well as most of the archer and Tashek, when a large number of his cavalry and foot-soldiers lay dead at the arab horse's feet. It seemed a very hollow victory.

Al'den stopped his horse at his destrier's resting place and dismounted. He reached out to lay a grieving hand on the bay's blood-matted cheek, running his fingers over the horse's familiar features. "Rest well, my friend." He whispered as he stroked the silky hair of the horse's cheekbone and smoothed back the black forelock. "You were so very good. I pray you find some peace in those green pastures beyond." A tear escaped Prince Al'den's eyes.

"It is good that you honor your mount so."

Prince Al'den turned to find All'ani Cum'ar was behind him. The small, willowy Tashek-man came to stand beside him. "Phoenix had been with me since I was a little boy. He was the best warhorse I ever rode, steady and courageous. I've never had another like him."

"And I'm sure, if he was anything like his rider, he would not have wanted to go out any other way than fighting alongside his master. Your Phoenix goes happy."

Prince Al'den allowed a small smile of thanks to flitter across his lips then he stood. He sobered at the carnage around him. "Too many have died today."

"And yet, the victory is won. Their deaths are not without meaning. They will rest in peace knowing they protected their people. That is enough." Prince Al'den did not answer. Cum'ar diverted the conversation, hoping to distract the royal—if only temporarily. "I see you have Kesh. He is Tem'arid Mall'ock's. Unfortunately, Mall'ock is no longer, so Kesh will need a master. You should take him for the time being." Prince Al'den murmured a thank you. He reached out and collected the stallion's reins and mounted. Cum'ar joined him a moment later on his own steed, whom came trotting at the Tashek's whistle. Together, the two leaders joined the line of soldiers heading back to the Citadel.

The weary army walked through the large, arched gates to the waiting city beyond. The townsfolk were very kind, applauding the soldiers and helping them walk back to the barracks. Many others streamed out of the main gates to help carry the injured and begin the grievous task of lining up the dead. The atmosphere stayed subdued.

The men finally reached the military yard. King Maushelik had been waiting to congratulate the men on their return. The aging man did not do so cheerfully, more with a respectful sympathy. He finally saw his son trailing the men and hurried forward to Al'den. The prince dismounted and the two Starians embraced, grateful he had survived. No words needed to be said. King Maushelik had seen the battle; he shared his son's grief.

Finally, the king pulled away. "It is done, son. For now, it is done. Go, take care of yourself, Al'den. I will take care of everything here."

Prince Al'den was too saddened and fatigued to answer. Touching his arm one last time, Maushelik left his son to Cum'ar's watchful guard. The Tashek took Al'den's elbow and steered the prince away from the crowd. He found Al'den a quiet place by the stables and sat him down. He began to create stripes for bandages from his outer robes, keeping one separate to dip into a nearby water bucket for a cleaning rag. Then, he attended to Prince Al'den's wounds. The cold water brought the Starian out of his stupor.

"You need not dote on me, All'ani."

"Just Cum'ar, Your Highness, and I do have to. The doctors are very busy caring for the wounded. You, prince, are only slightly so and should not take up their time; though, if they saw you, you would be first in line."

Prince Al'den looked weary. "I know. I need to be their prince. I should appear strong and courageous..." He ripped his own clothing to stop a minor cut on his wrist. "And, I should be helping my father, not sitting here like some mindless buffoon."

"I think you hardly count as a buffoon."

Al'den chuckled. "I guess not." He paused and studied the Tashek thoughtfully. "I need to thank you, Cum'ar." The Tashek did not reply. "You saved me by knocking Phoenix to the side. I..." Sadness flashed over his face but the prince banished it. "Just, thank you."

"You are the prince favored by the Stars. My people would not be very happy with me if I let you die."

"I don't understand why you think I'm so important to the deities when I only prayed once."

Cum'ar looked mischievous, like he held a secret. "Time will answer that for you, my prince." He finished cleaning the royal's wounds. "We should go see how everyone fares." Prince Al'den nodded in agreeance.

Together, the two men went to help with the chaos; first, to the military yard to greet the remaining soldiers and help direct them where they needed to be, then afterward, to the hospital to see if they could help with the wounded. As they neared, Prince Al'den was, once again, struck at the toll the war had wrought on his men. The main medical building had already reached maximum capacity. The nurses and doctors had been forced to lay many of the men outside in the streets or in the accompanying buildings. The more critical soldiers had been singled out to go the barber shop down the way, where they were immediately taken into surgery. The least injured men were left unattended until the worst off were looked over.

"If you'll excuse me," Cum'ar said, "I will get my men to come back here and help administer to the wounded."

Prince Alden nodded to the request, knowing that the Tashek were knowledgeable in medicine. He watched the desert warrior hurry away, then left alone, Prince Al'den wove his way to the main hospital area and found the head physician. The man, after hearing the prince's request to help, waved him to a nurse that thrust some heated water and clothes into his hands and sent him out to the next building.

The adjoining room had been set up with rows upon rows of cots, each one filled with soldiers in moderate condition. Some had dismembered limbs or deep wounds that needed stitches but did not require surgery. Still, the bloody sight and sounds of pain made the prince's chest ache. Moving to the closest cot, the prince began the demanding task of helping his wounded men.

By the fifth stitching, Prince Al'den felt he had gotten down the basics of first aid—and was very grateful he had taken the dreaded embroidery lessons his aunt had forced on him as a child. He was just about to leave to refresh his hot water bucket when the familiar face of the Golden Kingdom's prince hastened him to the next cot. "Kent! Kent, are you okay?!"

The usually exuberant scholar had his eyes closed and looked very pale in the shadows of the room. His eyes fluttered open at his name, however. "Al'den? What—what are you..."

"I should ask you the same thing. I was helping clean and bandage up the wounded."

"Oh, good." Kent let a pained smile light his lips. He struggled to sit and looked like he would pass out when Al'den reached out to steady him. "I was wondering when I would be gotten around to." It was then that Al'den saw the other prince's arm held close into his side and the deep gash along his shoulder.

"What happened?" Al'den asked alarmed. He started to look for other wounds.

"A battle, of course." Kent managed to joke. Al'den was not amused; worry was etched on his face. Kent sobered up. "No, I had been targeted and Lieutenant-Commander Sloane jumped in the way to save me. Five others were killed defending me. Sloane is in surgery. He may not make it, and all I got was this stupid cut on my shoulder."

It was not a little "cut". Al'den was not be sure but Prince Kent could have lost the use of his right arm. If not, it would have to be in a sling for a good while. The prince was lucky to be alive. "You wait here, I need to refresh my water and get more supplies. I will be right back."

"I ain't going anywhere." Kent replied wearily and laid back on his cot. The other prince hurried away.

Prince Al'den returned shortly with All'ani Cum'ar in tow. Together, they helped the wounded prince to a stable sitting position and inspected the laceration. Cum'ar deemed the arm savable, with good rest, and took out a bottle of Tashek herbs to sanitize the wound. Though the dark liquid stung, it also staunched the bleeding and numbed the wound. The desert man then waved the Starian prince to take his turn. Prince Al'den carefully stitched the injury closed, silently admiring the twenty-six-year-old for not even crying out as he worked. He finished his last stich and Cum'ar helped him bandage the injured shoulder. When they finished, Prince Kent sighed, exhausted, and allowed the two men to lay him back down.

"Thank you." Kent said weakly. Al'den nodded. "I'd like to sleep here awhile while you tend the others. I'll see you in a few."

"That's fine. We will come get you when we head back to the Citadel."

Prince Al'den and Cum'ar worked well into the evening. When the last of the soldiers was tended, they finally allowed themselves to drop their tools and head back to collect Prince Kent. The injured prince roused quickly enough, the mention of food and a soft bed being good motivation. It was just as they reached the steps of the Citadel of Light that the news came: the Crystine and mertinean had arrived—too late to fight against the maunstorz and just in time to bury the dead.

Part II

§

(Year 110 SC, near the end of Growing Time)

Chapter Sixteen

§

A Chained Dog Still Bites

Two days had passed since Zyanthena's fever, and Doctor Murnin finally deemed the Tashek woman healthy enough for a trip to the stables. She still had not regained her fiery disposition, much to Darshel's disconcertment, and followed her captor like a subdued dog. The Shekmann hoped seeing her black charger would liven her up again.

The Kavahadian lord led Zyanthena down the stairs to the first floor then through the main entranceway to the courtyard. Though the Tashek woman expressed mild interest in her surroundings, she mainly kept her eyes on Darshel's hand, just inches away from hers; she ignored their guard escort completely. If Darshel did not know better, it seemed like the desert woman was enamored with him like a beaten bitch-dog to her master. Just the image was enough to make Darshel wary of some escape plan on the warrioress's mind.

The small party passed through the west inner wall, entering into the military yard. Originally, Lord Darshel had debated allowing Zyanthena to see the grounds but the Crystine warhorse had not allowed them to move him closer to the keep, forcing the lord to bring his rider to him. Despite the issue that Zyanthena was seeing a large portion of Kavahad, Darshel felt there was little harm in the venture. Yet, as the very perceptive, brandy eyes scanned the military yard, the lord-governor had a moment of doubt.

Zyanthena was quick to place the barracks on the southern wall. Some soldiers were sitting casually around it. They cast curious glances her way. Beyond, a troop of soldiers was performing drills, taking up the large space between the barracks and the rest of the yard. To the north was the armory, its occupants busy with weapons inspections, inventory, and repair; twelve pages seemed to make up the main staff there. The pages were of little concern to the desert woman. Finally, it was the long stable, straight across the grounds, that held her attention—or, more importantly, the tall stallion trotting loose in the corral in front of the barn. The gorgeous black courser stopped his pacing, standing stock-still, nostrils flaring at the approaching humans. Zyanthena seemed to mirror the stallion's expression.

Doctor Murnin was standing inside the gate as Lord Darshel, Zyanthena, and the guards neared. He rose a hand in greeting. "This is the first I have seen this fine animal calm himself enough to stand still."

Lord Darshel agreed, as he had seen the horse at his worst. His emerald eyes turned to study the woman beside him. Zyanthena seemed like a coiled snake ready to strike from anticipation, her eyes locked on her mount. "Go to him, Zy'ena." She was moving as soon as the words were spoken. Before anyone had a chance to process her actions, the desert warrioress was up and over the corral fence.

The Tashek and horse greeted each other gleefully, the stallion dancing around his rider, nickering happily, until she raised her hands to embrace his muscular neck. He stood, quivering, while the Tashek held him; but, all the while, his head bobbed in barely-contained exuberance. Zyanthena finally released him and the black stallion wheeled away to buck and kick out. The desert woman waited out the horse's play until the stallion returned to his master's side and allowed her to inspect him head-to-toe.

As the Tashek examined the arrow wound, Doctor Murnin spoke out. "I redressed his injury, though your quick action and skills as a healer have saved him from worse harm. He should recover nicely. I would like to consult with you on what herbs you used and how you designed the patch. Your medicine intrigues me." Zyanthena bowed her head in response but continued her inspection without further reply. Doctor Murnin forgave the woman her rudeness, as she fussed over her mount with apt attention he rarely saw in people.

The horse master interrupted the horse and his rider's reunion by stomping out nosily from the stables to complain to his lord. "I hope you've come for this bloody bloak! This desert horse nearly killed one of my men and laid two unconscious. A page, he broke his arm. I don't want this beast to set a foot in my barn again!"

Lord Darshel ignored Zyanthena's insulted glare. He turned to face the vexed man, stern frown on his features. "This Crystal-bred war courser is worth more than all the horses in my stable, Brice. But, seeing as none of you can handle him, I will have him moved to my private barn… Just as long as this horse is the only problem you have to discuss?" Lord Darshel's tone hinted a warning that the stablemaster had better not be complaining of some other foolish thing—as he was apt to do.

Brice's face reddened but the horse master knew better than to cross words with his lord. He glared at the black stallion, who once more laid back his ears and would have charged the fence in response had Zyanthena not steadied him with a touch. Brice cursed and returned to his job.

Zyanthena visibly relaxed, her stallion following suit.

Lord Darshel noticed the change. "We should take the stallion over before Brice returns to list more of his grievances."

"Yes. He wasn't the best guest." Doctor Murnin explained with a chuckle. "Your horse was very unruly. Except from me, he would not let anyone near him." The desert woman looked pleased.

A stable hand brought out a halter and lead and passed them to the doctor. Murnin, in turn, walked over to hand the equipment to the Tashek. Zyanthena rolled her eyes and ignored the offered halter. She stepped toward the gate and pushed it open before the others realized what she was about. Walking out, Unrevealed following her as docilely as a lamb. Zyanthena stopped near Lord Darshel, a smug glint in her eyes, as she waited for the Kavahadian lord to order them to his own stable.

Lord Shekmann rose his eyebrows skeptically, but motioned the guards to fall in line. Besides the blatant stares from the soldiers, the walk over to the private barn was uneventful. Unrevealed was the picture of perfect obedience. "He's just like his owner." Doctor Murnin commented, chuckling, as the horse and Tashek inspected the private stable grounds. "He could easily kill a person with a bite or strike but holds himself in check when his master is around, feigning innocence."

"They are far from innocent, Murnin." Lord Darshel eyed the aging physician.

"Yes, but I have seen how she trails along behind you." Murnin returned. "Zyanthena yields to higher authorities. If you kept her unchained, she would remain faithful and, perhaps, in a better mood."

"You trust her far too much, old man."

Zyanthena had kept close enough to hear the lord and doctor banter. She risked a glance at the two men and found them both watching her intently. She averted her eyes quickly to inspect the fencing, making sure there was nothing for the courser to hurt himself on. As she bent over, Unrevealed joined her to sniff at the rails, looking for something to eat. Finding nothing, he whuffed boredly and bumped his nose against Zyanthena's side, knocking her off her feet. The desert woman cursed lightly, faking annoyance, and got to her feet to chase after the stallion. The tall black horse arched his neck and tail and pranced away, very smug with himself. He stopped on the other side of the pen and dropped his head to lip at the water bucket, his ear cocked in the warrioress's direction. Just as his rider neared, he wheeled around to face her and reared up, hopping up and down a few times. The Tashek waited the stallion out then rose a hand, beckoning him near. Unrevealed walked up and sniffed her palm, calming himself.

The pair seemed ready to continue their play when a movement caused the two of them to turn and tense. A moment later, a young page came scurrying down the keep steps. The young, sandy-haired boy ran to Lord Darshel and bowed as well as he could while puffing for breath. He thrust up two scrolls. Lord Darshel accepted these with more grace and gently dismissed the page. As he studied then broke open the seals, Zyanthena and Unrevealed wandered closer. The handsome lord read the letters to himself, re-reading some sections before continuing on. By the time he was done, Doctor Murnin and Zyanthena were waiting with curious anticipation; though, the warrioress covered her interest by seeming to be preoccupied combing her fingers through the black's mane.

Doctor Murnin was not so self-effacing. "What is it, lad?"

Lord Darshel passed the scrolls to the old physician. "A letter form King Maushelik, another from Princess Éleen Éldon-Tomino. The first states that the king is wondering where the Kavahadian army is and why we did not respond to his last correspondence. It asks us to travel to the Citadel of Light."

"You left out the part where the maunstorz have been defeated at the Gap." Murnin pointed out, reading the letter.

"I am more concerned that I never received a letter from His Majesty. If I had, I would have sent my forces to help the king."

Zyanthena had slunk up to the fence. "Perhaps, Your Lordship, the letter had been intercepted? I would not put it past the maunstorz. They have been known to shoot courier pigeons and lone riders leaving battlefields before."

Lord Darshel's mouth tightened at the thought. "I should have just headed out when I heard about the attack on the Citadel. The king will think less of me now that we go after the battle is won."

"King Maushelik is a fair man. If you explain his letter did not arrive, he will pardon you." Doctor Murnin tried to console his lord. Lord Shekmann did not look convinced.

Zyanthena, however, dismissed the matter, moving on to what really piqued her interest. "What did the Havenese princess have to say?"

"Rather curious, aren't you?" Darshel teased. The desert woman shrugged and schooled her features into indifference. Darshel loosed a crooked smile, amused at the Tashek's attitude. In answer, Zyanthena rolled her eyes and turned away. The Kavahadian chuckled. "Princess Éldon is on her way to the Citadel to meet her betrothed, Prince Maushelik. She was advised to wait until the fighting was over. The princess requests a stay here in my "lovely" keep until she can continue on to the Citadel."

"Well, you should write her immediately and say Kavahad is traveling to the Citadel as well and will wait to accompany the princess. You could win back some regard with the King by protecting his son's betrothed in a war zone."

"Who is in charge here?!" Lord Darshel berated, exasperated. "Now, I'm taking orders from a doctor, yesterday from my prisoner. Next, it may be a page boy!"

"You did not hear it from me." Doctor Murnin smoothed over lightly.

The Shekmann grasped the offered scrolls and arranged his features into a serious countenance, strong and untouchable. Zyanthena blinked at the sudden change. The tall man turned his emerald eyes on her, narrowing them in consideration, then spoke his mind. "I need to meet my friend for lunch." He motioned to the balcony and gardens he had shown Zyanthena earlier. "I will allow you to stay here with your horse until you wish to join us. My guards will escort you up." He did not wait for a reply, turning to Doctor

Murnin. His easy dismissal was a clear reminder that Zyanthena was his prisoner and not worth much concern. "I will see you around, Murnin. Thank you for taking such good care of the Crystal warhorse. I would like to invite you to dinner tonight to reciprocate the great service you offer me."

"Of course sir."

Lord Darshel walked off then, leaving the doctor and Tashek alone in his private paddock. Doctor Murnin sighed once the Kavahadian lord-governor was gone. "He is a puzzle, that man. Get him alone and he is almost good company. Get him thinking of his duties as a lord of this demesne and he is as cold as his father." The aging physician turned to the Tashek woman. "I am sorry that his cruelness is directed toward you. You have been a joy as a patient and very respectful, too. Such conduct is untowardly."

Zyanthena softened her features, okay with talking with the aged physician. "He has not been as bad as he was initially, or, perhaps, I am just getting used to the stench of his foul attitude. If I had been captured by his father, I am certain I would be suffering more so."

Doctor Murnin nodded his head but didn't agree out loud because of the guards nearby; even the doctor knew when not to be outspoken about his lord. Instead, he waved a hand toward Unrevealed. "Go on and enjoy the time with your stallion. I have other patients to attend."

Zyanthena Sheev'arid bowed deeply to the physician, earning one in return. "May the winds blow gently for you today."

"And you as well, Tashek." He waved and walked off, leaving the desert woman alone with her horse and the guards.

The warrioress watched him go, wishing she was able to do the same. Unrevealed bumped her shoulder and she reached back to caress his cheek. "Yes, boy, I know. What would I pay to be as free?" Her mind cast back to the Kavahadian lord's gloating words. "Obviously, not that high. Come, boy, let's get you settled."

§   §

"Who is that cunt?"

Lord Darshel glanced at his friend, Markus LaPoint, who had stood up to look down at the private paddock. The spindly, rough-shaven rogue was sipping his brandy with little attention to its taste, his sharp, brown eyes locked on Zyanthena as she brushed her stallion. The way the man's eyes critiqued the Tashek made the hairs on the back of Darshel's neck rise defensively. Markus was a known womanizer, regularly debauching respected ladies then tossing them aside once his fun was through. It was a fault Darshel had learned to turn a blind eye to, as his father had cultivated the prurience in his friend long before Darshel had any thought to argue the pastime. Yet, the certain lubricity in the look Markus had trained on the desert woman had the Kavahadian ready to defend his prisoner; however, Lord Darshel knew he had to do so carefully.

"Oh her," he faked boredom and waved a hand to dismiss Zyanthena's presence. "That is a Crystine scout staying here while her mount heals from a war injury. She is horrible company and even worse to try to woo. I swear she is missing the correct gonads by the way her tastes run."

Markus licked the fine coating of brandy from his lips, in a way showing where his thoughts lie. "She looks Tashek. Lord Shekmann said they were the best, so wild and deliciously hateful. Do you think—?"

"I most definitely *do not* think you would enjoy her." Darshel interrupted shortly. "I do not exaggerate her lack of interest in men. You would have no fun with her. She has no sense of feminine wiles."

"Hm. I like a challenge."

"Not that one." Lord Darshel tried to steer the conversation away from Zyanthena. "How did you like the brie? It had been ages since Kavahad had good cheese, and I was hoping this type would be a good choice to introduce here."

"Since when did you take such an interest in cheese?" Markus asked, overly suave. He eyed Darshel keenly. "It is not like you to forego a conversation about a woman. Unless…" His eyes wandered back to the Tashek and warhorse. The look was calculating. "It is intriguing, yes? A Tashek in Kavahad?"

"As I said, she is a Crystine scout."

"Yeah, a likely possibility." Markus replied, not believing. He pulled back his chair, sat down, and leaned toward his friend in challenge. "You haven't touched her yet, have you?"

"I would prefer to not sign my death warrant."

Markus threw his head back and laughed loudly. "She intimidates you! Of all the...I never thought I'd see the day when you were cowed, 'Shel. I have got to meet her." Before Darshel could stop him, Markus was leaning back over the balcony, yelling down to Zyanthena. "You, sweet thing, Tashek! The Lord of Kavahad need you up here now." Darshel could only imagine the knife-like glare the desert woman returned. She must have by Markus's enthusiastic, amused whoop.

Much to Lord Darshel's surprise, Zyanthena appeared a few minutes later, escorted by his guards. As she walked across the balcony to their table, Lord Darshel was struck—once again—by her fiery pose. She had somehow managed to not even dirty the hem of the white dress she wore; the look made her seem more a desert apparition come to life than normal. The old Zyanthena Sheev'arid was back—curtesy of the black stallion, he assumed. Maybe, she could hold her own against Markus's rakish ways. "Zyanthena, this is my friend, Viscount Markus LaPoint, who holds some of the Shekmann lands near the Shoal Lake. Markus, Zyanthena Sheev'arid, scout of the Crystine." Zyanthena looked wary, tipped off to the lord's concern by the formal title Lord Darshel should not be using with her stripped station.

Markus did not fail to look charming. "Zyanthena." He tested the foreign name. "What a lovely name, the way it slips off the tongue." The Tashek's face immediately hardened, becoming unreadable. She did not reply to the statement. Markus seemed to have expected as much, as seen by his amused smile. "Darshel was just telling me of your lack of enjoying the Shekmann hospitality. It seems odd that a woman of your stature does not wish to exploit it."

"If you are referring to his lust, there is little he could give me that would satisfy the smallest hint of pleasure I have known." She replied drily. Lord Darshel swallowed a pleased cough, despite the fact that her words were meant to insult.

Markus gasped and sucked back his surprised chuckle. "She is indeed a challenge." He turned his eyes back to Darshel. "And, she is most definitely not into you. I never thought I would see the day a woman eluded your charms."

Zyanthena responded, calling Markus's attention back to her. "The Lord Darshel has no charm just the Shekmann reputation. Only squirrelly, infatuated town girls, too young to know any better, have found any appeal in his lordship's bed."

The insult was so ridiculous that Markus could not help his snorting laugh. He was crumpled over in his laughter, acting very unviscountly. Doubled-over, he didn't see the glances exchanged between the Kavahadian and Tashek, one displeased and the other smug.

Lord Darshel knew it was time to reign in the desert woman's tongue; she had had enough fun at his expense. "Sit down, Zy'ena. Your time in the stables is done for the day." The reprimand was not lost on the Tashek. Her victorious glint vanished from her brandy eyes and she pulled out a chair to sit down on it woodenly. Just like before, it seemed Darshel had doused the fire in her soul with just a command. Interesting that.

By then, Markus LaPoint had regained his composure. "Well, I guess I have my answer. Sorry that it comes at your expense, 'Shel." His glimmering eyes passed back over the Tashek beauty, the fact that she had been subdued not diminishing her exotic pulchritude.

Lord Darshel dismissed his friend's behavior. "As I said, she is not worth your interest. Now, would you like more brandy?" As the two men returned to other, less provocative conversation, Zyanthena finally regained some semblance of civility to eat the wonderful spread of foods; however, Lord Darshel had an inkling of warning that there would be more to come, if Zyanthena and Markus were spending the afternoon and evening together.

§ §

The day passed, uneventful. Before dinner, Markus insisted on a round of archery, of which he convinced Darshel to let Zyanthena join. The Kavahadian lord had been nervous about the Tashek woman's behavior, but she performed unerringly, beating both men in a skillful display of her superior technique. It was obvious from the open stares of the watching soldiers and Markus's murmured approval that she had proven why she was such a valued scout. They had, then, finished off with a round of drinks before the evening meal was served, going to the private dinner only when Doctor Murnin appeared from his rounds.

Three young women joined them around the table. By the suggestive giggles and silly responses they gave the men, Zyanthena guessed that they were that evening's playthings. She was only slightly shocked that the doctor had his own lady, though the aging man seemed to make the woman aware that she was only there as a dinner acquaintance and nothing more. As for the other two men, it was rather blatant that the women would be getting some attention after the meal. Zyanthena sighed at the inevitable. The dinner spread was nice, however. There were two appetizers, mushrooms stuffed with thin meats and cheese and crackers served with a vegetable butter and roe eggs. Next came a beef and barley soup, followed with the main course of a slow roasted lamb in red wine sauce and a sprig of parsley. A lemon custard and minced meat pies finished off the meal.

Zyanthena could not remember when she had such a decadent meal, and neither could the ladies, it seemed, by the way they gushed over the courses; the women took up most of the dinner conversation. The Tashek could not help feeling a little put out. She had been placed between Lord Darshel and the doctor, but both men were preoccupied with the ladies' converse. For a brief moment, Zyanthena thought back to the wonderful meal she had shared with Lord Gordar, Priest Anibus, and Decond, remembering fondly how excited the banter had been as they had spoken about topics that interested the desert woman: horses, wine, military strategy, and politics. The silly exchange at the table Zyanthena found herself at seemed so shallow and imprudent on contrast.

A while later, Doctor Murnin was called away on an emergency for a pregnant woman. His polite exit seemed to signal to Lord Darshel that the meal was through. He called a servant to him to whisper an instruction and a guard followed the man in shortly afterward to take Zyanthena back to the alcove. She knew better than to protest. Her time of relative freedom was over.

Not long after Zyanthena was chained to her small bedroll, Lord Darshel and Markus entered the lord's bedchamber, the three women in tow. Before long, the five of them were having a grand old time; the women's pleasurable moans grating on the Tashek's nerves. The two Starian men seemed to be every bit the lovers they were rumored to be—much to Zyanthena's disgust. It was many long, loud hours before the deed seemed accomplished. Once it was, Zyanthena heard the women crawl up on either side of Lord Darshel; the third was already asleep at his feet. The threesome drifted off to a satisfied sleep.

The silence was a welcome relief.

The warrioress had almost drifted off to her own sleep when she heard the distinct footsteps of a man slinking closer to the alcove. Her brandy eyes snapped open and she pinned them to the entrance. To her distaste, Markus's wispy, naked frame was outlined in the near-darkness. He was watching her! The smell of his lust floating across the room to warn the desert woman. What Zyanthena had mistaken as the viscount in a slumber had been the man's patient wait for the others to drift off to sleep. The thought chilled her.

Markus drew near, his prurient eyes shining passionately as he took in Zyanthena's form. Slowly, he lowered himself to the desert woman's sitting height. "I learned something about you from a guard." He began, whispering. Zyanthena schooled her features into a cool glare, hoping to silence the pounding of her heart. Markus continued. "He said, Zyanthena, that you are Darshel's prisoner, captured when you defied the treaty and crossed his lands. Your people have forsaken you to Darshel's care. I find it intriguing, then, that 'Shel lied about you to me. He is keeping you for himself."

"The only one who lied was the guard."

Markus chuckled. "I think not. 'Shel has always been one to try to keep his favorites from my hands, lest I ruin them. You would have to be the best treasure he has kept thus far. A Tashek." He reached out to caress the lower leg that was nearest him. Thought the touch was gentle enough, its warmth sent Zyanthena's anger coursing through her body. If it wasn't for the chains that limited her reach, she would have knocked the viscount's hand away. Unaware of the fact, Markus continued. "Lord Shekmann, Darshel's father, always spoke of what erotic lovers your people were. He boasted he had a Tashek in bed every week before the treaty was introduced. The Tashek lovers never relinquished their fire to him."

"What you heard is that we never gave in to the man's disrespect and carnal abuse. He plundered our villages with his own father and violated my people numerous times."

"You were prisoners of war."

"His war. That does not make it right."

"But now *you* are the prisoner and one who seems to be well-cared-for by my friend. It seems he does not take the liberties with you that Lord Shekmann Sr. would have. It is a wasteful shame and I cannot stand by it."

"You will anger His Lordship if you continue down this path."

"Oh, I doubt our friendship is worth less than a Tashek wench." Markus sneered. He began to lean forward, tracing his fingers up Zyanthena's thigh, pulling up the hem of her dress. "You would be wise to keep quiet and let me have my way with you. I am the best, you know. 'Shel won't have to know about our little exchange." His hand slipped upward, well into range of Zyanthena's hands and far too close to what she considered an "out of bounds" zone on her person.

"You are an impertinent swine." She hissed. "I do not consent to your touching me." Quick as a coiled rattlesnake, Zyanthena's hands reached out and grasped Markus's wrist. She twisted quickly, hearing the bones snap like broken twigs.

Immediately, Markus was wailing in agony. His pained voice reached Lord Darshel and the ladies. Battle trained, the lord-governor was awake and instantly on his feet, the ladies sprawling around him. His alertness quickly turned to fury when he found his friend clutching his injured wrist to his person. Infuriated, Lord Darshel stormed out, Markus in tow, to find a servant to take his friend to Doctor Murnin. Ten minutes later, he returned, still in a huff, and ordered the women to leave. Frightened by his outrage, the ladies picked up their forgotten garments, not bothering to cover themselves, and high-tailed it from the room. Lord Darshel slammed the door shut behind them and slid the deadbolt home.

Zyanthena tensed as she heard him stride near the alcove. She came to her knees as he rounded the wall and rose her hands to ward off the furious lord, lest he swing a punch her way. Instead, the Kavahadian grabbed both her wrists and slammed her into the wall. The desert warrioress felt her healing back cry out at the new assault. She winced at the pain. Pinned to the rough stone by Darshel's forearm, Zyanthena found she was thoroughly trapped. "You broke his wrist! How fucking dare you!"

"He was touching me." She replied icily.

"Touching you! Touching! That is all you have to say for your actions!" In his fury, he clenched his jaw then slammed her against the wall once more. Zyanthena withheld that hiss of pain. She averted her beautiful eyes to the floor, feeling how completely hopeless it was to convince the infuriated Shekmann of her self-defense against the wrong-doing of his friend. But, His Lordship was not done with her, though. "Markus is a dear friend to me. Yet today, you insult me in front of him—twice!—and now you break his bones in two. I do not accept such behavior! You are my prisoner, under my roof and my laws. Your people gave you to me to punish for your crime. I think it is time you learn your place."

He yanked Zyanthena down to the bedding and pulled her arms up overhead, holding her wrists tightly in his left hand to bind her there. The warrioress instinctively revolted, trying to knee his lordship's groin, but the Kavahadian was ready for such a ploy and the blow landed too weakly to do any good. Darshel growled at the failed attempt and took strong fingers to the front of her dress, tearing it open. His long limbs and pure, naked muscle pressed down upon her, making the Tashek unable to do more than squirm underneath the lord's weight, preventing further attacks.

Fully hog-tied, Zyanthena could do little for herself as Lord Darshel began to feel down her exposed body. Strong fingers kneaded roughly over her battle-hardened figure. Lord Shekmann groped her breasts, forcing them to peak, then descended lower to find her right hipbone. This, he grasped assertively. His lips joined his hand, then, nipping at the sides of Zyanthena's neck and chin and began to move up to her face. It was only as Lord Darshel reached her lips, finding them held firmly closed, that his mind overrode his anger.

Once he became aware of the tension in the Tashek's body, Darshel realized his folly. Zyanthena was trembling beneath his touch; the usually tough warrioress was trying to keep herself together against his onslaught. Suddenly aghast at what he had almost done, the lord-governor stiffened and released her wrists. Darshel pushed himself away from the bed as if he had been burned.

Never before had he touched a woman so. Ever. That was his father's way, not his.

The Tashek warrioress hugged her arms to her body and turned her head away from Darshel, but not before he saw the single, silent tear slide down her left cheek. She looked scared and defenseless in the tatters of her clothing. Lord Darshel rose a hand to wipe the wetness from her face. Zyanthena flinched but allowed his touch. Slowly, she turned her face back to look at him, sensing his stare. In the candlelight, the Shekmann lord saw how completely open and vulnerable she was at that moment. If he dared ask, Darshel knew Zyanthena would give him any part of her just then, only to have the deed done.

"He tried to rape you." Darshel stated, finally grasping what had really happened. Zyanthena was too nervous to reply, though the answer was clear in her dark eyes. Lord Darshel felt pained at her look, for he knew he had almost done the same—despite his promise to not touch Zyanthena unless she allowed it. He suddenly felt very guilty.

Gingerly, Darshel reached out once more; this time to offer comfort; but Zyanthena still recoiled from his hand. She did, however, finally relent to his fingers on her cheek. Brandy-colored eyes met his after a long pause. Compelled by the depth of the emotion in her look, Lord Darshel leaned back down, moving slowly as if she was a deer about to jump away. His lips came to touch hers again. He pressed in softly, feeling them still trembling. Only when she was able to steady them and yield to his mouth did Darshel withdraw his kiss. As his face floated just breaths from her own, Darshel whispered, "I am sorry, Zy'ena." He pushed himself away then and walked out of the room.

Chapter Seventeen

§

Kavahad

After the other night's drama, Zyanthena was even more withdrawn. Whatever fire had been rekindled in the reuniting with Unrevealed was doused. Ashamed, Lord Darshel found ways to occupy his time, steering clear of the desert woman. He kept his eye on her indirectly, usually a quick glance from time to time through a window or when passing a doorway. The Kavahadian even allowed the Tashek free rein of the keep, under the watchful eye of his guards. Under the lord's orders, she was only chained at night. Zyanthena responded to her new-found freedom by spending all of her time with the black courser, usually just sitting apathetically near him and sometimes joining in his exuberant play.

Doctor Murnin would visit the Tashek now and then to check up on the black stallion and the warrioress's scars; however, even the physician could not get her to speak with him. After two days of the slight, the doctor began to limit his time, sensing Zyanthena just wanted to be left alone. Of course, the doctor had more than an earful to offer to His Lordship on the whole disgusting manner. Lord Darshel was wise enough to let his respected senior lay into him.

As for Markus, the viscount cut his visit short, feeling his friend's displeasure, and had slunk away the morning after the offense knowing only too well the temper the Shekmann could rain down on him. Viscount LaPoint's leaving showed Darshel who had truly been at fault—making his remorse grow.

Lord Darshel was angry with himself and just a little contrite. The staff of Kavahad felt the misdirected regret through sudden snippets and outbursts of anger. Soon, they avoided the lord-governor as much as they were able, keeping their heads down and busy to circumvent Darshel's mood. The tall, strong-statured Shekmann knew his behavior was churlish and took to locking himself in his study to avoid further abuse of his staff. He began to count the hours until Princess Éldon and her escort arrived, knowing that once he and his men were busied with their protection detail and far away from the site of Darshel's offense, the better his own attitude would become.

Day three of the wait finally brought the Havenese flags, seen by the regular patrol in the late morning. Lord Darshel was relieved at the news; however, he was not entirely consoled. During the preparations, Commander Raic had brought up a point the Shekmann had been trying to ignore: the route the procession needed to take went through Tashek lands, barren and uncharted as they were. No one in the party knew how to take the princess safely through the Aras Desert—with the exception of one. To avoid the inevitable, Lord Darshel had tried to piece together the old routes his grandfather had collected, but there was no guarantee that the outdated maps were accurate. With Princess Éldon's escort nearing, however, the twenty-eight-year-old lord-governor knew he could no longer put off begging the Tashek woman. Zyanthena would be the best choice to lead the ensemble, no one else would do. Steeling himself one last moment of solace, the tall, broad-shouldered Starian left his study to find the desert warrioress.

Zyanthena had been taking a bath in the connecting room to Darshel's quarters. Ms. Tika was there assisting her, having given a hard-won argument on why she should help the Tashek. As Lord Darshel entered of his own accord and stepped to the large window on the far side of the room, the young maid gasped and flushed at the improper intrusion. She raced for something to cover the bathing Tashek. Zyanthena, however, was more or less unfazed by the lord's appearance, though it was obvious by the tingling along the lord-governor's spine, that Zyanthena had her eyes in wary curiosity to his turned back.

"Forgive the intrusion." Lord Darshel began, remaining turned away. If he expected a reply, Zyanthena did not give one. "I just came to inform you that the Havenese banners have been spotted just south of here. The princess should be arriving by early afternoon, at the latest. I have arranged for her party to stay one night in the western corridor, longer if she requests such, and a feast will be held in her honor. You are invited to attend. We will, if all goes according to plan, leave by first light tomorrow morning."

"Thank you for the invitation, Your Lordship." Her emotionless tone intending to pronounce that the lord's conversation was over and that he should leave.

Darshel held his breath, feeling poised at the edge of a cliff. What he needed to say caught in his mouth like aged toffee chews. Behind him, he heard Zyanthena continue her bath, the splashing and dripping of water giving the message of disinterest. Damn! It was hard sucking up to a woman he had mistreated. Beratingly, he dug his fingernails into his left palm to push himself to speak. "I need you to lead our forces through the Aras. It is your people's place not ours. I do not want to endanger the Princess of Blue Haven through any negligence or hubris of mine."

Silence, then he heard the Tashek rise from the tube, water streaming off her body to the bath. Ms. Tika gasped again, this time at her lady's boldness. "I will finish my bath after speaking with His Lordship." Zyanthena informed the young girl, motioning for her robe. A moment late, the desert woman joined the Shekmann by the window, her brandy eyes wary and distant. Lord Darshel was surprised that she stood as close to him as she did; a test, maybe, to see how well behaved he could be with a barely clad beauty by his side.

His Lordship continued to be polite, his emerald eyes taking in the view beyond the open window. "Ms. Zyanthena," he began softly, feeling her intense eyes shift over his face, "I know I have done wrong by you and no amount of groveling can fix my transgression; however, for the sake of the safety of our Highness Prince Maushelik's fiancée, would you please accept my apology and lead the procession? We... I do not know the way through the Aras Desert. Please, I will do anything." The last he finished quietly, his usually rich, baritone voice meek and humble.

Zyanthena stood still, contemplating. The Shekmann dared not breath in fear that any movement on his part would discourage the desert woman's consent. Finally, she stirred. "For His Highness, I will do as you request, Your Lordship. But," the one word had Lord Darshel frozen in anticipation, "You will give me full control of the forces. There will be no Kavahadian banners furled, no crests or emblems of any kind to show you are from Kavahad. It must look like the procession is from Blue Haven, for if it does not, my people will not hesitate to attack. Your forces must also be battle-ready without appearing to be so."

"Why?"

The Tashek hesitated, unsure if she wanted to reveal what information she was privy to. Yet, she reached into her robe sleeve. After a moment's pause, she pulled out a small slip of paper. "I received this missive this morning." She held out the note for Darshel to take.

The Starian read the short message quickly. "Where did you get this?" He asked, distrustful.

Zyanthena made light of her response. "My father, the Shi'alam, sent a falcon to me at dawn to warn of the circumstances in North Point. Believe what is written there, Your Lordship, no matter how outrageous it seems. We must all travel with caution, for if the maunstorz can slip around so unearthly, an army of that size could trounce us if we are unsuspecting,"

Even though it seemed preposterous, Lord Darshel shut his mouth and nodded. "As you say, Zy'ena. Is there anything else I should know before I leave you?"

There was a pause as the Tashek thought. "Not in regards to the preparations, except of what I already spoke of, but... I would like to select a horse for the journey. I will take Unrevealed but do not wish to ride him until he is healed."

"Very well." The Kavahadian gave a short smile, amused at the Tashek's deep concern for her mount. It was an easy request. "We will go to the stables once you are done with your bath. I will be in my study until then." She bowed her head slightly, the first sign of respect Lord Darshel had seen from her. The deference causing a warm feeling inside him, deep and low. He bowed deeply in return and politely excused himself.

Lord Darshel's courteous departure had Zyanthena staring after him considering the subtle change in the man. She shook her head to clear her thoughts and turned back to the waiting maid. "I will finish my bath now, Ms. Tika."

The rough, brown walls of Kavahad came into view of Princess Éleen's company by mid-afternoon. The Havenese woman eyed the place critically, finding the earthen walls and high, plain spires of the keep to be rugged and alien compared to the contrasting luxurious estate they had left....it made her chest constrict in apprehension. The tired, heat-leaden townspeople of the place streamed in and out of the main gate, a reminder of the strong desert sun her travel coach managed to keep at bay.

"It is such a dreadful sight." Prince Connel muttered across from Éleen, his own face crinkled in slight disgust. "I hope the inside is better managed."

Princes Éleen would have agreed, except she found the Sunarian's contemptuous snub rude. "I am sure the place will do to keep out the desert sands and sun. I heard such constructions as these adobe walls are well-suited for the dry climate."

Prince Connel loosed a fake smile. "I still prefer the Sunarian architecture, M'lady, though I can accept such dismal quarters for one night, as necessary."

Éleen rose her eyebrows incredulously and turned away to watch their arrival. She took note that there was no escort party waiting to lead them in and that the front gate watchmen had to send a young boy scrambling to the keep to alert the lord-governor of their arrival. The small entourage was beckoned through the gates, a cavalryman leading the way up through the inner city into the main courtyard. There was no bright assembly of horns or honor guards at the main stairs—like Sunrise had procured—nor did there seem to be much interest in assembling any fanfare. Only the lone court advisor, closest to the Lord of Kavahad, stood on the steps to greet them.

Prince Connel scoffed under his breathe.

Lord Nexlé cued his horse forward and dismounted in front of the advisor. The two men spoke at some length then shook hands before the Havenese returned to speak with Princess Éleen. From Carrod's face, Éleen wondered what might be wrong. "Highness, the advisor wishes you welcome to Kavahad. Our rooms have been arranged for us, as well as, baths for all and a light snack to take away the exhaustion of our travels. He, Advisor Abrus, is calling some staff to take our trunks to our rooms."

Éleen nodded and began to climb out of the coach, but Prince Connel stopped her. "Princess, please." He held out a hand to halt her. "Where is the Lord-governor?"

Lord Nexlé paused, hesitating, before answering. "His Lordship is further preoccupied at this moment in the stables. Advisor Abrus had sent a page to alert him of our presence."

"Well, I am sure that what matters have the lord engaged must be important." The princess reasoned. "I am confident he will meet with us as he is able and I am quite ready to be out of this coach and refreshed." She took Lord Nexlé's hand and stepped out into the blaring desert sun, ignoring Prince Connel's irked look. The princess, too, found the lord's absence to be a slight, but she was too travel weary to argue the point. Besides, it seemed all affairs had been taken account of despite the lack of the lord-governor's curtesy.

Advisor Abrus proved to be a charitable host, making sure every room was to their liking, that all their belongings were correctly placed, and that the baths and food were to each person's specifications. The rest of the Kavahad staff were equally amiable and hurried to change anything that arose. Though the time passed without Lord Shekmann's appearance, Princess Éleen was put at ease that her stay was not going to be as uncomfortable as she had assumed.

An hour later, as the princess, Prince Connel, and Lord Carrod sat enjoying the shade from their private balcony and sipping glasses of chilled tea, Lord Darshel Shekmann was finally announced at their door. The tall Starian entered, a cautious-eyed woman trailing behind him. Princess Éleen could not help staring at the Lord-governor. Lord Darshel had been rumored to be a well-favored bachelor but none of the stories she had been whispered spoke of just how handsome the twenty-eight-year-old rogue really was. Aristocratic barely covered the lord's features; he was tall, broad-shouldered, and boasted a chiseled facial structure that would make any lady swoon (and many did, the princess had been told).

If Lord Shekmann noticed the princess's staring, he made no notion of it as he swept into a courtly bow and introduced himself. "Greetings, Your Highnesses and Lord. I am Lord Darshel Shekmann, governor of Kavahad. I apologize for my absence at your arrival but I hope Abrus was an acceptable stand-in for my nonattendance."

"Your Advisor was very accommodating, thank you, Lord Shekmann." Princess Éleen replied. "The service offered us has been first rate."

"Excellent." Darshel smiled charmingly and indicated the empty seat at the table. 'May I sit, Your Highness?" The princess nodded. Once the lord was seated, he waved his hand toward the raven-haired woman behind him. "I asked Zyanthena to join us this afternoon. She is a Tashek scout who will oversee our trip to the Citadel of Light." Zyanthena bowed gracefully to the royals and lord, her features still looked wary but very respectful. The three guests looked intrigued at seeing the desert warrioress; possibly, it was the first time they had ever met a Tashek. Lord Darshel understood the fascination. Zyanthena still seemed a mystery to him with her unnaturally lithe movements and cultured wildness. She was an exotic beauty for certain. The desert woman took the last available seat to his right. "I apologize if your stay seems rushed, Your Highness," Darshel began, pulling Éleen's eyes away from the Tashek beside him. "But, if we are all in agreeance, I would have us traveling to the Citadel as soon as we are able."

"You will get no argument from me. Advisor Abrus informed us that your militia is being assembled to leave in the morning. I am impressed with your speed and organization on such short notice."

"It is nothing, Your Highness." Lord Darshel answered suavely. "My men have been on war-readiness for weeks. Your correspondence and King Maushelik's were just the orders needed to get us moving."

"In any case," Princess Éleen said, "Your quick response to my letter and understanding for the need to be at the Citadel of Light as soon as possible is appreciated."

"What time are you expecting to leave in the morning?" Lord Nexlé asked.

"By dawn." Lord Darshel responded to Éleen's escort directly, sensing the man had a background in military training and would appreciate the candid response. "All of the horses and carts are being inspected and will be ready to head out upon first light. If anything needs to be addressed with your party, I will have you meet with my militia commander, Raic."

"I would like to meet with this commander anyway, Your Lord, as I would like to know what protections are in place for the journey."

Zyanthena shifted next to Darshel, reminding him of their agreement. "Well, if you are wishing to know what defenses we have in place, I would recommend you speak with Zyanthena." He nodded to the Tashek." She is responsible for all that during the trip." The Havenese looked skeptically at the desert woman, his prejudice against women as fighters showing in his eyes. Zyanthena's eyes flashed in annoyance. The glare had Lord Carrod sitting back, cowed, in his seat. "I see your uncertainty with my choice of command, but I assure you, Lord Carrod, Highnesses, Zyanthena is qualified."

"What experience do you have in this area?" Prince Connel questioned, finally joining their conversation.

Zyanthena met his stare evenly, her voice cool. "I have been a scout for the Crystine for six years. I personally, have taken out three maunstorz raiding camps on the border, and have killed a count of eighty-seven enemies this year alone. I have been trained in the deadly art of She-koum-o, ranking in the ninth level, and have the highest marks in marksmanship [archery] and swordsmanship. My horsemanship skills put your cavalry to shame. I believe, Your Highness Sunrise, that I am proficiently qualified."

Prince Connel seemed to be in shock at her words, but he quickly recovered, a pleased smile on his face. The man knew when he had been ousted. "Yes, I think you will do." Zyanthena nodded resolutely.

The conversation did not last much longer. The princess and Lord Carrod inquired on some details about the procession and the route to be taken. They seemed satisfied enough with the supplied answers that they drifted away from the journey to questions about Kavahad. Soon, the demands of being lord-governor had Darshel excusing himself. Zyanthena dutifully followed him out. The Kavahadian left with the invitation for an evening meal and went on his way.

Once the room was theirs again comments about the lord and the Tashek ensued. "He seems to be a very exceptional governor." Princess Éleen began.

"He seems to be more than that." Prince Connel meant the quip as sarcasm about the man's charms but the princess did not catch the undertone.

"Indeed! Lord Darshel had been very organized and punctual with his preparations. I am impressed with his work, and his staff had been top-rate. This keep is very well run."

"The Tashek is an interesting character," Lord Carrod said, "If not a tad bit intimidating. I have heard stories of their exploits in battle but have never seen one before. I had not known they allowed women to fight. It seems reprehensible."

Prince Connel nodded his agreeance. "I can't imagine she is as good as she boasted. A woman soiling herself with blood? It's nearly sinful."

"Well, I think she is to be applauded." Princess Éleen spoke out in the woman's defense. "It is commendable to see a woman who can more than hold her own in this world run by men. I am impressed with her bravery."

Prince Connel smiled falsely. "Of course, M'lady, a woman with a little mettle is to be commended; however, I am not sure a battlefield is the place to express it. Imagine, the disorder that would ensue with more women fighting. Could you see yourself doing such actions? Or one of your sisters?"

"Indeed, My Highness." Carrod agreed with the Sunarian. "The battlefield is not the place for your gender."

Princess Éleen knew she had no argument against the two men, as she was sure she would never take up arms and fight on a field, but she could see the Tashek woman doing just that. Zyanthena was the picture of pure strength and prowess, and, though the princess could not fathom what it would take to fight and kill another person, she could believe that the Tashek did. The desert woman had that aura around her. So, with the conclusion that some women were battle-capable, she asked the matter be dismissed. "I am going to my rooms now for a nap. Please, come see me to the dinner tonight." She rose and the two men bid her a good sleep. Lord Carrod escorted her to her guest quarters and informed her that he was going to check on the preparations and familiarize himself with the commanders and the chosen route. Princess Éleen wished him good fortune on his inquiries and turned into her rooms alone.

With a sigh of relief, the twenty-four-year-old allowed herself to relax her royal facade and sank onto the comfortable queen-sized bed like a child. She grabbed a fluffy pillow and curled up around it, feeling her weariness sink away in the downy cushion. Slowly, she drifted off to sleep, lulled by the soft breeze coming through her window and the small, glass windchime that sang out a calming song.

§   §

The knock came too soon to Éleen's door. The princess groaned at the insult and snuggled deeper into the soft linens. The door creaked open, with a polite greeting by a maid, and Princess Éleen regretfully pulled herself awake. The young maid who greeted the Havenese royal had soft, curly brunette hair and a cheerful smile. Her courteous bow and shyness had the princess instantly apologetic for her bad behavior. "Come in. I am sorry, I was still dozing."

"I apologize, Highness," the girl said demurely. "Lady Zyanthena was concerned that you would miss your dinner and asked me to help you get ready so you could make a timely appearance. She was most forward on that point."

"Well, thank you, miss..."

"Tika, Your Highness."

"Tika, for coming to assist me. I was unaware of the time. Is it really so late?"

"Well, not dreadfully late, M'lady—I mean Your Highness. Lady Zyanthena just wished to make sure you were not late. She made sure I came twenty-minutes to the appointed dinner hour."

"Twenty minutes!" Princess Éleen panicked. "I should have been preparing ages ago." She was quickly to her feet and scurrying to collect the needed garments and beauty supplies. She felt frantic. How she could possibly get herself together in such short time?!

Ms. Tika giggled at her antics, despite herself, and calmly stepped in. "It is okay, Your Highness. Lady Zyanthena assured me this is an informal banquet. Only some of the commanders, your lord, the Prince of Sunrise, and His Lordship will be there. Oh, and maybe Doctor Murnin and Advisor Abrus if they are not further disposed. The meal is being taken in His Lordship's private supping room and not in the lesser hall."

Princess Éleen was only slightly consoled but allowed the younger woman to direct her to a less formal outfit and jewels, and, though she still felt somewhat underdressed, the princess admitted Ms. Tika had done a fine job of putting up her hair and powdering her face in the short time. She let out the breath she had not realized she held and took one last look in the mirror. Ms. Tika had picked out her china blue frock, a choice the princess had overlooked because she had deemed it too casual. It now seemed to make sense in the still warm, desert night. The maid had piled Éleen's long, brunette hair into a casual bun atop her head, allowing stray curls to fall down around her face. It had not been a style Éleen would have tried on herself, as it would seem too "casually put together" for her family, yet the princess found it flattering in its simplicity.

"My, you are simply gorgeous!"

Princess Éleen jumped at the unannounced intruder and turned quickly to find Prince Connel standing part way into her doorway. "Why, Connel, you surprised me!"

"My apologies, Ms. Éleen. I seem to have a horrible knack for doing that to you." He motioned to see if he could step further inside the room and walked toward the Havenese woman upon her invitation. "May I say your choice of attire is most stunning, princess." Éleen was about to inject that the dress was of Ms. Tika's choosing but she glanced toward where the maid had stood to find the young woman slipping meekly out the door. Without the girl there to praise, she had to smile and say, "thank you". Prince Connel beamed. "May I be your escort this evening?"

Princess Éleen balked, wondering where her guardian was. "I...but...Lord Carrod." She muttered, finding herself flustered.

"The lord is preoccupied in his conversation with Commander Raic. He has thought of little else since they started speaking and taking cups." Princess Éleen knew that Carrod was prone to over drinking and forgetting his responsibilities on occasion but her man had been very controlled on their trip thus far. She was slightly suspicious that some other reason had the lord occupied but with no real excuse to turn down Prince Connel's hospitality, she held her tongue and took the other royal's arm.

As they entered the small dining hall, Éleen had to pause in wonder. The room had an elegant simplicity to it that spoke of both wealth and comfort. Three elaborate chandeliers hung down from the tin-tiled ceiling, casting a coppery light on the wooden table. The walls were decked in a rich mahogany wood that was both warming and calming. On the far distant wall, a small chamber orchestra was set up and playing quietly for the guests. The long table sat foremost in the room and was adorned in heirloom chinaware, delicate glassware, sterling silverware, and an array of delicacies. Éleen identified most of the items on the table; there was a tray of stuffed mushrooms and another with breads and cheeses for appetizers. Fresh fruits and finger-vegetables sat in numerous places about the giant cedar table and small dessert goblets, holding chunks of jelly-like balls to cleanse the palate between courses, sat by each plate. There was even four select sauces on individual silver trays for each "couple" set between the dishes. Éleen had never seen the use of such a setting before and she found herself curious as to what flavors were offered.

Yet, what surprised the princess the most was the number of guests dining that evening. There were twelve officers from Lord Darshel's militia, five of his advisors, four of Éleen's personal envoy, four from Prince Connel's, and all of the wives or ladies for each man. Including the princess, she counted fifty-four people who had been invited to the feast! This is what Lord Shekmann felt was "casual"?

"Your Highnesses." Lord Shekmann greeted them, coming over from a conversation with an advisor. "You are just in time; the meal is about to be served. Please," He flourished a hand to indicate where to go. "Have a seat on this end of the table, as our most esteemed guests." As the two royals moved, the other guests also found their seats. Lord Darshel then took the seat to Prince Connel's right and had assigned Lord Carrod to sit to the princess's left. From there the others allowed on the royal's end were Commanders Raic and Gordon, a beautiful blonde that accompanied Lord Darshel, Advisor Abrus and his wife, Doctor Murnin, and the Tashek woman to the doctor's left. Beyond them sat those of lesser station. The princess found she was actually quite pleased with the setup. Lord Darshel's staff had certainly done well to make her feel comfortable in the desert outpost.

The first round of courses came out. It was with a lovely dumpling-soup accompanied by a dish of Starian herbs. Though most of the plate was unidentifiable to the Havenese, the dish of herbs was tasty when eaten with the soup. Éleen commented on the surprisingly mild taste.

"I am glad you enjoy it, Highness." Lord Darshel replied. "These greens are picked fresh from my garden. If ever you stay again, I will have to show you the place."

"Oh, yes, that would be nice to see." The princess found herself almost cooing over the handsome Shekmann. Where did that come from? "So, you enjoy gardening yourself?"

Lord Darshel chuckled. "Well, I do not really have a "green thumb" when it comes to such exploits, Your Highness, but I do enjoy collecting plants that are rare and exquisite. Besides bringing sustenance, they provide a little greenery to such a drab countryside. As for their care, I leave them to my master gardener. Less likely to shrivel and die, you see."

Princess Éleen joined his laugh. "Yes, I see."

Prince Connel cut in then with a question, to steer some of Darshel's attention off of the princess. "Speaking of rare and exquisites, Lord Shekmann, I noticed you keep trophies of game you hunted in the eastern study. There are some exceptional catches there."

"Ah, yes, the foreman's brown bear and snow leopard being the most of note. Those are creatures my father killed come near twenty-years-ago now."

"Those must be fascinating tales!" The prince hoped he could steer the conversation in a direction that would deter the princess from long converse.

"Yes, actually they were. I was sixteen the year that snow leopard was brought in…" Lord Darshel spoke at great length of how this father had tracked the cat in the Noway Mountains on one of their yearly hunting trips. The two royals listened aptly to the tale, even gasping at the parts were his father had lost his weapons and had to fight barehanded while Darshel scurried to retrieve a crossbow and knife. The Starian continued on to the brown bear hunt; which had not been planned; and how the bear had been forced down before it mauled more than two retainers in a base-camp. "It was ironic that we have gone bear hunting and came back to a bear at the camp!"

"Indeed! My, that must have been a thrill!" Lord Carrod had been listening in on the second story, having finally exhausted his questions with the two Kavahadian commanders. "It sounds like the Shekmann family are quite apt hunters. Not many men I know would face off with a brown bear."

"Yes, our lord has made quite a name for himself amidst his ancestors." Commander Gordan supported. "And, he had even places in high rankings every year at the annual weapons championships, too. We are proud to serve under such a dedicated and talented leader."

At the remark, Princess Éleen noticed the dark look that came over the Tashek woman, three seats over from the Lord of Kavahad. While the others at the table were chuckling and bantering away, she seemed subdued and wary, an unusual character in the warm setting. As she observed the desert woman, Éleen became aware of the warrioress's features darkening at the praise the commanders gave their lord. Commander Raic got an especially callous glint. Why was she so unlike the others? Princess Éleen would have asked but the woman was too far away. Prince Connel steered her attention back to him as the third course, which consisted of a roasted pork tender, parsley, and a desert fruit were placed in front of the royal.

"So, princess, how is the evening going?"

Éleen turned back around to address her seat-mate. "It is wonderful. I am quite enjoying the food."

"Well, that is good." Prince Connel flashed a smile. "I have been impressed with the meal myself. These kiwano are delicious."

The Havenese looked back at her yellow fruit. "Is that what they are called? I have never heard of them before, but they are tasty."

"It is a desert delicacy. My father used to order them in when they were in season so that the court could try out new cuisine. I particularly like them steamed or in a pudding." He spoke to her at length of the delicacies the Sunarian court got to entertain. His converse was long enough to take care of the time until the fourth and final dinner course came out. Prince Connel stopped talking long enough for a small dish of chocolate soufflé in a raspberry sauce to be set down in front of him. A bowl of fresh fruits and a vanilla iced-cream was set to the left and a warm mug of tea to the right. The Sunarian breathed in a delighted sigh. "Kavahad had indeed done a fine job with this small banquet. The representation far exceeds my expectations."

"Thank you, Your Highness," Lord Darshel replied. The two royals were pulled back into the conversation with the Kavahadian lord, learning more about his town and ancestry. During the exchange, Prince Connel inadvertently stumbled upon the sore issue of Shekmann senior's death. "So, Lord Shekmann, how long have you been governor of this outpost?"

Lord Darshel, his two commanders, and the advisor paused in their eating. Tight-lipped glances were exchanged among the party as the men waited uneasily to see how their leader would respond. Would he keep his words light or respond honestly? The twenty-eight-year-old lord dropped his napkin on the table, after wiping his mouth politely, and sat back. From the expressions around the table, Princess Éleen wondered what blunder Prince Connel had made. It seemed odd, the sudden tension. Sensing it, Lord Darshel relaxed his visage and chuckled. "I apologize, Highness. We forget that the southern kingdoms do not receive many updates of the "doings" in the North. I have been Lord of Kavahad for nine years, since my father's death at the hands of a Sheev'anee."

"I am sorry," Éleen asked demurely, "But what is a Sheev'anee?"

The group looked pointedly at Zyanthena, their animosity rising to simmer beneath the surface of decorum. Only Lord Darshel and the doctor kept their calm. Doctor Murnin reached out a hand to clasp the Tashek's forearm, both to calm her and to remind those at the table to be careful on how the conversation turned. The desert woman rose her eyes defiantly and answered the princess's question. "The Sheev'anee are the main clan of the Tashek and the highest order of my people. Most who refer to the Tashek really refer to us."

Understanding began to dawn at the words. Éleen realized, with some unease, why Zyanthena was not popular with Kavahad. The royal felt that there was more to the issue than the few sentences spoken and, whatever the situation was, it festered among the Kavahadians and Tashek as an underlying resentment.

Lord Darshel continued where Zyanthena had left off. "My father's death by the Sheev'anee was not entirely unexpected. Our people have been at war for over a century. My grandfather started the feud when he burned a Tashek camp he "claimed" plundered vital food-stuffs from one of his caravans." A dark glare from Zyanthena said the lord had left out a part and Lord Darshel added the revision. "My grandfather not only destroyed the rebel camp; he also took their horses and women as payment for his losses. In doing so, he gravely insulted the Tashek, who launched an attack on our city days later, thus starting our continued conflict. The discord between us became so damning that the former King Maushelik had to intervene---was it seventy-six years ago now? He created a treaty, in which mapped out the borders of our two lands. Neither party is to trespass on the other's without permission from our king. Any actions against the other side is dealt with swiftly by the offending party, unless the situation is too substantial—in such cases, the offense is brought before King Maushelik." Lord Darshel paused his almost too-calm account to take a sip of wine before continuing, "There are, of course, many enactments to the treaty that would be too long and cumbersome for a dinner such as this, but that is the overall gist of our contract. Nevertheless, our two nations still carry the scars and hatred brought on by the feud. My father's death at the Sheev'anee was just another casualty in our war."

Princess Éleen sympathized.

"How exactly did your father—I mean Lord Shekmann—die?" Prince Connel asked, intrigued by the scandal.

"It was retribution." Zyanthena replied coldly, despite the vile glances shot her way.

Lord Darshel motioned her for silence and supplied more information. "My father had taken a Tashek woman prisoner, abusing her to death. The Sheev'anee demanded payment, which my father did not give. In retribution, a tenth-level Sheek'ala, a death-dealer, snuck in that new moon and took my father's life then his own. Since then, neither of our peoples have defied the treaty."

"Until now." Commander Raic added, his voice tense and malicious. His eyes swept over Zyanthena. There was a dare in the man's eyes, as if he was wanting to anger the desert woman enough to push her into something stupid.

Lord Darshel pushed back his chair and rose to his full, intimidating height. He glowered at his cavalry commander in warning and glanced over to the Tashek woman. Under his stare, the beautiful warrioress crumbled into a submissive head-bow.

"Zyanthena's intrusion is taken lightly by me, in account that she was working under orders of Prince Fantill of Sealand and her Crystine Commander Matar." He told the two highnesses, knowing that, at least, the Prince of Sealand would be familiar to them. "Zyanthena is a scout of the Crystine and was trying to get word between the two armies. Her failure was being caught by my cavalry, nothing more. However, she is bound to the treaty. As her punishment, she is my prisoner until the time I release her."

Princess Éleen could not believe the reasoning behind Zyanthena's capture. "Why not release her then, Lord Shekmann, if she was only doing her duty?"

Zyanthena spoke before Lord Darshel could reply. "It is okay, Your Highness. As one bound to our treaty, I accept the punishment for my offense, as declared by His Majesty and His Lordship. It is my fault to bear, as I knew the consequences." She left out that her people had already decided her fate lay with the Shekmann. The Tashek's integrity impressed the Havenese princess.

"But why have her lead us to the Citadel when she is only a prisoner, then?" Lord Carrod asked, his question rude, considering the circumstances.

Lord Darshel answered shortly, unhappy with the dangerous direction the conversation was taking. He wished to end the discussion quickly. "Because tomorrow morning we travel through Tashek territory." The words sounded ominous. The table became quiet, all eyes on the Kavahadian lord. The dark-haired man schooled his features into a disarming countenance. "Guests, men and ladies, seeing as our meal is drawing to a close, I want to offer my wishes for a good night's sleep. We will be leaving before dawn and heading north to the Citadel of Light. So please, enjoy your desserts at your leisure and have a peaceful evening."

The meal ended shortly afterward. The guests and army men dispersed to their own businesses. Lord Darshel apologized to the royals for not having an after-dinner sit, begging off to finish his own preparations. He left with the blond woman in tow and Zyanthena following a distance behind. Six soldiers followed after the warrioress, a reminder of the Tashek's situation. Princess Éleen's group was among the last to leave; all were ready to find their beds and escape the tense turn of the evening.

§   §

Without preamble, Kavahad became quiet, filled with the slumbers of the occupants. The lingering traces of the intense evening flowed away as the gentleness of the night breeze lulled the people to sleep. Alone in the silence, only Zyanthena stayed awake, finding peace in the night. Her mind, though, fluctuated between consternation over her situation and the treaty and the anticipation of the coming day. Keen eyes wandered to the sleeping Lord Shekmann across the way. Prisoner she may well be... but tomorrow that status would change. Did the Lord of Kavahad realize that? In the morning, they would be in Sheev'anee territory. Then, it was up to her how the story would be written and how she would to make her case to the King of Staria. "The Princess of Blue Haven is a Star's send." She whispered to the dark. "I ride to the Citadel. There is hope yet where there had been none."

Chapter Eighteen

§

Counting

"And eighty-two."

The pen tallied another stroke.

"Eighty-three."

And, once more the pen scratched out the count.

"And five-thousand-six-hundred-and-eight-four. That's the last one."

Commander Matar tallied the last count and set his quill down in wearied sorrow. He leaned back in the old, squeaky chair, sighing deeply, and rubbed the tiredness from his face. Beside him, cast in the shadows from the flickering candlelight was Wix, Matar's second. He looked just as haggard as the Crystine commander felt. The two veterans had been up all night counting the lines of the dead outside of the Citadel's walls; first with a quick tally then with this long, repeated marking when the tremendous number of the dead had astounded the old commander. Even repeated, Matar was cursing the horribly high number of bodies. And, there was still the tallies from Commander Kins and Madden, who had gone to collect the numbers from the Starian cavalry and Golden Kingdom's archers. Their tally would not include the Tashek, who had requested to count their own. Matar was not looking forward to the total head-count. If the number of dead foot soldiers were any indication, the full result would be atrocious.

"You may find your bedroll now, Wix." Matar gently excused his second. The older man looked ready to fall asleep on his feet, despite his stubbornness to look alert. Wix nodded and stood to leave. "Also, sleep in, if you are able." Matar bid the man. "The best we can give Staria at this time is our fresh energy." Wix didn't bother replying to his commanding officer. The disappointed vexation in Matar's voice was enough to let the other man know how his commander really felt—the counting of the dead was no small task. The Crystine leader waited for Wix to leave before bringing an angry fist down on the flimsy desk, cracking the wood with its force. Matar welcomed the pain from the blow, wishing it could dull out the ferocity of his frustration. "Damn it! Why couldn't we be just a few hours sooner?!" The cool air of the desert night held no answer. Matar stifled an irritated growl and rose from the uncomfortable seat. Hoping to find Commander Kins, Matar stalked outside of the small tent to the ghastly sight of brining pyres and the sickly stench of the cooking bodies that wafted from them. There were so many fires… enough to make the night bright enough to walk comfortably without any other aide. The funeral pyres stretched out across the desert sand like a burning plain.

Matar's heart clenched at the sight.

A long walk later, Matar found Commander Kins speaking with a Golden Kingdom soldier, next to the line of dead archers. The tall, red-haired Rubian looked stoic and impervious admits the carnage, though Matar knew better from the tightness around the man's emerald eyes. The other commander was just as affected by the sheer mass of the bloodshed as he was. "Ethan." Matar greeted.

The other man finished his conversation with the soldier and turned to the Crystine commander. "Matar." Weariness etched his voice. "I guess you've finished your count?" The other man nodded. Commander Kins clenched his jaw and looked away before his sadness showed up in his eyes "Eight-two archers. Eight-hundred-and-twelve cavalry." He spoke grimly. "There is little left of the Starian cavalry or Prince Kent's archers Most of the archers died of complications in surgery just a few hours ago. Very few of the soldiers in critical care are expected to survive. The Tashek have been hesitant to say what their loses are, but I am guessing around one-hundred-and-fifty-to-eighty were killed. I do not even want to know how many horses I have had to put out of their misery."

"That puts our total around eight-thousand-five-hundred-and-twenty-nine." Matar concluded hollowly. "Over half the foot soldiers are dead."

"Blessed Stars!" Commander Kins cursed quietly. "If only we'd—." He stopped himself from going into the "if onlys". "The only good thing with us being here now is that the remaining army can get some rest…now that it's over."

"And we are keeping this city safe." Matar finished. He, at least, had not forgotten that there were five thousand maunstorz running unaccounted for from North Point. Stars only knew how Staria would fare if they attacked now.

"Yes, there is that." Ethan replied, sounding far from cheered. "Well, I doubt that there is anything more to do here. King Maushelik asked for us to come to him right as soon as we had the tally. He was not going to take any sleep tonight while there were men to be buried and soldiers to care for. I believe we will find him at the hospital."

The overcrowded hospital seemed to be a different world from the fires outside. The air was stuffy with the smell of blood and sweat, thankfully dampened by the night temperatures, and eerie groans of pain and suffering ghosted through the large rooms as men, unable to find relief from their wounds, could not get the release that came from sleep. The sounds from the suffering men was worse for the two commanders than the sight of the deceased because there was nothing to be done to ease the soldiers' pain. The doctors had long reported the lack of pain-relieving medicines by the first hours of the night—most of the analgesics having been used in surgery to try to save those of the men worse off, and, though the mertinean, Crystine, and Tashek had given what medicines and herbs they could, those amounts had gone just as quickly. The only relief left to the soldiers had been a massage-pressing therapy the Tashek knew. The healing touch had helped some of the soldiers, but, alas, for the ones with severed limbs or injuries to their organs or deep wounds, no relief was to be found.

Kind Maushelik had taken up the head physician's office, the only space not filled with the injured. The doctor and king were the only occupants, having taken a short reprieve from the on-going task of checking and tending to the wounded. The thirty-some-years-old physician looked harried, as if for all his skills and talents he was at a loss at the butchery to the soldiers. The king looked little better, though at his old age he hid the distress well. Only the deep craters of lines on the king's face showed what discord was under the stoical, tired expression he wore. Commander Matar and Kins respectfully entered the room.

"Come." King Maushelik stood from where he had slumped against the front of the physician's desk. He cast his weariness aside as he waved the two men in. "Sit. Sit, please. I know you both have been working since your arrival. Take some rest for your feet."

They obeyed, more out of respect to the Starian king than because they wanted to sit. The king waved the physician back to his seat and crossed the room to a pitcher of rose water and small cookies of oats and honey, set there to help the doctors and nurses have some refreshment on their shifts. Ignoring the three men's protests, King Maushelik poured the glasses himself and handed them and the cookies out. "Thank you, Your Majesty. Under the circumstances, this is not needed but welcomed."

King Maushelik frowned sternly. "This is indeed needed!" His voice sounded scolding. "I have done very little for my people while they died on the field because of this curse-ed, battered body of mine. Hell, I'd have been out with them if I had been able. Since I could not, I was forced to watch as my men got butchered out on that field. So, do not tell me my waiting on you is not needed. It is the least I should do for you men who fight. And, I want to hear it least of all from you both." King Maushelik jabbed a finger first at Matar, who had known the aged king most of his life, then at the mertinean. Both men had fought alongside the king when they had all been younger men.

The Crystine commander looked contrite, his apology in his eyes. "I understand what it is like to feel helpless, but you are not helpless, Majesty. You are Staria's king. As king, you keep your kingdom as peaceful as you are able. I have witnessed your justice many times and know you are a good king." Matar referred to King Maushelik's injury. "You have done your share for your people."

Matar's words seemed to console the ruler. His countenance relaxed, becoming replaced by weariness. "Pardon me." He gave a wan smile. "I should not put out such an attitude. Your condolence comforts me."

"We are all tired. It is expected that our fears may slip under such conditions."

"Yes, but as you said, I am king." King Maushelik drew out some of his breathe and straightened. "If I cannot appear strong, my people will lose their hope and fortitude. I must hold back my own insecurities for their sake."

The two commanders finished their refreshments and stood as well, setting their used china cups on the doctor's desk. The rose water and cookies had restored some of their energy, enough that they felt they could make it a few more hours. They followed the king as he indicated his wish to walk to the funeral pyres.

"I hesitate to ask but I must know," King Maushelik said as they walked next to him, "What the final count came to?"

Commander Kins' lips tightened grimly. "It is not good. We do not have the numbers from the Tashek but the Starian army fares ill." The king gave a stern eye, not wanting to wait out the worst any longer. Ethan continued his monologue, sounding unfazed. "Eight-hundred-and-twelve cavalrymen, eighty-two of the archers (fifty of those Prince Kent's), and five-thousand-six-hundred-and eighty-four foot soldiers."

"The supposed total is around six-thousand-five-hundred-and seventy-eight." Matar continued. "Though I suspect the number will rise another five-hundred-some when the Tashek report."

The king's face aged further at the full account. His usually strong eyes looked sad and dull. He closed them a moment. When they opened, Maushelik seemed to have resigned to the horrible facts before him. "I had hoped for better but under the unfortunate odds the men were against, I cannot say I am much surprised. Are the burial preparations going okay?"

"Everything was set up before the last light of dusk faded. The mourners are left tending to the flames and their prayers. Your men's souls leave in peace."

"Very good." The king answered shortly as they finally exited into the cool, desert night. "I will go now to pray with them. Continue as you will or take your rest. Your assistance has been appreciated." The two commanders saluted respectfully and turned to go. King Maushelik stopped them for one final moment. "Matar, Ethan." They turned back. "Thank you, for your friendship and your support. It really helps to have you here. The Stars bless you for this. I will see you in the morning."

Chapter Nineteen

§

Port Al-Harrad

The two search parties had run into each other just east of the Noway Mountains. Terrik Sheev'arid's Crystine force pulled their tired horses alongside Siv'arid's more rested men. The two cousins greeted each other respectfully as their men merged together and turned back toward north.

"Have you found traces of the maunstorz?"

Kor'mauk Siv'arid shook his head, sending his plaited hair flying. "They are gone with no trace. Kinda like the stories of old about Ravel, eh?"

Terrik glared in reprimand and glanced about at the handful of Crystine that were with him. "You will hold your tongue." He hissed.

Kor'mauk looked revoked. "It is not like they remember. There is no worry of anyone outside of the Guardianship understanding what we speak of."

"Yet I say there will be no talk of it!" Terrik ordered, using his position as the Shi'alam's son to silence the other man. Angered, Kor'mauk turned his mount away, giving room for Decond to ride up beside his Tashek tutor. Terrik set aside his own annoyance to acknowledge the young man. The desert man sensed that Decond had keen senses, ones he did not advertise and may not be aware of; the seventeen-year-old had picked up on the confrontation between the two Tashek and was being polite by not bringing it up. "Port Al-Harrad is another one-and-half-day's ride." Terrik informed his new charge. "How do you fare?"

Decond looked tired. He was not accustomed to marching at the mertinean's slow pace and the Crystine riding at cavalry pace had been much harder on him. Terrik knew he should sympathize with the youth, but he was still sour over having to baby-sit the farrier. The lad, however, had the sense of preservation about his person not to complain. "I am well enough." He replied quietly, stroking his grey mount's mane absently. If someone could look as lost and forlorn as Decond, Terrik would be surprised. When the Tashek did not comment, the young man continue, as if that was expected of him.

"Will there be a place to rest sometime soon? I noticed Lieutenant Durham's' mare needs to be reshod."

Terrik hid a knowing smile. "See ahead on the horizon, that dark shape?" The farrier nodded. "That is the tip of the Noway Mountains. We will stop there, where it will be cooler. However, it will be in about one hour. Do you feel the mare can wait that long?" Decond considered and nodded. The mare's shoe hadn't been that bad, it had just made a valid excuse. "Then you can take care of the mare then. Our party will rest for an hour then continue to Port Al-Harrad. The Prince of Sealand is meeting us there."

Decond looked surprised and suddenly nervous. "The-the prince? Why?"

It seemed the lad had not expected to meet any of the royals. Terrik was amused. As a Tashek, being highly respected by his own king, he was accustomed to being called to the Citadel. It had been one of the perks of being high-up in his people's ranks. Though it would be his first time meeting the Heir of Sealand's throne. Word was, Prince Par was a man of high regard. Terrik was thrilled at the prospect of meeting him. Knowing he had lapsed too long in silence, Terrik addressed Decond's question. "Prince Par Fantill and my father, the Shi'alam, are going to head to the Citadel of Light. Apparently, now that the threat has subsided, representatives of other kingdoms are amassing there to discuss this threat on Syre's northern boarders. Finally. Prince Fantill and the Shi'alam want to join this discussion, but they were waiting for our scouting party to give the clear on the missing enemy."

Decond looked confused. "I heard no announcement that there was going to be discussions held at the Citadel." Wow, the kid could be bold when he wanted to, and very perceptive!

"It is informal. More, they are having it because of who is travelling there. I heard Princess Éldon-Tomino, betrothed of Prince Maushelik will be arriving, as it the second prince of Sunrise. Plus, with all of the commanders of the norther kingdoms present, the king called an impromptu "war council". This is the first they have been able to get together in over two years." Decond nodded his understanding, making Terrik a little less annoyed with him. The orphan had a good head on him; maybe, their "apprenticeship" would not be so bad.

§   §

The sun was beginning to set over the city, casting long rays through the alleyways and junctions of the wind-weathered buildings. Seagulls floated lazily on the cool sea breeze, their bellies having been filled by the fishing boats' scrapes. The brazen beat of a bell called across the port, notifying sailors of the final barges and sea-faring craft arriving at the docks. Beyond the bustle of the main port were the markets, packing up for the evening. On a typical day, those stalls lined the lower streets of Port Al-Harrad, separating the docks from the rest of the city.

The rest of Port Al-Harrad had been built up the slow incline of cliffs. The governor's and city officials' buildings were on the top-most point, overlooking the wandering town below. Since the port was mainly on an upward angle, its streets were want to being a confusing maze, running hither and yon to adjust to the multiple levels of cliff faces. That evening, they were relatively quiet, as most of the townspeople were back home eating their dinners. Without the usual crush of bodies on the streets, the large Tashek cavalry had an easy time reaching the northern gates of the governor's walled compound.

Young Decond's ice-blue eyes were wide in wonderment as he took in the unusual sprawl of the city. The farrier had never been to a port city before—not to mention any cities except those in the Crystal Kingdom. He took in the sight with innocent eyes. Terrik leaned closer to his charge. "You will need to stick close to me." He informed the youth. "People here are not to be trusted on their word. They like to take advantage whenever they see a chance." He let his warning hang in the air. Decond acknowledged the appraisal, though Terrik was not sure if he really took it seriously.

Kor'mauk kneed his horse ahead of the group to speak with the guards at the gate. The rest of the cavalry halted their mounts a short distance away and waited patiently. A few minutes passed, as if the guards needed verification from inside, but, finally, the wrought-iron gates were swung open. The band of sixty-two horses trotted inside.

The grounds inside held just enough room for the Tashek and Crystine horses, but not by much. The clop of shod and unshod hooves echoed off the cobbled courtyard and stone walls of the buildings, being an announcement to the city of the Tashek's arrival. The horsemen stopped in a perfect line and dismounted, just as the doors at the west end of the yard opened and a group of soldiers, Tashek, and pages strode out to greet the newcomers. Kor'mauk and Terrik stepped forward to address the governor's captain, stating why they were there. The plump man saluted them in respect when he realized who they were; Tashek had a good following in most of Staria's cities. The captain informed them that Governor Thornhoff was awaiting them in his den and that the Shi'alam and Prince of Sealand were also there. The rest of the Tashek and Crystine men were waved toward the stable to put the horses in the hands of the stablemaster. A lieutenant was instructed to show the men to the mess hall and then their bunks. The captain then waved the two Sheev'anee with him. As they headed off, Terrik motioned for Decond to follow. The farrier joined them hesitantly.

The captain led them up the small staircase and into the west wing of the governor's large manse. He continued down the long hallway to the belly of the house, taking a left into the parlor just off the spacious reception room. The common room beyond was warmed by a fire, keeping at bay the damp chill that had begun to permeate the air as the sun set beyond the ocean. A small table was against the eastern wall, adorned with a silver tray of pastries, a pitcher of wine, and a decanter of fine honey-whiskey. On the other side of the room, plush leather chairs and a loveseat were arranged around the fire, a small oak table between the furniture. Four men were already sitting, enjoying their drinks and talking. They looked up as the captain led Kor'mauk, Terrik, and Decond inside.

The two Tashek bowed respectfully, Decond quickly following suit as he realized the men in the chairs must be the governor, the Prince of Sealand, and the Shi'alam. The captain saluted shortly, announced them then dismissed himself. Once the man was gone, Governor Thornhoff stood and waved the three men to join them. The governor struck Decond as a pompous, flamboyant official, with his curly wig and expensive clothing. He smiled, overly-friendly, at the new-comers, waving about a ring-studded hand that was partly obscured in the long lace at the cuffs of his sleeves. Decond was surprised the man didn't knock over his drink, or somebody else's, in his overly exaggerated motions. However, the man's invitation to sit and recover from their long journey was sensible enough; maybe looks could be deceiving...

While Terrik and Decond joined the others, Kor'mauk went to the small refreshment table to respectfully procure a drink and food for the Shi'alam's son and his new apprentice. He brought the items for Terrik and Decond then went back for his own drink. Meanwhile, the Shi'alam and his son greeted each other, not displaying much affection despite both being happy to see each other alive and well. Terrik introduced Decond to his father as his new apprentice. Decond was astonished when the Sheev'anee leader accepted him warmly. He had expected the elder Sheev'arid to stare at him sternly or unapprovingly, but neither judgement flavored the desert man's greeting. The Shi'alam then proceeded to introduce the other men, starting with the governor, then over to Prince Par Fantill and his Lord Protector Gordar Farrylin.

Prince Par was a very open and honest person, Decond sensed right away. The blond-haired Sealander stood as he was introduced, offering his hand to greet them. He smiled kindly. His genuine hello was disarming and personal, as he looked both the Tashek and orphan in the eye. Decond could not help liking the prince right away; after all, he had learned throughout his hard life that it took a very special, kind-hearted character to stand up and treat a nobody like they were a somebody. Immediately, the tension Decond had held since Terrik had first announced the prince would be at Port Al-Harrad dissolved, leaving the farrier feeling less uncomfortable with the thought of being around royalty.

The Lord Protector shook Decond's hand just as respectfully as his prince had. "It is good to see you have made it safely across the Aras, young farrier."

"Ah, th-thank you, Your Lordship." He responded quickly. Without Zyanthena next to him, Decond was acting more bashful. "I am glad you made it across safely as well." Stars, he felt his words were said so poorly, denoting his low, uncultured status!

Lord Gordar did not seem to note the poor response. "Thank you, Decond. I was able to reach my prince quickly, all thanks to the Tashek." That time, the lord looked to Terrik, who responded with a graceful head bow. "Your people's skills with the horses and Star's speed had us arriving at North Point just in time."

"I am glad to hear that, Your Lordship." Terrik bowed. The four men took their seats.

Once they were all comfortable, Prince Par started in on the most pressing question. "So, Sheev'arid, Siv'arid, is it safe to travel to the Citadel of Light or have there been signs of the enemy that make passage concerning?"

Kor'mauk respectfully referred the question to Terrik, as rank demanded. "There have been no signs of the maunstorz, either by my party or Siv'arid's. It is as you reported from North Point, the maunstorz are simply gone. I could see the possibility of this being a trap to get you, Highness, away from the strength of your army but that is only stipulation. Beyond that, I see no other dangers. If you are still wanting to reach King Maushelik, it should be safe enough."

"I am." Prince Par answered, his voice commanding and direct. "The Shi'alam," he nodded his head in the Sheev'anee's direction, "And I have received word from His Majesty of Staria that the maunstorz at the Citadel have been defeated. While we have this small reprieve, he wishes to have a War Council. The commanders Matar and Kins are at the Citadel, too, as are Prince Argetlem and his lord protector, Lieutenant-Commander Sloane. Representatives from Blue Haven and Sunrise have been reported, too. With myself and Lord Gordar, and your Tashek clans, most of Syre's armies will be in presence in some form. This opportunity had not come around in years. I do not want to miss this."

The Shi'alam motioned his son for silence and sat forward in his chair. "We are in agreeance, Prince Fantill; however, my son's caution is warranted. I will consult with the oracle and her order. If they see no cause for concern, we will leave at dawn. If not, we will revisit our options." He looked into Par's ocean-blue eyes, his dark gaze having its own power, and it said for the prince to trust. The Sealander sucked back a breath and nodded, standing down to the authority. The Shi'alam rose from his chair. "Then, I will go immediately, Highness, Governor. Your answer will come shortly." He motioned for Terrik to stand but commanded Kor'mauk to stay with the prince and governor. The Shi'alam made for the door.

Terrik grabbed Decond's wrist and pulled the youth to his feet. Decond was confused, as he had not been invited in the Shi'alam's summons, but followed Terrik without comment. Once the three of them were away from the hearing of the others, Terrik questioned his father. "Why leave so quickly, father? There was very little discussed."

The Shi'alam turned to his son, his turbaned head lowered to meet Terrik's eyes. Decond stepped back, intimidated. He had not realized the Shi'alam was much taller than his son, though Terrik stood about five-foot-ten. The desert leader made a frightening figure in his dark robes and powerful frame. Terrik did not back down from his father, however.

"The time is pressing, and I, for one, am ready to be from the governor's manse. Stupid man, too cowardly to help Sealand or Staria when aid was needed but just pontifical enough to indulge us after the threat is gone." The Shi'alam shook his head at the insanity. He changed the subject before it irritated him overly much. "The maunstorz will return, of that I am certain. But the Stars have given us reprieve so that we can get the prince to the Citadel of Light safely. An event it approaching, one of great importance. The oracle is unsure as to what that is yet, but she warns that the council—including Sealand—must all be together before the next full moon."

"That is in three days."

"Yes. Which is why I make haste."

Terrik was not consoled. "Why though, father? The oracle had never been so vague. What is she keeping from us?"

Anger brought a flash to the Shi'alam's face. "Do not insult the oracle. She had never been wrong."

"You know something, don't you?" The statement was bold. The Shi'alam began to make a comment but then seemed to remember Decond, who was cowering against the wall trying to disappear from the heated conversation. Terrik also glanced the farrier's way. "Decond was ordered to be my apprentice by the Khataum. He knows about Ravel and some of the Prism. He is to be a Guardian. Whatever you have to say, you can say in front of him."

The Shi'alam dressed Decond down with his eyes. The look had the youth shrinking farther into the wall. He had never felt so completely stripped naked before, but the Shi'alam did so very capably. The farrier hoped what the man saw was not too damning. "The oracle's prophesy had begun. She said you would find your Khapta in the Crystal Kingdom and you have. You must have him ready by the last cycle of the next turning of the sun. Once we are done at the Citadel, you and Decond must go to the oracle. She had need of you to find the last three stones."

Terrik's eyes narrowed but he nodded at the order. "What else of the prophecy?"

"That is for the oracle to tell you." The Shi'alam sidestepped the question.

"Father—."

"Enough! I must go. The full moon is nearly upon us. Order the men ready; we will make haste to the Citadel. The prophecy requires it." He glanced back at Decond. "And get him some real clothing. The boy is no longer a farrier but a Guardian of the Prism. You should treat him better."

Terrik watched his father storm away in the billow of his dark, desert robes. "Well, that went well," he murmured sarcastically and looked back at Decond. "Come on, we have work to do."

Prince Par sat back in his chair, unnerved by how the Shi'alam had so easily overpowered him with just a glance. He kept the emotions off his face, as he had been schooled. It would not do for a prince to look weak, especially among men loyal to a different throne. The governor of Port Al-Harrad might strike an insensate facade but the Sealander knew it took a shrewd mind to hold the station of chief administrator for fifteen-plus years. And not to forget the Tashek in the other chair; Kor'mauk Siv'arid, cousin of the Sheev'arids, would most certainly note any weakness in the royal. All the Tashek seemed apt at picking out such characteristics in other people. It was unnerving.

Governor Thornhoff took a sip of his whiskey and picked up the conversation again. "It sounds like your stay will be quite short, Your Highness. A shame really. There are many sights here at Port Al-Harrad I would have loved to show the Heir of Sealand."

Prince Par pushed aside his thoughts to answer. "If we had been able to stay, I would have enjoyed seeing your city; however, recent events in Sealand and Staria call me to duties elsewhere."

"A shame that." The governor repeated, lips tightening unhappily at the fact that he could not milk a royal for some prestige. Though the man had been allowed to know about most of the details of the battles at North Point and the Citadel, both Prince Par and the Shi'alam had chosen to withhold the matter of the vanishing maunstorz army. The man had not been deemed worthy enough because of his lack of support to the forces when it meant something; having the man create rumors and panic was also a part of the reasoning for keeping the truth from the governor. Even if Thornhoff suspected that there were omissions, neither man indulged him.

"Well, may I suggest you at least take a stroll about my grounds as dinner is prepared? It has a nice panorama of the city." Thornhoff said. "I would join you but, alas, I have an appointment I cannot miss."

Prince Par felt tired. Tired from fighting and tired of having to be polite. The offer of being away from the governor—or any duties harder than a simple stroll—sounded too good to pass up. "I find that a fabulous idea, Governor." He replied. "I would love to see the view of your city at sunset. Have a man come get me when the meal is ready."

Governor Thornhoff stood and bowed, his torso bouncing up and down in multiple bows. "Yes, of course, Your Highness. And, I do apologize for not being able to stay and attend to you myself." Prince Par waved away the last statement. He really hoped the man would go soon; his civility was flowing away quickly. "Then I will call a servant to lead you around."

"There is no need." Kor'mauk stepped into the conversation before the governor could turn away. "I have been here before. I know the grounds well enough that I will take them."

Governor Thornhoff seemed flustered at that but accepted the Tashek's words. With more apologies and bows the man backed out of the room.

Lord Gordar sighed in relief, once the administrator was away. Par caught himself starting to mimic the action. Picking up his drink, the royal put back the last of his whiskey and stood. "Well, let's get to it then."

"We don't really need to go, Highness, if you are not up to it." Kor'mauk said, perhaps having sensed the prince's fatigue.

"No, Siv'arid. It is quite all right. A good stroll sounds nice and the cold ocean air may bring some life back to me." The Tashek bowed, acceding to the royal's wishes. He motioned them to follow and led the way through the large manse. He stopped by their quarters first so Par and Gordar could get their woven capotes before heading out into the evening costal air.

The Tashek led them through a small portico off to the right side of the large house. The cold stone of the area still had a small sliver of the golden rays of the descending sun but the rest of the structures were a dull grey. Beyond, a large, cobble-stoned veranda overlooked the cliffs. A bronze railing fenced off the drop of the cliffs, its once beautiful gleam tarnished a grey-green color from the exposure to the salty sea air. The prince stepped up to the rail and gripped the spade heads, feeling the cold metal, hard, against his palms. He breathed deeply of the brisk air and let go a breath, relaxing. Lord Gordar joined Par a few minutes later, after giving his prince some time alone. The two cousins acknowledged each other, then glanced back to the scene of the sprawling city spread out below them.

The darkness descended gradually, despite the sun having already slipped beyond the horizon. The calm silence of the approaching night soothed the two Sealanders. It seemed ethereal after the long three weeks of war. Prince Par finally stirred. "Tomorrow will be desert for as far as the eye can see." His breath followed his words in little clouds.

"Yeah," Gordar replied, knowing where his cousin's thoughts were going, "It'll be your first time in such a dry place, no water for miles around."

Par wrinkled his nose in distaste at the thought. It felt good to be able to act unprincely, sharing the action with his kin. "I'm not sure I'm ready for this."

The lord protector chuckled. "No, probably not. I'm sure you'll shrivel up like a cat fish on dry land without the taste of ocean air in your lungs."

"Right." He rolled his eyes.

Lord Gordar smiled broadly and laughed. "Well, maybe...I would hope you would make it through the council meeting before you completely dry to a husk."

"You're awful." Par teased. He shook his head, still amused.

"This is all very good and brave of you, Par."

The prince slowly sobered, feeling his cousin's sincerity. "It needs to be done, cuz. My father cannot risk the trip, but we need to secure the northern boarders again—and speak with King Maushelik."

"Still, there are others you could have sent in your place. I admire you for doing this, not just for your people, but because you hold yourself to such high standards. It is nice to see."

Prince Par regarded his cousin quietly. Lord Gordar rarely complimented him, though he often thanked his cousin and was always supportive. It felt comforting to know his cousin and lord protector regarded him so highly. "Thank you, Gordar."

"Highness." The blond-haired man bowed his head. "I would follow you anywhere."

Prince Par nodded to the declaration. "I'll hold you to that." His eyes gleamed in amusement, as he found he could not hold his solemnness for long. "A catfish? You really think I'm like a catfish out of water?"

Lord Gordar could not help laughing, too. "Yes, Highness, I do."

Chapter Twenty

§

Royal Procession

The distant haze of Paragon Oasis wavered in the heat, a green beacon in the golden-brown landscape. To the parched travelers, it seemed so far away. Only the enticing thoughts of refreshing shade, rest, and water had the Havenese and Kavahadian procession marching onward; however, after days of the heat and sand many of the men were cantankerous. Angry spats were less and less likely to be kept under the breath. Most of the irritable words were cast onto their Tashek guide.

Zyanthena, despite the disrespectful language thrown her way, had been true to her word, guiding the royal procession unerringly. She and her loose black stallion led the travelers during the cooler parts of the day, requiring the procession to rest during the worst part of the heat. The men were ungrateful, however, and the desert woman rarely spoke to anyone. She kept her words to her black companion alone as they led the way. She made sure that much of her time was spent near the front of the line, keeping a careful watch for other Tashek and even the unaccounted for maunstorz army.

Since the beginning of the journey, Zyanthena had earned her keep by steering away a small band of curious Tashek, under the command of a lesser clan, and diplomatically averting her people's attentions away from noting the Kavahad soldiers accompanying the Havenese; that brush had been very tense but she had kept the group safe. Yet, as the main desert oasis loomed closer, its palm trees becoming clearer in the evening landscape, the Tashek woman signaled her mount to a stop. She motioned for the other horses and carts to do the same. Grumbling ensued but her command was followed. Lord Darshel, Lord Carrod, and Commander Raic cantered their horses to the front to speak with her.

"Why do you ask us to stop, Zyanthena?" Lord Darshel asked. Beside him, Commander Raic sneered, satisfied that there was a reason to berate the warrioress.

"Your Lordship," Zyanthena began, ignoring the cavalry commander, "We are approaching Paragon Oasis. Beside it being the largest landmark used on the trade routes and a place to rest, it is the main encampment for the Sheev'anee." She looked over the desert sands, her brown eyes narrowed in trepidation. "It will be harder to blend in among the Havenese there. Your people will have to be extra cautious." She looked back at Darshel. "It would not be wise to start a conflict."

"A conflict? How would that happen?" Carrod asked from Darshel's offside.

Zyanthena gave Darshel a look that said she could not believe the stupid words pointed her way. The Kavahadian motioned for her to indulge the ignorant Havener. "We may not be at war, Lord, but under the circumstances—all of us being under the summons of the king and escort to Your Highness and the Sunarian crown—it would be rash to cause any grievances between Kavahad and the Sheev'anee. That is a fight we should not be willing to provoke. Are all the men able to withhold their impudence while we are Paragon?" She addressed Lord Darshel, "For if they are not, we would be wise to skirt the oasis."

Lord Carrod spoke before the Kavahadian lord could reply. "I think My Highness Princess Éleen and my men are in need of rest and shade. We are unused to this climate and already many days into our travel. The oasis had been a welcoming reward for our march. She would ask that you take her there despite the issues between your people."

Zyanthena nodded at the man's words but her sharp eyes were on Lord Darshel, waiting for him to make the final say. Her show of respect was not lost on the Shekmann. "I understand your concerns, Zy'ena, and yours as well, Lord Nexlé." Darshel's handsome face was very serious as he considered their options. "It would look suspicious if my men separated from the procession, correct?"

Zyanthena nodded. "It may even cause the Sheev'anee to attack them."

"Then I see no way around it." Lord Darshel commanded. "We will rest at Paragon and I will have my men behave themselves. Just tell us how you would like to approach and we will comply."

"Your Lordship." Zyanthena head-bowed. "Unfurl the Havenese banners, all of them, not just the one already in place. Have the Havenese soldiers on our perimeter, your men to their inside. I want

Lord Nexlé and Prince Sunrise to the fore. You and your commanders are to escort the royal carriage. None of your men are to reach for or draw a weapon and do not flash a single emblem or say any curses that will alert the Sheev'anee that your men are from Kavahad. And, Lord Shekmann," She paused, meeting his emerald eyes brazenly, "You should cover yourself. You look too much like your father, dressed as you are. They will recognize you."

"This is preposterous!" Commander Raic objected. "There are too few Havenese to escort us as there is. Having them at our perimeter makes us defenseless against an attack. Lord—."

"It will be done." Lord Darshel conceded, shutting his cavalry commander up. "I will allow you to speak with anyone who stops us and to pick out a spot to rest that is unobtrusive to the Tashek. Just keep us safe."

"Yes, Your Lordship. As long as your men behave, I will do my part."

The sheltered springs that made up the Paragon Oasis came into view just as the last light of dusk was receding. The tall palm trees swayed gently in the evening breeze, rustling calmingly. Two groups of travelers were already on the western side of the springs, nestled against the only short cliffs in the area. A stream wandered from spring to spring, having carved a sheltering canyon, until it ended in the last pool on the eastern side. Though the western area was the more sheltered place to camp, Zyanthena kept the procession to the east, among the numerous palm trees.

As the party stopped and began to set up camp, a Tashek wandered over to check them out. Zyanthena was quick to meet him, with Lord Carrod and Prince Connel in tow. Lord Darshel felt himself brace for trouble as the four of them met. The two Tashek spoke with each other in keshic, Zyanthena motioning to the two men with her as she conversed. The other desert man motioned repeatedly to the soldiers and to Lord Carrod and the prince. The conversation looked heated. Suddenly, the man yelled something Lord Darshel could only guess was meant to be insulting and the robed warrior jumped away from Zyanthena, sword in hand. Carrod and Prince Connel backed away nervously, their eyes flickering back to the procession. Instantly, there was a tension in the air.

"Do not move!" Zyanthena yelled back to the soldiers. She kept her body facing the other Tashek but motioned for everyone to stay calm with her left hand. She continued to keep a careful watch on the other clansman, her hand floating near her own sword—which Darshel had finally given her before their approach.

To their credit, the Kavahadian and Havenese soldiers obeyed her command.

The challenging Tashek spoke again, still sounding insulting, and leapt at the warrioress. Just as it looked like he would strike her down, she drew her blade, quicker than a flash of lightning, to perry his attack. The man jumped away and came at her again, beginning the deadly dance high-leveled practitioners of She-koum-o used to judge their skills. They circled each other, swords clashing, and pressed the swings to a faster tempo. Zyanthena broke the pattern by rolling out if it, kicking sand up toward the other's face. She spun back at him, changing the dance from a circle to a line, pushing the other Tashek backwards. From the outside, the two fighters looked to be in a well-choreographed display of spins, jumps, kicks, and sword perries but there was something about the energy of the dance that seemed deadly.

The challenger returned Zyanthena's push, forcing her back along the line. The young woman faltered in the sand. Seeing her missed step, the Tashek man called out some victorious whoop and increased his attack. Zyanthena barely got her kora up in time, the weak move allowing the other to knock the sword to the side. Somehow, the desert warrioress kept a hold of the weapon, though the shock up her arm had to be numbing. She waited the few breaths it took for the man to change his sword's direction. Then, just as he began to strike downward toward her, she leapt up and around the swing. Zyanthena's blade came to a stop at the man's open throat. Just like that, the two fighters froze.

The Tashek man said something in keshic and slowly backed away from Zyanthena. His neck wound began to bleed as he stepped out from her blade. He bowed deeply to her, his eyes and head downcast in a sign that she had his life in her hands. Without looking at her, he sheathed his sword and continued to back away. It was only as he disappeared into the tents of one of the other caravans that Zyanthena dropped her sword.

Immediately, Lord Darshel and a small handful of his men came out to surround Prince Connel and Lord Nexlé. They were still tense, eyeing the area for more challengers as they hustled the two men back into the safety of the group. As they rejoined the others, Lord Darshel and Commander Raic came over to Zyanthena. Nearing her, Lord Darshel finally got to see the aftermath of the Tashek fight. The desert warrioress sheathed her blade respectfully and tried to calm her heavy panting enough to say, "Your Lordship." She brushed the desert sand off of her clothes only to reveal how many slices the other man's sword had given her. There were enough marks that Lord Darshel was surprised none of the outfit fell off of her lovely frame. It also seemed a miracle that most of the sword touches had not drawn blood.

"Zy'ena, what just happened?"

The Tashek woman picked at her clothing to straighten it, finding the Kavahadian shirt and pants still uncomfortable. "He did not believe my claim to the Sheev'anee. Since I am not wearing my desert saer'rek nor my emblem, he said I could not be one of the Tashek. Such a claim can only be denied by the sword."

"Can he, or another Tashek, attack again?"

She shook her head. "No, Your Lordship. I proved myself by the sword. They should not question me again."

"Should not." Commander Raic muttered, unbelieving.

Lord Darshel glared a warning to his cavalry commander and asked the question himself. "You said should, Zy'ena. Do you have any worry of another challenge?"

The desert woman looked away from the Shekmann's imploring eyes. "There is a small possibility of another challenge, but only if they still doubt me. I almost lost, Sire." She said the admittance quietly, as if ashamed of the fact. "He had the fight. It is only by luck that I bested him."

Lord Darshel wasn't sure if it was her honesty or just how unnerved her eyes looked but he felt as if the Tashek woman had just diverted a very bad situation; she knew just how close they had come and was keeping everyone else unaware of the danger by passing it off as nothing out of the normal. He ordered Commander Raic to help organize the camp setup. Once the man left, he continued to probe Zyanthena with questions, hoping that their unstable truce would yield more clarifying answers. "I wish to understand what this challenge means to the safety of the procession. I did not know there were such things as these "challenges". Has my denying you certain items, such as your emblem, endangered us?"

With Commander Raic gone, Zyanthena seemed surer of herself. She still fingered her sword hilt nervously but met Darshel's emerald eyes. "Denying me my emblem and ruining my saer'rek had diminished my ability to pass off a Tashek but that alone does not excuse them from questioning me as a Sheev'anee. I gave a different name to him, one of my cousin's names, and he denied the station of that name over his. "She shrugged. "As a lesser clansman, he should have accepted my word. HIs dismissal of it, by my rank, is cause for me to petition my father to avenge the insult. But, seeing as I am your prisoner and disavowed from my people, I cannot pull rank. If we stay more than one day, he may suspect that I bluffed my station.

"As for these "challenges", any Tashek can challenge another if they feel the other has lied or overstepped themselves. I do not feel he had the right to challenge me, but, as it had already been done, there is little that can be changed. The man that provoked it was young, little older than myself, and looking for action. The only good thing with being challenged so openly is that I proved I am what I said. The problem is, if others were watching, they would notice how close I came to losing. If there are any others itching for a fight, there is a possibility of someone beating me."

"How long do you feel we will be safe here?"

Zyanthena replied curtly, not sugar-coating the situation. "We will not be safe until we reach the Citadel; however, I feel that, for tonight, we will not get any other inquiries. To avoid another challenge, we should leave before the sun rises and avoid venturing beyond our camp perimeter."

"You will have no problem convincing us to stay close after that display." Lord Darshel assured her. He let a charming smile soften his face. "Thank you for preventing a worse situation." He said sincerely.

Zyanthena bowed her head in acceptance of the compliment and motioned for them to join the procession. Lord Darshel walked with her, finding the change between them to be both intriguing and useful. Being away from Kavahad had seemed to lessen the woman's dampened spirit, though she continued to be vigilant and wary. The

Starian lord had been impressed by her self-control against his men's insults and at how skillfully she led the procession. Lord Darshel was beginning to see why she had been a valued scout for the Crystine; he was almost hoping he could see her in action on the battlefield—especially after the performance she just went through—but he also prayed it would not be too soon.

Princess Éleen had one of her bodyguards call Lord Darshel and Zyanthena to her tent. They came to the call out of respect for her position, though the Shekmann was not really wanting to speak to the royal to satisfy her curiosity. He thoroughly enjoyed playing with women but having to bow down to one he could not entertain was not something he wished to do; it was not wise to mess with royalty. However, Lord Darshel knew that, as long as he was the princess's escort, he had to play the generous host and ignore the royal's gender.

Beside the tall lord, Zyanthena seemed to be content to come to the princess's call. Perhaps it was that they were both women—or maybe some other reason—but Lord Darshel sensed the Tashek held the Havenese royal in high regard. The Kavahadian stopped the Tashek before they entered. "Do you wish to change your clothes first, Zy'ena?"

The Tashek seemed surprised at the question. Was it possible that she had forgotten that the outfit she wore was cut to pieces? "There is no need, Your Lordship. The Princess of Blue Haven wishes to see us right now and I've no pressing need to tend to myself. A disordered wardrobe is not cause enough to not present myself before Her Highness."

Lord Darshel frowned. "I will ignore your appearance for the time being, but when we are at the Citadel of Light, you must take measures to be more presentable."

She rose her eyebrows. "As you wish, Your Lordship." Zyanthena answered though her demeanor showed she was being coy. The fact that she was showing a little of her old, rebellious spirit almost had Lord Darshel relieved—if it wasn't for the fact that they could become at odds again as her disposition improved. He nodded to her before stepping up to the Havenese tent and pushing through the entrance flap.

Princess Éleen's small pavilion had a short entranceway leading into the main chamber. Two small rooms led off on either side, the princess's and Lord Nexlé's private bedrooms. The princess, Havenese lord, and a handful of bodyguards sat around a small table, nibbling on some meat pies and finger vegetables. As Darshel and Zyanthena entered, the royal greeted them from her seat and motioned them over. "Lord Shekmann, Zyanthena, please sit and help yourself to some food and drink."

They both sat but only took a small portion of vegetables and a cup of tea. Lord Darshel had not wanted either, not while his men worked to set up the camp outside, but he knew to not except the offered meal would be insulting. Zyanthena took her lead from him. The action had the Kavahadian wondering why the Tashek was being so respectful to his person, but it was not the time or place to ask. He stored the question away and took a sip of bergamot tea.

"That was quite the display out there," the princess addressed Zyanthena.

The desert woman's eyes looked guarded but she replied to the unasked question. "That was not a display, Your Highness. He was questioning our authority to be here." Lord Darshel found her choice of words intriguing. "Our right to camp had been won. They will leave us alone now."

"How barbaric." The Tashek tensed at Prince Connel's words and turned around to watch the Sunarian as he strode the rest of the way into the room. "Your people fight for space to camp. Isn't that a little old-fashioned and crude?"

Though her brown eyes flashed, Zyanthena held her composure against the insult. "Your Highness knows nothing of my people and yet you judge, so just who here is the uncivilized?" Her voice was pleasant, like she had just complimented the prince, but her words cut right back. It was entertaining to see how well the "barbaric" Tashek woman could throw back political insults. The Sunrise royal glowered but made no retort. Zyanthena continued unfazed. "It is common practice for my people to be suspicious until proven otherwise to anyone passing through our lands. What the man and I did out there was merely a "feeling out" sort of gesture, much like a handshake or greeting is to you."

"Some handshake." Prince Connel muttered as he picked up a cup of tea and leaned casually on a tent pole. Though his smug, royal arrogance was in check, there was no doubt in anyone's mind who held the highest rank in the room. It was almost a shame that such a youthful, comely face had to cover the Sunarian royals' callous mind. Ah, breeding at its finest.

Princess Éleen studied the other royal, as if she was trying to determine what the prince's end game was. When the twenty-year-old only continued to sip his tea in silence, she returned her attention to Zyanthena and Lord Darshel. "So, you are saying we passed their inspection." She reasoned. "I am consoled by that, though I must admit your people's methods are somewhat extreme. It was fortunate that you are our guide and able to understand the diplomatic steps needed to allow our passage."

Lord Darshel hid a smirk behind his cup. He found the Havenese princess's words naïve. Certainly, someone should have schooled her and the Southern Kingdoms about the Northern customs. Yet, it seemed all of these Southerners were unaware of the political blunders. No Northerners would have mistaken the Tashek she-koum-o dance as anything but a Tashek-to-Tashek challenge. The skills needed to survive the feat were beyond other people's abilities—a fact the Tashek did not flaunt. If Zyanthena had not been the one to speak with the man (say the prince or Lord Carrod has greeted the Tashek instead) the warrior would undoubtedly not have challenged them. The only reason he had was because of Zyanthena. The fact that she had accepted the challenge had been that she had not wanted the other Tashek to inspect the procession closely. She had distracted him by adhering to their customs. For all its danger, it had worked.

Zyanthena accepted the princess's words without correcting her. "Indeed, Your Highness. Now, with your leave, there is work to be done to the camp. May I be excused to do so?"

The royal hid her surprise at the Tashek's direct, almost rude, question of dismissal. It was a reversal of the woman's usually polite speech and Éleen was almost hurt that Zyanthena had been so abrupt. The princess noted that Lord Darshel also seemed taken aback by his prisoner's sudden commanding words. "Almost." Éleen replied. She hoped her men would not think less of her for appearing weak in front of the other woman and the Kavahadian lord. "I have some questions for Lord Shekmann. If he wishes for you to leave, then he may dismiss you." She hoped her tone didn't sound too offended but knew, as a royal heir, that she had to appear indifferent to those of lesser standing. To calm her thoughts, the princess fingered the topaz stone around her neck, feeling more relaxed as she felt the smooth hardness in her grasp.

"I apologize if I seemed rude, Your Highness, My Lordship. It is just that from the viewpoint of a soldier, it is imperative to get camp set up before night falls. My words were not meant to offend."

The princess bowed her head just enough to indicate she accepted the apology.

Lord Darshel, however, was staring at Zyanthena calculatingly. Never before had she called him by "*My Lordship*". The change in wording had him suspicious that she was up to something. "Zyanthena can stay until all your inquiries are answered, Princess. Though, she is right that we should be about setting up for the night."

"In that case, Lord Shekmann, I will be brief." Éleen replied reassuringly. "Mainly, I would like to know how much longer our trip will take. My men and I are not accustomed to this heat, and I am wishing to get through it as quickly as possible. Also, once we arrive at the Citadel, will you continue to escort us to the king? Do you feel that would be acceptable? I would also like to know about King Maushelik from your lips. I only know what I have been told about the Starian throne through my tutors. I feel I will know the situation better coming from words of a fellow Starian."

It was an unusual request, her last question, but Lord Darshel's evaluation of the princess's naivety went down. She had admitted to being uninformed, a fact some people would look down on as a political folly; however, Darshel was relieved to hear she was smart enough to know when she was lacking. He smiled a disarming, charming smile. "The first question I defer to Zyanthena."

The Tashek answered shortly. "Less than two days, Your Highness, if the winds blow true. We should reach the Citadel well before dusk the second day."

"Very well. I am relieved to hear that." She turned her china-blue eyes back to the Starian lord expectantly. There seemed to be some underlying tension in the room from the short answers. If anyone could dispel it, it would be Darshel.

The Kavahadian sipped his tea casually before beginning. "Once we reach the Citadel, Highness, you will be protected by the Starian royal guard and happily welcomed as the Royal Heir's betrothed. They will treat you most kindly." He almost felt as if he was talking to the princess as if she was a child. He brushed away the odd feeling and continued. "As you escort, I and a select handful, will accompany you to the king or his heir, as courtesy dictates. Once you have been proclaimed and received, you will be under the protection of the royal house of Staria. That is where we will part." Princess Éleen nodded to show she was keeping up. So far, everything was as she had been taught. "Staria's protocols are looser than yours in the South." Lord Darshel continued. "You will be announced at the door but not expected to wait to be called. You may walk to the throne. Your Lord Protector, Lord Nexlé, must wait until he is waved forward by the king because of his lesser standing. If you meet the king in private, it is his signal to be more lax about protocol. The rest you should already know." Lord Darshel paused to take another sip of tea, inviting the princess to speak if she desired.

"Thank you for making me aware of Starian protocol, Lord Shekmann. I am grateful that you wished to make me aware of it."

Darshel flashed his smile again. "Of course, Your Highness."

"Now, may you please tell me about King Maushelik himself?"

"Yes, I will." He leaned back on the travel stool. "King Maushelik had been our ruler for thirty-seven years, having taken the throne at thirty-five from his sickly father. That first year he sat the throne, he helped fight to save Crystalynian from falling into the maunstorz hands. He was injured in the battle, his leg and lower back. You may note a distinctive hobble when you meet him. Do not stare. Despite his impairment, the king had proven himself worthy of the crown. He had been a just and wise leader and he, like his son, is highly regarded by the people. He may strike an intimidating pose when you first meet him, but the king is known to be a kind man, firm but not rigidly so." Unsure what else to say, Lord Darshel shrugged and placed his empty teacup on the table. "If you had any doubts about the king, I assure you, Princess, you will not have any of them validated. He is a ruler I respect."

It seemed to mean a lot to Princess Éleen that Lord Darshel respected his king. The smile she returned the Shekmann was sincere and beautiful. "Thank you, Lord Darshel, for speaking with me. I know my questions were a little…unorthodox, but I am glad you answered me honestly. I will not bother you again. You and Zyanthena may return to your duties. Have a good evening."

Lord Darshel and Zyanthena rose at the dismissal, said their good-byes then exited the tent. It wasn't until they had the camp completely organized, the horses brushed and cared for, and themselves fed that Darshel bothered to speak with Tashek about the suspicion he harbored against her. All that evening—from the princess's tent on through their chores and meal—Zyanthena had been quiet, doing everything he had asked without fail. It wasn't that is was odd for her, she had certainly been less despondent than at Kavahad, but the fact that she had been extra respectful that day and used a different title to call him was peculiar. Lord Darshel had been working out his thoughts all evening about how to address the issue. Once everyone else was gone from his tent, he started in on the desert woman.

Presently, the Tashek was sitting on her make-shift bed of a thick pile of blankets and a coverlet next to the far wall from Darshel's cot. She had already allowed Darshel to chain her left wrist—it was one of the few things she still would not do for him—and was sitting, resting her head in her arms atop her knees. Darshel knew better than to think her harmless; though, sitting as she was, she looked very pretty and very benign. In the flickering lamplight, the desert woman looked younger in the curtain of her flowing black hair. So, why then did Lord Darshel still have a tingling of mistrust about her? Because her high-leveled display of she-koum-o earlier was reason enough to know that she was a well-trained Tashek warrior—and that training included deception.

The Shekmann lord walked over to her, stopping just short of the distance her chain limited her to. Zyanthena seemed to be lost in a thought, which was unusual. Once she realized the Kavahadian was standing over her, her brandy eyes slowly followed the line of his boots on up to his eyes until they finally met his emerald gaze. If she was unnerved by being caught unawares, she did not show it as she slowly straightened her frame.

"What are you scheming?"

She blinked. Zyanthena actually *blinked* at the question like she was surprised. "Your Lordship?"

"No, Zy'ena, Darshel. I am not your lord. You are my prisoner, as I dictated through the treaty."

"Lord Shekmann, then." She corrected herself smoothly.

Darshel sighed in frustration but let it go. "Earlier you called me "my lordship" in front of the princess. You have never used that title before nor do you ever need to. One would question your reasons for the sudden suaveness."

"Oh." Her eyes darkened and her face fell into its usual wariness. "I doubt you would understand. You are too much your father's son."

An angry hardness came to Lord Darshel's mouth. "What the hell does that have to do with any of it?!" He cut off the rest of his thought and sucked in a calming breath. Getting the inherited Shekmann temper involved would only strengthen her point. Slowly, he lowered himself to his haunches and looked into Zyanthena's guarded eyes. "As you have mentioned before, the way a person is addressed in situations denotes their rank. There is a reason you changed the wording today. I would like to know."

Zyanthena studied his face, only inches from her own. Very slowly, she let her wary expression fall away until she looked, once again, beautiful and young. She waited a few more breathes before answering. "It was a sign of respect and an apology, Your Lordship. In this procession, you are my commanding officer, so to speak. I had been overly forthright in front of the princess, enough so that I could have made both of you lose face. By using such a personal title, I was hoping to ease the tension."

"Why worry about me losing face, Zy'ena? They all understand why you are here. As my prisoner you are expected to be disdainful, contemptuous even, yet, you have done neither, being both respectful and accommodating. I do not understand your actions."

"I am Tashek." She said as if that answered all. She continued, "We do not do things the same as you. Respect is the highest mark of our people. We try for it in everything. A Shekmann would not understand that, raised as you were." She paused then added more, being thoughtfully, "However, despite that our people are enemies, I question what I have been told about you. Perhaps you are not incapable, after all. Yes, in ways you are vulgar, like your practices with women, but you also hold yourself to standards that are honorable—I've seen that on our travel. You have not used me like your father would have nor do you disparage me. You could act worse, too, but you do not. I can respect a man like that."

Darshel went quiet, surprised by her declaration. He sat back until his body touched the carpeted floor and crossed his long legs. Having assumed the more comfortable position, and one that was more vulnerable (a signal he knew Zyanthena would notice), he let the calm of the desert evening float between them in the flickering candlelight. He mirrored the Tashek's expression: thoughtful. The contemplative look had softened the lines around her depthless eyes. Almost, Darshel could see a different face behind the one Zyanthena usually wore; a face of a woman with no known past but content to fight for the present in front of her. She knew her home to be the unpredictable desert and she embraced the wild spirit of the earth openly. That was the reason she seemed so different, so exotic. Zyanthena Sheev'arid was made from a piece of the world the "civilized" nations had forgotten.

At that instant, Lord Darshel had his insight.

"You never would have gotten captured. You *let* my men take you in."

Zyanthena's right eyebrow twitched, as if was wont to do when Darshel said something that surprised her. "Word needed to reach the Crystine of the Tashek's progress toward North Point. Such would not happen if both I and Arimun were captured. Nor did it help that Unrevealed had been injured by an arrow. I could not allow the cost of losing either the message nor the soundness of my horse to my own whims."

"Yet, you would suffer your fate at my hands over the safety of freedom. You value Unrevealed very much."

"Yes, he is very special to me. He was a gift from the Crystine and chosen as my companion by his own volition. It is only right that I treat him with the best of care."

"But you must have been afraid? The stories of Kavahad and what my family did to your people..."

She gave a wan smile. "Yes, such fears did come to me; however... there is a kind of recklessness that goes along with being valiant in the face of danger that vindicates the utter stupidity one performs when trying to protect someone or something from harm.

I believe it was that that convinced me to risk the consequences at your hands."

Lord Darshel could not help letting go a brazen laugh. It was quite carefree and joyous, a sound he had not heard himself make in a long time. It felt good to let loose like that. The Kavahadian lord let it go on for a few more moments then slowly tapered it off. He noticed Zyanthena was smiling, amused at his actions. "I don't believe I have heard such an outrageously long sentence in my life! At least not one in such a befuddled mess that still made sense. You have quite the wit on you."

"Hardly, Your Lordship."

The formal statement sobered the lord-governor. They ended up staring at each other once again. Zyanthena seemed to feel his unrest, for she dropped her gaze to study her clasped hands, a pose that was nonthreatening. "I am still uncertain on what I want to do with you." Darshel admitted. The warrioress looked up, somewhat guarded again. "You still refuse my offer, I assume?" She nodded resolutely. "But you will remain my prisoner and follow my commands? I may never understand your reasoning when freedom is so easily obtained."

"Says the man who squanders his lust on any woman who is willing."

"It is because you do not that I made the "punishment" thus. Your refusal of me is intriguing." He smiled roguishly.

Zyanthena rolled her eyes. "It is not worth wasting myself in your arms when I am needed to be in top form for the war."

"Even the bedchamber can be a battleground, Zy'ena." He purred the words out. "You are just afraid of being conquered."

She rose her eyebrows doubtfully. "I am not afraid of congress, if that is what you are inferring, nor will I be conquered. I am not new to the act. I refuse to preserve my dignity—of which I doubt you have any."

Perhaps Darshel was getting used to her quips because he did not react to her insulting remark. Instead, he latched onto a different part of her words. "You've had sex? I would never have guessed." Zyanthena did not reply, unhappy where the conversation was being led. Without her taking the bait of his taunt, Lord Darshel found he had nothing more to add. He did keep his teasing smile, though.

"You're full of surprises, Zy'ena. I'm thoroughly enjoying having you as my prisoner."

"Well I am glad that makes one of us."

He chuckled.

"We will need to leave before the light of dawn." Zyanthena reminded her captor.

"Is that your way of getting rid of me?" Darshel teased. He was pleasantly shocked when she mirrored his amused look, with a twinkle in her eyes.

"I am nothing if not practical, Your Lordship. The night is growing late and we ae both in need of rest. It is foolishness to fritter away that which is necessary."

"It makes a good excuse to get rid of me." He continued cajoling her as he stood up. "You know, I could just stay and continue to have my fun with you."

The most perfect, intimidating glare was answer enough to his suggestion. "You will not."

"So sure you are." He grinned. "And here I was beginning to think we were getting along."

Her reply had Darshel instantly subdued. "Only to a point, Your Lordship. You are still your father's son. We may be able to speak more respectfully, even candidly, with each other; but, behind it all, you are still a Shekmann."

Sadness filled Darshel's heart but he kept the emotion from his eyes, lest Zyanthena see it and use it for her own purposes. She was very right. They were still Shekmann and Tashek, enemies. He doubted their truce would last long enough to change the course their people's hatred had created. Suddenly tired, he waved his hand lazily and said good-night before walking the short distance to his bed, where he sat down heavily.

Across from him, still bathed in candlelight, Zyanthena still sat and watched him remove everything but his pants and roll into his cot. Only when he stilled did she extinguish the two candles next to her. In the quiet dark that followed, Lord Darshel heard her soft voice answer him, "Goodnight, Lord Shekmann. May the Stars watch over you tonight."

Chapter Twenty-One

§

Conspiracy

"Hey, sir...Roland, it's time to wake up." Sage's softer, familiar voice cut through the Sunarian's muggy consciousness. Slowly, the merchant pulled himself awake with a dissatisfied groan. "Sir, it's late in the morning. Rio is waiting outside with Anibus. Brunch is to be taken on the patio."

"What?" Roland murmured as he pushed himself to a sitting position. He pushed aside the bed sheets. "Stars, Sage, I feel like I haven't slept much at all!"

"Six hours, sir." The nineteen-year-old grinned cheerfully. "From five am until eleven."

A tired groan was Roland's answer. "I was trying to forget about staying up all night moving dead bodies and debris." He ran his hands over his face in an attempt to wake up. Sage was already moving to pick out Roland's clothes, chatting away of the happenings of the morning as if his master was listening. The young man's voice grilled against Roland's nerves; he was bemoaning sleep and not in any mood to face the day. Sage was oblivious. "Sage. Sage, stop. Please, just stop." Roland finally ordered, rubbing out a forming headache. The other Sunarian paused in the middle of examining outfits to blink at Roland in surprise. "Look, just leave the garments. I'll dress myself today. Go tell Rio and Priest Anibus that I'll be to breakfast shortly."

Sage hesitated before setting down the russet outfit in his hands. "If that's what you'd like, sir." He began to head for the door but turned back, uncomfortable and unsure what he should do if he was not to help his master dress. "Ah, sir." Roland bit back an annoyed remark. "Would you like me to set out some elder flower tea? You look as if you might have a headache and—."

"That..." The Sunarian stopped himself from being rude. Sage was only trying to be helpful. "Would do me some good. Thank you, Sage." The auburn-haired assistant beamed in relief and bowed quickly before quitting the room. Once alone, Roland sighed heavily and stood. He trod to the wash basin and began to scrub his face in the lavender-scented water. He caught sight of his wearied features in the small, oval mirror on the wall. Dark circles under his midnight-blue eyes emphasized their deep color, making them look haunted against the paler complexion of his skin. His tangled, dark chestnut hair stuck out in an unruly mess around his face. "Hell, I look like I was drug across the face of Syre and back."

"You have been actually."

Roland turned to frown at Rio as the tall, dark-haired soldier stepped near, a towel offered in his extended hand. "Am I not to have my quiet this morning?"

"Just needing us all to keep appearances, sir." Rio replied smoothly. His light-natured smile only deepened Roland's frown. "Anibus already guessed to out nature. He warned me to be extra careful if you are to continue this ruse. That is all."

"And how long has he been in your confidence?"

"Over a week, but he suspected since the border."

"Dammit, Rio! You are supposed to inform me of these things when they happen." Roland snatched the towel from the soldier's fingers and began to dry his face with a furious vengeance. He turned away from the small vanity with a hairbrush in hand. He began in earnest to try to get his mess of a mane untangled and properly pulled in to a ponytail. The task, at least, held his temper in check. "Is there anything else I should know this morning? I'd like to get it all out now before this dreadful ache in my head becomes something real."

Rio tried to hide his amused chuckle under the clearing of his throat. "Ah, no, that is about it. Commander Matar and Kins are giving everyone the morning off. We're to help with the clearing of the field and sentry duties later today. Now that all of the dead have been properly laid to rest, the remainder of the tasks have been assigned in shifts. There was an announcement this morning that King Maushelik is preparing for the arrivals of Princess Éldon-Tomino, Prince Fantill, the Sheev'anee, and the cavalry from Kavahad. With seven armies and five cavalries all assembling here, His Majesty is having to organize the camps around the walls of the Citadel. Most of the rooms here in the palace are being reserved for all of the dignitaries that will arrive. We are asked to share our room amongst ourselves, so Sage, Anibus, and I will move our stuff in here…unless, of course, you would like to pull rank?"

Roland slipped into his pants and tunic and began straightening the loose garments around his muscular shoulders. "I thought you just said to keep up appearances?"

"Yes, I did, sir But, there is going to be a war council held at the end of the week. If you admit to the king and commanders who you are, they will make sure you are included."

"You're assuming we won't be."

Rio shrugged. "Who are we to them but the small party that accompanied Anibus to the Crystine? I'm just saying…"

"I'll think on your suggestion." Roland interrupted. "Now, can we please go eat? My stomach is threatening rebellion."

"Of course, sir."

The taller Sunarian led the way out to the back patio that connected Roland's room to its adjoining neighbor. The area itself could have seated three round tables, sitting six people apiece comfortably, over its red-toned tiled base. Large planters of flowers, all able to withstand the desert heat, were situated around the patio to bring some color to the desert tones. The Estarian priest and Sage were already at the table, enjoying the shade from the canopy hanging over it and the soft northwesterly breeze that floated by. The young assistant quickly hopped from his chair to begin pouring the other men's tea as they approached.

Anibus was slower to his feet, giving a casual hello and head bob. "Good morning. I hope your sleep was well."

Roland schooled his features into a polite smile, though there was a tightness about it that showed he would rather grimace. "As well as expected for marching all yesterday just to be up all night moving the Starian dead."

"Yes, it did take something out of me to be up doing prayers for the dead. I am glad that we were given the morning to recuperate." Anibus waved the two Sunarians to their seats and sat back down, his hand reaching for his tea cup.

"Rio tells me you are aware of my identity." Roland began without preamble. The priest paused in shock, his hand around his cup. He quickly ducked his head to hide his reaction behind a curtain of his unbound long, brown hair. Roland continued, "I am not happy to hear of my discovery outside of my two men, Sage and Rio, but I cannot say I am too surprised. As a companion of ours for over a month-and-a-half, you were bound to notice something amiss between us. I just want to thank you for keeping this to yourself."

"You are welcome.... Roland. I would never betray your confidence in this matter; though, I must ask: what is your purpose for your concealment?"

"There are those that are not happy with my nonchalanting across Syre. My...king does not want to involve Sunrise in this war, especially since the maunstorz have left us alone all these years. He will have little to do with the other kingdoms of Syre. As long as we remain prosperous and undisturbed, he will ignore the plight of the other kingdoms." Roland's eyes narrowed angrily and the bitterness in his voice betrayed his fury at Raymond Sunrise. "I do not want to be so indifferent over the troubles in Syre. While others suffer from this war, Sunrise sit in comfort, enjoying our pricey Havenese teas and pointless policy debates. One day, when Sunrise is in need, there will be no one there to come to our aide—all because we were stupid, spineless pigs! The people deserve better."

"It seems that the people will receive a just king once Prince Rowin is able to take the throne."

"It will not be soon enough." Roland replied. "And not at all, if the government officials have anything to do about it. Prince Rowin had already been sighted by two assassination attempts, the second of which he nearly lost his life. The officials will try anything to get the people's champion from the throne and put Prince Connel on it instead."

"That is grievous news to me." Anibus spoke in the way of an indirect apology. "I pray that such corruption never comes to pass; this I will do most ardently. Sunrise had a great king once, before Raymond overthrew the throne. The kingdom deserves that again."

Roland's eyes softened. "Yes, it does." His eyes grew distant as his thoughts drifted into a past memory. "There is a rumor that Sunrise's true king is still alive. A part of my being here is to search out his whereabouts—if such is true. I was too young to remember the king; I was only three when he was banished (or perhaps killed), but I still cling to the hope that the rumors of his being alive are not false. If King Richard is alive, he could help save Sunrise from the evils of the government."

"A grand notion." Anibus said truthfully." It is nice to see someone so strong in faith over a belief, but do not lose yourself or the people's needs over this quest." Roland frowned in contempt. "Sunrise will never have the king it needs if the prince is preoccupied and unavailable to fight for his throne. Remind him of that." The priest told Roland. "The quest you are on is a valiant one, just do not get so caught up in it that you cannot help save the throne."

"We understand." Rio interjected into the conversation. "We have not forgotten the issues at home. But until we heard the rumors about the former king, we had lost hope of safe guarding the prince and the throne. The prince's safety is crucial but he can no longer reside safely at the palace. What would you have us do? Prince Rowin refuses to take up the same tactics as his enemies deploy, and it seems I am not able to protect him from the dangers pointed his way."

"You should pray and pray hard. The Stars gift those who believe in a just cause. They hear your people's needs and will provide."

Rio nodded earnestly, but beside him Roland could not do the same. "I am sorry, Priest, but I have very little faith in what I cannot see. I trust in action and perseverance."

Anibus smiled, as if amused by the unbeliever. "And yet, you grasp at straws of a rumor of a person that may not be. You know more of Faith than you admit to. I pray you will come to know just how much you depend on Faith; for, in this reality, it is all you really have."

Chapter Twenty-Two

§

First Meeting

"The Havenese flags have been spotted on the southern horizon!" A young page came yelling excitedly into the prince's private study. Princes Al'den and Kent looked up from their reading in startlement at the abrupt intrusion. Their gaze had the boy quickly flushing in embarrassment and muttering his apologies for his unruly behavior. More subdued, the page repeated his message and bowed his way from the room, following Al'den's dismissal.

Prince Kent leaned back in his chair and stretched his good arm, hissing in pain as the movement jostled his injured shoulder. "Ow. Well, at least I was ready for a reprieve from reading all day." The Golden kingdom heir began. "Did you see the poor boy's face when he realized he'd burst in on the royal heir? The poor lad. It was priceless!"

Prince Al'den responded with an amused smile and stood, closing he thick leather-bound book he had been reading. "Jake is still fairly new to the staff. His naïve enthusiasm is a good change to the routine."

"Or a quick heart attack waiting to happen."

The tall Starian barked out a laugh. He shook his head as he put both his and Kent's books away. "Come on. Let's go to the bailey and watch the Havenese precession arrive."

"You just want to get a first-hand look at the lovely princess," Kent teased.

Prince Al'den ignored the quip as he led the way out of the palace to the southern wall. In reality he had been nervous about meeting the Havenese princess. Neither royal had ever seen the other. Their kingdoms' matchmaking had been planned as an act of friendship during their childhood. Knowing it was almost time for them to meet for real made Al'den's stomach twist nervously. Gulping back his nerves, the royal pasted a pleasant expression on his face as he greeted the sentries on duty on the baily.

In the distant south, the forward-moving procession was beginning to appear into the shapes of individual horsemen and travel carts. One of the sentries informed the prince that a messenger had reported three hundred Kavahadian cavalry and fifty Havenese royal guards making up the princess's escort. The Starian voiced his surprise that such a number of Kavahadian soldiers had marched safely through the Tashek territory but thanked the man for his service and settled himself into a comfortable lean against the stones wall. Beside him, Kent rested his good side of his body against the stone, angling himself toward the other prince. His blue eyes twinkled in their common mischievous way. Prince Al'den couldn't help asking, "What has you in such a good mood?"

"Just studying you." He grinned broadly. "You seem tense. I'm just trying to deduce why."

"You have an odd hobby." Al'den said, hoping the other man would not pry.

"It's amusing. Is it so unusual for the Kavahadian army to travel in such force? You sounded as if their number was unexpected."

The prince was fishing for information but he was being polite about it. "We had hoped for all of the Kavahadian cavalry to support us during the fighting—that would have been five hundred men— but with the enemy threat diminished, it was not wise for the Kavahadian cavalry to travel in such a high number." Prince Al'den paused to signal to the outriders waiting at the main gate to head out to meet the Havenese procession. He finished the thought, "There is a great tension between the Tashek and Kavahad. Even with both of their people under our rule, there is no guarantee either side will keep their unsteady peace this close together. I'm just concerned the large number of Kavahadian soldiers amongst the Sheev'anee will bring about unnecessary tension."

"I know the history between the Sheev'anee and Kavahad." Prince Kent stated, his announcement surprising the other royal. "But I think your people respect you enough not to cause any trouble while they are at the capitol. At least, I hope that to be true." He flashed a smile. "It would be a bad display on Staria's part as long as there are so many other kingdoms' representatives here. Your people should not be stupid enough to screw that up."

"If you were trying to cheer me up, it was the wrong choice of words."

Prince Kent chuckled. Al'den mirrored the amused look and the two princes turned their attention back to the arriving procession. As they watched, Prince Kent added one last thing to their talk. "And, don't worry about the princess, Al'den. She is an absolute sweetheart."

Princess Éleen cast her beautiful china-blue eyes to the solid Citadel walls as her procession passed underneath the mighty-stone gateway and entered the inner city. She had seen the aftermath of the battle already much cleaned up since the fight. It had been unnerving to see the full numbers of burial pyres that had surrounded the large out walls. The grief of the townspeople and the subdued workers clearing the desert grounds had been a forlorn greeting to the Havenese procession. The royal wondered what more despairing images would lead the large group up the main roadway leading toward the center, where the Citadel of Light towered above the surrounding buildings. Though it was late afternoon, the way was fairly clear, making the passage of the horses and carts quick. The two outriders paused at the inner wall's main gate and the second-in-command man called to the Kavahadian cavalry to follow him to the western stable yard. With the exception of Lord Darshel, his two main commanders, and Zyanthena, all of the Kavahad force was led away. Then, stepping his horse aside, the other outrider called for the inner gate to be opened and motioned Éleen's group through.

As the now-smaller procession moved into the large courtyard, the Havenese princess took in the sight of the Citadel of Light. The enormous fortress was made of the same sand-colored stone as they rest of the city. It was not majestic like Éleen had imagined it to be. Compared to the southern kingdoms' royal personages, Staria's was drab. To add to the princess's disappointment, only a small cortege of Starians were on the long, broad staircase leading up to the Citadel. The entire place was so unlike the south that Éleen felt herself choke back the fear forming in her throat. *"I don't know if I can do this."*

Her coach was stopped directly below the Starian party and Prince Connel and Lord Carrod dismounted and stepped toward Éleen's coach as she stepped down. The three of them moved forward to greet Staria. As they neared, two men came away from the stairs. The shorter man on the left, in lavish court clothes, smiled broadly at the three of them and made a very charismatic hello, complete with a partial bow. The taller man, also handsome but darker haired and wearing a military-style garment and long, sand-colored cape, echoed the other man's greeting and welcomed the Havenese and Sunarian to Staria.

Sensing that she was being greeted by the Starian prince himself, Princess Éleen let go of Lord Carrod's arm and stepped up to the two strangers. She extended her gloved hand to the shorter man and curtsied as demurely as she could saying, "Your Highness, Prince Maushelik, thank you for coming out to welcome me to your city personally. I am Princes Éldon-Tomino of Blue Haven and your betrothed. Please, accept my condolences on the loss against your people at the maunstorz attack." Éleen was so nervous at being under her betrothed's eyes that she was unaware of her terrible blunder. At the awkward silence, she raised her head to look at the prince that held her hand. The man's amused twinkle in his eyes and his vain attempt to keep a smile from his lips had Princess Éleen wondering what was wrong. A sideways glance to Lord Carrod showed her Havenese escort was in a blazing red blush of embarrassment.

"Ahem," Prince Connel came forward to whisper in her ear, "Ah, princess, may I introduce you to Prince Kent Argetlem, heir of the Golden Kingdom. Prince Al'den Maushelik is the other man."

Comprehending her error, Princess Éleen gasped and pulled her hand from Prince Kent's hand. She quickly ducked her face to hide her own mortification and mouthed her apologies. "Prince Argetlem, I apologize. Prince Maushelik, I am terribly sorry."

Prince Kent could not help laughing at the blunder, he was too tickled by it all. The unabashed sound had Éleen blushing even more in her shame. She cowered into herself, wishing desperately that she was not the center of attention, though there was no way to disappear or cover up her oversight with so many eyes. "Well, I have to say I am quite jealous that you think me so bold and strapping enough to be mistaken as His Highness Al'den." The sentence was outrageous and casual enough to bring the princess's eyes up in surprise. The Golden Kingdom's heir was grinning devilishly at the Starian prince, unaware of the affect his words had on the others. His blue eyes were transfixed on the tall, battle-hardened royal, waiting to see how the other prince would react.

Prince Al'den's heart had been beating fast in his chest as the Havenese carriage had parked and the princess was helped out. It had nearly stopped in utter awe as the beautiful Havenese woman had straightened her small frame and accepted her escort's arm so gracefully. Prince Al'den had had to remind himself to breath as first Kent then he welcomed the princess and her party to Staria. It had almost been a comical relief when Princess Éleen mistook him for Prince Kent; in truth, Al'den was not sure he could have answered the captivating angel before him. But Prince Kent's unrestrained laugh had brought the Starian back to his senses. It was blatantly obvious that the princess was embarrassed by her mistake. Fervently, he wished to ease her discomfort and lighten the tense mood, like his friend was doing.

"Oh, I am not sure of that, Kent. I think you make a striking image to get mistaken for." He smiled disarmingly and stepped up to the princess to offer her his hand. "Princess Éldon-Tomino, I am very glad to make your acquaintance. Please accept that the fault is mine for not dressing appropriately for such an important meeting as this. Even I can see how my dreary, military outfit can be cause to dismiss me in a crowd. I pray that this faux pas is quickly forgotten, as it is already from my mind."

"Highness." Éleen felt herself blush again, but for an entirely different reason. The Starian heir was comelier than she had imagined him to be and so much taller than rumors claimed. She felt so tiny and delicate standing before the prince, his strong hand consuming hers in a surprisingly gentle but firm grip. Éleen felt herself go to liquid in his grasp, so unused to being treated by a man so (Southern men did not shake hands with a lady). How could such a perfect stranger bring her to such deplorable womanly woes?

Prince Al'den continued, sensing the lovely brunette before him was still shy. "And, I see you have come accompanied by His Highness Prince Sunrise," he nodded his head respectfully at the Sunarian royal, "And Lord Nexlé, is it? As well as, Lord Shekmann of Kavahad." Prince Al'den easily diverted the attention from Éleen to the men he had pointed out. The tall Starian released his hold on Éleen's hand to properly greet the two men with the princess. "I welcome you all to the Citadel of Light. I am sure you are all tired from the long journey north. Rooms and refreshments have been made ready. I hope they are to your liking." With his greeting out of the way the Starian heir motioned retainers forward and bade the group to enter the Citadel to find their rest. He was quick to get his men to find Prince Connel's and the princess's belongings first and directed the party to follow the servants to their quarters. Sending Prince Kent with the princess, Prince Al'den excused himself from escorting the others so that he could speak with Lord Shekmann. The others headed up the stairs and out of the heat with the Starian prince's promise to find them again shortly.

Removed of the duty of welcoming the other royals, the Starian warrior-prince turned to his Kavahadian lord-governor and his men. Lord Darshel and his Kavahadian men had waited patiently through the sudden chaos of the royals' unpacking. As the others were finally led away to be attended to, the strapping lord strode forward to his heir-apparent and made his proper introductions. "Your Highness. I am Lord Darshel Shekmann of your lower outpost Kavahad. I and my men lament the losses to your people and beg forgiveness for our tardiness to assist you at your dire hour. I regret to say, I had no word from you until just recently but would have come sooner had your missive reached us. I know my actions are late, but I have brought with me three hundred of my best men to be at your disposal until you have no more need of them. We are yours to do with as you see fit."

Prince Al'den came to stand before the other Starian. Their two heights, almost exact, made it easy for the royal to stare directly into the other's eyes. In Lord Darshel's defense, the Kavahadian did not try to puff himself up to try and impress his kingdom's heir. Instead, he chose the very military-like stare ahead and waited for His Highness to speak. Approving the move, Lord Darshel stepped around the Shekmann to inspect the others the lord had brought with him. Commander Gordon, a medium-heighted veteran with greying, auburn-hair, was familiar to the prince. Once a part of Al'den's own foot soldiers, King Maushelik had reassigned the man to Kavahad upon the former Shekmann's death. To find that Commander Gordon had been well-placed in Lord Darshel's ranks made Al'den think better of the Kavahadian lord—he had only the rumors circulated about the man to make any assessments. The other commander, Raic, was not as familiar to him, but he, too, seemed to have the air of a competent leader. Satisfied, Prince Al'den continued past Lord Darshel's commanders to the final member of the Kavahadian party.

The prince could not hide the shock he felt as his eyes fell upon the woman accompanying the group. The beautiful Tashek had placed herself a short distance from the others, being respectful. She stood between a towering, greyhound-like black stallion and a chestnut mare. As the Starian stopped before her, she bowed deeply, arms outcast and palms up, just as Prince Kent had done with Cum'ar. Though she was not dressed as a Tashek, there was no doubt in Prince Al'den's mind that she was of the Shcev'anee. He gave a small bow in return and greeted the woman in keshic. She returned the greeting and straightened her lithe body from its bow.

"Lord Shekmann!" Prince Al'den called out firmly. The other Starian responded immediately by stepping over and saying, "yes, Highness?". Al'den knew he would have been more impressed with the lord's very disciplined action if he was not so troubled by finding a Tashek with the Kavahadian party. By the tenseness of the Shekmann's jaw, there might be cause for his concern. "I see you travel with one of the Sheev'anee. I find this unexpected, considering the history between your two people." There was a question in his statement.

"Yes, Highness, I do understand your concern." Lord Darshel replied, his deep, emerald eyes going to the woman. They shared a glance between them and Prince Al'den wondered what the Shekmann would say—or if the man would lie about the circumstances.

To the prince's surprise, it was the Tashek woman who answered. "My Prince, my name is Sheev'arid Zyanthena, daughter of the Shi'alam but currently dismissed from the Sheev'anee. I was a scout of the Crystine cavalry, under direct order of Commander Matar. Now, I am under the control of Lord Shekmann. It was I who led the procession through the Aras and protected His Lordship's men from Sheev'anee detection. His Lordship and I have an…agreement of my employment under him."

Prince Al'den was not sure he had heard correctly. The Shekmann and a Tashek were working together? He knit his eyebrows together as he studied the two Starians, waiting for one or the other to amend Zyanthena' words. Though Lord Darshel seemed a bit uneasy under His Highness's eyes, he did not correct the desert woman. Prince Al'den relented. "That was an interesting account, Sheev'arid; however, I am appreciative that the Kavahadian cavalry and the Sheev'anee avoided any confrontations, by your assistance. I would like you both to meet with His majesty and myself to discuss your unusual situation further, especially with the treaty between your two peoples. But I am grateful that your goodwill has saved us from further bloodshed."

"Your Highness." They both bowed submissively to their prince.

"As for the Kavahadian soldiers, I welcome their numbers to the defense of the Citadel. Your men have been taken to the western walls. There is not room enough for all the men here so each group— Crystine, mertinean, Sheev'anee, and you—are assigned portions of the walls to watch for further maunstorz attacks." The prince stepped back toward the two commanders under Lord Darshel's command. 'Your men seem to be well disciplined. I am grateful for your added support to our protection. I will have Sir Jason take you back to your force. In two days, we will hold a war council, which I will see you attend. After, the people and nobles are asking for a ceremonial banquet to honor the dead and rejoice in our victory. Again, I ask you to come in your best. Welcome to the Citadel, Lord Shekmann."

They all bowed deeply as Prince Al'den turned away and headed back up the long stairway to the fortress. The tension drained away from the Kavahadian men, once their royal heir was gone. Without the prince there to see, Lord Darshel collapsed his careful countenance into an anxious frown. He turned to Zyanthena, finding her avoiding his gaze by applying herself to a job of adjusting her chestnut mare's tack.

"Zy'ena you—."

Knowing what the twenty-eight-year old was going to say, she interjected. "The prince does not need to know I am you Prisoner...at least not yet."

"But—."

"What do you think he will do if he hears the truth, Your Lordship?" She shut him up. "Executions between our people have happened for much less." Lord Darshel's frown deepened. Sensing the lord's consternation, Zyanthena stopped fiddling with her mare's girth to stare at the Shekmann. "Look around, Your Lordship. Our kingdom has just been through a devastating attack. Our situation is the last thing His Highness needs to be concerned with. The truth can wait, our kingdom cannot."

"His Highness could have granted you your freedom, if you had said the truth."

Zyanthena sensed that the Starian was perplexed at her actions, much as he had been the other night. He was still trying to figure her out; it was almost commendable. "At what cost, Your Lordship? The Kavahadian cavalry needs you to lead it and Staria needs Kavahad to help protect its heart city. Consider my actions to be that of practicality; I will not compromise the welfare of the Citadel over my own problems. I can deal with the issue of my own freedom after the people are safe."

Her words gave the tall, dark-haired lord pause. He ended up staring at Zyanthena's lovely face as the late afternoon breeze batted loose locks of her black hair around her face. The desert woman seemed to go completely still under his gaze and, yet, her depthless eyes looked untamed. It seemed as if Lord Darshel would say something more, but his chance slipped away as Commander Gordon guided his horse over to them.

"My Lord, Sir Jason is here to show us to our camp."

"Very well." Lord Darshel replied, accepting the reins of his courser, Tano. He stepped away from Zyanthena and her horses to mount his grey. The Tashek woman followed his lead, settling atop her mare. Nodding to his men and to Sir Jason, Lord Darshel commanded, "Show us the way." His final look to Zyanthena beside him said something different. It said, *"We will speak of this again".*

Chapter Twenty-Three

§

The Secret of the "Keepers"

"We should reach the Citadel by the setting of the sun, Highness," Terrik informed Prince Par.

The Tashek had fallen back from his spot by the Shi'alam's side to speak with the Sealanders. The young farrier had come with the warrior, learning how to be a dutiful Khapta. The two of them seemed to have been appointed the Shi'alam's personal run-between for all of his messages to his men and the prince. Par wondered if the Shi'alam's son felt honored by the job or demoralized by the decrease in rank. "Thank you, Terrik. I, for one, am glad to hear this long journey is about at its end. This heat is quite atrocious."

"It does take some getting used to," Terrik replied. The desert man seemed at home under the blazing sun. The Southerner could not understand how anyone could be so at ease in the dry intenseness. Yet, none of the Tashek grumbled about the group's daytime passage. "I apologize for having us travel during the worst of the heat," Terrik continued. "Usually—when time is not pressing—we rest during the highest hours of the sun and use the stars to navigate at the cool of the night. However, the Shi'alam feels we need to reach the Citadel of Light at Stars' speed."

"I defer my opinion to you and your people," Prince Par said. "I have not the knowledge of the desert to say what is or is not best to do in these circumstances."

"Thank you, Highness, for your confidence. It is my understanding that this is your first time in Staria?" The prince nodded. "Well, I know our kingdom is dissimilar to yours, as most of Staria is desert; however, I think you will find it less deplorable than the landscape first indicates. Our sunsets are especially a sight, compared to elsewhere in Syre."

The royal kept his skeptical opinion to himself. "I hope that you are right, Terrik. I do try to see the best in every place I travel to." Yet, the Sealander heir knew there was no lands like the peaceful, ocean shoreline that held a special place in his heart.

The Tashek seemed to sense the prince's mood, for he respectfully excused himself and Decond from the royal's presence and cantered his horse back up to his father's side. Prince Par watched them go then reached down to his waterskin to take a drink of the mixture made of horse's milk diluted with water and honey and boiled dates. The sweet, tangy liquid instantly wetted his parched mouth. The first time he had taken a swig, though, Par had not particularly liked the taste, but as the long hours in the sun had passed by, he had begun to welcome the relief the drink gave him. The mixture kept him hydrated better than water alone, a fact that made him appreciative of the odd Tashek decoction. Satisfied, he replaced the waterskin and straightened in his horse's saddle.

Lord Gordar spoke up from beside the prince. "Are you doing all right, My Highness?"

Prince Par shifted in his saddle to see his Lord Protector better. The golden-eyed man had taken a little snooze in his saddle. He still looked sleep-drugged astride his chestnut mount. "I should be asking you that, cuz. You look as if you need to sleep for a month."

"I feel like it," Gordar chuckled softly. "I don't think the nap did me any good, not with this heat."

"You've run the whole length of Syre twice and a quarter over. Once we get to the Citadel, I think you are well-deserved of a few days of idleness. In fact, I order it of you." Par added in case the other Sealander objected. "I've half the mind to do it myself. The war council isn't for two more days, so I don't care if we sloth around in our rooms until then. I'd rather be recovered and refreshed than half-dead at the council table."

"If it's your order, My Highness, I've no dissent against it. I'm too tired to complain."

Prince Par nodded resolutely. "Then it's settled. We will dally in our rooms as long as we can afford it." Lord Gordar smiled at his cousin and the two men rode along in silence for a few minutes. The sound of the many, trotting horses' breathes and the dampened swish of their unshod hooves in the sand created a lulling atmosphere. If it wasn't for the soft murmur of some of the Tashek speaking in keshic, the trip would have felt surreal.

"Stars, I hope this trip is worth it!" Par suddenly thought out loud, much to both of their shock. Lord Gordar looked as if he was not sure how to answer. "I mean," the Sealander heir reformed his statement, "I hope that something gets accomplished at the war council. It had been far too long since Syre's armies have spoken with one another. It would be a dreadful shame if we are not able to figure out how to get us all working together against the maunstorz again."

"I do not think, My Highness, that this meeting will be in vain." Lord Gordar replied, solemnly. "This opportunity, having this many of Syre's war commanders together under one roof, hasn't happened on over twenty-five years. Most of the men you will be sitting with will have had to face the maunstorz since the beginning. They have more insight into this stars-awful war than we can hope for in our lifetime. That they all get a chance to discuss this threat together, combining all of their knowledge on this subject, means that Syre finally has a chance to get our defenses right."

"We need more than to just defend ourselves."

The lord protector easily sidestepped the prince's sudden anger. "One thing at a time, Highness. Even you know that."

"Yes...yet, we have only ever responded to the maunstorz attacks instead of taking them head on. I'm just frustrated at our inability to attack the enemy offensively."

"That has not always been." The prince was interrupted by Kor'mauk Siv'arid, who came trotting up with Jacen Novano and Patrick Kins. The three men had been at the back but were sent forward to bring the prince and his cousin some food and refreshment from the pack animals. The Tashek had overheard the prince's conversation and felt compelled to say the truth. "There was a time in our history—if fact, not that far in the past—when we joined forces to fight the maunstorz." The desert man dropped the bombshell then proceeded to pass out the food as if he had not said anything out of the ordinary.

Seeing food had the prince's stomach growling but he would not let his hunger deter his questions—especially when such outrageous statements were made. "You were saying that Syre attacked the maunstorz before? Never in any of our histories have I seen such written!"

The Tashek closed his expression down, being careful. It seemed suspicious to the Sealand prince. Why was the desert man so secretive? However, Kor'mauk did reply, as much as he was able to—

and certainly more than he should. "I do not have the authority to tell you much, Prince Fantill, yet... I will say this, but only as long as you do not say from whom you received this information...." The twenty-seven-year-old gave his assurances that he would keep the knowledge to himself. He hoped it was enough to get the Tashek to talk, as he was beginning to tire of the tight-lipped nomads and their structured social orders; they were more serious about their respect and familial-honor than any of the royal houses of Syre!

With the others' consent as well, Kor'mauk finally continued, though he kept sneaking nervous glances toward the front of the line. "Syre has been fighting the maunstorz for over eighty years, mostly just small raiding parties as seen across most of the North; however, the last time the kingdoms stood together against the enemy in force was about twenty-five years ago, at the Battle of Bil'cordys in Crystalynian. You all remember it as the time the eighth kingdom was at the end of its power. For the Sheev'anee, however, it was when Syre fought the enemy and nearly wiped them out. If only King Trev'shel had not been killed all that followed would not have come to pass..." Kor'mauk seemed lost in a memory, his voice fading until the prince cleared his throat, desiring to hear more. The Tashek shook himself back to the present and continued as if he had not paused. "Weakened and alarmed at the calamity the king's passing and Crystalynian's sudden fall to ruin had the other armies forced into retreat. Had they not done so, they, too, would have fallen prey to the catastrophic earthquake that shook Crystalynian. Many of the maunstorz were not as lucky, truth be told.... their losses could be the reason we have not seen them in force until now, when their next generation was old enough to join the fighting."

The four Syreans had never heard this accounting of the fighting in Crystalynian, though all had been raised on the stories of the wars before their time. There were many gaps in the telling, making it hard to believe that version versus the one they had been told. In the written histories, Crystalynian had been a part of the forces protecting the northern border—much as Staria, Rubia, and the Crystal kingdoms did at present. There had been no mention of a large battle there only the devastation of the earthquake. That a full-scale war had transpired—and had been covered up from the histories—seemed ridiculous.

Prince Par was the most unbelieving of the Tashek's account. "There was never a war stated in our history books, especially one so large as recent as a quarter of a century ago. That this has been covered up in every kingdom in Syre is a feat I find far from probable!"

The Tashek's face darkened. "My people are the "Keepers of the Truth", much like your Priests of Estaria. Everyone else was made to forget the past. Your kings lied to you all and thus kept the people at a peace of mind against the horrors of war."

"You can't take those kinds of events from people's mind! No force in the world can do that." Par argued.

Kor'mauk paused to look at the four men in turn, his gaze deep and penetrating. He gave an unhappy smirk at what he saw. "Oh, how sure you are that there does not exist the means to take away the memories of people—and how naïve! What lies you all live by. If I were you, I would learn to question all you know...the time may come when your eyes will be opened to the truths that hold Syre. I hope that, on that day, you are all ready for it." He let his words ring ominous and prophetic as he turned his horse away, leaving the others to the seed he had planted.

Chapter Twenty-Four

§

Impressions

The inside of the Citadel of Light was more eloquent than its exterior portrayed. The many halls and stairwells were carpeted in long, rich nut-brown rugs embroidered in the Starian amber and charcoal grey. Matching golden drapes were pulled back from the windows to let in the glorious sunshine. The hallway walls were decorated with oil printings of the former rulers of Staria, depicted in both portrait and landscape scenes. Simple but costly pieces of yellowwood furniture were placed in the many rooms, allowing visitors comfortable areas to rest, eat, or sleep. Overall, the fortress had been designed for comfort and practicality over extravagance, but without losing the feel that it housed the Starian royal family.

Princess Éleen's own apartments were just as comfortable as the rest of the Citadel. The nut-brown theme was still present around her room, such as the soft sheets and canopy of the four-post queen-sized bed and the pillowcases; however, there were more variations of desert tones in the walls and adornments, as if the decorator had decided the practical, royal colors were less important to the space as a whole than the need to feel at ease. The Havenese woman was beginning to let her guard down in the calming tones of the room, despite her overall feeling of overwhelm and embarrassment.

Prince Al'den had asked that the princess be given a chance to rest, without the constant presence of her escort or servants; it was an unusual request for someone from a royal household from the South. At first, the Havener had been alarmed to be left so completely alone, but as the refreshing silence in her quarters soaked into her pores, Éleen realized what a luxury it was to be able to explore her new surroundings without watching eyes. She found that, though she was tired from the long journey, there was too much to see and touch to find rest on the large bed. Instead, the royal spent her time unpacking (when had she ever done so herself?) and putting her things to rights on the large vanity that took up the southern wall. Finding all of her belongings placed thus, Éleen took to resting on the window seat.

The view from her perch looked out over the eastern courtyard and beyond to the inner city. There was very little activity on that side of the building. A little disappointed, Éleen began to turn away, but a movement on the grounds below brought her attention back around. A boy, of about the age of ten, sprinted out of the fortress to kick a small, red-colored ball across the courtyard. Thought the boy was alone, he seemed to be content with his play. Éleen could not help smiling at the lad's enthusiasm as he kicked his toy as hard as he could at one of the walls then raced to intercept its rebound path. So preoccupied was she on the scene, that Éleen did not hear the knock at her door and the man's entrance.

"I see Jake has found an activity to take away his robust energy. It will be a relief when he gets back to his duties."

"Oh!" Éleen startled and brought her hand to her chest in surprise. Turning, she found Prince Argetlem just beyond arm's reach. "Goodness, Highness, I apologize! I had not realized you came in."

The Golden heir smiled charmingly and motioned if he could sit beside the princess. "The apology is all mine, Ms. Éleen, for sneaking in so. It was impolite of me and, perhaps, too bold." He settled himself casually against the windowsill, one leg drawn up so he could rest a forearm on his knee. The princess could not help but gap at the man's easy air; Prince Kent did not seem to notice her rudeness. "I just met the lad myself this morning," he continued, "I guess Jake is the youngest on the staff and in his first weeks as a page. Oh, the simple cares of the young! I envy it so."

"You seem to not have lost you youthfulness yourself, Highness." Éleen commented lightly, finding the handsome royal easy to talk to.

Prince Kent looked away from the boy, his eyebrows lifted in surprise. "Well, I'd like to think so sometimes, Ms. Éleen, but my role as the sole heir of the Golden Kingdom does put a damper on such dreams."

"Oh? I did not realize you were an only child, Highness." The princess could not imagine how such would feel, as she had four siblings herself.

"Please, call me Kent, Ms. Éleen." His relaxed smile followed again. "And, I'm surprised you had forgotten I was an only child. You and I were introduced to one another on your youngest sister's birthday, four years ago. I had been visiting your family to discuss some trade propositions."

Éleen felt herself blush as she was called out on another blunder. She really was making so many awful mistakes that day! "I...I am sorry, Highness—I mean Prince Kent."

"Just Kent."

"Ah...Kent." Her face color deepened. It was strange to address another royal so familiarly. "I am sorry I forgot about that. That I did not recognize you earlier today, too, though we have meet previously, is so unseemly of me."

"It is okay, princess, you know?" Kent assured her. "I was not a memorable lad back then, of that I am sure. Shorter, less mesomorphic, very uncomely." To add to his joke, Prince Kent rose his good arm in an unprincely fashion to show off his now-developed bicep muscles. "I'm not hurt in the least that you dismissed me from your mind after all these past years."

Éleen could not help giggle at Kent's playful nature, though she did hide it behind a raised hand. It was unbecoming of a princess but it was too hard to be stoic and proper when the man across from her was so carefree. "Still," she managed to get out, "As a Havenese royal daughter, I mistook you for His Highness Prince Maushelik. I should not have done that."

"I do not think it is a matter you should dwell much upon." Kent replied, his mood becoming sincere. "His Highness was surprised at the misjudgment, to be sure, but he is most certainly not snubbed by it." The royal could see the doubt in the princess's eyes but was unsure of how he could erase her skepticism. Yes, Kent knew how insulting the princess's blunder would be if done in the South, and even here rumor would spread quickly on how the Havenese princess had mistaken Prince Maushelik. But Kent had heard Al'den: the other prince had wished the matter forgotten. He had forgiven the faux pas. How could Kent convey that to this demure princess? He was going to say his thoughts on the matter when another knock resounded on the door and a Starian retainer popped his greying head into the room to announce Prince Maushelik's arrival. Princess Éleen's blush returned and downcast her eyes, still embarrassed; however, she stood with Prince Kent to receive the Starian heir.

Prince Al'den had changed into garments better suited for a royal heir. Once the princess saw his lavish cashmere tunic and pants, though, she realized the ensemble did not go with the man wearing them. The Starian was a military man to the core, well-muscled, and as carefully-contained as a caged lion. Though he looked fetching in the royal clothing, there had been a completeness to the military attire the new one lacked. Still, the prince's respectful action was not lost on the Princess. She was glad to see her betrothed had been concerned enough to change.

Prince Kent looked between the two betrotheds, caught between their shy assessments of each other. He could tell that the royals needed some kind of catalyst to break the ice—and he was conveniently available to provide assistance. "Has the tea and biscuits been set out on the balcony?"

"Ah," Prince Al'den snapped his ice-blue eyes away from the princess's face. Recovering himself, he nodded and motioned the way to the sitting area. "Yes, I asked for it some time ago. The refreshments should be outside." Finding his courtesy again, the tall Starian waved the princess to follow Kent outside and he shadowed them out onto the large landing. As the royal had predicted, the staff had set out three cups, a teapot, a bowl of fruit, and a tray of biscuits.

Prince Kent pulled a chair out for Éleen, complete with his charismatic charm then he seated himself. Knowing Al'den well enough, he did not ask where the other prince would sit. Across for Éleen would give the man the best placement for viewing the princess and surveying their surroundings; it was a general rule that all military men wanted the one seat that gave them access to all entry and exit points; safety and security were always first over correct mannerism. As Kent sat in the last chair, he asked if the princess was fairly situated out of the sun and began to peel a fruit for her. As he worked on the fruit, he observed from the corner of his eye as Al'den came to the table and began to fill their tea cups. The Starian passed them out with skill that had the princess staring back, wide-eyed. His ease would have had the Havenese Ladies' Court put to shame. Éleen felt herself blushing again—this time in astoundment—at being served by two dashing princes.

"Life is more lax here in the North," Al'den explained as he poured, "And I am not up for letting people do for me what I am capable of doing myself. You have just come from a arduous journey. Relax now and we will take care of things."

"Ah..." Princess Éleen found herself at a loss for words. No man in the South would abase himself below a woman, especially to do the work only ladies or servants were for! Being treated by two men—both higher in status than her—had the princess befuddled.

"That's Syre's greatest military genius for you." Prince Kent joked as he set down the pieces of fruit by Éleen's biscuits. "Al'den is not used to having women-folk around to take care of him; and neither am I, come to think of it. But, don't you worry, Ms. Éleen, I promise he is quite capable of acting his part when it becomes him."

"I am not sure if you are complimenting me or graciously causing insult." Al'den bantered back, finding chatting with Kent was easing his insecurities with the princess. Who could believe such a decorated war hero as himself could be reduced to a simpering, tongue-tied fool in front of the Havenese princess? "Though I many lack certain...cultured airs...as my scholarly friend here, I am not as unschooled as I appear, Princess." It was the closest he could come to an apology for himself. Al'den took his seat and proceeded to eat a sweet biscuit.

Silence hung over the table as the three royals partook of the late afternoon tea. Princess Éleen found it uncomfortable but she was at a loss for how to break it. Her mind seemed incapable of conjuring forth any subject deemed acceptable to speak upon. In her discomfort, Éleen forced herself to pay extra attention to how she presented herself as she sipped her tea and nibbled on the biscuits.

Across from her, Al'den found himself transfixed by the Havenese woman's delicate airs. Never before had he witnessed such practiced eating habits: the fine, slender fingers holding the teacup and lifting it to rose-petal lips only to drink as if the cup would shatter if pressed too strongly or how, when tasting the biscuits, she barely took a bite so as to minimize any crumbs from falling. How did the fair lady not starve eating in such a state? Prince Kent kicked Al'den's shin none too gently to remind the other man that he was rudely staring.

Quickly, Al'den averted his gaze and cleared his throat. "I hope your quarters are acceptable, Highness. If there is anything you need that would make the room more to your liking, please do not hesitate to ask. My staff will provide anything you require."

"Ah, thank you, Your Highness." Éleen replied, setting her cup down. "The room is quite agreeable and to my liking already." She found herself struggling to say more and finally settled with, "I find the yellowwood furniture to be quite a novelty. We do not have such soft-toned wood in the South, nor any that match the color."

"Yes," Al'den gave a gentle smile. "It is a wood found only to our north, in a dead-wood forest. The place is somewhat haunting, all those acres of upright, bare trunks, but the furniture they create are always one of a kind." Éleen smiled back shyly but was unable to reply. Al'den spared a glance at Kent to see if the other man would intercede again but the Golden heir would not avail him. Prince Kent was beginning to see the two royals would have to figure themselves out on their own. "Do you play any instruments?" Al'den asked, trying to latch onto a subject.

Princess Éleen looked startled at the question but, finally, she nodded. "Yes, I was taught to play the harp, though I am not sure one would say I am proficient at it."

Prince Al'den very much doubted that the princess was a novice player, so he ignored her comment. "Well, in that case, I will have a wind lyre brought to your room. It is similar to your harps but is made in the same yellowwood you admire in your rooms. The sound is very…shall I say demure?… compared to your harps. You may well enjoy the sound. It is quite soothing."

"Thank you, Your Highness, I would very much like to hear your lyre. I will look forward to playing it." She sipped her tea again, to clear her dry throat. "Do either of you play…or, ah, I mean what do you like to do?" Éleen quickly caught herself. Again, in the South, men did not play instruments. That was an activity for sophisticated ladies and country bumpkins.

"Actually, I do play." Al'den replied and found even Kent surprised. "I took it upon myself as a young boy to play the flute. I learned from my mother before she passed away. It was her favorite instrument and she used to play for me when I was little so I bothered her to learn so I could duet with her. Hearing the flute gives me solace on days when the weight of all the fighting and deaths take their toll."

"I am sorry to hear of your mother." Éleen said sincerely and politely.

The Starian gave her a wan smile. "It is all right. She passed a long time ago." However, he quieted at the grief.

"I also play." Kent jumped in before the sadness of the moment stole the progress of the conversation. "I was instructed in the Se, a twenty-five stringed zither. You know the instrument kind of like a harp but laid on its side with a base board underneath? My teacher said it was important for a scholar to know music. *"A true man must never lack in any of the skilled disciplines"*, he used to say." His impersonation of his stern instructor brought a giggle to the princess and lightened the mood. "But I guess we are just men of exception to you, yes, Ms. Éleen? For it is not true that men of Blue Haven and Sunrise do not pursue such activities? Even parts of Sealand find it odd for men to take up an instrument."

"Yes, that is true. Until just now, I have known no men whom played. I always thought it strange that men did not wish to know the joy of such amazing inequity."

"That is because they are not men enough to admit they wish to join the women in such entertaining pursuits."

"Ha," Éleen laughed, "That would be quite the insult to them, to be sure!"

"Indeed." Kent grinned devilishly.

Al'den chuckled as well and shook his head. He cleared his thoughts by eating a piece of fruit and following it with a chaser of tea. Finding it becoming easier to speak with the princess, he continued to ask about herself. "So, what else do you enjoy doing, Highness, besides playing the harp?"

"I am much like other women, I am afraid." Éleen replied. The tall Starian rose an eyebrow to show his doubt but waited for more details. "I do needlepoint, sew gowns, practice my calligraphy, and read. On occasion I go for a hack on my mare before practice dancing or etiquette. Nothing out of the ordinary for a Lady of the South."

"And what do you like to read?" Kent asked, latching onto a subject he, too, enjoyed.

"Kingsley Barker, "The Tales of the Tradewinds", is my favorite. I have quite a liking for his stories of his travels through Syre back when the trade routes were just getting charted, and, Margaret Lynn

Symlie's sonnets are always a cheerful read, especially during the long winter."

"So, you are less into the Classics, then?"

"Classics are all right, but I much prefer the freshness of more contemporary writers. They inspire me more." She blushed, hoping she wasn't too forward in her convictions. Kent's agreeing nod soothed her fears.

"The Citadel has the largest library in Syre." Al'den interjected. Éleen flickered her lovely, china-blue eyes back to him. "Kent and I have been making a habit of visiting it in the afternoons. You are quite welcome to join us." He frowned slightly at a thought that maybe the princess would not appreciate the company and added, "Or, you can go there any time you wish. It is open to you at any hour."

"I would very much like that."

"Excellent." The Starian royal took the last sips of his tea and ate the last of his biscuits. Finished, he pushed back his chair and straightened, as if to stand. "If you are finished with your refreshment, Highness, Kent, my father King Maushelik had asked I introduce you."

"Oh!" Éleen felt herself become flustered again. She tried to shoo away the sudden nervousness. The abrupt change had caught her by surprise. The princess felt her stomach begin to flip-flop at the mention of meeting Maushelik senior. Inaudibly, she reminded herself that not two weeks past, she had behaved well in front of the Sunarian king. Certainly, the Starian king must be as easy to address? "Yes, yes. I am done, Your Highness. If you would, please, give me a moment to freShe up, I will be ready."

Prince Al'den wondered in what way the Havenese beauty could possibly need to be put to rights but set the thought aside as just another womanly action. He half-stood as the princess rose from the table and watched as the twenty-four-year-old maiden hurried inside to her vanity and mirror. Once she was out of hearing range, Kent leaned over and whispered, "You should get her some flowers for her room."

Al'den eyed him, confused. "Why on earth would I do that?"

The Golden heir looked back despairingly. "Trust me, she will very much like it."

"Okay." Al'den replied, not convincingly.

"You are not a romantic, are you?"

"What does that have to do with anything?"

Kent sighed. "She is a very gorgeous lady, Al'den. Treat her right. Get her roses and court her as if she was the only woman in the world."

"I do know about courtship, *sennie*, but the circumstances between the princess and I are not about love. I accepted her proposal for political reasons, not romantic ones."

[Note: Sennie is a Tashek word for friend; Starian royals use keshic on occasion when other words don't seem as inclusive enough.]

"All the more reason," Kent replied before the other man could say more. The playful flash came to his eyes again, as if any deep thought he had had to be preceded by the look. "What I ask is not hard to do, you know, especially for a man already showing signs of being smitten. Political or not, she is worth the effort of a real courtship, don't you think? If I was in her position, I know I would desperately hope the person I was arranged to would be courteous to such actions."

Al'den stared across at his friend, thinking the scholar quite amorous. "You seem to doubt my abilities to woo a lady."

"Oh, I do not think you incapable, not really," Kent replied, "But, I see the princess has an effect on you that completely boggles your senses. I am just pointing out my concern that you will forget to treat her like a lady you agreed to pay court to."

"You really needn't worry about that." Al'den stood. "A lady as fine as her I would want to treat with the highest of regards." He looked in the direction of the princess's room and his eyes got somewhat cautious, in a very characteristic Al'den sort of way. "You are right about two things, Kent. She is a sweetheart, and she is so very far away from what she knows. I cannot imagine what dreams of love and romance such a maiden can conceive, but I do understand the uncertainty of meeting someone given for betrothal only for political means. For her, I can tread gently."

§ §

Éleen batted her stray, wispy brunette bangs around to try to get them to settle just right on her image in the mirror but the strands would not do as she wished after days of travel. The issue was causing her anxiety to mix with frustration. Oh, how the princess wished to make a good impression on the Starian king—especially after her debacle with his son! She may have ruined her chances with Prince Al'den, he had to think of her as a silly, pampered ingénue; but she had yet to do so with Maushelik senior. There was no telling what Al'den had said to his father of their encounter, but it would not do her any justice. Éleen vowed to try harder to prove to the king and his heir that she was worthy of becoming the prince's wife—but darn if her hair and powder would just behave!

Éleen heard the two princes enter her room. Reluctantly, she pulled herself away from the mirror—to almost run smack-dab into Prince Al'den's powerful torso. The tall Starian caught her by the shoulders. "Easy, Highness," he said calmingly. Éleen felt her face burning as she backed away from the intimidating height of her betrothed; being only five-foot-three, she barely made the prince's chest. Éleen had not realized that the rumors of the Starian leader being so tall and handsome had also meant that he towered six-foot-two inches and was well-endowed in all the ways that made a woman swoon. Having the prince's touch on her tiny shoulders was too much. She felt herself go shaky again. "I apologize, Your Highness," she managed to say. Stars, she kept making so many mistakes around the royal heir of Staria!

To make matters worse, the Starian seemed unaffected, while Éleen was completely flustered. "No harm done, Highness, as long as you are not hurt. I have asked your escort, Lord Nexlé, to join us as we meet my father."

Éleen nodded. "And Prince Connel, Your Lordship?" She asked.

Al'den knit his brow, as if trying to decide whether to be concerned with the princess's friendship with the other royal. "I will invite him to dinner, where we will be joined by others of high rank, but I would like your audience with my father to be in private."

"Yes, of course." Éleen chose to agree with the prince and hoped she had not just made another blunder. Would her concern over another prince make her betrothed think even less of her than he already did?

Prince Al'den stepped away from the Havenese princess and motioned for Kent and Éleen to follow him to the door. He opened the heavy yellowwood and motioned the other royals passed. He joined them in the hall. Lord Carrod was waiting for his charge. The Havanese lord bowed at the Starian prince then straightened to his height of five-foot-eight. Al'den could see he was still tight-lipped, as he had been earlier when the royal heir had said he wished for time alone with the princess. Kent had been there for Stars' sake! Only the mention on the other royal had kept the man from arguing that such action bespoke of improper etiquette. The Havener had changed into appropriate stiff, military-styled tunic and pants and washed his short-cropped yet curly auburn hair for the meeting with the king. Freshly scrubbed and refreshed, the twenty-five-year-old looked the part of a royal escort. Al'den noted that Éleen seemed to find relief at seeing the familiar face.

Satisfied, Prince Al'den motioned for Kent to follow him down the hall, barely giving Lord Nexlé time to offer Princess Éleen his arm and trail along. Though Al'den had felt the desire to offer his own arm to the lady, he knew custom dictated that he act impartial to her, especially in public settings, until they were properly wed. The only reason he had been given any credence to the tea and biscuits was because Kent had been included; however, both princes knew it would not be a wise idea to do such again. Rules of engagements required chaperones. Trying the stunt again could result in political folly, even this far away from southern customs.

The princess kept finding her eyes falling back onto the Starian heir's strong back as he led the way to the King's private chambers. Though Éleen felt safer with her arm threaded through Lord Carrod's, she could not make her worried mind still. Her thoughts continued to run over everything that she had done wrong since encountering the Starian prince. No amount of coaching exercises were able to stop the demeaning dialogue. By the time they had crossed the length of the Citadel of Light, Éleen was on the verge of a silent panic attack.

A retainer was at the king's private chamber doors. He bowed to the royals as they neared and hurried to open the heavy wood. The four of them passed through and stepped into the private quarters of King Maushelik. The Starian king was much like his son in that he did not flaunt his wealth in fancy royal trappings, choosing instead simple styles that represented his reserved, military-like lifestyle.

Only a couch and two chairs were around a small yellowwood table making up the first room of his apartments. Beyond, in the next room, was a side alcove for his personal servants to wait, rest, or sleep when not doing their king's bidding. A large study desk took up that left wall of the room, stacked with numerous letters and official papers and documents. Ahead, another room led to a serviceable bed and vanity, barely seen around the corner of the doorframe. The aging king was in the last room, across from his study. The largest room by far, it led to his own private balcony and sitting room.

As Prince Al'den, Kent, and the two Havenese entered this final room, King Maushelik turned away from a parchment he was revising and stood to greet his son and Prince Kent fondly. The Starian prince hurried to his father's side so that the crippled king would not limp over. He returned the hello with affectionate regard just as strong as the king's. Prince Kent came forward with his friend and bowed deeply. King Maushelik welcomed the Golden heir just as warmly as his had his son then waved the two princes to seats near his own.

Princess Éleen and Lord Nexlé held back as the other royals greeted one another. The princess used the time to calm her frantic heart and steady her thoughts; she preoccupied their skipping by concentrating on comparing the elder king to his heir. King Maushelik was nearly as tall as his son and just as intimidating, though both had a charming smile that could make women swoon. Too, he had the airs of a warrior and it was evident in the deepening lines of his face that the king had witnessed many hardships, but the eyes that focused on Éleen still held a vitality and fighting spirit that time had not erased. The look stilled her. "Princess Éldon-Tomino." The king said in a low, powerful voice.

Éleen felt her breath leave her but she managed to get through a fluid curtsy and utterance of "Your Majesty". The king offered his hand and she managed to walk toward it and kiss the topaz ring without err. "You are absolutely lovely, dear. "King Maushelik said as she lifted her china-blue eyes to his own of steel-blue. His large, calloused hand was surprisingly gentle as he squeezed hers. "I am grateful to see you made the trip from Blue Haven safely. I had been concerned when your correspondence informed me of your journey. I had worried that misfortune might befall you, what with the maunstorz attacks and the like. I had heard that I have Prince Sunrise and my man, Lord Shekmann, to thank for your safe passage on the roads coming north."

"Yes, Your Majesty. Both Prince Connel and Lord Shekmann were able to lead my men and myself through any harrowing areas. It was a relief to have Your Lordship's offer of protection and guidance through the Aras Desert. He and his guide, Zyanthena Sheev'arid averted many such mishaps on the journey from Kavahad to here."

King Maushelik exchanged a glance with his son over the princess's last statement but he did not pursue the matter. "I will thank Lord Shekmann personally for receiving your party and taking over your protection." He waved her to another chair and released Éleen's hand, once she was settled. The Starian then waved Lord Carrod to join them and ordered a servant to get refreshments before relaxing himself back into his own chair. "I wish to extend my thanks to your father, King Éldon, for sending his condolences and support. To have asked Al'den's proposed betrothed to make the journey for our cause was an unexpected surprise. That you have arrived safely gives me relief; however, I must ask: what are King Éldon's intentions for your being here?"

Éleen felt her anxiety return at hearing the Starian king's query. He had every right to question her father's allowance of her coming to Staria. In fact, as she thought about it, she could see how her coming instead of her elder brother or one of the advisors with an army behind them could look suspicious. Yet, to say the truth of the matter would be worse. What would King Maushelik do if he found out that the King and Queen of Blue Haven did not really care about Staria's plight? The only reason Éleen had felt she could volunteer herself was because of Prince Al'den's reply about the betrothal proposal—though their correspondence had been last Snow Melt. The heir had seemed accepting of the match in his letter; had Éleen been too forward to believe his words had meant anything, and—if she said the truth—would it make their proposal nulled? Summoning up her courage, she chose to lie by omission. "I come with King Éldon's blessings on His Highness's acceptance of a political marriage. As my dowry, I have brought with me fifty of the kingdom's best fighters and six hundred gold dreites to offer Your Majesty." [Note: Dreites = gold bars]

King Maushelik rose his eyebrows at her price. "Indeed, that is a worthy dowry to offer Staria." His face became a careful mask, void of any clue as to where his thought's lay. The perceptive, steel-blue eyes stole over the princess's face then slid away to study the Starian prince. A tightness formed in Éleen's gut as she waited for the king to speak. Finally, the aging king stirred. "I will not accept Blue Haven's marriage proposal or dowry just yet," he declared. "I know my son already sent you a gift and letter of his favor, but I am not the kind of man—or king—who forces my son to marry to suit a political advantage. As Prince Al'den has expressed his interest in pursuing this union, so I will allow you to be courted by my son. If by the ending of the Deep Snows, my son still wishes to accept the proposal, you may be wed."

Princess Éleen felt her heart fall in her chest. After all the mistakes she had already performed in front of the prince, there was no way he would accept her—especially as he came to know the princess. Before, she had felt secure enough with her decision to come as Prince Al'den's betrothed. To be denied by the king had Éleen feeling like the ground had been pulled out from under her feet. Without a marriage to Staria, she would continue to be looked down upon by her family in Blue Haven; she would stay the different one, the unwanted one.

The princess was too lost in her own worries to notice the others in the room were just as astounded by the king's proclamation. Prince Al'den had turned to his father and was grasping the king's forearm in shock; both Prince Kent and Lord Carrod were being unsuccessful at hiding their own surprise. The Starian heir left his chair and knelt in front of his father. "Majesty...father, I do not understand this. I said I would accept the marriage and the dowry would help us repair our kingdom. To change our minds to Blue Haven—."

"I do not care about the political advantage Blue Haven can afford us, nor in making good wishes a king who will not grace us with anything unless it is his advantage alone." King Maushelik took his son by the shoulders. "All of my years as a ruler has taught me that there are certain agreements between kingdoms that are worth the effort and some that are not. Your getting married to a woman you do not know and have only just met today to mollify a king that is over one thousand miles away is not one of them." Al'den sat back on his heels, his father's words subduing him. "I married your mother, the Duchess of Port Al-Harrad, for political reasons alone, and, though I came to appreciate her as a partner and mother, I never loved her. I know how you are my son, about being loyal to your duties as the prince of Staria. I was just like you, after all. But...I would have you marry for love, Al'den, not for duty."

The king rose his eyes to include Éleen in his discussion. "You are both young enough that you should be given the chance to find love and pursue dreams of such. I do not wish you to be duty-bound to this union. I would have you be given the time to find if such is possible for you. This is what I would ask of you on this." He sat back in his chair. "This is my final decision on the matter. I gladly accept the Havenese soldiers into my army and welcome Princess Éldon-Tomino as a guest of this house. Lord Carrod, we are having a war council in two days. I extend my invitation for you to attend as Blue Haven's representative, with two of your men. Afterward, there will be a celebration banquet, of which Princess Éleen and my son may announce their courtship to the public. Now, if you will all excuse this old king, I have much to do. I will expect to see you all at the dinner tonight."

Chapter Twenty-Five

§

Who the Stars Favor

The camp had been arranged in record time, the Kavahadian army finding reserve energy to set up with the call of rest and food close an enticement. As the sun began to set, the small campfires and food wafted outward. By the quiet of Lord Darshel's command tent, Zyanthena was tending to her horses and ignoring her two always-present guards. She had proven her usefulness to the army by setting up the camp day in and day out efficiently and without complaint; yet, no matter her obedience, none of the men trusted her without the escort. During their trip from Kavahad, Zyanthena had learned many interesting things about the cavalry, including their insistence that she not be allowed food until the rest of the army had eaten. Knowing such, she regularly took to tending the chestnut mare and the doctoring of Unrevealed—a task she would have been doing before repast anyway. The task kept her from thinking of the stomach-grumbling and appealing smell of food she was long denied. It also meant the Tashek stayed predictable to the Kavahad men, especially Commanders Gordan and Raic and to Lord Darshel. It was always more comforting for the captors if the dangerous captee did nothing that would raise alarm. It was her predictability that had allowed Zyanthena even that much freedom. The only saving grace from the two men assigned to her were that they were just as content to ignore the warrioress as she was them.

A low, commanding voice greeted the two guards before his footfalls came closer to the Tashek's turned back. Zyanthena waited for the man to talk, staying calm by continuing her long brushstrokes over the mare' muscled hindquarters. A moment passed and the commander picked up a finishing brush and stepped up beside the desert woman to start on the mare's neck. "I just came to give my thanks, Zyanthena."

The young warrioress looked out of the corner of her right eye to the veteran as he stroked the mare, his movements fluid from years of practice. The auburn-haired commander had not spoken with her much during her time amongst the Kavahadian force; yet, she had learned that the Starian was both a very strict and a very reputable soldier. Feigning ignorance of what Commander Gordon was thanking her for, Zyanthena continued her brushing with careful attention. "Sir, I am not certain as to what you are referring to have gained such respects."

The elder man chuckled and gave her a knowing smile. "Sheev'arid Zyanthena, I am not a native-born man of Kavahad. I trained in His Majesty's foot soldier army for over twenty-five years. As such, I had the privilege to fight alongside many of your own people. I know, with certainty, that none of the Sheev'anee are dimwitted. You all catch details the rest of us would miss. You know exactly what I speak of."

Zyanthena paused in mid-stroke and dropped her arm. "Then you must understand why I did it, Commander."

He nodded solemnly. "Yes, and for that I wanted to speak to you of my gratitude. Many a normal people would only think of themselves and getting their freedom back, not the consequences that come from such a choice."

"I am not like other people."

"No, you're not." He grinned again. "Hell, you're not even like most Tashek I've known. Very few of them would go through all of the shit you have received while being "captive" ...I've heard the stories of what happened between Kavahad and the Sheev'anee. Most Tashek died once they were captured, usually by their own hand. Not a single account had one of you agreeing to an "employment" of sorts with the Shekmann."

"None of those accounts involved Lord Darshel."

"Most would say that doesn't matter. Even you have quoted the "like father, like son" line."

Zyanthena continued her work, avoiding the unspoken question she sensed Commander Gordon wanted to ask. "Did you know Lord Shekmann Sr.?"

The answering disgusted frown said all that words could not. "There is no comparison, as far as I am concerned. Lord Shekmann loved the thrill of the hunt, the bloodlust of torture that his own father cultivated in him. I had been offered the opportunity to serve him in 69 but declined. There were some things I did not want to be involved with. His army was one of them."

"And, yet, you are here now."

"As I said, there is no comparison."

A distant look came to Zyanthena's brandy eyes as she thought over something deep and compelling. The commander let the silence linger. He had kept an eye on the Tashek woman enough to know how insightful she could be when left to her own devices. She finally seemed to stir from her state, as if something had taken her soul and pulled it back into her eyes. "History does not need to repeat itself as long as there are those willing to change it." Hope flashed onto the commander's aged face. It asked the question, *"do you believe, then?"* Zyanthena turned away from the look and her voice became quiet. "There was something said the other night that makes me think differently of His Lordship. It is not that I see him as more than a Shekmann," she said as warning, "But that he is not assenting to the role his father and grandfather created as lords of Kavahad. By that will alone, he may create a different way."

"Then you have even more of my gratitude, Zyanthena. By whatever Star wished your paths to cross, it was fated to be. I have never witnessed a Shekmann and Tashek that could last more than an hour with each other, let alone nearly two weeks. Something up there seems to think you two will be different."

Zyanthena knit her eyebrows together creating a frown. "I doubt fate had anything to do with this. It is just that the politics behind the treaty and my people's wish for peace have kept me in the position I find myself."

"I thought all Tashek were heavily influenced by their belief in the Stars and fate and Karmic effect?"

There was a hint of irony in her voice as the beautiful warrioress responded. "I just like to think that the Stars would not play such a cruel joke on one of their own."

"I do not see the suffering you claim." Commander Gordon replied. "Compared to what has happened to other Tashek that were captured, your imprisonment had been a slight discomfort at best; however, I'm not standing where you are. What I see as an opportunity for change looks like an invisible cell to you."

Zyanthena finished grooming the chestnut mare and started on Unrevealed. The tall, black stallion leaned into her to direct her to a scratch at the base of his neck. Despite his pleasure, however, he cocked a hind leg in warning at the Kavahadian commander; his way of saying don't come any nearer. Zyanthena waved the Starian back and continued their conversation; though, there was an edge to her words that showed the anger she felt at the commander's last comment. "The price Lord Shekmann wishes on me is heinous. If I was not a woman, it would never be a part of my release. Tell me, then, how is that not barbarous?"

Her choice of words had the elder man chuckling, which elicited a piercing scowl from the Tashek. "Sex. He wished sex to be your deal. We all wondered what His Lordship's demands were…as for them being "barbarous", I have heard rumor that his abilities are anything from uncivilized." Zyanthena muttered a comment on how disgusting it was that everyone thought Lord Darshel's pleasuring was his best quality. Commander Gordon chuckled at her repulsion. "Trust me when I say this, Zyanthena. If that is the only cost he had laid upon you, you are very lucky. Especially if he had given you the choice. None of your people were treated as justly."

"Justly." She scoffed. "You have a skewed view of justice. But," she sobered as she thought over the other's words, "I know what you warn me of; the atrocities against my people cover a long list. However, that does not change the circumstances. Even you would not subjugate your own daughter to such a price." There was a sad tone to the words that Commander Gordon had not expected from the woman. More interesting was the fact that Unrevealed responded to her emotions by wrapping his neck around her wispy frame as if to hug her. The two stood embraced, lost in their comfort of each other. For all of Zyanthena's fiery nature, there was something very tender about the act that made her seem young and feminine.

"I am sorry, Zyanthena. I came here to say thank you for saving My Lordship's face in front of High Highness and have instead ended up judging your ordeal as if it is trifling. It is poorly done of me."

Zyanthena twisted around to look him in the eye. There was so much raw emotion there that it took Commander Gordon's breath away. Seeing his startlement had the Tashek instantly masking the look. Her eyes settled into their customary keenness, as if the other expression had never existed. "I thank you as well, Commander." Her voice seemed distant. "Your gratitude is acknowledged as is your sympathy."

Commander Gordan recognized her Tashek version of a dismissal. He had been on the receiving end of it many times before. Giving Zyanthena a formal salute and good-bye, he turned heel and walked away, taking a quick stop at her guards to remind them to get their dinners. He didn't look back. There was no need. Zyanthena would have her wary eyes on his back until he was long gone. She really was made of something unearthly.

Zyanthena unwrapped herself from Unrevealed's comforting embrace to finish grooming the stallion. She was angry at herself for showing such weakness to the commander—no matter that the man sympathized with her plight. The long, steady brushstrokes over his coat eased the emotion, however. By the time the Tashek reached the stallion's injured hip, she found the feeling pacified.

Doctor Murnin had copied her sticky poultice and herbal compresses. Peeling away the leather strip, the Tashek found the wound healing well, both her and Murnin's daily administrations having paid off. The flesh still had a small section, in its center, that would need more days of medicine, but the diameter of the arrow wound hat not been large and was closing at a good rate. The long ride up from Kavahad had not worsened the wound. Within the turning of the moon, Unrevealed would be healthy enough to be her mount again.

The smell of food wafted over to Zyanthena just as she reached into her kit to get her herbal supplies. Turning, she found Lord Darshel standing there, almost touching, with two plates of food in his hand. She jumped at finding the tall, dark-haired Shekmann so near and wondered how he had come so close without her hearing or Unrevealed flashing warning. To settle her nerves, she turned back to the stallion's injury.

"I figured you would be hungry after today." Lord Darshel began, not mentioning how he had snuck up on her so easily. "I just came from a meeting with Commanders Matar and Kins and Cum'ar All'ani."

Zyanthena whipped her head back around at the other Tashek's name. "All'ani Cum'ar." She corrected. "He is here with the Crystine and mertinean?"

"He claimed to be under the direct authority of the "Prince of the Yellow Star". It was assumed he meant Prince Maushelik's command, for he knew most of the details of the attack on the Citadel, at least since the Tashek arrival."

"The All'ani are one the strongest tribes under the Sheev'anee. Cum'ar is the youngest leader they have ever had. His declaration means that he believes the Yellow Star has specifically blessed High Highness."

Lord Darshel shrugged. "I do not understand the Tashek hierarchy or beliefs. All I wanted to say is that we met and discussed security for the Citadel. I told Commander Matar that you were here and well and that I will send you to him for an update when you can be spared." The look of shock (mixed with suspicion) on Zyanthena's beautiful face was priceless. "We need all the information we can get to keep this side of the wall safe. You have friends elsewhere who can provide it. I would be a fool to waste your talents."

"I would have thought you unreasonable and stubborn but not a fool."

"And now?" He challenged with a grin.

Zyanthena averted her eyes at his teasing. "Not so unreasonable but still bull-headed. Your trusting me enough to let me go see Matar has me revising my opinion."

"I never said I trusted you." Lord Darshel stepped away to sit in the sand and lean against his command tent's pole. The action was casual and very unlordly, though it seemed to fit the man. Zyanthena stared at the Shekmann, finding him peculiar in action. The Starian laughed. "Come now, I can't have baffled you, Zy'ena."

Her eyes narrowed. "No." She turned away to finish the poultice.

Lord Darshel continued to chuckle to himself. "When you are done, come eat with me. Sooner so your food will not be cold."

The Tashek woman did not reply, though she finished her doctoring in good time. She finished by giving Unrevealed some sort of pressed-grain bar as a treat and came to settle herself near the Kavahadian lord. Without a word, Lord Darshel passed her plate over and continued eating his dinner. Zyanthena kept a wary eye on the brawny lord as she ate; however, Darshel gave her no reason to be concerned. Slowly, she sighed and began to enjoy the warm food. "Was there anything Commander Matar or Commander Kins said that you found important?" *To tell me*, she had wanted to add but did not want herself to seem too personal with her captor.

Lord Darshel finished his last bites of dinner before answering. "They did not have much to say; just gave the count of the dead from the battle; and explained how they have been running the camps. The shifts are well-thought out. I have no reason to change any of it. Other than that, they asked that any who will volunteer should help repair the city's damaged properties and help clear the field. Most of that has been done already; helping out now would be more courtesy than necessary."

Zyanthena was slow to respond, but when she did, she voiced her suspicions. "If the really was nothing to mention then why are you here? There is much you should be doing."

"And taking time to eat is not one of them?" He teased, thought his face was all serious. Zyanthena's eyes flickered over Darshel's chiseled features, showing that she doubted that was his reason for bringing her food. Darshel sighed in disappointment. "Never easy to console." Reaching into his military jacket, he took out a folded letter from the inner breast pocket. He held it in front of Zy'ena's face until she reached out and grabbed the expensive paper. "His Majesty and His Highness wish us to a private audience."

Lord Darshel watched the desert woman as she read the flourished letter. Her sharp eyes did not show her emotions, keeping them locked off her face. Lord Darshel could not tell if Zyanthena was elated at the coming opportunity or not. He waited for the Tashek's response. Finally, Zyanthena finished reading. She dropped her hands to her lap and stared thoughtfully away, as if enjoying the sight of her war courser instead, lost in thought. "They request an audience the date of the celebration ball."

Lord Darshel was confused by her choice of introduction. "Perhaps they are preoccupied with other proceedings? Our situation was only recently known."

"That is not why I am concerned." Zyanthena shifted to sit facing the Kavahad lord. The sudden sign of respect was not lost on him. "I wish to be a part of the war council."

"I do not see how you would not be. You were one of the most important Tashek scouts of the Crystine, were you not?"

"I am with Kavahad now." She replied, as if it answered everything.

"And I will ask you to be a part of my party, just as you were meeting His Highness. You have proven your use to me on our journey. I can afford to give you that respect." Her eyes showed her skepticism. Lord Darshel continued, "What is your real concern, Zy'ena? You focused on the celebration ball, in five days. Is that it? Five days before you are granted your freedom. You were hoping for sooner."

Zyanthena stilled, as if Lord Darshel had said something that hit very close to the heart of the matter. Only someone so wild could become so still. The twenty-eight-year-old felt his breath stop as she froze. Then, the warrioress took her own, steadying breath. The action released her hold on the Kavahadian lord. She spoke her mind. "It is just that I feel the repeating of the past. Not two week ago, I stood before you and said I would be free of you by the command of Matar and the Sheev'anee. Now, I find I might again. I am hesitant to hope for such. You were right..." she paused, uncertain to finish. Lord Darshel waited, not wanting to ruin the moment with a smart-ass remark about his being correct in his judgment. There was something deep in their discussion that had him cautious of being too rude. "...the Stars favored you then. I fear they may favor you now."

Lord Darshel chuckled, unable to stay serious any longer. A Tashek afraid? He was rewarded with a sharp glare. "I am sorry, Zy'ena." He curbed his amusement. "It is just that I remember you saying I am not that religious. I doubt my lack of piety will be rewarded a second time. You are a people of the Faith, that gives you higher clout with the powers that be. Besides, His Majesty will, without a doubt, find my reasons for holding you inadequate. You are a scout of the Crystine and daughter of the Shi'alam. That gives you power over me."

"Some power." She muttered, unhappy with the circumstances. "My father already gave the word over my predicament. He has no need to change his mind. You have been...more civil...than your father. The king will take that into account, as well, and the Shi'alam's decision."

"King Maushelik has not been known to tolerate the situation between our people. You are as good as free."

Zyanthena became still again, her eyes attentive to the Shekmann's face. Lord Darshel wondered what she saw there. "You are still not inclined to letting me go free despite this new conviction of yours." Darshel's face became carefully blank but he did not offer a rebuttal. "You will let me go if His Majesty orders you to, but only if he does. You find me a fascination, a difficult beauty to unravel and conquer. You will not release me until I have been won by you."

Now the lord's face dropped into an irritated frown. "You are exotic to be sure, Tashek, but you are not so captivating as to be an obsession. On that you are too self-consumed of your allure. I have no need to win you; the number of beautiful, willing women I have to my bed is proof enough of that."

"Willing is not a challenge, Your Lordship, and you like a challenge very much." Zyanthena sat back, her brandy eyes confident in her assessment. "You cannot let go of that which challenges you the most—a woman who denies your advances. Less than a direct order from your king will not get you to release me."

"Then he better order it." Darshel replied, wishing to end the discussion. How had they become so perspective of each other and so quickly?

Zyanthena's face smoothed out into a neutral blankness as she stood. Looking down at the Shekmann, her face was cast in shadows of the falling light. She seemed like a distant, otherworldly desert apparition come to life. "Yes, Your Lordship, he must. We will answer his call. I can do as he bids—but will you be able to do the same?"

Chapter Twenty-Six

§

Courtesies

Princess Éleen could not breathe; she was fairly certain she was in shock. It had been almost two hours since she had been denied the prince's hand by King Maushelik. In her mind, however, she had lost all sense of the minutes gone by. In her defense, she had kept her head through the dismissal and all the way to her new quarters. Once Éleen had reached the rooms, however, the princess had requested she be alone and had locked the door. Since then, she had sat on the edge of her bed and stared at the far wall, not taking any notice of the cheerful desert sunset painted against the regular tones of the décor. Her mind continued reeling as the princess began to think of her predicament... the King of Staria had denied her hand and Blue Haven's favor. He hadn't accepted her royal dowry either—only the fifty guards she brought with her. Éleen's family would most assuredly look down on her for this blunder. There would be no forgiveness for missing this opportunity to gain an alliance with the Starian royal house; to go home was to become the permanent disappointment of the Eldon-Tomino name.

There would be no going home; there would be no home to return to.

Finally, Éleen became aware of the tears sliding, silently, down her cheeks. Once she did, she began to shake with unvoiced emotion, yet, the princess would not allow herself to make a sound. If she was to feeling sorry for herself, she would do so in silence. The emotions consumed her.

Éleen was so lost in her head that she did not hear the knock on her door nor the sound of someone tampering with the lock; even the loud click as the bolt came free and the wooden door was pushed open did not register. She jumped in surprise as large, calloused hands touched her gently.

"I apologize, My Highness, if I startled you." Lord Carrod responded immediately. Éleen sniffed and tried to wipe away the wetness from her face. It would not do for her escort to see her in such a state, but Lord Carrod captured her hands. "My Highness. It is okay. Everything will be okay." The words brought out a sob the princess had fought to control for so long. Just one, then she sucked back the sound. The Havenese man reached into his jacket and brought out a handkerchief. He began to wipe the tears from Éleen's delicate face. "You're messing up that lovely powder job, princess."

The statement was close enough to what Éleen's mother would have said that she was able to compose herself. "Thank you, Lode Nexlé. I'm done now." Her voice came out quiet but steady. Lord Carrod nodded and sat back on his haunches, though he kept one hand in hers. He did not attempt to say anything more to console the princess. Instead, he waited for Éleen to direct him. The respectful silence helped the Havenese woman remember her place.

Slowly, she pulled her hand from Carrod's and began to fuss over her hair and clothes, making them more presentable. Her face would require a mirror. She stood and began to collect the items required to fix her powder. As Éleen moved about the room, she forced her mind away from its fears by focusing on more present details. "May I ask how you got in here?"

Lord Carrod had the sense to look embarrassed but he answered. "Well, actually, there are a couple of men right outside your rooms that are worried about you. Prince Argetlem has the skills to undoing locks, it seems. They—Prince Argetlem and Prince Maushelik—both thought it would be best if I came in to see how you are, but they are waiting for my report."

"I—." Éleen looked shocked. Why would they care? Or did they think her unstable enough to hurt herself? She had never been treated so thoughtfully by anyone before. It felt foreign. "They are really outside?"

"Yes, My Highness." Lord Carrod gave her a soft smile and came to his feet. "They waited by your door, discussing whether to leave you alone. When the hours passed, they returned to check on you and were concerned that you had not come out yet. Finding me still locked without, His Highness Argetlem picked it and directed me to attend you. They asked I return with word on how you fared."

Éleen felt her panic return as she worried over the inconvenience she had caused the two princes. "Please, go inform them that I am well and that I will be out shortly to thank them for their worry. Tell them I am well."

Lord Carrod knew his princess too well to do her biding. "I am sorry to be so bold, My Highness, but you are not well. I will tell them so once you have a moment to compose yourself. Only then will I go."

The Havener sucked back her retort and turned away. It would not do for her to snap at her Lord Protector, especially when she was in such a teary-eyed state. Anything she would happen to say would come out wrong. Instead, she preoccupied herself with putting her face to rights and dabbing a wet cloth over her eyelids to decrease their redness. Behind her, Lord Carrod seemed to relax his vigil, enough so to take a precarious perch atop one of her chair's plush arms. Éleen flicked her eyes to his outline in her mirror then refocused on her face, feeling herself calm down as she set about powdering her delicate features. She finished her face as quickly as could be managed until she found the woman looking out from the mirror was more composed than she still felt inside; however, seeing the image helped Éleen pick up the shattered shards of courage she had in her heart and build up a strong facade. Turning around resolutely, the Havener went over to her Lord Protector to present herself. "I am ready, Lord Nexlé. Let us go together and thank Prince Maushelik and Prince Argetlem on their gracious concern."

Lord Nexlé blinked at her commanding presence before complying to her order. "My Highness." He offered the royal his arm and escorted her to the hallway.

The two princes had settled against the opposite wall. Prince Al'den leaned casually against the adobe, his arms crossed and a leg bent over the other. Beside the tall warrior, Prince Kent was fiddling with some kind of twisted wire contraption, bobbing it back and forth between his hands as he chatted gaily with the other man. The Starian noticed the princess first. He smartly straightened into a military-ready stance. The motion caused his companion to pause his hands and mouth and look up. It was the Golden heir that spoke first. "Ms. Éleen, we are glad to see you."

She answered his smile tentatively. "Prince Kent, Prince Maushelik, thank you for coming to check on me. I apologize for inconveniencing you." She curtsied.

Kent pulled away from the wall. "You are not anything of the sort, Ms. Éleen," he chided her gently. "Two men such as ourselves are not inconvenienced unless we want to be. And, as we have all had a shock from His Majesty King Maushelik's degree, I'd say we all are in need of a little loving care, hm?" Éleen blushed at the prince's choice of words, which could have been the scholar's intent, as indicated by the triumphant twinkle in his eyes. He chuckled and turned away to include Al'den into the conversation. "So, we were just seeing if Staria's guests were in need of anything as we passed along on our way to meet the final arrivals."

Prince Al'den cut in before Kent could ask if the princess would like to join them. "The Shi'alam, the leader of the Sheev'anee, and the Heir of Sealand have sent word of their pending arrival. Seeing as there was a little time before they get here, we wished to call on you and make sure you were faring all right. That is all." He ended with a warning glance at the other prince. Kent smiled back cheerfully. "I have asked two ladies, Miss Coltrine and Miss Ansley to be at your bidding." The tall prince motioned to two girls of barely sixteen, who had been skulking down the hallway, to come over. By the way the two girls hustled over and eyed the prince admiringly, it was obvious that they were smitten with the royal heir; however, it was evident to Éleen that the prince seemed to notice them just about as much as he did with her—which was not at all. Had she not been his proposed (former) betrothed and a princess, Éleen doubted he would have given her attention either. Bowing her head respectfully, Éleen greeted the ladies. They curtsied back politely but their eyes went quickly back to Prince Maushelik.

Al'den continued ignoring the ladies' flutter-eyed glances. "They will show you to the Bower whenever you are ready to meet more ladies of the court. Please, do not hesitate to ask them or any of my people for anything. Staria will accommodate your every need."

"Thank you, Your Highness."

Kent frowned at his friend, unhappy with how socially formal the two royals were being. "And, please, do know we are here for you, Ms. Éleen. We understand the demands of your station and how isolated it can make you. Do not feel inconvenienced to call on us. The pleasures is all ours." Discretely, he kneed Al'den's leg and indicated with his eyes for the prince to add his remarks.

"Yes, princess, do call on us," he managed a smile that would have most women swooning. "We can spare time to visit with you, and it is no problem."

"I will keep you offer in mind, then, Prince Maushelik." Éleen curtsied flawlessly, though she felt the affect the Starian prince's gaze had on her.

To her relief, the Starian heir turned away, quite unaware of his effect on the other gender. "May you have good evening, Highness. We will see you at the banquet hall after the hour." Éleen echoed the prince's formal good-bye and curtsied again as the warrior-prince strode away, a discontented Golden heir following suit.

Once they were departed, Éleen turned back to her new-found problem: the two Starian maidens who eyed her in barely-contained contempt. Pasting a smile on her face, Éleen waved the ladies toward her quarters. "May we sit and take some tea and become acquainted in my study?" She asked politely, beginning to lead the way back into her apartments.

Coltrine, the shorter, more homely of the two girls, whispered something to the other and they barely contained a rude laugh. Éleen felt the gesture was at her expense; whatever she had just said or done had made her their instant amusement. "Why, Ms. Éldon, of course we would have tea with you. How kind you are to offer."

Éleen knew, by the remark, what she had done. The girls were insulting her for treating them as above her station; however, Lord Carrod stepped in before she could make her own reply. "That is "Your Highness", Ms. Coltrine." He reminded sternly and assisted his princess into her room and to her chair. He ignored the two girls to find their own seats and began to fill Princess Éleen's tea cup before taking his seat beside the Havenese royal. His disapproving glare toward the two young women warning them to mind their manners. Coltrine tried to do her insulting, held-in laugh again but Ainsley elbowed her in the ribs. Gathering their composure, the two girls straightened in their chairs and sobered. Lord Carrod continued to keep his sullen glare on their two new charges, quite disapproving of their behavior. "Is there anything further you need, My Highness?" He asked Éleen, though his eyes strayed to the girls to make sure they were minding.

"No Lord Nexlé, thank you. Please, enjoy your tea." Her Lord Protector murmured his "Yes, My Highness" and set about following her command. Éleen did the same, carefully lifting her teacup and sipping from it in correct, courtly fashion. If the girls wanted to play that rude game, she could certainly comply. She made sure her movements were so precise and elegant that the two ladies blushed at their seemingly uneducated ways. Meanwhile, Éleen kept up the uncomfortable silence.

She had had quite enough of the day. The long travel, her many blunders, and the refusal of the Starian king had done their part to wear her down; however, Éleen refused to let the prince's gift of the two girls, however rude they were when he was not about, be her undoing. The Havenese princess would show Staria what the Southern courts were made of. She would get through the next hours, and her next months, and show that the Blue Haven marriage proposal was no sham.

As for Staria's uninterested warrior-prince, Éleen was quite certain she could get over her hopes of a happy marriage—just as long as the prince continued to treat her kindly and kept such good company as Prince Kent. If it took having to bear with the two love-smitten, condescending court brats and weeks of ostracization to do that, she would. Somehow.

Resolutely, Princess Éleen set aside her empty teacup and adjusted her polonaise so that she could stand without mishap, staying in perfect elegance. Lord Carrod was beside her immediately to offer her assistance. The two Havenese continued to ignore the two girls. "I will begin to change for the dinner tonight. Please, call the chambermaid and go prepare yourself."

"Yes, My Highness." Lord Nexlé bowed his burly frame. "And what of the ladies? May I escort them elsewhere?"

Éleen turned to look at the young Starian girls as if they were barely her concern—and indeed they weren't if they were going to treat her as laughing stock. "Leave them, Lord Nexlé. They may go change for their dinners when I have no more use for them. For now, they will entertain me with news of the Starian court."

"My Highness."

Éleen turned away from the table to go to her room and sort through her dresses for an appropriate gown. Though she wished to ask the objectionable girls to leave and give herself space to relax the false facade, Éleen kept her door open and allowed the girls to follow her into the bedchamber. It was obvious the Starian royal family had given her the best quarters by the way the maidens' eyes stared in awe about the room. The fact mollified the princess some; at least her status was expressed by the royal house. If that would help Éleen's standing in the foreign, desert kingdom, she would be grateful. "You may stand over there," she commanded, pointing them to a corner far enough away to not be in her way. Ignoring them, Éleen began to sort through the twelve gown she had thought to bring. By the time the chambermaid had arrived, she had selected a silver-grey evening gown adorned with white lace and deep blue piping, made of the finest materials Blue Haven offered. The elder lady quickly set about helping the princess into the dress and pinning her hair. As the woman worked, Éleen finally acknowledged the two girls in their corner. "The king must think highly of your families for young girls your age to be allowed free roam in the Citadel courts."

It was the more reticent Ainsley who answered. "Not at all, Your Highness. His Majesty follows customs much less strictly than the Southern kingdoms that is to be sure, but His Majesty only allows young ladies to be at the court if they have a well-established sponsor and have proven themselves responsible and level-headed. Miss Coltrine and I are amongst the youngest of the ladies, but we are not the pernicious sort."

"Of which you are referring that some ladies are."

"Well," Ainsley shuffled nervously and looked to her friend for help. Citrine scuffled, too, but prodded the other girl to answer. "There are some at court who are considered scandalous, but they are few. We are mostly good women of exemplary stock."

Éleen let slip an understanding smile. "Even the South had its ignominies."

Her statement seemed to put the Starian girls at ease. "Yes, I have heard there is no court without such disgraces." She even giggled some. "But we are mostly honorable. Lady Rosetta Greyson had been the anticipated Lady-in-Waiting for over a year. She had surpassed her family's already prominent position by being a voice of reason at court. Oh, and Lady Diana Levine, too; though she rarely participates in the political debates."

"And do not forget Lady Selena Durrow." Coltrine chimed in, bold again. "She's the most beautiful lady at court. It was expected that with her handsomeness and wealth that she would be one of the best candidates for queen…if His Highness Prince Maushelik shows any sign of choosing any of the ladies at court. His Highness must be waiting for someone new to catch his eye." The girl's tone suggested that she thought the prince had his eye on one of the younger ladies—and Coltrine hoped it was herself to get noticed.

"Coltrine!" Ainsley reprimanded. The other girl snapped her jaw closed but did not look at all contrite.

Éleen kept her cool, not wanting the girls to see her emotions. Surely, the Starian court had heard of Blue Haven's bridal proposal? But if they had, the girls would have said differently. Had Staria not accepted it after all and the letter had been a ruse to keep Blue Haven's favor? Or was it, perhaps, that the king and his heir were just very good at keeping a tight wrap on the information? It seemed odd that such a match as two royal-borns could be kept so quiet. Not, of course, that it mattered anymore since King Maushelik had voided the prince's acceptance of the marriage. Calming herself, Éleen stored the thought in her memory and returned her attention back to the two girls and to her appearance, the latter of which she found quite stunning from the chambermaid's experienced hand. "Could you tell me more of these ladies? I have heard their names even at the Azure Palace. I am anxious to know more about them."

Her question was answered with an enthusiastic account from both of the girls. Apparently, they wanted to outdo each other on conveying the gossip of the Ladies' Court. Princess Éleen listened carefully, taking in all she could. Knowing such information usually came at a more expensive price; but, if she was to live in Staria, Éleen knew it could better her chances of making it in the new court.

"Lady Greyson and her elder brother, Lord William, inherited a great sum and all their deceased father's lands not but three years back. Considered a young master at twenty-five, Lord Greyson was not expected to keep such a prominent holding his father had; however, both Lord and Lady Greyson have surpassed all expectations, including doubling their father's fortunes. Lady Greyson herself has been one of the most openly supported speakers in the court. Her position of unifying all of Syre's armies to defeat the loathed maunstorz—at first a preposterous idea—has become widely accepted in Staria and certain areas of Sealand and Rubia. She had been a diplomat between both kingdoms and had helped usher much support for His Highness Prince Maushelik's cause."

"She sounds like an exemplary lady." Éleen commented on Ainsley's account. In fact, Éleen was surprised that the Lady was not Prince Maushelik's choice for companion, what with all the accomplishments Ainsley named.

"Yes, she is." Ainsley replied.

"And this Diane Levine. What of that Lady?"

"She does little in the area of politics." Coltrine jumped in in her tactless way. "Her main focus is on education and religion, two subjects not granted to women of certain ages and status. Her influence is such matters has been to prove that society is greater as a whole if women are given more chances of education."

"She is a libertarian at the court." Ainsley continued quickly, as if slightly panicked that Coltrine had said such to a foreigner. "Most of Starian society is still conservative, especially on issues about womenfolk. Lady Levine only wishes to advance the society as a whole. Her take is that if women were given more education and allowed more spiritual practice that it would benefit all."

Éleen had never heard of such an unusually bold woman. In Blue Haven, she would be immediately cast down from high society for having such thought, let alone that the courts would ever let her preach such ideas. It was intriguing, then, that Staria's culture was more open; they seemed to be with many of their customs. It seemed odd to the princess to give women such liberties, but then, she was raised to think such things were wrong. It would be interesting to explore these new freedoms—if she could get past her discomfort with them. The Havenese royal stored the information for later and preceded on as if they had only been talking of the weather. "And this Lady Durrow...you say she is the favorite for queen?"

"Well, I think so." Coltrine announced. Ainsley cast her another warning glance, which she ignored. "She is stunning. No other lady is so comely...everyone says so. And she is always bringing in the latest fashions. You can never miss her at a ball. She is the eye of the party, between her beauty and graceful dancing." The young girl sighed as she remembered the way the woman seemed to float around the dance floor. There was no one else so alluring in her mind as Lady Selena Durrow.

"Lady Durrow is indeed the eye of the Citadel." Ainsley cut in before her friend could continue to fantasize about the woman. "And she does lead the Ladies' Court in fashion. Her wealth and prestige set her in high-standing at court, too. You will, assuredly, be meeting her if you are to stay here for any length of time, Your Highness."

Éleen felt her dislike of the woman already. In her experience, those who flaunted their wealth and physical assets tended to be social charms and behind-the-doors bitches. Nevertheless, the Havenese princess put her most sincere smile on and replied charmingly, "I cannot wait to meet her, then. Thank you, Lady Ainsley, Lady Coltrine, for your insights." The girls beamed back, their dislike for Éleen being replaced by her compliments. "Now, if you ladies would go prepare yourselves for your own dinners, I have mine to attend to. Thank you for your assistance."

The two Starian maidens seemed surprised at being dismissed so suddenly, but they did not seem to mind as they hurried away, giggling and coercing quietly with each other. Relived at their absence, Éleen let go a sigh and finished preparing her features for the banquet. Without the two maidens there, she found she felt less restrained in performing her tasks. Taking a final look at herself in the mirror, Princess Éleen collected her thoughts and prepared for the coming trial of being at the Starian court. "I am capable of doing this," she murmured to herself and unconsciously fingered the topaz pendant at her neck. Immediately, her resolve retuned. "The king wants his son to have true love; my family the favor of the Starian crown. I will not return home until I accomplish both...for however long it takes."

Chapter Twenty-Seven

§

A Lesson in Subtlety

Prince Par set his saddlebags heavily against the baseboards of the bed and fell onto the plush spread. In the antechamber, he heard Lord Gordar direct the Citadel pages where to set the rest of their belongings and shoo the men away. The golden-eyed Sealander appeared in the doorway a moment later and leaned against the frame. The two cousins stared exhaustedly at each other.

"You look fairly comfortable," Gordar commented.

Par huffed and sat up with a groan to survey the Starian décor. "It's such a stark contrast to the dreary weeks at North Point. I don't really feel right laying here."

"What, you don't enjoy the lavish pampering, cousin?" The Lord Protector teased and walked himself the rest of the way into the room to pick up a fine, jade cup for the nightstand. "It does seem odd, though, after the long nights in the rain and on the road. It's too quiet, too clean."

"Yeah." Par moved over to allow his cousin a place on the bed and took the cup of water and the sweet biscuit Gordar passed him. "At least High Highness Prince Maushelik did not keep us long."

"I think he sensed your lack of enthusiasm for introductions. You were a bit sullen during the reception."

"I know." Par grimaced. "May the Stars give him the compassion to pardon me."

The Shi'alam's party, accompanied by Prince Par, Lord Farrylin, and the knights Patrick and Jacen, had been received by the Starian prince and his companion the Prince of the Golden Kingdom in the western courtyard; as the southern one had been occupied by cleaning crews and wounded mounts—or so they had been told. The Shi'alam himself had introduced Prince Par; a great honor; and the Sealand heir was discontent with the lack of etiquette he had been able to give with his own greeting. Neither leader had shown any slight to his discourtesy, however. In fact, Prince Maushelik had called for retainers to take their belongings and stable hands for the wearied horses without any further comment. It was as if he knew how tired the arrivals had been. The lax protocol had been a welcomed relief.

"You will be more yourself after some rest."

"More myself." There was a note of sorrow coupled with forlornness in the prince's voice. "I'm afraid I do not remember who that was. I've lost too many good friends and loyal men these past few weeks. I cannot imagine being my old self after all that."

"That is your fatigue talking, cuz. There will be a time when you will know peace again."

"Was that your way of cheering me up?" Par looked over at his cousin. "It was very uplifting."

Gordar chuckled drily. "Yeah, that was pretty bad even for me. It's been a very long week," he said as way of excuse. They lapsed into silence, staring at their cups. Finally, though, Lord Gordar stirred to set his empty cup down. "I will take to my bed, with your leave, Highness."

"Oh, just go, Gordar, and forget the pleasantries." Par waved his cousin away. "And, hopefully, the retainers will leave us alone for some hours. Wake me if you arise before me."

"Rest well, Par." Gordar replied affectionately and turned away as the royal collapsed back onto the large bed. He, too, fell into his own accommodations and fell into an immediate sleep.

§ §

Prince Par awoke a few hours later to the pleasant sound of evening cicadas; the noise drifting in from an open window inlaid in the southern wall of his quarters. He yawned, stretched, and rolled to a sitting position against the high headboard so he could look about. Evening had set in as he had slept, and the slow-cooling of the desert heat had set his room to a comfortable temperature. The soft flames from two torches outside the window allowed a calm, golden glow to light his bedroom, making it surprisingly easy to make out everything in the unfamiliar setting.

The Sealander pushed himself from the bed and wandered over to the window to look out. His quarters were on the northern side of the Citadel, on the fifth level. It gave a wide view up over the Citadel of Light's towering walls. For as far as the eye could see was a dark plain of rolling, desert sand. It was gently illuminated by the almost-full moon. The stillness was captivating. The prince stood and took in the view, soaking in the solitude.

After many long minutes, he finally turned away to see how his cousin fared. His Lord Protector was still sound asleep in the antechamber. To see Gordar tired enough to relax his vigilant guard was rare and Par could not help smiling at the soft expression of the twenty-seven-year-old's face. He continued past the sleeping man and slipped out into the hallway, quietly shutting the door behind himself.

A young page came up to Par as he wandered down the hall. He stopped the Sealander with a flourished string of bows. "Your Highness, I was asked to bring you to His Royal Highness once you appeared. Please, come this way." Par withheld his disappointed sigh and motioned for the young lad to lead the way. The boy took his down into the floor level of the Citadel. They finally stopped at a tall pair of ornate doors. "Wait her, Highness," the boy said and slipped into the room beyond. Prince Par was left standing alone in the large, high-beamed hallway. A few minutes later, the large door groaned open and the boy appeared again, followed by Prince Maushelik.

"Thank you, Jake. You may go wait for his companion now." Prince Al'den dismissed the boy and turned to Prince Par with a friendly smile on his face. "And I apologize for Jake's not offering you any courtesies while you waited for me. The boy is still new to the staff here at the Citadel."

"I didn't mind, actually." Par replied honestly. He had enjoyed the short time alone.

Prince Al'den nodded, as if he understood, and motioned for Par to follow him down the hallway. "We are in the middle of dinner if you care to join us?" His stare carefully gauged the Sealander's reaction. Par was still tired enough to be unable to hide his unhappiness at the thought of entertaining strangers. "But I felt that you and your man were in need of some quiet after your journey. The Shi'alam informed me of the trials you faced at North Point. If it had been me, I would have wanted to hole up in my quarters for a week and not come out." The comment brought a grin to the other royal's face.

"Indeed, that is how I felt," Par admitted. He found it was easier to speak with the elder prince than he had imagined.

"I am a fighter first and foremost." Al'den replied. "I know how draining weeks at war can be. I hear this was your first major battle. I remember how I felt after mine. You may be here as a dignitary for Sealand, Prince Fantill, but I count you as a soldier of my equal. Do not dismay of needing to take yourself away from socializing. We all understand here."

The prince was surprised that he was being pardoned so easily. He was not sure he himself would have been so sympathetic to a guest a Fortress Opal if they had acted as he had earlier. "Highness—."

"Just Al'den or Prince Al'den, if you must Prince Fantill."

"Then you may do the same, Prince Al'den. Thank you for such curtesy. My man and I are indeed in need of some rest tonight. If you would excuse us from your party."

"Consider it already done." Al'den paused at another large door and waved the Sealander passed him. They stepped into a cool room lit by blue candles and smelling of dampness and sage. The Starian continued deeper into the muted light, going down a short hallway. Par followed, curious. The hall spilled into a large, oval sudatorium. Multiple alcoves led off into small, private baths. The warm steam clung to Par's skin in a pleasant reminder of the air back in Sealand. He breathed deeply of the moisture.

"I have reserved this sudatorium for you and your man's private use tonight. Mertle will be attending to your needs." The Starian indicated an elderly man Par had missed sitting near the entrance. He wore only a loincloth. "If you wish any refreshments, food, or entertainment, he will make sure you ae provided for,"

"I...thank you." Par found himself flustered at the Starian hospitality.

Prince Al'den smiled back warmly. "Just relax, Prince, and welcome to the Citadel. We will have plenty of time to properly meet each other on the 'morrow. I look forward to knowing you better. Now, if you will excuse me, I would like to return to my dinner. Jake will bring your man here if he awakens."

Par nodded. "Thank you for attending to me. I know it is an unusual matter for you to excuse yourself from your affairs to help a foreigner."

The tall Starian warrior paused at the entrance to look back at the other royal. His eyes looked sincere. "It is my honor, Prince Par, to assist you myself. May you have an enjoyable soak. I will see you tomorrow."

The tall Starian left Par to his private bath. The Sealander hesitated still finding a feeling of trepidation in his stomach; it did not sit right to be waited on by another prince. The other royal had been so at ease, acting the perfect host. Par could not help comparing himself against the other. No other kingdom acted so informal. However, from the Mausheliks' reputation, their actions had not made them in any way weaker. Of the seven houses of Syre, Staria was considered the strongest in military defense and combat. It was a small wonder, then, that such skilled fighters could be so hospitable.

"Your clothes, sir," Mertle startled Prince Par from his revelry. The Sealander turned to the elder attendant. The barely-clad man held his arms out ready to take his garments.

"Oh, right." Par turned away to busy himself undressing. To his relief, the man held out a robe and towel as he took off his clothes. Mertle returned to his perch as Par threw the robe about himself. "There is a bucket and soap to the left to wash with before you soak." The man directed the prince before occupying himself with scrubbing the far corner tiles. Left to his peace, Prince Par found the cold bucket of water, scrubbing brush, and soap. He quickly lathered and rinsed himself.

Refreshed and clean, he made his way to the large, central pool and waded into the hot water. Despite having been in the desert heat for the last three days, the hot water felt like heaven. Prince Par felt his wearied and knotted muscles loosen as he reclined against the tiled rim. Contented, he stretched his head back against the cooler wall and enjoyed the shifting shadows from the many candles in the room that danced the water reflection onto the ceiling.

Time passed in a healing silence.

He did not know how much time had gone by when Par finally shifted away from the shadow display, but elder Mertle was back to his former perch and was half-dozing in the steamy room. The entire walls had been scrubbed clean and the supplies put away. Prince Par groaned, finding himself languid from the heat and his hands pruned.

Despite his slow pace, he made it to the stairs and his towel. To his relief, a large pitcher of salted lemon-water had been set by his robe. The Sealander gulped the cool liquid greedily.

Mertle roused easily enough and came over to the royal with the prince's clothes in hand. He waited patiently by the door as the Sealander dressed then led the way back out of the sudatorium. In the fore-room, Prince Par halted, startled, to find a banquet of finger foods and cooling drinks set out for him, as well as, eight beautiful women reclining on a mountain of cushion. A well-rested Siv'arid, Kor'mauk was between them.

"Glad to see you are enjoying the Citadel baths, Prince Fantill." The Tashek greeted as he took a sip of Starian wine and leaned over to kiss one of the women he had wrapped around his arm. "I had assumed you had not eaten yet, so I asked for some repast be sent her. Come enjoy!"

Par went to the table and filled a platter high with Starian delicacies. He turned to find a seat to eat—away from the charming beauties. As he expected, the desert man crowed out that he should join the small troop of women. The prince graciously declined. "I do no partake in such activities, Siv'arid. I would prefer to eat my dinner in peace."

Kor'mauk guffawed the prince's action and continued to give his attentions to the women, but only for a moment as one last tease at the royal's chastity. He finally untangled himself from the women and bid them to leave him and Prince Fantill. "A darn shame, You Highness. They were especially delightful after such a hard ride."

"I had not imagined your people to be into such pursuits." And, indeed, he had not. The Tashek seemed to be such a dignified people, with an exotic nobleness that made them seem so otherworldly.

"We are still men," Kor'mauk replied as he readjusted his pillows to suit his now-lonely self. "Even you must have needs at some times, Highness. We encourage such comforts amongst ourselves and do not try to hide our natures as your people do. Coupling...as I believe you call it...is not seen as deplorable or "behind-the-curtains" as it is in your society. We embrace the sensual as a way to express the passions of life."

Par shifted, uncomfortable at the subject. The knowing smirk the desert man cast him was all at his expense. "And some things are sweeter kept in silence," he retorted, though even to him his comeback sounded weak.

"You are an odd princeling." Kor'mauk replied and tipped back the rest of his wine. "Most in your high station are quick to take their pleasures. You are much too sullen for your age. What fun you miss out on!" Siv'arid was quick to his feet, fluid as most Tashek were despite that he had been drinking. He refilled his goblet and one for the prince and sauntered over. "Are you one to deny a good Starian vintage as well, Prince Fantill?"

"I drink, Siv'arid." Par replied and accepted the wine. His answer seemed to amuse the man.

Kor'mauk returned to the table and danced his fingers around giddily as he thought over what choices he wished to feast on. The silly, almost childish action had Par rolling his eyes and chuckling. The Tashek cast him a sideways grin and picked out his meal before returning to settle back on his cushions. "Enjoy yourself whenever you are off-duty; that is what I believe, Prince. A good laugh feels great, do you not agree?"

The Sealander was too quick to sober. "A prince of Sealand's job is never truly over. The privilege of such joys, as you speak of, are not to be for me, Siv'arid."

"Too sullen." Siv'arid repeated. "You will grow old and die by the time you reach thirty with that attitude, Your Highness! You are in Staria now. Even our great prince knows life is not worth living without letting go of the reins at times and enjoying the wind through the hair—so to speak. You may learn much from our great "Prince of the Yellow Star" and his sire."

"Indeed, Prince Maushelik is a gracious man."

"He is pre-eminent."

Prince Par regarded the Tashek. Even the desert folk thought their royal heir to be an exemplary man. It made him, once again, wonder what his people thought of him. Did he rate as high in Sealand as Prince Maushelik rated in his own kingdom?

"Solemnness does not suit you, Highness," Kor'mauk commented. "Tomorrow, I pray you find some light-heartedness to ward off that somber heart of yours. 'Til them, drink and find your merry." Kor'mauk grinned, losing his seriousness as he saluted his wineglass at the prince.

Prince Par returned the salute and drank of the dark wine, still somewhat lost in his thoughts. He allowed the Tashek man to talk to him about paltry events, finding comfort in the common stories. The strong wine helped, too. Much to his amazement, he soon found himself loose-lipped on silly tales of his own. It felt both strange and revitalizing to laugh so hard after weeks and weeks of desperately trying to fight off the maunstorz at North Point. However, the Sealander only came to the realization as Kor'mauk Siv'arid left his at his guest quarter. Just as the first rays of dawn were filtering through the windows, it finally occurred to him that the desert man had not really been as drunk as he had appeared the entire night. The ingenious nephew of the Shi'alam had managed to cut through his sullen mood without the prince's being aware of the subtle working. It was almost eerie how easily the desert nomads could read and readjust situations. Prince Par was left wondering if that was a good thing—or distressing.

Chapter Twenty-Eight

§

Crossing the Line

Dawn had the Kavahadian army on its first watch atop the Citadel walls. Though the army was mainly cavalrymen, all the Shekmann's soldiers were able archers. Because of this, King Maushelik had asked their more-refreshed force to take the morning watch from his battle-wearied Citadel watchmen. The landscape from the West high-wall was empty; golden sands stretched endlessly, and only the dark shape of the mountains making up the Gap of the Forgotten broke the illusion that the Citadel was alone in the world.

A Tashek scouting party of forty riders was preparing to leave in the southern courtyard. Despite the distance between the two people, there was a tension in the air that spoke volumes of the Sheev'anee-Kavahad situation. Some of the Kavahadian men grouped together to gossip vulgar comments, all the while keeping a close eye to the activity below them. Shík All'aum, who was leading the Sheev'anee, kept a much more respectful line, keeping his men well away from the western wall of the courtyard. All of the Tashek stood at attention and did not glance up; though, there was no doubt they could hear all the slander the Kavahad soldiers spoke, as seen by the clenched jaws or hands resting lightly on their kora swords.

Amidst it all, Zyanthena Sheev'arid held her tongue. She stood just away from the Kavahadian soldiers, escorted by Commander Gordon. Just like the other Tashek, the warrioress kept up a disciplined stance. Only the brandy flash of anger in her eyes could give evidence of her mood. Beside her, Commander Gordon adopted a similar look, though he did try to order the men to shut their traps. "Ignorant, blathering fools," he muttered under his breath, knowing only Zyanthena could hear. Despite his rank, however, the soldiers did not put an end to their impolite grumblings.

Lord Darshel appeared shortly after. He came from the south-eastern bastion, where he had been speaking with Wix, the second-in-command of the Crystine, about fortifications on the wall. Though the Shekmann was tall and usually kept a noticeable presence, he seemed to slip behind his men unnoticed long enough to catch the insults his soldiers were saying amongst themselves. "Men, get hold of your tongues before I let the Sheev'anee have a go at them with a blade!" Darshel boomed out, startling a large number of the soldiers. Unnerved, they shut up and stood at rigid attention. Their hard-featured lord stepped up to the parapet on the other side of Commander Gordon. It was almost striking how quickly the energy shifted with Lord Darshel's presence.

To both armies' shock, Shík All'aum led his desert mount closer to the wall and entreated the Shekmann with a very courteous bow and a "thank you for taking your men in hand." Lord Darshel responded with a bow of his own and a safe farewell wish. Shík All'aum then mounted his bay and cued his riders away. As the forty horsemen exited the courtyard, Lord Darshel turned to his commander. "Gordon, see that all of our men understand, *explicitly*, that we are here under the roof of our king. Any and all transgressions to any of His Majesty's guests will be met with severe punishment. I will not hear of this malapropos talk again." Commander Gordon dipped his head and took leave to walk down the line of Kavahadian solders to repeat the words.

Zyanthena found herself alone with Lord Darshel. She glanced inquisitively at his chiseled features, as if trying to decipher his mood behind his stoic, domineering visage. But she was quick to turn her brandy eyes away to watch her people's departure. Her energy was on its usual guard. A sad longing filled her eyes as she watched the riders leave on the wind. Not having the liberty to go scouting in nearly a moon's turning brought out the restlessness she had been fighting since her "capture". So transfixed was the warrioress on the Sheev'anee scouting party, that Zyanthena did not notice when Lord Darshel fixed his gaze upon her and weighed her up as she had him.

"What is it about the flying of the dust from departing horsemen that has such an attraction to the eye?" Lord Darshel asked, startling the desert woman as he broke his commanding bearing by leaning casually against the stone parapet.

"Your Lordship?" Zyanthena turned her watchful eyes back to the Shekmann's face, wary.

Lord Darshel smiled back at her, his look both teasing and breathtakingly handsome. The casualness did nothing to settle the

Tashek's nerves, which seemed to amuse the lord all the more. "I have not seen you so riveted on something. Your eyes betray your yearning." Zyanthena responded with a sour frown as she looked away. It made the Shekmann chuckle. "You don't like that I'm getting better at reading you."

"Not at all, Your Lordship. You understand me very little."

"Even for you, that insult was weak." Darshel teased again as he, too, turned to watch Shík All'aum's party leave. "He was an interesting man."

"Shík All'aum is third in rank beneath the Shi'alam. For him to show you such high respects will cause word to travel through the Sheev'anee of what regards he wishes taken about you. Word will reach His Majesty of this."

"And may it. I wish it to be known that Kavahad is here under good will. We will put aside our grievances for the kingdom's sake."

"How noble," she replied. It was hard to tell if the woman was being sarcastic or sincere. "You are very unlike the descriptions of your father." Zyanthena commented off-handedly, her deep eyes betraying nothing of what was beneath her words.

Lord Darshel found himself trapped in the gaze. He shifted upright, feeling much too exposed. "My father was a valiant fighter. I cannot claim his valor nor his strength. I can only preserve my city's good name. Let that be known to all." He pushed away from the parapet.

"One would not have guessed the young Lord Shekmann to be modest."

"And one would expect Zyanthena to say that mockingly," Lord Darshel retorted. "Come, the show is over. I am off to meet with the commanders of the Citadel to discuss more of our fortifications and plans of action. Your Crystine commander will be there. I promised him you could be seen, as I suspect he is worried of ill treatment on my part."

There was almost a gloating air to the smirk Zyanthena returned the Shekmann. "Do I sense you are worried what report my Commander will make to the king? To hear your terms of my capture may ruin your "good will" with the Crystine."

"You learn one weakness of mine and you become arrogant."

Zyanthena rose an eyebrow and looked doubtful. "If you think you have showed me only one weakness, Lord Shekmann, you are sadly mistaken. And—I would be a fool to become too pompous, especially while still around you."

Lord Darshel scoffed. "Right." The Shekmann turned away and began to head back the way he had come, trusting or just assuming, that the desert warrioress would follow. She flitted up to his side as they headed down the bailey steps. In silence, they continued through the Citadel streets, cutting across the enormous walled city's main avenue. They joined the steady stream of townsfolk toward the Citadel of Light.

Lord Darshel paused at a street vendor to buy a fruit-filled pastry. He broke it in half to offer a piece to Zyanthena. "I used to have one of these when father and I visited here as a boy. Father disliked southern fruits, so the only time I could have them were when we journeyed here." The Tashek took the offered pastry, eyeing Darshel as if he had done something interesting and unexpected.

Zyanthena nibbled the treat, tasting the succulent boysenberries that grew south of the Pika Mounts. She, herself, had never tasted the tart berries before, and she found the dessert to her liking, not too sweet or too sour. "It is a splendid taste, Your Lordship," she said as way of conversation.

Lord Darshel nodded and motioned them on their way. "And here I had expected you to crack an insult about my taste in cuisine or something of the like."

"If it would suit you, Your Lordship, I may do so; however, from my observations, you have excellent preferences in food. It would be hard to find a fault to snub in your choices."

"Is that what you do?" the Starian replied, "Find my faults and denigrate them?" He teased her with a roguish grin.

Zyanthena's face stayed reserved, her brandy eyes assessing the lord. Darshel wondered what occupied her thoughts that time; the Tashek woman certainly studied him a lot. They continued walking, heading north through the markets. After a minute's passing, the Tashek voiced her thoughts. "You are in an unusually good mood today."

"I am, aren't I?" He shrugged and shook his head, as if with her words, he realized he was enjoying himself. "Yes, I guess I am." He grinned at her as if they shared a secret. "It's probably from the fond memories I have of this place…or, maybe, I find I am enjoying myself because you are here."

The warrioress's withering glare made him chuckle. It was her only answer but he had expected as much. Still, for some odd reason, Darshel felt like a young boy again, and he did wonder if the untamed woman beside him had some part to do with it. It felt almost comfortable having her with him now, Darshel realized. The epiphany came to him as he watched the beautiful desert warrioress fluidly shuffle around the crowded alleyway they entered, keeping up with his longer stride without effort. She never missed a step or a bite of her pastry despite the busy bustle of the market place. He found himself smiling at her despite himself.

Zyanthena finished her pastry as they took the steps up into the inner wall. She stepped ahead of Lord Darshel to announce themselves to the guards; an action she had not needed to do but showed her respect for Darshel's rank. The Citadel men did not question them long, waving them through after finding their purpose.

"This way," Darshel instructed Zyanthena. He turned to follow the inner wall around the Citadel and led the way to the east wing; the Starian war room had been moved there to account for the large number of guests. The glass doors leading from the outside patio into the Citadel were open and voices from the room's occupants reached the Shekmann and Tashek.

Nine men occupied the war room. They were clustered around the northern end, where the large map of Syre and smaller ones of the individual northern kingdoms had been laid out. All'ani Cum'ar and Sheev'arid Terrik seemed to have taken command of the small council; the two Tashek men stood in the center-most position around the maps and were arguing a point when Lord Darshel and Zyanthena made their entrance. The discussion cut off as the men noticed their presence.

Sheev'arid Terrik, being higher in rank, should have welcomed the new comers, but upon seeing his adoptive sister with Lord Shekmann, his mouth formed a hard line. He took his seat without word and poured himself a glass of Starian wine, waving to the Kavahadian lord to come over without curtesy. Cum'ar was much more pleasant, deftly filling the silence left by the other Tashek. "Lord Shekmann and Shi'ka Zyanthena, please join us. We have just begun the meeting. I know you only just arrived last night, so let me introduce you..." He paused long enough for them to find some room around the end of the table then began his introductions from the far left. "Jared Deed, Colonel of the Golden Kingdom archers and filling in for Lord-Commander Sloane while he is healing from his wounds, Siv'arid Kor'mauk of the Sheev'anee, Commander Matar and Lieutenant Madden Smith of the Crystine, Sheev'arid Terrik and Khapta Decond of the Sheev'anee, Commander Ethan Kins and Lieutenant-Commander Curtis Marx of the mertinean, and, of course, myself All'ani Cum'ar of the Sheev'anee." He made the introductions brief, expecting Darshel and Zyanthena to be apt at remembering the others' names. Really, he could have left out the introductions, in lieu of pressing time, but it was courteous of him to go out of the way for Lord Darshel. He went further by adding, for the others' benefit, "Lord Darshel Shekmann is the Lord-Governor of Kavahad." The men exchanged respectful hellos.

The conversation turned back to the matter at hand. Apparently, the three Sheev'anee had been arguing on where best to scout for the maunstorz. The point had been made that the few maunstorz that may have escaped the attack on the Citadel were posted up in the mountains around the Gap of the Forgotten. Terrik and Kor'mauk, who had been at North Point and had witnessed the vanishing, were less concerned with the stragglers and more with the missing eight-thousand-strong army. Terrik felt it a trifle silly that they were looking for an enemy that up-and-left like magic. "If you want to find them, you go look where we know they are. The maunstorz rarely split apart, so they would have joined together again—in the mountains. We have always suspected they make their home in the Valley of Death. We should be going after them there."

"Oh, right," Cum'ar scoffed at the Sheev'arid, "Even we do not know how far the desert stretches or whether any watering holes exist. I would not risk even a search party with odds as unknown as that. We need to stay here and defend the Citadel and the northern border. They will come to us."

"Prince Maushelik agrees with my opinion. He has defended this kingdom for over ten years and is loath to this sitting around anymore. The battle needs to be taken to them. It worked well this last time around."

"Yet, the Prince of the Yellow Star is wise enough to not risk the man power it would take to accomplish that." Kor'mauk pointed out, jumping in. "My clan is the most familiar with the norther territories of Staria, yet, even we are unable to mark the maunstorz passage through the Gap. We have never had the time to explore it properly..."

Terrik soured, "You're all so craven. We should—."

"Enough!" Commander Matar broke into the argument. The Tashek looked to him and slowly sat down into their chairs. Matar waited a moment more for the air to clear before he stood. "Ethan," he motioned to Commander Kins, "And I have long discussed the options we have. When we arrived, we had expected to join a battle; yet, the skirmish was already won. Our men have helped bury the dead for the past week and we know the toll the maunstorz did to this kingdom. More, we know what it had cost us to bring our forces across the expanse of Syre to come to Staria's aid.

"I have seen over thirty-five years of battles against the maunstorz. Our people are wearied and our men have been fighting with no reprieve for a handful of summers. Harvest-Gathering Time is already upon us; we see it most in the high country. The mertinean and Crystine cannot march once the snows set in. Plus, Staria and Sealand harbor the worst of the damage from this year's war. They need our forces to help them stay protected while the commons busy foods for First Snows. The Shi'alam, His Majesty, Ethan, and I feel it is best to try to find the maunstorz while so much of the north lays unprotected. We have a mind to take the Crystine and half the Sheev'anee north-east to camp out in the Red Hills and keep that flank protected. We will take the chance and believe that the maunstorz have yet to sneak around us to the east into Rubia or the Crystal Mountains. Word for continued vigilance from Raven's Den and King Raymond's Command Front have been sent—just in case we are wrong. But for now, our best defense is keeping our strongest forces here in the North-west. Kavahad is our freshest cavalry, then the Shi'alam's main forces. Our best defense is taking a stand here at the Citadel and sending out large scouting parties. It has worked best thus far and will minimize the toll taken on the fighters."

A pause followed as the men looked among each other to see who would argue with the words of the king and the Shi'alam. When none were raised, Commander Kins stood and began to address the issues of the scouting parties, the defenses still needing to be put into place, and the changes of watch. Most of what he said had already been passed around the armies. Trial versions were finalized with their council. The men listened carefully, asking questions when needing clarification on a point or directions to certain locations; however, most of the details were following along already established protocols.

The meeting came to a close an hour later, just as the late-morning bustle began around the Citadel. Lord Darshel pushed himself away from the table to stretch his tired muscles, finding the hard yellowwood chairs to not be to his liking after the long march from Kavahad. To his relief, the staff at the Citadel were quick to bring in refreshments for the commanders. He took two offered chalices of wine and turned to Zyanthena, knowing her to be dutifully by his side. "I know you are wanting to speak with Commander Matar," he said, as she took the drink. "Come, while we still have time."

The Crystine commander saluted Lord Darshel smartly as the Kavahadian neared. Lord Darshel returned the greeting and motioned to the desert woman beside him. "Commander, your Tashek scout, as you have requested."

"My 'Night Fox'," Matar murmured as he reached out to grasp Zyanthena's hands in his. The greeting was as loving as if the man was greeting a daughter. The warrioress returned his words with some phrase in high keshic and squeezed the elder man's hands in a rare display of affection. "And you are well?" Matar asked her, concern in his midnight-blue eyes.

The question had Zyanthena glancing back toward Lord Darshel. The Kavahadian became still as he waited for her to reply. The way she looked at the lord-governor made it clear she was his; like the way a slave would eye his mater if asked the question by an opposing nobleman. The thought that Zyanthena would call Darshel out to the Crystine master chilled him. What exactly would she say?

His musings must have been clear on his face for Zyanthena's eyes changed to a casual stare as she turned them back to Matar. "I am well enough, Master, for the concerns I know you must have for me. Lord Shekmann was true to his word of no harm coming to my person—as he vowed to you. You may mark him as being good on his promise."

Commander Matar looked shocked at the praise from the Tashek's lips. His eyes shifted over Lord Darshel, as if re-evaluating whatever assessment he had made at their previous meeting. "And his proposal, such as it was?"

The second question reflected plainly that the Crystine commander had been informed of what "deals" were usually made from a Lord of Kavahad—and that he found the practice detestable. Zyanthena gently squeezed the veteran's hands to bring his attention back to her. "You need not worry, my master. His "sentence", as it is, is still open to my choice—of which I may not have to make once the matter is taken before King Maushelik on four 'morrows."

"I would have the nonsense be done with to have your skills where they are truly needed, Zy'ena." Matar replied. He looked back to Lord Darshel with a scowl. "This foolishness between your peoples is rather nonsensical. Had it been I who could order you, she would be released from such an old disagreement. As it is, the Crystine are without one of their best scouts and the Sheev'anee and Shekmann are digging into an old pit so dark you can't see the filth that has piled up around you. There are much more pressing matters in Syre to be holding such a petty grudge long past its prime."

"Master," Zyanthena cautioned.

Lord Darshel replied, finding Matar's words nonthreatening. "As one who sees from the outside with eyes wizened from wars and years gone by, the conflict between our peoples had become a grudge of insurmountable proportions, but the pains from its wake still hold true. The Starian kings have been wise to keep the treaty. Without adherence to it, such grievances will only resurface; and, indeed, that would be an ill thing to happen while Staria had been weakened by the maunstorz. You are right to disapprove our actions but—for the sake of peace—even you cannot deny its importance."

"That speaks from the heart of a man still too fearful to step out from his cage when the chains that bound him have long been gone. Such cowardness."

The reply sounded just like a certain Tashek's that Lord Darshel could not help a chuckle under his breath, despite the fact that the situation called for anything but humor. "I apologize, Commander Matar," he was quick to beg forgiveness. "It is just that I finally understand where your fiery Tashek gets her tongue from. She speaks as poetically as you. I would never have guessed the source of her barbs."

Matar turned surprised eyes on Zyanthena. The desert woman averted her own almost-demurely, looking as innocent as both men knew her not to be. Commander Matar looked more taken aback from her oh-so-womanly actions than the fact that she had given insult to a Lord of Staria. "A sharp tongue she may have," Matar replied, after a moment's hesitation, "But from me she learned it not. Zy'ena is a Tashek warrior through and through, Lord Shekmann. Her place is on horseback, scouting and protecting the lands not skulking behind a lord's skirts. If you are as honorable as she claims of you, you would release her to her business." Matar brought himself up tall, reaching almost to Lord Darshel's six-foot-two height. He looked him eye-to-eye. "They say it kills a Tashek's sain'ya—their soul—to be held captive. If you do not hold her loosely, you will ruin the heart of her." He left the rest of his threat unsaid but Lord Darshel knew well enough the words that would have followed. The Crystine commander was very fond of the desert woman; he would not tolerate any harm done to her.

"It was said, too, Commander, that no Tashek could last more than a few days under the hand of a Shekmann, and yet, your Zyanthena stands before you these weeks later. You had my word of no harm coming to her, and I will continue that promise—until or passed the time of her sentence. But we are bound by the treaty. Until her amends are made, or the King releases her from the sentence, she remains mine."

Matar was not consoled, yet he knew his place and priorities. The elder veteran had made his arguments—including a private inquiry to the Shi'alam—to no avail. Neither the Sheev'anee nor the Shekmann would change their verdict. Zyanthena was still Lord

Darshel's. As a Khataum within the Guardianship of the Heavenly Prism, he knew well the rules that bound the Tashek. They believed the Stars created each individual's destiny and it was not for people to try to change the course. The Oracle had claimed Zyanthena was within a "circle of her destiny". The Shi'alam would not change her course.

Commander Kins and Colonel Deed called Matar away, then, before he could continue unloading his discontent on Lord Darshel. He gave a stiff good-bye to the Shekmann and a quick hand squeeze to Zyanthena and hurried off to the others. Lord Darshel let loose a sigh and tussled his hair with a hand. "That did not go as I had expected. Your commander was not so taciturn before."

"You happened to touch a sore spot by taking me captive, Your Lordship." Zyanthena replied. "He cannot respect you when he sees an injustice."

"You are both very alike." Darshel smiled at her fondly. "I think I like that man." Zyanthena's answering scowl showed she didn't like his new-found affection. It only made him grin all the more. He chuckled, "I have to meet with a friend of mine here at the Citadel. He is right across the way." Darshel indicated to some of the private quarters seen down the hallway from the new "war" room. Would you like to wait here or join me? We should only be a short while."

"I will wait, Your Lordship," Zyanthena replied. "The air is much clearer out here." She could not help adding the small insult. Darshel wondered if it was for his benefit, as the comment had him chuckling to himself as he departed. Zyanthena waited until the Kavahadian was admitted into his friend's apartments before settling herself against the frames of one of the large twelve-sectioned picture windows adorning the hallway.

A few minutes later, young Decond and Terrik exited the war room on their way back to the Shi'alam. The elder Sheev'arid caught sight of Zyanthena and turned abruptly around. "Wait here," he ordered of his young Khapta as he strode toward his adopted sister, who brought herself up tall as he neared.

"Brother," Zyanthena greeted neutrally.

Terrik stormed into her space, forcing her against the wall and frame. "That lecherous *caupt!* Why are you still with him, following him like his bitch dog? You should have done him his service and gotten away."

"You know not what his sentence is, brother—."

"I can damn well guess what he deems as "punishment". He's a filthy Shekmann! They all want the same: wet, submissive *kutt*. It's not like you haven't given yourself to a man before. I thought you smart enough to take the damn offer and get out of there—or is it, you are his for life?"

Zyanthena's face darkened. "You have been on spice." She observed, smelling the sweet flavor of the Tashek addictive clinging to Terrik's garments. "That would explain your foul attitude. You only partake of it when you are unhappy with an order from father."

"Keep him out of it. The Shi'alam will do nothing for you." Terrik snapped back. Yet, her words seemed to dampen his aggressiveness, for the desert man gave Zyanthena some room. "You have been ordered to be as a *faut'a*. The council will do nothing over this."

"The council is wise."

"They are a bunch of old, fattened men who will not protect one of their own from the Shekmann filth. They do not care if you're defiled."

"The council always protects what is best for the clan as a whole. That is our way, brother. The fault was mine. I will bear it as King Maushelik sees fit. Father is correct to let the king sort out what is his."

"That old king is just as bad. His son should have released you as soon as he saw you at the call of that swine."

"You have been insulting the crown greatly of late, Terrik. You, who stressed the greatness of our king. That is the spice speaking. You and your Khapta should go take Farwind for a run and come back when you've cleared your head."

"My head is clearer than it has been in weeks, Zyen!" Terrik replied angrily. "I was the one who told you to go while I stayed with Matar. My order made you the one to have to wander through Shekmann lands."

"Terrik." Zyanthena was startled to discover where her brother's words were leading. He was guilty over her capture? "I had the fastest horse. All know this. I was best choice to run point between the

Tashek and Crystine. Only I am to blame for the choice of the route I took. I took the risk and I got caught."

"You do not deserve such injustice!" Terrik slammed a fist against the window frame loudly, level with Zyanthena's head.

Young Decond gaped in worry and began to head over to the siblings. The Tashek woman kept a steady look on her brother's face but spoke to her farrier friend. "Stay back, Decond. I am all right," she told him. The seventeen-year-old would be no match for Terrik, even in his spiced state; she knew what damage her adoptive brother could do when he was in his numbed, uncaring disposition. To her relief, Decond had the sense to listen to her. As he stopped some feet away, Zyanthena focused all her attention of the fractious man before her. "The circumstances are as they are, brother. Accept them, unjust or not. It is not for you to worry over."

"Not to worry over!" Terrik spit back. "You—." He cut himself off in his anger and glared at his planted fist "There is another way for you to be admitted back to the Sheev'anee." Zyanthena's eyes narrowed, wary over what plans her brother had been decocting in his mind. None of it would be good. Terrik ploughed on, oblivious to the look. "I can challenge the Shekmann to the right to win your freedom. It's there in the treaty, just like a she-koum-o. I can beat him; you know I'm the better warrior. After he is slain, I will marry you. You cannot be refused as my wife."

Zyanthena wasn't sure what was more shocking: that Terrik had said out loud he would kill Lord Darshel or that he would marry her. Stunned, she could only get out her brother's name.

"Don't." Terrik replied, stopping her from any protest. "I love you, Zyen. You are one of us. You should be in truth, not just in courtesy. You would be my wife and be a Sheev'anee in full, as you are meant. With the Shekmann gone, there would be no more need for the treaty. All problems would be solved." Terrik took Zyanthena's silence as her agreeance. In his mind, he felt she would be thrilled at the prospect of being considered full Sheev'anee; it was a dream she had confided to him about, after all. Surely, she felt joy at the desire being so close to her reach? He looked at her beautiful face, then, the one he had studied for years at a respectful distance. She was so captivating, especially when her features were set in a cool, attentive mask. Taking her inaction as excitement, Terrik leaned forward and firmly pushed Zyanthena against the wall to kiss her. The warrioress reacted by trying to bring her arms between them to force him away but the elder Sheev'arid trapped her wrists in his own strong grasp and twisted them just enough to take her power away. In his sudden, head-rush of lust, Terrik smothered her against the wall and drank in his kiss hungrily.

Strong hands tore Terrik from his adoptive sister and flung him into the opposing wall. The desert man hit hard and staggered, fighting off the spice and his lust-crazed mind. His hand was already on his kora, ready to hack the defender to pieces. As his vision cleared, he found Lord Darshel and his nobleman friend standing in front of Zyanthena, both armed and in defensive positions. Young Decond was behind them checking on the warrioress. Angered, Terrik straightened and prepared to lash out.

"Don't!" Zyanthena commanded, coming around the Kavahadian lord, her own kora in hand. Her eyes were fiery. The stance she took in front of Lord Darshel was clear enough; she knew Lord Darshel may not be able to take on an attack from her brother and win—but she could, and would, if Terrik forced her hand.

Terrik dropped his kora, his eyes hurt but also disgusted. "So that is your choice. You really are his bitch."

Lord Darshel answered for Zyanthena. "Zy'ena is no one's bitch and least of all mine. She is not touched by me, which is more respect than it seems she gets from you. You would be wise to leave. Now, Sheev'arid."

The two Sheev'arids stared at one another, the silent exchange icy. The three observing men held their breathes, sensing the situation could turn poorly if Terrik really did decide to fight his sister. Zyanthena stayed steady, however, her body language reflecting her intent. It seemed enough to signal to Terrik that she would not back down, for he finally flicked a wrist to artfully sheath his sword and relax his stance. He bowed stiffly and turned heel to leave, not bothering to call for Decond. Zyanthena motioned for the farrier to follow her brother, murmuring an encouraging phrase to the youth as she sheathed her own sword, "Go, Decond. His Khapta must follow. I will visit you when I can. We have much to catch up on."

"Zee…" Decond's voice trailed off, torn between what duties he knew being a Khapta meant and staying with his friend. At the moment, Zyanthena was the gentler of the two choices.

Her lovely face softened in her fondness for the youth. "He is like a man on too much drink right now is all, Decond. The spice will wear off in short order. Go, be with Shytin. The old man will know how to handle him. You will be fine."

"But you—."

"My brother overstepped his place," Zyanthena interrupted softly. "I will not let him make such a mistake with me again. Once his head clears of the spice, he will regret what he did—and I will not forget. You need not be concerned about this." She added more gently, "I am well." Zyanthena knew they were the words that would calm Decond's real concern.

Decond's ice-blue eyes still looked uncertain under his unruly autumn-gold bangs but he accepted the desert woman's words and started off after Terrik. Zyanthena only relaxed her stance when the two men disappeared down the hall. Her quiet sigh showed how tense the Tashek really was.

"Zy'ena." Lord Darshel spoke behind her. He wanted to reach out and touch her shoulder as a reassurance but knew the action would probably set her off.

"Your Lordship," Zyanthena answered neutrally and turned around to give a polite bow.

"What was that about? Your relative was being quite familiar with you. I had not put two-and-two together that you had such relations with that man. At least, neither of you acted that way the day you were officially handed to me."

The desert woman's sour look said enough. "Terrik is my brother." She could see the scandalizing thoughts playing behind Darshel's emerald eyes. "I am not of his blood," she continued. "I was adopted by the Shi'alam over eight summers ago. I had known Terrik took an interest in me but not of that nature."

"For your intelligence, I would have thought you smart enough to know any man's thoughts go there around a woman like you." Her look showed the thought had never occurred to her. "In either case, I am surprised you let him overpower you as he did. You are always so apt at defending yourself. I would not expect that from you."

"He is Tashek, Your Lordship," she replied, as if that answered everything. "And he is higher-ranked more skilled than myself." The explanation was added to explain the wording. "I did not protect myself as I should have because he had been on spice…and my brother. It makes him reckless but not usually dominating. I was very careless."

"All his did was steal a kiss from your lady." Darshel's friend commented, finally including himself in their conversation. "Rude of him for sure and certainly not gentlemanly, but a far cry from anything overly serious. As I've seen it, it is not so unusual for the Tashek."

"It is highly unusual," Zyanthena replied coolly. "And quite disrespectful."

Darshel did reach out that time to calm the warrioress. Her face was dark in her anger over her brother's infraction, and he could only assume that would make her quick to lash out at insults. The warrioress schooled her features into a neutral expression at his touch. He felt relief at her self-control. "As little as we like the Tashek, even you and I know that was no innocent stealing of a kiss, Zale. Even you disapprove unrequited acts." To the woman beside him, he asked, "Did Terrik do anything else to you?"

"No, Your Lordship. You need not concern of it anymore. All he did was kiss me before you arrived. No other harm was done." But Lord Darshel, who was beginning to make sense of the beautiful warrior's words and actions, could see that what she had just told him was not true. Harm had been done: the trust she had had for her brother was broken. He knew better than to pursue it further, though, what with Zale standing there to witness them interacting.

"Well, that's a relief." Zale said, the bearded nobleman looked bored without any more excitement. "In that case, I best be going. I am to meet with Lady Catalina today." He winked at Darshel. "She's a sweet beut, if you remember, and my kind of perniciousness to boot. I'll be seeing you at the banquet."

"Zale." Darshel echoed back his friend's good-bye.

Lord Darshel studied Zyanthena a moment longer before turning away. He waved the desert woman to follow, and they walked back through the war room and to the Kavahadian camp. No more words were spoken about Terrik's kiss, but the Starian lord-governor could see her mind was still preoccupied over it.

As they entered the camp, Commander Raic met them and fell into place beside his lord. He handed a scroll to Lord Darshel and walked with them to the large command tent. "Just reports from the day, sir. Your orders have been spread throughout about the Tashek and actions toward them; this is a list of discrepancies from men who have overstepped your command since. They have been decisively punished, My Lord. The rest is old business."

Lord Darshel scanned the scroll then passed it back to Raic. "Thank you, Commander. If you would, relieve Gordon from his post for a while. Shifts will continue until further orders."

"Yes, My Lord." Commander Raic barely hid his shock at Lord Darshel's words being more of a request than a command but he was quick to salute and hurry away to the duty.

Darshel paused at his pavilion door and turned back to his shadow. "Zy'ena..." They shared a look; his emerald eyes indicated he had a lot to say. Instead of speaking, however, he glanced away. "My horse is in need of some attention, as are your mounts. Please see to them. I will be busy with a tailor, getting prepared for the banquet. My retainer will see to me the rest of the day."

"Your Lordship," Zyanthena replied quietly. She didn't bother waiting to see if the lord-governor had more to say. The Tashek woman drifting away near-inaudibly to the task. Her quick departure validated to Lord Darshel how truly scattered Zyanthena was from the earlier incident. He tried to shrug the thought away and pushed through his tent's entrance to meet the squat tailor within. The balding man bowed graciously to him. "I have one more request of you. I need a sapphire dress made to order..."

Chapter Twenty-Nine

§

Silence

"What would you like me to do about it?" King Maushelik turned away from the calming morning view out his chamber's western windows; it was not helping to take the edge off of his exasperation—only good sleep would do that now. The aging king could barely keep the edge out of his tone as he addressed the other two men: his son and the Shi'alam. "The treaty has been kept over eighty years. Kavahad and the Sheev'anee have dealt with minor incidents before this one with no problems. Why now?" He was too tired to care that he sounded sulky, like a naïve youth.

"It is because it is Zyanthena, my daughter, who is captured. The delicate circumstances that caused her to "overstep" the treaty have many of my people—and Crystine as well—angry over her mistreatment."

"Son, did this Zyanthena seem poorly treated to you?"

Prince Al'den straightened in his chair. "No, father. She was quite forthright that her involvement with Lord Shekmann was a matter of service not imprisonment. Her manner did not suggest otherwise. It was only that it seemed odd for a Tashek to be in employment of a Shekmann that I brought their situation to your attention."

"It would all be a lie," the Shi'alam interjected. "Zyanthena was captured about a fortnight ago on her way back to the Crystine. She has always been the fastest and most reliable out-rider between the Crystine and Sheev'anee; it was not unusual for her to have been picked to make the run. However, it is not like her to get captured so easily. According to Arimun, the other rider with her, her horse had been shot with an arrow. She had pulled him up to give Arimun a chance to escape and to save her mount further injury."

"And this Arimun can attest to that?"

"Yes, Majesty. She rides a Crystal horse. She would value his life over her own."

"Him? A black stallion?" Prince Al'den guessed, recalling the two hoses the Tashek woman had stood between when he had addressed her. It would have been hard to miss such a large and good-looking animal. The Shi'alam nodded to the prince's question. "The stallion was still with her, though it did not look as if she had ridden him. She was also with a chestnut mount..."

"The value of that Crystal stallion would make her careful with him—if he was still injured. For Zyanthena to bring him up from Kavahad comes as a surprise, but then again, she would not go anywhere without him—unless forced, of course." The Shi'alam's dark eyes bore into the king's, his presence commanding and bold. "She is the most-loyal woman you will ever meet and very talented besides. Zyanthena has been invaluable to the Sheev'anee, Crystine, and to me. It is a horrible shame for her to be under the treatment of a Shekmann. The only reason I and the council decided to keep her in the situation with the Shekmann was because Staria was under attack. Had the need not been so pressing, I would have ransomed for Zyanthena in some way." Both Mausheliks looked taken aback. Tashek never ransomed for any reason. It wasn't their style. The Shi'alam finished before they could ask. "Yes, she is that special to me...Zyanthena was found in a camp of Lost Ones. She was the only survivor to some kind of massacre; however, she bears the resemblance to a cousin near and dear to my heart. My cousin's family was killed years ago and I believe Zyanthena to be their lost daughter. The Sheev'anee bloodlines ran strong in her family."

[Note: Lost Ones, or the Nallaus, are a group of Tashek that refuse to follow the Sheev'anee doctrines or Prism of the Stars. They are "outcasts" and never allowed to settle in an area for long, always forced to move about the Aras.]

"Your cousin's bloodlines were of Xraxrain origin, were they not?" King Maushelik asked. "The Crystalynian royal family was traced through their women. Are you sure that this is so? Do you have any proof that Zyanthena is from Queen Kestrel's line?"

"No, I have none; and the girl had no memories from her time before the Lost Ones...but I have hope."

"It is not like you to make such strong assumptions on something with no facts, Shi'alam. I know you loved your dear cousin, Kestral, but the Xraxrain household did not survive the fall of Crystalynian." The Shi'alam persed his lips at the king's words, anger flashing in his eyes, but he did not reply to the king. Maushelik continued, "However, Zyanthena is your claimed daughter. That fact alone makes her more valuable. Too, I have heard of her valor in battle, and her skills in both warfare and tracking that have been paramount against the maunstorz. I will take those facts into consideration when I question Lord Shekmann and Zyanthena the day of the celebration ball. Unless there is a different solution either of you can see?"

The Shi'alam's eyes told a different story, but he shook his head. No. One thing about the Tashek leader was that he was loyal to the Starian crown. The king had named the day of his verdict; the Sheev'anee man would not question him. King Maushelik wished he could do better for the Tashek, but he was too wearied from the long days burying the dead and counseling the city to have spent any more attention to this new problem. Others were more pressing.

"Father...perhaps, there is another way." Prince Al'den rose, his ice-blue eyes afire in thought. "The situation between Lord Shekmann and Zyanthena, though delicate, has given us a rare opportunity. Lord Darshel was never a part of the bloodshed between his father, the late Lord Shekmann, and the Sheev'anee. Neither was Zyanthena. Reports I have received say that they get along well enough, despite some minor incidents. Maybe, this is the time to re-evaluate the terms of the treaty and see if any amendments can be made?"

The aging king looked thoughtful. The Shi'alam, however, did not. "There are still those alive who remember the atrocities committed to my people. They will not be so open to pardoning the Shekmann."

"And how much longer must Staria be chained to the wrongs of the past?" Al'den argued. "We are at war with the maunstorz. Why, then, should we still be among ourselves? Our kingdom needs strength from our members, not division from old grievances." He turned back to his father, who seemed more receptive to his plea. "Let us see what happens between Lord Shekmann and Zyanthena. They just might set a new example."

"I do not know enough of either the Kavahadian lord or Zyanthena to know if this is wise." King Maushelik began, "However, I too, have longed for peace between Kavahad and the Sheev'anee. Son, continue to have the Lord and Tashek monitored. Let us see what their actions bring about in the next few days."

"Majesty," the Shi'alam argued, "I do not want my daughter with that man longer than she has been. He is as lecherous as his father."

"And not without respect to the ladies I hear." Yes, the Shekmann's reputation had proceeded him all the way to the Citadel. "I hear he does not take any woman unwilling. That same courtesy should have been extended to your daughter, too. If it has not, I will deal with that when I know of it. However, word is your daughter is quite capable of taking care of herself and her affairs. She would not be one to suffer any wrong doing."

The desert man's face flamed in anger but even the Shi'alam could not deny the king's words. "No, Zyanthena was never one to allow any abuse to her person. My men know well that she would lay punishment on any who did her wrong..."

"Then unless I hear otherwise, your daughter had not been harmed by the Lord Shekmann. I have not the time to review her case until the appointed day. Until then, Shi'alam, Zyanthena stays in whatever arrangement Lord Shekmann and she have. And, you will leave it well enough alone. I need you, Shi'alam; Staria needs you; to be united with me on this. The Citadel is weakened by the last maunstorz attack, and there is still the chance of another. Are you able to serve despite this additional concern, or do I need to command All'ani Cum'ar to lead the Sheev'anee?"

The Shi'alam was quiet. Never before had his king had a reason to overrule his leadership of the Sheev'anee. The desert tribes had always followed under the Sheev'arids since the Second Age. They, in turn, had served the Starian kings as a courtesy; however, the Sheev'anee had never pledged fealty to the kings as the nobles had. It could almost be argued that they served Staria by their own volition. It could even be the Shi'alam's right to pull all the Sheev'anee from the Citadel that very day instead of taking the threat.

Prince Al'den began to protest, knowing how delicate the situation had turned. He hid his panic he felt as his father's words. "Father—." He began, in hopes of changing his mind.

"No need, Prince of the Yellow Star." The Shi'alam stopped him stiffly. "Your king may have been untactful in his selection of words, but I know, too, he rarely does so. This war had wearied all of our courtesies away." There was sympathy in his voice. "The Sheev'anee love this kingdom as much as you, Majesty," he returned to the king. "We... I have not forgotten who the real enemy is. The situation with Zyanthena will not distract me from defending it." His hard features broke into a brazen laugh, then. "And you are still as ballsy a king as you have ever been, Majesty. There are few who dare to reprimand me. The Stars thanks that there are some who still know their grit."

King Maushelik joined the Shi'alam's amused laugh. The tension broke as the men chortled. "And, I will not let you forget it as long as this heart still beats, al'ma [friend]. I am not through with you yet."

§ §

Prince Al'den was not sure if he was relieved over the recent conversation, but at least his father and the Shi'alam had left each other in cheery standings. He wandered back down from his father's private tower to the western apartments, where Kent Argetlem was staying. The other prince's assigned retainer said the royal was not about, however, when Al'den reached the Goldener's apartment. The man was unable to say where Kent had gone, as the prince had been unhelpful in supplying the information, so Al'den was left to find his friend by well-thought chance.

The library was one of the scholar-prince's favorite nooks in the Citadel, and Al'den's first choice. The enormous library was nearly empty, despite it being only midmorning. Amid rows and towers of old books and parchment, the Starian searched for his friend; however, as he came about the last section of books, he ran into the lovely princess of Blue Haven.

Princess Éleen gasped in shock as the tall Starian came around the corner she was about to turn. Instinctively, she crushed the heavy book she held to her person as she jumped to a halt. Prince Al'den, too, stopped abruptly, his hands reaching out to steady the princess and to keep her from falling. "Highness!" Al'den apologized at once. "I do beg pardon. Are you all right?"

Princess Éleen looked a bit breathless but she did reply. "No, Your Highness...I mean, yes, I am all right. I am just startled, Highness." She averted her pretty china blue-eyes to the floor, too nervous to look into Al'den's handsome face.

Al'den realized he still had his hands on her delicate shoulders. Quickly, he removed them. "We seem to have a knack for running into reach other," he commented lightly in hopes of diffusing the tension. The princess gaped at him, as if not comprehending the humor. Then, she seemed to remember herself. Éleen flushed an adorable scarlet and snapped her mouth closed. She looked back to the floor. "Well...again pardon me, Highness," Al'den began again. "I have been searching for Kent. Too quickly, it seems. I had not been watching where I was going. I am sorry for running into you." He started to back away to make an escape toward the exit.

"Um...You Highness." Éleen's sweet voice called after him. Al'den found himself turning around to the sound of the princess's lovely hail. She still stood there, shyly. "Ah, Prince Kent had been here not half-an-hour past. He was summoned by a page to go see his Lieutenant-Commander. There may have been something wrong..."

Al'den felt his brows knit at the news. "Thank you, Princess." He gave her a quick bow of his head. "I will be on my way then."

She nodded in return. "Please, tell Prince Kent of my sympathies and hopes that his man be all right."

"I will." The Starian gave her a smile and turned away, back to his task of finding his friend. At least the library had yielded up a direction. As he left, Al'den was not aware of the princess's worried eyes following him out.

The infirmary ended up being as empty of the Golden heir as the library. Prince Al'den searched the many rooms fervently, finally finding a nurse who knew what had become of the other man. The woman had seen to the Lieutenant-Commander personally. She did not herald good news, however.

"Highness," the elder woman looked sad. "His highness Prince Argetlem's Lieutenant-Commander passed away early this morning. We were finally able to find His Highness not an hour passed. He came to pay his respects and asked that the body be taken back to Greendale to be laid to rest with his family. Once he was done His Highness was seen going to the gardens, I believe."

"Thank you, Gladril." Al'den replied, "I will check there. Please, make sure the Lieutenant-Commander is treated with all respects. I will write a missive to be sent onto the man's family as well. And, please, inform me of any others' passing, if you would." It was not a harsh command but Gladril looked abashed that she had not thought to inform her prince over the Goldener's death. She bowed and hurried away to inform the others of the prince's commands.

Al'den let go a heavy sigh as she left. "Stars, that's not good news..." he muttered in anger but the feeling turned quickly to a stab of sadness that cooled the hot emotion. "I am going to miss that man. He was a great leader and swordsman..." Memories of Eric Sloane filled the prince's thoughts as he made his way to the small, public gardens in the southern corner of the hospital. The grizzled, battle-hardened knight had been a great swordsman and nearly as talented with a long-bow. It felt strange to think of the man as gone.

Prince Kent seemed to have that look, too, when Al'den found the other royal. He was sitting on a small stone bench amid a bower of winding mariposa lilies. His usually-vibrant, scholarly face was drawn and dismal. The Starian approached softly and sat beside the other prince without a word. The two of them sat amidst the flowers and hot morning sun, letting the silence of the day pass between them.

"He was a very brave man and the most loyal of fighters." Kent finally said, his voice soft and haggard. Then, he huffed sarcastically. "My words do not do him justice. That grizzled old geezer..."

Al'den reached out to clap his friend's shoulder. "He will be remembered well, Kent. Eric Sloane was a champion of the people and well-liked by many. He did more for the kingdoms than those who will live twice his age. We will pay him the respects he deserves."

"His family is in Greendale, east of Sardon. He leaves behind a beautiful wife, a daughter full-grown, and two grandchildren. They will do well on his estate. He made enough to sit them comfortably for years to come."

"We will host him a commemorative during the celebration ball, with the others that died."

At first, Kent looked confused. Then, his scholarly mind remembered why the prince had said such. In Staria, the dead were not mourned solemnly but thrown great parties in their honor. Other kingdoms had thought the practice vulgar, a blight to the dead, but Kent had thought it a grand idea. Why not celebrate a wonderful person's life with joy, not tears? It sounded more uplifting and healing. "Thank you."

The other prince gave a wan smile and settled back against the hedge to stare up at the blue sky, lost in thought. Kent followed suit, finding the position and reflective mood to be just what his saddened soul needed. Al'den did not rush away to other duties, which made Kent feel relieved. It was comforting to have the other man there not pushing or prodding but just sitting. It encouraged the grief to come as need. The Golden heir suspected the other prince was mourning Eric Sloane, too.

Prince Al'den knew well the value of treasuring grief. It was such a stark difference from the way the South viewed death and mourning. There was a kind of peace to the quiet air that seemed so powerful. In the rush of life, its struggle, and even death, there was a moment to just sit and be. Kent found the silence profound.

Chapter Thirty

§

The Dinner Party

If looks could kill, Terrik was sure his father's would have cut him down dead. The desert man had known the Shi'alam would hear of his incident with Zyanthena; the Sheev'anee leader heard everything; but the heir had not counted on his father being quite so furious. Usually, the Tashek leader had a good rein on his temper. That day was not the case. "...and how dare you think about touching your sister! We took her in with goodwill all these years, not as some hired whore-girl. This is unspeakable! What were you even thinking!?" Terrik opened his mouth to speak but his father glowered down at him with such ferocity, he quickly shut it again— for the umpteenth time that afternoon. They had already been at it for some minutes... "Oh, but of course you weren't thinking; you were on spice!" Terrik cringed. The Shi'alam had stayed away from that subject until now. "That deplorable substance! As if you hadn't learned what it can do to you before."

Five years ago, Terrik had his first lick of the addictive substance, only to have gone on a half-year's downward spiral into continued binges with the drug. He had done many stupid things that time around. Had it not been for Zyanthena's unwavering—if not overly strict—care, Terrik doubted he would have gotten over it. The Shi'alam had not forgotten or forgiven him, however. Since then, Terrik had partaken of the spice in small quantities on very rare occasions, thinking he was being secretive. The ploy hadn't worked on Zyanthena, who saw Terrik on a regular basis, but from the pure fury in his father' voice, Terrik knew this was the first he had heard of it. The elder Sheev'arid was so livid.

The tent became quiet; potently still charged with emotion.

The Shi'alam stopped his pacing to sit down at the small table across from the bedroll he had set Terrik on. His face was weary but still pinched from his anger. He stared at his son for long breaths. Terrik could feel the disappointment rolling off of his father. He swallowed nervously but refused to shift from his stiff, at-attention posture. Finally, the Shi'alam spoke again, "You are not fit to lead the

Sheev'anee. I will inform Commander Matar. Siv'arid Kor'mauk will be taking your place among the Crystine. I want you and your Khapta to leave the Citadel once the celebration ball is over. You are to go to the Oracle—and no place else. Do as she bid you."

Terrik felt his jaw clench. So, his father was dismissing him like he was ten-years-old and to the Oracle no less! The old, blind woman, for all her prophecies come true, was shriveled like a prune and senile—at least as far as Terrik was concerned. Youths were usually banished as punishment to her hole to do the menial labors she could not perform. The punch to his pride could not have been sharper. "Very well, Shi'alam." Terrik replied darkly. He came to his feet and hoped his words would hurt his father. "As you command, so I go." Staying distant and unfeeling, Terrik turned away without being dismissed and stepped out into the mid-afternoon sun.

He wound through the Sheev'anee tents, ignoring the looks from the other Tashek. No doubt they had heard all the recent events. Finally, Terrik reached Saulyn. The stallion sensed his rider's emotions and snorted warily at he approached where the desert horse had been picketed. Terrik collected his tack and quickly saddled up. Saulyn, not Farwind, was his feistier mount, and, right then, Terrik wanted the challenge to set his mind upon. Even though he knew he should not ride when in such a mood he did not care. He leapt ono the steel grey's back and spun him away. What would it matter for him to stay at the Citadel when he had been stripped of his station, anyway? Terrik pushed the stallion to a hard-gallop out of the Tashek camp and headed off into the wastes. He had lost the love of Zyanthena and the approval of his father in one day. There was no place for him except the rolling sands, desert winds, and his seething anger.

§ §

The Shi'alam watched his son go, thinking about a similar incident between his own father and himself many years past. They had never spoked again. Even as the elder Sheev'arid had laid dying, he had not gone to make amends. That was the Shi'alam's biggest regret: having not told his father how much the man had meant to him. To have the same image thrown in his face all these years later... the Shi'alam prayed to the Stars that such a fate would not happen again.

"Shytin!" he called out to the retainer.

His son's man was there in an instant, having been waiting on the other side of the tent frame. "Sir."

"I relieve you of your duties to my son on account of his behavior. But, before you go, would you search his tent for the rest of the spice? I wish to know how much he is hoarding and what dealer he used, if you are able to find out. As for his belongings, most can be packed away. He will only be in need of enough to make the journey to the Oracle."

"Yes, sir." Shytin bowed respectfully and began to back away.

"One more thing, shi'ah [loyal friend]," the Shi'alam called after. The retainer paused. "I thank you for making known to me what happened today. I am disturbed by these events but relieved to have them in the open. If you would, tell Decond he is at leave to see Zyanthena. I have heard they were friends, and I am sure he is worried about her." Shytin bowed again and left the Sheev'anee leader.

With the tent empty, the Shi'alam felt himself finally relax. He sighed. What a day he was having! First the Starian king's command to leave Zyanthena as she was, then to come back to such news about his son. The Shi'alam was both relieved and disappointed he had no other children to cause him grief. "Maybe I am getting too old for this," he grumbled as he rose from his chair to get a drink. "The young are getting too full of themselves and the old too tired and senile." He glanced at his kora hung on the wall and wondered if it would ever be passed on to his son. "Stars see that the Oracle can straighten him out good and even. I've had quite enough of delegating and fighting. I'd like to retire soon and enjoy a good woman and grandchildren. That's what your normal followers do!" He raised his voice to the empty air, his words for the Stars. Of course, none of them answered. The Shi'alam grumbled again and threw back the rest of his drink. "Enough of your bloody amusement at our expense! Some of us have work to do."

§ §

It was the first time in a long time that most of the kingdom's royalty had been under one roof, Prince Al'den reflected. He was the eldest of the royal heirs and even he could not recall when so many of the Houses had been in attendance. Too bad it was only one representative from each, but at least all but Rubia were there.

The Starian prince had invited the others to a private dinner on his personal balcony. Prince Kent and Al'den had shared the view alone for the hour prior, while the Citadel staff set the table with food and drink and straightened the garden. It had given them a chance to mourn the deceased Lieutenant-Commander. After, Princess Éleen and Lord Carrod had arrived first, followed ten minutes later by Prince Par and His Lord Protector. Prince Connel arrived last, looking far more decadent than necessary for the private setting—but, of course, no one was really surprised by the Sunarian's air.

The seven seated themselves around the oval table, and the staff came in to begin filling wine cups and helping with dishes. Prince Al'den had chosen Prince Kent to sit to his right with Éleen just passed him; the two royals would be good company. Par had been sat to his left, where Al'den could speak with the Sealander and become acquainted. Lords Gordar and Carrod were beside each other. Al'den had figured they would be more comfortable with each other's stations. Prince Connel finished off the circle beside Princess Éleen. Uncertain of sitting the young prince beside the princess—as Al'den did not trust the smooth-tongued and dashing Sunarian— he had had to console himself that no harm would come of one night's seating arrangements. Prince Maushelik had wanted Kent by his side due to the morning's loss.

Conversation at the table seemed stalled, what with the usually-charismatic Kent subdued and the others being mostly strangers to each other. Prince Al'den found himself at a loss, finding that he was rusty on courtly manners from too many years in the field. To his relief is was Prince Par who had the sense to make an opening comment. "I must admit, I have quite enjoyed my first day here at the Citadel, despite how unaccustomed I am to this dryness and heat."

"I am glad to hear that," Al'den answered sincerely. "I had hoped that the baths had helped to ease the aches of travel and fighting."

"Indeed, they did." Par's grin was infectious. His ocean-blue eyes were bright as he extended the conversation to the others. "Has anyone else been to the steam-baths yet? I haven't had a novelty like that since visiting the Crystal Castle, in my youth."

"I have been to the sudatorium," Prince Connel answered. "It was quite an experience—more than I had expected and a pleasant surprise. Sunrise does not have such an elaborate set-up as Staria."

"Not quite the "hole in the ground" as you'd expect, is it?" Kent jumped in, sounding more like himself. Connel agreed. "It seems we of the South have underestimated the affluence of our Northern kin."

"I'm never quite sure if you're being kind or if you jest," Al'den bantered with his friend.

"It seems he is being just kind enough." Éleen replied, her soft voice calling all the men's eyes to her. She blushed a pretty red but forged on despite her embarrassment. "I had imagined Staria as an anti-chromatic wasteland—excuse my bluntness, Highness—and not half as wondrous as it is. It is a unique sight from the Havenese grasslands and coastline."

Prince Al'den smiled encouragingly at the princess. "Yes, indeed. Though you are much too kind, princess. Drab and lifeless is how most people describe the Aras." The other men chuckled at Al'den's honesty. "I like to think we are civilized wastrels too stubborn to admit the grit between our teeth is not gold and too proud to call it anything else." The group laughed at that and the tension eased around the table as the seven found the dinner less formal than they had first imagined. Prince Al'den took a sip of wine and sat back in his chair. "So, Highness Connel, I heard you are an avid breeder of hunting dogs, yes?"

The Sunarian looked startled that Prince Al'den had done his research and knew his guest's favorite pastime. "I am, yes, and a trainer. My elder brother was already quite involved with horseflesh so I had wanted to have a reputable hobby that didn't tie so closely with his. Despite that horses are seen as more prestigious than canines in Sunrise, my hounds have quite a reputation." He looked smug at the fact.

Al'den replied with a nod, being politely interested. "You will have to forgive me, as I am unfamiliar with hunting dogs. Here in

Staria, we use falcons over other animals when we go out gaming," he explained.

"I am sure the concept is similar." Connel began. "We use the dogs to flush out the game then stand in a "point" as we shoot. A "steady" dog waits during the "wing and shoot" phase and only retrieves the bird when asked. My pack is special in that I usually hunt with two to three dogs at one time. I have the best "honing" dogs in the kingdom, meaning that the dogs that haven't pointed and flushed a bird will "stand at point" while the main dog finishes the job. Having two or more dogs working together is harder. That my own pack has a number of dogs that are good at "backing" makes them more sought after as breeding stock."

"That is very interesting. I usually only hunt with one falcon myself, so I can't imagine how much harder it is to manage multiple animals."

Connel shrugged. "With the right training, it is actually quite manageable."

"Did you compete at the Tri-kingdom Championships last season?"

Prince Connel seemed surprised that Princess Éleen knew about the hunting dog tournament. "Indeed, I did, Ms. Éleen. I was there with my top pair of dogs, Major and Wesson."

"The two liver-ticked, short-haired pointers that stole the cup in the end?"

"That is them."

Éleen's eyes were bright in her excitement. "My brother was cursing them for overtaking his hounds at the last. Ha, I can boast I know who beat them now!"

"You take an interest in bird hunting, Princess?" Kent asked, intrigued. He himself was not very fond of hunting—of any type.

"Not so much," she admitted smoothly, "But I am quite fond of dogs. I usually help my brother at the tournaments. Jace says I am being too soft on his animals, though."

"Sugar always wins more friends than vinegar," Kent replied with a fond smile at the young woman.

"That is what I say! Animals enjoy praise and affection as much as we do."

Connel's expression showed he begged to differ. "It just makes them lazy."

"It makes them try harder." Prince Al'den countered smoothly in favor of the princess. "At least, that had been the case with all my stock. A calm hand and some buttering up never hurt to boost anything's ego."

"I am sure either way of training will yield results." Prince Par cut in, sensing a force of wills going on between the others. "In the end, the way I see it, whichever way gives the best results is the one to go with. Sometimes, it takes a little bit of both."

"Do you have any experience with training, then?" Prince Connel asked.

Par's smile was patient. He would not be baited into an argument. "My interests run more in vintage wines and the intricate craftsmanship that goes into good weaponry, especially a well-made sword." He changed the subject smoothly.

"You do have an exceptional eye for weapons," Al'den commented. "I could not help admiring your rapier when you arrived. It looked to be one of Ferris Galandré's swords." Galandré was a famous Sealander swordsmith.

"Perceptive eye," Par commended the prince, "But that sword I crafted myself. I had the privilege of studying under Master Galandré. That sword was what I came away with." The other royal looked impressed. "It is not as well-tempered as Master's; yet, for you to recognize his style in my work, shows I must have learned something from all the back-handed, head-slapping I received from him." The table erupted in amused chuckles.

By then, the dinner had moved to the main course of twice-cooked roasted-and-brazened duck with russet potatoes and poached pigeon eggs in a buttery rosemary sauce. Accompanying the meal was a light cucumber soup and a goblet of prune-flavored gelatin balls (used to cleanse the palate between courses). A pitcher of fresh-squeezed, cactus-root water was set out among the two decanters of wine. Prince Al'den poured himself a glass, despite the nervous server behind him, and drank deeply of the desert drink. The others eyed the decoction skeptically as their own glasses were filled.

"Is this kiwano juice?" Kent asked curiously. Kiwano was a special cactus plant that came in bright colors of pinks and purples.

"No, just regular cactus." Al'den replied off-handedly.

The answer was good enough for the Golden heir, who threw back his drink. He found the taste to be mild, if anything lacking any real flavor. Yet he could not help laughing at the strange faces the Southerners made at the odd drink. "Oh, come now! It's not that bad."

"Yeah, if you are used to dog piss—no offense Highness." Lord Carrod commented. His words made the Starian and Golden heirs laugh.

"It has a certain taste to be sure." Lorre Gordar agreed eyeing the glass skeptically. "I think I'll take the Tashek horse's milk over this."

"Really?" The other Sealander eyed his cousin. "I'd take this. This juice is bland in comparison to that rich potation."

"This is bitter to say the least."

"Ah," Éleen countered the golden-eyes lord, "It is not half as bad as you make it seem. It's very...different is all."

"Uhuh, so you say, princess, always so tactful." Prince Connel bantered back, his words could be taken as either teasing or crude. They did spark a rather heated discussion, though, of what dishes and fare each kingdom had that were both far worse and better than the Starian drink. At least, they all had their share of "traditional delicacies" that were far from exemplary to complain about. It made the rest of the meal go smoothly.

As the last of the dishes were cleared from a custard pie, Prince Al'den asked the others if they would like to hang out in the sitting room for after-dinner entertainments. As the other filed into his private room, he had a servant fetch the princess's wind lyre, knowing she would be asked to play—if not from Kent then by another. He had another lady provide evening tea and pense-biscuits, in case anyone still wished to snack. When he turned his attention back to the group, he found Kent, Éleen, and Carrod sitting comfortably around the small fireplace; the rest were admiring the decorations and pictures adorning the room.

Prince Par was pointing out the old etching carved into the fuller of his family's original scimitar to his Lord Protector. The saying was in old Starian language, which was similar to keshic. Al'den didn't know if the Sealander knew the words or not but the blond-haired prince was enthusiastic about the weapon so he left them to admire it. The other prince was over by Al'den's private collection of books, leafing through one of the older texts of Syrean history. The young Sunarian had not seemed the scholarly-type to the Starian but he seemed interested in some subject or other.

"Come, tell us a little about your family." Prince Kent called to him, waving his hand to the oil painting over the fireplace.

The Sealanders and Prince Connel turned away from their preoccupations to join them on the comfortable leather chairs as Prince Al'den graciously began his narrative. The tall, military prince pointed to the first painting, the largest one, with a man, woman, and baby boy sitting atop a war charger. "My father, mother, and myself..." he began. The thirty-year-old spoke of his mother fondly and of what was going on during the time the painting had been created. It had been the summer before King Maushelik had injured his leg in battle and six summers before Queen Selene's death.

Once the prince finished with the last of the portraits, the group demanded music. To their surprise and pleasure, Lord Gordar took the lead. He sang in a gentle baritone voice an old Sealander hymn. Not to be ousted by his cousin, Prince Par followed with a jovial marching song that had the others clapping and singing along. Princess Éleen was then goaded into playing a few tunes on the lyre, of which she blushed over-modest as she finished a beautiful lullaby. To hide her embarrassment, she quickly asked the attention be given to Prince Kent.

"Please, Kent, would you sing that lovely song I heard the other day?"

"Of course, Ms. Éleen, but only if you and Al'den would accompany me again."

Al'den consented and rose to get his flute from its case on the mantle. He could feel the curious stares of the Southerners as he did so, knowing they were wondering what he was grabbing. As he turned back around to sit beside the princess, he could not help noticing the shock on the four men's faces. He felt smug a he fingered out a warm-up lilt and nodded to Éleen and Kent that he was ready. Then, the trio began a haunting song of love, loss, and holding on that would have had most people crying.

Silence followed the song as Prince Al'den let the last note hang in the air and dissipated it slowly. After some breathes, Prince Par began clapping and the others followed suit. "Wow! That was amazing!"

The trio grinned and Prince Kent gave a theatrical bow. "Thank you, thank you. We are here 'til closing and donations are greatly appreciated."

The group laughed.

Prince Al'den stood, then, as the jovial guests calmed themselves. "Well, the hour is getting late. Tomorrow is the war council, and I know you will all want to be well-rested for it. Thank you for making this an enjoyable evening." The others expressed their own gratitude at the great night and began preparing to leave for their own chambers. The Starian said his good-nights and turned away to pack up his flute.

"That was beautiful. Thank you, Highness."

Al'den turned to the lovely princess and found himself at a loss for words at her own loveliness. He caught himself smiling down at her and hurried to fill the silence. "Thank you, Highness. Your playing was very nice, too. You did not tell me you were such a gifted player." She blushed a cute scarlet. Prince Al'den forced his eyes away from her face to look back at Lord Carrod, waiting by the door. "May you have a good sleep, Princess. I will reserve a place for your man at the council tomorrow."

Princess Éleen followed his eyes to where her lord protector stood watching them. She returned her china blue-eyes to Al'den's face. "I will. Thank you, Highness. May the meeting go well. Good night."

Al'den bowed and kept his eyes on her small frame as she walked away. In the emptiness that followed, he whispered the words he had wished he had spoken, "You were beautiful, too."

Chapter Thirty-One
§
The Morning of the War Council

Lord Darshel unshackled Zyanthena in the early morning and went off to check on his lines. He returned some time later, an hour before the appointed council meeting, and found her training furiously with her kora sword in the vacant area behind his tent. The lord-governor leaned his brawny frame against a tent pole to watch. The dark-haired beauty spun, leapt, kicked out, and thrust in a wild abandon; her usual precision was swept aside. The Kavahadian lord could more easily picture what she would like during battle in her less calculating state. A final spin brought her around to Lord Darshel's viewpoint and Zyanthena froze in surprise. She quickly dropped her sword from where it pointed at his person and muttered an apology. "That was quite the display."

"Your Lordship." She dipped her head, eyes averted to the ground in total submission.

"You seemed entrapped in the form. I had not wished to interrupt." He straightened from his casual pose and stalked across the small space to the desert woman. She respectfully sheathed her sword as he neared. "I don't think I saw such fire since that first day we were introduced. It makes me wonder what could have prompted such liveliness." He let the question hang in the air. If Zyanthena wanted to tell him, she would; though, he guessed her intensity was left over from the incident with her brother.

She ignored the implied invitation. "Is it time for you to go to the council meeting?" Her brandy eyes shifted past the Kavahadian to where Commander Raic could be seen waiting in the lane on the other side of the tents.

Lord Darshel nodded. "I came to collect what is mine." Zyanthena's eyes looked back at his handsome face, wary as ever. "I want you to accompany me and my commander. Your experience as a Crystine scout will be needed for today's discussion. The council will be missing vital pieces without it."

"You are hoping to influence the king's opinion of you. By using me you put yourself in his good graces."

"No, I ask for the good of Syre." The Tashek blinked, as if taken aback by the answer. "What more can I say to convince you how much the council needs your presence? Do I have to bend a knee?"

Zyanthena actually looked amused; the hint of a smile played across her lips. "No groveling is necessary, Your Lordship. I am just…intrigued that you are going to let me come."

"I have not taken advantage of the skills you possess, and I should while I still have you."

"It makes you look the wiser," she replied saucily.

Lord Darshel rolled his eyes and chuckled. "You said it, not I."

"Indeed, Your Lordship." Zyanthena's eyes sparkled mischievously.

"Come on, before my men begin to think we have something going on between us."

"Oh, I wonder why they would think that." She muttered darkly but followed nonetheless. He returned to Commander Raic, who eyed Zyanthena with distaste but fell into line without complaint.

The Kavahadian lord led them through the Citadel streets and to the small sentry portal beside the western gate. The late-morning bustle in the inner-city walls felt a bit tense; townspeople stopped to mutter behind their hands as the threesome passed. All of the capitol had heard of the war council and would be waiting anxiously for the announcement of the council's decisions. Lord Darshel made no sign that he noticed the stares. The inner-gate guards let them through without stopping them, having come to know Lord Shekmann from his constant comings and goings. Darshel gave them a small nod in hello and continued onward to the Citadel's main entrance.

"Make all your weapons in plain sight." Lord Darshel commanded Raic and Zyanthena. "The palace guards will inspect us and any weapons that are hidden will bar you from entering the war room."

"Why not decree all weapons be confiscated?" Zyanthena asked. It seemed reasonable with all the royals running around. She had been surprised the king had not ordered it of every visitor.

Lord Darshel shrugged. He would have ordered such if the council had been at Kavahad. "Everyone present will be so by invitation only. Anyone not on His Majesty's list will not be admitted. Perhaps that made him feel secure in allowing weapons."

Eight Starian guards stood at the entrance to the war room. They were the king's most trusted honor guards. They inspected the incoming men with a critical eye. Lord Darshel walked up to them with a regal bearing, casual and haughty, to show there was no doubt that he belonged there. Commander Raic informed the guard of Lord Darshel's family name and status. Being unimpressed, the head-guard searched the lord and commander just as thoroughly as the others. "You are free to enter, Lord Darshel, commander." The Kavahadian lord began to step forward. "But you cannot enter, miss." The man brought his long spear in front of Zyanthena in warning.

Lord Darshel turned back to the guard. "She is with me; my other choice of my personnel."

"All due respect, Lord Shekmann, but we do not allow personal advisors *of her sort* today." He was hinting at a different word, though, as his eyes skimmed inappropriately over Zyanthena's slender body, made more apparent in the form-fitting men's pants and shirt she wore.

Lord Darshel felt an urge to punch the man's face. Why so many overlook Zyanthena's Tashek features all because she was not wearing her traditional saer'rek baffled him. He certainly couldn't. Her kora sword and very-wildish bearing left no doubt in his mind what she was. He could see Zyanthena had caught onto the undertone in the guard's voice, too, for she bristled and glared. Lord Shekmann's reputation had reached the capitol and she was not happy to be called one of his bed mates. "Zyanthena Sheev'arid is daughter of the Shi'alam, a scout of the Crystine, and under my employment for her expertise as a Tashek."

The man should have looked convinced by her positions of rank alone but a hard set of his full jaw showed he had already made up his mind on what kind of "employment" he thought Zyanthena had with the Shekmann. His brown eyes shifted to one of his guards to see if the desert woman was "on the list". The other man shook his head. "I am sorry, Lord Shekmann, but your lady-friend cannot be admitted into the *war* council." It was almost comical what the man suggested by emphasizing the word war, as if no woman could possibly be strong enough to handle the event. Apparently, he had not been informed what kind of fighters female Tashek were. Zyanthena looked like she wanted to educate him. Lord Darshel was getting a bit frustrated with the man himself. He had not foreseen having such problems with Zyanthena's status. His mind struggled for another reply. Just as he remembered the Crystine's Raven and Sword emblem he carried, he was saved by the appearance of the Starian prince and his own Tashek shadow.

Prince Al'den and All'ani Cum'ar had wandered to the door to see what was keeping up the steady flow of invited members into the war room. They exchanged a look of astonishment between themselves as they witnessed and heard the argument between the head-guard and Lord Shekmann. The Starian heir would have rolled his eyes at the ridiculousness of the head-guard's implied meaning to the Tashek woman's position—except for the dangerous glower in the warrioress's eyes at the insult. Sheev'arid Zyanthena did not take well to being thought of as a "whore". The prince was fairly disgusted himself that his father's man even thought the words. Zyanthena was beautiful, but head-to-toe Al'den would never think of her as that type of woman. "Sir Balion," he interrupted. The older knight turned upon hearing his name. He quickly bowed when he saw the heir-apparent. "Highness."

"Is there a problem here?"

"Highness... ah, Lord Shekmann wishes admittance for his lady. I was explaining to him that she was not allowed inside."

Prince Al'den looked to Zyanthena again, who had stilled at his presence. One thing could be said for the woman, she had a commendable self-control. No hint of her previous anger could be seen across her face. He knew, then, what would appease her. "Sheev'arid, Zyanthena. What a unique honor it is to have you among us today. I had hoped you would be invited to share your knowledge of the maunstorz. I am grateful Lord Shekmann had the grace to bring you."

"My Prince of the Yellow Star. All'ani, Cum'ar," she replied smoothly, taking the title the other Tashek had given the Starian heir.

The head-guard turned white. Prince Al'den ignored him. "Lord Shekmann, Commander, Sheev'arid, come join us. We will start shortly." The three of them bowed as Prince Al'den and All'ani Cum'ar turned back to the almost-filled-to-capacity room.

The Kavahadian party continued into the room; Zyanthena gave the head-guard a glare as she passed. Lord Shekmann turned away to hide his amused smirk.

Breakfast was taken on the patio again. The four men were still adjusting to sharing one room between themselves but had found they had come to enjoy their mornings together. The staff had set out a light meal of biscuits, fruit, and cheese, chased with some white wine and raspberry tea. Sage was busy filling the other men's cups as Rio, Roland, and Anibus seated themselves and began picking out foods for their plates. "The war council will be starting in an hour," the apprentice commented as a way to start a conversation.

"The tension in the air had been palpable for hours." Anibus accepted his wine glass and sipped the sweet drink. "I doubt many slept."

"The staff had been gossiping all morning."

Anibus thanked Sage for getting their drinks as the young, auburn-haired man sat down. The priest then addressed Roland. "Does it bother you that only Rio was admitted to the council? Surely, you could have gained entry if you had spoken with Prince Al'den or His Majesty."

Roland leaned back in his chair and brought his hands behind his head in a carefree pose. "I don't mind. Both you and Rio will be at the meeting so I will still know what transpired. While you are suffering through hours of debates, I will get to recline in the shade and sip Starian wine."

"'Cept you aren't very good at "reclining'," Rio commented. Roland grinned at the other Sunarian.

"Yet, a second-hand account is never as accurate," Anibus pursued.

"It will be enough to satisfy me." Roland came back upright to snag a blackberry. "Besides, Sage and I have business to conduct in town. It will take up plenty of our time."

Anibus's eyes narrowed but he was too polite to inquire further into the subject. "Well then, I guess I will extra attention today and give as many details of the meeting as I can."

"That is appreciated."

A polite clearing of the throat brought the men's attention around to the newcomers. Patrick and Jacen waved their hellos to their comrades as they neared. "May we join you for breakfast?" Patrick asked.

The others grinned and Rio stood up to greet his fellow soldiers and wave them to empty chairs. "Wow, it's great to see you!"

"The same." Jacen grinned back. "We were missing all the preaching and Sunarian bickering."

"Right. You were homesick for all that Southern charm. Did the Tashek treat you that poorly?"

"The Aras more like." The men exchanged chuckles. All were taking the desert heat a little hard.

"We are sorry for not dropping by sooner. We arrived with the Shi'alam's party just the other night. We needed a day to recover from the heat of the trip."

"Trust me, we understand." Anibus replied. "We had need of a few days respite from that ride ourselves."

The two soldiers accepted the food and drink Sage passed them. As they began eating, Jacen asked Rio, "So, are you going to the meeting today?"

Rio nodded. "Anibus and I, yes. His Majesty King Maushelik wanted more that Prince Connel there to represent the Sunrise Kingdom."

"The more the merrier." Jacen agreed.

"His Highness Prince Connel's snubbery probably proceeded him," Roland commented sarcastically.

Jacen eyes the merchant for his offhanded remark but didn't ask where it had come from. Even in Blue Haven, most knew the younger Sunarian prince was arrogant. "But, you are not in the meeting, sir?"

"I have business in town." Roland answered.

"Well, at least the market's good in Staria."

"That it is."

The rest of the meal jumped to lighter subjects, what had happened to everyone since they had spilt from the group and a whole host of new sights and experiences they had witnessed. The time passed quickly, and a page came to announce the nearing of the hour. The men finished their meals and the four who were to be at the meeting stood to leave.

"Enjoy yourselves." Roland teased, as he gave a casual wave good-bye and ate a succulent berry with thick cream—just for spite.

"Don't get lost in the marketplace or overburden your apprentice," Rio bantered back. "I'd hate to have to call a search party for you."

Roland chuckled, but there was a tightness to it that showed he was well-aware of the warning in the undertone of the other man's words. His good-bye nod was serious.

§ §

The four companions were among the last to arrive at the war council. The enormous room was nearly full, its many occupants squeezing around the enormous oval-wood table. The highest in rank (King Maushelik, the four princes, the lords, Shi'alam and his Shíks) were given the best seats. Then, the commanders filled around the remainder of the empty seats, their two accompanying officers behind them. The rest of the invited men were left to linger on the outskirts of the circle.

"There are so many!" Jacen whispered. It seemed more lords had shown up, each with their own officers. Most from Staria but some came from Rubia and northern Sealand. Too, the number of Tashek in attendance rivaled almost half of the other groups. It was both unnerving and astounding how many high-ranked desert nomads there were.

"Go to your kingdom's representatives." Anibus ordered of his friends gently. "See you afterward, in our chambers."

The three soldiers nodded and continued around the table to their places while Anibus came forward to greet King Maushelik. He was the only priest of Estaria in attendance; the king had asked him to bless the meeting. The king greeted Anibus warmly. "Priest, thank you for joining us. Come, I've reserved the seat to my right as your own." Anibus was shocked; only in Staria were holy men regarded so highly. That was because Starians took the signs and blessings for the Stars most seriously. As the young priest settled himself beside the king's chair, the Starian "master of order" called out to the room for silence.

Once the room came to attention, the Starian prince rose from his chair to address the assembly. "Highnesses Argetlem, Sunrise, and Fantill; Shi'alam and Tashek; lords, commanders, and honored guests; the House of Staria welcomes you and thanks you for leaving your duties to come to this assembly. It is the first official War Council since the fall of Crystalynian twenty-one years ago! Let it be known in your kingdoms of our discussions made here today, the eighteenth day of Growing Time during the Syrean Count of 110. Before we begin, we—the House of Staria—ask that the Estarian Priest Anibus Farryl bless this gathering." Prince Al'den waved a hand in the Sealander's direction and waited for the holy man to rise before seating himself.

Anibus pushed himself to his feet, fighting off his fear at speaking in front of one-hundred-and-forty men. Two-hundred-and-eight expectant eyes looked back at him. He gulped and closed his eyes to focus on his breathing. Preoccupied on the task, he felt his pulse slow its headlong rushing and a sense of calm came over him. When he opened his eyes again, they were an incredible, striking blue. "May we give praise to the Stars as we enter into this communion and remember their wisdom as we examine the course of the past and contemplate the future of our actions against the maunstorz. May the Stars protect our fight against our enemies. And may they steer us to correct actions as they see best fit of us, their faithful followers."

Anibus paused and felt the need to add the last to his prayer. "We lift up to the Stars those we have lost, knowing they are safe among our Creators. We ask for the Stars to hear our pleas to those injured and hurting from their wounds." The room was silent and heavy under his last words. Anibus gulped his own grief. The sorrow he had felt since burying so many dead rose to the fore. He forced himself to continued, "And for our wives and our children, we ask for the comfort of knowing they are sheltered by the Stars' light, wherever we and they are led; and whether we remain in this world or the next, may the Stars do the same for our loved ones."

The priest took a pause again and pointed to the center of the enormous table, where the large map of the kingdoms of Syre was spread open. The Mausheliks had taken their eight stones from the temple's center-alter and arranged them on the eight cardinal directions of an enormous, bronze compass-rose. Each stone fit snuggly into the arrow points. "And now, since we have lifted up our requests and concerns, we give name to the Eight Stars of Light and the eight stones that represent them: Morning Star, ruler of fire and stone of diamond; Evening Star, ruler of water and stone of sapphire; North Star, ruler of wind and stone of jade; South Star, ruler of earth and stone of crystal; Yellow Star, ruler of wisdom and stone of citrine; Red Star, ruler of war and stone of ruby; White Star ruler of life and stone of mother-of-pearl; and Black Star, ruler of death and stone of obsidian. As we recite your names, great Stars, we are reminded of your influence in our lives and we give thanks to the powers that are within and around us. Forever and always, we follow the Light of the Stars."

The room echoes back his ending and faded to silence. "Forever and always."

Chapter Thirty-Two

§

Rumors

Zyanthena lifted her sharp, brandy eyes from the compass–rose to recite the last words of the prayer, "Forever and always". She felt supercharged from the customary prayer; as if, with the combined observance of one-hundred-and-forty people, the space had been transformed into a sanctuary. Looking around, she observed similar countenances of ecstasy and knew her eyes had to be gleaming with the power, too.

The Estarian priest had the gift.

Across the large table, the Starian king rose from his seat and gave Anibus a bow of appreciation before turning back to the assembly. His strong voice carried across the room. "I have been at war against these maunstorz for nearly forty-nine years, most of my lifetime. It had been twenty-one years since I have sat at a full Syreans war council. A long twenty-one years since Syre had been able to call together the Houses of the kingdoms. Too long! I tire of seeing more generations come into this world only to learn that they must become a part of a fight older that their fathers. I look around this room and see many a younger man whose fathers and grandfathers I have fought beside. And, I ask myself: how much longer will this war go on? Is there no end? Can we even see one? I pose these questions to you.

"We have among us today, warriors who have fought nearly as many years as I. They remember the strength of Syre before it was broken apart at the horrible battle of Bil'cordys, before Crystalynian's fall. We have come full circle again, joined by others who do not know the world before Syre's kingdoms were divided. Men, this may be our only chance to speak like this. Do not hesitate—not one of you no matter your rank or odd your idea. I ask that we come to this meeting with open minds to find new solutions that may bring about an ending to this long, heart-wrenching war."

King Maushelik paused for a drink of water. He set his glass back down and motioned for the Crystine and mertinean commanders to step forward from their honorary places just three chairs to the left.

Though they had been offered seats, the two elder men had insisted on standing, wanting to be close to the head of the table and by the royal heirs and their protectors. Now, they made their way to the edge of the table, between the princes Kent, Al'den, and Connel. "I have heard the plans made between my son—Prince Al'den, Commander Matar, Commander Kins, and All'ani Cum'ar. I have asked these leaders to present their ideas to the council and seek your approval. Commanders."

Commander Matar bowed his head to the Starian king then addressed the assembly. "We, the four of us," he waved at the before mentioned, "have been discussing how best to proceed. With the Citadel army severely reduced in number and with the coming of First Snows only two divisions away, we are at a crossroads. On one hand, we must find the maunstorz and yet keep our forces strong in the North; on the other, we need to collect food-stuffs for ourselves and the people. The uncertainty is having the manpower for both."

"And what is the count on available men, commander?" A Rubian lord asked.

Ethan Kins answered, motioning his request to do so to his fellow commander. "Here stands of the armies: Staria's army had one-hundred-and-eighty-eight cavalry, two-hundred archers, and one-thousand-and-seventy-two footsoldiers." A few men swore. The Starian army had been the largest in Syre, now it was only over fourteen hundred. Commander Kins ploughed on despite the muttering. "There are two hundred Crystine soldiers here, with eighty Tashek scouts among them. The mertinean footmen number five-hundred-and-sixty-four, with another six hundred at Raven's Den and two-hundred-and-fifty at Carmine. Four hundred have gone to help hold North Point. There are forty-two Golden Kingdom archers and three-hundred cavalry from Kavahad. Blue Haven had brought fifty-foot soldiers; Sunrise has ten."

"Overall, that's only two-thousand-and-six men here at the Citadel." Prince Connel commented critically. "From what I have heard, there are five times that number of maunstorz running around."

"There are five-thousand-and sixty-eight men here at the Citadel and the surrounding area." The Shi'alam's commanding voice boomed out from the other side of the room. The soldiers bristled in shock at the higher number. Many uncertain glances were shared around the table.

Prince Connel refused to show he was cowed by the startling number. "You claim to have over three thousand men here at the Citadel, Shi'alam."

"And the surrounding area, Highness Sunrise. Some of the Sheev'anee are still at North Point, with the remaining two-thousand-eight-hundred-and-fifty Sealander soldiers; others are scattered in camps throughout the Aras Desert. I do not exaggerate our numbers."

"And we do not contend them." Prince Al'den replied, raising his voice over the sudden, nervous muttering. "The Sheev'anee are a strong nation. We welcome your gifted warriors to our cause." The Starian's words calmed the men, though it did not ease the tension. It was not helped by some of the younger Tashek men, who puffed up over their prince's praise. Not everyone was pleased to hear such high regards given to the wastrels. For a moment, the atmosphere was tedious.

"And what, then, are the plans, Prince Al'den, that you have been forming? Surely, some are about the fortifications already being placed around the Citadel, but there must be more?"

Commander Matar nodded his gratitude at Prince Argetlem. The scholar's ability to shift the conversation back to more important concerns was helpful. "Yes, indeed, Highness. As you are all aware, we have created shifts among the armies to protect the Citadel walls and keep a look-out to the horizon. The Starian army is at the northern wall and had been strengthened by Prince Argetlem's archers and the fifty Havenese soldiers offered by King Éldon. The Sheev'anee take the eastern wall and Kavahad the western. The Crystine and mertinean are spread among the southern and south-eastern walls. A quarter of each army is to be awake and on duty for two four-hour shifts a day. We believe this rotation will keep the men sharper; those that stand on watch. These shifts will stay the same throughout the celebration ball, so, please, alert your men of this.

"The Sheev'anee lead scouting parties into the Aras throughout the day. They welcome any who wish to join them. They are pressing closer to the Gap of the Forgotten and the Red Hills. Others send relays to Port Al-Harrad and Paragon Oasis. King Argetlem has agreed to send some of his men north to scout above the Pika Mounts and the Noway Mountains. As for the rest of the North, the remaining mertinean have been alerted of the unusual disappearance of the enemy at North Point. Careful watch is given to the Red Hills and Crystal Mountains. However, no sign of the maunstorz—not even the normal raids—have been reported."

"The North had been too quiet," Tem'arid Sid commented.

"We agree." Al'den replied. He thanked Commander Matar and Kins and skillfully took over. "That is what we have been discussing these past few days. The Citadel, and parts of the North, are well fortified; however, the sudden disappearance of the maunstorz, which had never occurred in this war with them—to my knowledge—is of great concern. Have any of you ever seen the enemy act this way?" There was a deep pause in the room as eyes looked around for anyone who would note the contrary—but none came. Prince Al'den's face was grave and his powerful shoulders slumped, as if, with the affirmation, he could not quite bear himself as regally as usually. "Shi'alam," he finally asked, "Have your people, the Holders of Syre's histories, ever heard of such an incident?"

The Sheev'anee leader rose from his chair across the far end of the table. "Highness, Prince of the Yellow Star, I have not. I even consulted with our Oracle, who herself had seen over one-hundred-summers. She did not recall such a reaction from the maunstorz. She felt the news was poor, considering it follows on the footsteps of the disappearance at North Point. She feels the two incidents are connected, though she cannot say how. She worries that this is the calm center of a sand storm. We have yet to see its other side."

Voices murmured worriedly throughout the room. Prince Al'den was quick to squash the distress with a question. "So, what do we do, gentlemen? How do we proceed against this new development?"

"Is there really no sign of the enemy?" Lord Carrod asked from his corner representing Blue Haven. "For all these years that the North had fought the maunstorz, it seems strange that none of you have any clues as to where they could be hiding."

"Oh, we have an inclination where they could be," Brash Terrik spoke out, despite the angry glares of his colleagues to keep quiet.

"What? We all know it, so why keep it secret any longer? This "secret" we all know but won't voice?" The angry stares did not lessen and the Shi'alam began to protest, which his son avoided by quickly talking over his father. "The maunstorz are in the Valley of Death, their home grounds, as they have always been."

"The Valley of Death is an endless, unmapped desert." Lord Gordar pointed out the obvious. "None in Syre know how large it is or any of its features. It's known only as a barren wasteland."

"Barren my ass!" Terrik replied acidly. "Am I the only one who begs to question its barrenness if the maunstorz are able to live there for over fifty-known-years?" A pointed stare over the council showed Terrik was not along in his thoughts. "Exactly. We are being foolish, careless *ket'fushka* by ignoring the pox in the room. Why do we never scout out the Valley of Death when it is the known homeland of our enemy?" Terrik's only saving grace was that he had insulted the room in keshic. Only a certain number of the group new the extent of his rudeness, which kept the ignorant half less fired-up.

"You assume, boy, that we have not thought of that course." Curtis Marx, Commander Kin's third-in-command, bellowed back. His face reddened as he pushed out of his chair. "Men have been sent before, multiple time even. None of the parties return. We are only stupid, prig, if we waste more men on that foolish errand."

A yelling match ensued. Too many insults had been thrown out. At the head of the table, the princes looked between themselves, their expressions embarrassed for the others. Prince Al'den was trying, in vain, to subdue the uproar. He slumped back in his chair, angered, when the room did not heed his words. "Bloody hell!" He muttered to his father, who mirrored his expression. "This war has wearied their discipline."

"Give them a moment," the elder Maushelik counselled. "Marx knows keshic, so it's really not a wonder he took offense; Commander Kins did warn he had a fiery temper."

"Of which I apologize, Majesty," Kins murmured. "I will be sure to reprimand him for this outburst." The king nodded back.

"Order! Order!" A brazen voice boomed out from Kavahad's section. The melee calmed to stare at Commander Raic, startled at his carrying voice. "You are all fools if you think getting into an argument and fist fighting is going to get this council anywhere!" The men in question slowly took their seats, voicing apologies as they did so.

Once they settled, Lord Shekmann rose from his chair and thanked his subordinate before addressing the council. "With your permission, my king?" King Maushelik waved him to continue, pleased with the respectful tone of his Kavahadian man. "The question posed, gentlemen, was what to do about the odd disappearance of our enemy. A reasonable answer was given by Tashek Sheev'arid, *despite*," he rose his voice over some discourse, "*Despite* arguments against it. I know the concerns of surveying the Valley of Death; it was some of my best men that were sent on those expeditions. They were good men, with families all, and none came back. Despite that, I believe, as others do, that all of the attacks from the maunstorz have been tracked back to that very desert. So, yes, young Sheev'arid is right. We will have to address that issue at some point. But—I caution the time be later and not made in haste. Staria's winters are mild in comparison to those in Rubia and the Crystal Kingdoms; however, its northern border is mountainous. Those mountains will get snow and will be unpassable until Snow Thaw. By then, the maunstorz may be attacking again."

"And how would you go about planning an expedition to a land known only to bring death?" Commander Kins asked of the Starian. "The snows give us time—as you have pointed out—but none have ever returned; another point of yours."

Lord Darshel continued to stand calmly, unruffled by the questions as he faced the assembly with his proposition. "I have thought long and hard on those very questions; ever since my men left Kavahad's walls to ne'er return. I have come to two conclusions: One is that the forces we asked to go forth were quite large, thirty to fifty in number. The other was that these men were military only. We have never sent a small force beyond the Gap that moved swiftly and could hide easily and were trained in surveying." He paused and shifted his reply slightly. "I have researched the most skilled men of the surveyors' guild and conclude that Peore Callé, instructor of geography to His Highness Argetlem," he matched gazes with the scholarly prince, "Is the most appropriate choice for a surveying expedition. Along with a small handful of men, they could go through the Gap of the Forgotten and follow the inner border of the mountains there, as I feel following the desert alone would be risky. Following the mountain range will give them more shelter and take away the problems of heat stroke or dehydration. It would also reduce the need to carry large amounts of water."

"Mater Callé would be pleased to hear he is spoken so highly of." Prince Kent spoke out and rose from his chair. "I will take your idea to him and see what he thinks of this plan; however, Callé is not a young man. If he cannot make the trip, I will ask for his opinion on who else is best fit."

"So, you support this plan, Prince Argetlem?"

"Yes, Majesty," Kent addressed the Starian king. "Lord Shekmann's reasoning is sound. We have the winter to prepare. The timing could not be better."

"But who would go with the surveyor and his apprentice?" Curtis Marx argued. "Hell, it just sounds like another death-wish if you ask me."

Eyes turned back to Lord Darshel, who wasn't quite sure how to answer himself. He had some names of men he thought capable of such a mission, but even they would see the writing on the wall and could refuse such a commission. Before he could answer the heated mertinean captain, a hand rested on his forearm. It brought his gaze around to meet Zyanthena's. Her touch disappeared as soon as he turned to her and she gave a bow of her head to ask for permission to step forward to answer in his stead. He hesitated for only a moment before stepping out of her way.

"The Tashek will answer your call, Curtis Marx." Zyanthena's voice was cool, almost piercing as she stared directly at the mertinean man. She had not had many dealings with the hot-tempered captain. The few times they had met, the warrioress had had an instant dislike for his character. That fact flavored her words. "Not once have we been asked to accompany such expeditions, despite out unrivalled skills scouting the land or fighting raids. You risk more men by not asking at least one of us to go."

"Like any group would want the likes of you in it." Marx replied. Others (who did not know Zyanthena's reputation) muttered similar assents about how unlucky it was to have a woman among their company.

"You arrogant numbskulls!" Commander Matar growled out, starling everyone. The beratement calmed the Tashek's fierce eyes. Matar came around the table to Curtis Marx's side and glared down at the man. His fury turned to embrace other naysayers. "You snicker at the Tashek before you without knowing her. Zyanthena Sheev'arid had been a scout for the Crystine for five years. She, personally, led thirteen successful fronts against maunstorz raids and scouted out twenty-five encampments along the Crystal Mountains and the Red Hills. It was she who single-handedly kept fifty enemies at bay at Wynward's Crossing last year when our forces got divided by other raids." Matar mentioned that because Marx had been there that day.

Zyanthena's record stood for itself. Most had heard whispers of her name across the North. What had been distain turned to awe as the assembly looked back over the slight, exotic form of the Tashek woman. She almost rolled her eyes. "We know of Zyanthena Sheev'arid's exploits." Prince Al'den said. "Her council is welcome here." He motioned for all to sit and calm themselves. Once the council settled, he addressed Zyanthena personally. "Are you suggesting yourself for this expedition, Shi'ka?"

"If it was asked of me, Highness; though, I had thought Siv'arid, Kor'mauk would be better suited for the appointment." The nephew of the Shi'alam sputtered in the drink he had been taking, surprised to be pointed out. He quickly dried his mouth on his sleeve and tried to act dignified beside his uncle. "Siv'arid's tribe patrols the mountains around the Gap of the Forgotten, so they would know the area better than myself, who has been away to the east. Siv'arid would know which warriors would be best to send along with Callé."

"It is true my tribe know those mountains well but—." Kor'mauk began but was cut off by the Shi'alam.

"Two of Siv'arid's warriors will answer your call, Prince of the Yellow Star. Zyanthena is correct in her assessment of their knowledge of the area and how best to survive the conditions against them; however, I request that others not of the Sheev'anee blood be sent as well. Seeing as we seem to be electing people, might I suggest two young men who have caught my attention: Patrick Kins, son of Ethan Kins, and Jacen Novano, son of Berret Novano of Blue Haven?"

It was hard to know who looked more shocked, the two men in question or Commander Kins. It was not often that the Shi'alam regarded other fighters over his own men, especially since he never had a reason to do so.

"Do you both agree to this appointment?" Prince Al'den asked, himself not sounding sure.

From their respective corners the two friends locked eyes. Jacen shrugged at the other and let Patrick speak for them both. "We will accept, Highness." None were aware of Commander Kin's fallen face as his son made his decision.

"Very well, Kins, Novano, you are officially being assigned to the next surveying expedition to the Valley of Death."

"That makes five people for the expedition," Prince Kent said. "How many do we want to send?" Eyes turned back toward Lord Shekmann, the unofficial organizer for the proposed trip.

The tall Kavahadian took his spot back from Zyanthena. "That is six, actually, since I do not know any scholar who passes up an assistant." His remark sparked a few chuckles. It helped to ease the tension. "Eight men were, to my best estimate, the number most adequate to travel the enemy territory and avoid detection. I would not appoint more than ten. A cook—with battle experience—would be a nice novelty, though not a requirement; for sure a medic, and maybe one blacksmith. I suggest the group decide the last men with more thought, as they will have the Snows to prepare the party. I offer them any supplies they require; if my provisions be accepted; and lodging at Kavahad if they so choose to do so."

"Thank you, Lord Shekmann," Prince Al'den replied gratefully. The council notary jotted down the offer, by the prince's suggestion. "I propose a break, gentlemen," he continued. "When we return, I would like us to discuss how we will separate the armies to defend the Northern borders and what care we need to take for provisions and food storage for the Deep Snows. Plus, we need to make the Southern kingdoms aware of our need for reinforcements… Please, take the time to discuss amongst yourselves before the second half of the day. We will meet back here in a half an hour."

Roland kept Sage and himself to the shadowed side of the street, heading for the large marketplace. He had disguised themselves in a garb of the Golden Kingdom tradesmen. Once they had reached the bustling market, he made sure to stop at enough vendors to make them seem like they were on the hunt for good merchandise. At a few places, Roland did purchase some items: Starian silk, spices, some desert teas, and a snack of grilled chicken meat on a skewer. All of these products, save the last, he had his apprentice carry in the bag slung across his back.

The southern edge of the marketplace was lined with permanent shops. It was at one of these that an aging man, ensconced by a heavy grey-laced beard, gave Roland the agreed-upon signal that he was their informant. Acting nonchalant, Roland paused at the goods displayed outside the shop. Roland commented that he liked the craftsmanship of the keeper's yellowwood bowls and if the man had any more merchandise than just the items on display. The shopkeeper waved them into the shade of his shop. He quickly closed the door behind them with an "out to lunch" sign posted.

The interior of the shop was not large, only about seven paces across wall to wall. Yet, it was well-kept and proudly displayed detailed wood-works; none of which Roland inspected. The shopkeeper was already leading the way to the next room, blocked from the main shop by a heavy, blue curtain. "Come, come." He motioned for quickness and had them into a small hallway leading to the back alleyway behind his store. As stone staircase was to the right of the door, once they came to the street, and the man hustled merchant and apprentice up it. The shopkeeper paused to bob his head from side to side, watching for unwelcome eyes, before joining Roland and Sage at the top. Alone, he welcomed them to his home.

"Tea?" The man asked as the two Sunarians eased themselves to the mates around his humble, floor-table.

"Please." Roland replied courteously.

The shopkeeper bowed and scurried to his kitchen, a tiny alcove just off from the main one. He prepared the pot, cups, and hot water on his stove. He brought out his most expensive tea, aged one-hundred-years and carefully seeped it. With the tea well-tended, he brought the tray back to the main room and set it on the floor table. To finish the refreshment, he added a bowl of cubed sugar and dates.

"Have you had any word from your grandfather?" Roland asked the man politely as he accepted his tea cup.

"Some time has passed, sir, since we last spoken. My grandmother has fared ill, you see, so he was busy tending her, but I received a missive that all had been better. He was thinking of traveling to Sideview next."

"Sideview? That is east of the Pika Mounts, right?" Roland shared a quick glance with Sage.

"Yes," the man smiled, "You know your geography well. Grandfather had said Sideview didn't use to be such a small, rundown bump in the road. Of old, it was a trading center of fine wares, not much different than in Deluge. But more, it was known as a stop for war washouts and spies. He felt he might uncover some old relic there in a side hovel."

"So, his search has not lent him much?"

The man's features tightened. "Oh, much can be troweled up, young lad, but seeing hide and hair of the lost "Ruby of Sunlight" seems to be a different matter. There are rumors of its whereabouts everywhere but nothing concrete. Your order is a tall one, sir."

"Then why did he want to check Sideview?" Sage asked innocently.

"Because, boy, sometimes you need to look through a whole lot of filth to uncover a gem."

Sage gave the shopkeeper a hopeless look, as only a youth not yet drug around by life could do. His skepticism had the senior clucking in reprimand and standing again to go to the only other room in the abode. After much mumbling and items being shuffled, the storekeeper returned to them. He plopped a coin down on the table in front of the auburn-haired apprentice. "A friend shipped that to grandfather, knowing he was looking for such items."

The coin was burnished gold. One side was stamped in the signa of the Sunarian crown; the other with the royal cornet of rubies and trilliums. The words: modest ambition led by vitality and passion will bring peace to those born by blood" was etched around the perimeter in the scrolling of old Sunarian. It was barely readable with its delicate size.

"It is an old Sunarian trid. What does it have to do with anything?" Roland asked as he took the gold piece from his apprentice to inspect.

"That is no ordinary hundreds-piece," the man smirked. "The likes of that coin have been banned since you were a wee one, and yet, it came back in circulation last month at Sideview." He leaned in to point out features to Roland. "The new coins and old are similar but there are differences between the change of reigns. The words, you see are important. The new coins read: meaningful ambitions led with vivaciousness and power will bring prosperity to those born from blood. Very subtle when you consider the scrolling of *modest* and *meaningful, vitality* and *vivacious, passion* and *power, peace* and *prosperity*, and *by* and *from* look very similar in old Sunarian—in fact, they share all but twelve letters different when written. It's only when read aloud that the changes are noticed. The new king did not agree with the saying, so he tweaked it."

"And the saying was only on one-hundreds pieces, which are carried by the nobility and court, all now loyal to or coerced by the king."

"Exactment! Few were none the wiser or did not bother to notice the changes. This coin is one of thirty-three pieces never recalled, melted down, and reprinted with the new wording. All were owned by the one man no longer in Sunrise." He lowered his voice to a whisper. "The one you seek used this in Sideview last month."

Roland's eyes flashed. "It is good to know your grandfather's work was not in vain. I always look forward to hearing about him." Roland paused and eyed the trid one last time. He let the silence fill the room as an invitation for the shopkeeper to say more, if he wished. When the man kept quiet, Roland finished his tea and said, "Alas, you must pardon us, sir. I have more items I need to purchase for my trip back home." He pocketed the coin and rose from the table, Sage following. The old man was quick to his own feet to show them to the door.

"Thank you for having time to visit while you were here at the Citadel. I will try to write you as I am able. You may also appreciate the hospitality of a woman by the name of Saida Newdōn. She is in the Green Light district. La Cont's. I told her you might be calling."

"Thank you again." Roland replied to his informer and followed Sage down the steps to the street.

At ground level, he murmured, "Follow the street to the next alley, we will enter the market at that corner." As casually as possible, they strode down the quiet back street and around its bend to the hubbub of the main street beyond.

"To the Green Light?" Sage asked, looking out amidst the crowd as he adjusted his partially full bag of goodies across his back.

Roland nodded and fingered the heavy coin in his pocket. "May our luck continue and we have more good news… I have waited a long time for leads such as this."

Chapter Thirty-Three

§

Accordance

The day wore on and the sun traveled to the west, readying itself to set; however, in the war room, tempers were getting a tad heated as the discussion dragged on. Despite grumbling, Commander Kins gave the agreed-upon orders to the individual armies. After a two-hour debate, it had finally been laid out how the North would set itself up for the coming snows: The mertinean would divide its army to cover Rubia from Wynward's Crossing to Carmine to Raven's Den. A rotational third of the soldiers would help with the Harvest. The seventy Crystine horsemen still at the Crystal Castle would assist in patrols in the Crystal Kingdom, reporting to Wynward's crossing as scheduled. The remainder of the Crystine would report to North Point, taking over the post from mertinean Commander Tyk; it would give Sealand a chance to regroup its injured forces at Ivor. Any of Prince Fantill's forces that were unharmed were to remain at North Point with the Crystine. Prince Kent's archers were to be sent back to Sardon to join with a fourth of the Golden Kingdom's army, led by Lord-Commander Ivance.

The remainder of the forces had been harder to space out. At first, the discussion had included Kavahad returning home, but King Maushelik wanted to keep Lord Darshel's fresh men at the Citadel, to relieve his own forces, so the council then discussed keeping a part of the Sheev'anee at the post instead—which did not sit well with either Kavahad or the Tashek. Prince Al'den tried to point out Kavahad's importance, for its location was centermost to the North's scattered forces, but, even with such a high claim, Lord Darshel would not budge.

"As you say, Highness," Commander Matar added to the discussion, "Kavahad is a vital city to our defenses, but I agree with Lord Shekmann that their dispute with the Sheev'anee must be respected. May I propose a different avenue then?" The council settled their hackles. Matar repressed a sigh, wearied by the constant issues that had colored the men's' tempers; it seemed over a third of the council was unhappy with the Tashek involvement—something

Matar had not expected. To him, the Sheev'anee were apt fighter well worth their boasts, but the surprising number of men opposed to the Tashek did so out of jealousy. The issue was not being dropped and it was slowing the council's plans considerably. He felt a headache forming behind his temples. The Crystine leader picked up the long pointing stick and used it as he spoke. "Right now, we have all our forces here at the Citadel. It, unlike other cities, is quite close to our enemy's lair—if they are indeed from the Valley of Death. Too, we have some very important dignitaries here, most notable Princess Éldon-Tomino, and three—I mean four—royal heirs." He met Prince Al'den's eyes to remind the brave hero he was the sole heir of his family. "All in all, we risk much by having met here, even if it was happenstance that the maunstorz showing up at the Gap of the Forgotten prompted all of our movements north or west."

"You are proposing—?"

"Kavahad should become our secondary base of command and main refuge for the citizens of the Citadel. It is farther away from the enemy lines and has access to food stuffs harder to cart up here."

The room filled with hushed whispers as the council conferred among themselves. Prince Al'den and King Maushelik were bent together in discussion, though Matar knew it was not the first time the idea had passed between them. The main issue had been that the Citadel was a better city to defend. It had never fallen to any attack since its creation in the Second Age, but Prince Al'den was known for his wisdom, not the steadfast arrogance many royalty could boast. Matar counted on the man's good sense of perspective to win out.

Father and son broke from their huddle. "His Majesty and I know our own council but we wish to hear from all of you of this. Is Kavahad to be our new command center and house to the people of the capital, as Matar suggests?"

"This is madness!" Lieutenant-Commander Terrance yelled out first. The rugged, battle-worn leader of Staria's footsoldiers stood with a huff. "The Citadel had never fallen to any army. Never! It is the safest place to be right now. What does that tiny, backwater military post have that these huge walls do not? They chase bandits from our supply wagons for Stars' sake!'

Lieutenant Raic began to stand and yell back in anger, but Lord Shekmann took hold of his man's arm and ordered him down, shaking his head for silence. "Let them have their proud words," he whispered the order to him.

Other officers of the Citadel voiced their agreeance at Terrance's words, ignoring the angry frowns of the Kavahadians. It was pointed out, many times, the great record of the Citadel of Light's walls to withstand heavy bombardments and scaling tactics. The strength of the mighty stone walls could not be disputed.

Finally, the last of the supporters for staying at the Citadel finished, leaving a break in the sea of voices. It allowed everyone to hear the Shi'alam's poignant words. "What good are walls, men, if its citizens are trapped inside? There are other ways to take a city, like waiting for all the food to eaten. The people would starve themselves to death." He paused. "My vote is for Kavahad and my reasoning is this: I have lived sixty-five seasons in the Aras desert, long enough to have known a Shekmann lord who made that "tiny, backwater"—as you so put it—post a terrible force to be reckoned with. It, the city of Kavahad, was once your king's greatest weapon, producing this kingdom's finest warriors and private fighters-for-hire. Perhaps, you have forgotten this? My people have not. There was always more than one reason our people did not get along." The Tashek leader could have expounded, but he chose not to. The Sheev'anee and Kavahadians knew what he inferred. Both nations were fighters as a trade. It was rare to find those matched to the Tashek she-koum-o; the fighters of the elder Lord Shekmann had been their match. The bloodshed, rape, and torture had been so profound and evil because the men behind it had known how to make things hurt more than the average man.

King Maushelik also knew. "I agree, Shi'alam." He started to say more but loud protests of "always siding with the Sheev'anee" cut him short. The rudeness was a horrible slight but the aging king, the royals, and high commanders on his end of the table were too wearied over the constant bickering to point it out.

Commander Kins finally yelled out, "Enough! Enough men, we have heard you." He and Matar exchanged haggard looks before he continued. His pause had, at least, settled the room. "If you cannot settle on leaving the Citadel can we not at least agree to move the women and children south to Kavahad? Can you not agree with me that they have seen enough of their share of this war? The maunstorz have not attacked as far south as Kavahad. The citizens would be away from the worst of the fighting there." Not a single complaint against the idea was voiced—much to the commander's surprise. His green eyes searched the room, unbelieving, but the men were subdued by the mention of the women and children. Ethan Kins returned his attention to King Maushelik. "I volunteer to lead the group with the women and children and will keep some of my men at Kavahad while the rest cross over to Rubia. I will sit as commander there, by Lord Shekmann's leave."

"Very well, Commander." King Maushelik accepted. "Do you also agree, Lord Shekmann?"

"I find it an appropriate appointment," Lord Darshel replied. "I will send a missive along with Commander Kins telling my people to recede the city to him until such a time as you relieve me and my men of our service here. I do insist one of my men hold joint-leadership with Commander Kins, however." He looked to the mertinean commander to see if the man agreed to the rescript. Kins bobbed his head, yes.

It was so refreshing to have such a simple agreement between two men that King Maushelik let slip his relief onto his face. He nodded at Lord Shekmann. "Do so and give your missive to Commander Kins at your earliest convenience." He sat down then to have a sip of wine. He motioned for his son to step in.

Prince Al'den looked less than enthused to take over, but he knew the next order of business had to be dealt with. "The last force we have to place is the Sheev'anee." Grumbles immediately seeped across the room. "Shut it, all of you!" He hissed; his patience worn thin. "As the Shi'alam has pointed out, he holds the largest number of our defensive. Because of this, I will have no arguments against my orders." He made sure he sounded very certain as he spoke. "The Shi'alam and his three Kala will stay here at the Citadel. I want Siv'arids Kor'moon and Kor'ar's men to travel to Port Al-Harrad; Tem'arid Sid's will go to Paragon Oasis. All'ani Cum'ar and his horsemen will join my cavalry. You have my permission to spread your forces beyond what I have just said, as your superiors see best. Do I have your agreeance on this, Shi'alam?"

"As His Highness the Prince of the Yellow Star decrees, so it is." The Shi'alam bowed to Prince Al'den, giving him the highest title of respect. The subservience was downright refreshing.

"Thank you, Shi'alam." Prince Al'den closed his eyes and took a deep breath to pause his thoughts. When they opened, he glanced at the list his "master of order" set beside him. Relieved, he saw that there were only two more points he and his father had wish to discuss with the council. He breathed a little prayer of gratitude. "Now that we have gotten clear on how we will deploy our forces, I have just a couple of smaller matters to pose. The first I direct to Highness Sunrise and Lord Protector Nexlé, our representatives of Sunrise and Blue Haven. King Maushelik, King Chível, and Highness Fantill have written a letter to your Majesties. In it, it asks for their aid against the attacks on the Northern Kingdoms. Any provisions and medicines that can be sent to help relieve us would be most appreciated. I ask," Al'den paused seeing Prince Connel's arrogant lift of his head, "No, I beseech you, to speak to Your Majesties of what you have heard today and seen of the devastation of our kingdom. Please, tell them of our great need for aid. We humbly await their reply and will provide any assistance they may require in getting supplies and men here."

Lord Carrod was quick to give his affirmation of his assistance to Prince Al'den's request—he was, after all, one of the closest dignitaries to King Éldon. Prince Connel, however, was not so easily swayed. The smug royal had a stubborn set to his angled jaw that Al'den remembered seeing in King Sunrise's own countenance. It spelled an arrogant remark coming. He braced himself for the trouble that was to follow. "Your forces seem to be stretched quite thin, Highness, to be offering assistance to our own people. It seems to me to be only a courteous dole on your part, though I applaud you on your artful demonstration of civility. I arrived with only a small entourage myself, as I joined Princess Éldon-Tomino's escort on her journey here. My men's numbers are not large enough to protect my person on a venture back to Sunrise with enemy afoot. Therefore, I will accompany the forces going to Kavahad and stay there until it is clear there will be no danger from the maunstorz on my return trip. That way your forces will have no need to be extended to assist me."

He smiled as demurely as a snake. "In return, I will write my father, King Sunrise, a letter of what I have witness at the Citadel."

It was clear the younger prince was snubbing Staria but Prince Al'den refused to be baited by the royal twit. He pasted a gracious smile on his face and thanked the other royal for his letter of support—even if the other had not directly said as much. He turned away before his expression could turn sour and pressed on. "Our last piece of business is about the food storage and Deep Snows preparations. For these, I turn the floor to Prince Argetlem, heir of the Golden Kingdom and Head of their Economics department."

Prince Kent's ideas on food storage and preparations were very thorough and well-thought out. For men more accustomed to war and defense, it was an opportunity to link their knowledge of fighting tactics to more mundane practices, of which Prince Kent was apt at making relevant. To Alden's surprise, his scholarly friend had the council's full attention. He answered all of their questions completely and with patience. The half an hour that the Golden heir took to explain his ideas passed with an ease that had been lacking the rest of the day.

Prince Argetlem finished answering a final question and returned the floor to the Starian heir to call an end to the war council. A quick, reassuring smile from the Golden prince gave his friend the final ounce of patience he had needed to conclude the meeting. "Gentlemen, in conclusion to this war meeting, I will recap our discussions: We have only two divisions to prepare for winter, one of which will be spent by some of you on travels to your posts. Your respective estates and cities will be notified on how best to store foods to accommodate our armies and their citizens alike. Each army will rotate workers to help with the harvesting.

"The Northern forces are grouped as such: here at the Citadel will stay the Starian army, the Sheev'anee main contingent, and Kavahad. The mertinean will head back to Rubia to protect its northern borders and will be met by the seventy Crystine horsemen still stationed at Wynward's. The rest of the Crystine will ride to North Point and relieve Sealand of its wounded and Commander Tyk to his post. The Golden Kingdom's archers are to fall back to Sardon. Commander Kins is taking a force to Kavahad to protect the Citadel's citizens. Finally, the rest of the Sheev'anee are to go to Port Al-Harrad and Paragon Oasis respectfully.

"A small expedition party made of two surveyors, Patrick Kins, Jacen Novano, two Tashek, and five others will prepare for their travels to the Valley of Death at Kavahad—or elsewhere, if they so choose. If any of you have more suggestions on any references to join their party, send the missives through Commander Kins.

"Our discussions of weaponry, added reinforcement to our defenses, and divisions of labor for these additions will be handled by your superiors, who in turn will send all missives through Kavahad to respective authorities. Communication fires will be laid across the various routes to alert the armies to any large attacks from the maunstorz. Any queries about the more common raids, I ask you to direct to the Crystine or mertinean, who have seen more of these than the rest of the North. Couriers will be sent regularly, on rotation, between all of the main army heads and spread among the different divisions as needed. Let us keep as open a communication grid as we are able.

"Any additional reinforcements we can get from your citizens and from the Southern kingdoms would be most welcomed. If it is within their graces to aid us, more support from the South would relieve the lack of defense and supplies we have here in the North. More so, it would show the maunstorz we are a united front against them. Remember, too, that over five-thousand maunstorz are out there somewhere that could strike at any moment...."

Prince Al'den paused to review the master of order's notes and found he had touched on all the key points he cared to reiterate. A lot had been discussed in seven hours but quite a bit had also just been bickering. He felt the weariness from many days of private meetings, fighting, and burying the dead go as deep as his bones, aching and hollow. Looking out across the room, he saw similar expressions that mirrored his own—especially on the veterans of the group. He doubted the council meeting had been as successful as he had originally hoped, but it was reassuring to see just how much of Syre was united against the maunstorz attacks.

The time had been taken (after twenty-one years) to get an inter-kingdom war council formed. Prince Al'den vowed he would make sure it continued; if it was in his power to do so. "In conclusion,

I thank you all for coming together on such short notice to form this council today. I propose we meet again at Snow Thaw to speak of our campaign for the next year, albeit at a location more south than this." A few that had travelled far chuckled at the notion; though, Al'den suspected it was from relief and not because it was amusing. Yet, it made him smile, too. "I bid you rest until the celebration ball tomorrow night. A commemorative shrine will be at the entrance, where you may lay tributes to your deceased. Doors will open at eighteen-hundred. Until then, forever and always, may the Light of the Stars guide and protect your way."

Chapter Thirty-Four

§

Le Cont's

The Green Light district was much like its neighboring Red Light, with whorehouses, dive bars, and gambling; however, it catered to a more opulent crowd. The streets were better managed; there was no trash or refuse allowed in sight; and were lined with large palm trees and yellowwood benches. Tiny candle-lights hung between each tree like colorful streamers, brightening the long main street as the sun's rays went away. Street bands were posted about, as well, in between the colorful tents of vendors. There were none of the more grotesque or awe-inspiring performers, like sword-swallowers, gypsies, or pyros found in the neighboring district.

For young Sage Cooper, the district seemed licentious and daring in how much it flaunted its less than law-abiding practices. The number of libertines walking the street made even Sunrise's one Red Light District look chaste. He gulped at the daunting spread before them and hugged to the shoulder of his master, who did not seem to be having the same discomforts he. "Are they really—!?"

"Yes," Roland cut in.

"Right here in the street!?"

Roland eyed his auburn-haired retainer with an amused smile. "As if you have never done such with a certain kitchen maid I know."

"I was a bit more discreet with it."

Roland chuckled. "I'll say, considering the clucking I heard from the kitchen staff for a week." Sage blushed bright red and Roland laughed. "Come on, I see Le Cont's just up ahead."

Sage made a face but followed dutifully. "I see you're not uncomfortable being here. Rather dismaying, don't you think?"

Roland arched an eyebrow. "You've never looked down upon my activities before."

Sage shrugged helplessly. "It's just worrisome for someone like you to be so well accustomed to this kind of place, is all."

Intrigued that his man was being so open with him, Roland was uncertain of how to retort. "Whatever," was the best he could come up with but it lacked any good defense.

They came up to the large, gilded doorway of Le Cont's and the doorman bowed to the two men before opening the door. Roland stepped through into the beautiful front room of the bawdyhouse. Sage came more timidly behind him.

"May I help you gentlemen?" A beautiful madam stepped around a blue screen patterned in flowers and leaves. Her hair was neatly piled atop her head and adorned with silver and sapphire pins. A stray brunette tendril fell seductively along her right jawline, distracting the eye lower to the tight, blue velvet bodice and white lace at its collar. She sashayed toward them purposely.

"Ms. Saida Newdōn?"

Her smile broadened. "I am she, Sir…"

"Roland Seagold and my man, Sage Cooper."

Her brown eyes roved over them slowly, taking in every detail as if drinking in a delectable liquor. Sage began to blush again. "A Golden merchant with a Sunarian name? Or a Sunarian and his servant in the guise of a merchant? Hm." She smirked and noticed Sage twitched at the later. "From the way Charles gushed about you, I was expecting someone more…enigmatic, yet you look too much like your father to not stand out. You're good at the perception you wish to convey, but that blue blood of yours will always win through."

"People tend to see what they wish to, madam."

"Indeed." Saida eyed Roland as if he was an especially delightful candy. She even went so far as to lick her lower lip suggestively. "And what I see in you is the pedigree that you are, and of what he is." She began to turn away beckoning for Roland to follow with a finger.

"I expect no disrespect taken to my man."

Saida looked startled at the directness of the order. She paused in her turn, eyes going to the assistant, considering. "As you wish, sir." Her suaveness dropped away at the response. Saida continued to lead the way deeper into her liar. Le Cont's was very distinguished; its walls were decorated in periwinkle-blue and silver silk wallpaper, the many rooms private and heavily walled, and the carpet thick and comfortable. It seemed more like a high-end hotel than a brothel. Saida Newdōn had certainly made sure of its continued prosperity and prudence.

It was nothing short of what Roland had heard of the woman, but he was impressed just the same. He made sure to mention his thoughts to the madam as she led them through her establishment to her most private rooms. His compliments seemed to restock her charm, of which was again turned onto him seductively. There was no question in Roland's mind who made Le Cont's such a popular stomping ground; its owner was just as ravishing as the other ladies.

"This room is reserved for my most distinguished guests." Saida Newdōn introduced as she motioned them into a large, circular room with a windowed dome that looked up into the night sky. The sound of water brought Roland and Sage's eyes from the window to find all the walls were made of blue glass, water trickling down it from the ceiling to a collection basin along the floorboards. Tiny, orange fish swam in the water, showing up brightly against the dark glass. The air was humid and sweet from the water. "As you see, it had a unique appeal."

The two men turned to Saida, who had gone to the middle of the room to sprawl on a lounge sofa with one armrest. The cream of the fabric enhanced her beauty and complimented her dark blue dress. Roland was amused by her chosen aire. She flaunted sex like other ladies wore their perfume. It just wafted from her. "You need not pull all the stops on me, Ms. Newdōn. I am not here to sample the wares of your establishment."

"So you say," her mouth quirked, "But you are still a man, and I am still a businesswoman. There is a price for which you seek."

"You know there is no limit to my pocketbook."

"Yes, I am quite aware of that." Saida propped herself up against the armrest. "But, maybe, I am not asking for money. I have more than enough of that. For all the men—and women—I've had, I have never had one of your blood, and I am rather eager to have a sample."

"Sire I don't—." Sage protested.

"Sage, I can handle this." Roland interrupted the young man with a small glare. "But thank you for your concern," he softened the command.

Saida laughed. "You two do not play your roles as well as you should. Someone's going to catch on to that." She stood and stalked over to Sage. "Do not worry little varlet, no harm will come to your master, and I have not forgotten your needs, either." She clapped her hands and two blond girls, both with similar looks, came from the doorway where they had been waiting. "Ladies, this young man needs to be occupied. Maybe a dinner as well. I am sure he had yet to eat." Sage looked worried and at a loss but Roland made no move to protest as the apprentice was being led away. "You offer no protection?" Saida remarked, looking at the Sunarian curiously.

"Sage is not as naïve as he sometimes appears, and I have no reason to believe you mean him any harm. He makes a poor bargaining chip."

"You act like that boy is nothing to you but the fondness can be seen in your eyes." Saida came near and raised one slender finger to Roland's cheek. She opened her hand to splay her fingers along his smooth jawline. "You are an intriguing Sunarian. Most of your station treat their servants no better than dogs, but you...you treat him like a close acquaintance."

"Some masters treat their dogs very well," he said as way of explanation.

She gazed deeply into his midnight-blue eyes; her own were sharp and perceptive. "That is not what you are doing. You're just like your father. He treated every man, or woman, as no less than his equal. You share his convictions."

Roland frowned. "You speak of my father as if you knew him well."

"I do...or did." Saida's smirk was back as she turned away, to return to the lounge sofa. She indicated the space next to her for Roland to sit. He finally accepted, though there was reluctance in his posture. The madame was already reaching for two wine glasses before he could settle himself into the deep plushness of the seat. "Your father wasn't one to accept my hospitality, either." She began as he took his wine. "He came for my other...talents. Besides the lucrative business you see here, I deal in the black market and intelligence."

"Spying."

"Yes." She gave Roland one of those deep looks again, as if trying to decide just how much she was willing to tell. "Your father had a secret he needed to protect at all costs. And, it isn't what you think it is." Roland opened his mouth to object but she stopped him with a finger to his lips. "Trust me on that, darling. Your father had quite a doozy as far as secrets go. Yet, like all secrets, it gets less relevant as time passes but no less potent." Roland looked confused but Saida did not expound. She had mainly said that statement for herself, looking wistful. Her expression cleared and she flashed Roland a smile. "And now, here you are. Like father, like son." She raised her glass in toast.

"You're not going to tell me anything are you?"

"That is not mine to tell." Roland began to stand, annoyed that he was unable to get what he sought. Saida stopped him by grabbing a forearm. "You seek the "Ruby of Sunlight"'. Her words were more an incentive to wait than her hand on his arm. "You need not worry about it. Where your father is, there it will also be."

"My father still has it? Where is he?" The intensity of his plea was surprising, even to Roland.

Saida's countenance became sympathetic. "Alas, even I do not know that. I have not seen your father in a year—or heard rumor of his whereabouts. He has always been good at hiding."

"That sounds like what I have heard." Roland slumped on the couch. "I feel like I will never see him again."

"Hm. Your father was always full of surprises. I wouldn't count him gone just yet; he is a survivor." She sipped her wine with lovely, red lips just slightly darker in color than the liquor. Saida caught the Sunarian watching her so she finished her drink with a charming smile.

"You tell me to hold onto a man that had been gone most of my life. Many say it's just foolishness to hold such romantic hopes."

"Romantic," she purred. "They are hardly that. Mostly stubbornness—which you take from your mother." Her voice dropped to a hollowness.

Roland caught the inflection and recognized the flavor. "You're jealous of my mother." Saida tried to feign denial by coming to her feet in a sweep of sapphire skirts but Roland caught her elbow, nearly disturbing her drink. "What, you finally ran out of charm?"

"Yes. I am jealous of her." Saida jerked her elbow away and set her drink on the side table. She faced Roland with fire in her eyes. "Your father used to stay here, back in the day. I was his constant companion, his beautiful lady, but that was back when I was still young, barely older than your young Sage. I loved your father—but then he married her. Since then, I have only been an informant of your father's. He never wanted to touch me, to hold me, as he did her."

Roland stood, forcing her to either look up at him or back up to a more comfortable distance. Saida held her ground and glared. "Your bitterness makes you a poor choice as an informant."

"On the contrary, dear, your father found me very useful—and so do many others. I keep personal vendettas from business."

Roland found her close proximity startlingly moving. Her perfume, some exotic sent, floated up to his nostrils to enflame his senses. He jerked back as his body responded and nearly stumbled on the sofa. Saida was suddenly there, pushing him down on the couch. She was uncaring of the dark wine that spilled across the furniture and the floor. Her lovely mouth was on his, devouring him mercilessly in a kiss that left him senseless and consumed by her passion. Roland finally pulled away, breathless, and regained some of his composure, enough to realize her hands were kneading him in delicate places. He was quick to capture her wrists and put a stop to it. "You have not given me enough for such a price."

"And who are you to decide what price I demand for the information you request!? The least, the secret of your father, the greatest, information of the "Ruby of Sunlight". Do you know how much people would pay for those two things alone? It's high enough to cost their lives."

"You have not told me about either, just rumors of."

"To tell you anything at all is risking my own life," Saida replied fiercely. "Having said anything, even to you, is too high a price for me. I like my own skin right as it is. Can't say the Sunarian king and his spies would say the same, if they caught me."

Her words sobered Roland and slackened his grip on her wrists. "I know what price they would demand for information on my father—and how they would extract it. To hear you sounding so defensive here, a thousand clicks away, concerns me as to what you know of Sunrise's spy network here in Staria."

Her keen eyes held his. "The king's spies are everywhere. He had one of the vastest networks I have ever seen, apart from the Sheev'anee. In fact, who is to say you're not one?"

"If I were, I would have been dead already; not that they haven't been trying."

"Yes," she licked her lips, watching as his eyes wandered there as if mesmerized. "I had heard rumors of assassination attempts on your life. It makes you more trustworthy but does not exempt you from paying the price for the information you seek. I have been told I lack a certain empathy for lost causes."

"Empathy is it? I certainly don't need your empathy. I need answers." Roland extracted himself from her lovely arms and moved away from the lounge to pace the room. "My informant spoke as if you could provide such to me, but you are as little a help as the rest."

"Charles did not exaggerate my usefulness." Saida replied suavely, trying to restore herself in his eyes. "It is the subjects you propose that I cannot grant you." She came before Roland again, stopping the Sunarian on his rounds. "However, I can give you something of equal value as to what you seek." Roland looked skeptical but he waited for her to continue. Saida reached into her bodice and produced a compact powder case hidden there. A quick turn of the lock then the preplacement of the cake of powder revealed a secret backing holding a tightly folded parchment of paper. "This paper holds information about your father's secret plus names of people in his circle and places he has frequented in the past. The little things I would note to keep track of him. I may not have heard hide or hair of him in a year, but this year had been especially difficult with the war with those maunstorz right on our doorstep. My people have been busy keeping alive. Perhaps you, not tied down in the same way as my network, can piece something out of this."

Roland took the paper and carefully unrolled the well-worn parchment. Flattened, it was larger than he had believed it to be...and not written in a language he knew. His perplexed frown made Saida chuckle. "And this helps me how?"

"It's coded. I could not walk around with such information without some assurance of its being protected. All you need is the key." She raised a lovely hand to flash a gold bracelet. Roland grasped the extended appendage to steady the adornment. There were three bands to the circlet, all with symbols like those on the paper. "Remove it." Saida coaxed and seemed to take delight in the feel of his fingers as Roland slowly pulled the bands from her wrist. She took back her jewelry to show his how it worked. "The three bands line up on the suns." She explained, pointing out the symbols of three circles with rays extending from them. "Once they align, the bracelet unsnaps. The top band, front and back, had the symbols I use as my secret code; the second has the letters of the Tashek alphabet; and the final band is in Sunarian. With the bands aligned, each letter stacks atop its translation. You will be able to correspond the Sunarian letters with my code and with the Tashek. Both are within the letter. With a little practice, you can read that letter as easily as you can a regular correspondence."

"You credit me a skill I may not possess," Roland muttered as he studied the two foreign languages, baffled at the intricacies of both.

"Oh, surely you jest. I have it in good faith that you are not as dimwitted as you falsely like to claim. To get as far as you have at the Sunarian court, you must possess the mind of the greatest deviant. Without, you would not have survived so unscathed."

"Perhaps I am just lucky."

"Humph. Lucky my sweet ass…if which is in need of payment for such a gift."

Roland tucked away the two items in a hidden pocket of his vest and returned his attention to the madam of La Cont's. He looked resigned and not the least bit happy about it. "If that is the only price I can bargain with you?"

"For such an item, it is." Saida replied matter-of-factly. "But you need not look so dismayed about it. It's really my pleasure to be given this night with you. You will not leave discontented."

Ethan Kins tipped back his fifth cup of mead and banged his glass down on the stone railing. The alcohol, which he rarely indulged, was not giving him a numbing buzz, let alone helping his mind slip away from its dour track. Discontented, he flicked the glass off the balcony into the bushes two stories below. Sadly, he gazed out at the whitewashed landscape revealed by the full moon.

"It just had to be him, my son, that the Shi'alam noticed. Damn it! It should be somebody else's—anyone else's—son but not him. Not Patrick." Ethan lamented. He felt a hot teardrop slide down his cheek and tried to wipe it away, as if his doing so could erase it and the whole damned day. However, another and then another followed and the elder commander was soon sobbing; his fears for his son braking passed his solid exterior. "Please, Stars, please…have I not already lost enough? You have my beautiful Marion and little Cecily and her sister Caylee...my brother, he fought for you in your name...and, still, you want me to sacrifice my son to your cause. Oh, isn't it enough!"

The Stars, hidden by the moon's light, did not answer.

Ethan let go another sob and hung his head to lean it against the cold railing, losing himself to his grief.

A strong hand clasped his shoulders, bringing Ethan out of his stupor. Glancing sideways, he found its owner. Through his hair, he saw a bottle of brandy extended to him. "It's never any use yelling at them. The Stars are far too busy with their own concerns to answer every plea cast upon them. That's why they invented friends."

Ethan turned himself around to slump against the stone, embarrassed to be caught in such a delicate state. "I would not have wanted to bother you with my woes," he replied sullenly as he took the offered drink.

"I would not judge your misfortunes, Ethan." Matar replied as he sat beside the other commander. "We've all lost a great deal. I, for one, can become quite bitter by it all. But it's not best to grieve so, all alone. If you're going to drink, it's always better with someone."

Ethan started to scoff at the idea but quickly stopped the expression, realizing it was his bleak attitude that was causing him to be rude. He took a swig of brandy instead and let the liquid burn the words from his throat. "I've gotten used to mourning alone," he admitted in recourse. "Patrick, my son, has been out of the house for eleven years now and since the...death of my wife and two daughters, I busy myself with the mertinean instead of keeping residence at my demesne. Sometimes, it lets me forget..." He let the thought fade and fill the air with silence.

The two veterans passed the bottle between themselves for a time before Matar spoke. "We've known each other for, what, thirty-five years now?"

"Yeah, that's about right." Ethan shook his head in disbelief.

"And we have seen a lot together." His words were sobering. "You know my history, Ethan, and you have kept it between us—but I am saddened to know you do not wish to share with me your own grievances."

"I know you would understand..." Ethan responded, "Because you deal with anxieties over your own lost child, but I cannot voice my feelings about Patrick. Not right now. My grief and my anger are too raw."

"He has volunteered for no small task, and there are no guarantees of him returning." Matar said, not one to sugar-coat situations. "But he is still your son. He does want to know how his father feels and that he is proud. Tell him, Ethan, before you no longer have the chance..."

The Rubian commander nodded solemnly and let the alcohol soak into his body, warming and calming it. "I know, I know." He studied the Starian architecture for a breath. "But Patrick...he probably thinks the expedition is a grand adventure, a chance to play hero. He won't think about what it might cost him."

"Sounds like another brash man I remember in '75."

Ethan chuckled. "Stars! You're right, he is just like I was. It's the endless curse: to have children so they can be just as reckless and hardheaded as you were to your parents."

"Isn't that the truth." Matar laughed and got a distant, contented look on his face. "I certainly gave my father a headache trying to keep me in line." He took another sip of brandy.

"I'm afraid for him." Ethan said suddenly, his eyes showing his concern. "I'm afraid of what will happen, that he will be killed in some far-off, uncharted territory and I will never get to say good-bye or that I am so proud of his courage."

Matar met Ethan's eyes. "Then all the more reason to do it now, while you have the opportunity. *"Tomorrow will come too soon and yesterday will fall quickly behind, but no regret will be begotten from words spoken in haste from love."*

"Helnesy. She was a beautiful poet."

"And wise. Talk with Patrick in the morning, Ethan. It will be good—for both of you."

Chapter Thirty-Five

§

Emissary

The Citadel of Light seemed quiet the next day. Most of its occupants were resting up for the evening celebration ball; however, the kitchen and Citadel staff were busy bustling around, arranging the ballroom and preparing the seven-course meal. The ballroom was to be held in the South Hall, where its entrance could be lit enough to see passed the iron gates of the inner wall to the town beyond. For that night, the gates would be open for the people to come and go freely, leaving gifts and mementos for the departed.

It was through the Southern gate that Lord Darshel and Zyanthena entered, on their way to the throne room.

Lord Darshel had been summoned by a retainer during a late breakfast of pigeon eggs and bacon. The young lad had come in somewhat pompously, as if he was unaccustomed to such a chore. It would have amused the Kavahadian if the boy had not also made a mess of his weapons' rack by the entranceway. After the debacle, the retainer had stammered that the king wished to see both Lord Shekmann and the Tashek—and that they were to follow the boy to the king.

Which was why Lord Darshel and the warrioress had to leave behind a pleasant meal and follow the boy through the camp—a quarter of the way around the outer wall. Darshel was beginning to suspect that the lad had no idea where the other entrances were and had taken the route he knew, despite it taking longer, or else it was the king's idea of a joke; to lead his guests around on a day when most would be resting. Zyanthena seemed not to mind the extra trek. She had dutifully followed the Shekmann from his tent and had kept a respectful pace behind His Lordship the entire way. Her keen brown eyes took in the mourning decoration of candles and flowers at the two entranceways and made a small sign of respect at the memorial painting on the left alcove in the South Hall.

"This way," the boy said, reminding them to stop staring at the memorial and continue on. The Starian king awaited. The small sitting room the ruler had chosen to meet was just four doors down from the South Hall. The youth was quick to show them the room and be gone.

"He lacks a sense of good manners." Lord Darshel muttered to Zyanthena as the boy hurried away.

"He is a kitchen boy." Zyanthena remarked as she passed by the lord into the sitting room. "Most likely, he doesn't have to worry about pleasantries."

"How'd you—?"

"Flour on his hands and a smuggled carrot piece in his trouser pocket."

Lord Darshel just shook his head, impressed at her eye for detail, and followed the desert woman into the private room.

King Maushelik was standing by the window, his back to the room, as he poured himself some tea from the pedestal table situated under the sill. By the false fireplace on the right wall, Commander Matar and the Shi'alam halted their conversation to acknowledge the entrance of the Shekmann and Zyanthena. The rest of the room was occupied by well-cushioned, yellowwood chairs and a coffee table.

"Please, be seated." King Maushelik welcomed as he turned to face them. "Gentlemen," he added to Matar and the Shi'alam. "If I could have you leave us. Please."

It felt a bit awkward for Lord Darshel to have the two men who disliked him to walk past on their way out. He suspected they had been discussing the situation between himself and the Tashek woman before their arrival. Their leaving, now that he and the woman had come, was marked by their silence. Darshel's thoughts raced back to five days prior, when Zyanthena had mentioned the Stars had favored him in keeping her captive. At that moment, he very much doubted her words to be true.

"I have called you here for the private audience I wrote you about." The Starian royal began. "Your...predicament came to my attention through the Shi'alam upon his arrival. As Zyanthena is his daughter, I felt the situation needed my review.

"It has been some time since any issues have arose between the Sheev'anee and Kavahad, and I find the circumstances surrounding your situation to be unique. I have collected what information I could from Commander Matar, the Shi'alam, and others, both from Kavahad and the Crystine, to piece together what they know leading up to and after Zyanthena's trespassing and capture on Shekmann lands. The question they debated was whether Sheev'arid had a pass for war-time necessity or if the treaty covered even that possibility." Lord Darshel shuffled nervously as the king looked at him with piercing steel-blue eyes. He felt a bit like a schoolboy having been caught misbehaving. He had to remind himself to buck-up and take whatever reprimand his king had for him like the lord-governor he was. King Maushelik continued, "I find the question less important than others I have wondered. With my inquires, I have heard tales about your interactions being quite unexpected between a Shekmann and a Tashek."

"Majesty, we——." Zyanthena was going to object, sensing some of the rumors included them being intimate.

"I will hear from each of you," the king continued, cutting her off, "One at a time. Tell me of the happenings over the last month-and-a-half. Leave out nothing and answer me as thoroughly as you can. I will start with Sheev'arid, Zyanthena."

§ §

King Maushelik led Zyanthena out onto the small veranda adjoining the sitting room. He took a seat on the stone bench and rubbed his aching knee absentmindedly. Zyanthena watched him until he bade her to "stop skulking like a shadow". She came to lean against the railing opposite the royal. "What is your opinion of Lord Shekmann, Shi'ka?"

"Your Majesty?" Zyanthena looked startled at the question.

"What do you think of him as a man and as a leader?"

Zyanthena licked her lips, looking unsettled. "Those are two loaded questions, Majesty."

He chuckled at her phrasing. "Just humor me. I have heard you are very perceptive about people. I merely wish to know what you think about my lord-governor. No holding back. I wish to hear it all."

The desert woman eyed him, wary of a hidden agenda but not seeing one. She sighed, finally coming to some conclusion and started in. "As a man, Lord Shekmann had two serious flaws—his love of women and his hard-headedness. Both products of his breeding, or so I have been told. The Shekmann men are a lecherous lot and have all the townswomen in their thrall. I think it vulgar that Kavahad has allowed such a practice, though perhaps, it is because it is seen as *customary* that I find it distasteful. But that is me judging the whole line of Shekmann, not just His Lordship.

"As a leader, there are few I can compare to him that equal him in refinement and respectability. His men do not question his authority or that he will deal out justice. He leads unequivocally, in a manner I have seen in very few. He is an exceptional leader. On that I have had no doubts."

"The man and the leader seem to describe two different persons," King Maushelik remarked.

Zyanthena looked up from the distant, glazed-over look she had fallen into as she had described Lord Darshel. "That is because my initial introduction to him flavors my assessment of Lord Shekmann as a man."

"Go on. Tell me what you mean."

"I will start further back...to when I was captured by Commander Raic and the cavalry." He nodded, prompting her to continue. "Siv'arid, Kor'mauk had sent me back to inform Commander Matar of our progress. Siv'an, Arimun accompanied me. We passed back through the Shekmann lands because it was the quickest route to the East Bridge. I made that choice." She wanted to make it clear that Arimun was not involved. "It was early morning when we came across the Kavahadian patrol party. We made a run for it, but Unrevealed, my mount, was shot with an arrow in a compromising location. I pulled him up in hopes of saving him further injury and to give Arimun a chance to get away..."

"Unrevealed is a Crystal horse, or so I am told."

"Yes. One of Valed Darkness's colts." Zyanthena knew His Majesty would understand the significance. "He is not a horse I would allow myself to lose, even if it meant getting caught by a man my people fear and loathe."

"Go on. What happened when you were brought to Lord Shekmann?"

Zyanthena continued, telling of their meeting in the lesser hall, her being taken away to Lord Darshel's private quarters and chained. She left out nothing of the treatment to her person. Her account continued on through her days chained up, the visit of Matar and Terrik, her getting a fever, and the days afterward. With more prompting, Zyanthena also included their trip through the Aras Desert, Kavahad's arrival at the Citadel, and her activities with Lord Darshel since. Through it all, King Maushelik listened intently, asking only a few questions for more embellishment. In return for his attention, Zyanthena covered every part of her capture in detail.

"I must say, you and Lord Shekmann certainly made a statement at the war council. Between his ideas for an expedition north and your electing Siv'arid, Kor'mauk for the job amid resentments toward too much Sheev'anee involvement, I would say you two made an interesting impression."

The Tashek grimaced. "An impression. Making a statement. You make it seem like we were in league together."

"Are you not?" The Starian king asked. "You are in his employment, as you so readily stated to my son. Plus, you were his second-in-command at the council meeting." There was a sense of an underlying question or a threat in his words.

For a moment, Zyanthena did not reply, making the king wonder if he had inadvertently insulted her. "His Lordship takes me with him most places these days; however, I was shocked when he invited me to the war council—even if he had said beforehand that he would do so. As for the other situation in question… I was in employment with Kavahad—but only to cross the Aras. They needed a guide and who better than a Tashek scout? I agreed to do it for Princess Éldon-Tomino's sake." She left unsaid that that was the reason she had told Prince Maushelik she was employed by Kavahad. Like most Tashek, she expected her words to be referred.

King Maushelik moved slowly to rise, making sure he looked nonthreatening. Even still, Zyanthena looked wary and strung-tight as the aging king joined her at the stone railing and gazed out across the Citadel's gardens. "Pardon me for sounding contemptuous. I do not mean to question your motives, especially in lieu of staying alive amidst a man considered by your people to be an enemy." Zyanthena glanced at him with her sharp, brown eyes. She studied him. He continued, "No other Tashek had been able to survive this long among the Shekmann and Kavahad. I find it peculiar that you have. But then, I question if it is because your situation involves Shekmann Jr. and yourself, and that that makes all the difference."

Zyanthena answered, as if he had asked a question. "Lord Shekmann does not match with the stories I have been told of the Shekmann family. He does not take women and rape them, nor does he take up torture. I was demoralized in the beginning, but he was quick to make amends for that—or at least seemed to." She shrugged as if finally at a loss for what else to report.

The king turned to face Zyanthena. He took in her features in as the warrioress sat facing toward the door. Her posture still looked wary and she kept a sideways glance his way; however, she portrayed every description he had ever heard of her. The fact that the desert woman had been captured by the Shekmann and not been changed was significant to him. "What are your thoughts on the treaty?"

"Majesty?"

The Starian began to understand that Zyanthena's use of his title was her way of asking for more clarification, so he elaborated. "How do you, personally, feel about the treaty? I do not want the thoughts of other Sheev'anee, just yours."

Zyanthena paused as she thought through her reply. "I do not quite know what to say, Majesty. My... situation is unique compared to other Tashek."

"Yes, so I have heard. You were found in a camp of Lost Ones, over... nine summers ago." She nodded. "And you suffer from...amnesia, was it?"

"Yes, Majesty." She continued so the king would not have to continue to fish for her story. "I was the only one alive in camp. Even now, no one is sure why only I survived or what caused the deaths of the others. It must have been bad for my mind to block out all of my memories of the events prior to it."

"And that is why you feel your view on the treaty is skewed?"

"Yes, Majesty." She almost smiled wanly. "I have but these past years to my memories. None pertain to the atrocities my people tell me of the Shekmann horrors. So, how can the treaty seem real to me? It had no bearing on how I live my life. The rules of the treaty were already in place long before I was born. I did not have to adjust to them or carry about the wounds that caused its creation." King Maushelik looked away, out across the gardens. He stayed silent long enough that Zyanthena asked her own question. "Why do you ask me on this?"

The king's eyes flickered back. "My son had been arguing with me about your situation—and about the treaty" He turned to the Tashek woman. "He sees it so differently than me...it makes me feel old to have my rulings sound so outdated."

"I thought the treaty was your father's?"

"Well...his and mine. I enforced it for him." He looked a bit sad at the admittance. "Al'den sees it as an obstacle to the future; that it prevents much of Staria from moving forward into unity. I am not sure if I agree—or if I am just scared to admit he has a point."

"You do not seem to be the kind of ruler who gets confused on issues like that."

"That would be nice to think so, Shi'ka." Maushelik joked lightly. He gave a deep sigh. "Honestly...I just want my people to be happy, prosperous, and at peace—but, how can that happen when two nations in my kingdom are still so bitter with each other?"

"You know that answer, my king," Zyanthena replied.

"Yes, I guess I do." He studied her with his age-tested eyes. Zyanthena held his gaze, unmoving. She let him see whatever he wished to see in her. There was such strength there in her depthless, brown eyes... and a hint of recalcitrance that made her test the boundaries of her world's agree-upon borders. In a way, the warrioress was the perfect mirror for what the king had needed to finalize the decree he had been tossing around in his mind. "Zyanthena." The desert woman seemed to come to attention as if he had ordered her; she was very perceptive to his changes in mood. "My son suggested a very...unconventional solution to the termination of the treaty. He proposed an emissary between the people of Kavahad and the Sheev'anee."

"An emissary?"

"Yes. Or more accurately, someone who could act as a mediator between the two nations. Someone who is respected and trusted by both."

"Respected, trusted..." She scoffed. "Those two words describe no one. The history between the Sheev'anee and Shekmann assured this."

"You sound so certain."

"Well, yes. To have that, you would have to have someone who is high-ranked in the Sheev'anee and someone who will not be insulted by His Lordship and his men..." The king rose his eyebrows and looked expectantly at the Sheev'arid. "It's..." she trailed off. "The Prince of the Yellow Star is impetuous!"

"Is he?" The king encouraged, seeing the knowing look in the woman's eyes. "I hear your people think he is an exemplary leader, ordained by the Stars themselves." The choice of words the king used almost sounded like a jest. Almost—except to a Tashek.

Zyanthena knit her eyebrows in consternation. She shook her head at the ridiculousness. "No. No, no, no...this is *shept'kelna*. He is *kelna*! I—." She reverted to keshic when no Starian word would suffice.

"You know you are in the position to do so. All of the inquiries into your interactions with Lord Shekmann suggest it."

"Except my father's and Master's."

"Most," he corrected smoothly, "And even they could see the importance of what my son suggests. An end to the treaty is no small thing." The warrioress turned away and rested her forehead against her fingers. She fought to control her breath as her mind raced. "Zyanthena," he continued gently, "I am not ordering you to do this. The choice will be yours to accept or not. I only propose it as a way to bring about a conclusion to the treaty. It could a way for the Sheev'anee and Kavahad to start anew."

Zyanthena rose her head and took a deep, steadying breath. "I am not sure if I can do that, Your Majesty." The Starian king nodded in understanding. "I—." She shook her head. "I am not sure I want to continue any interactions with His Lordship."

"Which is understandable. I do have to point out one thing, though, even if my words sound cruel. If you are not going to be an emissary, then I must still abide by the treaty. By it, I have no part in the dissolution of agreed upon punishments—except in circumstances of executions or unconsented acts." Zyanthena scowled as she comprehended what the king said. "It is written so in the treaty and agreed upon by all parties. You would have to uphold your end of the deal."

"You are the king," she replied woodenly, "And yet, you will not use your power for this one thing."

"If I had other solutions, Zyanthena, I would. But I must either adhere to the treaty or find a way to end it. If you have some other idea, I would like to know. Otherwise, it must stay as it stands."

"And you would not just release me?"

"Stars know that would seem the justified way to do it, but there are too many who worry that my doing so shows too much favoritism to the Sheev'anee. Even a king can be trapped in politics."

"No, just a benevolent king who wishes to treat all his people equally."

King Maushelik was not sure if her comment was an agreement to his words or an insult. He decided to ignore it. "You can go about your business. I will speak to Lord Shekmann now. Please think on my offer or find one to counter those already on the table. I need to do what is best for all involved. I know you, at least, understand that; for, it is what your people live by."

Zyanthena bowed stiflly and took her leave through the dutch-doors back into the parlor. King Maushelik was left feeling he had done poorly by her, as he watched her walk away.

Chapter Thirty-Six

§

Distasteful Reunion

The midday breeze coming from the distant mountains to the north took the edge off the desert sun above the six riders. Kesh, the fiery little Tashek mount Prince Al'den seemed to have adopted, tossed his long, white mane. The stallion was enthused by the cooling wind. He picked up speed at the front of the pack. The Starian gave the stallion his head, counting on All'ani, Cum'ar and the other warriors to keep up. It was the first real ride Al'den had had on his new mount, and, thanks to Cum'ar's suggestion, he was starting to appreciate just how surefooted the little horse was and how much stamina a true Sheev'anee-bred mount could have; the patrol had already run ten miles and the horses still felt fresh.

All'ani, Cum'ar's bay mount started to edge up alongside Kesh's right flank, close enough for the desert man to shout to Al'den. "Turn back toward the Citadel and let 'im go." It was all he could get out before Kesh pinned back his ears and put on a burst of speed, but Prince Al'den had heard and deftly pointed the stallion south. The two lead horses edged away from the rest. Cum'ar's bay made a valiant effort to take back the distance between them. The white and the bay sped across the golden sands, digging in for all their worth. They quickly ate up the distance back to the Citadel. Finally, the prince signaled a slowdown and eased Kesh back to a snorty walk. He laughed at the stallion's enthusiasm. "Wow, that was incredible!"

Cum'ar laughed too. "Kesh is one of the finest. The Tem'arid's pride themselves on their speed horses."

"Well, he certainly has that." Al'den patted the stallion's sweaty neck and reined him into an easy walk. "I've ridden many good horses but the stamina of your people's stock can't be beat. Now I understand why you insist on doing all the patrols; your horses are better suited for the long distance."

"They've been bred for this for six centuries. They have to be this good." Cum'ar replied as he turned his horse's head and slipped its bride off. Though Al'den thought the practice a little too daring, he had seen many Tashek remove their horses' bridles as they cooled them down. He didn't understand it, but all the horses would heave happy sighs and calm down immediately. Cum'ar's mount was no exception. "I'm glad you had time to come out for a ride."

"Me, too." Al'den agreed, thinking of all of the duties he had joyfully skirted through the invitation—not that they would not still be there on his return, but the reprieve had been welcome. "Having a nice breeze was welcome, too, and I got to see how your patrols operate first hand."

"Good things for a prince to know," the desert man joked. Al'den chuckled.

The two riders came back into the Sheev'anee camp. They rode passed the many, colorful tents and came to a stop at the long horse "barn" in the center—though expansive tent was what really came to mind when looking at it. The sheer, ivory-cloth barn stretched a good six hundred paces and forty paces wide. Horses were kept together on tethers run up by the "ceiling", which kept any from getting their legs caught on the ropes. The tethers gave some room for the horses to move by sliding on a central long rope spanning each fifteen paces between posts. What had, at first, seemed to be a jumbled mess to the Starian prince was actually a very effective and safe way to keep so many horses together.

Prince Al'den and Cum'ar attended to their mounts themselves, sponging them down and slowly watering them and feeding a grain mixture with salt and herbs before taking them to their respective areas to rest. The chore was a pleasurable relief for the royal, who usually had attendants, and a mandatory practice for the Tashek.

It was also another excuse for Al'den to linger.

"I should be getting back to the Citadel, Cum'ar."

"As you need, my prince." The willowy Tashek bowed to the Starian. "I will make my way there before the banquet fills, to attend you, as I would very much like to do, Prince of the Yellow Star."

The sudden formality took Al'den by surprise, as Cum'ar had been so causal that morning. Yet, he was quick to reply. "I would be honored, All'ani, Cum'ar. Come as the sun sets. Festivities start once candles can be seen. Until then, enjoy a good rest." Cum'ar gave a sign of agreeance and respect (bringing his fingers of his right hand to his third eye then sweeping it out toward the prince with a slight bow). Prince Al'den returned the gesture. "As you are," he said as way of parting and started his trek back to the inner walls.

§ §

The Starian prince decided to enjoy the rare coolness of the day by taking his time returning to his duties. His path led south, toward the Queen's Garden, where he often sat remembering the sweet memories of his departed mother. The Queen's Garden was in full bloom, with tall palm trees swaying—like raindrops—in the wind and shading some of the more delicate plants. Al'den reached up to finger the tough fronds before strolling down the center gravel way, leading back to the Citadel's walls.

His crunching footsteps drowned out the quiet voices of the five women until the prince was nearly upon them. It was Miss Coltrine, unrestrained as usual, who called out to the prince first. "Oh, Highness, are you out for a midday stroll, too?"

The tall warrior-prince paused in mid-step and turned to the group of women. He returned an easy smile and gave a curt bow to the ladies. "Just on my way back to the Citadel," he politely called back and acknowledged Lady Selena Durrow, Lady Kathlin Lepree, and Lady Rosa Quartlett by name. He tried to excuse himself for bothering their afternoon outing.

"Would you care to join us, Your Highness?" Lady Selena suavely invited. "We are just setting down for some tea after our walk."

Prince Al'den felt himself baulk. He knew well the traps the ladies at court would weave when given any chance. He was never fond of the gossip that spread with any interactions with the opposite gender, but astute Ainsley was already out of her chair and sliding in with Coltrine, making it near-impossible for him to refuse. The prince found he lacked the tact with women as he had in the field; men were never so complicated.

"Please, Your Highness. There is room for one more, if only for a short passing of time."

Al'den stole himself a prayer then sat down in the vacant seat. Immediately, the court women were all abuzz at him, questions on how he was and his day and, of course, about the ball that evening. He answered as smoothly as he could manage and accepted the cup of tea (in a very haphazardly, delicate cup) and plate of pastries. The prince found the later stuck in his dry throat. He coughed to clear it.

"Oh, dear, I hope you are not coming down with something, Your Highness!" Lady Rosa clucked in concern.

"Not at all, I assure you, just a catch in the throat."

"Or just a knot in the tongue." Lady Selena replied to his statement. As usual, Al'den wondered if she enjoyed sounding abrasive or if it was just at him—lady slighted and all that. She certainly had grown an attitude the past year, since he had refused to woo her and the other women at court. She continued, "But, since you do not claim any poor condition to yourself, may I ask then, Your Highness, do you have any lady to escort you at the celebration this evening?"

There it was... just as Al'den had expected. "I am unattended," he replied flatly, sensing the net being lowered around him.

"Indeed?" Selena's ruby lips persed making her stern but regal features tense. Her dark green eyes narrowed. "I would have expected the Starian prince to have many women clambering for such a privilege. Like, say, that Havenese princess?"

"Or you?" He could not help the short reply. Selena was fishing to add more gossip toward Éleen, he guessed.

"Why, Your Highness," she faked surprise, "Are you asking?"

"I am not, as I said, going attended." He mentally kicked himself to behave better around the ladies. In attempt, he pasted a smile on his face. "I felt it was necessary to have only my Lord Protector by my side until the dancing begins. Then, I will take the ladies that so please."

"Such a gentleman." Selena mirrored his smile with one just as ungenuine.

The other ladies seemed to sense the tension, for they cast nervous glances amongst themselves. Should Selena be talking to the Prince of Staria thusly? Should they intercede?

Al'den could read the concern in their expressions. "As an endearing Lady of the Court, I had assumed you would find such manners to your liking."

"Oh, we do, Highness," Selena assured thickly. "Though, such manners would be taken better if such a man meant them as they were. As for you, Highness, the ladies are left wondering when they will no longer be for show."

Ah, Al'den realized where Lady Durrow's speech was headed—the usual battle with her. "If I find such a woman that would be worth my efforts of courting, Lady Durrow, then I will surely make it known that I am doing more than being a fine gentleman. Until such a time, I hope that you, Lady, show more sense with your courtly fashion than you do with your tongue." He made sure his reply was tackless, even callous. The woman had shown him nothing less. "For it, at least, had not lost the favor of Your Highness." Selena paled at the insult. Al'den pushed his chair back from the table and stood, keeping his anger in check as he—politely as possible—excused himself from the women. The Starian prince made sure his escape to the Citadel did not show how furious he felt, though there was little he could do to unclench his jaw. Silently, he berated himself for his behavior. He knew from previous encounters that dealing with Lady Durrow and the others always left him in a foul mood. He should never let himself be baited thusly.

In the next breath, Al'den's thoughts turned to Princess Éleen, who had yet to bring the worst out of him. "Damn father for not allowing the betrothal! I was done with courting such womanly disasters. Stars, what does love have to do with it? An alliance with Blue Haven has its advantages." The last thought was followed with a sting of guilt. The Havanese princess was young and still had fancies of romance, or so he guessed. Yet, she was there because of the betrothal agreement, and he had accepted the proposition to get more support for the South. For all the distance she had travelled, Princess Éleen still upheld a brave front, while he looked like a callous, selfish heir who had used her for his own ends.

Al'den's anger returned as he mentally berated himself for being a selfish ass. Whatever happiness he had gotten from the morning's ride was gone, on the heels of a group of gossiping, scheming women and his own cowardly retreat. His only relief was in the duties and audiences he had yet to attend to, in the long hours leading up to the celebration ball.

Roland and Sage came plodding in, in the last hours of the morning. They found Rio pacing through the bedroom, distressed at their long absence. The Sunarian soldier was not placated by their arrival, even after Roland assured him of no harm to their persons. Though, he did let his man finger the gold bracelet Ms. Newdōn had given the merchant. "Such a piece is not worth your life."

"It's worth a great deal, Rio. If it leads me to my father, then all the more value to it."

"You tread precariously. Stars know what ill has gone on in your absence as you chase this crazy notion. The court will be—."

"The courts are happy to have me out of the way. The king can spin his webs around them and his favorite son all they want without any interference. Support for the royal heir will be at an all-time low, giving their "favorite" headway."

"Highness Rowin should be worried about that. He will need that support when he takes the crown—or he might lose it, deserving or not. There will be too many fires to put out when he returns."

"We are well beyond fires, Rio Ravesbend-son."

The two Sunarians were interrupted by the admittance of their travel companions, who trailed Sage into the room. Their entrance ended the private discussion and sent Roland scurrying to hide his gifts.

"I see you made it back." Jacen came up to clap Sage on the shoulder. "Have too much fun yesterday?" He teased good-naturedly and winked. "I got wind your master likes to enjoy his women." He whispered at the lad, despite the fact that everyone could hear.

"Err…about that." Sage blushed a deep red.

Jacen laughed along with the others and extended his hand to Roland as the merchant came over. "Never kiss and tell, boy. We've all been there."

"Not all," Anibus interrupted with a clearing of his throat.

"My pardon, father."

Roland settled his countenance, hoping his and Rio's expressions foretold nothing of their interrupted discussion. "What brings you over from next room?" He said lightly.

"We have been invited to lunch with my father and Commander Matar." Patrick replied. "They sent to us to joint them downstairs, as we are able."

"Well, then, we should not keep them waiting."

"You do not wish to freShe up first?"

"I think we have had all the freSheing up we need." Roland answered, seeing Sage blush further. "Ms. Newdōn made sure our cloths were cleaned and gave us use of her baths."

"Of that we call tell, at least." Rio teased. "You never smelled so strongly of lavender."

Roland chuckled as he ushered them out the door, not wanting them to speak further of his business at La Cont's. Besides, the offer of a good-hearted meal, better than the fruit and cheeses they had breakfasted on, sounded appealing to his stomach.

The dining hall—for the word *room* did not cover the place's huge expanse—was set up with many individual round tables. Most were already filled with diners. The group stopped, surprised, until Caleb Hadily, Commander Kin's second, came to lead them to their seats. "This hall will be used for overflow tonight," he explained, "So, King Maushelik has opened it for lunch, too, much to the cook's exasperations, I am sure." He chuckled, amused at his comment. Really, all the kitchen staff and servants seemed to be in gay spirits, not at all bothered by the extra work. "Actually, I hear they have made a very fine stew and bread with vegetables and meats not needed for the dinner celebration. Waste not in this kingdom."

Commanders Matar and Kins and Crystine second-in-commander Wix all stood as their group neared their table. Pleasantries were extended all around. Then, moments after they had found their seats, a young servant boy, very diligently, set out their eating ware and dished out steaming soup. He left just as quickly, leaving two fresh-from-the-oven loaves in the center of the table. Anibus, so accustomed to playing host, was already pouring glasses of water for everyone—the only task the boy had not done.

"You have all been faring well here at the Citadel?" Kins asked, starting the conversation.

"Yes, father. Though, I think I speak for Rio and Jacen, too, when I admit, I am not used to such fine sleeping arrangements."

Jacen agreed. "The king has us sharing an apartment in the west wing of the Citadel. Even six of us in that one place feels luxurious."

"If you boys are missing the camps so much, I am sure I could arrange something," Commander Kins teased. Truthfully, he was happy that his son and his friends had been given such nice living arrangements—even he had not been offered such fine fare. They all laughed when the Sunarian merchant choked on his water.

"I think they should enjoy the honors King Maushelik bestowed them." Matar added his own opinion. "The rooms of the Citadel are less lavish than most of the royal houses. They are well suited for these boys, who have travelled so far across Syre to warn the east of Staria and Sealand's plight. A warm bed and yellowwood furnishings are a small, welcomed comfort from such a long ordeal."

"Thank you, commander." Rio spoke for the rest. "We are grateful to His Majesty and Highness."

"And they are satisfied with your escort of Priest Anibus. The king told us himself. Your idea of using a merchant with bodyguards to help keep him safe was ingenious."

"We all came up with that one," Anibus admitted. "Though, it seemed more a flight-of-fancy at the time. The others were meeting at Deluge for some fun when they happened upon me and heard what I needed to do. One thing led to another and we ended up all going to the Crystal Kingdom then here."

"We might have been a little reckless."

Ethan Kins smiled at Jacen's words. "You boys were always that way, ever since you met." He referred to the three soldiers of the group. "And, you were never ones to let an adventure out of your grasp, no matter the danger."

"He means to say he is proud of you." Caleb said behind a hand, as if his commanding officer could not hear.

Ethan fought to keep the amusement from his face. "What he said."

They all lapsed into silence, their chuckles slow to fade for some. A few minutes passed as they focused on their palatable stews. "I dare say, we need to teach Russel to cook such a nice soup from his leftovers!" Wix said of the Crystine's cook.

"I think it would take quite a bit of persuasion." Matar bantered back and added, for the others' benefit, "The poor man barely mastered the gruel he serves. I swear he must have been trained to feed dogs, not people. If it weren't for the Tashek and their fine foods, we would have all starved!"

"It didn't seem so bad when we were travelling with you." Sage quipped, then seemed shocked he had spoken at all.

"Trust me, lad," Wix pointed his spoon at the auburn-haired youth. "If you thought the grub was good, you must have sampled Tashek fare. They make anything taste good. Cook's would damn-near kill you. Which makes me wonder why we haven't fired him yet?" He directed the question at his commander. Matar only shrugged and kept eating. "Anyway, Russel really can't cook."

"The man did not ruin any of the dishes I asked of him." Anibus countered smoothly. "He was good with the southern fish and meat pies. I would guess the man was from Lakeshore from the light spices and grains he preferred to use."

Matar seemed intrigued at the priest's words. "Well, he was originally from Greendale. I am impressed, priest, you could tell all of that from the dishes he made."

The Sealander shrugged off the compliment. "I make it a hobby to sample foods and fine wines from places I visit. You can tell a lot about people from their food." He chuckles at the comment. "I guess it is the Fantill blood in me that desires delightful things."

"It is a rare talent." Ethan replied.

"It is a preoccupation for a holy man that had little options else deemed worthy for the profession." Anibus said. "But—your cook Russel's dishes not being to your liking are probably from that. Crystal food is much heartier, the spices warming and robust. Sealand food would seem bland or too salty in comparison."

"You are a marvel, priest."

Anibus hoped Wix meant the words as a compliment. "What can I say? I am a marvelous holy man!" He jested lightly, pleased to make the others laugh, and doubly pleased when conversation turned to other things; of the coming ball and talk of Starian goods. Both were quite unique from the rest of Syre—as Staria boasted the only desert and a people more prone to hardships from the lack of water. The two commanders had much to say about it, as they had travelled across northern Syre many times over. They even hinted at being close friends of King Maushelik and knew details about his kingship that could be hard to come by any regular way. The group was enamored with the tales the Crystine and mertinean men could tell.

"I did not know you fought at the Battle of Bil'cordys," Patrick said to his father.

"Both Matar and I were there at King Xraxrain's last battle. Not long after, Crystalynian fell to the maunstorz then an earthquake." The two veterans shared a solemn glance, in respects for the deceased and a shared knowledge of the events of the past. "Bil'cordys was the last time so many armies of Syre marched together against our enemy."

"Texts say it was the bloodiest battle to date."

Commander Kin's aged face looked worn as he answered the Estarian priest. "All truth; every battle is as bloody, but yes, priest, it had many casualties and was the biggest reason we split the armies since. Syre threw all we had at the maunstorz—and we lost. It seemed safer to make sure some armies survive then all being decimated..."

"I thought the earthquake in Crystalynian killed most of maunstorz?"

"It did," Matar answered that time, "But it also took most of the population of Crystalynian with it. As natural disasters go, it did more damage than any of the battles we have been through. It may have taken a large number of maunstorz but the price of all those people's lives was not worth it." The way he said the last words made it sound like there had been a choice to prevent the earthquake; one that had not been taken. It seemed an odd choice of wording.

The group fell quiet after that, the somber mood taking up most of the last minutes of their meal. By then, most of the hall was empty and tables were being cleared by kitchen staff. Soon, their group would be in the way of the preparations for the evening festivities.

"I hate to leave you all under such heavy thoughts," Commander Matar said, finishing the last of his stew, "'Twas not my intent to lead the conversation that way."

"We understand, Commander." Anibus replied, polite as always. "There is much in the past that had been of hardships and heartaches."

"Yes, but not all of it, priest." Matar have a wan smile. "There were good times, too. I fear it is just the recent events that have my thoughts so dark." He stood, Wix at his side. "But it was nice to share a meal with you all, under circumstance less dire than before." The group all responded that, yes, they agreed that it was nice to meet under quieter circumstances. The others stood and all the military men saluted respectfully, as trained, while the rest offered polite handshakes.

As the Crystine leaders left, Ethan Kins also said his thanks and quietly pulled his son aside to ask him a favor. "My son, do you have time for a stroll with me while I visit Ellie?"

"Of course, father. I would not mind seeing the old fellow." The two Kins-men trailed off, in discussion on the old, palomino stallion, who had been Ethan's mount for some years.

Left alone, the others looked to each other for what to do. "Well… I guess we can go back to the rooms for a short nap?" Rio suggested. "After all, in a few hours we will have to be "primping" for the ball." He held up his fingers to emphasize the quotes around the word "primping", their new private joke against the maid who cleaned their quarters. She had used the term the day before, when she had come to clean and drop off their clothes for the celebration ball.

"I second that." Roland spoke up. "Balls can last all night. I am up for any extra shut-eye I can get."

"Especially after last night's escapades, I am sure." Rio teased back, for which Roland rolled his eyes as a reply. Bantering playfully, the remainder of the group headed back toward their designated room.

Since most of the preparations for the ball were happening in the Southern Hall, the companions took the Eastern stairwell, so as not to be in the way of the Citadel staff. They had not wandered that way before and found themselves marveling at the large paintings that adorned the hallway. Some were of royals passed; others were of beautiful desert landscapes or horses.

"There aren't many paintings in our wing." Sage commented, sweeping fingers delicately along one particular oil painting.

"That is because the East wing is reserved for the nobility or dignitaries from the other kingdoms," Anibus replied. He added when the others looked at him in curiosity at the tidbit, "I am the cousin to the throne of Sealand. I had to know certain things for visits to other kingdoms."

Intrigued by the priest's knowledge, Roland sidled over and started asking other questions about Staria, finding that the tidbits the holy man knew differed from his own. Lost in conversation, the two men idled down the hall, while Rio, Sage, and Jacen partially listened while they enjoyed the viewings of the large paintings.

One of the doors to a private apartment banged open ahead of them, startling the group out of their peaceful dallying. They shuffled aside to give room to the three nobles that came out into the hallway. Then, thinking them all out of the room, Roland and Anibus continued---only to run straight into the last man, late in leaving his quarters.

Prince Connel bounced backward into the doorframe with a furious curse. He continued to utter profanities as he righted himself and rubbed at an offended wrist. Roland and Anibus began their apologies, but Roland stopped as the Sunarian raised his face to them. Anibus's words seemed to fall on deaf ears as the two countrymen met each other's gazes. The younger Sunarian heir's face became angry and dark. "How dare you! How fucking dare you! You just can't stay away from my affairs, can you?! These were mine. This trip was mine."

Confused, Anibus backed off toward Jacen and Sage, finding Rio coming up to take his place by Roland—who did not seem the least bit intimidated by the royal prince. At the doorway, another Sunarian, Prince Connel's Lord Protector, came up behind his prince to see what the commotion was about. His eyes looked startled as he muttered, "Highness," and took to a bow, quick as a flash and not to Prince Connel's liking.

"Don't "highness" him!" Connel ordered, angered.

Rio came up to Roland's side and whispered something of which the other Sunarian quieted with a press his hand on Rio's arm. He turned to indicate the three nobles, who had waited out the prince's anger by the opposing wall. The three men alike seemed as confused as the companions—that was until they registered the face before them. They were abasing themselves then, too.

The elder Sunarian sighed and answered Prince Connel. "You and I came for different reasons, brother. Yours and "father's" affairs are all your own; though, I do not agree with your scheming. I am here on my own business."

Prince Connel scoffed. "You're so arrogant, thinking running hither and yon while I have to do your duties makes you justified. And—what are you wearing anyway?! Some half-docked peasants throw from Dabber? I'll just bet you have been out having the time of it, oh whore lover." He smirked when his comment darkened the other's face. He opened his mouth to say more when his Lord Protector stepped in with a "that's enough, Highness" and a "I beg your pardon, My Highness" to each man.

"Prince Rowin, we beg your pardon for not greeting you sooner." A nobleman spoke up, boldened by the Lord Protector and fearing the Sunrise temper.

Disappointed at his secret being so publicly known, Rowin held his breath and counted to five before turning to the three noblemen and his travel companions—the latter two gaping at him as if he had sprouted a third head. "You are pardoned Lord Darrow, Duke Mardom, Lord Edwyn." He greeted them by name; though, he had only chanced to meet them once, five summers ago in court. The men were impressed to hear him name them so. "I had not meant to avoid you. My business had taken me other roads." To Anibus and Jacen, the two companions who had not known, he tried to express an apology through his features—and a promise to explain himself later. He turned back to his brother. "I had heard of your accompanying Princess Éldon-Tomino as her escort. Stars know, you and father care not about Staria as much as King Éldon. I am sure both Majesties know that as well."

Connel's lips formed a thin, angry line at the remark. "As I'm sure your skulking around as a peddler makes your actions so noble." His Lord Protector tried to calm the royal again but he hissed out a "shut it" at the man's attempts. "I will have my say." He growled out and continued. "Visiting a kingdom's royalty under false pretenses gives a rather nefarious message; one that reflects poorly on father."

"Your father."

For once the other heir did not concede one way or another at the argument. "Your actions have jeopardized our welcome."

"I have already sent a request to His Majesty of my doings here. I had his full consent on the matter." Which was news to everyone—even Rio and Sage. None suspected Rowin of bluffing...and his brother was too flabbergasted to make a retort. Rowin kept his cool manner, refusing to be cowed by Connel. "But now—since you're making such a public display (of which I should have suspected from you)—I will go make my official appearance to His Majesty and his court." He made quick work to end the disastrous situation. "Please excuse me, gentlemen," he directed to the nobles, "Brother; it seems I have much to get organized now that I am attending the ball as Sunrise's royal heir."

Connel reddened. "Oh, we are so not done, brother!" His words fell on Rowin's hastily retreating back. "Rowin!"

The Sunarian heir had signaled Rio to him and offered his hand to his Lord Protector. Rio took it, sharing in the touch of telepathy Rowin had inherited from his mother, Queen Sylvia. "*Make haste to get a private audience with His Majesty Maushelik and His Highness. Word will be flying by the hour of my presence and I will not have them learning of it from a page. Use my seal if it helps speed my request. I do have documents signed by His Majesty of his permission—though they are over two divisions old.*"

"My Prince." Rio gave a small bow and hurried away on his errand.

"Highness, Prince Rowin." It was Anibus, following on the heels of Sage, Jacen in tow. Rowin slowed to allow them to catch up. "I must say, Rol—prince, I am a bit astounded at this turn of events. I know I guessed at your identity—but I missed the mark a few rungs short."

"I didn't mean any disrespect with the deception."

"Oh, I am not taking any, Highness." Anibus chuckled. "I thought you were a nobleman doing your biding, but it turns out you do your own. I am quite impressed. Really." Rowin was intrigued by the priest's good humor. He glanced at Jacen to see if the other companion was as forgiving.

"I, too, can say, I am equally shocked to find I shared a camp with a royal heir and did not recognize you for who you were. You handled yourself well, Highness."

"Maybe not that well," he confessed as they made their way back to their quarters. "I may have overstated my welcome to my brother. I did have permission by the king, but it is a little outdated."

"King Maushelik is a just king. He is rarely known to revoke an invitation, once given."

"I wish I had your faith, father." Rowin replied, as Sage went ahead of him to lay out cloths more fit of his station. "The coming hours will see if my blunder is pardoned."

Chapter Thirty-Seven

§

The Dress

The gossip spread like wildfire through the Citadel; two juicy rumors about two royal heirs. The first came to Princess Éleen on the conniving feet of Ainsley and Coltrine. The second spread more slowly of the Sunarian prince's official arrival to the courts. It was all about faux pas in the ladies' court.

Éleen took the first news with dismay; though, she was quick to hide how she felt about Prince Al'den's encounter with Lady Durrow and her group of followers. The prince would not ask her to attend him. It had her mind flitting about in worry that King Maushelik had forgone his favor to her to announce their courtship to the court of Staria. To preoccupy herself from more concerning thoughts, Éleen busied herself wondering what Prince Connel' brother looked like. Was he as handsome as Connel? Would Prince Rowin be as charming or viler in nature? Though Sunrise and Blue Haven frequently visited each other, Éleen came to the realization that the two heirs had rarely frequented the gatherings. She, had not been considered for betrothal to either, so they had never been formally introduced.

She was so lost in her ponderings that it took the maid five attempts to alert Éleen her assigned staff had the ballgown and jewels ready and a fresh bath prepared in the other room. Flustered, the Havenese princess allowed the poor woman to lead her to the bath and undress her. She came to her senses as her skin hit the hot water. "Oh!" She exclaimed at the heat. But it felt wonderful in the next second, so Éleen waived the concerned staff away from going for cold buckets of water. "It's okay. The water feels good now."

"Yes, Highness. Very good, Highness." The maid motioned the others away, to other preparations, and helped Éleen clean herself and wash her hair. Then, it was straight to the hairdresser and makeup artist to get fully made-over. A slip and undergarments followed, then the flowing ballgown. It was embellished with tiny pearls and lace, to soften the sea-green coloring of the silk. Finally, a string of pearls and jadestones were clipped around her neck. The troupe of helpers backed away to let Princess Éleen see herself and the ensemble.

Éleen was silent as she gazed into the mirror. In all the rush, she had forgotten which dress she had chosen—the Havenese green, made of the softest and mellowest colored silk. Though it was one of her favorites, looking at it now, it lacked the flare she had desired. How was Prince Al'den to notice her if the princess did not stand out? Yet, there was no time to remake the whole ensemble. Besides, her scalp ached from all the hair pulling it had endured from the intricate style she had requested. The sea-green would have to do.

The maid, still a constant shadow, did not hold Éleen's concerns. She cooed in appreciation at the fine lady before her, reaching timidly to pet the exotic silk. "How fine ye look, M'lady. How fine. Ev'ry eye will be on ye tonight, that 'ey will."

Éleen thanked her for the kind words. Inwardly, though, *she thought, I can only hope.*

§   §

The dusk light signaled the lighting of the hundreds of white candles at the commemorative entrance. Flames licked golden and orange, casting the bright murals in the archway and the multitude of flowers to dancing. The sight was stunning and unique to the three visitors as they walked about the memorial.

"They make a very elegant display for the deceased," Gordar murmured to his prince.

"That they do," Par returned. He reached out to gently touch a delicate rose petal. "We send pyres to sea, and Staria paints murals and lays out flowers…"

"Better than us; we bury our dead." Prince Kent told them as he came over; a frown was on his face. "I feel this display shows more respect than that." To embellish, he said, "We only give a quick funeral prayer then away they go. No time is taken to acknowledge who the deceased were." He fingered an emblem worn by his Lieutenant-Commander that he had laid among other such items. "It makes me relieved that Eric will be remembered so."

"Mr. Sloane was a great man, or so I have heard." Prince Par added his own condolences. "He will be missed."

"But not forgotten." They shared sad smiles then moved passed the memorial, giving others room to show their own respects.

"This evening's celebration is bitter-sweet," Par continued as the three men entered the domed hallway leading to the Southern Hall.

"Yes," Kent agreed, "But, as I have come to understand, Starians believe that no life is fully appreciated if there were not both grief and happiness; "for without one, there is not a way to know the other" … An interesting philosophy, the pairing of opposites. It made much sense to me. This ball is based on that concept. Celebrate their lives and accomplishments with merriment but also grieve—if that is what is needed. Many townspeople will go to the shrine tonight and pay their respects. All of the commemoratives will be divided between the households of the deceased on the 'morrow—a way of giving back. There will be many gifts."

"A unique custom and commendable." Prince Par replied, as he accepted a glass of wine Lord Gordar had snagged from a passing servant. "Much kinder than giving the grieving families a letter of regret and a bag of coins."

The two princes would have continued their conversation, but their arrival at the Southern Hall was met by a zealous heralder, who pompously flourished out their titles to the room beyond. Prince Kent let out a sigh and let the other prince see him roll his eyes, before he fixed his face in a jubilant smile and led the way into the room. Par followed behind, with a chuckle. The lords and ladies already present had paused their mingling at the announcement of their arrival. In shock—and some flushing, in Par's case—the whole room bowed to the two royals, acknowledging their status. "Wow," Par breathed.

"Weren't expecting that, huh?" Prince Kent whispered, as the room settled back into their festivities, with the Golden heir's prompting.

"They treat you as well as they do their own royalty," Gordar commented.

Kent nodded. "That they do." Then, he saw someone in the crowd. "Come, let me introduce you to Lord William Greyson. He and his sister have graced my father's court many tomes, acting as emissaries for trade between our two kingdoms; I think you will like the man." Knowing hardly anyone, the two Sealanders were grateful to be towed around by the charming Goldener.

Lord Greyson, it turned out, was very pleasant to talk with. The willowy lord towered over the Sealanders, but his height of six-foot-four-inches did not reflect his gentle nature. He had a mellow voice, as easy to take as sweet, summer honey, and a wit that sparked the imagination. He and Prince Kent vied for the title of better jester—a running joke between the two friends. The contest left Prince Par and his Lord Protector with wet eyes and sore faces from laughing too hard.

"Oh!" Gordar exclaimed at a recent bout. "Stars, it feels like I haven't laughed so hard in ages! I think my face is going to regret this in the morning."

"No, good Lord, it is the nice hangover you'll regret!" William reminded. Most would have more than their fair share of hangovers once the night was through.

"Ah, don't remind me!" Gordar replied, feigning a frown.

"Oh, on that I am sure I won't. Here, good sirs, have another glass of wine. Cheers all around!"

A trumpet sounded out as they took their sips of the beverage. Turning, they and the other guests witnessed the arrival of the Sunarian party—the two brothers entering at the same moment. "No love lost there." Lord William noted as the two royals paused at the entrance. The tension noticeable between them. No love indeed.

§   §

Prince Rowin felt the tension sing through his body the closer he came to the Southern Hall. Though his companions were still forgiving of his deception—and the Starian king had been, as well—he could not but help feel as if his new guise, even if it was his true one, was a lie. How could he walk into that room when he felt torn over having to reveal his identity?

Obviously, his distress was more palpable than he had assumed, for Priest Anibus came even with him and touched his shoulder. "Highness."

"Rowin, please, Anibus. We have travelled together long enough to be less formal with each other."

"Prince Rowin, then." Anibus amended, but only slightly. "Though in public, I will continue to use your title." Rowin reluctantly acquiesced. "I know that these last few weeks have been freeing for you and that having to don your rank must be disappointing, but maybe this will be for the best, Highness? Staria will get to know the Heir of Sunrise."

"It will help our relations; I have no doubt." Rowin replied. His mind was thinking it was good for Staria to see another side to Sunrise beside his arrogant, self-centered brother. And yet...

"It isn't that that worries you, is it?" Anibus guessed. Rowin looked at him quizzically. "Rowin, or Roland—which ever name you decide to be—we are not upset with your actions, nor do we feel deceived." He stopped the prince and glanced back to the others. Jacen, and Patrick (who had come back to them as speedily as he could once the rumor had made its way into the mertinean camp) both agreed. Patrick even added that Rowin had made such a good merchant that neither man would have suspected his royal heritage. It was a high compliment from the soldier. "There is nothing between our friendship. We will get through this event as we have with others: together."

Rowin's sculpted jaw clenched, showing he was still concerned, but he was consoled enough by their support to say, "Thank you, Anibus, Jacen, Patrick."

Relieved that his prince was receiving such support from their travel companions, Rio released the breath he had been holding and stepped into the conversation. "My thanks as well, to such loyal friends. Shall we continue to the hall?" He cast his question to Rowin.

Rowin nodded, then repeated it, more resolutely. "Yes. Yes, I believe we shall."

They began to start off again, but a hollow clap sounded from their right. It called their attention to the men there. Prince Connel rose from the bench he had occupied, coming through his small entourage of soldiers to engage his elder brother. "My, my, what loyal companions you travel with. They are so eager to please the skulking prince within their midst. It's touching." Rowin frowned but refused to offer a retort. His midnight-blue eyes looked beyond his brother to the eight men accompanying him—eight of Sunrise's finest royal guard, dressed in deep burgundy that clashed with the calm reflecting pool and yellowwood bench of the alcove. Elis Thorpson, the prince's Lord Protector, hung back with the others. A nasty bruise was on his right cheekbone. Apparently, Connel had felt him unfit to do his job. The elder prince was appalled. Elis had served their family for over thirty-five years; he was not a man easily cowed by the Sunarian temper.

"A reflecting pool does not suit you."

Connel sneered. He was not fooled by his brother's off-handed remark. "Elis ran into a door, at least, as far as anyone is concerned." He sidled up until they were almost face to face. Being that close, it was easy to see which father they resembled. King Richard had been a tall man, lean and dashing with eyes and hair the same color as Rowin's. His younger brother, Raymond, had honey-highlighted chestnut hair and a broader, lanky frame. Prince Connel's height came from his father; his delicate, comely features came from their mother, Queen Sylvia. Their attitudes, too, matched their fathers'. "I was waiting for you. Why else would I sit in such a place? I had to see how you fared after your news spread through the castle."

"It is a Citadel, and, as you see, I am just fine, brother."

Connel fixed him with a keen, arrogant eye. "Fine enough to beg pentatance from an Estarian priest." He let the insult be his parting words as he waved his men to follow him down the hall.

Rowin almost let his younger brother go, but he knew it would not end well if Connel went into the Southern Hall ahead of him. The dashing, young prince needed only a minute of one lonely lady's time to speed along nasty rumors of his brother. He waved to his friends and caught up to the other's side without looking like he was chasing him. "I had expected you to stay the charming lady's-man you like to portray at social events."

"And am I not?" Connel flashed an instant smile, transformed into such a man. "My annoyance at your interference will not change that I am Sunrise's most beloved prince."

It seemed beside the fact to point out that Connel was only loved by the noble class (and not the commons) so Rowin decided not to correct his brother. They were entering Prince Connel's playing field, after all. "On the contrary, brother, is it not best that Sunrise has both princes in attendance? There are so few Sunarians here at this function. Should we not be giving them [Staria] our best show?"

Prince Connel seemed to pause at Rowin's words. Finally, he conceded to the other's reasoning. "For Father, yes, it would be best to have more of Sunrise in attendance at this ball. Just don't go getting into my light, brother."

"Of course." On that settlement, the two princes entered the Southern Hall to join the festivities.

§   §

Commander Raic was unhappy with the task his lord had commanded him to perform, but he would not refuse the Lord Shekmann. "Find Zyanthena," Darshel had ordered. "We will not go to the celebration until I have talked with her." Nonplussed, the cavalry commander had set off through the camps, asking after the woman. In dreaded suspicion, he began to suspect that she might had found refuge with her kin. Almost an hour into the search, word got back to him—from a stable boy no less!—that the desert woman was back at the tents tending to her mounts. She was not gallivanting through Sheev'anee territory. Raic cursed, "And you could not tell me this an hour ago!" The boy cringed and failed a reply. "Dim wit, I was back at the camp at the start of all this." He fumed as he returned to the Kavahadian tents; really, Raic was pissed at himself just as much as he was at the others enlisted to find the Tashek. Of course, she was with Unrevealed, when wasn't she? Sure enough, there was the vile hauntress herself. Her raven hair as long and as dark as the stallion's she was nestled against. It was almost a pity he did not like the Tashek; for, Zyanthena was both beautiful and useful to His lordship—and very perceptive, he thought, as her brandy eyes fixed on him immediately upon his arrival.

"My Lord Shekmann has asked for you in his tent."

Zyanthena seemed to freeze, like an animal caught in the crosshairs—or a predator hiding from its prey. Commander Raic felt his own breath pause. He willed it to life, angry at himself for feeling her sway. He wondered if the Tashek would deny the order. If he understood the rumors floating around, Raic knew it was no longer His Lord's place to order the woman around; however, Zyanthena disentangled herself from the black stallion and came to him. "As His Lordship wishes." Raic was suspicious of her demure attitude, but he knew it was not his place to question the task he was assigned. The commander motioned the desert woman ahead of him and fell into step a few paces behind.

Lore Darshel was in his private pavilion. He nursed a glass of wine with Commander Gordon and Lieutenant Lendon, Gordon's man. The lord-governor seemed to be brooding over something, as his face in hard lines, but his countenance improved upon Zyanthena's arrival. He was quick to his feet as the Tashek woman entered.

"Your Lordship." Zyanthena bowed her head, her own features solemn.

"The Ball has started, and yet, my men tell me you were still out with your horse."

"Yes, Your Lordship. I have the mind to attend to him tonight."

"And I've the mind you don't." Darshel was rewarded with a flash of annoyance at his command. He quirked a smile at the desert warrioress's usual defiance. "Our king requested of me to remind you that your people will expect your attendance. You are, after all, one of Staria's greatest protectors and the Shi'alam's daughter."

She had that look of skepticism at the praise he gave. "King Maushelik says," she repeated. Despite how loyal she was to the Starian king, discontent still etched her brow.

Lord Darshel studied the beautiful woman before him. He had the feeling something the king had said to her earlier had scattered her hopes of her freedom. He, certainly, had heard a mouthful of the ruler's discontent with the Kavahad-Sheev'anee treaty, and other else. It must have been a grave verdict indeed for Zyanthena to keep such a look on her face. "I have something for you." Zyanthena gave the Shekmann lord a guarded look but followed him as Darshel entered his sleeping quarters, deeper into the pavilion. She hung back by the curtain that separated the large tent into two parts. Her keen eyes stayed on Darshel's back. "I was uncertain if you would accept this," Lord Darshel began, letting Zyanthena know his weakness, "But I had hoped you might find some way to…"

Curiosity gave way to suspicion and Zyanthena came closer to Lord Darshel's mattress—and the item atop it. She paused at the foot of his bed before reaching out with more conviction to touch the soft, rich-blue silk of the dress. Lord Darshel let go the breath he held. He had been uncertain of Zyanthena's reaction to the dress or if the

Tashek would don such an item. Seeing her eyes soften as she touched the fabric, her eyes in wonderment, eased his fears. Slowly, he bent and lifted the dress off the blankets.

The tailor had done well on the design, despite the fact he had never heard of such a dress. "Exotic," he had called it. "Exotic for an exotic woman," Darshel had replied. The torso was made to fit formingly around the wearer and fall in a simple, flowing cascade. Darshel had requested hidden slots be formed in the sides—all to accommodate Zyanthena's need to keep a weapon hidden on her person (not that he had explained it that way to the tailor). Elegant lace, nothing extravagant, framed the V-neck and piped down from the shoulder to the flowing sleeve to stop just short of the wrist. The last of the lace was around the delicate waistline. Lighter panels of blue brocade, in a velvety flower pattern, gave a delicate contrast to the rich blue of the silk.

"I know it is simple compared to what the ladies of the ball will be wearing, but I thought if it was overly constricting of your movements, it would not suit you. I also designed two thigh sheaths that can be hidden under the skirt and within reach by these slits." Lord Darshel showed her the well-hidden areas. "I thought it would be nicer than the clothes you have been wearing; unless I am very wrong and you wish some Tashek garments instead?"

Zyanthena persed her lips, appraising the unique dress. Her hand caressed the weapon slits then the brocade and finally the lace. "The Tashek do not have clothes as fine as these. We are a practical people, not prone to fanciful things, but this..." A pleased smile, there and gone again like the sun hidden behind a bank of clouds, showed her pleasure at such a gift. "This is most appropriate for a ball."

"And still represents where you come from, I hope. You will be the only lady to wear such an exotic ensemble. All of their eyes will be on you."

"And on you?"

"Still quick to find the heart of the matter," Lord Darshel teased, chuckling. "Only if you desire, Zy'ena; though, Commander Gordon is here to escort you—if you would prefer his company. Without you on my arm, I am more likely to be pursued by other women."

"So vulgar...as usual," she replied, but with a little humor in her own tone.

"A man has to be true to his nature."

"Uhuh," was her skeptical reply.

Darshel laughed and waved her to his dressing area. "Go, change. I have one more piece to give you when you are done."

Zyanthena took the dress with her behind the screen and changed out of her worn and hay-ridden garments. She lifted the dress over her head and let it slide, cool and lustrously smooth, down her skin until is pooled around her ankles; she could not remember a time when she had worn something feeling so delicate. It was like rose petals. All the Tashek clothing was made of plant fiber, sheep's wool, or horsehair; rough in comparison to this dress. Not a panel or seam scratched her or made her skin itch. It was so fine and lovely...

"Everything okay? Does it fit? I guessed on your measurements."

"Ah...um, no. It feels fine, I think." She found herself stammering uncharacteristically and hurried out from behind the screen. The dress felt like it molded to her body. It was better than any garment she had ever worn, but that made Zyanthena more uncertain of her appearance; tighter clothes could highlight any imperfections. From the way Lord Darshel stared as she walked up to him made the warrioress think something was wrong. "Well, maybe a seam's too tight or the colors make me washed-out?"

That sent Lord Darshel laughing, leaving the desert woman baffled. "I would never have expected you, of all people, to think about your complexion as "washed out'." Zyanthena shrugged in the wake of the lord-governor's amusement and waited it out. Lord Darshel finally calmed himself enough to wave her to a full-length mirror tucked into the corner of his make-shift quarters. "I think the dress does anything but wash you out. The measurements are perfect. This dress couldn't have been made better."

Indeed. Zyanthena barely took liberties to see herself in a looking-glass. The stunning woman it showed could not possibly be her. The deep blue of the dress brought out similar highlights in the Tashek's long hair, and it seemed to cause her skin to glow vibrantly—but not to distraction—in the softening light of the tent. The form-fitting dress made the woman in the glass seem taller and very elegant. And very much a woman. When had her hips and chest filled out and how had she missed the last traces of girlhood leave her face? "Oh," she breathed.

"Very much so, yes." Darshel agreed, appearing beside her in the mirror. "You are very beautiful." In response to the lord's sincere words, Zyanthena ducked her head. She was unused to such a claim. "If I may," Darshel asked, "I brought this silver hair clip and string of onyx to go with your dress. I am pretty good with hair, too, if you would like me to do it up for you?"

"Ah," Zyanthena eyed the brush Darshel held as if it would bite. She didn't want to say so, but doing more than putting her hair back in a ponytail or messy braid was beyond her skills. "Yes, maybe you should. I have no inclination of what would be appropriate for a Ball. It's—."

"Not something a warrioress deals with," he finished for her. "I understand that. Just hold still, okay?" Zyanthena seemed to freeze in place as the Kavahadian lord-governor started on her hair. She never once flinched, despite numerous tangles in her wind-blown strands. It took a good five minutes to smooth her long mane then another ten for Lord Darshel to add some decorative braids that formed a net around her head and kept the long strands from her face. In the end, Lord Darshel fastened the many braids together with the delicate silver clip. Lastly, he took dried baby's breath flowers— which Zyanthena hadn't noticed he had gathered—and placed them in bunches throughout the weave. "The final touch is the necklace." He lifted the single cord up and fastened it around the Tashek's graceful neck.

Zyanthena fingered the delicate chain and smoothed gems. "They are pretty but," she noticed the four onyx gems were offset to the sides leaving a gap at the middle of the chain, "The positions of the stones seem off."

"On purpose." Darshel reached out to the chain that rarely left her neck since its return. With the onyx stones, the two necklaces looked complete. The four stones being smaller than her main stone lent to the obsidian pendant being the centerpiece. "Now, you are complete."

Zyanthena fingered her obsidian, considering its position of honor amidst the rest of the ensemble. It felt right being there. "Why did you do all this?"

Darshel looked embarrassed at the question, much to Zyanthena's fascination. He cleared his throat. "I wish I could give you an answer that would sound reasonable, but nothing about my motives are from any logical provocation. I... our situation is nothing like I would have imagined it. I felt this would be the right thing to do. The dress...it felt like the best thing for you, as the Shi'alam's daughter. Anything less would be disrespectful."

The desert woman fixed the Shekmann lord with her keen eyes, as if she could see into his very soul. Lord Darshel felt himself held, like a tightened bowstring about to snap, in the brandy gaze. What did she see when she looked at him so, he wondered? A moment later and he knew. "You have changed your mind about us...Tashek, I mean. So many of the stories you were told were outdated and not truthful. There is something else, too..." Darshel was afraid he had been found out. Did Zyanthena guess at the feelings the lord had for her? "You have changed, Your Lordship. You are not as cruel as you were upon our meeting."

Darshel released the breath he held, relieved at her words. Perhaps, she was not as perceptive as he had thought. To think that she knew he lusted after her? —well, she may know that, but that he had begun to feel a fondness for her, finding her companionship comfortable and even anticipated it... that he hoped she did not suspect. Stars, his ancestors were already rolling in their graves at his private admittance! He gave a shaky laugh and pushed his thoughts away. "Changed, yes. Well, there were quite a few words exchanged between His Majesty and myself earlier. Our situation is very much in the royal spotlight. I cannot afford to look like a fool in His Majesty's eyes."

"Indeed, you cannot." But Zyanthena looked unconvinced at the Kavahadian's words. It was as if she knew he had made them up on the spot to cover up what he really meant to say. She turned away to collect the knives and sheaths still on the bed. "We best not be any later, Your Lordship, if you are to keep up appearances. I will accompany you—with Commander Gordan as my escort."

Chapter Thirty-Eight

§

Remembrance

As Lord Darshel had predicted, their arrival at the Ball stunned those in attendance. His arrival was only courteously remarked, as most Starians knew him by reputation if not by sight; however, it was the woman who proceeded him that drew the stares. Zyanthena was announced, belated by the crier (Commander Gordon had had to prompt the man to recognize the Tashek woman). The crowd looked up. Firstly, because a Sheev'anee name among the Kavahadian party was unheard of, and, secondly, because Zyanthena was so breathtaking in her exotic dress. More than a few tongues were wagging at the sight of it.

Zyanthena came forward to pose beside Lord Darshel. She looking very regal as her sharp gaze swept the room—Darshel knew it was to mark everyone in attendance and to locate exit points—and seemed to meet everyone's gaze individually. The warrioress left no room for questions in anyone's mind that she had full right to be there, looking and being however she chose. Lord Darshel withheld a pleased smile as their audience let out a collective sigh.

"May we, Your Lordship?" She asked. Her words broke the spell she had cast.

"Yes, we shall." Lord Darshel waved his commander back to Zyanthena's side and moved their party away from the entranceway. Commander Raic stepped aside to get His Lordship some refreshment as the rest of Kavahad drifted apart to mingle.

"May I introduce you to some of my old friends and squad members?" Commander Gordon asked Zyanthena.

The Tashek woman nodded and slid her hand out from his arm, no longer wishing to tolerate the silly custom now that they weren't in the spotlight. "I would be honored to meet them, Commander."

Gordon flashed a joyful grin on his aging face at her words. "Come this way, then. I know they will enjoy meeting you..."

Lord Darshel watched his commander and the Tashek woman as they wandered away, feeling oddly jealous that he could not find a reason to make the woman stay. He accepted the wine Commander

Raic brought him and downed a decent portion of it to ease his preoccupied thoughts. "Have you seen Zale?" he asked his gruff horse commander.

"Ah, I believe I spied him over by the sweet meats, Your Lordship."

"Then that's where we will go," he directed and followed the other man through the crowd. They came upon the bearded nobleman near where Raic had indicated. He was surrounded by lovely ladies. One, Lord Darshel recalled, was Lady Catalina. There were two men there, as well, that he had not expected to see at the celebration: his friend Markus LaPoint and his cousin, Jeremy Freedman.

"'Shel, you're here!" Zale called out as they neared, obviously drunk on wine and women. "I'd heard you were gonna stay at camp and sort out things with that dumb treaty you're entangled in."

"And miss you make a fool of yourself so I can steal all your ladies? I don't think so."

Zale brayed out a giggle and slung his arms around two of the ladies in question. "What'd ya think of that darlings? Lord Shekmann thinks he's more a man than I am."

"I know I am and so do they." Darshel bantered back, winning timid smiles from three of the beauties. He rose a glass in hello to those ladies and turned to include Markus and Jeremy. "Though with these two gents here, I am surprised you haven't lost a few ladies to their charms already."

"Oh, he's been really trying tonight," Markus said, keeping the tone light. Lord Darshel could tell his friend was nervous to address him, what with how they had left things the last time they had been together; the man's still-casted wrist was a blatant reminder.

"Has he now?" Darshel laughed and said hello to Jeremy, clasping Markus's cousin's hand firmly. "And how you have grown, Jeremy!"

"Yes, sir, ah, Your Lordship, sir." Jeremy stumbled on the words, awed to meet his family's lord-governor. "I am eighteen now, Your Lordship."

"Well now, that was a good age, was it not, Markus?"

"Indeed." Markus grinned, feeling more at ease with Darshel being so lighthearted. "But I promised Jeremy's father no antics, if he is to be staying with me. It's just work and study and maybe, just maybe, he will get to run a demesne of his own someday."

"Ah, that work and study stuff's overrated." Darshel teased and winked at Jeremy conspiratorially. "Send the lad to me when you get bored of him and I will show him the real way to run an acreage."

"Really?" Jeremy asked, pleasantly surprised to get the invitation at all. He glanced at his cousin, excited.

"We will see," Markus kept from being committal. "Maybe, I will have reason to visit His Lordship soon."

The three men turned their attentions back to the others to find Zale in full wooing mode. He was feeding sweet meats to Lady Catalina and her friend. The group of women, also most likely drunk, giggled and swooned at his affections and hung on the nobleman's every word. Two even petted his chest; they were so into him.

Lord Darshel caught himself staring and came to the startling realization that the women's actions repulsed him, where they would not have before. His mind leapt again to his now-constant shadow. He could not help comparing the ladies to the desert woman. The warrioress would not fawn over a drunken man so, no matter how handsome or rich. Zyanthena would never sink that low. Perturbed, Darshel emptied his glass and said, "If you will excuse me, gentlemen, ladies, I have others I need to visit. I will see you all later." Smiling politely, he backed away and motioned Commander Raic to him. "More wine, please, and much less intoxicated company."

"Yes, sir, Your Lordship." Even Raic seemed relieved to have Darshel come to his senses.

Prince Al'den and his father waited for the ball to be underway for nearly an hour—enough time to let any late-comers straggle in. Through the gossip of the Citadel servants, the Starian learned all the little tidbits on who had arrived and in what manner and what attire. He was privy, therefore, to the juicy bits about all the ladies' dresses; Lady Durrow's flashy new statement of pheasant feathers and russet, Sheev'arid Zyanthena's ostentatious form-fitting slip, and Princess Éleen's sea-green silk. The prince shook his head at the flutter the three women's attires created with the maids. Who else but women cared about styles so? Included in the gossip, were the four other princes and which lords and ladies had made appearances. There was even the amusing gossip of a Lord Lemont's housecat having gotten loose and found eating the stuffed goose. All the news made Prince Al'den antsy to see the celebration himself.

"We will go soon, Al'den." King Maushelik soothed, finding his son's pacing beginning to wear on him. "The staff is making one more sweep of the premises to hurry any stragglers, then we will make our way to the memorial."

"I know, father. It's just been a while since we have had such a gathering. I've forgotten how much I used to enjoy them."
"Plus, you have one other joyous event tonight." The warrior prince paused his line-making to look questioningly at his father. The Starian king chuckled at his expression. "I know you have been busy, my son, but have you forgotten so quickly that you wished to announce your courtship to Princess Éldon-Tomino? Perhaps, I should delay the announcement until a later date?"

"No, father." Al'den's face became etched in concern and... was it embarrassment? "No, don't do that. I hadn't forgotten. It would be wrong of us to make her wait any longer. I want everyone to know."

"Okay," the king agreed. "I was just making sure of your intentions—what with that crazy rumor going around the halls this afternoon."

Al'den ducked his head. "The gossip is Lady Durrow's way of scolding me, as per her usual."

"Such a lovely lady, if such a man loves lying with serpents."

Al'den looked shocked at his father, then they both burst out laughing at the absurdity. "She definitely is a snake."

"But she would make a wonderful duchess somewhere, I am sure. Maybe, I will suggest to her uncle to settle her with Duke Norsen at Oxford Manor."

"I would rightly approve. Let the cool, mountain air soothe that hot head of hers."

King Maushelik chuckled and settled his robe across his shoulders, unused to wearing its bulky weight. He spoke more seriously, "I just hope that this princess will make you happy, my son. She is delicate, soft like the Blue Havanese breeze and very unaccustomed to our harsh life."

"She is stronger than she looks." Al'den defended Princess Éleen. "Stars, how many women do you know that travel across Syre on a betrothal agreement, alone and without any of her estate?"

"Only ambitious ones."

Al'den gave his father an, "*oh, really?*" look. "And do you believe that to be her motive?"

"I do not know yet what I believe. I have not made up my mind, and neither should you. Be careful who you give yourself away to, my son."

§ §

The crier announced the King and Heir of Staria. The announcement made the whole room still. As the two men entered, the crowd bowed as one and held it until King Maushelik thanked everyone for coming and released them. The elder king then proceeded with a speech commemorating the dead. "This evening, we mourn the great losses we have suffered, some very recently on lands around this old Citadel; others in great valleys and fields all across the North. We have lost many wonderful men—fathers, sons, brothers, friends, and even those few, valiant women—who have fought alongside us." King Maushelik paused to share a lonesome, grieving smile with his son. "We are, every one of us, touched by these losses. Together, tonight, we recognize the departed and show our respects to all they have done and what they mean to us. Lift up your candles and light one with the other," the king instructed. He waited as servants passed out white candles to all in attendance and lite them. The other lights within the room were extinguished, to allow the smaller flames of the mourning candles to pierce the dark. "And now, let us give a moment of silence as my son, Prince Al'den Reddiar Maushelik plays the "Warrior's Song'."

Prince Al'den took his flute from his First Guardsman Meeg Thorson and made sure it was in tune. After a short adjustment, he steadied himself and brought the yellowwood flute to his lips. He played a sad, haunting tune. The notes slid across the room and brought more than a few tears to the audience's eyes. The mix of the candlelight and the music blanketed the ballroom in a thick, palpable shade of otherworldliness. The Starian prince finished the song and let the last, crying note drift away into the lonesome silence. The room stayed still, save for the flickering of the flames.

Finally, King Maushelik shifted and broke the tone of the room. He lifted his candle high. "We lift up to the Stars those that we have lost, knowing that they are safe among our Creators. Forever and Always we follow the Light of the Stars." The crowd murmured back the lines of the familiar Estarian prayer. As one, the candles were blown out. Darkness followed only long enough for the servants to relight the sconces. The king motioned to the musicians in the corner to begin more festive tunes. "Despite our grief, it is our custom to show our departed we remember happier memories of them by celebration, dance, and food. Please partake of the festivities as you will, together or alone, as the need take you. Peace be granted to you this night."

The celebration picked up again; the lively tune of the band took away the last traces of the somber attitude. Emboldened couples set about on a reel, pulling other ladies and gents into the dance until a majority of the hall was filled with dancers. The mood lightened.

Prince Al'den replaced his precious flute in the case Meeg held open for him and thanked the man for his assistance. He turned to the room and scanned the crowd, nodding to Kent and Cum'ar as they waved to him. Yet, he did not stop his search until his eyes lit upon the woman he sought. Smiling, Prince Al'den strode down the steps and into the crowd, being courteous as he passed lords, ladies, and soldiers, but not leaving his line until he came to stand in front of his intended target. "Has this evening been well for you, Highness?"

Princess Éleen blushed a lovely shade of rosy pink and turned her attention from the group of ladies she had been pulled into. She felt her throat catch as one of the ladies whispered something rude behind her, but she quickly amended her problem. "Your Highness," she curtsied gracefully and dipped her head carefully so as to not upset her intricate hairdo. "I have been enjoying myself."

Prince Al'den wondered at her lovely voice, trying to decide if the princess meant her words or was just being polite. Certainly, he knew she must not be fairing any better among her patrons as he was among his—what with the gossip that had been flying around all day. Perhaps, he should have waved the Golden heir over to translate "woman etiquette" for him. Nonetheless, the Havanese woman wore a brave and regal front that made her all the more lovely. "I am glad. I apologize for not being able to speak with you sooner. I hope my delay had not caused any misunderstanding between us." The princess seemed about to say something to that affect but her china-blue eyes cast about at the women around her. Their attentions kept her from saying whatever reply she had wished. Perturbed, Prince Al'den glanced at the other ladies, as well, and noticed how they looked at the two royals with eyes shining of keen interest. Two were close acquaintances of Lady Durrow and likely enamored to spread any tales her way. *A pit of fanciful vipers indeed.* "If I did, I do apologize, Highness. My day had not been my own, what with this ball and my duties and all."

"I do understand that, Your Highness." Éleen replied. This time she did mean it. She knew well all the duties an heir had to his kingdom. "Your people have done an amazing effort decorating this place." She swept a hand up to indicate the Southern Hall. "It is very beautiful."

An idea came to the prince upon her words; a way to save them both a continued awkward conversation in front of the other ladies. "There is a lot of symbolism to the layout of the ballroom. All is according to Starian mourning customs. Would you like me to tour you around the room so I may show you some of them?"

Prince Al'den was relieved when the princess beamed at him, as taken by the idea as he was. "I would like that, Your Highness." The Havener accepted the arm the Starian prince extended to her. She was relieved to be pulled away from the hearing of more gossip from the ladies she had been invited to join. Lord Carrod, her constant, protective shadow, trailed behind, also relieved for an excuse to speak with other guests.

"If you would be okay with it, I would like to meet up with Kent; to show him around as well. He would enjoy learning more of our culture."

"You two are together a lot," Éleen commented.

Prince Al'den looked down at her in consternation, worried he had upset her. "I do not have to invite him if it bothers you so?"

"No, no. That is not my meaning." Éleen replied quickly to reassure him. She let go a sweet smile. "I find it...endearing that two princes have such a great friendship. I am not bothered by it at all. Really."

"All right." Al'den smiled back. "It's just that he and I haven't been friends long; I greatly appreciate finally having someone so intriguing to talk with."

"The Prince of the Golden Kingdom makes a wonderful conversationalist," she agreed. "Though I have to ask," she continued more hesitantly, "Have you been so lonely? I...I don't mean to pry. It is just that you said "finally", like you meant you had been waiting for it a while."

She is very perceptive. Al'den thought. "I have no siblings, as you have come to see, and not even a Lord Protector. I was supposed to have a baby brother—but he and my mother died in childbirth." His eyes looked sad at the words and he skipped ahead to other details. "I find it hard, too, to make friends with the nobles, as I will be ruling them one day. Circumstances make them try to court me instead of acting on interests of friendship. The closest I come to having "friends" are the soldiers under my command, good men all."

"But even they are there to serve you and the kingdom," the princess finished, comprehending.

"Yes. So, Prince Kent's arrival has been a blessing to me."

The two royals and their shadow finally reached Prince Argetlem and All'ani Cum'ar, finding both men in a joyous discussion with Prince Al'den's Lieutenant-Commander Terrance. The three men turned, still laughing, to the new arrivals.

"Oh, you brought Ms. Éleen with you. Delightful!" Prince Kent smiled charmingly and lifted Éleen's hand to kiss her glove. "I am glad you came to join us, princess."

There was a fondness for the prince in the Havanese woman's returned smile. "Thank you, Prince Kent." The Goldener raised his eyebrows. "Ah...Kent." She amended, still finding it hard to address the man without his title. The young man glowed at her correction, satisfied he could get her to call him such.

Al'den introduced Éleen and Lord Carrod to the Sheev'anee and Starian solder then told the group of his plans to tour the princess about the room. "I was wondering if you would like to join us, Kent?"

Of course, the Golden scholar was eager to learn. The three royals headed off through the crowd, leaving the others to talk about military matters and war stories. Prince Al'den led them back to the entrance, where garlands hung in the archway. "We use the Southern Hall for all our mourning celebrations," he began his explanation. "The passage under the archway symbolizes victory over death, as do the willow flowers, rubies, and carved eagles that are tied into the garlands of ivy and acacia plants. To cross through the doorway means to recognize the courage everyone has within them to walk the labyrinth of life." He indicated the intricate labyrinth wound into the tiles of the floor, knowing most people would miss it amidst the other decorations. "As you look around the room, you will see most of the wreaths and sconces are held in either a carved hand, setting sun, or a mourning knot. All represent a part of death. The crossed swords are, of course, to express the military deaths of the recent battles."

The Starian then showed them the refreshment tables on the eastern wall. "As you see, even our foods are made in circular vessels; bowls or baskets; to symbolize eternity. Most of the bowls are made of jadestone for remembrance, or bloodstones, jet, and carnelian for sorrow."

"And the baskets are woven by certain trees?" Prince Kent guessed sensing a theme.

Al'den nodded. "Yew and willow trees for sadness or dogwood and oak for eternity. We used willow and dogwood this year because the Crystine was kind enough to bring some boughs to use, knowing their significance to our people."

"They are beautiful," Éleen commented softly as she ran her fingers along some of the weaves.

Al'den smiled down at her, admiring how considerately her fingers touched the baskets and bowls. He checked himself from staring too long and continued on with his tutorial. "We celebrate with certain foods, too. We like our themes around here—if you haven't noticed," he chuckled. The two royals graced the Starian with a laugh. Al'den reached into the bowl nearest him and grabbed a handful of almonds. "Most of the food represents hope, peace, or long life—to remind mourners these aspects are still available to them despite their grief. Almonds, figs, and noodles are made with corn and wheat for grief and long life respectively." Al'den handed the princess a delicate round cake. "Poppy seeds, for your peace."

Éleen blushed shyly and nibbled on the cake. She found its flavor to be mild and crunchy. "It had a delicate flavor."

"It is one of our milder dishes," Al'den agreed.

"No kidding!" Kent said. Al'den turned to find the prince had moved down the line. "This meat is hot!"

"That's *russen*." Al'den walked over, collecting some pear juice on his way to help cool his friend's throat. "Snake meat flavored with our hottest peppers."

Prince Kent's eyes widened. "Wow, really? Snake, huh? I have never had that before."

"It's a Tashek favorite, as are these frog legs spiced with rosemary and wrapped in bay leaves."

"Let me guess, to symbolize long life?"

"Not quite. Frogs are about resurrection, rosemary is for remembrance, and bay leaves follow our idea of *Kavannen*, the idea that death is only a change of the spirit becoming ethereal and not taking physical form."

"You people think too much about all this."

"We probably do, but living in a desert gives you much to think about."

The younger royal shook his head at the silliness of the statement. "Sure, it does," he teased and drank down the juice Al'den had given him. The feeling of heat receded. "Anything else I shouldn't touch? I am a lightweight when it comes to hot foods; my poor, delicate stomach."

"Ah...any of the meats and noodle dishes that have these red flakes in them. Everything else is safe."

"Well, that's good because I love a good bread loaf and butter," Kent replied. He supplied himself with said items. "Overall, I think this is all great. Not every kingdom is so thorough with their mourning customs. I feel that Staria, at least, is very respectful of the dead."

"Well, we do what we can. Birth and death are very significant events in people's lives. Both are honored just as equally."

"I think that is commendable," Éleen stated.

"Thank you, Highness," Al'den returned. He was about to say more but a familiar song began to play and his head snapped around to listen as dancers began to clap out a rhythm. "Would you two like to learn some dances?" He asked, excitedly. "The song playing is a communal dance, no partners needed. It's easy to learn. Come," he grabbed their hands without giving them much a chance to deny him, "Let me teach you!" He dragged them to the floor. "Trust me, this will be easy to learn." Just as the Starian said the words, the dancing began.

Commander Matar spotted his "night fox" through the crowd and made his way to her; Zyanthena was surrounded by Starian soldiers and some mertinean men—a place she would be quite at ease. The beautiful Tashek was speaking to a Starian and Commander Gordon, the Kavahad commander. Her lovely dress and necklace made her seem even more alluring than the Crystine commander remembered. Matar was impressed at whomever had convinced her to wear the sapphire dress. It would not have been an article of clothing the desert woman would have chosen on her own.

The said warrioress turned her sharp, brandy eyes to him, as if she had sensed Matar nearing. "Khataum," she greeted him respectfully and gave him a small dip of her head. It was the closest Zyanthena had ever come to bowing to Commander Matar. He was surprised.

"My Night Fox."

"Master," she said with more affection. "May I introduce you to Commander Gordon of Kavahad and Colonel Foller."

The military men saluted each other. "It is a pleasure to meet you, Commander." Gordon said, as he dropped his arm. "Ms. Zyanthena was just telling us about her career under your command. The Crystine have an impressive record against the maunstorz."

"Well, we have fought them for nearly twelve years now. In that long time, I would hope we are effective. But, don't credit us too much. It has been the Tashek that have made the biggest difference. If we had known the enemy was so cowed by them, I would have called for their aid earlier."

"Oh really?" Gordon rose his eyebrows at Zyanthena.

The desert woman persed her lips at being the center of attention again. "Master exaggerates. Yes, the maunstorz have a tendency to run from our forces, but, individually, we are no more a threat than any other people. It is my theory that the maunstorz dislike horses—as they do not use any—and are unnerved by their immense power."

"That would not explain their attacking the Starian cavalry, however."

"Yes," Zyanthena replied. "But I think that that is due to their large numbers—more than we have seen for nearly," she glanced at Matar to confirm, "Twenty-five years? Ten thousand is a number to be confident against any cavalry. Would you not agree?"

"Oh, touché." Commander Gordon responded. The others chuckled. "And did Zyanthena learn her way with words from you, Commander?"

Matar smiled affectionately at the warrioress. "Her tongue is all her own, I assure you; though, some of my men believe she learned by my example." He shrugged. "A Tashek with the ability to be both diplomatic and very direct served me well. I could not have asked for a better warrior to assist me."

"And does this warrior also know how to dance?" Colonel Foller asked.

Zyanthena seemed shocked, certainly she stilled at the question. So far in her life, she had never been treated like a lady. Usual questions toward such a woman were rarely turned upon herself. She blinked at the unfamiliarity of it. Her sudden change of demeanor reminded the military men that she was a different creature from the other women in the room. Colonel Foller looked embarrassed, as if he had made a faux pas—though he was not sure how. However, a breath later, Zyanthena replied. "Yes, I do, Colonel. I am quite proficient at dancing."

"Oh, well that is good then," he shifted, uncomfortable.

Zyanthena's lips curved into an amused smile. "I don't bite—that hard. Colonel," she teased, "Would you like the next dance?" She eyed him boldly.

Colonel Foller gulped, finding her directness suddenly intimidating. "Ah, I apologize Sheev'arid Zyanthena. I hadn't meant to be—."

"That was not rude, Colonel. Any lady would like a dance from you."

The Starian looked uncertain, like a cornered rat.

Commander Matar cleared his throat. "Well, I would like to take your next dance, Zyen." He extended his hand, inviting the Tashek to follow him to the dance floor. "If anyone else wishes afterward, I will hand my "night fox" over without a fight." He made the comment to Colonel Foller. The two bid the other men a good evening and Matar pulled her away. "You really shouldn't toy with them so, My Night Fox. These poor souls cannot handle a woman who is both superior and intimidating—and you can be both, usually at the same time. Most ladies are demure, soft-spoken, accommodating; none of those attributes you own."

"I am a Tashek warrior. When would any of those attributes be a help to me?"

"No, you are right...they are most certainly not needed in your nature." The elder Crystine commander chuckled. He spun Zyanthena into his arms and they flitted into a graceful waltz. "Have I mentioned how stunning you look this evening?"

"You are changing the subject." Matar shrugged. "It makes me wonder what you are implying, master."

"Just as I said, you look stunning. Not every person says something without implications behind their words."

"But you are not every person, Khataum. Usually, such a phrase means you disapprove of something."

"Well, I did not mean to. The look is not one I had expected for you to don..."

"Ah, see I knew you didn't mean it," Zyanthena interrupted.

Matar fixed her in his midnight-blue eyes, making sure Zyanthena could see how sincere he was. "No. I really do like the dress, Zyen. Whomever made it for you did a fabulous job. It just isn't something you would wear regularly."

Zyanthena averted her eyes. Her next words would, most likely, change Matar's mind. "Lord Shekmann had the dress fashioned for me and the onyx stones to match. He thought I should have a dress for the ball."

"I had suspected as much." The desert woman glanced back at Matar, intrigued that he was not saying more in reproof. "Lord Shekmann is a man of very good taste and has an eye for style. He knew what would make you stand out."

When he did not say anything worse, Zyanthena replied, "Yes, he does. His Lordship did not wish me to be swathed in a ballgown, nor in the clothes I rode in on. He compromised. I am not without a weapon—which fits me—and not bedecked in that finery." The way she said finery was not meant as a compliment.

"He allowed you weapons?" The commander stepped her back so he could look about her figure for any knives, but he could not note any.

"They are well disguised." Zyanthena reached into the concealed slit along her right hip to demonstrate.

"Well then. That feature I approve." Matar smoothly whirled her around and had Zyanthena in his arms again, as if he had never been studying her dress. "Perhaps Lord Shekmann does understand who you are—if just a little. I am not sure I would have been trusting enough to let someone, like yourself, carry a blade. I would understand, however, that by doing so shows I trusted you to use them judiciously. He is smarter than I gave him credit for."

Commander Matar led Zyanthena through two more dances before his body forced him to take a rest. "I need a break, Zyen." Matar had to admit after a fast-paced round. "I may be in shape for horseback riding and fighting but all this jumping around has me trying to catch my breath."

"Of course, master. I had not meant to pull you into that last round."

"Sure, you didn't," he teased. "You're just half my age and as spry as a lamb." Matar allowed Zyanthena to find him a bench to sit on. "A glass of wine, if you please," he asked of her.

"Of course. I will be back, master."

Zyanthena eased herself through the crowd, slipping through it like a shadow. She reached the refreshment table and began to collect up a glass of wine and one of thistle tea plus a small plate of crossed-buns, cakes, and figs. Just as she was ready to pick up the three dishes and return to Commander Matar's side, a strong, calloused hand grabbed her on the elbow. The startled voice asked, "Princess Zerra?!"

Chapter Thirty-Nine
§
Memory

Prince Par and his cousin found themselves more at ease since the Golden heir introduced them to a number of guests. The Sealander even found himself bold enough to ask two ladies to dance; though, he had no interest in conversation with them afterward. Lord Gordar approved the exchanges, happy to see his prince finally take any fancy toward the other gender. His Highness, however, kept from his Lord Protector how out of his element he felt—having just spent eight months among his soldiers and nowhere near any nobles. It was that fact, among a few others, that had the Sealand heir returning time and again to polite converse with Kor'mauk Siv'arid. He had developed a friendship with the desert man in the few weeks they had travelled together.

"Being too sullen again, are we?"

Par laughed at Kor'mauk's question. "Maybe I am, Siv'arid. Truthfully, I haven't been at a function in some time, because of the war. I had forgotten how tedious some etiquettes can be."

Kor'mauk shook his head at the ridicule. "I may not be invited to many of these posh events myself, but I do know Starian balls are less stifling than those in the South. You, young prince, should be living up the night not sulking around like a penned-up pup."

"I am hardly sulking," Par retorted, defending himself. "I will have you know I have danced thrice now and spoken with at least half of the groups in the room."

"Oh, thrice is it?" Siv'arid wasn't done teasing. "And that number is perfectly respectable for a handsome young lad such as yourself? Try another ten of those and you just might make shy of a decent count."

"May I remind you, Siv'arid," Par replied, "That I am here as a dignitary and have not had the pleasure of knowing any of your kingdom's dances. Your people have a way with footwork I dare say I have never seen."

"Fancy and upbeat, isn't it?" Kor'mauk grinned devilishly and tramped out a lick of steps from the most recent round. Like all the desert nomads, his footwork seemed effortless and gliding—and far too difficult to emulate. The desert man laughed gaily at his feat. "It really isn't the steps that are hard, Prince Sealand," he admitted. "See, here are what those steps were...the only reason they seem flourished is the spirit in which they were taken. Our dances that celebrate *Kavannen* are more about the passion put into them than the steps. You move as you feel called to; the rest becomes its own majik." The Tashek man took the simple steps in sequence then repeated them with the intent of passion. The dance became lively. "You see? Not as hard as you thought."

"In theory," Par responded, still skeptical.

"T'ha!" Kor'mauk sighed. "You really need to change your perspective, young princeling. I'm telling you, there is so much fun to be had! Where is you Lord Protector? Gordar? Yes, yes bring him." Kor'mauk waved them to follow him out to join the dancing. "I will instruct you in our three basic dance sequences, which all else comes from. Now, don't give me that, Prince! I want you to learn these. You are going to enjoy this night."

In no time at all, Prince Par was able to learn the sequencing, finding it really wasn't as hard as he assumed. Three dances later, he felt he understood what the "passion" of the dances was about. The upbeat rhythm of the music encouraged jumps, twists, and dips that made him feel very much alive and enlivened. He was well-spent by the end of the third set of rounds. "That was great!" he proclaimed as the dance came to end and the three of them were attempting to catch their breaths. Prince Par leaned forward, his hands on his thighs, as he panted.

"That is a very interesting sapphire."

Par's hand went automatically to his neck, finding Serein had slipped out from under his collar. He clutched it protectively and straightened. "It's a family heirloom, passed to me on my Berneisse."

"A rare stone to be sure." Kor'mauk seemed to be hinting at something. "One of only eight stones gifted to the Kingdom's leaders by the First King of Syre."

Par's eyebrows knit together. "You know that?"

"Yes. The Tashek are the "Keepers of the Histories" of Syre. Your "Water Holder" is a very special piece."

Par frowned. "How did you know Serein's translation?"

"I do know ancient Landarïan, Prince. I have to. There are few that remember it, however." The Tashek looked Par straight in the eye. "You will need one of us as your council eventually, Prince of the Evening Star. May I suggest myself for the position?"

"What?!" Prince Par blinked, confused. He backed away from Kor'mauk, suddenly suspicious of the man. He had heard the title the Tashek had given Prince Maushelik but had never expected them to name him, too. The timing seemed somewhat odd and Kor'mauk had been very serious on the matter of being his "council". "I...excuse me. I—I need a drink." Par turned away and pushed himself through the crowd, leaving the desert man and his cousin on the dance floor.

"Is he all right?" Gordar asked. He had not heard their conversation, as he had been commenting on the dance with a lovely lady to his right.

"Just a little winded, I think," Kor'mauk replied. "He went to get a drink."

"I should follow."

"In a minute." The Tashek stopped the golden-eyed Lord Protector. "Can I ask you something?"

§ §

Prince Par made it to one of the long, yellowwood benches near the refreshment tables and sat down. He felt dizzy. Was it the heat, the physical exertion, or just the fact that the Tashek man had unnerved him? The prince was uncertain. A warmth flared over his breastbone, as Serein was wont to do when he became upset. The royal clutched the stone. A vision flared into his mind, letting the noise of the band and conversations drift away; as usual, Serein was going to show him an image that always assuaged him in times of stress.

Suddenly, the prince found himself caught in a memory many years past...

The cold, stone walls, vaguely familiar, sprouted up around his vision; candles lighting his way in their iron-wrought sconces. A lovely girl with long, raven-hair pulled up in tiny, braided buns formed into a crown on her head, turned to Par with a gleeful smile. She dared him to follow as she flitted ahead in her sapphire dress through the quiet halls. She called for Par to hurry along with her as she ran through the moonlit garden. The Queen's Garden at the Crystal Kingdom, *Par remembered. Zerra, my precious, precious Zerra. His heart ached to go back to that night. It had been the best memory he had of the princess.*

The image jumped ahead to them standing by a stream. The moonlight caused both the flowing waters and the princess's eyes to dance. There was no words, though the prince remembered they had spoken; however, there was the sound of Serein's song, soft and soothing as the ocean, pouring into the scene. There had been more after—he remembered—a kiss that had ended that night in a fever. Yet, the image began to fade away around the edges before the scene came to pass...

In its place, Zerra's beautiful face, older but still just as lovely, stayed. The girl, now a woman, stood only six paces in front of the prince. She was before the refreshment table, selecting three platefuls of delectables. The Sealand prince was on his feet and reaching for her long before his mind could fathom how the Crystal princess could possibly be there in Staria. "Princess Zerra?"

The woman stilled at the pressure on her elbow and slowly turned to face the royal. Prince Par blinked as the image of Zerra changed. The Tashek's depthless brown eyes did not fit with Zerra's softer expression. Zyanthena saw her look had affected the Sealander. She was quick to make herself less dispassionate, softening her countenance into a small, polite smile. "Prince Fantill of Sealand," the warrioress acknowledged with a small bow. She was careful to not upset her load of plates and cups.

"I, ah..." Par gulped as he felt himself flush with embarrassment. "I—I apologize Sheev'arid, Zyanthena." He pressed the heels of his hands to his eyes and blinked. "I do not know what came over me. I—I..."

"Thought you saw someone else," Zyanthena replied. "Someone you wish I had been."

He chucked nervously. "Yeah. Yes, that was it. I had not meant to mistake you."

The desert woman looked thoughtful as she studied the befuddled prince. "I am not sure I have ever been mistaking for the royal princess of the Crystal Kingdom. It is almost flattering."

The remark brought on the laugh the Tashek had hoped to elicit. "Again, I greatly apologize for my mistake. I hadn't meant to stop you from returning to your party." Prince Par hoped Zyanthena knew he was trying to excuse himself from the awkward situation.

The desert woman did not pardon him to leave, however. Instead, she set her dishes down and gave the Sealander her undivided attention. "You must have been very fond of the princess, to be looking for her in a crowd all these years. I never got to meet her myself, as the royals of the kingdom had been many years gone upon my arrival into the Crystine. I...I have seen her portrait in the castle. Zerra was a most beautiful girl."

"And as rebellious as the stories claim," Prince Par continued; as Zyanthena had hoped her words would prompt him. It was a time for grieving, after all. The Tashek sensed the man needed to grieve the loss of his betrothed. "Zerra would have been content to be like you. If you had met, you would see she could have made a good fighter—if society had dictated she could." The desert woman smiled warmly, but Par looked away. He was momentarily lost in a sad thought. "But perhaps, she would still be alive if she had been more able to be like you. She would have fought the maunstorz if she had known how."

"And would have died with many of the Crystine that day," Zyanthena countered. "There had been no definite evidence that the princess—or any of her family, excluding the queen—are dead. Maybe her not knowing how to fight saved her, and the princess is alive somewhere..."

Prince Par felt tears threatening to show in his eyes at the words. Hope, still so raw and achingly strong came to the surface. "Eight turnings of the seasons she has been gone—and yet, your words make me hope. It shows I am forever the fool to cling to such notions."

"There is nothing foolish with having hope, Prince Fantill. Indeed, sometimes it is all we have left at the end of a long day." A tear slipped from the royal's eyes and he averted his face so the warrioress would not see his weakness. "Do not close yourself off from your grief, Prince. We are here to mourn all our losses—the new and the old. You would not be looked down upon for having your sorrow or the need to be by yourself. Everyone had their own ways of grieving. Be true to your own." Zyanthena bowed respectfully and touched him on the forearm before collecting her items and excusing herself. As she stepped away, the Tashek met eyes with the prince's Lord Protector. Zyanthena offered him a head-bow in acknowledgement.

"Thank you," Gordar said softly as she passed him.

"Your Lordship, take care of your prince. He is a gentle soul."

The Sealander rose his eyebrows, surprised at her choice of words, but nodded to them all the same. He watched the alluring woman leave before turning to the heir of Sealand.

"I think I am ready to retire, cousin."

"Yes, Highness," Gordar agreed. "I think we both are."

Chapter Forty

§

Jealousy

Zyanthena returned to Commander Matar's side. Her thoughts, however, were still occupied with the encounter she had just left. Something about the situation had struck her. It was as if there had been some hidden purpose—or message—for her in the encounter with the Sealander prince. The warrioress may admit to not being as religious compared to other Tashek, but the moment she had turned to meet the prince' stare, Zyanthena had felt a prickle of anticipation to be *aware*. It was as if fate was handing her a sign that should not ignored... The feeling did not leave her despite the distance she walked away from the royal. Perhaps it was her own words to the prince, the ones to mourn, that ghosted after her? After all, Zyanthena knew she had never grieved the person she had been— not that she remembered who that past girl was. Sometimes, the losses were not so easily seen as felt.

Commander Matar was not alone, the Tashek discovered, as she neared. The Crystine man was in conversation with the Shi'alam. The desert leader's bodyguards was a short distance away, and a bored and out-of-place youth stood to the Shi'alam's right. Decond, who had been glancing around the room in small snatches, was the one to acknowledge her arrival first. "Zee!" He called out, relieved to see a familiar face.

"Decond." Zyanthena responded, finding herself smiling back at the youth's contagious grin. "Father," she continued more reverently and bowed to the Shi'alam.

"Zyanthena," the Shi'alam responded curtly. His brown eyes assessed her; disapproval etched in his brow. "Your...dress is quite revealing."

The desert woman passed Matar his beverage and plate of food, to steal a few seconds of peace before responding. The Crystine commander thanked her in keshic. Zyanthena took the small courage he offered as she returned her attention to her father. "I desired something more of color for the ball than the desert brown. You always said blue would be my shade."

"It's designed by someone with a pernicious attitude."

The younger Sheev'arid did not rise to the bait her father's angry statement tried to initiate. She knew he was fishing to see if the dress had been designed by the lord-governor of Kavahad. Zyanthena did not feel like bringing up Lord Shekmann to the Shi'alam. "It has its charms," she replied instead. Subtly, she showed her father a knife through one of the slits, knowing the desert warrior would approve of the well-designed defenses. Indeed, the Shi'alam seemed surprised to find her armed; he had not been able to tell she wore two weapons under her blue slip. "To deceive the eye, the dress had to be the most flattering." Her answer was enough to acquit her from anymore cutting remarks.

Relieved to be out from under her father's disapproving gaze, Zyanthena skirted around the two men to speak with her friend. "Decond," she greeted the seventeen-year-old again and allowed the farrier to embrace her.

"Zee. Man, I was hoping I would get to see you tonight."

"The Crystine that bad, huh?" She teased.

"Not the Crystine, your brother." Decond made a face. "He's been trying to teach me hand-to-hand combat, weaponry, ironwork. It's torture more like! I have never been so sore in my life!"

"And here I thought you would never pick up a weapon."

"I didn't really get a choice. Terrik found out my reasons for my dislike, but it wasn't enough to persuade him against the notion. He said, 'I must learn to conquer my beliefs before they own me'."

"That sounds like something he would say—if only he would take his own advice. Do not let Terrik's bullying dissuade you. He lets his jealousy rule his pride." Decond seemed baffled over her words, and, indeed, Zyanthena admitted to herself she had been uncommonly "Tashek-cryptic" compared to her usual casualness with her friend. "I just mean, there is much you could teach my brother, my kind-hearted friend."

"Oh." Decond beamed at her, elated to be talking with Zyanthena. "Well, I'm glad you think so highly of me."

"I do," the desert warrioress replied. She was oblivious to the fact that her words had made the orphan believe she had meant something more beyond a sisterly affection for the youth.

A lull came to their conversation; Zyanthena found her attention beginning to focus on others' words around the room until, suddenly, Decond took her by the hand. "Come, dance with me," he said and began to pull her to the dance floor without excusing himself to the Shi'alam and Khataum. Stunned, Zyanthena barely made the words of pardon herself before she was whooshed away. They raced into the next dance as couples began to move in the line, and the Tashek was swept away into the reel before she had time to think of anything more.

§ §

It was rare for Zyanthena to allow herself to let loose and enjoy herself, but, with Decond there with her, the reserved warrioress found herself swept along to the dizzying pace of the music. For a long four sets, she allowed the jaunty orphan to lead her about in the reels. By the end of the last set, Zyanthena became aware of how much her cheeks hurt from laughing so hard. The realization unsettled her and she was quick to back out of the next dance, leaving a startled Decond to chase after her.

"Zee?" Decond called out as he raced to catch the desert woman.

Zyanthena caught herself and slowed for her friend. "I apologize," she said before Decond could ask. "I...think I am done with the dancing for now. Shall we return to my father and Commander Matar?" She started back that way before Decond could ask on her sudden change of attitude. Zyanthena was grateful that her autumn-haired friend was not as perceptive, or as demanding, as the Kavahadian lord-governor she had to shadow; the warrioress was not sure she could have answered about her reaction to having too much fun.

Making matters worse, the other Sheev'arid had finally made his appearance by the Shi'alam's side. His knowing eyes would not leave Zyanthena and Decond's direction, as the two of them rejoined the group and made their comments on the dancing. Zyanthena became distinctly aware of her brother's attentions. She became more disquieted as the elder Sheev'arid signed to her that she *"had seemed to be quite enthralled in the dancing."*—meaning he had been watching them on the dance floor for some time. "*My Khapta seems very taken with you,*" Terrik continued.

Zyanthena felt her chest clench at the words. "*You know not what you talk about,*" she signed back. She did not want her brother to have any reason to be jealous of his new apprentice. An eye roll was Terrik's response. The younger Sheev'arid tried to give her attention to the present conversation but Terrik's words had her occupied—as Terrik had, perhaps, intended. Zyanthena caught herself catching glances at her autumn-haired friend, observing how he reacted when he was around her; the way he stood pointed her way and how he kept bringing his eyes back her direction. It wasn't enough for her to believe that the boy was smitten, however.

Annoyed that Terrik's words had such an impact on her, Zyanthena asked pardon to go relieve herself and subtly cued her brother to follow—a feat made harder with the Shi'alam and his constant shadows present. No doubt, their father would want them to stay chaperoned, what with how Terrik had behaved upon their last encounter. Terrik appeared in the muted hallway a minute after Zyanthena had arrived and pretended to admire the reflection pool his younger sister had chosen to stand by. Silence hung thickly between them until Terrik opened with, "My Khapta flirts with you. Don't deny that you see it, too."

Zyanthena kept cool-headed, not letting her brother's words show their effects on her features. Inside, however, her heart paused in concern over young Decond's well-being. Terrik had a history of letting his jealousy lead his reactions—to ill effect. For that reason, Zyanthena knew she should tread carefully. "You use your envy against the wrong person, for I am the one you wish to lash out at."

Terrik scowled at her response. "You evade—."

"And you deny," she interrupted. Zyanthena turned her gaze at the elder Sheev'arid directly. "You always resort to petty feuds when you are not given your way. You, who is known as the steadier of us, has a great flaw of casting off blame where it needs to go."

Her brother's lips became a hard line, showing Zyanthena had hit a cord inside him that rang true. It also pissed him off. His eyes flashed. "You...you are a self-centered, cutthroat *kutt*. After everything we did together, all the secrets shared...and you cast aside my most sincere offer for a man who treats you lower than filth. You are the one in denial. Denial for who you are—or could be. I gave you a chance for freedom—and to be Sheev'anee in full—but how do you pay me back? By letting My Khapta have what should be rightfully mine."

"Decond had nothing but your jealousy. He is an orphan, without any relations to call his own. It is you who is trying to cast him off as more fortunate. You, the one who has not lost anyone close. Until now. I cannot claim you as my brother so long as you hold such discontent toward one I call my closest friend. You are not worthy of such a title. We are through, Terrik."

Zyanthena began to turn away and rejoin the celebration, but Terrik's strong hand grabbed her arm, stopping her. For a brief moment, the desert woman debated taking hold of one of her knives. Yet, the love for her bother stayed her hand. Her brandy eyes cast sideways toward Terrik. His angry expression was formed into pain over her declaration, but the look was not enough to melt her resolve. "Zyen," he breathed. The air from his breaths fluttered across her neck, he was that close. Zyanthena tensed, her right hand slipping into her dress to finger one of the knife hilts. Her brother noticed and slowly released his hold on her arm. He stepped away. "As you wish, Zyanthena. This man will no longer confess to being called your brother."

"And your Khapta will be treated fairly, as the Stars decree all apprentices must be," she demanded.

Terrik sucked in his breath, understanding the unspoken threat behind her words. He bowed; his eyes averted in total submission. "As the Stars will it, so I will."

Zyanthena nodded to the proclamation and turned away. She left Terrik to his own, lonesome company. The warrioress did not bother to give him a good-bye.

Of all the ladies to attend the Starian ball, Prince Rowin would not have expected Ms. Saida Newdōn to be one of them. Just finishing up a conversation with a Rubian dignitary, the Sunarian royal had turned and nearly run into the beautiful Madame. Still, he spilt red wine all over her silk dress. "Ms. Newdōn!" He gasped and quickly pulled his cup away. He was aghast at the ruin he had done to the dress.

Le Cont's Madame chuckled seductively, finding his concern charming. "Oh, you are the gentleman," she purred and accepted the handkerchief extended to her. "Luckily, I wore my red dress tonight, darling. It's hardly worth a docet compared to others of mine." Saida's lack of concern eased Rowin's embarrassment. She rolled the soiled handkerchief through her fingers suggestively, calling Rowin's worries to more intimate concerns.

He shook his head clear, unwilling to let the lovely lady control his thoughts so easily. "I will still have my man send over a bill to cover the cost of the dress."

"I will await his visit," she replied playfully and stepped closer to the prince to take a hold of his forearm. "But—it would be more to my pleasure if you joined your servant, Highness," she whispered the words in his ear. Rowin's blue eyes shifted to her face, sizing the woman up like one would with a venomous snake. The look had the Madame chuckling. Saida pulled away. "I heard the most interesting rumor this afternoon; that the true Heir of Sunrise had surfaced amongst his brother's party. Well, certainly most of the populous doesn't know of your keen dislike of each other or the rumor would not fare so well."

"We can be cordial to save face for our kingdom."

"Oh, indeed. The Sunarian court is very good at playing the game. Say, have you made sure your Shield-man had tasted every drink of wine?"

"I take none without him." Prince Rowin looked to Rio Ravesbend, who kept a careful vigil without appearing to do so, protecting His Highness's back. Rio nodded at his prince to show he had heard. "I have learned that lesson since I was eight-years-old and my man-servant became ill from a drink sent to me by my stepfather."

"Hm, ah yes. King Raymond that sly, scandalous bastard who usurped your father's throne and married his woman. Even your mother did not deserve such a fate."

"Ms. Newdōn," he cautioned.

"I know, Highness. Even away from your kingdom, my words are slanderous—but oh so true. And from yours, I suspect your brother had not been aware of your stay here at the Citadel but was quick to put his stamp on it. Connel was always one to take credit, whether it was his due or not."

"And he can have it, I care not."

"Only as long as he does not get the throne…"

"My, you are the conspirator."

Saida grinned and sipped a glass of brandy she had snagged from a passing server. Her eyes scanned the room, falling on the man of their conversation. The other prince's eyes were upon her. "It seems your brother had his eye on you, too."

"Making sure I do not steal his thunder."

"Or jealous of your woman." Saida wiggled her eyebrows at Prince Rowin, seductive as always. "Oh look, he is coming this way! I just love getting between two brothers and their affections." She giggled when Rowin sighed at the inevitable encounter.

It didn't take long for Connel to make it across the room. Apparently, harassing his elder brother was more important than wooing it. He laid out his most charming smile to Madame Newdōn as he sidled up beside Rowin. "Brother, I am not sure I have met the Lady's acquaintance yet. Please introduce us."

Rowin suppressed another sigh but obliged. "Brother, Ms. Saida Newdōn. Ms. Newdōn, my brother, Prince Connel Sunrise."

Saida allowed the younger Sunarian to kiss her offered hand and giggled at his charm. Whereas she would play the seductive mistress with Rowin; with Connel, Saida pretended to gush at his sweetness. It rolled off her tongue as thickly as the prince's suaveness. To Rowin's surprise, her sudden "cuteness" seemed to soften his brother's usual snobbishness. "I am delighted to meet you, Highness Sunrise. It had been some time since such dashing Southern men have graced the Starian court. I quite enjoy your countrymen's charms." She splayed her fingers across Prince Connel's, grasped around his goblet. Her eyes rose to meet his own. Her flirting worked to draw the prince into her seduction.

Rowin suppressed a triumphant grin when he noted his brother's tight jaw and thin blush that appeared upon the Madame's touch. It felt good to be an observer to his brother's discomfort—as he was certain, having been on the receiving end himself, that Connel was trying to squelch his body's impulses. He became more satisfied as his brother stammered out a "thank you." It lacked any of its usual authority.

"Ah yes, Lady. Indeed, we Sunarians have not been this far North in some time. It seems we are long overdue, if we have left you without men such as ourselves. Our sincerest apologies." Rowin spoke for his lost-for-words brother.

Saida batted her handkerchief at the prince's chest. "Oh, you are such the sweetest! I will certainly have to have you two brothers over to my establishment before you leave."

The invitation alarmed Prince Rowin. He and Connel at Le Cont's? He could not dream of such a horrid thing. He rushed to protest before Connel could reply. "Ms. Newdōn! Certainly, I think my brother and I will have too much to arrange here at the Citadel to make the visit. You will have to accept our condolences for a later date."

"Oh, posh!" Saida waved his words away, knowing she could win the argument by getting the other prince on her side. "I know you royal men have your duties but surely you can spare an hour or two for the likes of me?"

"Of course we can," Prince Connel replied. He frowned at his older brother and mouthed "*don't be an ass*" before returning to smile at Saida. "We can make it three days from now, midmorning. I will make a point to bring you some Southern comforts."

"Oh, that would please me greatly, Highness. I will send for you through Highness Rowin's page—as we are already acquainted; if you do not mind, of course."

Usually having Rowin given more courtesy would make Connel annoyed, but the way the seductive Madame posed the question kept the younger prince civil. "Yes, that will do. Thank you, Lady."

Saida preened, victorious. "Lovely, so very lovely. Ah, you brothers of Sunrise are the most genteel of the gentlemen here! Trust me, there are a few and far from in between." She added the last like she was sharing a secret with Connel. The Madame and prince shared a laugh. "But it seems I have the best in the room." Saida situated herself between the two Sunarians and grabbed each by arm. Rowin was at a loss for words and Connel seemed thoroughly charmed. "So, Prince Connel, tell me more about yourself. I fear I have exhausted your brother by my questions. Perhaps, you can entreat me longer...?"

Prince Rowin quietly extracted his arm from Saida's touch and stepped away to his Shield-man's side. He was shaking his head with the ridiculousness that had just transpired. "She's a cunning little fox," he commented to Rio.

"She certainly knows how to use her charms, especially on your brother."

"She likes being able to screw with royalty." *Literally.* His words made Rio chuckle. "As it is, Saida had made an invitation for the Sunarian princes to join her at Le Cont's. Together."

"Oh, boy."

"Yeah. That is going to end poorly. No way I could get out of it by feigning a headache, do you think?" Rio shook his head. "I didn't think so. Stars pray that something transpires that can prevent the inevitable."

"Perhaps the Madame will catch the clamps." Rowin gave his Shield-man a warning stare. "Or just be under the weather," Rio amended with a helpless shrug.

"Perhaps," Rowin replied. He glanced back at his brother and the lovely mistress as they chatted away. "Else, I fear it's going to be a very, very long day I'm in for."

Chapter Forty-One

§

Mark of the Nallaus

It was late when Lord Shekmann decided to retire. He sent Commander Gordon to collect Zyanthena and met them at the Southern Gate, just as the night was beginning to recede to the light of dawn. Though he had partied to the full extent, Darshel was still alert and ready for more socializing; however, it was the exhaustion of his two best men, both soldiers over twenty-years his senior, that had him heading back to camp.

As the elder soldier and Tashek neared, Lord Darshel reached out to the beautiful woman, inciting a cool stare and sidestep from his reach. The desert warrioress was still as fresh as he. Darshel chuckled. "Still alert I see."

"I am a Tashek scout. Long hours awake do not affect me as much as most."

"So I see," he motioned his small party off, leading the way down the slight hill into town. Zyanthena shadowed him quietly. "Did you have a good evening?" Darshel asked, after a time, finding himself compelled to speak with the alluring woman.

"It was fairly memorable," Zyanthena replied politely, to which the Shekmann's look bade her to expound on. She added, "I was able to meet with some few friends and acquaintances that I have been unable to see for some time. It was good to speak with them."

Lord Darshel nodded. "Very good. I am glad your outing was a success." His emerald eyes ran along the woman's dashing figure, thrilling some as he thought back to how she had moved earlier, during one of the reels he had happened to catch sight of her performing. Zyanthena had been a sight to behold, so lithe, light, and entrancing. He had been caught staring by one of his Citadel acquaintances. Fortunately, the man had not known what had held his attention; unlike the woman of his reoccupation. The warrioress cast a calculating glance his way as she felt the heat of his stare. Lord Darshel looked away but could not shake his thoughts off the Tashek. Finally, he worked the question out of his lips. "Have you...or," he cleared his throat, "Would you accept a place in my bed tonight?"

The dark look that followed told the Kavahadian her answer. Zyanthena stopped in her tracks and took on a cautious stance, as if expecting the lord to force her into his desires. Certainly, Darshel could if he ordered his two commanders to help (not that he ever would; but the desert woman did not know that). "My answer will always be no."

Lord Darshel clenched his jaw and gazed around the town, anywhere by at the woman who tormented him. His eyes picked out a trio of fire pits at the end of the lane they took. The flames gave shape to some of the townsfolk still out and about partying. It was not hard for him to identify the figures: two old drunken men by one small pit, a group of rowdy teenagers at the second, and women—very likely prostitutes—at the last. The less-fortunate in the city taking advantage of a royal decree to celebrate and mourn. The Shekmann's anger cast itself outward, looking for a way to relieve itself. "Well then, you won't be minding your usual sleeping arrangements. Raic, see to her." Zyanthena frowned, uncomprehending, until their party neared the fire pits and the cavalry commander was quick to take and bind her wrists. Her brandy eyes followed the lord's brawny frame to the third pit. "You are such a lecherous pig." Lord Darshel heard the warrioress mutter as he walked up to the huddle of women and spoke with them.

The women were working and eager to take a lord's money. They fawned conservatively, excited by the prospect of better payment. In the end, though, Darshel found himself interested in only one prostitute—an olive-skinned woman barely out of girlhood with black hair and brown eyes. "You," he pointed at the beautiful wench and offered her his hand.

§ §

Commander Raic pushed Zyanthena through His Lordship's tent and into her small alcove where he dumped her unceremoniously onto the floor-height cot set up for her. The desert woman glared and arranged herself more comfortably on the blankets, though the cavalry commander barely gave her time to do so before asking for her right arm. "My Lord may still trust you, but I do not. Likely, I never will." Raic declared as he shackled her wrist in the chain they had not used in a week. "You anger His Lordship, so I take pleasure in whatever restrictions he asks against you."

"King Maushelik will not allow such treatment."

"You're not free yet." Raic threw back at her. "Now give up your daggers." Zyanthena didn't move to comply. "I know you have two, and I also know you would not like me to take them off your person. Now hand them over." That time the Tashek complied, pulling the weapons from their sheaths on her thigh. Raic grabbed them. He checked the cuff one more time and stood. His eyes looked over at Lord Darshel's bed, just across the room. He smirked. "You'll get a nice view."

The commander took his leave.

Lord Darshel and the young prostitute entered shortly after. The tall lord-governor took his time lighting candles around the room as the woman viewed her surroundings. The girl's eyes were perceptive but nervous—an emotion made more prominent when she realized Zyanthena was within the tent. Lord Darshel came to her, upon her sound of protest, and steadied her with his hands on her cheek. "That woman is a prisoner of war, handcuffed to serve her punishment. She is on no concern." He turned the woman away and led her to his bed.

They started soon after.

Zyanthena sighed and rolled onto her back to stare at the ceiling. The tent was still darkened; the light of dawn had yet to bring any color to the blue canvas. With only the candlelight from across the room, there wasn't enough detail to the tent's top to distract the Tashek for long. Feeling the need for more distraction, she turned instead to the cold, iron shackle around her wrist. Commander Raic had been thorough in making the cuff tight; she hadn't been able to fool him into keeping it slightly larger. The lock, too, was designed to be harder to pick—a feat made more difficult since she couldn't spy anything useful to lock-pick the dumb thing. The shackle left her few options. She sighed again and rolled back onto her side to cover her ears in her arms.

The minutes ticked by following the rhythm of hard breathing and moans. Lord Darshel seemed less careful and less caring about the woman, however. He finished their "session" much quicker than he ever did with the Kavahadian ladies. Zyanthena concluded he had wanted to vent his frustration on someone and had not cared who or how they were treated. It must have been a relief to the prostitute, as it was for her, when the Kavahadian conclude and rolled onto his side of the bed to sleep.

In the quiet that followed, the Tashek woman let her arms slide back to her sides. She breathed into the welcoming silence. Soon, she found herself drifting toward sleep—but a muted sound of cloth sliding called her attention back. Zyanthena opened her eyes but stayed still, listening to the room. Lord Darshel slept but the girl—the girl!—was slipping out of the bed softly and tiptoeing across the carpeted tent. She did not stop to grab her clothes. Her focus went farther to something by the entrance of the tent. Zyanthena rose enough to watch the prostitute. The young woman paused near the tent's entranceway and stayed close to the tent's side to keep the guards from seeing her. She waited a breathe to make sure she was not found out then reached for an object near the flap. The deed done, the prostitute turned back around and headed for Lord Darshel's sleeping form. Her footsteps hastened.

Zyanthena was fully alert by the time the woman turned around. There were only two pieces of furniture by the door, a small desk and the cache of Lord Darshel's weapons. The latter was the only one of any concern. Alarmed, the warrioress worked against her shackle, fighting off the feeling of futility as each second gave the prostitute more time to reach Lord Darshel. Ignoring the pain, the Tashek twisted her thumb and yanked on the cuff, crying out a warning to the Lord Shekmann to cover up the scream she would have preferred to release as her hand slipped free. Not knowing if the Kavahadian would be awake enough to respond, the Tashek rushed across the tent and sprang to tackle the woman as she was poised to thrust a knife into the lord-governor's heart. The prostitute screamed out in defiance as Zyanthena's weight knocked them into the ground.

Lord Darshel came awake at the sound above him, his hand was clutched to a small dagger he kept hidden in the pillow. He cast around in confusion until he made out the two women struggling on the floor. In the darkened tent, Darshel found it hard to know which was which—both being dark-featured and seemingly adept at fighting. The women tore at each other, rolling, punching, and kneeing at the other. Both tried to gain the upper hand. Their keshic and the prostitute's defiant screams alerted the guards, who came running in with lit torches and unsheathed swords. The men stopped to gawk at the unusual show they came upon.

Zyanthena felt the woman hesitate at the appearance of the reinforcements. Using the moment of distraction, she managed to roll the would-be assassin off of her and slid in behind the woman to lock an arm around her throat. The warrioress pulled the naked length of the prostitute against her. She clenched her teeth against the weakening blows to her sides. The tight hold made Zyanthena acutely aware of the moment the woman made an unusual working and biting with her jaw. The next moment, the would-be assassin went limp, a noxious, bubbly spittle foaming from her mouth. Zyanthena pushed the dead woman away with great haste.

"She's dead." Zyanthena panted out as a soldier came near to check the prostitute. "Poison. She bit down on a pill of poison." The man was quick to back away, as thrilled to touch the stuff as the desert woman had been. "Lord Shekmann?"

"I'm here and I'm fine." Lord Darshel walked to the tired Tashek and knelt beside her. "You saved my life!"

"Don't sound like it's so unbelievable."

He chuckled and glanced away toward the dead woman. His humor faded away. "She tried to kill me."

"Tried, yes. At first, I did not know what she was doing, then she picked up one of your weapons..."

A soldier retrieved the said knife. "She was smart. She knew she wouldn't get in here with one. Must have assumed there was something in here to use as a weapon."

"Or she knew there would be weapons in here," Zyanthena replied.

"She had an informant?"

"Possibly." Zyanthena looked to Lord Darshel. "She walked straight to the rack." The lord-governor of Kavahad swore. "Rouse Commander Raic," he ordered and began to cast about for his clothes.

A man complied.

The first guard—who had picked up the knife—bent over the body again. He was careful to not touch any of the dribbled poison. "She was a pretty thing," the man commented, "And very Tashek."

"She might be." Zyanthena reluctantly agreed as she came forward to also study the woman. The dark, desert features could not be denied, but it didn't seem right for a Sheev'anee to try to assassinate Lord Darshel in the capitol. Zyanthena used her left hand to roll the woman's limbs around then rocked her side to side, closely investigating the torso and neck. The guard reached to help when he realized she was looking for something. Behind then, still cussing, Lord Darshel finished dressing. He muttered words of betrayal from the Sheev'anee. "It wasn't my people," Zyanthena said. Her words incited Lord Shekmann to begin cursing her, too. "It was the Nallaus."

The odd word stopped the lord-governor's tirade. The handsome Shekmann came to kneel beside the desert woman to look where she pointed. A mark was inked into the woman's mastoid, behind her ear. A smaller one was beside it. "The Mark of the Nallaus, the Lost Ones. They are a group of Tashek who refuse to follow the ways of the Sheev'anee. They are a small tribe that wanders the wastes. Behind it is a mark I have seen only a few times; the emblem for Mansocan, general of the maunstorz. She works for the enemy."

Lord Darshel lightly touched the marks. "How do you know? This looks keshic to me…" Zyanthena balked and he looked at her more sharply. "Zy'ena?" Hesitantly, the beautiful warrioress turned her head and pulled her hair aside to show the Shekmann her scar behind her ear. "They wait to initiate new tribesmen until they have proven themselves. I hold the scar used before initiation. My father found me, the only one alive, in a small camp of Lost Ones…" She released her hair to cover the wound. "My people do not talk of the Nallaus. I only know because of the scars."

Her words cooled the Shekmann's temper. He could see the memory seemed painful to the desert woman. "Then this is a matter for the king?" He posed it as a question to get the compelling brown eyes to look up at him.

"Yes, My Lordship. It is." She began to rise.

Lord Darshel reached for her arm, to stop her and turn Zyanthena back around. His grasp insighted a hiss of pain. "Zy'ena?" He released her wrist and rose to join her.

The Tashek tried to hide her injured hand into the slit of her dress but Lord Darshel caught her elbow. He pulled her arm into the torch light. "It was not from the fight," Zyanthena protested.

The Kavahadian ignored her as he and his guard inspected the bloodied mess of her wrist and disjointed thumb. "Your hand is broken."

"I dislocated it," she replied. Despite the pain she must feel, Zyanthena's voice was monotone. "It was the only way I could get the shackle off in time."

Realization dawned in the lord's emerald eyes. "You were bound. Even bound, you wouldn't let her kill me."

Zyanthena averted her eyes. "It was necessary to stop her, Your Lordship. Had I the choice, I wouldn't have sacrificed the hand so."

"Zyen." Lord Darshel's voice softened in affection over her show of loyalty.

The warrioress looked up at him, then, and something changed in her expression. They stared at each other as if meeting for the first time. This time, they did not stand facing each other as enemies. Zyanthena's actions had changed that. Lord Darshel came to a realization as he gazed into her eyes: he was finally beginning to understand the untamable Tashek woman.

"Let's get you cleaned up," he ordered gently. He asked his guard to get a bucket of hot water while he led the desert woman to his bed to sit. Darshel turned away to collect her bag of herbs and ointments. The Tashek reset her thumb herself, despite Lord Darshel's request to help. Her thumb repositioned, Zyanthena let the lord-governor wash her hand and apply the needed medicines before binding the injury. She never protested once.

Going unnoticed, Commander Raic watched the whole process before announcing his presence. Having seen both the damage to the Tashek's hand and how calmly she handled the pain awoke a respect in the cavalryman. He stepped up to them more humbled. "I heard what happened, My Lord."

"Yes. I foolishly let an assassin into my mist," Darshel replied, taking the blame himself. "Had it not been for Zy'ena, I would be in the afterlife right now."

"Sir—."

"Next time, she will remain unbound."

"Yes, My Lord."

"As it is, I want to know who's been telling prostitutes stories beneath the sheets. Our assassin was too well informed." Raic nodded. "And in the meantime, I need you to make sure all is all right in our camp. Zyanthena and I need to see the king immediately."

"I will get an escort ready then."

"No need. Between the two of us, we will be armed well-enough."

The horse commander looked shaken at his lord's disfavor. Zyanthena stepped in at his behest. "Take four guards, Your Lordship. The commander is right to let us have some protection. I am down a hand." She rose her hands to emphasize her plight. "I would feel more secure, if nothing else."

Lord Darshel sighed but did not disagree again. "Okay then. Let's go."

§   §

The small group from Kavahad had expected the Citadel to be quiet by that hour. Indeed, there were few people still up and about from the festivities; however, they did not need to wait for a night-guard to rouse the king. King Maushelik was awake and ready to receive them in his smaller East Room. Accompanying the king was the Shi'alam, his protector, Captain Sean Woodman, and Commander Matar. All of the men looked harried and concerned.

"Have you lost men, as well?" King Maushelik asked without preamble. The aging king's face pinched in anticipation to more bad news.

"Majesty, sir, yes. Almost. Zyanthena stopped an attempt on my life not half-an-hour ago. My men are searching my camps to see if there were other attacks." Lord Darshel replied. "By your face, I assume there were others in other camps?"

"Yes. Captain Woodman had found five accounts to our foot soldiers; the Sheev'anee had twelve to some of their night watch and scouts; and the Crystine had three. My guards assure me there have not been any losses within the Citadel. Yet. The attacks seem to be in the camps outside."

"Were they all women?" Zyanthena asked. The men seemed shocked at her question.

"In fact, yes." Woodman answered. "Those caught were, at least. Some got away."

The second question was more alarming. "And were they all Tashek?"

"Ah..." Woodman cast about at the others, uncertain of the answer. The possibility that the desert people were involved would inflame the forces across the Citadel. It was a bold question.

"Of those that attacked us, yes. But no one claimed them as kin," the Shi'alam replied to his daughter. His face was hard at the admittance. The Sheev'anee leader knew how damning the situation would be.

"I would have to say all the women looked desert-born to me, too." Matar said softly.

"They weren't Sheev'anee." Zyanthena reassured them. "The woman who attacked Lord Darshel had the Mark of the Nallaus behind her right ear." She said the words, looking directly at her father.

The Shi'alam was stunned. "The Nallaus? Here?"

"And aligned with Mansocan, it seems."

"No," the Sheev'anee leader breathed out. He closed his eyes at the thought. "The enemy has collected a bold hand if that is true."

The others were confused. Even King Maushelik and Commander Matar had not heard of the Nallaus. Only Lord Darshel, now privy to the secret Zyanthena knew, did not bark out questions to clarify what the desert woman said.

It took the Shi'alam some minutes to calm himself before he could speak. "The Nallaus are Tashek, but they are not aligned with the Sheev'anee. Many years ago, they chose to disagree with our laws and disbanded from us. We've driven them to the wastes, far away from good settling ground. We don't allow them to make any permanent camps. They're wanderers, numbering about two-hundred-and-thirty members. They do not usually band together in mass, expect on auspicious occasions. They are, by all rights, as talented as the Sheev'anee."

"And you're saying—or Zyanthena is saying—these Nallaus just attacked us?" Captain Woodman clarified. "Why would they have cause?"

"They wouldn't," Zyanthena replied, "But the maunstorz would. The Nallaus are a perfect weapon for them. Fighters, survivors, master at infiltration..."

"Not to mention that they look just like the Sheev'anee," Matar finished. "It was the perfect ruse. No one would have suspected an enemy within the Sheev'anee until it was too late."

"It is too late!" The Shi'alam barked out. He could barely control his temper at the helplessness of aftersight. "The damage is done. There will be more deaths reported in the coming hour."

"Majesty, the defenses are weakened." Matar turned their attention to the immediate problem. "We must wake everyone and be on full alert."

"Yes." Maushelik was quick to consider all the matters that needed to be done. "In case the enemy has planned another attack. The men will be tired from just finding their beds, but it must be done—delicately," he ordered of Captain Woodman. The man was ready to speed off. "Leave out the issue of the Tashek—the Nallaus. I do not want fights starting."

"Sir." The army captain nodded and hurried away.

Zyanthena was considering the king's last words as the men around her conversed about everything that needed to be done with the new problem at hand. She mused over the small map on the table to her left, studying the Citadel and its surrounding areas. Old battles against the maunstorz swirled in her head about the possible attacks the enemy could bring against them—only, Zyanthena did not know of any attacks (except the most recent) where the maunstorz had amassed enough men to fight Syre directly. The Citadel was a stronghold not lightly taken on.

"It's a ruse," she mumbled. When no one paid her any attention, she spoke louder. "It's a ruse. The attack to our forces is a ruse." The others quieted, looking at her in skepticism but willing to listen. "Look, they aren't dumb. If I was them, the Citadel of Light would be one of the last places I would attack head-on, especially with a dwindled force and the Citadel reinforced. The city can stand a siege of one hundred-and-twenty days before needing to consider breaking out of it. Once our armies are inside the walls, they can't do anything. So, why attack us at all?"

"See how our defenses hold?" Matar spoke up immediately. He was used to conferring with his "Night Fox" over battle plans. "Looking for weaknesses or—." He stopped, his intense midnight-blue eyes locked with Zyanthena's, "Or, they wanted us to squabble with each other, thinking the Sheev'anee are trying to take over the Citadel."

"Exactly, master. The Nallaus were working as a decoy for them. If our attentions are kept here, they could use the distraction to move what was left of their forces passed us, going back east again." Her fingers traced along the space between the mountains, the Red Hills, and the Citadel. "They stand a better chance of regrouping and gathering food in the Hills than the wastes or the mountains this close to the First Snows. They are affected by the weather, too."

The Crystine commander bent over the maps with his "Night Fox", considering the advantages and issues with her idea. If the Nallaus were indeed acting as decoys, he could see how their distraction would help move a maunstorz force. There was not much room to maneuver an army to the north of the Citadel of Light. The dust from the foot soldiers would be spotted by the capitol. "Zyen could be right. At this point, the Citadel has been reinforced from its previous losses. It wouldn't make good sense to attack it again, not after Prince Al'den and All'ani Cum'ar's last fight. The enemy took many losses."

"I cannot afford to make assumptions," King Maushelik stated. "I have lost too many good men to bet on Zyanthena's idea. I want everyone woken."

"Indeed, Majesty," Matar soothed. "I wasn't saying that, but it may be a good idea to check Zyanthena's suggestion, too."

The king agreed, "We will send out the scouts then."

"Your Majesty," Lord Darshel stepped forward. "With all due respects, I would like to offer my cavalry to that end."

It was clear that the king had been thinking of Tashek scouts to do the runs, but the aging king looked to the Shi'alam to make the final say. The Sheev'anee leader shrugged. "I am all right with that. My scouts have been at runs for nearly two weeks; they are not as rested as Kavahad. And, it may settle our forces to have someone who is not Tashek leading a run."

"Very well. Lord Shekmann the task is yours. I will give each of your men a second mount in case you find yourselves in need of farther travel than expected."

"Thank you, Majesty."

"And I will go with them."

The men were taken aback at Zyanthena's boldness once again. Even Lord Darshel could not help staring at the desert woman. He had not expected her offer. The Shi'alam, however, was quick to protest. "Zyanthena, I forbid—."

"All due respect, father, Majesty," the Tashek warrioress interrupted with some emphasis. "The Kavahadian cavalry had not ventured the lands east of here—or at least not for some great time. I have. The maunstorz enjoy setting traps and sneaking up on forces. They are fairly skilled at it in the hills and forests. If Kavahad happens to venture those areas that far east, they would fare better with a scout who had traversed those places. Therefore, I volunteer myself for that position."

The others could not find a fault with Zyanthena's logic. It was a good idea. In the end, even the Shi'alam gave in—grudgingly. Having come to the decision, they conferred over the best areas to send the Kavahadian cavalry and decided on how often the Shekmann should check in. The king then ordered everyone back to their posts so he could deal with other matters.

As they began to leave, the Shi'alam hurried to his daughter to pull her aside. In an unusual display of affection, he held her tight. "Zyen, my beautiful, beautiful girl. It's too much to bear to think I am losing you again."

"Tai'en [father]. You are not losing me, as I have never been lost from you." Zyanthena replied, calming the leader. "And, there is nothing in this world that could ever separate me."

"Oh, my sweet, fierce Zy'ena." The Shi'alam blinked back tears that threatened to fall. Every day since the first I held you in my arms, I felt like I was on borrowed time…Now you are leaving with a man of such…" he could not finish the words.

"Tai'en." Zyanthena gave her father a warm smile, rarely given to the man who had raised her. "He is not the enemy his father or fore-father were. You look for the evil that is no longer there." She stepped away from her father, seeing Lord Darshel still waiting for her by the doorway. "I will come back, father, at Star's speed."

"At Stars' speed," the Shi'alam murmured back. He stood watching as his strong, wild daughter left with the Lord-governor of Kavahad.

Part III

§

(Year 110 SC, Harvest-Gathering Time)

Chapter Forty-Two

§

Burned

The Kavahadian cavalry packed quickly, efficiently getting all their gear and supplies compacted down into loads that would fit on their second horses. Anything unnecessary was left behind in the keeping of Staria's armory master. Though they were finished by the next hour, Lord Darshel had his forces wait a half-an-hour longer as he and Commander Gordon reassessed their supplies. He wanted to make sure they only took necessities but that nothing important was missed. Finally, the Shekmann knew he could not dally any longer. He signaled his horsemen to move, and they all headed to the main stairs of the Citadel to bid their Starian king farewell.

Zyanthena joined them there. She had been away to her father's camp to acquire another Tashek-bred mount to help relieve Unrevealed, who had been pronounced healed and ready to ride. Despite the happy prognosis, the desert woman insisted that she take a second mount, in case her black was lacking conditioning. Secretly, Lord Darshel suspected the request was really to say good-bye to her father and Commander Matar one last time.

It pleased Lord Darshel to see his men respond respectfully, some even cheerfully, to the Tashek woman as she made her way through their ranks to his side. Having saved their lord from death seemed to have thawed any dislike for her. Even Commander Raic greeted her civilly. "I have gathered what information the other scouts have of our eastern route; though, I expect it had changed some if the enemy is indeed crossing us to the north."

"Good. It is appreciated, your volunteering to stay with us."

Zyanthena gave a small huff. "Who else would do it, Your Lordship? I fear you would have been stuck with me even if I hadn't stepped forth."

"Your Stars' decree," Darshel replied, nodding. "If you are really more pious about such things than you admit." The Tashek woman answered with a shrug.

The trumpets sounded, then, pronouncing the Starian king's arrival. The Kavahadian cavalry came to attention and saluted their king as he and his son descended the steps. Lord Darshel, accompanied by his two commanders and Zyanthena, came forward to meet the Mausheliks. "I know that you understand how grateful I am that you have taken up this call of service," the king told Lord Shekmann. "This is beyond the fealty you swore to me and I will not forget your actions."

"Majesty," Lord Darshel bowed, "I am and always will be at the service of Staria's king. My men have long been restless for a part in this war. We will make sure to come back only if the north and eastern lands are completely combed through, on my word."

"I know, Lord Shekmann." The king extended his hand so Darshel could clasp it and kiss his ring. Then, he moved his attention to the desert woman at the Shekmann's side. "Zyanthena." He reached out to her and she allowed him to take her hands in his. "I know what sacrifices you make by volunteering as you have. You are exemplary. I understand now why you are spoken of so highly by the soldiers. Upon your return, I will have a document signed of your release from Kavahad. No one can argue it now."

"Majesty. I am forever indebted to you and your son."

King Maushelik smiled. "No, it is I who is indebted, Sheev'arid Zyanthena." He stepped aside and motioned a man forward. "Your father send you some support."

"Aerrisson." Zyanthena breathed, knowing the desert man. She strode to the man's side and they bent together, foreheads touching, in a display that suggested an intimate connection. They seemed lost to the eyes that fell upon them. Zyanthena finally pulled back. "Father sent you?"

"I go where the Shi'alam bids me."

"But your family?"

"Cannot complain of a direct order from the Shi'alam. I am happy to protect his daughter."

"I don't need protection."

Aerrisson laughed. "Never did, but you will appreciate having another scout around. I know why the cavalry is going."

"Yes." Zyanthena agreed, reluctantly. She finally turned to introduce her friend to Lord Darshel and the Kavahadian commanders. "Lord Shekmann, this is Re'shaird Aerrisson, a scout of the Sheev'anee, under clan Sheev'arid. The Shi'alam gives him to you on loan for his abilities."

Lord Darshel greeted the man with arms wide, bowing forward as he had seen others do in greeting. Aerrisson seemed surprised but he did greet him back. "We are pleased to have your assistance, Re'shaird."

The king and Prince Al'den seemed pleased with the exchange. They both noted how respectfully the Shekmann had handled the situation. Lord Darshel was certainly not his father. They bid the Kavahadian cavalry a safe passage and blessed them on their way. By full sun-up, Kavahad was leaving the Citadel of Light, heading north and east.

§   §

By late afternoon, the cavalry had crossed the edge of the Aras Desert, feeling relief from the change in altitude as the sands began to disappear into the border of the mountains and hills. Just to the east, the beginning of the Red Hills could be seen—and something else: smoke. Lord Darshel pulled up his men and motioned the two Tashek near. He took out his looking glass to view the horizon. "Over that way is a village—Teem, was it?"

Zyanthena nodded her pretty head. "Yes, a small village of only about three hundred, farmers mostly."

"Smoke does not bode well," Aerrisson commented.

"No, it does not." Lord Darshel shared a glance with his commanders. "I had hoped to bed down for the night by that village, but now I fear what we will find when we get there."

"You should let us go ahead." Aerrisson told them. "Zyanthena and I will make sure the maunstorz are not still near."

Lord Darshel wished to protest but he knew that was the purpose for bringing scouts. Reluctantly, he nodded them away. "Be careful," he said to Zyanthena. The desert woman nodded to him and turned her grey mount away with Aerrisson's. "We will follow them at walking pace." Darshel instructed Commander Raic. "I would like to reach Teem by nightfall, if it is safe to camp."

"Sir, yes. My Lord."

Aerrisson and Zyanthena met back up with Kavahad on the outlying farms of Teem. They carried grim news. "There is no sign of the enemy but their footsteps head east. Of Teem…no one is left alive." Aerrisson stated stoically. "The houses are burned though some food-stuffs may still be salvaged. The animals were slaughtered, as well."

"Stars!" Commander Gordon exclaimed. "What madness made the maunstorz start that? And when?"

Zyanthena shook her head, grim. "They have never attacked a village so savagely; not that I have seen. Something's changed."

They looked among themselves, concerned. Finally, Lord Darshel asked the more pressing question. "Is it safe to camp there tonight?"

Aerrisson nodded. "There is no sign that the enemy has been there for two days. They had no reason to stay."

"Okay," Darshel motioned to his commanders, "So, we will head in and make a make-shift camp. Tomorrow, we will keep heading east. Send a pigeon back to the king. He will want to know of this tragedy."

By the falling of the sun, the Kavahadian cavalry had made a small camp by the edge of Teem. The men were put onto two hour watches and everyone stayed in their armor. Enough food was found around the destroyed town to make a passable dinner without delving into their own supplies. Anyone not on watch duty was ordered to sleep.

As the quiet of the town surrounded them, Lord Darshel sought out Zyanthena. He found her and Aerrisson by the embers of the burning worship-house. They had been speaking in keshic, but their words ended as he neared. Zyanthena turned to face the Shekmann. "I wanted to know what you've found, if anything more." Aerrisson touched Zyanthena's arm softly, whispered something. The he turned away to give them space to talk alone. "He doesn't need to leave."

"He knows." Zyanthena answered. "It's not so easy for him to forget about your family. He had a sister…" She didn't finish, knowing Darshel would understand.

"Oh…I am sorry." Darshel became subdued, weighed down by his father's legacy.

Unexpectedly, Zyanthena stepped closer and gave him a small smile, catching his attention and bringing his emerald eyes back to her. "He also knows it was not you." She waved toward the worship-house, getting back to business. "We found evidence that a majority of the people were massed here."

"They were attacked during a town meeting or service?"

"Worse, I think." The desert woman kicked at a burning log in front of her. "They may have been locked in here. It's the largest building in town. Usually, these types of houses do not have locks, yet, this front door, the windows, and the back door all have these large beams across them."

"Stars! You think these people were burned alive?!" The Tashek's expression answered for her. Darshel felt his bile come up his throat. "This isn't the way the maunstorz have attacked in the past."

"No, it definitely is not. They always attack places of power: military camps, castles, on occasion some river crossings—but never have I head of this kind of atrocity, this mindless murder. Except for some of the footprints and a broken sword showing it's them, I would not have guessed this to be maunstorz attack. Something or someone had changed how they operate."

"Or, they are desperate."

"Perhaps." She did not look convinced.

"Either way, we won't know until we catch up to them. By daybreak, we are going to head out at a speed tolerable to the horses."

By midafternoon the Citadel of Light had an accurate accounting of their losses. The Starian army had suffered thirty-three injuries; twenty-nine of them were fatal. Their cavalry had only three men killed. The mertinean found twelve soldiers dead and two missing. Eight of the Crystine were in critical condition but only the original three found men were dead—yet. None of the Golden Kingdom's archers had come to any harm, and only one of Blue Haven's contingent was injured. The Sheev'anee's final count came down to forty-three casualties, between the night guard and scouts. In the end, the only good news was that the Nallaus hadn't attacked inside the walls of the city.

Knowing his people were uneasy with the recent tragedy, King Maushelik opened his throne room to a public hearing. All of the forces protecting the Citadel had their leaders attend, as the king declared them in a state-of-emergency. A large portion of the Citadel's leading citizens also attended, begging to know what their great leader was going to do about the recent attacks.

King Maushelik let his court attendant announce the tally of their recent losses. Worried murmurs arise as the total became known. He knew the numbers would scare some of his citizens but he refused to lie about it. The people would have to learn to be strong enough to deal with the tragedies of war. Once his man was done, the king rose from his throne and motioned for silence. "This recent event had me concerned for Staria's people. You all are what make up the heart of this kingdom and I would see you all safe. This attack only emphasizes the need. At our war meeting, we agreed that the Citadel is not the best place because it presents as a target. The women and children must be moved to safer ground. Commander Kins!" The mertinean commander came forward from his place by his Crystine friend. "Commander Kins has agreed to act, in my authority, to lead the groups travelling to Kavahad—our designated command center. Some of the mertinean and any man who volunteers from my army will go under his command. I also decree all nobles go with Commander Kins and make Kavahad their temporary home. Only the military will stay here at the Citadel."

The aged king continued on before anyone could pretest. "The heirs of Sealand, Golden, and Sunrise will accompany these groups until Paragon Oasis, where Sealand will split off from the force and travel back to North Point with the Crystine, under command of Matar. The Golden heir will continue to Sardon with his men and the heirs of Sunrise will return to their kingdom through Kavahad. This is not up to debate!" He added roughly, to settle any arguments that could ensue. "The rest of our forces will be separated according to the plans we laid out at the war council. I want everyone to be ready to move by tomorrow night. By the next dawn, I want the forces to leave in groups." The ruler began to turn away, but the gathered crowd erupted in questions, complaints, and accusations. Tired, King Maushelik sighed and turned back. He rose his voice as his temper began to flare. "Quiet! I am not here for a discussion. My words are final. Go back to your homes and prepare. I will not let my men wait for stragglers. Now go!"

The room became hushed; the people were unaccustomed to their king being angry and not open to queries. The moment passed, however, and the crowd began to file out in a more subdued manner. Some still muttered among themselves. It was only as the last of the citizens and military men left the room that King Maushelik allowed himself to collapse onto his hard throne. His son and most trusted advisors had stayed. Prince Al'den kneeled by his father's chair, finally allowing his disquieted emotions to show now that the others were gone. "Speak your mind, my son."

"All'ani Cum'ar's men are concerned of attacks coming from the west. Scouts have picked up tracks in the sand there. Does this mean Sheev'arid Zyanthena's guess that they are travelling east was wrong? Have you heard from Kavahad about it?"

"I am expecting a bird by evening to tell us if Kavahad has found evidence of the enemy, but it may take a few more days for them to be sure." The king rubbed his temples, feeling a headache forming from the stress of it all. "We must expect the worst, though. Have all the Sheev'anee battle-ready and available to protect the groups that are leaving the Citadel. The rest of our forces will be stationed along the walls in case of an attack to us directly."

"Father." Al'den had stood up by then. Yet, he seemed hesitant about what he wanted to say next; which was unusual. "They seem more persistent this time with their attacks. Are the maunstorz hoping we will fall like the Crystal Kingdom? Are you and I targets now?"

"My boy," King Maushelik smiled wanly and patted Al'den's outstretched hand. "They may think that we have been weakened, but the forces that have come to our aid have me confident that the enemy is wrong to assume we can be conquered. They will come and they will try, but Staria will not fall."

"But you are saying you suspect that is their plan?"

"It has always been. Though their motivation to conquer us had never been clear, they are always picking away at the kingdoms. Sometimes war does not make sense. But we will fight to protect our own." King Maushelik looked at his only son squarely in the eye, wanting to convey more than he could ever say with words. "Syre will need you in the end, Al'den. It's time I share something with you—in case my time comes to an end too soon."

Chapter Forty-Three

§

Paramour

Another town burned; its people and animals slaughtered. Lord Darshel looked at the carnage with tight features and a heavy heart. The small town of Starlight had been home to Estarian monks and a wayfarers' tavern and inn. It wasn't even a place of influence to be targeted. It just happened to be the only town on Staria's northeastern border that fell in line with the maunstorz chosen route.

His men and the two Tashek scouts had found little left to salvage. Starlight had been more thoroughly ransacked than Teem. None of the company could understand why. Kavahad stopped for lunch outside of the small town while Lord Darshel sat with his commanders and the Tashek around the map of Staria, discussing their options.

"The trail still leads east," Zyanthena told them, tracing the probable route of the enemy. "Now, they are most definitely in Rubia."

"And we have orders to stake out Staria and make sure we have swept the area north and east of the Citadel. We are far from the capitol." Raic pointed out, disgruntled to be pulled away from familiar territory. Here, only the two desert warriors had any knowledge.

"But we found them!" Gordan argued. "We found the damn bastards burning villages along their merry way. The king would not fault us for hunting them down."

"Bah! Rubia is the mertinean's business. We only answer to the King of Staria and Lord Shekmann."

"Rubia cannot stay unprotected. Not while half of the mertinean is at the Citadel helping King Maushelik."

"Only one-third of the mertinean." Zyanthena replied to Aerrisson's plea. "But, still Raven's Den may not yet be aware of this threat. They should be warned. Lord Shekmann?" She glanced at the Kavahadian, wondering why he had yet to speak. "What is your decision, Your Lordship?"

Darshel's mind had been preoccupied on the burning villages not too distant from where they rested. He had not seen such carnage in some great while. It infuriate him. At Zyanthena's call, he pulled himself out of his thoughts. "Though it seems unlikely, we have to make sure that the north and eastern lands of Staria are not hiding more maunstorz. Commander Raic is right that our duty is to the King; however," he continued before his cavalry commander could gloat, "My conscious cannot let more innocents be slaughtered. We need to send a man to Raven's Den."

"Send a damn bird," Raic muttered.

"If the enemy is near, a bird will be shot down. It is their way. I will go to Commander Grant at Raven's Den." Aerrisson volunteered. "I know the way best and have one of the fastest horses."

"A man will be more of a target than a bird," Lord Darshel pointed out, gently.

"I know, but it is not the first time I have done a run while eluding the enemy. I will get through."

Lord Darshel nodded to the Tashek man's words. He ignored Raic's muttering of "arrogant, desert bastards". "I give you leave to go, then. Take what provisions you need. I will send a bird to Grant and King Maushelik of this plan, in case either gets through. As for the rest, half of the men will turn around and continue surveying the lands of Staria. Commander Gordon, I would like you to take this task. The rest of the men will continue on with me in pursuit of this enemy."

"My Lord!" The commanders protested together. Surprised, they paused to look at one another, then Raic took the lead. "My Lord, you cannot compromise yourself so. Send me in your stead and return with Gordon."

"No, commander. This, I feel, is something I must do. Gordan is a far better diplomate than you, a skill he will need as he comes upon towns on his search. Your skills I need to watch my back; Zyanthena know the territory and will guide us, but I know you two will not agree without me there to intercede. I need all of your cooperation on this." He stood to make sure his words were final. Darshel looked to Aerrisson. "I will write a missive for you to carry."

Commander Gordan stood to follow as Lord Darshel strode to his horse to get parchment and pen. He waited until they were out of earshot before confronting his lord. "My Lord, I respect you—perhaps more than any man I have served under—but to let you risk yourself—."

"Commander, I know your concerns, I really do. But—I need to do this. People's lives are at stake."

"These are not your people."

"They are Syreans being attacked by our enemy. They are all our people. This is what I can do and what we have been trained to do. I want to help where I can."

"I don't doubt your fighting abilities, but—."

"Then you need to believe that we will all survive. And if we don't then I need you to give this," Darshel handed his elder commander a sealed missive, "To Markus LaPoint or his cousin Jeremy Freedman. Do you understand?"

"My Lord!" Gordan exclaimed.

"They will know what to do if anything happens to me, Gordan. Please, this is crucial." He looked his commander steadily in the eye.

Commander Gordan nodded solemnly. "My Lord," he finally agreed and took the missive. Still, his face showed some trepidation. "Come back soon, My Lord."

§ §

Zyanthena stood by Lunier's head as Aerrisson blanketed his silver stallion. She was quiet, unable to speak the words she knew she would regret not saying later. Somehow, her concerns would not voice themselves. Aerrisson eyed her as he worked, knowing the look. Whereas a younger Zyanthena would have spoken the thoughts in her head, however, this battle-hardened warrioress was quick to keep her tongue. Oh, how four years had changed her.

"My Desert Rose, what is on your mind?" Zyanthena looked startled to hear her old pet name but it did little to elicit her into talking. A cautious look came to her eye. "Zy'ena." Aerrisson turned from his rigging to take the desert woman's hands in his. He felt her stiffen at his touch. "Zyen, what is it? Are we no longer friends enough to speak our minds to each other?"

"Friends..." She licked her lips. "You were once more than that and now much less, but comrades we are still."

"Then speak to me as Zyanthena would."

"It is not Zyanthena's heart that has the words."

Aerrisson's face softened. "Then as the Desert Rose."

She paused then nodded. "She would ask that you would not risk yourself when others could be sent. There is no need for such valor."

"And a Desert Rose of old would have thought everything was for valor."

"That was before she found out the cost of such rashness."

"Oh, Zyen," he touched her face, cupping her cheek. "Where has all this bitterness come from?"

"Ironic that it is you wondering when you know what the first instance of my learning came from."

Zyanthena saw Aerrisson's eyes flinch at her words. "And you know—."

"Yes, I do. It doesn't make it feel any better." She stepped back from her former lover. "I am only asking for you to reconsider this task, for your safety if nothing else. I know your answer but I had to say it nonetheless."

"Zyen," Aerrisson reached for her, pleading for her to understand.

But the strong-willed woman evaded his touch. She bowed in high-clan fashion as she bid him farewell. "Then go safely on the winds, as the Stars' will, Aerrisson. The people your success will save will be forever grateful, even if they are not aware of your actions. Until again…" Zyanthena spun away before Aerrisson could answer. For once in her life, she did not turn back to give him one last farewell.

§   §

Five days passed, with more villages in ashes, and still no sign of their enemy. The Kavahadian cavalry was becoming restless, concerned by being so deep into Rubia, and confused on how the maunstorz could have eluded them so long. Even Zyanthena, as she returned from a short scouting run, seemed disquieted by the fact that—even at horse speed—the maunstorz managed to outpace them. Yet, they continued to follow the trail in hopes that the next village could be saved.

"There is more smoke ahead." A scout reported as he returned with Zyanthena.

"It should be the village Sackett, fifty miles north of Carmine. I am not sure why they chose the smaller target, but I am afraid it's been ransacked, too," the desert woman said.

"And the maunstorz?" Commander Raic asked.

"The tracks are fresh but they are not there."

"We missed them again! Bloody hell!"

Zyanthena gave a tight-lipped nod in agreeance and stepped Unrevealed closer to Lord Darshel's mount. She turned herself away from the others so they could not see her speaking. "A moment alone with you, Your Lordship?"

Just for her to ask for privacy was concerning enough. Lord Darshel consented quickly and sent his men to prepare to enter the burned village. He gave the Tashek woman a few minutes alone to stare down the hill they had posted out on. "What is it?"

"Poor news. I found horseshoe tracks mixed with the maunstorz ones and this," she passed him a thrown horseshoe. He inspected it, finding it made of a different metal than those used in Staria. He glanced at the desert warrioress expectantly. "It's not worked like any in the mertinean or Crystine. If I didn't know better, the farrier-work is from the South."

"Way up here? We are nearly to the northern-most border of Rubia."

"I am more concerned that the horsemen seem to have been with the enemy."

"You don't think they were with the village?"

"Horses like that? No. I would expect heavy horses for plowing and work, not light cavalry. It was two whole infantries. The horses went south from Sackett, toward Carmine; the foot soldiers north and east." Her brandy eyes stared off the way the maunstorz went. "They are close. Maybe even up in those hills just at the edge of the mountains. They could be aware of us…"

Her words sounded ominous. Lord Darshel felt his pulse quicken to think the maunstorz could be watching him and his men right then. His eyes studied the tree line just to their north. "You think we should go south?"

She shook her head, face serious. "I do not trust having a Southern force this far north without a sign of the mertinean. I do not like the feelings I get over this." She stared deeply into his emerald eyes. "We should have heard back from the Citadel or Aerrisson by now; even the mertinean should have crossed paths with us; but there have been no birds nor no runners. We have sent six missives with no return word. I'm concerned..." She paused her words and Lord Darshel wanted to reach out to steady her.

"Concerned of what?" He asked instead, though he thought he knew.

"My Lordship," she took the most familiar title as she admitted her deepest fear, "We are very alone and may well have gone straight into a trap. Surely, the maunstorz had expected someone to search the lands north of the Citadel after the assassinations. Any force, either Staria or Rubia, would have chased then down because of the village burnings. The lands north of here become very wooded. They make up the southern edge of the Forbidding Forests of Crystalynian. I've been here. There are many places they can hide and ambush forces...I should have seen this coming."

"What would you have us do, then?"

The question helped steady her and put Zyanthena in a strategic frame of mind. "My first instinct is to get to Wynward's Crossing and the remainder of the Crystine and mertinean stationed there but—." Her eyes searched the hills again. "If we are being watched, I would have us find higher ground and a place more secure. With it nearing nightfall, we cannot risk getting surrounded here."

"Then, we will do it, Zy'ena," Darshel told the desert woman. "Find a place that we can hold."

"Yes, My Lordship."

The Shekmann's pigeon finally arrived at the Citadel on the third day, just hours before the king sent out the first wave of townspeople. Prince Al'den was the one to spot the bird first, having posted himself near the bird tower in case any were to arrive from any of their forces out scouting. "One comes," he tapped Kent on the shoulder to wake him from a short doze.

Prince Kent groaned at being woken and pushed himself up to sitting. "Who's it from?"

"Hold on." The Starian collected the tired bird and fed it before removing the missive attached to its foot. "It is Lord Shekmann's seal."

"Took them long enough to send us information."

Al'den ignored the quip as he unrolled the paper and read its contents. His face hardened. "Kavahad reached the Red Hills and found two villages burned. They followed to the border village Starlight. Half his force is returning west to keep scouting the desert. Re'shaird Aerrisson goes south to Raven's Den to warn the mertinean. Lord Shekmann continues pursuit. He saw more smoke; more villages burn."

"Holy shit!" Kent took the missive and read it, too. "The maunstorz are burning villages now?! How many people dead? Wait—!" He looked at Al'den in alarm. "This is marked his third message. We never received any others."

"I saw that." Al'den pursed his lips and looked out at the desert. "The maunstorz are killing our birds. We have no idea how many messages we have missed. They are keeping us in the dark on their movements. I have no choice but to send out more scouts."

"And risk more men? If they are killing birds then they will most certainly take out scouts."

I know." The Starian prince gripped the stone in frustration. "I must speak to Cum'ar and the Shi'alam to see how we can safely call the men back. Can you give that missive to my father?"

"Yes, I can. Al'den," Kent stopped his friend, "The first group of townspeople going south leave soon. They could be a target."

The princes looked at each other, their thoughts jumping to another concern. "Princess Éleen. She was to go with the first group to Kavahad," Al'den murmured. "Kent, after you go to my father, can you find her? I...I need to speak with her."

"Yes. I can do that, my friend." They clasped hands once and turned to their tasks.

§   §

An hour later, Prince Al'den made it back to his private rooms to find the other two royals waiting. He thanked his Goldener friend with his eyes as he walked over and took the princess's offered hand. He grasped it tightly in his concern.

"Your Highness?" Elene asked, surprised at the urgency in the handsome warrior-prince's touch.

Her lovely voice reminded Al'den to mind his grip and to control his fears. "Princess. There is concern that the parties leaving the Citadel could be targeted by the enemy." Her china-blue eyes widened in fear. "So, I have arranged for a larger escort for you by All'ani Cum'ar's men. I would have asked you to stay in the Citadel longer but I—or the King and I—cannot have you so close to danger. We would have you go south as quickly as possible."

"Your Highness...I understand." Éleen made an effort to look brave, though the news unsettled her.

Al'den nodded, matter-of-fact as a typical, military man should be. "And I will have you go all the way to the Golden Palace, if you are able. The maunstorz have not gotten passed the Pika Mounts. You would be safest there."

"I—." Éleen was confused at the request. Staria did not want her? Al'den did not want her? "Highness, am I not to be courted by you then? Did His Majesty dismiss the Blue Haven marriage proposal?"

Prince Al'den had been so concerned over the princess's safety that he had forgotten her reasons for being there. It was evident enough to his friend, who spoke up when Al'den stayed quiet. "That was not Staria's intentions, Ms. Éleen. Indeed, it is my fault for offering my father's palace for your winter stay. Concern for Your Highness's safety has been our concern, not your kingdom's proposal. Rest assured Staria has no intentions of dismissing it."

"But in Golden how am I to know His Highness?"

Kent smiled fondly. "His Highness Prince Al'den will make sure to write you as often as he is able."

"Yes, princess, I shall." Al'den stated. "Letters to gain your affections will be most acceptable to the courts, as well. I know you desire their affections. Too, I will make sure you have some ladies with you at the Golden court."

Princess Éleen felt the chains of her station bind her again. Indeed, the princes were correct to protect her reputation, but she felt her hopes breaking as the fates separated her from the man she had expected to be betrothed to by spring. How could she fulfill her role to her parents and kingdom so far away from Staria? "As His Highness wishes," she finally conceded.

A relieved smile formed on Prince Al'den's lips. He grasped her hands more gently. "Thank you, princess." He then looked past her to Kent. "Lord Carrod is waiting in the hall. Could you send him in?"

"Of course." Kent grinned and joked to the couple as he passed. "Just don't let out that I've become Al'den's personal assistant, okay, Ms. Éleen? It wouldn't reflect well when I return home." He winked and walked off.

Al'den waited for his friend to leave the room before asking the princess his most pressing concern. "Do you still have my betrothal gift?"

"Yes," Éleen replied. Her hand went to the citrine hidden in her bodice. She clutched the yellow stone afraid the prince was going to ask for it back.

Al'den breathed a sigh of relief. "Good, good. Please, keep that safe, princess. It's a...a family heirloom, very precious. *Never*, I repeat, *never* lose it or show it to anyone. Will you do this?"

"I...yes." Éleen was startled at the prince's conviction. How precious was it that it must be held so secret?

"Thank you." Al'den reached out to grasp her delicate shoulders, the only familiar touch he would allow himself. "I will ask you for it sometime. Maybe, not too far in the future. I will expect you to have kept it safe."

"Yes, Highness," she replied. Éleen was confused on the Starian prince would be so adamant about a simple stone, but to have such trust bestowed on her strengthened her resolve. "I will keep it secret and keep it safe," she promised.

Lord Darshel came to Zyanthena after his men had settled down to their suppers and half to their beds. The Tashek had found the cavalry a small knoll within the forest that butted up to a cliff face on one side and an open meadow on the other three sides. A small brook, adequate to water the horses and men, flowed from the rock face and had helped to carry away the earth around the hillock, making it a good lookout.

As the Shekmann neared the desert woman's chosen post, he heard her singing. "I do not know much keshic, but that sounds like a lullaby. Is your horse unable to sleep?"

The lord-governor was rewarded with a rare, soft smile from the warrioress as she stroked Unrevealed's silken neck. "It is more for me, Your Lordship."

"And we are back to "your lordship" again, all of a sudden."

"No, My Lord...Darshel."

The Shekmann had never heard Zyanthena say his name before. The way it rolled so smoothly off her tongue struck him at how melodious the desert woman's voice was. He caught himself staring. "Zyen," he returned her most-familiar name. Darshel cleared his throat and stepped to the black stallion's head to pet his nose and offer him a hard biscuit as a treat. "You are unable to sleep?"

"As long as the maunstorz are out there, I do not trust the night—no offense to your men. The enemy loves to sneak up upon forces in the cover of darkness. Their sight is better than most at night, that is why," she explained. "I feel better staying awake with your watch. At least, the maunstorz have yet to sneak up on me."

"Just don't let my men hear you say you have such little faith in them...I know I, at least, feel safer with you awake."

She bowed her head at his sign of good faith. "I know this forest from here to the Crystal Kingdom. I may not know where or when the maunstorz will strike, but I promise you, until we are safely at Wynward's Crossing, I will continue to be alert for an ambush."

"*Ahnamen*," Darshel replied, surprising Zyanthena with a keshic "thank you". The handsome Shekmann turned away and found a seat on a small boulder. He leaned back to look up at the stars. The sounds of the night filled the gap in their conversation.

Zyanthena finally dropped her brush and came closer to the Shekmann. She sensed he was waiting for her to make the next move at being friendly, especially since he had offered her kind words in her own tongue and gave her space to be alone. "You have no wish for sleep yourself?"

"Not yet. Perhaps soon."

Zyanthena settled herself on another boulder bedside him. The warrioress curled her arms around one knee and rested her chin on her forearms as she listened to the forest. Lord Darshel found himself glancing over at the Tashek, his mind circling through questions he had about his now-constant shadow. Zyanthena must have felt his gaze, for she turned her perceptive eyes to his. "What is it, Lord Darshel?"

The second use of his first name gave him some encouragement. "I...I was wondering about something... Aerrisson. He and you—."

An unexpected chuckle came from the desert woman. "Careful, My Lordship. You are close to making yourself sound jealous."

"I haven't said anything of the sort—yet," he retorted.

"No, but you are going to." She laughed quietly but it was short-lived as her thoughts centered on the man of their conversation. Zyanthena's sobered. "I was wondering how long it would take for you to inquire about him...us, as we have been quite familiar with each other."

"If I did not know better, I would say you two were—."

"Lovers. We call them paramours."

Darshel blinked at her directness.

Zyanthena continued, "We were, nearly five summers ago. The Tashek view such matters differently than most societies. Youths coming-to-age are allowed a paramour—an experienced lover—for their education of such adult matters. It is looked down upon for a paramour to—what is your term, "knock up?"—a girl in her first years of womanhood. Only a woman who is amalgamated is allowed the privilege."

"Amalgamated?"

"Ah...married?" Darshel nodded at the term. She continued, "Boys with paramours are taught the arts of pleasuring, respectively. Our society deems a healthy knowledge of such relations best for everyone in the tribe."

"And you were calling the kettle black."

"Having a paramour is not as feckless as what you do. To enter into a relationship with a paramour is an agreement of mutual respect and preservation of dignity. It is not about squandering lust on anyone willing."

"Sure, you keep telling yourself that," he teased. Zyanthena gave him a scowl then shook her pretty head, letting it go. "So, Aerrisson was your paramour?" He prompted.

"Yes—and almost more... but for his mother. Being the Shi'alam's daughter would have given Aerrisson higher status, but his mother was suspicious of me. She knew my father's wife had died giving birth to Terrik. Because of this, she questioned who my mother was. Despite my father's efforts, she finally learned of me having been found with the Nallaus... She sent Aerrisson away. He was married off to one of the Cum'eri women a summer later."

"Your people do arranged marriages?"

"Some, it depends on the tribe."

Zyanthena became quiet and Lord Darshel sensed she was being withdrawn with sadness. "I am sorry to hear you lost your lover to the prejudice of his mother."

She gave a wan smile. "It has been over four summers since...I have become someone more. His leaving gave me the freedom to become the Crystine scout you found me as. I do not regret the road I have had to travel."

"Still...such trials leave a scar."

Zyanthena looked into his emerald eyes, hers full of the knowledge of loss. "Spoken from one who understands the same?"

"Now, that we will leave for another night." Lord Darshel stood up so that Zyanthena could not question him further. "I am going to retire. Please, try to not stay up all night."

"I will not promise that, Lord Darshel."

"Very well, Zy'ena. Goodnight nonetheless."

"Goodnight, My Lordship."

Chapter Forty-Four

§

Declaration

Commander Kins looked out at the gathering crowd. Their growing numbers emphasized the enormity of the task he had agreed to. The mertinean leader was a military man through-and-through. He knew how to get his men through even the toughest of skirmishes—but these people were townspeople, not used to day-long marches in the sweltering heat and eating trail rations. There, too, were the elderly and children to fend for, and the livestock that had been approved to take along. Ethan Kins could feel the start of a headache form at the base of his neck from the stress.

"All is ready," Lieutenant-Commander Marx informed him, coming through the back of the horse stables, where his commander had taken refuge with his golden mount.

Commander Kins thanked his man and idly fingered Elliscandero's flaxen mane, trying to buy himself a few more minutes of peace.

Marx had not left, however. "Sir? Commander, even All'ani Cum'ar's men are readied and standing by with Princess Éldon-Tomino and His Highness Argetlem."

That detail was the final straw to start the headache going. The worst stress to the trip was the two royals he had to protect before all the others. "Yes, thank you, Lieutenant. I will be out shortly. Let me finish with Ellie's tack."

"Commander," Max saluted and walked away.

A chuckle came from the barn aisleway as the mertinean lieutenant-commander took his leave. Ethan turned to find his son standing there; Candor, his mount, was saddled and waiting boredly behind his rider. "Patrick."

"Father." Patrick left Candor tied to the rail and stepped inside the stall. The two Kinsmen embraced. As he pulled away, Patrick said, "You seem rather touchy today. I wasn't sure I should stop in."

"For my son, my disposition will always be lightened," Ethan replied. "Especially to set eyes on you one more time."

"Oh, it's not the last time, father. Jacen and I decided we could head out with you and your group. We are to travel with Prince Argetlem's men to Sardon. Part of our journey can be with you. Plus, I'm sure you could use two more able-bodied men to cross the Aras."

Ethan Kins felt elated to hear the news. Yet, as a proper mertinean commander, he reserved his joy. "I could definitely find use for you—if you would be first at my side for the journey."

"And be the first to get yelled at? I wouldn't miss it for the world," Patrick joked.

They grasped forearms, their usual display of intimacy since Patrick had become a man. Before they released, Ethan could not help saying, "I am glad to have you with me, my son."

"I know, father. Me too."

The Mausheliks came to bid Commander Kin's group off. They waited for the entirety of the townspeople and militia to disappear out the gates before turning to other duties. Prince Al'den, with his now-constant shadow, All'ani Cum'ar, took to wandering the town, making sure the other three groups were finishing their packing. The second group was to leave by the third position of the sun, the third by high-noon, and the last by the ninth position. By nightfall, the Citadel would be quiet and filled only with the Starian and Sheev'anee forces that remained.

"You are quiet, Highness," Cum'ar observed.

"Hm? I guess I am. I just miss Kent's babbling already."

"His Highness of Golden had quite the knowledge to share. A great mind indeed. He will be sorely missed, as will Her Highness Éldon."

"Don't probe, Cum'ar." Al'den commanded lightly, though he let his face form a smile. "I know you want to hear me say how I feel about her leaving—of both their leaving."

"Who said I was probing, Highness?" The Tashek placed the innocent. "I just note your change of expression."

"Yeah…that." Al'den chuckled, though he didn't feel the humor in it. "I've never seen the Citadel so empty of its people. It has an air of hopelessness to it."

"Or, perhaps, the poignancy of possibility?" Cum'ar turned the thought. "Now Staria can hold its front without the fear of injury to its people. Your force will attack with a vengeance now that its most vulnerable underbelly is being protected."

"We will see."

Cum'ar stepped in front of his prince to look him forcefully in the eye. "You know so, Prince of the Yellow Star. You—and you alone—command the Sheev'anee. Order us and we will descend on the enemy in full force, more than we have ever done before. You are leader of a force to be reckoned with."

The Starian prince looked perturbed, unsettled by the Tashek's words. "My father—."

"King Maushelik is still the King of Staria, but you know he is waning. How many years had it been since he has led his armies? How many years had he given you many of his tasks? Your father knows it is soon your time to lead. The Sheev'anee see this, too."

The declaration did little to ease the tension in the warrior-prince's heart. His father's words, three days past, had reflected a similar tone. Since, Al'den had felt the futility of his father's mortality looming like a constant companion. King Maushelik had not said a word but he seemed to feel in his bones his time was coming. Al'den felt fear at the thought. "And, is that all or does your devotion have to do with Amun?"

The Tashek did not bat an eye at the name. Of course, the Sheev'anee man was privy to the knowledge of the Stones of Syre. "You are its master and thus the Mater of Staria. Your father, the king, knows that it is your birthright. I see he has finally told you, now that the time is nearing. The stones may be reawakening. Indeed, Ravel may already be in use. To have Amun in play would strengthen our odds against the enemy."

"Amun is not awake nor is it with me. The Citrine is being kept safe."

"Safe," Cum'ar echoed unhappily. "The stone is only safe with its master. Certainly, you keep it near?"

Al'den's mind flashed to its keeper and he struggled to hide his affection to the desert man before him. It would only vex the Sheev'anee to know how far away Amun was travelling from its master. Instead, he defended his choice. "The enemy seems privy to the knowledge of the stones, as well, Cum'ar. In fact, it could be their main reason for attacking us so. If all these stones exist amidst the royal houses then they must have procured Ravel from the Crystal royalty. Am I not correct?"

It seemed the idea had not presented itself to the man. All'ani Cum'ar was quiet, deep in thought on the matter. Finally, he conceded. "Perhaps, you are wiser than us to have come to such a conclusion. It explains their plunder of the Crystal Kingdom. The stones were almost the maunstorz undoing twenty-eight years ago. It would make sense for them to seek out the stones for their own gain."

"And it is the reason I do not carry Amun with me. If all my father had told me is true of the stones then having even one— Ravel—in the hands of our enemy is disastrous. I will not let them be so rewarded the second time around."

"You are brave and quite wise—and very well informed for having just learned of your destiny."

"It is my father that is so full of knowledge and wisdom. It was he who came to the conclusion about Ravel, especially once he learned of the unusual happenings at North Point. I am but his vessel."

Cum'ar rocked back on his heels, considering the Prince of the Yellow Star. Whatever conclusion the desert man came to, he seemed satisfied with the heir to Amun. "You are indeed correct to keep Amun hidden, as you are the only child of Staria's king. The maunstorz know who to target to capture the stone. Perhaps, your actions have saved us a worse fate."

"Perhaps," Al'den replied, though he thought afterward, "*Or maybe I sent away my best weapon at hand and Staria will fall just like the Crystal Kingdom. Stars, I hope this does not leave us undone!*"

Chapter Forty-Five

§

The Promise

The first traces of dawn began to halo along the mountains, showing the hours were leading out of the deepest part of the night. It was the time Zyanthena feared the most; the earliest hours were when sentries would be more lax and more easily taken advantage of. The desert woman danced around to rouse herself and to keep the night coldness at bay. She refused to surrender to her own fatigue as she knew the cavalry men would be trying to do. Some would fail; she would not be one of them.

Zyanthena busied herself preparing Unrevealed's tack, wanting her black stallion ready for anything the day might bring. Though the chestnut mare Yenamein the Shi'alam had given her was sounder, the warrioress trusted her ebony charger to take her through any challenge. The tall stallion, too, seemed pleased with the prospect. He lifted his head high and snorted in excitement to be readied for a day in the saddle. "Easy, boy. The day is still young and we've many miles left to run," she murmured as she adjusted the last piece of his tack and gave the stallion a piece of apple to preoccupy him.

The desert woman surveyed the forest again before starting on Tano, the grey mount Lord Darshel usually rode. She did so less to please the Kavahadian and more to assuage her growing sense of restlessness. The morning was quiet, too quiet, and a nagging feeling kept her attentive to the movements of the camp and the forest shadows.

The cavalry's cook lit his fire across the camp, anticipating the men awakening. The first whiffs of a morning porridge came across the expanse toward the Tashek, who nibbled on a piece of dried meat to settle her hungry stomach. Across the camp, she could see some of the men rising from their tents.

—And, just like that her tired senses became alerted to a shifting in the trees beyond the cook's commotions. Zyanthena stiffened, casting her eyes more directly to the forest there. She made sure she wouldn't just be sounding a false alarm from frayed nerves—.

The shadows moved again and the Tashek knew she had not misconceived the shapes. "Awake! To arms! The maunstorz come from the east!" She yelled out, startling the men and sentries who should have been as vigilant. "Look, look to the east! Gather your arms!" Zyanthena jumped onto Unrevealed's back as she commanded the cavalry. She reached across to Tano's reins, asking the grey courser to come with them. As she and the two horses raced across the knoll to Lord Darshel's tent, the rest of the force took up the cry and hurried to their weapons.

Commander Raic was standing ready at his lord's tent, armored and ready to defend the Shekmann. He grabbed Tano's reins as the desert woman stopped by his side and yelled for Lord Darshel. The Shekmann came out a moment later, armored too, as he had taken the Tashek's concerns to heart. He nodded to the commander and the Tashek. "To your horse, Raic, if you are able. Zyanthena will stay by my side as you mount." The horse commander didn't argue, as he was wont to do. He just saluted quickly and rushed away amidst the chaos.

Left alone, Lord Darshel steered himself and Zyanthena toward the fighting. Some of the cavalry men had been well-prepared and armored, others had not. Those not properly shielded were falling more quickly to the maunstorzs' jagged weapons. The butchery of the enemies' strokes would have made the Shekmann gage if he had had thought to it. "Your assessment, Zy'ena?" He barked as they closed in on the fighting lines.

The Tashek warrioress blanched, a characteristic the Starian did not know the woman possessed. The sign was not good. "In short, I believe we are quite screwed, My Lordship." She unsheathed her kora sword and spoke no more, charging the enemy on her black steed.

It had been remarked at the Citadel of Light how incredibly skilled the Tashek were at fighting, but, up until that point, Lord Darshel had barely been witness to Zyanthena's abilities. Seeing the desert warrioress and her horse charge into the fray, weapon singing and the dark steed striking out, the Shekmann finally understood all the hype. In moments, the Tashek and Crystal horse had taken out five of the enemy men for Kavahad's one.

In a whirlwind, Zyanthena pushed through the enemy's outer defenses, cutting back the line enough for the cavalrymen to regroup and form a more effective line. It spared them more losses and time for Commander Raic to come and reinforce the defensive with the men who got to horseback. As she had hoped, seeing horses seemed to deter the maunstorz from a stronger attack; their aversion to the four-legged creatures being their one, large weakness. Satisfied she had held the line, Zyanthena hacked her way back to the cavalry and Lord Darshel's side, where she could more readily assess their situation.

What had seemed a valiant effort, and had even strengthened the men's resolve, began to seem insignificant when Zyanthena had time to study their situation. The maunstorz were coming at them from the east and south, in a number far greater than they usually amassed. Usually, the maunstorz travelled in groups of fifty to one-hundred men, the latter number a rare account. That morning, she estimated nearly two-hundred-and-fifty coming from the forest. More were more possibly held back in the trees. They were not a skirmish raid. With the Kavahadian army cut in half, the one-hundred-and-fifty men were now outnumbered and unprepared.

"Shit," she muttered under her breath, comprehending just how grievous their situation had become. "We must get as many men to horseback as we can." She yelled to Lord Darshel. "Bring the horses near and cover the men."

Lord Darshel didn't question her. He ordered ten men to do as she bid. Calling out to the rest, he asked they double their efforts holding the enemy back. The lord-governor joined the fighting where he could. Zyanthena stayed back with Commander Raic and a few of the men already mounted; they defended a small circle where cavalrymen were called back to mount. As most of the men became ahorse, she called back the few remaining men afoot and ordered the rest of the riders forward. The exchange from foot to horse would have been a commendable act, as very few men fell, had anyone the time to note its efficiency. Zyanthena herself was relieved when the last man was astride.

"Organize the line!" Raic called out as all the men lastly to horseback gathered. The men complied quickly. "We take the right flank! Force these bastards away from His Lordship!"

With all the remaining men ahorse, it seemed the tide was turning. The first wave of maunstorz began to be pushed back, until the enemy line broke and they began retreating for the trees. Commander Raic called men to follow him, to cut down the maunstorz running in retreat; the rest of the cavalry stayed to guard Lord Darshel. Raic and his men ran down the enemy, taking one after another of them down. His force neared the trees—and suddenly a wall of lances were lifted in front of the line of horses from enemies lying in wait at the forest edge. The horses ran straight into them and both man and horse fell.

"Stars!" Zyanthena heard Lord Darshel swear at the annihilation of the cavalrymen. Other swears came up too. "My Lordship," Zyanthena appealed, "We cannot stay here. Your men are too few. We must flee to the north. My Lord!"

The Shekmann was battle-hardened enough to not let the shock take his senses. He was quick to respond. "Yes. Yes, we must. Zy'ena lead on. Get us out of here." He barked orders to the men.

Zyanthena cued Unrevealed to the front. She glanced across the meadow, looking for the quickest path. Despite her misgivings that the northern end could possibly lead to a trap, she saw no other way. "We must run hard! Push your horses as fast as they are able. Our only hope is to outrun them. Now, now!" Zyanthena asked Unrevealed forward, the black horse leaping into stride. Lord Darshel, his men around him, followed.

They raced for the trees.

§   §

Zyanthena pushed the horses for nearly five miles before letting the group fall back to a walk, and only long enough for all the horses to catch their breaths. Once the mounts seemed collected, she ordered them on into a trot; a pace well-suited for long-distance travel. Just before noon, their vector crossed with a stream and she had the men slowly water their horses and refresh themselves.

As the men and horses rested, Lord Darshel and Zyanthena talked. "The men are losing faith. With Raic gone..." Lord Shekmann slapped his hand with his riding gloves, frustrated. "We don't have any of our provisions nor our extra horses, both probably being fought over right now." Zyanthena did not comment. She knew the horses would either be slaughtered or left to wander by the maunstorz; the first point a distressing pain to her heart, the latter not so much. Lord Darshel did not need to know any of it. "What am I to say to them now? They've followed me foolhardily to their deaths."

"They followed out of loyalty."

"Well, they shouldn't have!" Darshel growled back. Zyanthena stayed calm. The Shekmann stopped his angry pacing. The look he gave the desert woman was a mix of surliness and despondency. "What am I to do?!"

"The "great" Shekmann can't surely be at a loss." The returned snarl alerted the Tashek that she had pushed heartlessly. The man had really felt at wits end. "Nothing is hopeless, My Lordship. Not yet," she softened.

"I took my men beyond my kingdom's borders and now most certainly beyond Rubia's. I never should have."

"Your convictions were not wrong."

"My convictions," he muttered, not yet soothed.

"I thought them admirable, beyond reproof." The statement brought Lord Darshel's gaze back to the Tashek. He seemed genuinely surprised. She continued, "You were willing to risk your life and your men's' lives in aide of farmers and peasants and townspeople you don't even know. That I find remarkable. So, no, I do not think these men judge you for your choice, but they do look to you to lead them."

"And therein lies the problem. I don't know these lands."

Zyanthena paused, considering, then said, "You were right, My Lordship. We are beyond Rubia now. We are entering the Forbidding Forests of Crystalynian, where it is rumored many beasts of unusual, colossal size reside. The woods are haunted so they say, whomever "they" are." She shrugged. "But, to me, this forest seems healthy, unruined by human hand for a quarter of a century. The wilds have consumed any of the remnants of the old kingdom."

"And none of what you just said consoles me."

Zyanthena chuckled. "I thought I was the one with the "smart" tongue."

The Shekmann's features softened. "Two can play that game."

"Indeed. Well, Lord Shekmann, you don't look so helpless now. Are you ready to tackle the wilds?"

"As long as you know where you are going."

"North and east, My Lordship, north and east. As long as we do not encounter more maunstorz, I plan to head for Wynward's Crossing."

"North and east it is then."

§   §

Before they left the stream, Zyanthena had all the injured men and horses cared for. Three of the horses were fairly lame; two were stone-bruised from the long trek; a third had a large gash on its hind leg. Zyanthena showed the cavalrymen a shoeing technique that took pressure off of the bruised areas on the hooves that relieved most of the horses' discomfort. She stitched the third horse's leg herself. Despite her skilled work, however, Zyanthena warned that the horses might not be able to make the distance they had yet to travel.

As for the men, the Kavahadian cavalry was down to eighty-eight me. Forty-three of them were wounded. The group did their best to patch up the injured and clean off the blood, but some of the cases looked poor. If twelve of the men didn't get gangrene before they reached Wynward's Zyanthena would be pleasantly surprised. "That is the last of them," she announced to Lord Darshel, as she woke him from a nap she had insisted he take. "We should be going now."

§   §

The cavalry continued at a trotting-pace until the first touches of dusk. Zyanthena slowed the horses to a walk as she kept a lookout for a place to rest. The part of the forest they travelled through was wooded in high-mountain pines that smelled of vanilla and evergreen. Small clumps of aspen trees, their leaves turning golden-orange and burnt red, dotted the small drainages between the hillocks. A short way ahead, Zyanthena thought she heard a river flowing. She let Unrevealed direct the way, knowing the horse would be drawn to the water. Behind her, the cavalrymen followed, whispering about the alien landscape around them. Zyanthena smiled at their awe; for, indeed, the Forbidding Forest was a sight after the Aras Desert.

Unrevealed did not fail to lead them to water. Though the water-source turned out to only be a small stream, Zyanthena was grateful to find water for the tired men and horses. She called a halt and let the men dismount, stretch, and drink before reminding them to set a camp. Then, leaving Unrevealed with Tano, the desert woman padded away in search of food.

A make-shift camp was fully created by the time she returned. The men had not been idle in her absence. Horses had been brushed down with grass and beds had been created out of the saddle blankets, brush, and pine needles around the stream. The injured were already asleep, while other men were set to watch; another group had gathered twigs and kindling in case a fire could be tempted.

Zyanthena brought what she found to the area with firewood. Some of the men gathered around to see what she had collected. "I will need a small fire for some of these." Zyanthena suggested as she opened up the cloth to show them. Unwrapping a second, she revealed four squirrels and one rabbit she had managed to kill. As expected, the men were excited at her bounty. "Nick, we will need a small fire and water. You can use the leather pouch from my bag to heat the water in. The rest of you can help me prepare." She separated out plants she had collected into piles and pointed to each. "We can make an herb salad with these: porcini mushrooms, dandelions, wild garlic, and lettuce, even the goat beard and onions. The chickweed, too, if anyone cared to try it. I found some raspberries and gooseberries. Unfortunately, the pin cherries seemed unripe yet and the strawberries were too small to feed everyone. As for the rest, I want to make a tea from the aspen bark and yarrow. The rose hips can be added, too; though, hulled they don't taste bad." She paused and looked at all she had brought then looked around at the men. "It won't seem like much of a meal but it's all I could gather. Maybe tomorrow we will be able to run down a deer or something."

The men were too relieved to have any meal—and some even guilty that they hadn't thought to contribute—that they all expressed their gratefulness. They set to work preparing the meager meal, letting Zyanthena rest near the fire as they worked.

"Wow, I never would have guessed you could forage so well." Lord Darshel commented as he came to sit beside the Tashek.

"I've had to once or twice within the last few years. Matar was gracious enough to teach me which plants to look for. The knowledge beats starving to death when food it to be had."

"That's about right." Darshel nibbled on a rose hip, not finding the tart taste unpleasant. "Still, it's good to have someone who knows what is safe to eat in the company. I'll have my men ration out their jerky and hard tack to help fill everyone's stomachs."

The desert woman nodded and sat back on her hands, lifting her head to the last rays of the evening sun. She seemed to be enjoying the stillness of the wild forest. Soon, though, she shifted. Her mind was too occupied on keeping Kavahad's men alive to dally long. "We will need to seek out an animal carcass tomorrow, or let some flies land of a piece of meat."

"Why?" Darshel asked.

"I need to collect maggots." The Starian lord wrinkled his nose. "There are a number of men with severe wounds. The maggots will eat the festering flesh and keep them alive better than any herbs I can collect. With us on the run and so far away from a doctor, that is the only way I know to keep these men from dying."

Darshel sobered. "If it's the only way, I will make sure we find some. Thank you for caring so much for my men."

"Trust me, My Lordship, I am doing what I can. I have seen too many gruesome deaths. I would do anything within my abilities to prevent seeing another man go through such again..." A distant memory had her shivering slightly. "There are worse things than seeing men getting hacked up on the field."

Lord Darshel was about to comment on the desert woman's statement when one of his soldiers came over to them with some greens and meat for their meager dinner. The interruption put an end to where their conversation had steered, leaving them quiet as they ate their suppers. The food was consumed in short order; however, it did ease the hunger pangs in their bellies. Lord Darshel finished his last raspberry with a relieved sigh. "It's my turn to insist you sleep, Zy'ena. I know you've been up for nearly forty-eight hours."

To his surprise, the Tashek did not argue. "Very well, My Lordship. Wake me if you become concerned of anything—even if it seems minor." She stifled a yawn, her body relieved that she would finally let it rest. "I do not want you to be up the whole night, either. Wake me for my shift." She barely acknowledged the Shekmann's nod before she slipped away to lay at Unrevealed's feet. The Tashek was asleep by the time her head hit her pillow of soft stream grasses.

§   §

The next day found the Kavahadian cavalry following a course through a steep gorge dug out by spring snow melts. The way became tricky, and there were few places large enough to go more than two horses abreast. Yet, Zyanthena was not ready to force the horses to turn around, the time lost would allow their pursuers to corner them again.

The gorge finally opened up into a larger canyon surrounded by straggly pinon trees. Evidence of a creek, dried up by mid-summer, dogged their way down the wash. Some estranged cottonwoods dotted the trailside like haunted skeletons of a wetter time. The desert woman took the signs of trees and creek bed as a hope of lusher ground farther ahead. The Tashek veered them northward toward what she believed was the mouth of the canyon. The way opened up three clickes later into a long, flat valley. Mountains slowly rose above the hills that ringed the green pastureland. The untouched, lush plain looked quite inviting to the cavalry. It was a stark contrast to the dry canyon they left behind.

The warrioress edged them out into the open land cautiously, her sharp eyes to the hills surrounding them; however, no danger showed itself as they passed through. Relieved, the Tashek allowed the soldiers to rest their mounts in the shade of some pine trees on the other side, beside a tiny trickling creek. She dismounted from Unrevealed and stretched her aching body, finding the ground unstable after hours on horseback.

The Cavalrymen all seemed as relieved as the desert woman to have a respite from the saddle. They groaned and limped around the horses as they slowly pulled the injured from their mounts and sat to eat a meager lunch of hard tack and jerky. Some fell quickly to sleep, taking advantage of a nap on solid ground.

One of the men, Lieutenant Dawson, sidled over to Zyanthena as the other men settled into their lunches and naps. The young lad had been shy with the Tashek until then and the warrioress sensed he wouldn't have come over for just a simple reason; the lad must have something he felt was important enough to say to come over despite his leeriness of her. She greeted the lieutenant kindly and encouraged him to meet her eyes with a soft smile. Lieutenant Dawson gulped nervously but finally came up beside her as she eased herself into a relaxed seat by the creek.

"Are you doing all right, Lieutenant?"

A hurried nod then the lad spoke. "Ye—yes, ma'am. A little saddle-sore but good besides, ma'am."

"Me, too." She admitted. Her words seemed to surprise the man. Zyanthena took out a few pieces of Tashek sausage and offered the lieutenant some as she ate her portion. Then, the desert woman let the silence take over, biding her time for the young man to find his courage to speak his mind. As always, her brandy eyes were evaluating the company and the surrounding landscape, missing little about the men or wilderness and always calculating each condition; however, Zyanthena kept her vigil casual, not wanting to spook the lieutenant by any unusual Tashek mannerisms.

Dawson shifted before he spoke. "Ah...Ms." He cleared his throat. "Lady Sheev'arid."

"Just Zy'ena, please."

"Zy'ena," he repeated. "I—we actually—wanted to ask something of you." His eyes darted across the company to Lord Darshel, as if anxious that the governor would yell at him for speaking with her.

The Tashek signaled Unrevealed to move around herself and the lieutenant to partially block the view. "Yes, Lieutenant. You have no need to worry about speaking your mind with me. I appreciate your candor."

He chuckled nervously but was quick to sober. He licked his lips. "Well I [the cavalry] want you to promise us all something, if things go ill." The Tashek rose her eyebrows but allowed the lad to go on. "We...want you to rescue Lord Shekmann at all costs if the enemy is upon us again. We all agree that we would risk our lives to get him to safety and know you would do all you could to get His Lordship out of danger. Please," he turned and grasped her hand startling her with his desperation, "Please, promise us that you will make sure His Lordship is saved when it comes to it. His Lordship would not leave us willingly, but we know you could make him go. Please, say you will!"

Zyanthena blinked, stunned at the request but also finding the reasoning sound. She, too, looked to Lord Darshel and knew the truth of the matter. Indeed, Lord Shekmann would not leave his men easily; his soldiers knew him well. "Lieutenant Dawson," she returned her eyes to the cavalryman, "I will do this but—," she gave him a stern look, "Only as a last resort. I will not leave you to be slaughtered willingly either—not if I have a choice. You understand this?"

Dawson nodded and gulped again. Zyanthena realized the youth was scared to death but putting on a strong front. She touched him gently, in an uncharacteristic display of sympathy. "I promise you, Lieutenant, I am doing all I can to make sure you all survive this; I am far from thinking our situation hopeless. Do not lose your faith yet."

Chapter Forty-Six

§

Captured

"Highness, the first group had reported reaching Paragon Oasis. There was no sign of the enemy." One of All'ani Cum'ar's scouts reported to Prince Al'den.

The Starian let go the breath he had been holding since Princess Éleen's group had left the Citadel's safe walls. "Very good news. Thank you, Tem'id." He accepted the scroll the desert man offered him from the falcon. "And the second group?"

"No word yet, Highness. But the third had also reported safe passage."

Al'den nodded and waved the man away. The worry in his gut eased some. With the Stars' help, all the groups having left the Citadel of Light would be spared any hardships. Though his mind was mainly on Éleen's procession, the Sunrise royals were among group two, and the Sealanders among the last group. Politically, interests rested with all the people reaching their destinations safely. Silently, Al'den sent up a plea to the Stars for their protection, then he directed himself to more pressing matters; those he could deal with.

Dusk came to group two. Wearied townsfolk set down their burdens to ready a camp for sleep. Amidst the people, a tent of royal scarlet was set up for the Sunarian princes. The Sunarian escort surrounded the pavilion and scared the Starians from coming near. The silent, threatening men did little to help the other Syreans. Worse, it made the accompanying Tashek bristle.

"Brother, you could have your men stand more at ease. It does us ill to vex those we travel with." Rowin said as he sat at the small table of his brother's, filled with dinner plates.

Connel snorted as he lifted a grape to his mouth and bit down. "Seriously, leave off, Rowin. I've no intention of giving these people much more than the honor of travelling in my procession, and what with those dark-haired and slanted eyed warriors that "escort" us, I will keep my men at ready. I have no trust of their kind."

"The Sheev'anee are more than for show; they are the best defense we have. I would trust them to keep us safe; more than your handful of men can handle. The Tashek have fought the enemy, yours have not. I would urge you to not humiliate yourself to them."

"Humiliate? Please." Connel scoffed. "And play soldier with them, like you? No, I will not stoop to the level of once-a-month baths and living in the stench of days-old-worn armor. I will be free of these people soon enough and back to the more civilized levels of our kingdom."

Rowin rolled his eyes, fully annoyed with his brother. He shared a glance with Rio, who stood just off to his left. He rose his plate to offer his friend and Lord Protector some chicken, not caring that his younger brother did not approve of him sharing his meal with his man. "We are not free of Staria yet, brother. You are unwise to lose your graces so far from home. His Majesty would disapprove."

"Father would feel the same as I," Connel disagreed. "He would urge that we get free of these people immediately. They slow us down."

"Well lucky, then, that it is I who is the elder prince, for I do say we remain civil until such a time that we part ways with Staria." Rowin spoke as he rose from the table. He leaned closer to his brother to emphasize his point then took his glass of wine with him as he turned away. "I'm off to bed, little brother. See you in the morning."

§   §

Screams in the dark, fire, and smoke woke Prince Rowin from his sleep. Across from him, Rio was already standing, sword in hand, ready to investigate the trouble. A much-shaken Sage stumbled through the tent toward his prince with Rowin's armor and weapons in hand. "The camp is being attacked!" Rio informed him hastily. "What little I can make out makes me think it is the enemy."

"Get all the weapons you can. Sage, get to my horse!" Rowin thrust the lad away as he took his weapons in hand. He spared only long enough to put his breastplate on before joining Rio at the tent's flap." Where arc our sentries?" He asked his Lord Protector.

"They ran to defend Connel. They are fucking loyal only to him!"

Rowin cussed and gripped his friend's shoulder. "No matter, we've had worse. If we get through this night, I will remind those men who the real Heir of Sunrise is. Where is Sage with my horse?"

Rio shook his head. "I don't know, Sire."

"Damn it! Let's go outside. I will not cower here waiting for this tent to be burned to the ground."

Outside was a living hell. Most of the tents were burning and too many of the townspeople lay dead. Though there were Sheev'anee who still fought, the Sunarians could see the remainder were outnumbered. Of Sunrise's men, there were none to be found. Rowin waved Rio to follow him toward where the horses were tethered around back from his tent.

As they rounded the corner, they ran into three of the enemy hovering over the bloodied form of young Sage Cooper. The leader, with red-stained-and-tangled, white hair, finished skewering the good lad with his ragged-edged sword. The two on the other side of the Sunarian's corpse, looked up at their movements. Blood-red eyes centered on Prince Rowin and Rio. The leader turned at their excited hisses. "Ah…" he breathed out. He faced them with a twisted smile. "Those are the ones Mansocan requested."

"Fucking bastards," Rio muttered beside Rowin. The Lord Protector had not cared much for the enemy man's words but seeing Sage cut down had his blood boiling. He adjusted his sword and stepped in front of his prince to protect him. "You will stay behind me, Rowin."

"Rio—." Rowin made to protest but his Lord Protector had already advanced on the maunstorzs.

The maunstorz leader perried Rio's first attack and swept the blade aside. He struck out with his fist to catch the Sunarian a glancing blow on the temple and chuckled when Rio fumbled. Rio swung carelessness for three strokes before seeming to find his thoughts. By then, the leader had walked past him toward Rowin. The other maunstorz stepped in to subdue Rio as he tried to leap after the white-haired man. A few punches and one arm twisted back farther than anatomically possible and Rio was forced to the ground.

"You fight like paunch-faced Southern men." The leader taunted as he advanced toward Rowin. "Only you people's machinations make you worth any while."

"Like you know anything about us," Rowin replied back just as jeering. He bid his time as the leader smiled a mouthful of crooked teeth and continued to creep near. "Third in line of Syre, your first king was; hardly a man of aptitude. He knew only of ways to fill his coffers on his people's bread and monies. Most that succeeded him were just like that, as is your court today. Pampered, dollified puppies your "men of prestige" are, lost now without the one king that knew of your histories and had true greatness. Like him you are, Prince Rowin of Sunrise, but not destined to have his throne—at least as far as your usurper desires… your head on a plate, perhaps? But Mansocan had other needs for you."

Rowin faltered, taken aback by the maunstorz words. He almost let the man close ground with him before Rio's cry of warning, quickly silenced, spurred him into action. As the leader reached out to grasp his arm, he yelled out and danced back, striking downward with his sword. His blade, Tengrand "Sword of Kings", was extra sharp and strong. It bit cleanly through the enemy leader's wrist in one swing. Yet, before Rowin had time to finish the maunstorz off and go after Rio's captors, a glancing blow from the butt of a club knocked him unconscious.

The white-haired maunstorz straightened and held his stump to his chest. As he worked a piece of cloth around his wound, he nodded stiffly to his warrior who had snuck around the Sunarian's guard and knocked him out. "Good work. Take these two to the prison cart. I will bring the other princeling soon. We leave none else alive."

§   §

Prince Connel had called all his men to him and had them douse the lighting so only six candles chased the shadows away. The thick, scarlet cloth of his tent kept out the flames consuming the other tents and muted the terrible screams of the massacred people beyond. His ten loyal soldiers and Lord Protector stood in somber silence, swords at ready. He knew they would fight to their deaths to keep him safe.

The screams became less frequent as the battle outside came to a halt. Still, the Sunarian tent lay untouched. The royal guard tensed at the potent possibility that the Sheev'anee had successfully taken care of their attackers. Certainly, Prince Connel desired that to be the case, but he kept himself collected and would not court hope until a loathsome, desert man came to announce their victory.

What came through the tent flap, however, stilled the twenty-year-old's breathe.

A white-haired maunstorz, his red-colored eyes especially shocking against his long mane, signaled with his recently-made, blood-soaked stump to his twenty soldiers that followed after to spread out around the tent. The ragged group of enemy soldiers stood jeering at the small force of Sunarians but waited dutifully for their leader to command them. "I am Chornauk, commander of the third battalion of Mansocan's army." The leader spoke, his common tongue much smoother than most of the maunstorz speech. "You are now my prisoner, young prince."

Connel gulped back his fear and set his jaw. He would never beg to any man (or creature) below him, no matter how dire his circumstances. Slowly, he rose from his chair, as if it was he that commanded the room and not the fearsome enemy spawn. "I am Prince Connel Sunrise, vested heir of the Sunarian Court. You will not harm me or my men or you will suffer retribution from my kingdom. You will allow us safe passage to Sunrise's border. Our kingdom had no quarrel with you; unlike these Starians. We will remain thus as long as you give us no cause. Your great haste in this will not be without reward."

Chornauk was quiet. For a moment, Connel thought the man was going to accede to his authority, but then the leader stirred and the Sunarian realized the maunstorz was laughing at him. The other maunstorz joined in until Chornauk waved them to silence. "You Sunarian princes are so cheeky—and so much alike. Too bad you are not the real heir of Sunrise, young Connel. Your brazenness makes you quite becoming of a Sunarian king. But, alas, young cock-start, I already have your brother. He makes a much better bargaining piece. You're chicken-fodder compared to the First Prince of Sunrise."

Despite his blushing cheeks, Prince Connel would not be cowed. "You may have Rowin, but, to the Sunarian Court, I am the venerated heir to my father's throne. My death will enrage them more than Prince Rowin's capture. Sunrise will retaliate."

Chornauk chortled. "Ah, how little you know young, pampered princeling. Sunrise has already tipped its hand without you. Pity your

King Raymond did not bargain for his two "courageous" princes better. Mansocan will enjoy having you to loom over his pretty, bald head. Men!" He called out and signaled his warriors. "Kill them all," he ordered as he stepped up to Prince Connel. "I have somewhere I need you to be, prince. Mansocan is eagerly awaiting you."

Chapter Forty-Seven

§

Ar'heim

An outrider noticed the haggard group first and sent back a falcon to the Citadel of Light to alert the Mausheliks of the horses. Then, knowing an army on horseback was not the enemy, the Tashek rider had ridden out to meet the one-hundred-and-fifty soldiers.

Prince Al'den and All'ani Cum'ar stood on the eastern parapet as the cavalry approached. The royal worked his jaw. "That's Lord Shekmann's flag but not the number of his cavalry. Damn, something happened!"

"We don't know that for sure, Highness. It is best to not jump to conclusions until we hear His Lordship's account." Yet, Cum'ar was also disturbed by the number of horsemen and the exhausted plod of their mounts.

The Starian prince cast his Tashek companion a doubtful look. "This is one conversation I am not looking forward to. The one bird we received was concerning enough but half the force coming home...no, there is not going to be any good news." He turned to wave a soldier over. "Officer, go inform the barracks of new arrivals. Ready food, baths, and beds." He looked back toward the Kavahadian cavalry. "Stars pray all of them are in one piece."

§ §

It was more alarming to find Lord Shekmann was not with the company, nor were Re'shaird, Aerrisson and Sheev'arid, Zyanthena. Commander Gordon, too, seemed disturbed to find Lord Darshel had not reported back from Rubia. When he asked after His Lordship and received news that no bird had come, Gordon turned aShe and crossed his chest. "Stars preserve us that was eight days passed! His Lordship kept sending birds back with word twice a day. Zyanthena worried that none were getting through when no word came in reply."

"What happened, Commander? Why did you split from Lord Shekmann?" Al'den refrained from putting his hands on the tired man's shoulders and shaking him—it certainly would not be princely and definitely not worth the effort.

"He ordered me to, Highness." The veteran seemed physically pained by the admittance. "I begged him to come back west and finish our patrol but we kept following the trail of smoke from one ransacked town to the next. His Lordship would not turn away when it was obvious where the enemy had gone. He continued into Rubia. There was no sign of the mertinean or else he would have turned 'round."

"And Re'shaird and Sheev'arid?" Cum'ar demanded to know. "What of them. Did they agree to pursuit?"

"Zy'ena did," Gordan replied. "And even I. Commander Raic wanted His Lordship to come back—but, Highness, we knew where the enemy was! We were following their path like a beacon in the night!" His eyes pleaded with Al'den to understand. "So, His Lordship asked me back—more 'cause Raic would never leave him—and so I came. And Aerrisson," he looked to Cum'ar. "Aerrisson volunteered to run to Raven's Den to find reinforcement with Commander Grant. Please tell me you've word from him, at least?" Cum'ar's answering keshic curses were answer enough. "Stars! I knew it was poor to leave him so few men; I felt no good would come of it. Highness, I ask leave to take my men after His Lordship immediately."

Al'den rubbed his hand across his eyes in frustration at the hopelessness of the situation. Worse, he had to say the words he knew he would hate himself for. "Denied, Commander. I will not have you risk the rest of Kavahad's cavalry by going after Lord Shekmann into most certain demise. Until I hear word otherwise, I will not let you go nor send out more men into uncertain circumstances. The enemy may most certainly be east…but none of our birds have made it back. I will not risk men in their stead. Your men will stay here at the Citadel until we know more."

Al'den and Cum'ar left Gordon, then, to finish his meal without their grilling. As they left the barracks, Prince Al'den suddenly let a fist fly at the outer wall and he yelled out his frustration. All'ani Cum'ar stood back, blinking in wonder, and waited for the royal to finish venting, As the anger slowly settled, Al'den straightened his cape and garments and took in a deep breath. "Cum'ar," he said, "We have to find out where those bastards are hiding before we lose more good men."

"Yes, Highness, we do. I will go see what more the Sheev'anee can do."

Al'den nodded and closed his eyes. "That's all I ask. Thank you...friend." The warrior prince knew the desert man was gone before the last word had left his mouth. Alone, he found himself staring at the setting of the sun as another day past with Staria still occupied by maunstorz harriers. In the twilight, the first star, bright Yellow Star (the Teacher of Wisdom) gleamed above him. Still angry, Al'den found himself talking aloud to the Star. "Of all the good you're doing, setting up there cold and uncaring as can be. Why choose me anyway if I can't protect these people? I'm as helpless to them as you are to me sitting silently snug up there. I need your help, damn it!" He waited a breath but all was quiet. Al'den growled in his frustration. "Typical! You ask for piety and send one sandstorm to our aid then sit up there smug at yourself for good work while we suffer down here in your name! I've had enough I say!! You hear me?! I've had enough of sending my people up to you before their time. So, it's your turn or so help me—." He closed his mouth, unwilling to finish the thought. In the deepening twilight, Prince Al'den finally felt his anger drain away to leave him empty and exhausted. He looked up one more time to the star then decided to walk away.

They had left on the morning after the celebration ball, just as the fear of a maunstorz attack had quieted down and the first tally of killed men was brought to the leaders. Sensing the Shi'alam would be distracted, Terrik had called Decond to him and loaded up four horses to take with them on their journey to the Oracle. He didn't bother to speak with anyone, except to be let out of the western gates. Afterward, the only time Terrik paused was when they reached the first, large dune and only long enough for Decond to look back at the Citadel of Light with longing.

After that, Terrik pushed both young man and horses across the desert, heading north-west. He stopped them at small Tashek posts and watering holes along the way. Rest periods lasted only as long as the hottest hours of the day or at the indication from the horses that they needed to catch their breathes. Little concern was shown to Decond despite the fact that the youth was not accustomed to the dry, desert heat or long hours of intense horseback riding.

By the third day, Terrik finally let the horses slow to an even pace and lightened his mood toward Decond. He even shared a bag of mare's milk with his Khapta, infused with energizing herbs, white ginseng, and dates. "This will rehydrate you," he said when the orphan looked skeptically at the offering. Then to try to be more polite, Terrik pointed out the landscape that was slowly turning into craggy bluffs ahead of them. "You see those rock pillars ahead of us? That is the Ar'heim, the holy place of my people. Within the deepest canyons dwell the Seers and most reverent, the Oracle. We will make it there before nightfall."

The Ar'heim slowly grew closer until sharp crags of teeth and chimney shoots could be made out in the grey rock formations. Sparse clumps of grasses, tough and hair-thin began to nestle themselves against the stones fighting for a purchase in the arid landscape. Most was barren; however, at least to the unacquainted eyes of the mountain-born farrier. Unbenounced to him but noticed by Terrik, a few shadowy shapes followed them as the Tashek led the way through the winding canyons.

"Just ahead is the sacrellum." Terrik announced just as the deepest canyon opened up to a large, carved-out bowl. The entire span ran one-thousand-meters around and fifty-meters tall. Across the sacrellum, a deep crevice continued, with a fresh water stream trickling into the bedrock. Two desert guards, dressed all in black, stood at the entrance. "This is where we leave the horses," Terrik instructed his Khapta as he started his dismount. As if his words were a cue, ten other Tashek suddenly descended from caves carved into the tall walls. These men reached for the horses and came to block Terrik's way, speaking to the Sheev'arid in keshic. Decond felt himself cowering behind his Guardian teacher as the men spoke. He felt certain that they were unwelcome in the Sheev'anee's most holy of holiest places. "They say the Oracle is awaiting us, but we must give up all our weapons before we go further—and anything she deems a danger." Decond was quick to unsheathe his battle-ax from his back and the two daggers from his belt and hand them over. He noted Terrik was not so forthright. The main guard standing in front of Terrik said words that sounded harsh. The man reached for the Sheev'arid's pouches to sift through them until he found the one he wanted. The other pouches were tossed roughly back to Terrik as the last of his weapons were confiscated. Neither Terrik nor the guard looked happy with each other. "We go this way," Terrik said to Decond shortly and started off without looking back. Nervously, Decond made his way through the black-robed guards and followed.

The deep crevice was just wide enough for a grown man to walk through without needing to turn sideways. There was barely any foot room, however, on the meager trail trod beside the small stream that ran down its center. More than once, Decond's feet slipped into the water, eliciting a scowl from his teacher. To the youth, the crevice seemed to go on forever. They had certainly been without direct sunlight for a good ten minutes when the long crack finally ended abruptly—into open air. Beyond, the Ar'heim stretched across as far as the eyes could see, into many arroyos and steep mesas. The expanse looked easy to get lost in.

"We climb down." Terrik directed Decond's eyes to a small step carved into the rock to the right of their ledge. The way looked impossible to scale until Terrik took a rope, also inlaid into the stone, in his hands and used it to help balance himself on the shallow stairs. "Come, dusk is upon us. We will lose our sight unless we hurry."

At the bottom, ten robed guards awaited them again. These, at least, seemed more pleased to see Terrik than the first. They greeted both visitors warmly and motioned them to clean themselves in the waterfall they had just climbed down beside. New clothes and fresh drinks were offered, as well. "Ahnamen, En'ril." Terrik thanked the leader. "Decond, this is Savam'eed En'ril, son of Shík Savam'eed, who attends my father as one of his closest Three. He is also my closest cousin, beside Kor'mauk, in the Sheev'anee." Decond was lost with the introduction, besides the words "closest cousin", but he did well in a formal bow of greeting. En'ril laughed and said something to Terrik in keshic, of which Sheev'arid bantered back then returned to Decond in common tongue, "He said you look more like a mountain goat than a desert rat—meaning mountain-born—of which I told him you were from the Crystal Kingdom and an orphan." En'ril spoke some more, looking solemn and gave Decond a half-bow. "He says he is sad to hear of your loss but welcomes you as a brother to our camp."

"Tell him thank you," Decond replied. He bowed to En'ril again. Terrik seemed pleased by how his Khapta spoke to his cousin. He gave his own half-bow to Decond and spoke with En'ril at great length as they rested and refreshed themselves. Then, at nightfall, all of the Tashek stood and torches were lite. "We go now to the Oracle," Terrik told Decond. "She is old and blind but do not stare at her. Here, she is master of Sight and she will know you look."

Decond gulped, unnerved, but followed his teacher as they were led through the maze of rock deep into the Ar'heim.

§   §

They were finally given the word to stop. En'ril motioned them to sit and wait. Young Decond felt himself sink heavily against the cold sandstone wall, the long trip and endless maze of the Ar'heim weighing on him. His eyelids felt so heavy as he fought to keep them open, trying to be as alert as Terrik looked. Yet, time passed in the coolness of the night and still no one else directed them to do anything more.

"Sleep." Terrik broke the silence, startling Decond some. "They are up to their tests of will. You need not try to honor them, tired as you are and unaccustomed to such trials. They will not think less of you." He did not add his thoughts that he, the son of the Shi'alam, would not be treated as kindly if he was to do the same. "I will wake you, come time."

Decond was more than happy to comply. He was breathing heavily almost as soon as Terrik gave the go-ahead. The Tashek was left to his silent envy of his Khapta's innocence; yet, he sat tall as the hours of the night passed by; Terrik suspected he would need to fight his tired body until the light of dawn. Indeed, not long before sunrise, a lone wisp-of-a-seer came out from deeper into the cavern from which entrance they sat. Terrik slowly came to stand in front of the frail girl and prodded Decond awake with the toe of his boot.

The girl bowed to them both and spoke in a high, quiet voice, "Welcome Sheev'arid, Terrik and Khapta Decond. The Great Seer calls you to her now. Come, follow." She turned around and headed back into the bowels of the cave, unhindered by the scant lighting. She didn't look back to see if her charges followed.

"Awake with you," Terrik murmured to Decond as he helped the stumbling youth through the darkened and uneven cavern. "They need no light here, so it is we who must adjust. Keep close with me and do not speak unless spoken to…"

Decond felt the flutters of nervousness again in his stomach and he choked it back, trying to wet his suddenly dry throat. His deepest apprehension was seeing the revered Oracle—and for her to find him somehow lacking. Terrik squeezed his forearm and the youth focused his attention forward.

The girl led them into the largest cavern of the Ar'heim. Its wide depths stretched into the dark beyond sight. The robed guards and eight seers were present around the room that glowed softly in orange-red light from burning oil lamps. They were all chanting in keshic softly as the young wisp-seer led the two guests through their ranks toward a raised section of floor, where the Oracle sat amidst a bundle of horse-hide blankets. The girl stepped below the rise and sat down, not giving Terrik or Decond any indication if they should do the same.

"Sheev'arid's-son." The old woman's voice rasped out and the huddled form of the Oracle shifted. She lifted a clawed and deformed hand toward Terrik. "Incestuous, undutiful, addict, unfit for hegemony." She stated without preamble, throwing out insults to the Tashek—and yet expecting him to take hold of her offered hand. Terrik stiffened at the words but still reached out to accept the fragile limb. For a brief moment, he relished the thought of breaking the bird-thin bones of her fingers but common-sense stayed his hand. He quickly released the Oracle's limb back to her and backed away; Terrik had learned long ago, he did best if he didn't argue with the old bag-of-bones or throw out his own insults. At least, he got to leave her sooner if he behaved.

If the Oracle had expected her words to infuriate Terrik to the point of a scandalous outburst, she was sorely disappointed. She frowned and her head turned toward Decond. Burned-out holes where her eyes had once been focused on the Crystal farrier. "Orphan, seeker, all-hearted, misplaced. You are Decond, now Khapta to Sheev'arid. I call you now foreordained, destined to follow the inner circles of all that is to be. You are reborn." Decond felt himself shaking, his eyes locked on her stark blindness. Somehow, he seemed to be pulled into those hollows as if by majik. He swayed and Terrik had to catch hold of him. "He is the One, Sheev'arid Terrik. The One you will need for the quest we have told you would be before you. Your Khapta is innocent-born. He will be able to bear Sevén without corrupting it and use it to find the last of the stones— until such a time as Sevén finds it rightful wielder." A small, round object flashed into the Oracle's hands and the pearl gleamed, as if happy with the choice. "But you will stay and learn until both are ready for this undertaking. We will speak of this again." Her tone sounded dismissive and yet Terrik did not move to leave. Decond glanced at him, looking for a cue to follow. The old crone had shifted backwards into her blankets and lifted a hollowed-out horse hoof with shaking hands. Smoke rose from the hollow in pungent waves of a substance very sweet and thick. She began chanting in a haggard keshic, her aged vocal cords raspy and thin. The others soon followed the song, even Terrik obediently joining the chorus. The Oracle waved the smoke over herself with a horse-haired switch. Then, with the help of two seers, she rose to her feet and tottered to the edge of her rise to waft the smoke at Terrik and Decond. She said words as she proceeded passed the two men to bath the others in the cleansing smoke.

"She said, "may no spirits not welcome here cling to you'." Terrik translated in a whisper to his Khapta. "She also said "may you find comfort here in your new life [among us]." The smoke chases away "spirits" attached to you that you may have brought here. Is she offers you any powders or herbs accept them. Never argue the choices of the Oracle."

The whole event seemed scary and sacrilegious to Decond who considered himself devout Estarian. He huddled in on himself as if he could will himself to disappear and hide himself from the Stars' wrath. He felt Terrik eyeing him—and perhaps the others too—and sweat beaded on his brow. The Oracle returned to the dais and loomed over him once more. She spoke in keshic then in common tongue. "Young Decond, you will be first to bear a Crystal of the Prism, an honor above all the wielders. Do not cower so at the privilege. You are held most high in the great Stars' eyes. They favor you. Sheev'arid's-son, you will take up Their righteous task of teaching him of the Guardianship—and you will cast down your envy. Your people, Syre's people, need this task done or all will perish in the shadows of our enemies. Savam'eed and his Khapta will help train you both for the Trials you will meet. Sevén requires a steady companion, quiet and thoughtful. Decond must become so. You have forty days to make him so."

"Forty days?!" Terrik objected, out of turn. "Even forty years would not make it so. There is too much of our ways he does not know."

"Then you best get started." The Oracle seemed to gaze at Terrik in disapproval. "We are done. Go, train! Time is always pressing and Syre cannot wait for fools."

Chapter Forty-Eight

§

Lure

Day eleven of their harried march came wet and despairing. Eighteen of the wounded men had died in the night; their fight with gangrene, exhaustion, and starvation exacting its toll. Two of the horses had to be put down, as well, though the promise of food helped to sustain the men—all but Zyanthena, who refused to eat the meat. She let twelve of the horses go to wander free, using the task to not think of the men butchering the wounded mounts or burying the soldiers.

Lord Darshel found her still watching the last of the loosened horses wander away. "For all your practicality, I am surprised you will not eat the food the horses will provide us." He offered her a watered-down version of coffee, the last of their stores.

"It is of our people," she said as she took the offered drink. "Horses are our wealth and power. Without, we become nothing. It would take worse than this for a Tashek to kill a horse, and we are not there yet."

"The men lose hope—hell, even the will to survive—entailed to get us to safety. You see that, I know you do."

Zyanthena brushed damp strands of hair from her face and stared off at the distance, as if the wild mountain terrain held more interest than the remaining seventy cavalrymen. Lord Darshel bit his lip in annoyance but held his tongue as the desert woman kept her gaze to the forest. "They do not believe they will survive long enough to make Wynward's Crossing," she admitted her voice low. Darshel looked startled. "With how the men fare, even I doubt more than a handful will. It is Harvest-Gathering Time and foods grow plentiful enough for me to sustain them for them to not die of starvation. But more men are sick and more horses fail." She paused and added other thoughts. "None have been this far north, at least in my time, so my estimation of our distance to Wynward's is scant guesses at best." Her sharp eyes turned to the Kavahadian lord. "And your men are people of the desert, unused to such cold and unpredictable weather. They fare ill from multiple stressors. Yes, My Lordship, I dare say that *now*

I worry. Would you have me risk leading them back south? I would if you asked. The lands I know better but so do our pursuers."

The Shekmann looked thoughtful, his emerald eyes reflecting intelligence and tact. The leader had all the skills to survive and knowledge of how best to deal with enemies, so Zyanthena knew his answer would have been weighed for days already past. She knew the words before he spoke. "South. I would have us start to go back south. I will collect the men. And Zy'ena," he turned back to her on a second thought, "Do not show them you worry. Only you have gotten them this far."

She nodded dutifully and watched the lord-governor walk away. Alone, she spoke her mind. "I will do as asked, Your Lordship, but there is worry in my heart. I fear I am leading you and your men to doom…" Zyanthena gazed southward. A nagging feeling clenched her chest in doubt. Was it just the rains and the deaths that had her so apprehensive that morning or did she sense something her eyes had yet to see? The Forbidding Mountains stretched large and dark in the south. They were still veiled in smoke rings of low-hanging clouds. The scene seemed ominous that morning, whereas previous days it had seemed an untouched sanctuary.

A warm nose touched the back of her neck and velvety lips wiggled against her skin. Zyanthena raided her hand to Unrevealed's cheek at his playful comfort. "I worry too much of what could lay ahead, do I not, my friend? And yet, I have gotten us this far. You think we will make it through to the end?" He black stallion sighed and shifted away to nibble on grasses still wet with dew. She huffed at his reply, so uncaring of the future and concerned with breakfast and comfort. "What a war horse you are," she teased and stepped closer to swing up onto his back. "And so practical. Come on, then, let's get these men back to civilization."

§   §

Their chosen path took them directly into the downpour headed southeast. The fall rains were biting cold and soaked though the men's tattered clothing in minutes. After the half-an-hour dump, an eerie mist descended into the trees making visibility difficult. Wearied soldiers huddled into their sodden coats and fretted. The Tashek woman felt the distress of the men behind her but willed herself to keep up appearances. She led them southward as straight as she could, but the new rains made the clay of the foothills slick and dangerous. Multiple times Zyanthena had to tell the cavalry to stop as she went ahead to find different approaches though the steep gorges. By noon, they had only made six clicks.

"Stop here," Lord Darshel commanded as they were given a small break in the trees. "Rest the horses. Zy'ena a word, please." The cavalrymen gratefully obliged being allowed a rest from horseback; the desert warrioress did not look so pleased. "Zyen, have you been leading us in circles? I see the same landmarks as we've had one hour ago."

Zyanthena scowled at his poor remark. "You wish to lead, Your Lordship?" She quipped back; her temper as short as everyone's because of the trials. "Or do you think I am not trying hard enough? I could certainly pick up the pace if you would like to lose more horses to the footing."

The Kavahadian lord worked his jaw and had to remind himself to not lash out with his temper. He knew that if Zyanthena saw him respond more thoughtfully, she would do the same. "No, I do not think any of that. But we are going in circles?" Her sharp eyes averted—he had caught her hiding some truth. "What is it, Zyen? What have you seen that you tarry so?"

His change of wording had the desert woman in a more cooperative mood. "I have seen evidence of the enemy, My Lordship. Twice, in fact. They have camped here no more than three days ago but I am uncertain which direction they took. They could be down any number of these drainages. With the rains, evidence of their passage had been ruined. Ours will not be."

Lord Darshel frowned. "And you kept this from me."

"Have you—we not had enough to deal with? We already knew they were pursuing us, just not how close. From here southward it's going to be a tedious balance of stealth and speed."

Darshel turned away to kick at the earth and pace. Exhaustion etched itself on his face before he could wipe it away. "You're feeling like this is it? They have found us?"

"That I cannot tell you, My Lordsh—."

"Darshel, please. We have been through enough together."

She persed her lips and conceded. "Lord Darshel. But I am surprised we have evaded them thus far. The maunstorz have gotten closer than I had suspected; however, even I am having trouble maintaining vigilance after little sleep and food," she admitted.

"Are you doubting we can make Wynward's?"

"The enemy is all to our south. Seventy-two men and horses are not going to be easy to hide anymore."

"What are you suggesting?"

"I am not suggesting anything!" Zyanthena replied curtly, exasperation clouding her words. "There's few options open to me. I say you ask your men their advice. They had shown how loyal they are to you. Now, give them your respect and ask them how they want to make their end."

Her declaration seemed to startle them both, for they ended up just staring at each other in silence instead of escalating to a yelling match. Slowly, Lord Darshel began to nod. "Very well, Zyanthena," he replied coolly. "We will ask them." His body language made it very clear that the Tashek woman had crossed a line neither of them had known was there—until that moment. Too long they had spoken frankly with each other, letting the walls that defined their positions down until they had forgotten they were there at all. But just then, Lord Darshel remembered. "*I will* tell them what you suspect is out there waiting for us, but *it is you* who will be honest of their chances."

Zyanthena nodded, conceding.

They returned to the men. The wearied soldiers tried to stand in respect for their lord but Darshel asked them back to their seats and gathered the cavalry around him—minus the four men on watch. The Shekmann took a moment to gather his thoughts as he assessed the huddled and bedraggled forms of his cavalry. Finally, he spoke, "Zy'ena had marked two occasions now of recent passage of our pursuers; however, the rains have washed out their trail. She does not believe we will be as lucky with the mud." He turned to point at the forest and mountainous terrain to the south. "From here onward, we will be within the territory the maunstorz know. The enemy numbers are unknown; we could run across a scouting party or a whole troupe." He motioned for Zyanthena to continue.

The men looked to the Tashek with the same amount of respect on their faces as they had shown their leader. The warrioress seemed to take pause at their belief in her. Zyanthena shifted on her feet, a wild and nervous reaction to the attention, and fingered her kora sword. "You have followed me across the lands of Rubia and far beyond the borders of your homelands. You have taken your lord's case of saving innocents from the wrath of our enemy to heart and come farther than any good man would have been expected to come. He—," she looked to Lord Darshel, "We—know that you have followed out of loyalty and duty this entire way with no questioning of what you may lose. Your courage and strength is well noted, but now...now we ask what it is you men would desire from us to do from this point." The men shifted around, surprised at her wording and request. Zyanthena forged on. "Perhaps our asking comes too late, but I would hear what you have to say. Yes, I have seen signs of the enemy, and I am unconfident from here where we can descend safely into the valley below." She shifted, uneasy, and added the last, an admittance of her own mistake in their predicament. "It was my fault that I led us too quickly toward Carmine and realized too late, the danger I had led you into. I should have kept your cavalry at a safer distance and realized the ambush sooner. I—."

"You did no such thing!" An older cavalryman spoke out of turn. He rose from his seat. "We are seasoned men, having seem more wars than I am sure you yourself have." Zyanthena did not argue the man's truth; he was correct. "I know what information you kept from us." He pulled a horseshoe from his jacket and held it aloft. "You understood how odd this shoe was; it being found in the ruins around Sackett. Maunstorz do not ride horses, so there was another force that had helped sack the town, a Syrean army." The horseman blushed at the admittance. "Forgive me, Ms. Zy'ena, I saw the shoe flash when you tossed it."

Lord Darshel stepped over and took the shoe from his soldier. "Yes, this is the ill news that had us turning north." He fingered the metal horseshoe that had changed their course and fate. "So, you all understand then?" Many of the men nodded. "Then you know, too, that if the maunstorz were in league with a kingdom of Syre that their pursuit of our cavalry may be two-fold. We could have stumbled upon them learning new tactics from their new association or maybe unearthed a coup not yet sprung. Either way we have been hunted…it is the later news troubles me. Perhaps only we know of these new developments."

"We must get word to Wynward's and back to the Citadel."

"Yes, we must," Darshel agreed with his man, "But we are already taxed beyond our means and out in the middle of nowhere. We will be unable to adequately hide from the enemy with our numbers, if we do continue south. Only having stayed as north as Zy'ena has taken us has helped to hide us from them this long."

"Then we have to travel in smaller groups." Young Lieutenant Dawson suggested. "For is it not paramount that at least one man makes it back to the King or the Crystine?" Others nodded at the soundness of the young man's reasoning.

Lord Darshel closed his eyes, saddened that their situation had come down to such a dire idea. Yet, he knew it would be an action Zyanthena would support. He glanced to his right at his wild companion. She was looking back at him, waiting for the Shekmann to take the lead. "Yes, I do fear and believe that is our best option. Groups of four to ten will travel more lightly through the forest than one of seventy."

The men stood and organized themselves immediately, unbidden, but with the training and understanding of seasoned soldiers. They saluted and spoke their readiness to their lord-governor. Lord Darshel still stood where they had begun talking, as if shell-shocked that his men would move so quickly to act (of course, he had had less time in the field of late as he had had with his advisors—men slow to act and long to argue). A touch of Zyanthena's hand on his forearm reminded him to respond. "Right…well, our main goal should be to reach Wynward's Crossing, south and east of here."

Six of the groups raised their hands and voiced that they would continue to head for that destination. Each would take a different drainage and following the landmarks Zyanthena provided them to mark their direction. The last three groups volunteered to risk the longer trek back west, toward Raven's Den or the East Bridge. None of the soldiers would let Lord Darshel continue east to the Crystal Kingdom, saying, "there is a whole city back home needing you". They also would not let Zyanthena leave their lord's side. If anyone was to get the Shekmann back to Staria alive, it would be her. The cavalry's executive decision was made up without Lord Darshel's or Zyanthena's say-so.

Disturbed by the change of events, Darshel found himself without much ordering to do. His cavalrymen were quick to settle up on saddlebags and sort out food, all without him. With final handshakes and back-slaps good-bye, the different groups gathered up and headed their separate ways. In the end, Lord Shekmann was left with his handful of soldiers and his desert woman alone in the Forbidding Forest. The sudden quiet and solitude was deafening.

"What just happened?" He asked himself.

"It seems your men have taken matters into their own hands. You really ought to commend them and reward their efforts well, if any return to Kavahad." Zyanthena handed the Shekmann Tano's reins. "I, for one, will never question their abilities after this. It may have taken me a long road to get to this point, but I do believe I respect your cavalrymen at the upmost."

"Yeah," Darshel chuckled softly. "I have seen a different side to them, too." He sobered, then. "I am not the kind of leader my father was. He could have kept this cavalry together, all the way to the end."

"And killed off all his loyal men in the process," the Tashek countered. "Even my people would not rush headlong into the situation to our south. They would try covert groups, too."

"I am a Shekmann and my men Kavahadian, not Tashek. This strategy is deemed cowardly by my people."

Zyanthena huffed. "I do not seeing your men saying that. They may not live to see their families again, but even they believed that more of them would survive travelling that way. Most certainly, they will not be found as easily, which is more than I can say for us if we do not leave soon."

"Your subtle way of making me move my ass?"

"Hey, especially a lord-governor needs his dignity caressed. You still have five of us to command as you will—and only I will be bold enough to counter you on our way home."

"Home. Now, I like the sound of that." Darshel put his foot in Tano's stirrup and hoisted himself aloft. "And more time through these Stars-forsaken woods...I'm really looking forward to this."

Zyanthena gave a soft chuckle and let the Starian cue his horse to the lead. She waited for the five men to start their trek back the way she had just led them before turning away. She pulled out a flint and stone from a pouch and started them against a small handful of leaves and twigs she had kept dry for the purpose. A small flame licked out, quickly eating the offered food stuffs. Hurriedly, Zyanthena stoked the small fire, making sure it would send a smoke trail into the air—a diversion for the maunstorz to follow leading away from the men heading south. The deed done, the desert woman swung atop Unrevealed's back and cantered to catch up. Her return was barely noted, the men used to her comings-and-goings. She nodded to Lord Darshel in greeting and fell into line at the back, content to let the Shekmann follow their tracks northward.

Behind them, the smoke began to rise skyward.

§   §

"Some dinner, Your Lordship?" Zyanthena offered, coming up beside Darshel with a small bowl of watery stew made of rabbit meat and wild onions. The Kavahadian accepted the meager meal tiredly and sipped of the warm broth.

"How do you think they fare?" He asked, looking to the south.

"As fair as us, I suspect, and getting closer to their destination every hour." She stayed somewhat curt in her reply as she watched him for a change that said he was not angry at her any longer.

"You're not one to think about others much are you?"

He was still mad. "I am not selfish, Your Lordship, I just do not waste my energy thinking of other's situations when mine requires such attentions. You do enough for both of us."

Lord Darshel snickered at the remark. "Indeed." He finished the rest of his stew in silence, the weight of their earlier disagreeance making it harder for him to be overly-cordial with the Tashek.

Zyanthena, astute as always, shifted off of her heels to stand. "I will take first watch while you all sleep. There will be a full moon tonight. We should try to make some headway once it rises." She turned away without waiting for the Shekmann's reply.

Darshel watched her retreating back then caught himself staring and turned away sullenly, resolved to not let his thoughts run around with his annoyance at the woman's commanding and awe-catching demeanor. He shrugged deeper into his coat and rolled into a tight ball, letting the warm soup in his belly persuade his body it was good and ready for sleep. Soon, his heavy eyelids closed and he fell into a dreamless slumber.

Zyanthena sat on Unrevealed as she kept watch over the tired men. She used her horse's body-heat to keep her warm as the night deepened. The tall black dozed beneath her; his breath sending out small puffs into the moonlit night. Despite her own fatigued body, the calm moment with her horse alone, in the woods, kept Zyanthena awake and content—enough so that she did not bother any of the men awake to take spot.

A wolf's howl, quite close, startled Unrevealed and the men awake. Zy'ena soothed her horse and kept her eyes to the darkened forest in the direction of the sound. The five Kavahadian men leapt to their feet, unnerved by the wild creature. They collected their things in a rush and quickly mounted their horses, feeling a little safer off of the ground. Another howl answered farther away. "They are hunting," Zyanthena stated as the men gathered around. She could see the fear in their faces, though all kept up a strong front. "They will find easier pray than us; though, only if we do not let the horses run... Seeing as we are all awake, let's get some more road behind us. Keep your eyes open. I will lead." Not one of the men argued.

The going was well lit now that they were in the subalpine forests of Crystalynian. Pine needles blanketed the ground, making the passage soft on the overworked horses' feet. The night was alive with the chirp of cicadas and crickets and the calls of night creatures. The occasional howl of the wolves kept the trespassers on their guard.

"It sounds like they are dogging us," Officer Orin muttered.

"They're hungry, man, just like we are." Another officer, Aaron, replied. "I'll bet we look mighty tasty right about now."

The third cavalryman glanced about nervously. "Oh, keep it quiet! I don't want them to get any ideas."

"They don't understand what we say," Aaron said. "Though if they did, I'd tell them you have the most meat on ya."

"Hey!" Officer Cade retorted. "I do not!" Just as he spoke, another howl, this one sounding just yards away, called again. "Shit! They are right here!"

"Keep it down, men!" Lord Darshel ordered them. "And keep the horses clumped. Zyanthena?"

"We can stop, Your Lordship." The Tashek turned her stallion back to the group. "Keep your weapons out and do not let the horses flee. The wolves won't attack a group of prey that doesn't run. They prefer fleeing prey, so that they can cull out sick, old, or slow animals."

"Sure they do." Officer Cade didn't agree but he huddled atop his sorrel mount with his weapons gleaming in the moonlight.

The six of them waited in the lightened dark, their eyes cast about for moving shadows. Two shapes moved then a third, this one larger than the rest. Two of the officers cursed at the close proximity of the large predators. "Keep the horses together!" Zyanthena ordered as she turned Unrevealed to face the large grey wolf that stalked toward the group. Her black stallion snorted a warning and pawed the earth, rearing some to slash the air with his hooves. His warning made the wolf pause. "Remember, do not let them run. These wolves are trying to bait them." It was easier said than done, what with the other two pack members pacing around the horses, but the men held the small bunch together.

"This is madness!" Officer Orin repeated under his breath.

"Keep it steady," Lord Darshel said in response. He waved his sword threateningly and held Tano in. He locked his eyes on the smaller black wolf that eyed his mount and gave a gruff shout at it, intimidating it to step away.

"Three is not a pack. If we get them to back off, they will join the rest in search of easier prey."

"So says the Tashek," Darshel replied to her remark. For a second, they shared a frown at one another before they returned their attentions to the predators. Lord Darshel yelled again. This time his men joined in, feeling more empowered by the sounds of their voices. The wolves skittered back to pace behind a stand of trees.

The lead grey wolf still stood eyeing Unrevealed. His large eyes glowed slightly in the reflective moonlight. A vast intelligence marked his eyes; this wolf had to be an alpha. Zyanthena stared back, willing herself to be strong; strong enough to convince the leader she was just as capable as it. The grey blinked his eyes and turned his head away. His ears moved to catch sounds in the distance. His attention focused elsewhere and he turned away to blend in with the night. His leaving signaled the other two to vanish as well.

"Shit, shit, shit!" Officer Cade trembled. "Too close, too close!"

"Did they circle around?"

Zyanthena kept her eyes to the trees as she replied, "I do not believe so, but keep the horses huddled. I would rather not assume."

"What made them move?"

The Tashek woman shook her head. It hadn't been anything she had done. The leader had heard something that had made it leave. Her eyes searched the direction the wolf had looked. Her breath paused—there were torches in the distance, coming over the next hill. "Lord Darshel—!"

"I see, I see! Run, run north. Now!"

Zyanthena held her stallion back as the men wheeled their horses around and took off. Quickly, she counted the number of torches, now close enough that she could make out the faint red coloring of the nearest enemy's eyes in the firelight. A small troupe of maunstorz had finally caught up to them. "Unrevealed, run, run!" She cued the black into a gallop and followed the Kavahadian men northward, deeper into the Forbidding Forest.

Chapter Forty-Nine

§

Returning Home

Under Matar's command, the Crystine made short work of the distance between Paragon Oasis and North Point, using the cool, moonlight nights to keep the horses and men from overheating. The Crystine travelled in war-time cavalry style, each rider having two horses apiece. The Crystine leader made good on his promise to the Sealander heir to have him back by a fortnight—he did it in nine days.

Compared to Prince Par's last journey across the Aras Desert, this one was spent in cool breezes and starlight. Besides the first few nights desiring sleep, the princeling found their travel quite pleasant. It was a very welcoming sight to see his northern army still alive and healthy and well-defended under Commander Averron and Tyk. The two leaders came out to greet the Crystine and prince as the cavalry neared the fortress walls.

"Highness, it is so good to see you again!" Averron said. He saluted his prince and his Lord Protector. "I feared you would be swallowed up by the desert."

"Me, too." Par returned, grinning. "But, alas, my cousin would have probably walked a thousand leagues just to see me through."

That brought the Sealander commander's attention to Lord Gordar, who he praised at length for his daring run to the Crystine. The Lord Protector denied his bravery saying, "I knew that the Crystine have always been out closest allies and most reliable friends. I did what you yourself would have done to find us reinforcements."

"And we will always do so; if ever Sealand had need again." Commander Matar promised. He shook hands with the two commanders—all having known each other for years. "The North had always been stretched thin against the enemy, but we will never hesitate to take them down wherever they decide to raise their heads."

"Just so," Tyk agreed, "I quite enjoyed giving them a whopping. It was almost a shame them Tashek had to ride in and steal my thunder, but those horsemen really had those cowards turning tail and running. Handy, that was."

"The Tashek have that way about them," Matar agreed. "Has there been any sighting of the maunstorz since their disappearance?" He refrained from using the word *vanished*, though as a Khataum within the Prism of the Stars Matar new the word was more accurate.

Averron shook his head. "All had been quiet. Besides the hundreds of graves we have had to dig, there is little evidence left of their having been here. Outriders, even those from Port Al-Harrad, have not seen any hide or hair of their passage. From the birds you sent, it seems there is nothing found west of the Citadel?"

"That seems correct. Of the maunstorz themselves, they have not been seen. Only the destructive attacks to the camps around the walls of the Citadel of Light by the Nallaus gives us any indication that they are still present."

"It seems so strange, them disappearing so suddenly after such violent attacks." Averron replied. He indicated the cavalry move inside the fortress walls. "I've a wish to know more about these Nallaus." He slipped on the keshic word. "There was little detail about them or the attacks to the camps. What little I gleam makes them seem like rogue Tashek."

Matar understood the confusion; it was the reason his "Night Fox" had been quick to warn King Maushelik of the danger. "If you would let us partake of your ale and some bread, I would be happy to settle this fallaciousness."

"That can be arranged." Prince Par spoke for his commander. "Averron, if you would, please see that someone be appointed to host the Crystine in the western quarters? We will settle these commanders with drink and food as you conclude such business."

"Aye, sir."

§ §

Their bellies filled and all the commanders' questions answered, Prince Par bid all the men to find their beds. The cavalry had ridden over half the night before reaching North Point and the Sealander was sure they were all just as tired as he. "Rest the day away. My men keep a quarterly change of command and can do without need of your men until they have satisfied a decent night's sleep; we can sort out the integration of the Crystine into the ranks at a later hour. So, please, take time to freShe up and sleep. I will meet you all again by the evening meal." The men rose stiffly and filed away to the rooms prepared for them, leaving the prince with his Lord Protector and commander. The golden-haired Sealander stretched and yawned very unprincely-like.

"You should rest, too." Gordar told his cousin.

"I will, cuz, I will. Just not until I see the keep." Par rubbed his eyes to clear his head and stood. Apparently, he must have done a poor job of seeming capable of walking the grounds because golden eyes stared back at him, unconvinced. "Really, I mean it! I want to see how everything fares—then, I promise, I will take to my bed."

"My Highness, I assure you all is fine. The men can wait seeing you until you've rested." Commander Averron backed up the Lord Protector. Both men knew the royal heir could be stubborn when it came to certain duties. The Sealander commander gave his prince a different task in hopes of changing the prince's mind. "The men and rounds can wait, Highness, while there are correspondences that have been awaiting your attention in your study. Two are from His Majesty, Highness."

The change of subject—and priority—convinced the prince. "Very well, letters it is then, Averron. Thank you for keeping them for me."

The old veteran bobbed his head. "Of course, My Prince. I remember the Shi'alam saying, "send no birds", and I couldn't risk a man through that desert or else I'da had sent you His Majesty's letters."

"No, it was all right, Averron. Indeed, His Highness Maushelik confirmed that it is erroneous to send letters by bird; you did right keeping them here. I will see to those, then." Over the prince's head, the two men shared a relieved look.

"Well, let's go then." Lord Gordar pulled his cousin to his feet and helped him to his quarters. He pulled out the wooden chair and readied an oil lamp for his cousin. "Now, not too long, right?"

"Par chuckled. "Yes, mother hen." He smiled at his cousin, tired. "Just a few, I promise, then to sleep with me. Now off to bed with yourself! I can handle a few papers on my own." Lord Gordar still looked skeptical but he did leave Par in peace.

Par stifled another yawn then reached for the bundled stack of correspondences Commander Averron had organized for him. On top were the blue wax seals in the royal crest of seagulls and eldlaus flowers. He picked the blue wax seals and unrolled the fine parchment. The first letter must have arrived just hours after the prince had left for Port Al-Harrad with the Shi'alam's party. King Fantill had received word for the Citadel of the heavy losses of the men and the possible reinforcement of the Crystine and mertinean, who at the writing were passing Raven's Den. His father warned that, with the decrease in defenses, the Citadel could fall—of which point, North Point or Port Al-Harrad could be their next target. Par's father also wrote of his trying to gain more assistance for his son but that, with Sealand's forces spread from north to south, it could be at least a fortnight to reach the keep.

The prince crumpled the outdated letter, not bothering to read more than the first page before tossing it aside. He turned to the second one, hoping it was newer. The script was less flourished than the first, his father's writing in haste after hearing the events. The king had just learned of both the victory at the Citadel of Light and the vanishing of the maunstorz at North Point. The first point was written with relief and caution; King Maushelik had sent a bird to Fortress Opal to extend to them the invitation for representation at the war council, any man they wished. At the time of his writing, King Fantill had not known his son and only heir was on his way across the Aras Desert to do just that. Though Par felt guilty at having not told his father his plans, there was little he could do now that he had gone and come back. However, it was the rest of the letter that had him thinking twice on his actions.

The second part of the king's message urged Par to come home as soon as he was able. King Fantill feared what the vanishing of the maunstorz meant—hinting at the Stones of Power that he had told his son a small bit about when Par had turned seventeen. He said he didn't want to explain over a long-distance correspondence but that the incident at North Point was not from natural causes. He warned that another stone must be active, besides Serein, for such an occurrence to happen. The maunstorz could strike again wherever Par was, as long as he-the wielder of the sapphire—had it on his person. "Come home now, my son. I will tell you more when we are face to face. Be careful."

Suddenly concerned, Par reached for the blue stone that hung around his neck. Its soothing ocean song came into his mind, its repetitive breath reminding him that there was still calm somewhere—even amidst chaos. A warmth entered his hand as Par lifted the silver chain over his head. In the lamplight, Serein glowed a faint blue against his palm. "I need to give you up, though I do not want to. Father says I am in danger with you and I know I need to trust him to know what he is talking about." The thought clenched the prince's heart; he had not been without the stone since he was gifted it at age thirteen. Would it be erroneous to keep it just over the night? Yet, Par knew there was much about the Stones of Power he had yet to discover.

Torn, the Sealander prince found himself still in his chair by sun-up, his precious sapphire sitting on his wooden desk in front of him, untouched. The first beams of the morning light hit him at eye level from the partially closed window. They caused Par to blink his ocean-blue eyes. Somehow finding himself refreshed, Par rose and, taking Serein with him, went in search of Averron to tell him to prepare a boat for him on the coast.

His northern wing of the keep was quiet as most of the men were to post, so it came as a surprise to find the elder commander awake and staring at the sunrise. "Commander!"

Commander Matar turned away from the view to give the prince a bow. "Highness Fantill, a good morning to you?"

"Ah, of that I am not entirely certain. I slept nil since our dinner."

"A shame." The Crystine man regarded the prince with an astute eye. For a moment, Par felt as if he was being sized-up by a Tashek again, "I suspect some news had kept you preoccupied."

Par started, surprised the commander could guess so close to the mark. "I—."

"I assume because Averron reported there was news from Fortress Opal."

"Oh, yes…from my father." The heir-apparent made to walk on but the leader stepped into his path, startling him. Par suddenly felt intimidated by the commander's taller height and imposing energy.

When had the respectful cavalryman become so domineering? Matar's sharp, midnight-blue eyes focused on Par's right hand. Par clenched his fist, suddenly remembering he held Serein.

The words "water holder" were whispered under Matar's breath—or so Par thought he heard. Matar's eyes wandered to the prince's face. "King Fantill's letters were of a more pressing issue, were they not?" He looked back at Serein, who the Sealander was now trying to shield. Par gulped, unsure how to keep secret what the stone was that he held. Responding to his nervousness, Serein began to glow the blue cast again. Matar saw and stepped back. "She is active!"

"Sh—she?" Par stammered.

"Serein. The sapphire's powers are awake."

"Ah," Par licked his lips but finally answered, "For some time now, yes."

Matar rose his eyebrows. He continued to stare calculatingly at the prince. "You know much about her, then?"

"I should ask you that." Par sidestepped, knowing his father would be panicking if he heard the conversation.

Matar replied with a startling laugh. "Boy, I know more about the stones than you may ever. Now, unless you plan on using her, I suggest you relax your emotions so Serein doesn't respond in kind. She can be a little dramatic."

Par wasn't really certain he wanted to, but, since he was already in the process of ruining his concealment with the Crystine man, it felt silly not to try to calm himself. In response, Serein's color dulled to a lifeless-looking rack.

"That's better," Matar commented. He looked to be breathing more freely, too. "Now, did your father warn you that having Serein active can point a target on your back thousands of clicks wide if you do not shield yourself?" Par's confused look was answer enough. Matar swore under his breath. "Stars, Highness! I should have you hand Serein over to me right now—if I thought you would trust me to keep her. Can you give her to your Lord Protector...does he know?"

The questions were railed out, poundingly quick, and Par hesitated before saying, "He knows only that she is an heirloom I wear at all times."

Matar looked aghast. "Highness, you need to, *now*, on both accounts—and I hope you are planning on setting forth to Fortress Opal very soon—."

"I am, Commander. What has both you and my father so spooked?"

The Crystine leader paused. "I—or King Fantill and myself—will tell you more when we are farther away from the North. Had I or the Shi'alam known you had an activated stone—with no real knowledge on how to use her!—we would never have let you come north to the Citadel."

"The Shi'alam—."

"Later, prince. When do you plan to leave for Fortress Opal?"

"Tomorrow morning."

"Make it today, afternoon. I am coming with you."

"You—wait, what?"

"With the force you have at North Point, I am comfortable leaving my men in Averron's care. You and Serein are more important to our cause. I would see you safely home. Now, you should go give Lord Farrylin your stone and make arrangements. Time is pressing on this, Highness. Go, go!"

§ §

The Sealander was still wavering in confusion four days later, when his warliner ship neared the docks below Fortress Opal. The Crystine commander had avoided him the entire trip—an interesting feat seeing as the prince's horse-transporting vessel was only slightly over twenty-five-and-a-half-meters long. Prince Par felt frustrated to be treated so indifferently by the Crystal man. The commander was keeping details about Serein close to the chest. Plus, the fact that there were more people that knew about the stones than Par had supposed came as an unsettling shock. Were the stones really as secret as his father claimed?

Lord Gordar had tried to be supportive of his cousin. Yet, since learning of Serein, he seemed to regard his prince with wariness; almost as if he suspected the Sealand heir of having a mental break. It was almost comical to see how Gordar stared at him when he thought the prince wasn't looking—except it really wasn't when the prince felt slightly crazy himself. It was a welcome relief when the

high, craggy walls of Fortress Opal were above them. Now—
finally—King Fantill would ease both Par's and Gordar's minds once
and for all.

"Are you ready?" His cousin came up on his left shoulder as Par
gazed out at the familiar worn walls of the fortress.

Par turned his ocean-blue eyes to his Lord Protector. "As ready
as I will ever be," he replied, feeling a flutter of uncertainty.

The two Sealanders headed for the disembarking area. Not to
the prince's surprise—but much to his irritation—the Crystine
commander was there to walk to the fortress with them. Matar gave
them a respectful bow and fell in line with Par's guard. He seemed
not to care that he had been dismissive of the royal heir until that
moment. Par suppressed a sigh and headed down the gangway.
Horses were waiting for the party at the bottom. The twelve of them
were quickly mounted and two of Par's men led the way up the
winding cobblestone hill to the main gates, then through the inner
bailey's own gates to the main ward outside of the keep.

Fortress Opal had been built right into the high cliff walls of the
only strong buttress on the whole Southern coastline. Thus, it stuck
up into the air like an enduring stone crown amidst a sea of rolling,
smoothed stones and sparse clumps of green seagrass. Within the
walls, very little native grasses remained; most were a part of the
large ward the small party were let to. The rest of the keep looked
more like a military outpost, which was deceptive. The interior was
made of mother-of-pearl and guilt in silver and came with the
highest in royal comforts. It was not until the very doors of the
keep—which were wrot in intricate Landarïan scrollwork that the
cloistered finery of Sealand was noted.

Two guards greeted the prince and his party at the door, bowing
deeply to the royal highness as he passed through. Another guard,
acting more as the king's page, intercepted them in the main
anteway. He, too, bowed and spoke courtesies to his prince and bid
them to follow to the king's chambers, on the south-western corner
of the Fortress.

The middle-aged King of Sealand received them in his private
billiard. He was a medium-built man with salt-and-pepper colored
hair and tanned skin. Compared to his son, who had gotten his
delicate features from Queen Kesnia, King Fantill had a strong jaw

structure and muscled-yet-somehow-wiry frame. It was only their calming ocean-blue eyes that father and son shared. These lit up as his only heir and the other guests made their way into the billiard. "I am relieved to see you safe with my own two eyes!"

Prince Par smiled warmly at his father and embraced him. "It feels good to have ocean air back into these lungs, father. Though I apologize for having not seen your missive calling me back sooner."

"I am just grateful you got it." King Fantill waved away Par's guards and motioned the other two men near. "Gordar, thank you for keeping my son safe. I hear you have quite the journey with him this time." He grasped both young men in affection—as Gordar was as much a son to him as Par. There was almost an undercurrent of worry to the king's touch, however, as if he feared that, if he were to let go, both boys would disappear.

Par shared a glance with his cousin then waved his father's attention to their last guest. "Father, Commander Matar of the Crystine."

The two men's eyes met and they seemed to still. King Fantill's eyes slowly widened in shock and then elation. "Son of a—. You're..." He strode forward to grasp Matar's hand with both his own. "I don't believe it! All this time and you, you've been—."

"A commander of King Lanar Starkindler's cavalry, of which I would prefer to stay, William, please. I have no intention of being anything else as long as I am needed as Khataum of the Guardianship."

"I understand," his face grew solemn. "I had heard rumors but thought of them very little until now. You gave up a great deal to become a Guardian. I only hope your sacrifice has been well worth it."

"Everything had its prices, but I do not regret what I have had to do to keep the secrets all these years."

"We all know, too well, the sacrifices. I am just in disbelief that you are here! Stars, sir, stars...!" It was obvious that these had been an old kinship between the two men. King Fantill was moved enough by the reunion to have a hint of tears sticking to his eyelashes. "Look at me. I am getting enough years on me that I have become a bit sentimental."

"I am sure you will tire of me soon enough, William."

Prince Par and Lord Gordar were stunned. Never would they have expected such a scene as they witnessed. The two men from different sides of Syre knew each other—and what was more, the Sealander king let the Crystine commander call him William?! It was highly unusual. The prince cleared his throat. "Okay then...seeing as we are obviously lost on something, or a number of somethings, can we get to the reason why you needed me back here so quickly. And why the commander sounds as concerned as you?"

King Fantill and Commander Matar turned to the two young men. "Sit down," the king said to them and motioned to Matar. The Crystine man proceeded to "secure the room" before joining them. Prince Par had never felt so secretive in his own house before. "There are many secrets kept from the public, certainly even most of the classes of the royal houses." The Sealand ruler turned away to what looked like a wall and tapped a sequence in the paneling. A hidden space was revealed as the king lifted away the front. "It seems that the years have turned long enough to rejuvenate the Stones of Power. Your Serein is not the only one to have come back to herself." The ocean-blue eyes turned to stare at Par, wanting to convey just how significant the words were. "You know some of Serein but you know very little of the other stones, their origins, and powers. If indeed the enemy had procured a Stone of Power and someone to use it, then Syre is in worse trouble than we thought."

"Wait, what are you talking about, father?"

"Do you really believe that a force of nearly eight-thousand-strong maunstorz can just pack up and disappear over one night? There was no natural means to that event."

"Nothing like that is possible," Lord Gordar argued.

"And yet, you witnessed it with your own two eyes." King Fantill went to retrieve something else from the hidden alcove then replaced the false front and returned to the chairs. "And still you deny that what you saw was majik."

"Magic has been banned for nearly three-hundred years."

"That is what you are meant to believe," Matar chimed in. "In reality, the Stones of Power were actively used until twenty-five years ago. After the fall of Crystalynian, the stones became dormant."

"Much seems to involve Crystalynian," Par noted.

"Yes," Matar replied. "It was the high-seat of power. All stone-bearers would meet at Crystanian. It was the one kingdom that embraced majik freely."

The Landarïan king set down a very old and cumbersome codex on the table before his son and Lord Protector. He flipped to an old map of Syre, lacking the eight kingdoms. "At the end of the first age, all of Syre was ruled by one king, his throne being at Crystanian. This king had nine children, his youngest—a son—his most favored. Before his death, the king named this son, Ressön, as his predecessor. The other eight siblings resented this, of course, but did nothing until their father's death."

"I know that." Par said, fingering another map. "The eight children denied the succession of their brother. They took Syre and broke it into the eight kingdoms. Some books say the ninth son was killed; others that he and his supporters were banished."

"Indeed, that was so. I believe the latter to be correct. Though we know little of the regions beyond the North, there must be more lands beyond our knowledge." King Fantill traced the wilderness beyond Syre's boundary, lost in thought.

"That's all good and dandy to have a history lesson, Majesty, but what has this to do with the stones?" Lord Gordar asked.

The king came back to himself. "Ah, yes, these Stones of Power. Not much is written of how they came to be—except one tale of them coming from the monoliths that mark the boundaries near each castle and each kingdom's strategic entry points. That aside, the existence of the eight Stones of Power marked the beginning of the Second Age. Majik flourished, Syre flourished. We have never seen a golden age like that before or since. The stones gave the eight rulers near-instant access to each other, even over vast distances of the country, and protected our norther borders from outside dangers."

"I thought there was nothing beyond our north?"

Matar answered for King Fantill. "There are a few records of skirmishes beyond our borders, usually with small tribes that have come south. Those records can only be found with the Sheev'anee and at Crystanian's library. The rulers made sure to keep this information quite so as to not arouse the populous. Until the maunstorz arrival, Syre did not have a threat they could keep contained and secret."

"What?!" Par was stunned. He and his cousin shared a glance. "You're saying that all of Syre is not aware of these previous attacks? We've come to see ourselves as all these is in this world."

"But we are not. Though, supposedly, old surveyors found very little in the unknown regions. They tried to map some parts during the Second Age. They reported "primitive peoples, unfit to speak with and in small number", found on some occasions but nothing else. Their conclusions made Syre's rulers end any other expeditions and pursued matters here. Had they persisted in mapping beyond these regions, perhaps, they could have discovered the maunstorz before they threatened us so boldly."

"That's hearsay, Matar, and of no importance here. You're leading my boys astray with your wild ideas."

The Crystine commander shrugged. "I felt they needed more of an explanation. I found it a tad interesting when I first learned of it."

Kind Fantill frowned at that and returned the conversation back to its original course. "Beyond that point... I believe I was trying to explain about the stones." He collected his thoughts by flipping to another page in the codex. "There are eight stones, each used by one member of the royal family. Most pass from parent to heir, though sometimes the stones may respond to a different family member. Originally, whomever wielded the stones were given the most elite status—as the stones can do many unimaginable things. Stone bearers were called to services kingdom-wide for many tasks. This was the reason for the golden age."

"But the stones are all but unheard of. Until Prince Par gave me Serein, I knew nothing of even it."

"Yes." Matar smiled sadly. "One bad seed ruined it all."

King Fantill continue, filling in for the commander's cryptic answer, frowning at the unnecessary quip. "Near the end of the Second Age, a Havanese prince was gifted Bellor, the jade stone, on his seventeenth birthday—late for a royal. Usually children were trained from a young age how to use the stones. This prince was not, as he inherited Bellor after his elder sister (its true bearer) died in childbirth."

"To Syre's peril."

"Yes," King Fantill agreed. "This prince had a lust for blood and terror. He was the first of the stone bearers to use his for warfare. He had pure enjoyment for killing people and scaring subjects into submission. His reign was full of atrocities. By the time the fool was stopped, the populous had learned to fear the stones and their powers. The stone bearers were ostracized, some even killed. The stones were hidden away from two generations because of this."

"I can understand that, father, but how did they convince the populous the stones no longer existed?"

The king and Crystine shared a glance and Matar indicated he would answer. "As we have conveyed, the stones have many powers. During those years trying to subdue that renegade prince, the other bearers discovered other...uses for the stones. One such use was clouding memories—even to the point of full removal of them if made to make sense enough. Once the prince was killed, the other bearers focused the stones' powers on masking the existence of the stones over all but select few people. They then turned the stones over to the Guardians of the Prism, with assurance that the stones be given back to the royal families after a number of years and new bearers passed along the information of the stones. Supposedly, the seven bearers then killed themselves, ending the chapter of the Second Age."

Par looked stunned at the news. "Then these stones are too dangerous!" He looked down at Serein, which was clutched tightly in his hand since its return to him upon their arrival to Fortress Opal. He found himself staring in horror at the stone he had been entrusted with for fourteen years. "Why did you give her to me? I can't—."

"The stones are neither good nor evil, my son, and much good can come from them. I would not have given you Serein had I thought you could not use her for just purposes."

"But I am one of eight able to use them. Not every man would use something so powerful for good. Didn't that old prince teach Syre that?"

"Which is why it is important that we know where all the stones are, Prince," Matar said.

"You don't know!" Lord Gordar, too, sounded alarmed. He had been reading over each stone's many powers and had been shocked at all he had learned. Never before had he feared a weapon so, as much as, what some of the stones could do.

"We know where Kevel, Sevén, and Vauldin are, and, too, your Serein. King Maushelik had promised that Amun is also safely accounted for. It's the last three we do not have knowledge of; though, Ravel, we assume, is now controlled by someone working for the maunstorz."

"Someone with Crystal blood." Gordar put two-and-two together." Someone with ties to the Starkindlers."

"He's a smart one," Matar commented to King Fantill. "I see why you have him protecting your son." To Lord Gordar he then replied, "And, yes, young Protector, I do believe one of the Starkindlers is still alive or else Ravel would not work. In faith, I am counting on it."

"This is preposterous!" Prince Par muttered. His mind spun with all that he was learning. "Those stones were made to be forgotten for a reason, and now you (however many all of *you* are) want them back in use?! I have a choice and I will not do it."

"My son—."

"No, father, I will not hear of it. I will not use Serein for whatever reasons you wish me to."

"Even if it saves Syre?" Matar countered.

"Save her from what?"

"The maunstorz, Prince. We almost won the last time all the stone bearers came together against them. Had King Trev'shel not died in that last battle..." Matar would not let himself finish the thought, unwilling to voice the mistakes of his generation those twenty-five years past. Sad eyes met Prince Par's. "The stones have been our only chance. Syre can't keep fighting these maunstorz forever. We will lose if you [the stone bearers] do not find a way."

"You may believe that, Commander, but I do not. I have fought, too, and I have seen us win—without the use of magic. There will be a way, but not this one. Not this one! You give me other options because I will not do this. And, Syre will not fall. I believe that."

Chapter Fifty

§

Betrayed

It was raining outside, as shown by the ever-deepening puddles in his dark and mold-smelling cell. There was a high vent overhead that let in too little of the wet scent. It was not low enough for the commander to reach for and pull himself up to smell the simple delight. Instead, Commander Loris Ravesbend was forced to find the least wet spot in the dusty straw lining his swamped prison and hunker down to wait out long hours alone.

The commander had lost count of the days he had been kept in the cell; certainly, the king's men who attended him were too loyal to King Raymond to offer the caged commander-in-arms any solace on the matter (or any matter, for that matter). They rarely spoke to him at all, except to order him to do something. It could have been a month for all Loris knew.

Whatever time had passed, Commander Ravesbend did know that he—and those most loyal to him—had been carried out from the Sunarian forces in the middle of the night and made example of by the next dawn. King Raymond had sent his most ruthless guard— those that did their ruler's "dirty" work—to the Command Front to "clean-up" the royal army. Any of the men who tried to save their commander were subdued and tied to stakes to be burned alive in front of the whole troupe. The vile punishments had quickly put the army in line. A Thane Cornell now commanded Loris Ravesbend's men, while their leader rotted away in an ill-kept cage.

An iron door squeaked open from the landing above the cell and meek steps came down the staircase. Mousy Bradon came up to the small barred opening of the cell. He glanced back at the two soldiers that had stopped at the edge of the stairs. It was the first Loris had seen of the man since he had been imprisoned. The nervous man gave a partial, uncertain salute at his one-time commander. "Sir," he said.

Loris came slowly to his full, lanky frame, not too certain he wanted to speak with his former second-in-command when the man was still walking around free and he was not. There must have been resentment written on his face because Bradon squeaked and backed a few steps away from the bars. Loris schooled his features to a less-threatening countenance and came forward. "Bradon."

"Sir Ravesbend." The man swallowed nervously and came back to the bars. "How—how do you fare, sir?"

"I'm in a five-star establishment," he motioned to the slop and straw around him. "How do you think I fare?"

"I meant about your health, sir. You have enough to eat, too, sir?"

The Sunarian commander gave his inferior a shriveling stare. "I am as good as I'm sure you suspect, but still at a need for explanations." Loris doubted he would get anything of importance from Bradon but never hurt to nudge the man.

Bradon's beady eyes scurried back and forth—the balding man at his most insecure. Loris waited, his own hungry for answers. "They're here," he whispered, almost inaudible.

"They? Who, King Raymond and his son?"

"No, *they*." Bradon spoke louder then jumped as if bitten and looked back at the two guards, who were ignoring their conversation. "They are here."

Loris frowned. "You're not being very clear, Bradon."

"They. *They* they. You know: the evil, take-over-the-world they."

The commander's heart stopped. "The maunstorz."

Bradon bobbed his bald head. "A whole contingent of them, under a pact with our king. Apparently, they have agreed to aid His Majesty in taking over Rubia in exchange for using Sunrise as part of their territory—no more raids! The Red Palace has been taken already with some of Thane Cornell's men and one of the maunstorz generals."

"What!?"" Loris swore loudly too angry to care that he had alerted the guards. The men started to come down to end their conversation. "Bradon, my men…they aided him in this?"

"No, sir. They are being held here, too. All of your force." Bradon hurried to say the last. "They were furious at this betrayal, too. All are loyal to you." The guards grabbed Bradon's shoulders and started to haul him away. "Sir, sir! Please take care of yourself, sir. We will wait for you!" Bradon was silenced and led away, leaving Commander Ravesbend to ponder over his second's words. Loris doubted he would ever see the plucky man again. He was certain Bradon had been allowed in to dishearten him with the information—but the truth had emboldened the commander.

Loris sank back into his wet straw and hardened his resolve around the small tidbit he had learned about the king. King Raymond would not get away with such a betrayal to Sunrise's people. Even if it was not Loris himself, someone would take down the debauched king...all it took was time.

Chapter Fifty-One
§
Awakening

Zyanthena's main fear came to pass; as the six of them filed down a steep bank along a small river, Officer Orin's horse slipped into a hidden hole and fell. The sickening crunch told the story before anyone assessed the animal's leg. There was little doubt that his horse had broken it. Still, Zyanthena slid off of Unrevealed to check on the injury. The others, too, dismounted. "It's a serious break. He can't keep weight on it," the Tashek decreed. "There's no way he can be ridden, if even moved."

The men shared a glance and Lord Darshel finally had to say the obvious. "Then, there's only one thing to do." He walked over to the horse and took out a long dagger. Zyanthena cringed but nodded to the logic. "I will stab its heart. It will be as quick as I can make." The desert woman nodded and turned away to soothe the gelding as Lord Darshel positioned himself and thrust deeply into the horse's side. The ailing gelding sank heavily to the ground and its eyelids fluttered. Finally, the life left its chestnut-colored eyes. Zyanthena moved away, back to her black, to hide the tears in her eyes.

"We keep moving," Darshel ordered. "It's dawn. We should make good miles if we trade off who rides double. Hopefully, we can save the other horses." More privately, Lord Darshel touched Zyanthena on the shoulder and quietly asked, "Will you be okay?"

The Tashek nodded back sullenly, "There was nothing to be done, but we need to preserve the other horses as well as we can."

"Ah…sorry to interrupt, My Lord, but now the enemy will know where we were, once they come across the carcass." Darshel and the warrioress turned to address the new problem. "I'd doubt the wolves will finish it off before they come across it. They seem to have efficient trackers."

"They do," Zyanthena agreed.

The six of them became quiet as they thought over their options. Then, Officer Mercer spoke out, "I think we should separate. Let Zyanthena and His Lordship head north up the river while the rest of us go across the water and keep heading westerly. It will draw them our direction and let His lordship get some distance between our pursuers."

"We are not separating again. I have lost too many of you already."

"I agree with Mercer on this one, Your Lordship. All your men want you to get home alive. A distraction can help us on that."

"Not without them!" Lord Darshel repeated. "Not this time."

"Okay... then, I say we fake a river crossing, come back, and head upstream. That could give us some extra time." Officer Aaron contributed.

"Any other ideas?" Lord Darshel asked. He didn't appreciate felling like a tracked deer. The men and Zyanthena all shook their heads.

"Okay. Let's do it."

§ §

It took a good twenty minutes to create a false crossing and head up stream. By then, the sun had risen and their way was easily lit. Zyanthena still led. Unrevealed being long-legged and sure-footed made the best choice to follow. Even in barrel-deep water, he did not seem fazed to keep marching forward. Two of the other horses were not as willing and both Zyanthena and Lord Darshel had to assist their riders by holding the horse's bridles.

"How much farther before you feel we are enough upstream to go back to the bank?" Lord Darshel yelled up to Zyanthena. He gauged they had already gone over a half-mile in varying water depths. Tano certainly seemed tired of the charade.

"Not yet." Was the desert woman's reply. "I hear heavier water ahead. This next bend may lead to a small waterfall. We will cross to the north bank there." True to her prediction, the next bend revealed a fall coming down off of a steep drop in a canyon formed in the hill. The pool it created at its bottom was deep and Zyanthena moved the men to the bank, as even her black stallion refused to go forward. "Let me scout ahead as you all rest. I will see if this gorge is passable by horse." The Tashek slid from Unrevealed's back, spoke to him, and left him with the others as she scouted ahead on foot.

Time passed and the men became anxious. "She usually doesn't take this long." Officer Cade worried. The others voiced similar concerns.

"Easy men," Lord Darshel ordered trying to keep himself calm. "She hasn't failed us yet. Zy'ena will be back soon."

Indeed, the beautiful warrioress did return soon after—at a hurried run. "We need to go now! The maunstorz trackers guessed our diversion too quickly. They are not far behind." She swung atop Unrevealed and motioned the way to go. "The way get tricky but we have no choice now. Come!" The way out was laid in flat stone boulders, slippery to the shod horses of Kavahad. The black led, surefooted, but the others balked and quivered at the unsure obstacles. Officer Aaron and Mercer dismounted to guide their mounts and returned to help the other two. Zyanthena held their horses leads as the soldiers rushed back for Cade's and Darshel's mounts.

Arrows started raining down on the men as they tried to coax the horses over the rocks. Aaron yelled out as one hit him in the upper back and he fell backward into the gorge. Another three hit Cadet Cade and his horse. Both rider and mount flailed. "My Lord, hurry forward!" Mercer begged of Darshel as he rushed to get to Cade and his horse.

"Lord Darshel!" Zyanthena cried out as well, urging the Kavahadian to reach her. She felt defenseless to help as there were no arrows for her to return in response. Too, she knew that if she cued Unrevealed back out onto the rocks, Tano would not be able to move forward.

"Run, My Lord! Run! To Zy'ena." Mercer yelled again as he hoisted a dying Cade on his shoulder. More arrows were shot at their small force. Lord Darshel urged Tano forward with all the will he could muster. He refused to look back to see if his loyal soldiers followed. From Zyanthena's release of her two chargers and urgent yell to follow, they had not.

Grimly, the Shekmann urged Tano onward and followed the black stallion up the ridge. By the top, the grey and black were panting hard, lathered, and barely making a trot, but with the enemy so close the two riders could not afford to rest them. They forced the animals on as they followed the top of the ridge and looked for a safe

enough place to head down the other side. "The way levels out ahead
and to the right. Go there," Zyanthena pointed and led the way
down. They didn't let the horses' pace slow despite well disguised
rock, downed trees, and matted clumps of grasses that lines the side
of the ridge. It was a small wonder neither of the mounts stumbled
by the time they reached the bottom.

"We must hold to a trot," Lord Darshel said as he found room
enough to ride abreast with the Tashek. "We could lose both animals
if we don't."

Zyanthena nodded. Her sharp, brandy eyes went back to the
ridge they had just descended. "They closed rather quickly. I'm not
confident we will be able to make enough distance to lose them."

"We will cross that bridge when we get there. For now, we will
follow this draw northward."

"Farther away from Rubia."

The Shekmann persed his lips. "We have no choice."

"We could fight." The look in her eye was that rare fiery one
reserved for the battlefield. It unnerved the Shekmann. "No. Not yet,
Zy'ena. We aren't that desperate; not yet."

The look the wild woman returned sunk the Shekmann's heart.
"Perhaps, My Lord Darshel. Or, maybe, it is exactly that kind of
time."

§   §

The way they took became easier, as if under the undergrowth,
the path they took had once been a road. Tano and Unrevealed
recovered their breaths and trotted on willingly enough, relived with
the ease of the footing. The sun, now late-day, beat down warmly
and soothed the anxious riders. Both Lord Darshel and Zyanthena
began to find a reflective silence, lulled by the calm of the mountains
around them. Neither spoke of the new losses or the threat that
dogged them. It seemed too hopeless a situation to discuss. Only the
desire to get free of their pursuers held any fleeting feeling of
aspiration.

As evening began to form, they found themselves travelling into
a more wooded area. Shadows began to grow long within the
deepening pine forest. Passing through the narrowed clump of trees,
the two horses began to get edgy. Lord Darshel found himself arguing

with Tano to calm down. The Shekmann had almost succeeded at containing his prancing steed when a grey shape rose up from the high grasses next to the large pine trees they passed. Instinctively, Tano leapt away sideways, catching his rider unprepared. Lord Darshel was thrust from the tack and into the hard tree trunk on his right.

The flight instincts triggered in the two horses at the motion, and they took off. Zyanthena, who had been ahead of the Shekmann, was unaware that Tano ran with them riderless. She kept her seat as her black surged forward, knowing better than to stop the stallion until his feet outran his innate desire to flee. It wasn't until Tano rushed by, his saddle empty, that she tried to slow her mount; however, whatever had spooked them had both horses in a panicked run. Unrevealed refused to slow.

Around two bends in the trees the horses ran. Then, suddenly, the way opened up into a field of ruins. A large, crumpled wall was before the horses and rider. Zyanthena prepared herself for the horses to jump it. Instead, Unrevealed slip to a stop in front of the stones and his Tashek rider was tossed over. Dazed, Zyanthena lay and let her mind catch up with what had happened. It was only as her senses returned that Zyanthena realized something devastating: she could not feel or move her body! The disconnect was empty and disturbing. Her immediate panic was worsened as darkness began to descend into her vision. The head wound she had sustained from the fall was bleeding out...

Zyanthena Sheev'arid blacked out.

§ §

Lord Darshel groaned and pushed himself to a sitting position against the hard tree he had smacked into. Slowly, he moved his right hand to touch the bloody lump on his skull, wincing at the pain. "Ah," he muttered, "I haven't been thrown like that since I was a child." His body protested the fact.

A crunch of leaves had the Shekmann looking up. When he did, he froze. The enormous grey wolf stood mere yards from him, its golden eyes staring intently at the human. Around it, a pack of twelve wolves circled around the proximity of the pine tree. "Holy shit!" Darshel whispered. He slowly released his breath and began to reach for a dagger.

Sharp teeth nipped at his movement, a surprised feint from behind. The small brown-tinged she-wolf who had done so was quick to skitter away but her intent had been clear: the dagger was not an option.

The lead grey wolf waited until his packmate settled then paced closer to Lord Darshel. Its eyes bore right into the Shekmann's green ones, as if trying to communicate something. Oddly, the large predator came to sit in front of him, just out of reach, and cocked its head. An unusual vocal groan was issued and the wolf stood and walked off. It paused, looking back at Darshel and stepped farther away to look back again. The Kavahadian lord was baffled; he had never seen such behavior in a predator before. The alpha wolf huffed, came back to stare at Darshel again and repeated the process. By the third time of this, Lord Darshel wondered if the wolf meant for him to follow...

"Here goes nothing," Darshel muttered, finding his feet. He could be dead in an instant anyway; why not become a walking lunch?

The group of wolves became excited by his standing. Some pranced around, rubbing against others, some rolled over; that was, until the leader chortled. The wolves all fell into a semicircle around Lord Darshel at the signal. Still unnerved, the Shekmann took a few steps toward the alpha and stopped, afraid to be attacked. When nothing happened, Darshel took more steps, finally catching up to the leader.

The alpha grey wolf had sat, waiting, until Lord Darshel neared. Then, huffing again, he turned away and walked off, only to pause again to see if the human was following. "I get it!" Darshel muttered, feeling weird to be following a dangerous predator with its pack milling around him. Yet, the alpha seemed pleased. He turned away again to lead the way up the grassy path through the forest.

And, so it went: the wolves leading the Shekmann through the Forbidding Forest.

The pack led His Lordship to an open field littered with old, overgrown ruins. It was there that Lord Darshel found Tano and Unrevealed, the former's saddle having slipped half off his side, the latter riderless. "Tano," Darshel said. He rushing forward as the alpha wolf moved aside to lay by other ruins. His grey charger rose his head and whuffed into the lord's offered palm. Darshel ordered his horse's reins and righted his saddle. Next, he turned to Unrevealed to make sure the black stallion was all right. "Where is your master?' He asked of the warhorse as he checked him for injuries. Unrevealed bobbed his head and walked off, as if understanding the question. The black went around the partial wall and dropped his head to sniff something on the ground there. Darshel hurried after the stallion to find the Tashek woman on the other side.

Zyanthena lay still. Too still. Darkened blood pooled in the grass around the stone her head lay upon. "Stars! Zy'ena?! Zyen!" Darshel stopped himself from the desire to shake the desert woman awake. Carefully, he reached out to a wrist and then her throat to feel for a pulse. It was there but oh so faint. "Zy'ena, damn it! Zyen…please, please wake up for me. Please!" He leaned over to feel for her breath on his cheek but wasn't certain it was just hope that had Darshel thinking he felt it. "Oh, Stars, come on!" He yelled out to the sky. "Not now, damn it, not now!"

The Shekmann's yelling scared Unrevealed away and alerted the wolves to his failure. The alpha neared again and began to sniff at Zyanthena's body. "Go away!" Darshel screamed at the predator. The wolf's ears flattened to its skull and he growled. The Shekmann lord-governor felt himself cringe but he refused to leave Zyanthena with the beast. "Get back I say!" He said again, making himself big. The alpha backed a few steps and sat with its intense stare again. "What?!" The grey wolf began its same "follow me" cue. "I'm not leaving her," he told the alpha. The leader huffed—Darshel was starting to believe it was the way the wolf showed his exasperation at the human's stupidity—and came over to, very slowly, take Darshel's shirt sleeve in its teeth and pulled. The golden stare continued afterward. "Okay, give me a minute." The alpha chortled and gave the Shekmann space.

"I'm sorry if this hurts you, Zyen," Darshel whispered. He refused to believe the desert woman was dead. "I'm gonna lift you as carefully as I can." He removed his jacket and pillowed it under the woman's blood-plastered hair. Very carefully, Lord Darshel lifted Zyanthena and clung to her. Silent tears crept down his cheeks at the limp feel of the warrioress in his arms. Gingerly, he turned to face the wolf. "Okay, I follow now."

The other wolves rounded up the two nervous horses and ushered them after the alpha and lord. As a motley group, the wolves, horses, and humans filed around the ruins in the field, heading westerly towards the edge of the meadow. The ruins at that end seemed different, more solid and less damaged. The alpha came to a stop near the final wall of that area and sat watching Lord Darshel, as if expecting something.

Unsure, Lord Darshel stepped onto the flint stones of light-brown jasper that made up the floor of the once-grand room. As soon as his boots touched the old stones, *something* felt different. Six more steps confirmed his feeling; the more steps Darshel took onto the jasper, the lighter Zyanthena felt. A haunting song began to steam out from the air. Just like that, the obsidian pendant around the Tashek's neck floated into the air. A pulsing, pale-golden light began to pound out inside the black stone, slowly growing in size and intensity. "Holy shit!" Darshel exclaimed, his arms opening unbidden at the sight. Yet, the Tashek did not fall. Instead, she stayed suspended in the ever-growing light from the stone.

Terrified, Lord Darshel found himself back-peddling off of the flint stones to fall in a heap at the paws of the wolves. Neither the wolves nor the horses skittered away, however, and the Shekmann found his eyes were drawn back to the extraordinary event unfolding before him.

Vauldin pulsed brighter and brighter; its power growing as it awakened from its long slumber. Pounding like a heartbeat, its light and song continued to build until it encompassed the old ruins of Crystanian. It continued outward to include the forests of Crystalynian. The ground started to shake with the force and large sections of crumbled palace lifted into the air. Everything built and built until the pressure of the stone's power made all spectators' eyes avert away.

The pale light became an intense gold until Lord Darshel could no longer see a thing. Then, the loudest pop the Shekmann had ever heard sounded. He was blasted backward into the ground, into quiet oblivion.

§   §

There was a tremor that passed over the entirety of Syre, like a deep yawn after a long nap. Birds were roused from their nest and animals jittered uncertainly. In houses, people reached out to steady themselves and outside the citizens fell to their feet. Though the earthquake lasted only a few seconds, it left panic in its wake.

Not even a half-hour later, a queer rolling of darkened clouds amassed in the north-westerly skies. It built and leeched south and east from its point of origin, coming to cover the northern lands of Syre. By evening, a heavy snowstorm, far too early for the First Snows (as it was still Harvest-Gathering time) let loose over the North and brought a cold wind as far south as the Pearl River in the Golden Kingdom. Crops and animals froze during the night from the unusually cold temperatures. People scrambled to prepare for what should have been three moon-cycles away. Snow hung over Syre in a deathly embrace.

From the norther parapet of Fortress Opal, four men observed the supernatural events. "What is happening?" Prince Par asked of his father as the tremor gently rocked the walls of the castle.

The two aged men looked at each other; that shared glance they gave when they were about to say something grave. "From the direction and intensity of the shaking, I would say the obsidian stone, Vauldin, has been activated."

Lord Gordar offered a curse and Prince Par finished with a, "Stars! The obsidian stone is that powerful!?"

"Not usually," Matar admitted. "Most stones don't come alive so willfully, but the last time Vauldin made the ground shake, it completely destroyed Crystalynian."

"Let us hope that is not the case this time," King Fantill declared.

"Hope? You hope?!" Gordar sputtered. "You're saying these stones can wipe out an entire kingdom!—wait, I thought Crystalynian was sacked?"

"No," King Fantill said quietly. "It was Vauldin. Queen Kestral used the stone in a way it should never be intended… Instead of the result she wanted, the stone brought the kingdom to ruin."

"But how?"

"Another time," King Fantill said. He was unwilling to tell all of the past—yet. He continued, "But, if Vauldin has awakened then the other stones will, too. It being that violent a re-birthing, it should not be long."

A chill wind swept into the window-less parapet. The men shivered and wrapped their coats tighter about themselves. In the setting sunset colors, the crawling snow clouds were highlighted in reds, oranges, and blues. It took some few minutes for the men to grow suspicious of the sight. Yet, as the winds grew stronger and the clouds more ominous, the spectators started to understand.

"That's not normal either, is it?" Par looked to the elder men.

"No." Nope." Both said together.

"Vauldin?"

Matar shook his head. "That would be Ravel. Whomever controls it must feel threatened by Vauldin's display."

"Ravel controls land weather, especially mountain weather," King Fantill explained. "And whomever it is that controls her is quite strong themselves to cover so much of the land like that. I worry what that kind of weather brings out-of-season…"

"The North only recently started gathering for First Snows. With the fighting, stores are running low." Matar's lips tightened in concern. "Our forces will be in trouble in the North. The Citadel should handle it okay but the rest of Staria, Rubia, and the Crystal Kingdom? They will be hard-pressed."

"I know what you're *not* asking me, friend, and you know I cannot promise. My priorities are first to my kingdom. Once I know our limits, I can better tell you what I can provide."

Matar frowned but knew better than to press the Sealander king. "Make it a priority, William. The North stands between you and *that.*"

"As they have always stood! I do not forget. But what I said stands." The two men argued. They looked away, sullenly.

"Ah, okay…" Prince Par began. "So, you're both concerned then of what will come of Syre with this new development? Father and I will make sure to find ways to help the North, Commander, that I will promise you." Matar turned back to nod a thanks at the prince. "And, as I have no choice now, I will learn of these Stones of Power.

It seems Syre is in need of Serein's power; if only to counter Ravel. She can, can't she? Counter Ravel, I mean."

They were grave again. 'Yes, prince, she can," Matar replied. "But it will take a lot of your will to be stronger than the bearer of Ravel. You have much to learn…and no time to become as good as he."

"Then I am at your disposal, Commander, father."

King Fantill looked sad at his son's brave commitment. He reached out a hand to clasp his only heir around the nape of his neck. William Fantill pulled Par into a strong embrace. "I would not have wished this power on you like this, but thank you, my son. Thank you."

"We will need you both ready to face whatever the enemy has coming for Syre." Matar told both prince and protector. "That weather cannot last forever; even nature is averse to such inordinate actions. You will have to be ready by that time, brave Prince of the Evening Star." Commander Matar glanced northward, at the evil clouds. "The Stones of Power are awakening, kindly prince. It has begun."

Acknowledgements

Books are always a process; this one was no less. I have to thank those few souls who read this manuscript when it was hand written and then the first typings: Rachel Rheam, George Cowherd, Mattie Cowherd-Sutter, Carole Perry, and Katie Chouinard. You got through this in different stages and know how far it's come!

Thanks goes, too, to my family who continuously supports me; yes, even these books that do take up a lot of space in my mind! I love you all!

To the artist through SelfPubBookCovers.com/Shardel who made the cover of this book. It was just the artwork I had imagined for this first Crystals book...of course, those of you [readers] who have reached this page now understand the picture! (Or at least I hope.) And lastly, to the authors who have come before who have been a reminder to me that if we all love to write we should share it with the world!

Author Bio

Lindsey Cowherd lives in Salida, CO, where she was born and raised. She lives with her sweetie, Michael, who somehow tolerates her horse-craziness and love of all-things-Asian.

She started writing "novels" at a young teen; this book being one of the first she ever thought up that was beyond her normal obsession of horses. Turning to a world immersed in martial arts, codes, and "places not of this world" allowed her an outlet from everyday living and circumstances out of her control. Now, they are a place to allow her imagination to run wild.

Licensed as an acupuncturist since 2010, Lindsey still finds time for the small stuff: writing, watching almost anything Asian on Netflix, singing and playing guitar, but especially enjoying her two horses, Bricco and Tyrra, and two dogs, Ms. K and Huffington.

Connect with Lindsey at www.authorlindseycowherd.com
Also on Facebook, Instagram, Twitter, Good Reads!

Follow author Lindsey Cowherd on Facebook. Giveaways are announced on her page throughout the year. Just like her page to keep up with new releases and giveaways.

(Free books? Of course!!!)

Made in the USA
Lexington, KY
24 November 2019